WITH FATE CONSPIRE

(A Novel of the North West Highlands)

Robert O Scott

Pen Press Publishers Ltd

Published in Great Britain by
Pen Press Publishers Ltd
39, Chesham Road
Brighton
BN2 1NB

ISBN 1-905621-03-5
978-1-905621-03-3

Cover design Jacqueline Abromeit

Born in Glasgow in 1927, Robert Scott developed a love of climbing the Scotish hills; this eventually took him to ASSYNT where he became a gamekeeper.

Retired, he now lives in Pitlochry, still walks the hills and writes poetry. *With Fate Conspire* is his first novel.

This book is dedicated in memory of my wife,
Eileen,
who loved Assynt and its people.

"Ah Love! Could thou and I with fate conspire,
To grasp this sorry scheme of things entire,
Would not we shatter it to bits - and then
Re-mould it nearer to the heart's desire!"

From - The Rubaiyat of Omar Khayyam.

Chapter One

For what seemed an alarmingly long time, the sound of that rifle shot loudly echoed and re-echoed around the high corries of Craig Mhor.

With a smooth flowing movement which revealed experienced skill, Ron MacDonald eased back the rifle bolt, ejected the spent cartridge then slid a fresh bullet into the breech. He was now ready, if necessary, to take a second shot.

Lying in the thick heather beside Ron, Ian MacLean lowered his telescope and exclaimed, "Good shooting, Ron, a perfect heart shot!"

So a second bullet was not required. Death was instantaneous. Struck through the heart, the red deer stag collapsed with a clatter of hard antlers against harder rock. Its savagely jolted lungs exploded a sharp gasp. It seemed a gasp of terrible surprise – this sudden blow was incomprehensible; what invisible predator had struck it down?

The keenly watching poachers rose from the concealing heather. Ron MacDonald, slim and sinewy, was the taller. He was 'correctly' dressed for deer stalking in matching fawnish tweed jacket and neat plus fours. A deerstalker hat adorned with a few salmon flies completed his outfit. His clothes blended perfectly with the browns and bronzes of the September hillsides in this wildly rugged landscape of the North West Highlands of Scotland. Ron did not look like a poacher. With his expensive clothes and his greying hair neatly trimmed, he looked more like a 'gentleman stalker', one of the many wealthy, tweed-clad sportsmen who invaded the Highlands every autumn. One hint that Ron was not – at least not on this occasion, not on this September day of 1983 – a truly pukka gentleman sportsman was the fact that he was not wearing a tie.

Ian MacLean was a man of middle height. His solid bulk made him look smaller and gave an impression of real strength. He was sixty-three years old, exactly ten years older than Ron. From a distance his bushy grey beard and abundant white hair made him look older, but, close up, his dark brown eyes, well sheltered under each eyebrow's thick thatch, belied his age as they vivaciously sparkled with eager love of life. He wore an old ex-army anorak, its confusion of camouflage patterns further confused by the marks of many old bloodstains. His raggedly disreputable faded blue jeans also showed what looked suspiciously like old bloodstains. His tattered cotton shirt, lacking a few buttons, flapped open and revealed a mass of grey hair matting his broad chest. He looked what he was – a carefree poacher of a happy disposition; one who was well content with his careless disorder, one who was in his true element here in his native Highland hills.

Together the poachers walked over to the dead stag. Inspecting it, they admired the nobility it still retained, despite the sombre rudeness of death.

Grinning broadly, Ron thrust out his right hand and said in his pleasant New England accent, "Many thanks, Ian, you've done real swell helping me get my first 'Macnab'"[*]

"Aye, well I'm sure it won't be your only 'Macnab', Ron. You'll get more in the future, especially if you do buy your own Highland sporting estate and live here in your ancestral homeland."

After warmly shaking Ian's hand, Ron handed over his small hip flask. Never backwards about coming forward to accept an offered dram, Ian saluted 'Slainte Math' (good health), then took a generous gulp. Delighted with the excellent malt whisky, he smacked appreciative lips and beamed, "My, but that truly is the nectar of the Gods!"

"I sure am pleased it meets with your expert approval. Is it a really good whisky?" Ron asked, reaching out for his flask.

"Aye, it is that. It's a braw whisky. But of course you know my opinion… there is no such thing as bad whisky, some whiskies are better than others, that's all!"

Laughing, Ron again handed over his flask. Ian eagerly gulped another generous dram. After examining the intricately engraved small silver flask, he remarked, "That's a real braw wee flask you have, Ron, but it's not nearly as precious as what it contains… or rather, contained." Ruefully, almost reproachfully, he corrected himself as he shook the now almost empty flask. "Anyway, you've done real well getting your first 'Macnab'; getting it despite the extra difficulties of poaching it on a hostile estate. Many landowners find it hard enough to achieve a 'Macnab' on their own Highland sporting estate even with the expert help of their own gamekeepers."

"Yeah, but I only got it thanks to your poaching skills and your great knowledge of this land. I could never have done it without your help."

Ian nodded in modest agreement, "Aye, that's as may be, but you were very skilful yourself, quickly catching that salmon, then shooting those two brace of grouse, and now accurately shooting this stag after a fair stalk out on the hills, and all poached on this 'enemy' estate in less than six hours. Not bad… not bad at all!"

"Such praise from you is high praise indeed!"

"Och, you deserve it. Although for a while I thought you weren't going to get your stag. Yon auld bitch of a hind almost spoiled the stalk for us."

Ron vividly recalled that anxious time when, as they cautiously stalked towards a group of stags, they had suddenly come upon a herd of hinds and calves. Instantly both stalkers dropped into the heather and lay apprehensively still. They fervently prayed that the grey faced old hind, the matriarch of her herd, standing alertly apart, had not seen them. Every moment they expected to hear that ancient hind give her loud alarm bark, which would instantly send all

---

[*] *'A Macnab' – fairly and sportingly getting a salmon, a brace of grouse and a red deer stag, all in the one day.*

hinds and the nearby stags into precipitous flight. She might well spoil Ron's chance of getting a stag to complete his first 'Macnab'.

At last, Ian and Ron exchanged quick smiles. They had been lucky; the old hind had not seen them.

Slowly, inch-by-inch, they cautiously slithered backwards through the heather towards a rocky outcrop that would conceal them from the deer. Before reaching that cover they had to traverse a stretch of sodden black peat and a vivid green carpet of spongy sphagnum moss.

Exchanging rueful smiles, they started squirming over this bog. Smiles quickly turned to grimaces of dismay as peaty water icily soaked through clothes.

Once concealed behind the rock outcrop, they thankfully rose to their feet. They then descended the hillside and made a long detour to avoid the hinds. Eventually, undetected, they got within range of the stags. Ron shot this stag and thus completed his first 'Macnab'.

"What was it you called that old hind?" Ron asked.

"Och, I called her a good few things; not very polite things either! But my usual name for such an ancient matriarch is 'An Auld Dowager'. Aye, we were really lucky she didn't see us. Auld Dowagers like her are so alertly and nervously watchful that it's almost as if they were endowed with more than one pair of eyes, ears and nostrils." Ian grinned, "Och, I suppose we shouldn't stand here blethering all day, we better get your stag gralloched and cut up, then start on the long trek home. The sooner we're safely home the better, just in case anyone does come to investigate that shot."

"Is anyone on this estate likely to come and investigate?"

"Och, no, not now, not since the present bastard of a laird took over and rapidly started ruining the estate. All the gamekeepers who used to be employed were sacked one after the other and their estate owned houses sold as holiday homes to wealthy incomers, all those alien 'White Settlers'. Pre-war, when my father ghillied on this estate, it was a different story entirely. Then your shot would have had this ground swarming with gamekeepers in no time at all, all searching for the poachers responsible."

"Gee, that sure must have made it much more difficult to poach successfully, didn't it?"

"Aye, it did; but it made it much more exciting and challenging too!"

"How does the present laird manage then without any gamekeepers working on his estate?"

"Och, he hardly manages the sporting side of the estate at all."

"Then what do those who rent out the stalking do? It must be very difficult for them without the expert guidance of a gamekeeper – or of a tough old bugger of a poacher like you – who intimately knows the land and the habits of its stags."

"This laird hires a deerstalker each season. But he can't get any good stalkers to work for him. He only gets the worst type of chancers."

"Chancers?... Cowboys, you mean: I know all about 'cowboy' builders, but I've never heard of 'cowboy' deerstalkers before," laughed Ron.

"Aye, that's right, all he can get are 'cowboy' stalkers. This season he's excelled himself; he's got a real cowboy."

"Oh, really? An actual cowboy from the States, you mean?"

"Yes, a cowboy from Texas no less. He was supposed to be an expert hunter, but, according to all reports, he's useless. Those who've been out stalking with him reckon he can hardly tell the difference between a stag and a steer. They reckon he's got about as much chance of getting a stag with his lasso as with his rifle. Anyway, I believe he's handed in his notice and is heading back to his own sunshine state."

"What will the laird do now without any stalker at all?"

"Och, God knows! I suppose he'll just continue to blunder along somehow until he drags the entire estate down to some final disaster!"

"Does he do any stalking or grouse shooting himself?"

"No, not him. Those sports are much too strenuous. He rents them out and squanders the money on his only real interests... drugs, drink and fancy young whores. He rents out the salmon fishing as well, although he still does a little fishing now and again, but even then he fishes for money. He sells most of the salmon he catches."

"Gee, he sure sounds an obnoxious character." With quiet irony, Ron dryly remarked, "Somehow, I get the impression that you don't care for him much, Ian."

"Don't care for him much?... That's a monumental understatement... I hate him!" Ian's ruddy face flushed even ruddier and his eyes flashed anger. "In fact he's the only person I've ever really hated."

Ron was startled at the strength of feelings his few light words triggered.

"If that bastard of a laird did come out himself to investigate, it would be very dangerous, not for us, but for him. If I met him here with that loaded rifle so handy I would be sorely tempted to use it on him. It would be just like killing any other vermin – a good riddance!"

"Gee, you really are wound up about him, Ian. You wouldn't really shoot him if you had the chance, would you?"

"Perhaps I would, perhaps I wouldn't, I'm not sure... Och, I don't suppose I would, after all. And yet some of the Germans I killed during the war must have been much better men than him, and I never felt any hatred for them." Ian paused; he had a sudden flash of memory. He corrected himself, "Well, only very rarely did I really hate any of those Germans." His flush of anger faded as quickly as it had flared. His eyes regained their usual bright, happy expression. He smiled, "However we better get moving, just to be on the safe side."

Ron readily agreed. He quickly unloaded the rifle and slipped it into its canvas cover.

With jacket and anorak thrown off, with shirtsleeves rolled above elbows, they set about their butchery work. After half an hour of steady labour, skilled labour on Ian's part, much less skilled on Ron's, they were finished. They

4

dragged the unwanted remains of the stag away and partially concealed them under an overhanging peat bank. Those gory remains would not be wasted. Alerted by the sound of the shot, four ravens flew in ragged circles high overhead. Occasionally they gave impatient croaks in anticipation of the promised glory of the feed awaiting them.

Ian smiled as he looked up at them, "Och, don't you worry, my glossy dark beauties, you'll soon get your feast, the feast you yourselves foretold." Then, still smiling, he turned to Ron, "Remember. I said you'd have a successful stalk when we saw these ravens when we started out this morning?"

"Yes, I sure do remember. You were real pleased to see them, weren't you?"

"Aye, I was. I always like to see ravens at the start of a day's stalking. I like to have them predict a successful stalk. It's just an old tradition of Highland stalkers; only an ancient superstition I suppose, and yet how often it comes true and the ravens get their foretold reward. Other days, when we don't see ravens, we often have unsuccessful stalks."

"Of course that happening is mere chance, isn't it?" Ron asked, smiling.

"Yes, perhaps it is mere chance, right enough," Ian quietly replied, then solemnly added, "but then on the other hand, perhaps it's not."

They now gathered handfuls of lime green sphagnum moss. Ian squeezed the water and the colour out of the moss and, now an anaemic ghost of itself, efficiently used it as swabs to mop up the blood on the parts of the stag they had retained. Having admired the almost surgical skill with which Ian had gralloched and cut up the stag and was now swabbing the blood away, Ron grinned, "You've surely missed your true vocation, Ian, you should have been a surgeon."

"A surgeon?... A bloody butcher, more like!"

Finally they used fresh wet moss to sponge clean their hands and arms – arms bloodied to the elbows.

"Gee, this sphagnum moss sure is very versatile," Ron said as he finished cleaning himself.

"Aye, it is, and it has great natural antiseptic qualities too."

"Oh, really?"

"Aye, it has. It was collected in vast amounts by Highland women and children during the First World War and used as excellent medical dressings for thousands of wounded soldiers in Flanders. Its healing qualities were supposed to be much better than any man-made medical dressings."

"Oh, really?" Ron repeated, "I didn't know that."

"Och, there's a lot about the Highlands you don't know yet... for instance, what kind of birds are these?" Ian pointed to a group of dark birds gathered at a safe distance on a rocky knoll.

"Are they crows?... some kind of crows?" Then suddenly remembering, Ron added in triumph, "They are Hooded Crows, aren't they?"

"Yes, well done, Ron. They are Hoodie Crows, right enough."

Seven of these ever keen, ever ruthless, opportunist scavengers, nature's ugly undertakers, waited, noisily impatient, to join in the promised feast. Like a mob of drunken louts they squabbled amongst themselves and viciously stabbed the innocent air with filthy curses from their chisel sharp beaks.

Ian again pointed, "And what's that animal over there?"

Ron caught a fleeting glimpse of a reddish, dog-like beast before it disappeared behind a heathery ridge. "Was that a fox?"

"Aye, you're right again. You're learning fast. That fox has come to investigate what these ravens and hoodies are so excited about."

"It seemed to be going away from us though, didn't it?"

"No, not really, it's only making a wide detour to get well downwind of us."

Out of sight of them, the fox cautiously advanced on wary paws. With all senses set at hair-triggered alert, it circled until it was truly downwind. Then, how sensitively those quivering nostrils tested the wind, how accurately they read the story so clearly written there. The fox's brain analysed every whiff of information. Its long, bright pink tongue licked drooling lips. Saliva flowed in response to the gloriously strong scent of stag's fresh blood. But with that delicious scent was mingled another strong scent – the disgusting smell of humans. That, the most loathed and feared scent in all nature, warned the fox to stay well clear. It would patiently wait and only move cautiously forward under the protective shield of darkness. It would still get the lion's share of that succulent feast. Perhaps its pleasure would be all the greater for the long, mouth-watering delay.

Ian now shouldered the heaviest burden, the stag's large, solidly firm haunches. Ron, having slung the rifle over his back, struggled with the lighter, but more awkward burden of his sporting trophy, the stag's head complete with thickly-maned neck and wide, nine pointed antlers.

"Are you ready?" Ian asked.

"Yeah, or at least I'm as ready as I'll ever be."

"All right then, let's get going. The sooner we start the sooner we'll be finished and then we can start celebrating. I hope you are going to celebrate?" Ian anxiously asked.

"Yeah, I sure am! My first 'Macnab' is surely something worth celebrating, isn't it?"

Resolutely they started out on their long journey over that austere wilderness of shaggy heather ridges and brown peaty moors which stretched from the slopes of Craig Mhor to the back of Ian's croft.

All day a pleasant South Easterly breeze had steadily blown and gossamer clouds had sailed high across the September sky and veiled and tempered the sun's warmth. Now, in one of those frequent changes in this unpredictable Northern land – changes that can condense almost an entire year's weather into a single day – the welcome breeze completely died. The last remnants of thin clouds evaporated and left a clear vivid blue. Now the brave afternoon sunshine furnaced down. All nature welcomed this warming sunshine. The two poachers did not.

Toiling and sweating under their heavy burdens, they regretted the loss of the cooling breeze. Salty rivulets coursed down scarlet faces. Saturated shirts clammily clung to damp bodies. Dark patches sweatily stained through jackets and mingled with blood oozing from the dismembered stag. Plodding on determinedly they gasped in the breathless air.

The many rests they allowed themselves were most welcome. They did not say much as they lay resting. Words were not required to confirm their true companionship. Ian felt something akin to the comradeship of his wartime army years. That sincere camaraderie remained the best memory of those long years in North Africa and Italy. The sunshine warming his face further reminded him of those distant, yet still vividly immediate years. It seemed impossible that forty years had passed since that time of "blood, toil, tears and sweat." Smiling he thought, "Well at least it's not quite so bad today, all we have is blood, toil and sweat – but no tears."

Sometimes they were not given peace to enjoy those rests. They cursed in annoyance as they felt deer ticks crawling in lively exploration over their heads. Those loathsome small parasites were deserting the dead stag for the excitingly warm and sweaty human prey. For Ian it was easy to find and remove the ticks from Ron's neatly trimmed hair; but his own mass of hair and bushy beard were hirsute paradises for those pets. It took Ron's keen eyes and quick fingers some time to locate and remove Ian's ticks. Despite their annoyance they were amused at the strange spectacle they made – a couple of apes engrossed in eagerly searching one another for parasites.

"Have you got them all yet?" Ian asked.

"Yeah, I think so… Oh no, there's another one. Hold on just a minute!"

Ian laughed, "Surely you mean, hold on just a tick!"

Once more they reluctantly got to their feet, once more they wearily shouldered their heavy burdens and set out on what was, thankfully, the final lap of their journey.

At last, with heartfelt relief, they dumped their bloody loads near the summit of Cairndhu, the small craggy hill, which rose steeply behind Ian's crofthouse. While Ron stayed to rest and guard the precious booty, Ian made his sure-footed way down the familiar path which contoured round the hill and led directly to the back of his croft.

Soon he reached the small wood that cosily sheltered and hid his house. Entering this oasis of shady woodland unfailingly gave him a thrill of pleasure. This was his own wood, his own garden, his own croft and crofthouse; he felt proprietary pride of ownership firmly linked to strong family ties. He was the third generation to have planted trees in this mini forest.

Today its pleasant dappled shade was especially welcome after his long and sweaty trek through the vast expanse of sun-bright treeless landscape. This was a fascinating place of undisciplined, un-regimented trees and shrubs. Massed rhododendrons dwarfed urgently competing clumps of gorse and broom. Tall, un-pruned buddleias sent slender fingers spiking up towards the sky. Varied trees – birch, hazel, rowans – were haphazardly dotted around, while thirsty willows crowded along the small burn which ran through the croft and gave it its name, 'Altdour' – the burn of the otter. Mixed conifers growing along by the

7

enclosing fence gave protection and seclusion. Grouped companionably together outside the garden three rugged Scots Pines reared their wrinkled and grizzled massive might. Those ancient giants towered high above all other trees and presided over them with solemn craggy dignity.

Ian now came to a large thicket of wild raspberry canes that rioted too, and aggressively invaded, a generously productive vegetable plot. From out of this dense jungle of lush canes the head of a tiger fiercely glared. Years ago, when he had discovered William Blake's fantastic poetry, Ian had crudely carved this savagely grotesque wooden head. Almost subconsciously he murmured:

"Tiger, Tiger, burning bright,
in the forests of the night."

He repeated those lines every time he passed that tiger. It was now a well-established ritual.

Beyond the vegetables, lawns sloped gently downwards and flooded round to the front of the crofthouse. They surged like green waves trying to engulf the outcrops of sandstone rock which formed the heart of two rockeries. A margin of white flowers splashed their frothy foam between lawn and rocks. Bright clumps of many coloured heathers tartaned their autumn glory over the rocky outcrops.

Ian's wife, Helen, lovingly tended this front garden. She was there now contentedly engrossed, stooping and pottering in the largest rockery. She straightened and turned as their two dogs noisily bounded to greet Ian.

"Quiet Glen!... Quiet Corrie!" he commanded, stooping and patting the excited dogs.

They fell obediently silent, but continued their wildly ecstatic welcome.

Helen also welcomed him, but in an undemonstrative, though no less sincere, manner. A warm smile spread from her mouth, radiated her entire face and brightened her pale blue eyes.

"Well, did Ron get his stag?" she eagerly enquired.

"Oh aye, he got it all right."

"Good!... So that means he's got his first 'Macnab'?"

"Yes, he has – and very expertly he got them all... the salmon, the grouse and the stag."

"That's great!... He will be delighted. But where is he?"

"He's waiting with the stag until I make sure it's safe to bring it down here. There's been no one about, has there?"

"Oh no," Helen assured him, "I haven't seen anyone all afternoon."

"Good! But I think I'll go down and have a look from the front gate."

Helen and the dogs willingly accompanied him. They passed, and again admired, the two large old rowan trees, which, one on each side of the track, stood like a pair of alert sentries and spread their mysteriously obscure benign influence over the house and garden. Each tree was a flamboyant sight. Both were a mass of scarlet berries that vied with the autumn reds the leaves were vividly displaying. Dragged down by burdens of berries, thinner branches sadly sagged and seemed to weep drops of crimson blood. Blackbirds greedily feasted on this succulent fare. They made no appreciable impact on the vast number of berries.

Continuing along the rutted track which drunkenly meandered down from the front of the house, they passed many more trees and large clumps of unkempt shrubs. The track now curved sharply round a group of birch trees whose silvery bark gleamed brightly in the sunshine, then it staggered to an abrupt halt at a five barred wooden gate. From there a roughly tarred and badly pot-holed road took over. Altdour was the last and the highest house in Glen Aldrory. From it that narrow road slid down the slope through the attractive glen.

Leaning companionably side-by-side on the sun-warmed gate, Helen and Ian silently gazed at the familiar, well-loved scene stretching entrancingly before them. Familiar, too, was the sound of the flooded River Aldrory. Although near them, that wild river kept itself well hidden under the dense tree cover darkly cloaking its steep banks. After recent heavy rains the river deep throatedly growled its way through narrow, sheer sided rocky ravines and menacingly roared down its five and a half miles to the small village of Inveraldrory. There it met the sea. There it was swallowed by that ever-insatiable predator. It left nothing of that savagely proud river but a peaty stain that dyed the estuary an iodine brown.

Ian knew every pool on that river, knew them intimately. His knowledge of these pools went back to, and formed a memorable part of, his happiest boyhood years. Illuminated by strong imagination and bright memories he pictured each pool's unique character. Clearly he imagined the many salmon enticed from the sea's deep calm by that furious spate's irresistible call. He saw them leap high in silver splendour, felt them fight their way with urgent eagerness against that thundering flood. He almost felt the spawning madness wildly surging through their blood and echoing the river's mad, tempestuous rush.

These imaginings were interrupted by Helen gently murmuring, "What a lovely afternoon."

"Aye, it certainly is," Ian quietly agreed.

Although so familiar, that view down Aldrory Glen with its rugged, birch clad ridges enclosing it and the sea sparkling in the distant West, was a scene of which they never tired. Helen unobtrusively glanced at a now pensively silent Ian. Effortlessly she read his mind. She knew that for him the beauty of this scene was marred by the knowledge that most of the houses dotted throughout the glen were now merely holiday homes, which lay unoccupied and desolate for much of the year. He remembered when at least one cow and a pony had been kept at each of these houses and numerous hens had fussily scraped and pecked in engrossed self-importance. Now Range-Rovers and Mercedes were parked there, the obvious expensive status symbols of well-heeled Southerners escaping for a time the stresses and pressures of their hectically demanding affluent lifestyle.

After a time, Ian, feeling Helen's gaze on him, turned his head and with a sigh and a smile said, "It's all quiet enough now, there's not even old Nell to neigh her usual welcome!"

"Yes, that's exactly what I was thinking. I always expect to see her come galloping up for titbits when I come to this gate. The field seems very empty without her, doesn't it?"

Nell was the only pony left in that glen. She was a greyish white, sturdy Highland garron, sure-footed, steady and reliable. She belonged to their nearest neighbours, Kenny MacLeod and his sister, Kate. For most of the year old Nell contentedly grazed in the rough pasture, stretching for a quarter of a mile between the two houses. She was kept more as a pet than as a working pony. Her only local work was to carry panniers of peat from the moors a few miles above Aldrory Glen. However, when it came to autumn's deer stalking months she did work: she worked hard and earned her keep. She was hired out to Lord Kilver's Ardgie Sporting Estate to help carry home shot stags.

"Aye, the field is real empty, right enough, but it won't be long before she's back home again!"

Ian was not in the least surprised that Helen and he had been thinking of exactly the same thing at exactly the same time. During their thirty years of marriage, not only their bodies had come together in wonderful intimate happiness, but also their minds had also happily come together; had understandingly joined together perhaps as much as it was possible for the male mind and the female mind ever to truly merge. In their early married years it had not all been plain sailing. There had been many savage squalls as Ian, guided by his reasoning masculine logic, and Helen, guided largely by her intuitive feminine feelings, had struggled to understand one another. Gradually they had adjusted to and had come to terms with each other's strangely novel way of thinking.

It had been especially difficult for Ian to understand the amazing depths of Helen's strange intuitive powers. To him, a mere male, her powers were disturbingly inexplicable. They worryingly defied all his attempts at finding any possible reasonable, logical explanation. It was only after experiencing many proofs that he was completely convinced that Helen possessed some unique powers – powers that could only be described as paranormal... some form of psychic gifts that, as yet, could not be explained scientifically.

Ian smiled, "Och, I suppose I better not stand gawking here all day. I better get back to Ron and help bring his stag home and get his 'Macnab' finished at last."

"I'll have tea ready for you both when you get back. You must be parched."

"Aye, I am a bit thirsty, though perhaps we'll be needing something stronger than tea! Anyway Ron will be pleased to get finished with carrying his awkward trophy. He was looking a wee touch weary when I left him.

"We won't be long," Ian said as he left Helen at the front of the house; then, noting the pleading expressions in both dog's eyes, he smiled, "They may be merely dumb brutes, but their eyes can speak as eloquently as any words, can't they?... Aye, all right, you can come along with me."

They needed no second telling. Both dogs gave joyous barks and bounded ahead of Ian in an exultant race. Glen, the neat, slim black and white collie, fleetly led the way. Corrie, the hardy, rough coated tan and white fox terrier determinedly followed.

At a steady pace Ian climbed back up the steep Cairndhu path. Soon he reached Ron who was lying resting where he had left him. His eyes were closed. He seemed fast asleep.

"Oh, it's all right for some folk. You're gae comfortable there. Have you had a good sleep?" Ian mockingly enquired.

With an apologetic smile, Ron admitted that he might have dozed off, "But just for a minute or two, no more!"

"You don't expect me to believe that, do you? You've not been a very reliable sentry, have you? And you know it's a court martial offence to sleep while on sentry duty, don't you?" Ian again mocked, with mischievously gleaming eyes.

Ron smiled another apology, "I'm sorry. I was lying admiring the view when I must have dozed off."

Ian, suddenly remembering a certain wartime incident in Italy, laughingly relented, "Ah well, perhaps the less I say about sleeping on sentry duty the better." In answer to Ron's enquiring glance, he added, "Och, maybe I'll tell you that story some other time."

They lay in contented silence. Then, with sincere emotion, Ron quietly said, "These views from here really are great, are truly something special. Surely they must be some of the best views in the entire world!"

"Aye, they are a wee bit better than your usual views at home in New York, aren't they? At times you must surely get terribly weary of being amongst those huge skyscrapers; don't you feel completely overwhelmed by them? I know I could never live there. Being in that hideous city, or any other city, amongst all the ceaseless traffic and the forever grimly hurrying crowds would kill me... would kill me or else drive me mad." Ian grinned, "Perhaps the latter would be much more likely, eh?"

"Gee, Ian, do you think I don't know how you feel? I often feel something approaching deep despair at having to work in that huge, mad, hectic, and ever more crazily hectic city. It was different when I was younger; then I thrilled to the tremendous excitement of working in Wall Street. It seemed wonderful being an insider, being in the know, working with, and learning from my father; meeting those who had the real power... not the politicians, but those who controlled the world's purse strings. Then, too, it was thrilling to jet around the world, to rush to Tokyo, to London, to Hong Kong, arranging deals worth hundreds of millions of dollars. I truly admired my father then. I admired him for building up such a successful financial business of his own. I admired him for achieving his goal of becoming a wealthy man. But, when I see him now, almost seventy-five years old, and still a workaholic, much of his life seems such a waste. He has always been too busy making and increasing his wealth to have had any time to really enjoy it. He has not taken a real holiday for twenty years. He even grudges me the two weeks annual vacation I have over here salmon fishing with you. Now that I'm over fifty years old I increasingly, feel I'm just following in my father's footsteps, will, like him, work till I die. I seem to have lost any true purpose in life. Every one of those once exciting cities I visit on hectic business trips now seem more and more the same. Ever the same Hilton type hotels; ever more frustrating traffic jams; ever more crowds all desperately hurrying with pasty grey faces grimly unsmiling."

Ron now paused (for breath?) then with a wistful smile said, "It's only when I'm over here, in the Highlands, that I feel truly alive. I envy you, Ian. How I envy Helen and you the simple, natural life you so wisely lead here."

"Yes, a simple life for a simple couple, perhaps?" grinned Ian, then added seriously, "Why don't you give it all up then, retire early and buy a place over here in the Highlands? You could afford to, couldn't you?"

"Yeah, I could. I often feel sorely tempted to do just that, but there are problems. There are a few problems which prevent me."

Ian remained diplomatically silent. He knew that one of those problems was Ron's wife, Cynthia. She certainly was a problem!

They once more fell silent. They once more swept their gaze over the vast panorama of mountains. Each mountain towered individually; each had its own unique character. They thrust themselves out of the rugged expanses of purplish brown heather moors with immense primeval strength and reared like savage dinosaurish giants. The many lochs scattered over the moors sparkled in the sunshine and the distant sea brightly glittered its silvery sheen.

The silence was broken by Ian reverentially murmuring, "Aye, they are grand views, right enough." This quiet understatement concealed the real depth of feelings this superb landscape unfailingly awoke in him. True to his Highland upbringing and ancestry he was instinctively reticent about openly expressing his deepest feelings. Only in his attempts at poetry did he allow something of his deeper emotions to be – guardedly – revealed.

Ron, too, disliked being over-demonstrative. He, too, remained true to the much remoter, but still strong, ancestral Highland nature he had inherited. He again thought of the many visitors he had met briefly at the Inveraldrory Hotel over the past nine consecutive years that he had stayed there. How false and superficial sounded the gushing outpourings of so many of those tourists who stopped for only one night before rushing off to the next posh hotel. He regretted that so many of them were from his own country; were the worst type of American tourists who 'did' Scotland in two days, 'did' Europe in twelve days. The type who breathlessly exclaimed, "If this is Tuesday, then I reckon this must be Belgium!" How could those transient visitors know anything of what he felt for this place; this his own ancestral land?

Still less could those desperately trivial tourists know anything of what someone like Ian, a true native, felt for this land. What countless memories this place held for him.

One of his earliest and brightest memories of infancy was being carried up to this summit on his father's shoulders. Even then, at that tender age, something of this place's fantastic wild magnificence seemed to make a profound imprint on his infant consciousness.

And how vividly he remembered the first time he climbed up here on his own feet. He must have been about four years old on that great occasion. He had climbed unaided all the way, apart from his grandfather's strong hand firmly and reassuringly enveloping his trusting small hand and encouraging him on the roughest and steepest sections of the narrow path. How happily he sat beside his grandfather almost in exactly this very spot. It had seemed to him then that there were just the two of them, his grandfather and himself, with their two dogs, in all the glorious wide world.

Then he was overwhelmed with pride when his grandfather, with one of his gentle, almost shy smiles, quietly said, "You did well, Ian boy, climbing that steep brae, not many bairns of your age could have managed it."

Shyly he returned his grandfather's smile. He remained silent. He could not trust himself to speak. Such intensity of emotions he had never known before. Overcome by these feelings his eyes blurred, were swamped by tears that threatened to overflow. Resolutely he blinked back these tears and quickly, instinctively, turned away to hide his emotions. Leaning over, he caressed the five-month-old collie lying at his side. The dog rolled over on to its back. The young boy and the young dog wriggled and quivered together in an ecstasy of joy. Innocently they rejoiced in the sheer wonder of simply being alive. Life was marvellous!

The wise and gentle old man pretended not to notice his grandson's profound emotion. With quiet deliberation he started the pleasant procedure of preparing to smoke his pipe. This familiar routine was unvaried, was unhurried, as it had been for sixty years. From one pocket of his old tweed jacket he removed his pipe, from another he brought out his knife. Methodically he scraped out the commodious bowl. Holding a solid plug of jet-black tobacco in the palm of his left hand, he engrossed himself in shaving delicately thin slices from it.

The boy glanced out of the corners of his eyes at his grandfather. Once again he was amazed at how he managed to slice up that tobacco without ever cutting his hand. Lovingly, painstakingly, the old man rubbed the tobacco slices into a loose heap. Fascinated the boy watched his grandfather's right hand steadily move over the rough, toil-hardened palm holding the tobacco and, like a millstone, grind the slices into loose flakes. He knew that his grandfather's huge hands were as strong and as tough as any granite millstone.

The old man teased out the tobacco to his entire satisfaction. He then filled and lit his favourite old pipe. Once it was drawing properly, he securely fitted the perforated metal cover over its bowl. He lay back in sighing ease. He puffed out clouds of utter contentment.

The boy gazed unobserved – so he thought – at that wise and venerable patriarch whom he worshipped with a dog-like devotion. His grandfather appeared truly godlike. In fact just now he seemed God himself. He was the exact replica of that benevolent, caring God, complete with breeze blown white hair and beard, depicted in those glowing pictures in the large family bible at home.

For some time – childhood's immensely long time – young Ian continued silently gazing with shy adoration. Suddenly he solemnly asked, "Granda, does God smoke a pipe?"

Slowly, thoughtfully, his grandfather removed his pipe. He gently smiled down with amused wonder. Eventually he replied, "Bless me, boy, what a question. No, boy, I don't think God smokes a pipe. But I'm not really sure… after all, if God does not smoke, why did he create tobacco?"

But he had lost the boy's attention; it had abruptly switched to the two bright butterflies frantically fluttering over the heather near his feet. With wide-eyed wonder he stared at those gaudy beauties as they rose and fell, fluttered one way, then restlessly winged another way. He turned and asked, "Granda, why do they fly like that? Why do they try to go every way at once?"

"Bless me, boy, what questions you ask. Goodness knows why they fly so crazily like that. I suppose it's just the way they're made – butterflies have to flutter by!"

Giggling with delight, the boy repeated, "Butterflies have to flutter by!"

"Do you know what butterflies are called in the Gaelic?"

"No." The boy shook his head and stared expectantly.

"They are known as 'Amadan-dei' – 'God's fools' – because of that foolish way they flutter about."

How clearly those glorious memories flashed before Ian's 'inner eye'. How wonderful had been that time of simple, deep, contentment with his grandfather. Age and infancy had joined in profoundly innocent harmony, both had inarticulately gloried in the simple wonder of being alive and of being an integral part of that vast landscape spread out all around them.

Ian was abruptly jolted out of his pleasant reverie by Ron exclaiming, "Gee, look at those butterflies, aren't they beauties? What kind are they?"

"They are large Tortoiseshells. Aye, they are real beauties."

Spellbound, they watched those two gaily-fluttering fragile creatures as they rose and fell in carefree gyrations above the scented, glowing heather. With feathery lightness they occasionally touched down on that inviting pinkness and had their freckled wings delicately powdered by the heather's pollen.

"Why do they try to fly in every direction at once?" Ron asked with a smile.

Ian did not reply, but stared at Ron in wondering silence.

"What's the matter?" Ron asked.

"I am just surprised by the coincidence, that's all."

Ian explained that coincidence; the fact that he had been remembering that incident with the butterflies all those years ago. The coincidence that he as a boy had asked that same question in almost exactly the same words in almost exactly this same place.

"Gee, that sure is a real coincidence, isn't it? How do you explain it, Ian?"

"Och, I don't know… pure chance? Just a chance in a million?"

"Do you believe that?"

"No, not really, not now. I used to think such things were mere chance, but that was when I was much younger. That was before I was married to Helen."

"Oh, of course, Helen has strong ideas about such things, hasn't she?"

"Yes, she has, and after thirty years married to her, I have learned to respect her ideas."

"'There are more things in Heaven and in Earth than are dreamt of in our philosophy', eh, Ian?" Ron laughed. He knew that this thought of Hamlet's was Ian's favourite quotation.

"That quote seems vaguely familiar, I seem to have heard it before," Ian laughed in turn.

"Yeah, yeah, it should be familiar, I've heard it often enough from you."

For some moments they fell thoughtfully silent, then Ron said, "That coincidence sort of raised the age-old question of whether there is such a thing as fate, with everything being predestined; or is there free will with everyone being able to make their own destiny, doesn't it?"

"Aye, I suppose it does. Of course we've discussed this before, but this is hardly the time or the place for any further discussion, is it? It's much better to debate such profound questions sitting comfortably at home with a bottle or two of whisky to stimulate one's imagination and illuminate – or confuse – one's thoughts. Anyway our immediate concern is not with such questions, but with getting your 'Macnab' finished at long last. Come on, we better get moving."

With some reluctance they rose from their comfortable heathery couch. Once more Ian eased the stag's heavy haunches on to his aching shoulders while Ron again wearily struggled with the rifle and his ungainly trophy. Cautiously they made their way down the steep path leading to Ian's croft. The two dogs joyously led the way.

Thankfully they entered the welcome shade of the small wood. Many branches arched over and met above the path. Sunlight filtered through and created a greenish tunnel – a strange ethereal world.

"Those trees provide good shelter for your house, don't they? And I suppose it's no accident that they also give cover to hide us from any unfriendly prying eyes," Ron said.

"Aye, that was one of the reasons my grandfather first planted them."

"He must have been a real character. I remember you telling me he was regarded as the best shot and the best poacher in this district when he was in his prime; and yet he was also a very well read man, something of a scholar."

"Yes, he certainly was really a great character… 'Take him for all in all, we shall not see his likes again'."

"Still, I think you make a darned good job of keeping his spirit alive, Ian."

"I try!… I try! I do my humble best to keep something of his good old ways alive. But over the last number of years, he must surely be wildly birring in his grave. He must be so dismayed at how things have changed for the worst since his time, especially at how this estate has so terribly degenerated under the present bastard of a laird, bloody Campbell-Fotheringay."

Spurred by his own violent words, Ian's anger started to rise, he paused, he smiled in self-mockery, "Och, take no heed of me, Ron, I'm just mounting my usual old hobbyhorse again. It's little wonder that Helen worries that my hatred of that laird is becoming something of an obsession with me."

"Perhaps she's right... I have heard you curse the hated Campbell-Fotheringay many times recently myself," laughed Ron. Then to change the subject, he said, "Of course you've planted many of those trees yourself, haven't you?"

"Yes, I certainly have. Over the years I've added many to the ones my grandfather and my father planted."

"Gee, it must give you a wonderful feeling of continuity to carry on with the work your grandfather so wisely started. No wonder you feel so strongly this is where your ancestral roots are firmly planted."

"Aye, that's true. My own roots are securely intertwined with the tenacious roots of all those trees. It is a most satisfying feeling to be aware of those successive plantings of trees which now shelter the old family home from the fierce winter gales. Also, there's the extra bonus which you noted, Ron, that these trees effectively hide me whenever I'm returning to the house laden with my illicit booty after being out on one of my unofficial sporting exploits."

"Your 'unofficial sporting exploits!" gee, that sure is a dandy expression for your poaching expeditions."

As they passed the carved tiger peering out from the jungle of raspberry canes, Ian again laughingly repeated Blake's lines. Joining in his laughter, Ron exclaimed, "This sure is an unexpected place to see a tiger!"

"Aye, I suppose it is... but then perhaps it's not; after all, surely all nature is a savage jungle, all 'red in tooth and claw'!"

"Yeah, Ian, I suppose that's true, right enough."

"Yes, of course it is; but most people nowadays refuse to face up to this fact. So many, especially city dwellers, prefer to have a false, saccharine-coated sentimental view of nature. They refuse to recognise the reality of the ruthless deaths incessantly taking place in nature and which are an essential part of it and which must be fully accepted if we have to have a correct understanding of nature."

"Yeah, of course that's undoubtedly true," Ron readily agreed. "And yet surely it's understandable that many people cannot face up to those harsh facts and need a more falsely rosy picture of nature, isn't it?"

"Och, yes, I suppose it is. But the trouble is that they try to impose their false, over sentimental ideals on those who have to face the hard practical realities of living and working with nature in the countryside."

Both dogs ecstatically greeted Helen as she came from the front garden and met the returned poachers.

"You would think they had been away for a week, not for just an hour," laughing, she stooped and lovingly returned their greetings. Then she warmly greeted Ron, "Congratulations on getting your first 'Macnab'. You've done really well today."

"Many thanks, Helen. Yeah, I've done well. But you know I would never have managed it without the expert help of this fine man of yours. He sure is a really fine poacher, isn't he?"

"Oh, yes, I have to admit he does know quite a bit about poaching; but I don't believe in over praising him, we don't want him to get too swollen headed, do we?"

"Och, there's damned little danger of that. I certainly won't get big-headed from your excessive praise of me," grinned Ian.

Helen mischievously smiled, "Och, all men are vain enough without having their vanity boosted by praise from women!" Still smiling, she said to Ron, "Anyway, my congratulations once more on getting your first 'Macnab'. I'm sure that over the years you'll get some more once you've bought your own Highland sporting estate."

"Aye, that's exactly what I told him as well," Ian said.

"Yes, I know you did," Helen replied.

Ian almost asked, "How did you know?" but wisely he stopped himself and kept quiet. But Helen had noticed, she had heard his unspoken words. Gently she murmured, "By now sure you know better than to ask, or even think, such a foolish question."

Ron laughed, "Anyway, it's more a question of if I ever buy my own Highland estate, surely?"

Resolutely Helen corrected him, "No, Ron, it is not a question of if you buy it. It is only a question of *when* you buy it!"

Ron opened his mouth to speak, then he too thought better of it and stood silently staring at Helen. For some long moments all three stood silent. They all felt in the presence of something mysterious, something shadowy insubstantial, yet something very real. For Ian such strange moments with Helen were not rare and he had learned to calmly accept them. He had long since given up attempting to explain them.

Ron was the first to speak, "Yeah, anyway if – oh sorry, Helen, I mean *when* – I do buy my own sporting estate, I will certainly need to stop a certain person from poaching on it, won't I?"

Ian laughed, "Ah well, you know the best way to stop me poaching on your estate, don't you?"

"No, I don't; what way is that?"

"It's simple; just you employ me as your gamekeeper. The likes of me, an old poacher who turns gamekeeper becomes the best of all 'keepers, he knows from long experience all the ploys poachers get up to."

"Oh, really? Well I'll keep that in mind once I do have my own estate."

"In the meantime, you both must be parched. I've got the tea ready, shall we take in the garden, in the 'sitter-ootery'?" Helen asked.

It was pleasant to sit out in that aptly named secluded corner of the garden. Shrubs and trees concealed it yet allowed afternoon sunshine to smile into the small patch of lawn. The sun's warmth coaxed out alluring scents from the masses of late flowering climbing roses which rioted in unrestrained exuberance through the shrubs and eagerly climbed the trees. Wild honeysuckle competed with these roses in parasitically exploiting the trees and shrubs. The honeysuckle was much more ruthlessly efficient than the roses. True to their ancient name of 'woodbine', their tendrils gripped and strangled with boa-constrictor strength. Coiling up and around hazels they deformed the vertical shafts into corkscrewed Harry Lauder walking sticks.

Helen, Ron and Ian comfortably settled themselves on the large wooden seat. Helen poured the tea. They drank and ate. Contentedly they watched the bulky bumblebees drift from flower to flower and drowsily enjoy the autumn afternoon's bright warmth. Half a dozen gaudy butterflies more actively enjoyed the warmth and brightness. Rising and falling and fluttery chasing they performed their final erotic mating dance.

Grinning, Ron asked, "What's the collective name for a number of butterflies like these?"

"A flock?… A flight?" Helen tentatively suggested.

"What about a Flutter of Butterflies?" Ian contributed.

"A flutter of butterflies?" Helen tested the sound of it, then smiled, "Oh yes, that's perfect."

As Helen happily poured their third cup of tea, Ian apologised to Ron. "It looks as though we're going to get nothing stronger than tea just now. Do you mind? Would you like some whisky?"

"Oh no. No thanks. This tea's just fine and dandy. It's truly a perfect drink. It's amazing how refreshing and thirst quenching it is. No wonder you British are so inordinately fond of it."

"Aye, I have to admit it is a good drink, right enough. Truly it is, 'The cup that cheers, but does not inebriate,' as they used to say at temperance meetings."

"Oh, really?" Ron laughed, "I'm surprised that you know anything about temperance meetings, Ian, I wouldn't have thought they would have been exactly your cup of tea! Surely you're not speaking from personal experience?"

"Ach no, certainly not!" Ian cried in mock indignation. "Temperance is a faith – a misguided faith (like so many others) – which I'm delighted to say I have never believed in."

"Aye, we ken that, all right," Helen laughed. "Perhaps it would have been better if you had believed in temperance."

"Och, don't blether, Helen. You really wouldn't want me teetotal, would you? You wouldn't want me like my miserable teetotal brother, would you?"

"No, perhaps not," she conceded. Then with heavy irony added, "No I guess not; I suppose you are just about perfect as you are."

"Ah well, many a truth's spoken in jest." Ian grinned. "You know, I used to be conceited, but now I'm perfect!… However, Ron, I'm sure we'll make up for this present dearth of whisky when we celebrate with you this evening. And, although it's very pleasant sitting here, I've still some work to do. I better get those haunches skinned and hung up."

"Yeah, and I want to get a few photos of all my trophies before the light goes."

Ian carried the stag's haunches into the old stable that was now partitioned off into workshops. One contained a neat pottery, where Helen spent many happy hours turning out imaginative small clay models of Highland wildlife – both the animal and the human variety. The other workshop was Ian's. Here he crafted varied items from native wood and from stag's antlers. Clearing a space on the crowded workbench, he dumped the haunches there and with deft skill skinned them. He now hung up that fine, dark fleshed, fat free venison to season. It hung from the rafters in the company of stag's antlers, slim hazel sticks and many large, well-established, dusty cobwebs.

As he admired that hanging venison, Ian grinned and thought, "I don't suppose conditions here exactly comply with all the stringent food hygiene regulations being imposed from Brussels." Each year the Brussels bureaucrats brought out more and more ridiculous new rules and regulations. One of their latest crazily impracticable ideas was that every deer carcase had to be inspected by an approved vet (a vetted vet?) soon after being shot. That might seem a good idea to an overpaid bureaucrat cocooned in the overheated comfort of his Brussels office, but was an impossible idea to put into practise, especially in the remote environment of the North West Highlands.

Again Ian grinned as he looked up at the swallows' nests in the roof above the rafters. At least these birds were no longer constantly flying in and out to feed their young as they had done all summer. This old building had been used by generation after generation of swallows. Now in mid-September these birds were gathered in one large flock of ceaselessly twittering parents and youngsters. As they perched on the wire between the crofthouse and the stable they looked like a row of animated clothes pegs. Some youngsters, tired of too much sedentary leisure, excitedly launched themselves into joyously bright seductive air. They soared high, then swooped and scythed space with curved, sharp-edged wings. Eager beaks gaped wide, then snapped shut on succulent flies. In this ethereal flight each swallow was a perfect embodiment of beauty combined with ruthless purpose.

It was incredible that such small, slim and frail looking birds could soon be taking off on a long and hazardous migratory journey to Southern Africa. The sudden silence around the croft after the departure of those attractive birds always came as something of a surprise to Helen and Ian. That silence lasted only a short time until it was overwhelmed by the riotous noise of the first of autumn's gales. Each year they wished these swallows well on their long journey and eagerly looked forward to their return the following spring.

As Ian again admired that hanging venison, he had a sudden glorious vision of a large dinner plate generously heaped with steaming hot venison stew. He licked his lips. He could almost smell and taste its luscious, mouth-watering promise.

His terrier, Corrie, also gazed up at that venison with longing eyes. He, too, licked drooling lips until he was sternly ordered out of the building.

19

While Ian was busy in the stable, Ron got his day's sporting trophies together and set about arranging them on the front lawn. Eventually he had the stag's wide antlered head, the salmon and the two brace of grouse arranged to his satisfaction. He admitted to himself that there was something almost reproachfully sad about those dead birds and the stag's decapitated head, but he felt there was nothing in the least sad about the large salmon. In death that noble king of fish still retained its truly impressive majesty. How beautiful was that firm shape of silvery bright streamlined perfection.

As Ron hurried over to his hired car for his cameras, he heard Helen's amused shout of, "Stop that, Glen!... Come here!"

"What was he doing?"

"Och, obviously Glen doesn't think much of your trophies, Ron, he was lifting his leg to piddle on the stag's head."

Then with further amusement, Helen shouted, "And Corrie, just you come here as well."

"What was Corrie doing?"

"It was what he was thinking of doing. He was planning on snatching one of your grouse and sneaking away with it. That's what he attempts to do with any dead trout left unattended while Ian and I are fishing."

Corrie now sat at Helen's feet and steadily gazed up at her. "And don't try to win me over with such an innocent expression. You can't fool me, you rascal, I know what mischief you were planning," she laughed. Corrie dumbly joined in her laughter with his stump of a tail in frantic action.

Ron got busy with his cameras. He arranged and rearranged his trophies on the lawn to get different effects. He then placed them amongst the bright flowering heathers in the rockeries to give them a truly Highland background. He was photographing one grouse neatly set in a lifelike position between red sandstone rock and pink heather, when Ian strolled over. "I like the way you've arranged that 'Famous Grouse' of yours there, Ron, it happily reminds me of a certain whisky."

Ron laughed, "Oh, trust you to be reminded of whisky, Ian."

Helen's laughter joined in, "Och, everything reminds him of whisky!"

Watching Ron eagerly using both cameras, Ian grinned, "You're certainly going to town with your cameras, Ron. You're behaving like a true Yankee tourist."

"Yeah, well I want a good pictorial record of my first 'Macnab'."

Finally Ron was satisfied that he had a complete record.

"Och, thank God you're finished with your damned cameras," Ian said. "You're keeping us away from our dinner, you ken, and – what's much more important – from our after dinner drams."

As Ron got into his car and prepared to leave, he keenly anticipated the many delights awaiting him at the posh hotel in Inveraldrory: a bath, a cocktail or two before dinner, a fine wine to complement the excellent meal, and yet all the hotel's delightful luxuries faded in comparison to the keen anticipation he felt at the prospect of returning to Altdour later that evening to celebrate with those true friends. "I'll see you later, then," he called. "I'll bring something to celebrate with."

"Aye, you better or you won't get past the front door?" Ian shouted.

Chapter Two

Some two and a half hours later, Ron drove cautiously up the narrow and twisting road through Aldrory Glen. He was mellowly aware of the drinks he'd enjoyed before, and with his substantial dinner. All the way up the glen he followed a van that now stopped in front of Altdour's front door. As it was illuminated by the house lights, that dark green van looked vaguely familiar. Then, with genuine pleasure, he recognised the two figures emerging from it. They were Colin MacDonald and his wife, Jeannie.

All their visitors were warmly greeted by Helen and Ian.

"Oh my, it's a real gathering o' the clans tonight," Helen laughed. "It's a long time since I've seen sae many braw bare knees here."

Ron had changed into his MacDonald tartan kilt and both Colin and Ian were wearing their old ex-army Seaforth Highlanders kilts of MacKenzie tartan.

"Gee, it sure is a real gathering of the clans right enough," Ron cried delightedly.

"Aye, it is," Ian laughed. "Thank God it's dark or you'd be keeping us out here for ages posing for your damned cameras. You'd keep us away from the really important things – the celebratory drams."

"Aye, and it's a special occasion for a real Highland celebration," Helen added.

"What's the celebration for? Is it someone's birthday?" Colin asked.

"Seeing as you're a gamekeeper, perhaps the less you know about why we're celebrating the better," Ian said, grinning.

"Aye, just you drink up and ask nae questions," Helen said.

"Och, I'll drink up all right. You ken me, you need have nae doots about that," Colin laughed. His ruddy face beamed, his honest eyes merrily twinkled, "Just you try and stop me!"

"Aye, we ken you fine. We've shared many braw drams together over the years, you and I," Ian said.

"Perhaps they've shared far too many drams together," Jeannie quietly remarked to Helen.

"Aye, that's true. They've shared far, far, too many!" Helen nodded in amused agreement.

"Och, stop your havering, wifies, there can be no such thing as too many drams," Colin beamingly objected.

"By God, that's true, Colin, we have never had too many drams at all, have we? The only thing too many are all the years passing far too quickly. We're both getting old and perhaps not quite so able to drink the way we used to."

"Och, I don't know about that, Ian, I think we can still manage to get through a bottle of whisky in fine style yet, can't we?"

It was getting on for sixty years since Colin and Ian had been at Inveraldrory Primary School together. They had caught their first trout together. Later, as older schoolboys, they had shared the excitement and the glory of catching their first salmon together. They had successfully poached that glorious fish from the River Aldrory despite the river being guarded by alert gamekeepers. That poaching triumph had been an unforgettable achievement. It was only much later, when Colin became a gamekeeper himself and Ian became a skilled poacher, that they realised just how amazingly lucky they had been not to have been caught red-handed that day.

Shortly before the outbreak of the Second World War they joined the local Territorial Army unit together. They enjoyed improving their already considerable skills at rifle shooting and fieldcraft. They also enjoyed improving their less impressive skills at whisky drinking.

Then in the Seaforth Highlanders they had endured the long, weary, war years together. They had shared the dangers and hardships of the terrible 'dry' North African campaign where all kinds of drink, especially whisky, had been so very scarce. Once they got to Italy, the abundant local vino compensated, to a certain extent, for the continual scarcity of whisky. As often as possible they vivaciously enjoyed war's brighter times; but there were many grim times when they were deeply saddened by the cruel death of brave comrades.

Ian now turned to Ron and reproachfully, almost accusingly, said, "Talking about whisky, I notice you've arrived empty-handed."

"Oh, really? You think I've come here empty-handed, do you? Well just you… and you, too, Colin, come with me and we'll see about that."

Eagerly they followed him. Eagerly they watched him open the boot of his car. Delightedly they saw him lift out a case of malt whisky.

"Is that better?" he asked, handing the case over to Ian.

"Oh aye, Ron, that's much better."

"Oh aye, that's much, much, better!" echoed Colin in an awed, reverential voice.

Ian's and Colin's beaming faces glowed their approval, glowed with appreciation and glorious anticipation.

As they quietly looked on, Jeannie and Helen exchanged sympathetic glances. They gave gentle, profoundly feminine, profoundly understanding smiles and resigned sighs.

Chattering happily they all entered the house. Ian brought up the rear. With firm strength, yet with gentle loving tenderness he hugged that precious case to his broad chest.

The small, comfortably unpretentious sitting room warmly welcomed them. In the centre of one wall a glowing fire of peat and birch logs gave out a bright radiance that the clear-varnished pine panelling on the walls and ceiling cheerily reflected. Under the weight of their feet the old floorboards wearily sagged and noisily creaked them a knottily arthritic welcome. A large, old, and handsomely carved solid oak sideboard gleamed darkly in sombre contrast to the pale pine's surrounding brightness. On that sideboard many glasses glittered in neat array. As the floorboards protestingly sagged those glasses vibrated and tinkled merrily against one another as if shivering with excitement at the prospect of once again being filled with malt whisky, of once more joyously coming alive with that marvellous golden elixir, that uisge beatha – 'the water of life'.

Jeannie and Colin settled themselves with familiar ease on the comfortable old sofa that faced the glowing fire. Ron was about to follow their example by lowering himself into the large armchair which stood cosily inviting at the left of the fireplace when Colin shouted out an amused warning, "Och, you better not sit there, Ron, that's Ian's special chair. No one is allowed to use it but 'Himself'."

"Sit there, Ron, you can use my chair," Helen said, pointing to a matching armchair on the opposite side of the fireplace. "I'm not as fussy as 'Himself'."

"But what about you? Where will you sit?"

"Och, she can sit here on the sofa beside me. There's plenty of room for a neat wee craitur like you, Helen, isn't there?" Jeannie said, smiling, as she eased herself closer to Colin.

"Aye, there's plenty of room. We'll all be brawly cosy here," Colin happily agreed.

Giving a mischievous smile, Jeannie playfully moved her leg against Colin's bare knee, saying, "Aye, we're braw and cosy, right enough, but it's about time you went on a strict diet, Colin, you take up half the sofa by yourself."

Ian ignored them while they were sorting themselves out. He was happily engrossed devoting his entire urgent attention to getting the case of whisky opened. Victoriously, he lifted out the first bottle. He gloated over the bright attractive label 'Glenlivet Fifteen Year Old Malt Whisky'. Lovingly he held the bottle up and the fire's cheery brightness glowed through the golden liquid and brought it voluptuously alive. As if mesmerized, he gazed at that enticing treasure with reverent admiration.

From where he sat, hemmed in by Jeannie on the sofa, Colin could not turn round to see what Ian was silently getting up to, instead he anxiously asked, "What are you doing, Ian? Haven't you got that whisky opened yet?… or are you drinking it by yourself there?"

For answer Ian removed the bottle's cork and with well practised skill accurately threw it over Colin's head and into the centre of the fire, disdainfully remarking, "Och, we won't be needing you again!"

For whisky-loving Highlanders the thought of keeping a cork to re-seal an only partially emptied whisky bottle on any occasion of celebrating was utterly abhorrent. Any suggestion of such a course was regarded as a terrible insult.

Colin laughed his loud approval, "Ah, that's much better! I was just wondering what was delaying 'Himself'. I was thinking he was taking an awful long time getting the first cork into the fire!"

Ian ignored that implied rebuke. He wasted no more precious time. He poured out five generous drams then hurriedly handed them around.

Once Ian was comfortably settled in his own armchair, he raised his glass and gave the usual Gaelic toast, 'Slaine Math' (Good Health).

All the others eagerly lifted their glasses and returned that toast.

Colin gave a sigh of profound contentment and, smacking appreciative lips, exclaimed, "My, but that was worth waiting for. My, but that's a real grand malt, man!"

"Good! I'm delighted it meets with your expert approval as well, Colin. It received Ian's wholehearted approval this afternoon when we got our stag," Ron said, forgetting that Colin, the gamekeeper, had not been told of today's exciting poaching exploits.

Colin noticed that slip of Ron's and gave Ian an amused questioning glance but diplomatically said nothing.

"Aye, it certainly is a grand malt. An there's plenty more, so drink up," Ian happily enthused. "If that's all right with you, Ron, after all it's your whisky."

"No, no… not at all. It's your whisky, Ian. I gave it to you as a present for all your expert help today."

Again Colin gave Ian a smiling enquiring glance, but again tactfully said nothing.

"Thanks, Ron, thanks a lot. That's very generous of you. There's enough whisky there for more than one really good celebration."

"Aye, there certainly is… even at the rate that Colin and you can get through it," Helen said. "As long as Ron won't suffer too much from a hangover, after all he's not so experienced at knocking back the whisky as you two hardened old sinners are."

"Och, I thought Ian would have trained him to knock back his whisky in the approved Highland way. After all, Ron, you are truly a Highlander at heart, aren't you? You're a MacDonald like myself, a member of the largest and the best of all the Scottish clans… a much better clan than the MacLean's anyway."

As Colin made this declaration he raised his glass and again toasted Ian MacLean before once more drinking deeply.

Generously fuelled and smoothly lubricated by the free flowing whisky, the hours pleasantly and imperceptibly glided by. The tide of conviviality flowing around that cosy small room rose in waves of animated talk and often burst in a bright foam of glorious laughter.

Slumped back in contented ease, Ron let his gaze wander around this homely room. Thankfully, this crofthouse had not been over-modernised when electricity and piped water had been installed some thirty years ago. It retained most of its original character. All its rooms were lined with clear varnished pale pinewood that kept intact the bright, warm and cosy old atmosphere. This pleasant sitting room had been the kitchen. The massive iron cooking range, which had needed so much painstaking work to keep proudly black-leaded, had been removed. Ian, with much weary labour, had replaced it with an open fireplace and a large and attractive natural stone surrounding. Above the fireplace hung one of Ian's largest oil paintings. That painting of a group of

Scots Pines vividly afire with sunset's pulsing reds, glowed almost as brightly as the fire beneath it. The room's furniture was comfortably old-fashioned. There was no television set and no telephone in the room – nor anywhere else in the house.

Ron felt utterly relaxed and completely at home here as he happily basked in the glorious atmosphere of this room – this haven of warmly sincere friendship. It was such a contrast to the large and luxurious, but soulless, New York apartment where his wife and he uncongenially lived.

Suddenly, loudly, Ian demanded to know what he was daydreaming about, "Were you re-living today's events?"

Coming to with a start, Ron smiled, "No, I was just admiring this room. Gee, it's by far the most friendly and welcoming room I've ever been in."

"You've been in it often before, haven't you?" Jeannie asked.

"Oh yeah, often. I've enjoyed its hospitality for the last nine years, ever since I first came salmon fishing on the River Aldrory and got Ian to ghillie for me and to share his expert knowledge of the river with me."

How clearly Ron remembered that time when, on enquiring at the hotel, he had been directed to Ian MacLean as being the best local man to inform him about the salmon fishing. Wisely heeding further advice – advice given jocularly, but with serious undertones – he had taken a bottle of malt whisky with him when he set out to find Ian. It was impossible to judge just how influential that whisky had been on him securing Ian's advice and services. It was certain, however, that it had not harmed his chance of success.

In a short time Ian had become not only Ron's almost indispensable ghillie and fishing companion but also a real friend. Each successive year Ron eagerly returned to fish the Aldrory River and each year that friendship between him and Ian and Helen was ever further strengthened.

"Och, he's not too bad a ghillie and salmon fisher," Colin laughed, "as long as you can manage to keep him reasonably sober."

"I'm as good a fisherman and ghillie as you any day, drunk or sober," Ian laughed in reply.

"Aye, perhaps… perhaps. That's as may be, but what I want to know is, what are we all so pleasantly celebrating here tonight? Although you've not told me, I noted a few unintended hints that Ron's let slip, so I can make a gae shrewd guess at what ploys the pair of you have been up to."

"Shall we tell him?" Ian asked Ron.

"Yeah, sure, why not?"

"We're celebrating Ron getting his first 'Macnab' today."

"Congratulations, Ron, well done!" Colin smiled, "I hope it won't be the only one you get. Did you get it legally or were you poaching?… or need I ask? With Ian as your guide and companion nae doot you would be poaching… is that right?"

"Yeah, that's right, we were poaching."

"Aye, he was poaching when he got his salmon fairly caught on the fly, then he bagged not only one, but two brace of grouse neatly shot in fast flight and then the stag was accurately shot out on the hill after a long and fair stalk," Ian confirmed.

"Och, that's all very well, but where were you poaching? Not on Ardgic Estate, not on my ground, I hope?" Colin smilingly enquired.

Colin was one of three gamekeepers employed on Lord Kilvert's Ardgie Estate. This large sporting estate covered over seventy thousand acres. Apart from the more fertile land by the seashore, especially by the beautiful white beaches whose lime rich shell sand generously enriched the surrounding soil, most of those seventy odd thousand acres consisted of sour, impoverished, waterlogged peat. This fragile cover, this thin skin, of peat and heather constantly struggled to retain their precarious grip on the underlying rock. In many places it had lost the battle and huge slabs of grey gneiss lay tortuously exposed – lay revealed as the stark skeleton of this ancient land.

For many centuries people, too, had tenaciously struggled to make a living from this inhospitable land of rock, peat and bog. But those people, having been cruelly betrayed by those who should have protected them, had lost that struggle and now for square mile after square mile this wild landscape was entirely unpopulated.

Almost the only commercial value this land now possessed lay in its sporting assets: its deer, salmon, grouse and trout. But it possessed a much greater non-commercial value. Those many miles of moors and rocks, those countless lochs and reedy lochans, all those windswept mountains rising in isolated majesty, surely possess an aesthetic, a spiritual, value which transcends all other values.

The greatness of this landscape now lay in the very fact of it being so fiercely untamed, of it being such a primitively elemental wilderness. And yet, and yet, people had lived in it before… might not people live in it again, even if only a hardy few, without spoiling its wild beauty?

"Och no, don't worry, Colin, we didn't poach on any of your ground," Ian assured him. "We did all our poaching on bloody Campbell-Fotheringay's estate."

"Och, that's all right then. You can poach there as much as you like as far as I'm concerned, on the ground of that friend of yours."

"That friend of mine?… That devilish fiend of mine, more like," Ian retorted.

"Och, I thought he was everyone's friend," laughed Colin, knowing full well how that laird was hated, was justifiably hated, by the local population and that Ian's hatred of him was especially strong.

Helen glanced uneasily at Ian. She hoped he would not over-react. Over the last few years she had begun to worry about his increasingly expressed hatred for Mr Campbell-Fotheringay, the laird of Aldrory Estate, and for what he had done, and was still doing, to ruin this estate. While she agreed with Ian's outspoken views and, to a considerable extent, shared his feeling of hatred for that laird, yet she was conscious that he seemed to be allowing his hatred to grow into a real obsession – a possibly dangerous obsession.

But not allowing Ian's feelings to build up any further, Colin – with characteristic natural diplomatic skill – quickly asked for details of Ron's

'Macnab'. Soon he had Ian engrossed in giving a detailed account of the day's poached exploits on Campbell-Fotheringay's estate. His Aldrory estate covered only some twenty thousand acres. It spread South of Ardgie Estate and the five-and-a-half mile long River Aldrory formed the boundary between these two sporting estates. Lord Kilvert owned the salmon fishing on the top three miles of the river, while the bottom two-and-a-half miles was owned by Campbell-Fotheringay. That lower part of the river flowed most conveniently and most temptingly close to Ian's croft at Altdour. The small village of Inveraldrory was included in Aldrory Estate, as was the mountain, Suileag, which reared its fantastic steep shape from the rugged moors some miles inland of the village. That mountain's unique shape dominated this entire landscape. It was inescapable.

While listening with real pleasure to Ian recounting the day's memorable adventures, Ron again let his gaze wander around this homely room. It came to rest on Colin MacDonald. He was the same age as Ian, was of the same medium height, but of even sturdier build. With advancing age he had put on quite a bit of unwanted weight; he was now a stout, jolly, droll character. Yet he was still remarkably fit. His deep and resonant voice rolled up from the depth of his impressive chest and his unrestrained laughter resounded like eruptions of thunder. His broad forehead was unlined and his clean-shaven chin was strong. His jovial good nature benignly beamed.

As she sat beside her husband on the sofa Jeannie also listened with real interest. Colin and she were a perfectly matched couple. They were like a happily contented couple in an old Dutch painting – a stout, prosperous, jolly old farmer with his cheerily buxom, rosy cheeked wife. Only Jeannie's hair, its grey rapidly turning to white, and her increasing stoutness betrayed her age.

Helen, sitting on the other side of Jeannie, also eagerly listened to Ian graphically describing the day's exciting events. She admired the clear and vivid way he related the story. It had been her encouragement that had persuaded Ian to write down his fund of memories, humorous anecdotes and old, almost forgotten local tales. When some of his short stories and articles were published, her delight had been even greater than his.

Jeannie and Colin's combined solidly comfortable stoutness took up most of the old sofa, leaving Helen's much smaller body dwarfed and happily ensconced in its cosy corner. The years had been kind to Helen. Although now sixty years old, her small body was still as attractively petite as it had been thirty years ago. Despite now being grey, her hair was still thick and naturally curly.

Ian paused in his narrative, paused to gulp more whisky and plaintively complain, "All this talking is very dry work."

Helen smiled at Ron, "Are you falling asleep there?... You're not saying much."

With a start Ron opened his eyes wide, he smiled, "Gee, no, I'm not sleeping, I'm just resting my eyes! I really do enjoy listening to Ian recounting today's sporting adventures – and he has not exaggerated any of the events either."

Ron now turned to Colin, "It's sure great for me to listen to Ian and you. Both of you know this land so well. It must be wonderful to know the rivers, the lochs, the moors and the hills in the intimate way you so obviously do. Perhaps only the likes of you can ever really know and truly love this fantastic land."

"Aye, perhaps that's true. Certainly we've known this land from our infancy and we have been learning about it ever since. And even yet, in our experienced age, we are still learning about it. Every now and again we experience something new and unexpected which reminds us that even we don't ken it all."

"Yes, that's true, even auld craiturs – auld bodachs – like us are never too old to learn," Ian agreed. "I suppose we are part of this ancient land and it's a part of us. I know that often at the end of a long, hard and wet day's stalking I do truly feel like a part of this landscape; my wearily aching rheumaticky old bones feel almost as old as the drearily soaking hills and the cold grey rocks."

"I ken exactly what you mean, Ian," Colin said. "Often I've also been tired of, and have cursed, this wild land and its savage weather."

"Och, yet despite all that there's no other place either of you would want to live, is there?" Helen asked.

"Oh, I know… I know. This is our own, our native land," Ian said. "I suppose love of it is bred in our blood and bones."

"Aye, and in return it breeds aching rheumatics in our bloody bones!" Colin thunderously laughed.

"I suppose all of us here have a sort of love/hate relationship with this land?" Helen pondered. Her roots were not here in Aldrory. She was a native of Aboyne in the North East of Scotland. That pleasant small town had been her home until she moved to Aberdeen during the war to train as a nurse. After the war she spent a few years nursing in Africa then had returned to Scotland to become a district nurse at Inveraldrory. A few years later she married Ian and since then had lived with him at his croft at Altdour. Although not a native, Helen loved this district as deeply as any actual native.

"A love/hate relationship? Aye, that's true, Helen," Colin said.

"Only, it's much more a love relationship than a hate relationship!" Helen passionately declared.

"Aye, that's right enough"… "Aye, that's true!" Colin and the others heartily agreed.

"That's our ancient, our anc… ancestral Highland blood speaking; it's proudly proclaiming our love of this, our own, our true ancestral land!" Ron loudly declared with both hands wildly gesticulating to emphasise, to encourage, his whisky slurred words.

"You've got true native Highland blood in you, haven't you, Ron?" asked Jeannie.

"Aye, I sure have!" he proudly and excitedly exclaimed. "My great, great, gran'parents came from here, from Aldrory. They were forced to emigrate to Canada in the nineteenth ch – century during the Sh – Sutherland Clearances. So my ancestral roots are truly here. That's why I love coming back here every year. It's like coming back home! I love this place!" He paused for another sip of whisky then animatedly continued. "I love coming back to meet you all again; all my good, true friends. My true auld, auld, friends." His arms again wildly swept out to include them all within friendship's warm embrace.

"Och, there's no need to emphasis the 'auld' of you auld friends so much," laughed Ian.

"Och, gee, it sure is great for me to be made so welcome here with you all in this hosh – hospitable wee housie, this cosy wee but an'ben." With deep emotion Ron benevolently beamed all around.

Everyone glowed with sincere emotion. Every whisky-flushed face genially beamed mutual friendship.

Ian quietly smiled to himself. He was amused at how, under the influence of the malt whisky, Ron's vocabulary was becoming sprinkled with Scots words. Even his American accent was acquiring traces of a Scottish inflexion. "Oh Ron," he said, "If you do buy this estate and live here as laird you'll soon really get to know this land, especially with Colin and I to instruct you. You'll soon become one of us, one of the true natives!"

"Would you really fancy buying this estate, Ron, in the unlikely event of it coming up for sale?" Colin asked, thinking that if he could afford to buy and run this sporting estate then it certainly put him in the multi-millionaire bracket. He understood from Ian that Ron did belong to that wealthy strata of society. In that case, then really it was amazing how friendly and completely unpretentious he was, so perfectly relaxed, so perfectly at home drinking with them, all equals, in this humble crofthouse.

How different he was from the really wealthy British gentry like Colin's employers, Lord and Lady Kilvert. Although Colin had worked for them as a gamekeeper for twenty-five years and he got on well with them, finding them good employers, and they in turn genuinely liked Colin, still there was always a barrier, invisible but real, between them – the British class system. That deeply dividing system came between employer and employee, between gentry and commoner. While they were all companionably friendly together when sharing the often strenuously demanding pleasures of deer stalking, when sharing the often midge-tormented pleasures of salmon fishing, still, even if at those times it was for a while apparently forgotten, it was never quite forgotten – the consciousness of class differences was always there on both sides of the great divide.

How different it was here with Ron, who, true to his democratic American ideals, had no class-consciousness. How natural, how relaxed, they all were in this friendly small room. No one felt under any constraint; no one was in the least conscious of any barriers of wealth or class dividing them.

Colin smiled as he remembered another – a very different social occasion of a good number of years back.

Lord and Lady Kilvert, having returned from an around the world business plus pleasure trip, had graciously invited the gamekeepers and a number of other estate employees, with their wives, to view the cine-camera films they had made of that trip.

Promptly at the arranged time on the appointed evening they had all, with some trepidation, presented themselves at the large and impressive front door of Glen Ardgie Lodge. There had been some animated debate as to which door they should use. They were all accustomed to entering the lodge by the kitchen or the gunroom, however Colin insisted that, "On this special occasion we are invited guests, so we are expected to use the front door." The wives wholeheartedly agreed with him. To enter by the kitchen would most definitely be demeaning. It would sadly dim the glory of this unique social event.

John Williams, the stout and stately butler, greeted them. He held the door open and ushered the party in. Formally attired in his butler's immaculate uniform of grey striped trousers, black jacket and stiff white shirt, Colin thought he looked like a freshly laundered penguin. In the handsome front hall he politely disembarrassed them of their hats and coats. His experienced eyes rapidly appraised the party. Carefully arrayed in their best Sabbath finery, their hair recently permed, he thought the wives were really quite presentable. But the men were obviously very uncomfortably ill at ease in their sombrely dark best suits – suits which they normally only wore at funerals. With nervous agitation they ran thick fingers around inside too tight collars and straightened up unaccustomed ties. Delicately the butler's nostrils sniffed. Almost superciliously they quivered as they detected the faint, but definite, unpleasant and unmistakable camphor smell of mothballs. Crossing the hall he knocked at a door, opened it wide, and with impressive dignity, and in a deep, sepulchral voice announced, "Your guests have arrived, my Lord."

Lord and Lady Kilvert rose, came forward, and warmly welcomed them into the large, bright and comfortable lounge.

As he turned and closed the door the butler surreptitiously gave Colin a wink and a grin. He whispered, "I see you're moving in high society now!" Over the years they had shared many a fine dram together. Colin only dared reply with a quick, cautious wink.

Lady Kilvert soon got the ladies comfortably settled while Lord Kilvert busied himself pouring out drinks that the butler took round on a silver tray. Each lady received a glass of sherry; each man received a dram. Slowly and abstemiously they sipped their drinks. Apart from being polite this was wise, for once the glasses were empty, no offer came from their host to refill them. Likewise, when cigarettes, in a silver box, were handed around, they were passed around only the once.

The curtains were drawn and the cine-show began. Some of the films were very interesting: films of trout fishing in Argentina, Brazil and New Zealand and big game fishing in the Indian Ocean. The audience dutifully maintained an air of great interest even during the less engrossing films. At the end of the show they politely expressed keen appreciation.

The butler reappeared, wheeling in a laden trolley. The ladies delicately sipped from dainty teacups and, carefully avoiding dropping any crumbs, genteelly nibbled at stylishly thin sandwiches and delicious, but tiny, cakes. There was nothing in the least graceful about the men as they valiantly endeavoured to eat and drink. They precariously balanced a valuable plate on one broad knee and an elegant cup and saucer on the other. The delicate teacups were dwarfed in their large, rough, hands. They appeared to be awkwardly playing with a child's toy tea set. Before starting out each man had been told by his wife to be on his best behaviour; had been warned to say or do nothing to give her a showing up before 'the gentry' and all the others. Despite these severe warnings and their best efforts, many crumbs and larger pieces of cake were dropped on the luxurious carpet. Each time this happened the clumsy man responsible received an angry glare from his affronted wife.

As the guests rose to take their leave the butler gathered up cups and plates and placed them on the trolley. He gave annoyed frowns at the large male feet, which blithely unaware trod crumbs and chocolate cake into the carpet. Lady Kilver also noticed her favourite carpet being desecrated, but she hid her feelings better; she merely unobtrusively exchanged a sympathetic glance with her butler.

Colin gave a few words of thanks on behalf of the entire party. He said they had all thoroughly enjoyed the evening – he even sounded convincing!

Yes, that had been a truly memorable evening. Not one they would want to repeat too often though. It had been much too politely formal, and awkwardly constrained for the men to get any real pleasure from it. At least their wives had really enjoyed it, or so they – not entirely convincingly – assured on another afterwards.

In answer to Colin's question, Ron said, "Oh yeah, I sure do fancy buying this esh – estate. It would be great being laird here. Aye, and I'd be a darned good laird, too, so I would!" He declared this almost belligerently, as if daring someone to contradict him.

"All right!… All right! We believe you. We all believe you would be a great laird," Ian laughed.

"Yeah, I will be a really great laird. I'll be a much better laird than the present laird, anyway."

"Aye, well it would be damned difficult to be a worse laird than the present bastard!"

"Yeah, but you know, Ian, I might have to get tough with a terrible old bugger of a poacher like you, though," Ron grinned.

"Och," Helen quietly said, "between the two of us, Ron, we'd keep him under control. We'd make him lead a nice respectable life in his old age."

"Heaven's forbid!" cried Ian. "To be dully respectable and drearily good would be no life for me… I'd rather be dead! In fact that would be death – a slow, weary, dismal death."

"Wouldn't you like to grow old gracefully, Ian?" grinned Jeannie.

"No, I wouldn't. I would much rather grow old disgracefully!"

"No, I could never imagine you becoming dully respectful, Ian, and I hope I never get like that myself either," Colin said. "In fact I'll propose a toast to us… to us all, staying just as we are… perfect, chust perfect!"

32

Ian struggled to his feet, stood erect with head held high, with grey beard defiantly jutting, and said, "Aye, here's a toast to us all and to personal liberty, to individuality, to freedom to poach." He beamed at Ron and Colin, "Aye, and tae hell with bloody lairds and their damned gamekeepers!" With solemn dignity he recited lines from The Jolly Beggars:'

"A fig for those by law protected!
Liberty's a glorious feast!
Courts for cowards were erected,
Churches built to please the priest."

"Gee, those are great lines," Ron enthusiastically cried.

"Have you read much of Burns?" Jeannie asked.

"No, I'm sorry… I'm ass-ashamed… to admit I've not. There are so many books I've been meaning to read for years, but I never get the time. I'm always too darned busy working all the time."

"Aye, we know. You're far too busy making a living, a very affluent living, to have time to live – to really live," Ian said, with a smile.

"Yeah, that's true, Ian, that's only too true. It's only when I'm over here with you all that I really live!" Ron passionately exclaimed.

To relieve Ron's sudden seriousness, Helen smiled, "Anyway, don't encourage Ian or he'll recite Burns all night."

"Aye, and given any encouragement, Colin will sing Rabbie's songs all night, too," Jeannie said.

Engrossed in all the eager talk, the joyous laughter and no less joyous drinking, Ian had neglected the fire. He had allowed it to fade to a dull, grey smouldering heap of peat and wood ash.

"We could do with some more wood on the fire, Ian, it's nearly out," Helen said. "It's getting cooler, now, isn't it?"

"Aye, it's a bit colder right enough," agreed Jeannie.

All three men disagreed. They were warm enough.

"Oh, it's all right for you men, you're centrally heated with all the whisky you've taken," Helen said. Wisely, Jeannie and she had only taken a moderate amount of whisky and had supplemented it with a few mugs of coffee. "Go on, Ian, put some wood on the fire."

"Oh, all right… all right."

With reluctance he heaved himself out of his armchair's deep comfort and gathered an armful of firewood from the large wicker basket in the corner. Passing in front of the sofa where Jeannie, Helen and Colin were companionably ensconced, Ian bent to attend to the fire. He raked out some of the dead ashes and gathered together the few remaining glowing embers. Completely engrossed in this task he stooped even further. The more he stooped the higher the pleats of his kilt rode up the back of his thighs.

"Oh, Ian, watch what you're doing. You're almost exposing yourself!" Helen warned in a loud, serious voice, but with her eyes brightly, merrily twinkling.

"Well, it was you who wanted the fire seen to, wasn't it?" he replied, with a touch of annoyance. He hurriedly threw wood on the fire, straightened up, and spun round with his kilt's whirling pleats fanning out a cloud of smoke from the fire. In mock alarm, he cried out, "Oh, Jeannie, I hope you didn't see my war wound!"

"Och no, don't worry, Ian, I didn't see it. I tried my best, but I couldn't quite see that famous war wound of yours!" Jeannie's face beamed, her body shook with mirth.

Once the laughter had somewhat subsided, Ron asked, "Do you really have a war wound, Ian?"

It was Jeannie who answered, "Oh aye, Ian and Colin still carry the scars of their old war wounds, right enough."

"Oh, really? I didn't know that."

"Aye, we both proudly carry our honourable old scars of battle," Colin laughingly confirmed. "We both received minor wounds in Italy. But trust Ian to be different. Trust him to get wounded on his backside!"

When the renewed laughter died down, Ian indignantly exclaimed, "Och, it was all right for you, Colin, you auld bugger, with your slight wound in your shoulder. You had a fine time going around with your arm in a sling, with all the lovely Italian signorinas worshipping you as a brave, wounded war hero. They nearly overwhelmed you with their sympathy and their most generous and voluptuous favours. But when they, or everyone else, discovered where I was wounded I got no sympathy. I only got laughed at and ridiculed for having two wee bits of shrapnel embedded in my left buttock."

"Gee, that sure was tough luck, Ian. But surely you would have had some fun when the beautiful young nurses were dressing your embarrassing wound?" Ron suggested.

"Beautiful young nurses?... What beautiful young nurses? My wound was dressed by rough, tough, male army medical orderlies."

"Aye, that's right. And those medical orderlies really were a pretty rough lot, weren't they?" Colin said.

"Aye they were. Some of them were more like bloody butchers from a knacker's yard than male nurses! But there were a few exceptions. Remember yon wee corporal?... I forget his name. He was soft and gentle, in fact he was quite effeminate."

"Oh yes, that's true... I can't remember his name either. He really was a bit soft, wasn't he?"

"Aye, he was very soft. I was thankful I was in a ward with ten other soldiers, there was safety in numbers. I would not have been happy having him dressing my backside if I'd been in a small ward on my own," Ian laughed.

Colin laughed, too, "Aye, I suppose he was a wee bit queer, wasn't he?"

"A wee bit queer? He was very queer! He was as queer as a three pound note!"

Once more hearty laughter cascaded around the room. All were happy. None were aware of passing time until Jeannie suddenly noticed the clock and exclaimed, "Goodness, look at the time! Come on, Colin, we better be getting home and into bed." Smiling, she loudly and playfully slapped her hand on Colin's bare knee.

"Unhand me, Wifie! Don't be in such a shameless hurry to get me into bed with you," roared Colin with his ruddy face beaming and his laughter again thunderously reverberating.

"Och, what a fool I saddled myself wi' when I married you," Jeannie laughed in reply with tears of merriment glittering her quivering rosy cheeks. "Och, come on home, you great muckle fool." Mischievously, she started sliding her hand upwards from Colin's knee.

As he clamped his large hand restrainingly over hers, he laughed, "That's enough... so far and no further."

Together they struggled to their feet and Colin said, "Och, I suppose I better take her home before she gets completely out of hand. I think the whisky has made her frisky!"

Ian laughed, "You know what we used to say in the army, 'Whisky makes you frisky!... brandy makes you randy!'"

With a gleeful grin Colin asked, "Well, in that case, do you have a big glass of brandy for me, Ian?"

Jeannie chuckled, "Och, you should manage to rise to the occasion without the help of brandy... you usually do. There's life in the old dog yet!"

Colin complacently beamed then disparagingly shook his head. "Och, be quiet, wifie, you're embarrassing Ron."

Ron grinned, "Oh no you're not. I'm not embarrassed. Once again I'm pleasantly surprised, that's all. You are so different from what I had been told that most Highlanders were like. Many years ago I heard that you were supposed to be a rather straight-laced and narrowly Calvinistic lot. But I've discovered for myself that not many of you are like that."

Ian laughed, "None of us here are straight-laced and certainly none of us are narrowly Calvinistic. We are not like the 'Wee Frees' – thank God!"

Jeannie and Colin resisted Helen's efforts to persuade them to stay longer. Colin beamed, "Och, it's all right for you idle parasites, you can sleep late in the morning. I've to get up early for my work. I expect I'll be out stalking again tomorrow."

After a few abortive attempts, Ron finally managed to extricate himself from his armchair's seductive depths. Staggering, he only just saved himself from collapsing back into the chair. "Gee I su-suppose I'd better get back to my hotel as well. Is it late? What time is it anyway?"

Ian laughed, "It's still early. It's only just after half past midnight."

"Gee, that's too early... I'll stay on a while, just a wee while longer. That's if it's OK with you Helen, my bonnie wee Helen," Ron said as he draped his arm companionably over her shoulder.

"Of course you're welcome to stay on, Ron. Anyway, I don't think you're in a fit state to drive."

"No, you're certainly not fit to drive," Colin grinned. "I'll give you a lift back to your hotel now if you like."

Although Colin and Ian had drunk at least three times as much whisky as Ron, they, astonishingly (astonishing that is, to anyone who did not know them), seemed almost completely sober, while Ron was certainly far from sober.

"No, och, it's too early yet. I'll stay here awhile yet."

"How will you get back to your hotel, then?" Jeannie asked.

"Och, I think he'd better stay here tonight," Helen suggested. "He can have the spare bedroom, it's always ready for any welcome visitors."

"An – and do I fit into that category… a welcome visitor?" grinned Ron.

"Och, of course you do, Ron, you know that by now surely."

"Aye, you're a welcome visitor. And you'll always be a most welcome visitor as long as you arrive laden with malt whisky," Ian laughed. He then turned to Colin, "Perhaps you better call in at the hotel on your way home and let them know that Ron won't be coming back tonight."

"Aye, I'll do that. I'll call in and let 'Blue Assed Angus' know."

"You'll let who know?" Ron asked.

"'Blue Assed Angus', the old head porter, surely you know him?"

"Yeah, I know the old porter all right. He's sure quite a character, isn't he? But the hotel guests call him, 'Anxious Angus'."

"Aye, that's right. That's what the posh, polite hotel guests – like you – call him. But to the locals he's knows as 'Blue Assed Angus'," Colin explained.

"Oh, really? Is he? Why? What's the story behind that quaint nickname?"

"Well, you know what he's like don't you? He's always anxiously running about, almost in a panic, attending to the hotel guests ceaseless and endlessly varied requests, isn't he?"

"Sure, that's right, Colin, that's why the regular guests affectionately know him as 'Anxious Angus'. I like him, I've always found him most friendly and helpful."

"Aye, that's right. He's a fine old man who's well liked locally. It's when he's off duty and having a few drams that he complains about the exacting posh guests and how they constantly keep him running around, keep him frantically buzzing about like a 'Blue Assed Fly'."

"Aye, he worked in the united States for twenty years, hence that American expression," Ian further explained.

"Oh, really? Well Colin, ch-chust you tell 'Anxious Angus' – or rather 'Blue Assed Angus', not to be anxious about me. Tell him I'll come back to the hotel sometime tomorrow," Ron cheerily requested.

With their two dogs again eagerly leading the way, Helen and Ian strolled through the front garden to open the gate for Colin's van. Swaying unsteadily, Ron used up the full width of the track as he happily accompanied them.

After having bid Jeannie and Colin a cheery farewell, Ian closed and fastened the gate, then Helen and he leaned companionably on it in relaxed ease. Ron was happy to cling to the security of the gate's firm support.

After the lights and noise of the van had vanished, had been replaced by the slumbering glen's dark stillness, they continued lingering at the gate. They allowed the calm of the night's mild darkness to silently and solemnly engulf them. There was no whisper of wind to disturb the shadowy trees around them. The pale light glowing along the Northern horizon was not bright enough to dim the myriad stars glittering throughout the crowded vastness of the sky.

Gently, reverently, Helen whispered, "It really is a lovely night."

"Aye, it certainly is," Ian quietly agreed.

Helen gave a contented sigh and snuggled up to him as he slipped his arm around her waist. Silently they continued gazing at the countless stars. How coldly remote these stars seemed, so self-sufficient, so indifferent to these staring humans.

The silence was broken by Ron asking, "What's that strange glowing light along that horizon?" He raised both hands and waved towards the North, then quickly grabbed the gate's reassuring support.

"That's the Northern Lights. The Aurora Borealis," Ian said.

"'The Fairy Dancers', you mean – that's our name for them in Aberdeenshire, and it's a much better, a much more romantic name, than that scientific name of yours, Ian," Helen declared.

"Yes, I agree, yours is a more descriptive name, especially when there's a real vividly flaring luminescent display. What you're seeing tonight, Ron, is nothing. Often we've seen the entire Northern sky ablaze with fantastic displays, see it all lit up as if by hundreds of multi-coloured searchlights."

"Gee, that sure must be quite some sight."

"Well, you'll see it for yourself, Ron, once you're living here," Helen promised.

Once more silence enveloped them.

This silence was again ended by Ron. In a subdued voice – a voice touched with awe – he murmured, "Gosh, it really is fantastic here under all those remote and mysterious stars. It sure is great to have ample leisure to quietly stare at the vastness of this night sky… to be strangely moved by unfamiliar feelings of… of contemplative wonder."

Helen and Ian nodded in silent agreement. Then, unable to resist the opportunity for an appropriate quotation, Ian recited:

"What is this life if, full of care,
We have no time to stand and stare?"

Ron laughed, "Trust you to have a suitable quotation ready to hand, Ian."

Helen chuckled, "Aye, if you ever want a quote come to Ian MacLean – he has a quotation for every occasion."

Ian smiled, "I remembered when, as a youth, I first quoted these lines to my grandfather. That wise old man was silent for some moments, then came out with a true Highland thought; with a gentle chuckle he asked, "Och, lad, why *stand* and stare when you can *sit* and stare?"

Their laughter faded, was drowned in the night's profound silence.

For Ron, happy in his not quite sober state, his confused body seemed to follow his confused mind as it swept and soared through the starry sky's infinite space. With desperate effort he tried to reason his vague, soaring feelings into calm, logical thoughts. It was impossible. He gave up the useless effort and allowed his ethereal body to wander freely wherever it desired. Another part of that body firmly held on to the solid reality of the wooden gate.

As Ian gazed at the incredible vastness of the firmament's hushed space, at individual star's glittering brightness, at the combined starlight's incandescent splendour, he too was touched with awe. He too felt himself swept away; he felt himself an integral part of all this mysterious splendour.

Like Ron, he tried to rationalise his confused feelings into logical thoughts. He wryly smiled as he mused, "To think of us infinitesimally petty humans as being a significant part of this immense universe is surely only to once again confirm our ridiculous, our boundless conceit." Struggling with his elusive thoughts, Ian suddenly felt that, after all, perhaps there was something not entirely ignoble in the vastness of human conceit when it could send the unfettered human imagination effortlessly soaring through that starry vastness to visualise fantastic new universes far beyond this one. Again he smiled, "Yes, there is truly something indomitable in the vastness of human conceit."

As she leant by Ian's side, Helen was also wondrously entranced by the universe's timeless mysteries. Motionlessly she stared in awe at the silent flowing, the luminous glowing immensity of the Milky Way. She was moved to the utmost depths of her soul. Her lips were slightly parted as if they whispered secret prayers. She felt in touch with vague, unknown, but immensely potent universal forces. Guided by her sensitive intuitive gifts she sensed the trembling touch of profound, ancient mysteries. With instinctive feminine wisdom she did not attempt to rationalise these feelings. She left it to foolish males to unwisely try to dissect and painstakingly analyse. With wonder, with awe, she accepted every emotional marvel her inexplicable powers brought her.

She turned her head and gazed into Ian's eyes. Her own eyes brightly glittered with reflected starlight. She murmured, "Isn't it fantastic how, in spirit, we petty humans can reach out through vast space and venture far beyond the remotest of these stars to create fresh new universes of the imagination? Surely there is something truly glorious in the indomitable human spirit?"

Ian nodded in silent agreement. With no surprise he accepted the fact that Helen had once again read his thoughts. Or had the same thoughts risen in both minds at the same time? There was no doubt that a strange affinity linked them.

Suddenly, savagely, shockingly, the screech of an unseen owl ripped the silence apart.

That screech stabbed a stiletto of fear into each human heart. All gave startled jumps. All exchanged foolish, shamefaced grins. Somewhere in the dark distance a tawny owl unwound its more lingering, more eerily quavering solemn sepulchral call in response to that other owl.

Silence again descended. The humans once sensed, rather than actually saw, the stealthy feathery presence of an owl as it silently ghosted between dim, shadowy trees.

As they waited – heron silent, heron still – these tense humans became acutely conscious of tiny rustlings and scamperings and muffled murmurings. These secretive sounds were the anxious thudding heart of the night's dark silence.

That living silence was again violently torn apart... not by the owl's fearful scarlet screech, but by the high-pitched squeals of a terrified mouse. Those agonised squeals rose high as the owl's powerful talons squeezed life out of the small mammal.

These sounds, symbolising the ceaseless, the ruthless, conflict between predator and prey, brought the humans back to normality, back to everyday life, back to everyday death.

Helen shivered, "It's getting cold, isn't it? Let's go back home."

As always, the cosy small sitting room warmly welcomed them.

"I'll make some coffee and sandwiches," Helen said.

"You better make it strong black coffee for Ron," Ian laughed.

As he slumped deeply into the old armchair and sprawled in undignified ease, Ron indignantly declared, "I don't need black coffee, Helen, I'm as sober as 'Himself' – well almost!"

A few minutes later his head slumped to his chest. He was soundly and snoringly asleep.

After an hour they woke Ron from his deep sleep. He seemed pleasantly refreshed. He eagerly accepted the mug of strong black coffee and the toasted sandwiches filled with succulently crispy bacon.

After some minutes of hearty munching he remarked, "Gee, Ian, you're real fortunate having a wife like Helen, she's a real wee gem."

"Aye, Ron, that's what I keep telling him," Helen laughed. "He does not appreciate what a real treasure I am!"

Before Ian could respond, Ron, with solemn seriousness said, "Oh, how I wish I had a wife like you, Helen, then maybe my marriage would have been successful."

Attempting to make light of this, Helen smiled, "I suppose you'll be telling us that your wife does not understand you?"

Ron, however, took her seriously. He leant forward and, getting more solemnly confidential, gravely declared, "That's the truth. Yeah, that's the truth. My wife, Cynthia, she does not understand me. She doesn't understand me at all."

Helen and Ian felt slightly embarrassed at Ron saying things he wouldn't say when he was completely sober. Ian, in turn, tried to lighten the solemnity, he smiled, "And do you understand yourself, Ron?"

"Sure I understand myself. At least I know myself much better than she does." Then, with a wan smile, he added, "At least I think I do!... Yeah, I do know myself. I do know what I want out of life: but if I'll ever get it, well that's another matter altogether."

Ian and Helen gave Ron understanding sympathetic glances; they remembered the one and only time his wife had come here on holiday with him.

Chapter Three

It was six years ago that Cynthia had come with Ron on her memorable Highland sporting holiday. It had not been a successful vacation for either of them.

Against her better judgement she had allowed Ron to persuade her to forego her usual yachting holiday in the Caribbean sunshine and to accompany him on his Scottish holiday. She had read several articles in glossy magazines explaining how, since the time of Queen Victoria, the British Royalty and British gentry had gone shooting and fishing in the Scottish Highlands. With considerable surprise she read that they returned year after year and seemed to really enjoy – even love – their sporting holidays in that wild and often wet country. She had finally been persuaded to go with Ron after hearing that some of her wealthy friends were going to the Scottish Highlands. These friends stridently boasted that for two weeks they were renting a large flat in a centuries old Scottish castle (complete with ghost) and they were to be guests of the titled laird when salmon fishing on the River Spey, grouse shooting on his moors and dear stalking on his hills.

The start of Cynthia and Ron's holiday was a disaster. Their plane was two hours late arriving at Glasgow Airport and then their hired car broke down on the outskirts of that dreary city. It had taken over an hour before their replacement car arrived. Eventually, exhausted, and Cynthia with a thumping headache, they reached Aldrory. Torrential rain poured and dark clouds swept with dreary monotony over the dismal dull landscape.

Cynthia's deeply depressed mood was further depressed. She mourned with the mourning rain. Why, oh why, had she so foolishly given up her Caribbean sunshine for this?

At least they received a warm welcome at Inveraldrory Hotel. After giving a few comprehensive, critical glances around the hotel, Cynthia noted with satisfaction that it appeared to be comfortably luxurious – as it should be at the prices they (or rather Ron) were paying.

After taking some aspirins and enjoying a lengthy, relaxing soak in a steaming bath Cynthia felt much better… felt almost human again. Once she got into her expensive new evening dress of figure hugging black chiffon (it was a present from Ron in appreciation of her sacrifice in foregoing her Caribbean holiday) she felt increasingly better. Her recovery continued when she fastened a string of expensive pearls (Ron's wedding present to her) around her still reasonably slender and smooth neck. She noted with complacent pride how well the black of her fashionable dress showed the pearls to advantage. Once the matching pair of pearl earrings were securely fastened, they too contributed to her recovery. There was something unfailingly wonderful about the reassuring feel of these expensive pearls.

Sitting at the dressing table she gave her smooth flowing dark hair a final gentle brush, then completed applying her make-up. With self-confidence fully renewed, she now felt fit enough to face meeting Ron's fishing friends who were staying at the hotel. As this would be her first meeting with them, naturally she wanted to feel and look her best. With quiet self-indulgence she admired herself in the mirror. She was pleased with what she saw; well groomed and well made up she did not look her age. Her figure in that clinging black dress was still reasonably slim, was still attractive to men. She smiled and gave a gentle sigh. Only she knew just how much time and effort it took to achieve this pleasant result, how much strict diet and vigorous exercise it took for her to, if not entirely halt, at least keep at bay the insidious advance of middle-age.

Satisfied, she rose, turned, and bestowed a bright smile on patiently waiting Ron. Silently, expectantly, she awaited his approval.

Delighted to see her in much better mood and genuinely attracted to her beauty, Ron unstintingly lavished praise on her. But when he attempted to embrace and kiss her she hastily drew back, exclaiming, "Oh, don't, Ron, you'll mess up my hair and make-up."

He limited himself to merely taking her hand. Eagerly he led her downstairs to dinner.

Cynthia immediately felt at home in the large, comfortable and warm dining room. She mellowed further as attentive waitresses hovered and an obsequious headwaiter led her to a table by one of the many large windows at the far side of the room. The waiter pulled out a chair for her and smiled apologetically, "I'm afraid there's not much of a view this evening, madam."

As Cynthia peered through the film of rainwater cascading down the windowpanes, she could just make out a vague, distorted view of land, sea and sky. In the rapidly descending dusk, the sea, the oppressive low clouds and the land were all varying shades of grey. The only spot of brightness in this dismal scene were the vivid orange colours of the Inveraldrory lifeboat shivering at its moorings in the centre of the sheltered bay.

Cynthia gave a slight shudder. She turned from the window, sat in the offered chair, eagerly lifted the leather bound menu and revelled in its promised pleasures. Smiling, she decided to self-indulgently treat herself. Surely after all today's miseries, she was entitled to console herself with a really good dinner and for this once to hell with her diet.

Ron repressed a sigh as he stared out of the window. How much more pleasant it would be for Cynthia if evening sunshine had been bringing that scene glowingly and glitteringly alive. He remembered admiring many glorious sunsets over that now dismally dull bay. He remembered watching dark otters playfully disporting and grey seals solemnly staring only a little distance out from this dining room.

Soon the excellent food and wine completed Cynthia's rehabilitation. By the time they had finished their leisurely meal she felt fully relaxed.

Ron now led her into the cosily crowded smoking room and introduced her to his friends who were companionably gathered there. Like Ron, those friends were all keen salmon fishers who returned year after year to the River Aldrory. Like him, they never tired of fishing that river which was one of the wildest and most challenging rivers in all Scotland. After being further mollified by a velvety smooth 'Drambuie' liqueur, Cynthia looked around this room with interest. She liked the quaint old world charm of its comfortable settees and deep armchairs all covered, she noted, in rather shabby and faded floral chintzes. On a small table beside her armchair there was a large blue and white bowl of pot pourri. Its pleasantly subtle scent unsuccessfully tried to disguise the strong aroma of many after dinner cigars. She liked the nineteenth century sporting prints decorating the dark oak panelling. She was not so keen on the large old plaster-of-Paris salmon interred in a glass coffin above the fireplace. Its glassy eye seemed to stare down at the carefree revellers in this room with icy Calvinistic disapproval.

With pleasure, Ron saw that Cynthia was leisurely drinking, smoking and brightly holding her own with these new friends. Every time he glanced over at her from where he stood talking, one of a small group of men, she appeared to be entirely engrossed in gaily chatting to those new female friends. Little did he guess at the intensity with which, as she pleasantly chatted, she was keenly scrutinising these ladies.

While in the dining room she had noticed with considerable surprise how plainly most of the ladies there seemed to be dressed. Now, seeing them at close quarters, that impression was confirmed. Most were quietly dressed in tweed skirts and plain jumpers and wore little, or no, jewellery. Some of the older ladies were not just 'quietly' dressed, but were dowdily dressed. "Yes," Cynthia thought, "there was really no other word to describe them – they were most unattractively dowdy."

The frocks which some of them wore were by no means new and were of styles which Cynthia thought decidedly unfashionable and would not dream of wearing herself. Later, she was amazed to be informed that two of the most dowdy of these ladies were actually very wealthy and titled aristocratic English ladies.

As she continued to study them, Cynthia could not fail to notice, and be impressed by, the self-assured ease with which these women wore their comfortable old clothes. She was well aware that she herself was also being keenly scrutinised. Every woman in that room was taking in the details of her fashionable frock and expensive pearls, all were shrewdly guessing their value. All were trying to guess her age. They noted, many with envy, how that black frock showed her still fairly slim figure to advantage. The more charitable ladies – the younger ones who still retained trim figures – guessed her to be about forty years old. The more uncharitable ones those who had long since lost their neat figures – guessed her to be well on the wrong side of forty-five years. The two plumpish, late middle-aged, aristocratic English ladies thought her to be in her fifties. Secretly they scathingly condemned her as being a typical, grossly pretentious example of the all too numerous, nouveau riche.

With an intuitive flash of insight, Cynthia realised that in the eyes of all those women, it was she – not they – who revealed poor dress sense. She was too grossly overdressed in that fashionable expensive black dress, which too ostentatiously displayed her string of large pearls, to fit properly into the quietly unpretentious luxury of this Highland hotel. She realised that she was meeting with an unusual class of people such as she had never encountered before – the uniquely British (mostly English) extremely keen type of wealthy, fishing and shooting sportsmen and sportswoman.

The hours passed quite pleasantly. The numbers in that smoking room gradually dwindled until there was merely a handful all comfortably seated around one table beside the fireplace where a few birch logs cheerily glowed. The women had passed the stage of being formally polite to one another. Cynthia now felt them to be genuinely friendly. The husbands too were friendly; they found her very attractive. One husband was inclined to be just too friendly until he noticed, and was warned off by, his spouse's icily disapproving glare.

Cynthia had been astounded to learn that these people, the women as well as the men, had been out most of the day in the pouring rain 'enjoying' their salmon fishing. She wondered at how tough and determined – and foolish? – they must be to continue fishing despite the atrocious weather. Apart from being most unpleasant she would have thought it rather boring, just as she found their interminable talk about fishing very boring. Smiling grimly to herself, she thought, "Gee, I sure am a fish out of water here!"

Whenever Ron noticed her boredom getting rather too obvious he quickly changed the conversation to subjects of more interest to her.

When they returned to their bedroom and started to undress, Cynthia suddenly felt utterly exhausted. Her headache had come back and was adding its thumping misery to her exhaustion. She shuddered as an angry gust of wind battered rain against the windows and shook and rattled them as if furious at being denied admittance.

Petulantly she exclaimed, "I hope you don't expect me to go fishing with you tomorrow if this ghastly rain is pouring like this, do you?"

"No... no, of course not. You can stay in the hotel while I might try an hour's fishing."

"And what am I going to do here by myself, might I ask, while you take the car and go off enjoying yourself?"

With an effort Ron, also quite exhausted now after all that day's travelling and driving, controlled his annoyance and quietly and reasonably replied, "After all this rain the river will almost certainly be too high in flood for any decent fishing tomorrow, so you will not be left by yourself for long." With conciliatory patience he added, "Anyway, we're both tired after our long day, let's get some sleep and we'll see what tomorrow brings. After all it might be blazing sunshine tomorrow."

"Blazing sunshine! Blazing sunshine here? I don't believe it! That's about impossible, isn't it?"

"Yeah, perhaps it is. But you never can tell here. The weather can change amazingly quickly. But let's leave it, for God's sake, and get some sleep."

"Oh yeah, it's all right for you; you can fall asleep at once wherever you are, but I won't get a wink of sleep all night. I'll be kept awake hearing that hideous rain battering against that bloody window all night." A combination of anger, weariness, and increasing self-pity made her voice querulously tremble as she continued, "And then after a dreary sleepless night, you expect me to be happy left in this damn hotel on my own for most of the day while you are enjoying yourself at that bloody river. No doubt you would much rather be with those fancy English friends of your than with me. Or rather, those dowdy friends of yours… my God, I've never seen such dreary clothes! And don't they think they're the cat's whiskers in them too! You might have warned me not to wear a too fashionable and expensive frock. But no, I'm just your wife, you don't care how out of place I look in this damned antiquated moth-eaten hole, full of your dear old tedious fuddy-duddy buddies."

Ron clearly remembered that as he handed over the cheque for Cynthia to buy clothes for her Highland holiday he had tried to advise her not to get anything too obviously fashionable to wear in the comfortably unpretentious hotel. As usual, she had eagerly accepted his cheque but with a frown had summarily disregarded his advice.

By now they had got into their separate beds. Ron was about to reply to his wife's complaints, but instead he sighed, turned away from her, pulled the bedclothes high about his head and composed himself for sleep. After many years of uneasy married life, he had learned that it was more conducive to peace to let his wife have the last word.

Late the following morning, Ron pulled back the bedroom curtains and was delighted to be greeted by sunshine joyfully pouring into the room. In one of those marvellous transformations that make the West Highlands a wonderland of infinite variety, the heavens were swept clear of clouds and entrancing blue sky stretched from horizon to horizon.

For the next five days the sun shone. The sunshine effectively combined with a pleasantly fresh breeze to keep the midges at bay. Under these attractive conditions, Cynthia's spirits rose and she tolerated – it would be stretching the truth to say that she actually enjoyed – sharing the fishing with Ron. She complained about the strenuous efforts required to laboriously clamber about from pool to pool on the steep and rocky banks of the wild River Aldrory. However, she complacently enjoyed posing beside Ron as he held up the magnificent twenty-three pound salmon he caught on his third day fishing. It was his largest salmon ever. He was delighted. Its fresh, firm, streamlined, silvery body shone and glittered in the sunshine. It was a glorious hymn to bountiful nature. It was a glorious hymn to transcendent beauty.

How smugly Cynthia looked forward to showing off these photographs of this salmon to her boastful friends back home.

Ron was pleased, and surprised, at how well those five fishing days had gone. Cynthia kept in a reasonably pleasant mood most of the time. As long as she was well fortified with alcohol she even seemed to quite enjoy the cosy after-dinner chats with the hotel's other fishermen and their 'dowdy' wives. Ron assiduously saw to it that before, during, and after dinner she was generously supplied with drinks.

But then came disaster.

Colin MacDonald informed Ron that a day's deer stalking was available on Lord Kilvert's Ardgie Estate, and knowing how keenly he had enjoyed stalking there in previous years, he was offered it.

With some trepidation, Ron broached the possibility of his taking up this offer with Cynthia. As expected, she was not enthusiastic. However, after lengthy and at times rather heated discussions she finally agreed to go with him. Two things persuaded her to make this venturesome decision. The first was the assurance that she could ride one of the hardy stalking ponies all the way up Glen Ardgie, some seven miles, and all the way back. She would only have to walk after the ponies had been left at the end of the track. If all went well, she might only have two or three miles to walk in search of stags. Cynthia was keen on riding; at home she was a member of an exclusive and expensive riding club. She had brought a pair of jodhpurs with her and quite looked forward to riding up that long glen to the far hills, always providing, of course, that the weather was good.

The second thing that had decided her was the information that they would start out from Lord Kilvert's Glen Ardgie Lodge. The ponies would be waiting for them at that shooting lodge and, knowing his wife, Ron had strongly hinted that there was a good chance of them meeting Lord and Lady Kilvert there before they set out. Cynthia had eagerly swallowed that tempting bait. It would certainly be something extra to boast of to her friends back home; the fact that she had met, and had been a guest of those titled English aristocrats.

When Cynthia and Ron drove up to Ardgie Lodge on the appointed morning, two ponies were awaiting them, one was fitted with a large deer saddle while the other had a neat riding saddle for Cynthia's use. As Colin MacDonald and Ian MacLean greeted them, they noted that Cynthia was suitably dressed in jodhpurs, a woollen jumper and a fawn shower proof jacket, they also noticed that she was wearing a string of expensive pearls and matching earrings. Discreetly, Colin had a whispered word with Ron, advising that these pearls should be left behind. They were hardly suitable for taking on a strenuous day's stalking.

"Yeah, I know, Colin, I know. I've told her that, but to no avail," Ron sighed, "Perhaps you could have a word with her?"

Although he did not fancy that rather delicate task, Colin resolutely squared his shoulders and – metaphorically – girded up his loins before manfully approaching Cynthia. He broached the subject using his best diplomatic skills. Gently he explained the very real danger of her pearls getting lost while she was out on the rough moors and hills with the stalkers. She listened to him silently and stonily until he ended by warning, "It would be only too easy to lose them if we have to crawl through thick heather."

Forcing the semblance of a smile to her lips, she gasped with dismayed disbelief, "Crawl through thick heather! Good heavens, what have I let myself in for?… Or rather, what has my husband let me in for?"

There was no hint of a smile in the accusing glare she stabbed at Ron as, with scarcely concealed annoyance, she agreed to leave her pearls behind. Removing them, she silently handed them over to him. He quickly hid them in the car then securely locked it.

Then, fortunately, Lord and Lady Kilvert appeared. Eagerly, Ron introduced Cynthia to them. Delighted, she switched her smiling charm full on.

For some minutes the four of them cheerfully chatted together. As Cynthia vivaciously joined in the pleasant chatter she again keenly, but unobtrusively scrutinised. She reckoned Lady Kilvert to be about sixty-ish; she had attractive, well cared for pure white hair; she was of middle height with a full figure. Her plump cheeks glowed as friendly and lively smiles animated her mouth. Lord Kilvert looked a number of years older. He too had a fine head of well-groomed white hair. Tall and slim, he held himself erect with unselfconscious elegant dignity. Cynthia was delighted at how perfectly he fitted the picture of how she imagined an English aristocrat of ancient lineage should look.

Cynthia noted that his Lordship's noble dignity was in no way diminished by the old clothes he was wearing – clothes that many an American scarecrow would be ashamed to wear. His faded old tweed jacket was much darned at cuffs and elbows and both knees of his matching plus fours were even more extensively darned. Smiling secretly to herself, she thought, "Gosh, I'm darned if the very darns aren't themselves darned!" With a sudden flash of insight, Cynthia was pleased that she was not wearing her pearls; she now realised just how out of place they would be on this special sporting occasion. She also clearly saw that someone like Lady Kilvert had no need of pearls or of showy fashionable clothes to proclaim her assured place in society. She was always a true lady, no matter how old or dowdy the clothes she wore.

Cynthia was learning.

After wishing them a pleasant and successful day's stalking, Lord and Lady Kilvert left them.

Put in a much better mood by this meeting with these true English gentry, Cynthia cheerily mounted her pony and the stalking party set out. Colin and Ian led the way, while Ron, walking by the side of her pony, kept Cynthia company. The pony-man, leading the second pony, brought up the rear.

After glancing behind to make sure he could not be overheard, Ian, with a broad grin, whispered to Colin, "That was quite a shock to her, telling her about possibly having to crawl through thick heather. It was not one of your best diplomatic efforts, Colin."

"Aye, I ken. I ken that fine. But she left the pearls behind; that's the main thing. I didn't fancy the idea of having to spend day after day searching the moors for her lost pearls, did you?"

"No, I didn't. Why was she so keen to wear them, I wonder?" Ian, much too innocently, asked.

"She hoped to impress Lord and Lady Kilvert with them, I suppose," Colin said with a smile and a shrewd glance.

"Aye, that's exactly what I thought too. But it only shows how little she knows about that class of people, doesn't it?"

"Aye, it does. I feel quite sorry for poor Ron, he deserves a better wife than her. He's so genuinely unpretentious himself."

A quarter of a mile beyond the thick belt of trees that sheltered the shooting lodge, Colin halted, pointed with his stick and grinned. "You'll get your stag today, Ron. Our glossy black friends are telling us that."

They all stopped and stared at the welcome sight of four loudly cawing ravens circling above them. Ron, smiling, explained to Cynthia the old Highland stalking superstition that seeing these birds foretold a successful stalk.

"Yeah, well I sure hope their prediction comes true. I don't see much point in you dragging me all the way up this place if, after all the effort, you don't shoot a damned buck."

Colin and Ian hurriedly strode out again and continued leading the way along the stalking path that led into the heart of that magnificently wild and starkly treeless land.

As Cynthia expertly rode the sturdy placid, sure-footed Highland pony she quite enjoyed the leisurely journey. The mountains rising on either side of the long glen were truly impressive.

A few miles further on, Colin stopped and again pointed, exclaiming, "Eagles!"

They watched two golden eagles rise from the ground a little distance South of the path. With heavy wings they laboriously beat upwards until, having found aerial updraughts, they spiralled higher in effortless lazy circles. As they circled, their keen vision remained steadily focused on the staring humans.

"Oh gee, aren't they magnificent! They are so noble and majestic," Cynthia enthused.

Quickly, eagerly, Ron agreed with her.

Ian and Colin nodded their agreement, "Aye, they truly are impressive birds."

Then they exchanged meaningful glances, both thinking the same thing. Cynthia would not think these eagles so "noble and majestic" if, like them, she had seen these birds with their powerful and greedy curved beaks tearing and pulling at the stinking guts of the decomposing carcase of a sheep or deer. Here, in the North West Highlands, eagles were mostly opportunist scavengers, feeding on carrion. Last week Colin had noticed a group of excited hoodie crows where these eagles had been, and on investigating, had discovered a dead sheep. That was what these eagles were feeding on today. Wisely, he said nothing of this to Cynthia.

For the last hour Colin and Ian had been uneasily aware that the early morning's pallid sunshine was being overwhelmed by tired grey clouds that now wearily rested on the hills and blanketed them in misty sadness. Nothing stirred;

all was gripped in a humid windless hush. As the stalking party climbed higher the mist grew ominously thicker. Cynthia's apprehensive, drooping spirits drooped even further as a soft rain began to fall. Though falling with sluggish silent gentleness that drizzle soaked with determined persistence. Soon the heather was soaking, was mistily bedecked with myriad droplets of moisture. Soon the stalker's plus fours took on their all too familiar heavy wet feel and gave out their distinctive damp, tweedy scent.

At the end of the path the two ponies were left in charge of the pony man and all the others started climbing through the wet heather. Ron stayed close by Cynthia's side and anxiously encouraged her. They were now completely enveloped by the oppressive, steadily drizzling mist. Whenever they stopped in that humid wilderness they were immediately assaulted by swarms of ferocious midges. Seeing Cynthia's distress as she waved a large silk scar about her head, vainly trying to repel the midges, Colin hurriedly set out again through the obscuring mist. With all his years of stalking experience, he knew how nervously alert and restless the deer were in such windless misty conditions. Normally he would have advanced slowly with extra caution, but for Cynthia's sake he walked faster, for only by keeping moving could they obtain some relief from these hellish midges.

Suddenly, inexplicably, for there was not the faintest whisper of a breeze, the mist thinned and gave them a reasonably clear view of their surroundings. Simultaneously, Colin and Ian spotted a group of five stags standing motionless, barely seventy yards from them. As one, they dropped soundlessly into the heather and lay still. Ron immediately followed their example and urgently motioned Cynthia to do the same. Not seeing the stags, not understanding the men's strange behaviour, she continued to stand. With urgent excitement Ron hissed, "Stags!… Get down and lie still or they'll see you."

With great reluctance she inelegantly flopped into the soaking heather beside her husband.

Very cautiously Colin, Ian and Ron raised their heads and searched for the stags; they did not expect them still to be in sight. But they were; amazingly the five stags were still there, all were gazing intently in their direction as if mystified by the sudden disappearance of these humans.

As the stalkers lay silently motionless, masses of midges gleefully descended on them. Valiantly trying to ignore these tiny, maddening insects, Colin urgently whispered to Ian, "Hurry, get the rifle out and Ron can try for a quick shot."

Ian was sliding the loaded rifle out from its canvas cover even before Colin spoke.

Concentrating on the stalking, hoping for a successful hasty shot, Ron, Ian and Colin stoically endured the countless midges which blackened their faces; whined their mocking singing in their ears; cruelly stung sensitive eyelids; got into eyes, nostrils and mouths, and crawled, so many tiny dark specks, all over their hands. Frantically, each female midge stung and with lusty eagerness sucked the blood of their helpless victims.

These midges, these whining menaces, were everywhere. Heather and air vibrated with their evil presence. For a few more agonising moments Cynthia endured their maddening torture then with a gasping, half-strangled scream she jumped to her feet, shouting, "Oh Christ, I can't stand this!… This is bloody hellish!"

For bemused seconds the stags stared at that strange apparition which had so suddenly, so menacingly appeared. Then, as one, they turned and ran. That fast flowing line of agile red bodies trapezed gracefully over patches of soggy bog; their high bounding hooves leapt through soaking heather and cascaded a slipstream of fine white spray. The thickening mist quickly swallowed them.

Ron had just raised the rifle to his shoulder when Cynthia jumped up. With commendable self-control he contained his annoyance. He only gave expression to his frustration and anger in a deep, heartfelt sigh and a wry smile as he apologetically handed the rifle back to Ian. He then stood up beside Cynthia.

Tactfully, Colin and Ian moved away, turned their backs on Ron and Cynthia, lit their pipes and urgently puffed out clouds of midge deterring smoke.

Ron lit two cigarettes and handed one to Cynthia who was frantically waving her silk scarf about her head and desperately using it to wipe midges from her agonised face. Ian and Colin could not help hearing some of the furious words which flowed from her; such phrases as, "This hellish place!… These bloody gnats!… This is bloody madness!"

Ron, puffing furiously at his cigarette, tried to mollify and calm her. After a short time, he shouted to Colin, "Cynthia would like to go back on the pony now and make her own way home while I continue stalking. Will that be all right?"

Colin and Ian walked over and they stood together, all desperately puffing clouds of tobacco smoke, all frantically scratching at their maddeningly itching midge bites. Colin replied, "Yes, of course." He then apologised to Cynthia, "I'm very sorry you've had such a terrible time. These midges certainly are awful just now. Let's hope we get a breeze soon to disperse them." He turned to Ian, "Will you take Mrs MacDonald down to her pony and see her safely start out on the path for home? Then you can wait with the ponyman while Ron and I try to find other stags."

As he guided Cynthia down through the thick and drizzly mist towards the ponies, Ian sympathised with her as she almost apologised for having scared the stags and spoiled Ron's chance of a shot. But then she resolutely declared, "Honestly, I just couldn't stand it a second longer, lying there and being eaten alive by thousands of those bloody gnats. I really don't know how you can stand them. Don't they drive you mad too?"

Ian laughed, "Aye, they are terrible wee brutes, right enough. I find that if I keep lots of whisky flowing in my blood these midge bites don't itch quite as much. That's my excuse – one of my many excuses – for drinking many drams!"

After continuing for a while in silence, Ian asked, "Is this your first experience of deer stalking, Mrs MacDonald?"

"Yeah, this is my first time out deer hunting, and I'm darned sure it's my last time as well!"

Passionately she vowed, "All my future vacations will be in the Caribbean. I would be there now enjoying its glorious sunshine if I hadn't foolishly allowed Ron to persuade me to come with him to his beloved Scotch Highlands. He can come here on his own in future. The only thing Scotch I ever want to see again is the Scotch that comes out of a bottle!"

Ian gave her a sympathetic smile, and thought "Poor Ron, I wouldn't fancy being in his shoes when he faces her wrath this evening."

For what seemed an age to Cynthia, she tottered, stumbled and slithered through the blinding dense mist and the persistent soaking drizzle as they slowly continued their downward journey. Cursing the treacherous thick heather, she gasped, "I'm sure it's got a spite at me... I swear it takes a malicious delight in tripping me up!" Bravely she managed a tortured smile, "God-damn-it, to think that only yesterday I really admired this Scotch heather for being so picturesque."

As she got more exhausted, Cynthia began to despair of ever finding the ponies. Gradually her despair increased to real fear... to a fear which could very easily turn to unreasoning panic at the thought of being completely lost in this strange, unreal, ethereal world. The reassuring solidity of Ian's body (the only solid object in this unsubstantial world of spectral gloom) as he, with steady and seemingly assured certainty, guided her was the only thing which kept her calm, kept her from giving way to that threatening panic. Although he was careful not to allow any concern to show, Ian secretly began to wonder if he had gone astray in this thick and confusing mist. He hoped not. He did not really think so, but he could not stop some slight doubt creeping in. He wished the mist would clear, if only for a minute, to allow him to check his bearings.

Suddenly a strange loud sound, startling in its unexpectedness, cut through the mist. Cynthia stood motionless in fright. Then her anxious face broke into a relieved smile as the neighing of a pony was repeated not far from her. Ian gave a delighted grin. Although the two ponies could not see them in the shrouding grey mist, they sensed some unknown creatures approaching and repeatedly neighed their nervous unease.

Cynthia wasted no time in mounting her pony and starting down the path. Ian guided her down the steepest section until they got clear of the mist. From there she had merely to follow that path all the way back to Glen Ardgie Lodge.

Ian climbed back up to the other pony, which, having with sad, longing eyes watched its companion set out for home, stood most reluctantly waiting with its despondent head drooping miserably and the experienced pony-man securely holding its rope halter.

Although pleased to be out of that obscuring mist, Cynthia was still depressed by the miserable scene all around her. The heavy layer of dank mist pressed low and menacingly on the hills on either side of the path and formed a miserable grey ceiling over the entire glen. The drizzle steadily continued to soak. Dejectedly she moaned, "I'm sure pissed off with this God-damned persistently pissing drizzle."

Obstinately ignoring Cynthia's belabouring heels, her loud commands and bad tempered curses, the pony continued at its own steady plodding pace which made the dreary journey down that long glen drag on interminably. As she wearily jogged along Cynthia longingly imagined soaking in a hot bath; imagined – could almost taste – a large gin and tonic. It seemed to her that it was only those enticingly vivid mirages that kept her going.

Eventually these mirages became realities.

How voluptuously she gloried in that foaming, luxuriously scented bath. How recklessly she poured the gin. How eagerly she gulped from the brimming glass as she sat before the dressing-table mirror and applied soothing lotions to the midge bites disfiguring her face.

As she lay on her bed she fortified and consoled herself with another generous gin and tonic and awaited Ron's return in a not altogether unpleasant self-righteously bellicose mood. After a time, sleep timidly crept forth and tentatively touched her exhausted body. While physically she drowsily drifted towards relaxing rest, mentally she was still active, her mind vindictively kept 'nursing her wrath to keep it warm'.

Despite the poor stalking conditions, Ron managed to shoot a stag late in the afternoon. When Colin drove him back to the hotel, he persuaded Colin and Ian to come into the bar with him for a celebratory dram. They were easily persuaded.

Ron bought one round of drams. They were quickly and appreciatively disposed of. He bought another round. As these drams were more slowly drank, he again thanked them for a successful day's stalking. "I didn't really think I would get a stag today under these appallingly poor conditions."

"Aye, the conditions were gey bad, right enough. You were really lucky to get your stag," Colin said.

Ron grinned, "Yeah, sure I was lucky. But you're being far too modest, Colin, it wasn't just luck that got me that stag, it was mainly your expert and quite amazing skill that got me it."

Ian grinned his agreement, "Aye, Ron, he's not a bad deer stalker... not a bad stalker at all."

To Ron, these remarkable stalking skills of Colin's seemed little short of miraculous. He remembered how as he peered into the thick grey blanket of mist, he had very doubtfully asked, "Do you really think we've any chance of getting a stag in this?"

"Och, why not?... why not? As long as we gang real cannily," Colin replied.

And they did go really cannily. Slowly they silently moved forward with every sense acutely alert. Often visibility was no more than a few yards, at other times they could see for almost seventy dim yards. Occasionally Colin stopped, wet his right index finger and held it up to feel for the merest hint of the stirrings of a faint breeze. Then, slightly changing direction, he again slowly moved on. His strong ancestral hunting instincts were allied to more than thirty years stalking experience and intimate knowledge of this land. He had an accurate, an almost intuitive, feel for what deer were likely to do, where they were likely to be, under all the infinitely varied weather conditions to be met with in this wild landscape.

Once again his intuitive feelings – his sixth sense? – were proved correct.

Motioning Ron to follow him, Colin silently crawled to the edge of a heathery knoll and peered over. He grinned triumphantly. Ron stared in almost disbelieving amazement. Nine stags were nervously and hesitantly grazing less than sixty yards from them.

Sitting in the hotel bar, Ron again raised his glass and again toasted Colin, "Here's to you, Colin, the best deer stalker in all the Highlands!"

Ian eagerly joined in that toast, "Aye, there are not many stalkers and gamekeepers like Colin left now. He's one of the last of a rare breed, a gamekeeper whose father and grandfather were gamekeepers before him on the same Highland estate."

"Yeah, and your son is a gamekeeper as well, isn't he, Colin? Where does he work?" Ron asked.

"Aye, Alasdair's a gamekeeper too. He's working near Gairloch, in Wester Ross."

Ron was about to buy another round of drams, but Colin and Ian refused them. With gallant and uncharacteristic self-denial they resolutely refused, declaring that they had to get back home to their wives and their dinners. Almost certainly an urgent need for their belated dinners was a much more potent reason for their refusal than any urgent need to be with their waiting wives.

As Colin drove Ian home, he turned and with a broad grin said, "Ron is very generous, he's very liberal with the drams, isn't he? But I wonder if he had another reason for wanting to stay drinking in the bar?"

Ian grinned in reply, "Aye, I'm sure he had. I'm sure he had a very good reason; he was putting off as long as possible the dreaded moment when he had to face his wife's wrath!"

"Aye, that's exactly what I was thinking myself."

Smiling, they sympathetically exclaimed, "Poor Ron!... Poor Ron!"

Ron laboriously forced his leadenly reluctant feet up the hotel's brightly carpeted stairs and then slowly made his way along the corridor. He wryly grimaced at the face grimacing back at him from a mirror. His entire face was angrily measled with midge bites.

With grim determination he entered their bedroom. Cynthia woke at once and immediately started berating him for waking her from her much needed sleep. That was only the start of the outrush of her long damned and careful hoarded grievances. Her violent curses poured forth. She cursed this miserable country; she cursed the hellish midges; she cursed the mist and rain, cursed the maddeningly slow pony, but most of all she cursed Ron. She savagely cursed him for having insisted on her coming on this terrible holiday with him. This was the most miserable day of her entire life!

Ron knew better than to attempt to justify or excuse himself. He confined his response to occasionally interjecting a few soothing, apologetic words. Any lingering elation he still felt at having completed that long, exhausting, and eventually successful day's stalking rapidly evaporated – cruelly melted by the heat of Cynthia's wrath. Finally, feeling that he could not contain his temper much longer, he broke into her venomous tirade, exclaiming, "I'm soaked and tired. I must have a bath."

He turned tail and ignominiously retreated to the bathroom. With a loud sigh of relief, he locked himself into that sanctuary.

That unhappily memorable stalking expedition marked the end of their Highland sporting holiday. The next morning the rain poured. To appease Cynthia, Ron agreed to take her to Edinburgh. They spent three days there – three days in which Cynthia indulged in a mad orgy of revengefully expensive shopping.

Five days after their return to New York they were both once again at Kennedy Airport. But they left on separate planes. Cynthia was en route to the Caribbean and, she hoped, to a repeat of the illicit affair she had enjoyed there last year. Ron, at his father's insistence, was on his way to Hong Kong to sort out problems that had suddenly arisen with a large and complex loan their company was negotiating there.

As he clearly remembered that time six years ago, Ian reflected that that had been Cynthia's one and only holiday in Aldrory, which was surely just as well for all concerned.

Suddenly, Ron's voice brought Ian out of his reverie and back into the present, back to his own comfortable sitting room. "Neither of you really cared much for Cynthia when you met her here on her memorable visit, did you?" Ron asked.

Helen and Ian exchanged glances; no, they certainly had not taken to Cynthia. She was so pretentiously false. She was the exact opposite of Ron, with his deeply sincere warm friendship. They were not surprised that their marriage was not very successful. Helen quietly replied, "That's an awkward question, Ron, how do you expect us to answer it?"

"You don't need to answer it – in fact you have answered it by that question, Helen. Anyway, I don't care much for her myself either now. You know, I made the biggest mistake of my life when I married her. We were never really suited to one another. We had almost no interests in common, apart from our strong mutual sexual passion for each other. That was fine for our first few years together, but it is hardly enough to make a long and successful marriage out of, is it?"

"You are still living together, aren't you?" Helen asked.

"Oh yeah, we're living together. At least we live in the same apartment, but we see very little of each other. We go our separate ways. Cynthia has her own foolish lady friends and spends most of her time with them, all frantically keeping up with the latest fads and fashions. As for me, I spend almost all my time working, working, working." Ron smiled ruefully, "Not much of a life, is it?"

"Well, for God's sake, why don't you give it all up and retire to your ancestral home here in the Highlands?" Ian – not for the first time – asked.

"I know… I know, Ian, I would love to do just that, but as I've said before, there are problems. The main problem is my old father. He has his mind set on my continuing and expanding the financial business he spent his entire life founding and building up. It would simply break his heart if I were to retire and give up the business. It would kill him as surely as if I had plunged a dagger into his heart."

"What about your brother, he's a bit younger than you, isn't he? Couldn't he take your place in the business?"

"No, Ian, I'm afraid there's no chance of that. My brother, Bill, is three years younger than me, but he has absolutely no interest in entering the family business, or any other business. He is a lecturer in English and Literature at Delaware University. His only real interests were always in the more abstract artistic studies, especially literature. Despite our father's urgings, he had no interest in any business studies. My father and he had many fierce arguments over this, but eventually Dad was reconciled to Bill doing his own thing. As long as I was in the business with him and seemed almost as wholeheartedly engrossed in it as he was, then he did not so much mind his younger son becoming, as he described him, 'an arty lefty, divorced from reality in the cosy ivory tower of his university'."

"So it seems there is no way you could retire early, then?"

"No, I'm afraid not, Ian. Not as long as my father is alive. I repeat it would simply kill him if I was to retire early."

They now became thoughtfully silent. The same thought was in both minds. That thought came unbidden, but powerfully insistent; the awareness that Ron's father was old, that he could not live forever. They were not cruel; neither of them wished for that old man's death, and yet surely it was pure hypocrisy not to admit, if only to oneself, the thought that the death of that old man could be the solution to quite a number of problems.

Ian had noticed Helen's complete silence for the last few minutes. Now observing her more closely, he saw how stiffly motionless she held herself; how steadily and solemnly she stared at Ron. A faint tremor whispered through Ian's body, then he too became tensely silent. He waited expectantly, remembering similar past experiences.

Ron opened his mouth to speak, but no sound issued, he also sat silent and still with his lips slightly parted and his questioning eyes returning Helen's unflinching, unblinking stare.

At last Helen broke that profound silence. She spoke slowly and distinctly. She spoke with her normal voice and yet there was something extra in it – a touch of unusual authority, as she stated, "Ronald MacDonald, within two years you will be Laird of Aldrory."

As Helen made that statement – made it with absolute certainty – it seemed to Ron that her steady gaze pierced to his soul and that she clearly saw his future. It was an uncanny feeling. He shuddered slightly.

For some moments profound silence again descended. Then suddenly Helen jumped to her feet and with a self-disparaging impish grin said, "Now let's get to our beds. It's very late."

The two dogs followed Helen's example and eagerly leapt to their feet as if they too were pleased to be back in familiar, reassuring 'normality'.

Ron was shown to the spare bedroom and was soon comfortably settled in its large double bed.

Helen and Ian lay quietly and snugly together in their own bed's familiar intimate cosiness. Helen, most unusually, was the first to fall asleep. As Ian lay restlessly listening to her steady gentle breathing he consoled himself that at least she did not snore; he was accustomed to her regular complaints of lying sleepless listening to his loud and violent snores. That distinct and definite prophecy of hers kept swirling and whirling around and around inside his head:

"Ronald MacDonald, within two years you will be Laird of Aldrory."

Ron, too, could not sleep. Those same prophetic words of Helen's kept revolving inside his bemused and weary head. They seemed to revolve in rhythm with the unsteadily and queasily revolving room. But the words themselves were perfectly clear:

"Ronald MacDonald, within two years you will be Laird of Aldrory."

Chapter Four

At ten minutes past eleven next morning – or rather, that same morning – Ron's full bladder woke him with its insistent demand for urgent relief. Slowly, cautiously, he raised his throbbing head from the pillow, sat upright, then slid his legs out from under the blankets. Each of those gentlest of movements added to his anguished head's pulsing pain. He shuddered wearily as his sad stomach queasily churned.

Obeying his bladder's ever more pressing demands, he unsteadily slithered to the bathroom. After having thankfully finished, he flushed the toilet and quietly quoted to himself, "For this relief much thanks."

Despite his sorry and delicate state, he managed a smile – a wry, wintry smile – at having remembered that quotation from when he had studied and acted in Hamlet at college. Probably Ian's habit of quoting on any suitable occasion had influenced him to dredge up that quote from the depths of his memory. As he stared at the ghastly pale sickly face grimly peering at him from the mirror, Ron shuddered and thought, "Oh God, I look more like Banquo's ghost than like Hamlet!"

Returning to the bedroom, Ron manfully resisted the temptation to get back into the seductively inviting warm and cosy bed. Instead he laboriously buckled his kilt around his waist, then stood listening outside Helen and Ian's bedroom door. Absolute silence reigned in that room, so he slowly and cautiously groped his way down the steep stairs.

He entered the sitting room. It, too, was silent and deserted. The entire house seemed unnaturally still and lifeless. He noticed that the fire's old ashes had been raked out and fresh kindling was set ready, awaiting a match. On the table behind the old sofa stood a full bottle of Glenlivet whisky with five clean glasses neatly and invitingly set out beside it. With a grimace of dismay he quickly averted his eyes from that sight. In his present sorry state, the sight of, the thought of, whisky filled him with disgust. He turned his thoughts to more pleasant things. He recalled the boisterous laughter of last night's many hours of convivial friendship. He thought he could detect echoes of that laughter joyously lingering around the room. Certainly, despite the wide-open window, the stale reek of last night's cigar smoke still persistently lingered.

Ron suddenly shivered. He had a frightening feeling that this house's human and canine occupants had suffered some terrible inexplicable fate; had suffered a fate similar to that which befell the crew of the mysteriously deserted ship *Marie Celest*. That waiting whisky, those waiting glasses, that fire set and waiting coldly unlit all seemed as if they might wait forever. Standing silently and forlornly in his pitiful hung-over state he felt as though he too might wait here forever.

A sudden loud sound made him jump. Then he smiled in relief as he recognised that clattering noise. It was made by Ian using his ancient and very noisy typewriter in his 'study' across the narrow passage from this room. Ron knocked at, then opened the door of that 'study' as Ian cheerily bade him enter. "Come in, Ron, come in. So you're stirring at long last. How are you this fine morning?"

"Oh, for God's sake, Ian, please don't sound so darned bright and cheery. Gee, I've got some hell of a hangover this miserable morning."

Ron moved his lips in what he intended as a courageous smile, but which appeared to Ian more a desperate grimace. Ian noted the details of Ron's dishevelled and sadly woebegone state: he had no shoes on; his stockings were rumpled about his ankles, his kilt slanted unevenly and hung over one knee. His uncombed hair straggled and his unshaven jaw bristled. Dull eyes blearily squinted from a sickly, pale, unwashed face like a couple of black raisins sunk in a pasty pudding. He was a startling contrast to his usual neat, well-groomed appearance.

"Well, you've given me a darned good scrutiny, Ian; what do I look like?"

"You look like death warmed up... like something the cat's dragged in."

"Thank you, Ian... I guess I asked for that, didn't I?" Raising another ghastly spectre of a smile, he ruefully added, "Anyway that's exactly what I feel like."

"Well, you better take a seat and quietly rest yourself for a while."

"Yeah, thanks, that sounds a swell idea."

As Ian rose from his seat at the large table and cleared the heap of newspapers and magazines from the rocking chair, which was the only other seat in the room, Ron anxiously asked, "Won't I be disturbing you too much, Ian? Won't I be keeping you from your work?"

"Och no, not at all. As long as you just sit silently there and rest you won't disturb me."

"That's all I feel like doing; sitting quietly and letting this fantastic den of yours weave its wonderful, restful spell over me."

"My 'study', you mean... not my 'den'," Ian corrected, grinning.

"Sorry!... Yeah, your study; although to me it will always be your marvellous den."

Ian pushed the large and heavy ancient 'Imperial' typewriter to the back of the untidily cluttered table then sat down and took up a pen, remarking, "I won't use the typewriter just now. I'll have pity on your sore head and not batter its loud clattering din into your poor, throbbing brain. I'll just check over this article about trout fishing before I post it."

"Thanks, Ian, that's most considerate of you."

Ron settled more comfortably into the rocking chair then slowly let his weary gaze wander around this fantastic room. He knew of no other room that could compare with this unique den of Ian's. The most overwhelming impression this room gave was of being a truly masculine place – a gloriously untidy, most interesting male den. Obviously it was well used and well loved by its owner.

The most dominant features in the room were the books – hundreds upon hundreds of books all tightly packed together on shelves which stretched across the entire length of the back wall and, rising one above the other, proudly carried those massed books from floor to ceiling. There were books of all types, all sizes, all colours. Crowded companionably together, they were a richly glorious company.

Numerous gaudily coloured paperbacks vied with the bright dust jackets of hardbacks. Their combined jaunty brightness was in brash, almost flippant contrast to the rows of darkly sombre old leather bound volumes that, with grave dignity, graced the library's bottom shelf. Those old volumes had an air of dull respectability, of attempting to keep up appearances despite their brittle leather binding's mouldering decay and their tired pages' unhealthy jaundice pallor. Those large old books were solidly heavy, were drearily heavy in content as well as in physical weight. They gave out a dustily dry smell – the smell of the previous century's death. They had no literary merit. Ian kept them for nostalgic reasons; for fond memories of boyhood when on miserably dreary winter days he had lain, elbows propped on carpet, face cupped in hands, and pored over those old books, legacies from his mother's parents. Wisely, he ignored the thick volumes of infinitely dull sermons with their endless oceans of small print and no relieving pictures. He gloried in the histories of the British army as its ever-victorious soldiers expanded and defended the glorious Empire on which the sun never set. These books were vividly alive with many colourful pictures. The heroic exploits of the gallant kilted soldiers of the Highland regiments stirred his eager boyish blood and the wild tunes of the pipes of war thrilled hereditary nerves in his excited brain. Those heavy, dusty old books were fortunate to have this comfortable and friendly home to slumber away their senile old age in.

As Ron let his gaze slowly wander and longingly linger over this truly loved library of Ian's he suddenly had a clear vision of another library – his father's luxurious library in his large and imposing country house. That house stood secluded in fifty acres of the tamed wilderness of New York State's sprawling forests and rolling hills.

Ron's father had spared no expense in building and furnishing that house. The library was also his study and it was here that he spent most of his time on these rare occasions when he gave himself the, to him, somewhat doubtful pleasure of a weekend away from his New York office and his town house. This library was very impressively furnished and fitted. Row upon row of leather bound volumes stretched in imposing matching sets. The collection of great American literature was bound in glowing red, while the larger collection of great English literature nobly gleamed in royal blue. Sadly, these books – each one a glorious tribute to the printer's and the book binder's art – were for show, not for reading. The hours that Ron's father spent in this room were devoted exclusively to working; they were merely a continuation of his hectic weekday work. The bulky Saturday edition of the *Wall Street Journal* with other financial magazines were all he ever read in this library.

On his elegantly carved antique desk, were two telephones, one bright red, one dark blue, both were elaborate many buttoned wonders incorporating all the latest marvels of electronic telecommunications. In a discreet corner a fax machine stood waiting with a self-important air of breathless expectation. Two computer screens were hidden behind the highly varnished pale pine panelling which lined the room. For most of the time those screens lurked silently and lifelessly hidden in dark obscurity as if ashamed to show their faces. It was only on those fairly rare occasions when Ron's father spent a weekend there that these screens came to life. Invariably his first action on entering this room was to slide back the concealing panels and impatiently resuscitate these screens into flickering life. Then, sitting in his black leather swivel chair behind the desk, he eagerly put on his viewing glasses and, cocking his 'good ear', gazed and listened intently at the urgent stream of electronic images flooding from both screens. His aged and stooped lean body bowed in reverend homage to those flickering icons – those profound oracles of our modern age's materialistic religion.

When Ron (leaving his wife to enjoy herself with 'the girls' at some fashionable horse show) did manage to escape with his father to that lovely country retreat, they were welcomed by Jack and Betty Williamson, the aged husband and wife team who as caretaker/gardener and housekeeper/cook, lived in and looked after the house all the year round. Ron often envied them their quiet, contented lifestyle in this pleasant countryside. They had an easy time of it, with Jack managing to put in a good many happy summer hours trout fishing in the nearby Delaware River. In many ways that contented couple reminded Ron of Ian and Helen with their similar easy going lifestyle in the Scottish Highlands. Ron very occasionally managed some delightful hours fly-fishing in the expert company of Jack, but those few hours of pleasure were resented by Ron's workaholic father who expected his son to work as hard as he did.

Usually, Ron reluctantly, but with good grace, obeyed his father's commands and the pair of them worked as industriously in that study as they did during the week in their Wall Street office. If Ron, with great daring, ever ventured to take down one of the handsome volumes from its sacrosanct place on the library shelves and admiringly inspect its voluptuous beauty, he immediately felt his father's displeased gaze silently stab at him. That frowning, disapproving glare made him feel like a naughty, disobedient schoolboy again. Sometimes he ignored that very palpable, though unspoken, disapproval and, lifting the book to his nostrils, sniffed its luxurious leather's pleasantly subtle, distinctive odour. Then as he gently, reverently, opened the book, its gleaming spine, stiff with disuse, leatherly creaked. It creaked as with sharp rheumatic twinges in which there was pain, but also an overwhelming joy at being opened and admired. Ron carefully rippled through and keenly glanced over these inviting pages. There was something pathetically sad about all those pages, all so pure, all so unsullied in their unread virginal state.

As Ron gently held that precious volume in his hands, he imagined that a tiny tremor ran through it. It was as if that book – one of Charles Dickens' greatest novels – was excited, was full of great expectations of at long last being tenderly held and lovingly read.

Then his father's voice would loudly address him and savagely shatter his dream of reading that book. With querulous impatience, that wealthy old workaholic brought Ron back down to earth: "I see the Yen's dropping further against the Dollar. That's what you were expecting, Ron, wasn't it?"

Stifling a sigh, Ron carefully replaced the book in its correct place in that violated space in the prim row of unread books. With a conscious effort he tore his mind from the wonders of literature, from the marvels of all that glorious fiction, to the wonders of high finance, to the hardly less fantastic fictions of much of international finance.

"How much has it dropped by?" he forced himself to ask as he turned and, following his father's example, gazed at those electronic oracles that, with unwearied insistence, flickered and flashed their golden revelations to a breathlessly agog watching world. He was back in the mad unreality of much of present day reality.

Coming back to the glory of where he sat in Ian's untidily cluttered den, Ron's gaze now wandered from all those well read books to the many heaps of old magazines and newspapers which towered in unstable stacks against the room's walls. In one corner a heap of glossy magazines soared mountainously while others slowly slipped and slithered their slippery way with the stealthy movements of a glacier, and gradually encroached further out towards the old faded carpet that dustily covered the centre of the room. Many of these magazines contained articles and short stories written by Ian.

Bravely and precariously perched on another of these heaps was a bright green stuffed frog. It stood upright and maintained an alert fencing pose with its left claw held high above its shoulder while the right claw firmly grasped a large, fierce darning needle sword. The sharp point of this sword was aggressively thrust at, and almost touched, the astounded nose of a stoat. Although also dead and stuffed that brown stoat recoiled in very lifelike fear and amazement.

The large and solid oak table where Ian sat working bore the substantial weight of an ancient 'Imperial' typewriter and was also laden with, almost overflowed with, piles of letters, yet more magazines and even more books. Behind the table, the room's only window was securely set in the crofthouse's thickly solid old wall. On the wide window ledge was another stuffed creature – a large, one-eyed wildcat. A white scar replaced its left eye and together with its staring right eye gave that cat the appearance of perpetually and whimsically winking. Its one glass eye kept an alert watch on the many dead flies and bluebottles littering the dusty window ledge. These ugly black corpses lay on their backs with rigid legs pointing vertically upwards; they had come to a truly ignoble dusty death on that un-dusted and cobwebby ledge. The wildcat's right paw reached out towards these small corpses, but this suggestion of action was belied by the cobwebs stretching thickly from that paw to the window frame.

Other cobwebs spread from its tufted ear and from the tip of its bushy, black ringed tail. Those constraining cobwebs held that wildcat a Gulliverishly helpless captive.

Ron quietly smiled as he gazed at these stuffed animals, all evidence of, and dumb tribute to Ian's skill as a taxidermist when, many years ago, that craft had been one additional hobby added to his many others. There were also a few stuffed birds in this room. From its perch high on the bookshelves a tawny owl stared with wide-eyed disapproving solemnity at the smaller birds fluttering frivolously on their lower perches.

On the wall above an artist's easel a large and plump plaster-of-Paris brown trout perpetually swam in a cracked glass case. Over the years that poor trout had suffered much disfiguring damage where many chips had been knocked out of its body. These wounds glared with vivid whiteness. Ron again smiled as he remembered once being in this room with Helen and Ian when Helen had declared that grievously chipped trout an eyesore – an ugly object which should have been thrown out ages ago. Ian had laughingly defended it, saying, "I think those chips suit that trout… after all, fish and chips always go together, don't they?"

In a corner was a small table, which was used exclusively for fly-tying. Its entire surface was cluttered with the many varied bright and glittering materials used in this painstakingly finicky skilled craft. All sorts of bird's feathers glossily gleamed and tangled with coils of gauzy fine wires of gold and silver which, mixing with threads of every shade, combined in a fantastic kaleidoscope of colour. Securely held in the fly-tying vice a large salmon fly was slowly taking shape. Its gaudy feathers, its bright tinsels and threads were combining to form what would be a perfect "Jock Scott" salmon fly. It would be virtually a work of art which, hopefully, would irresistibly appeal to some keen and wealthy salmon fisher who would buy it, hoping in turn it would appeal just as irresistibly to some large salmon.

Some half a dozen trout and salmon fly rods rested on racks above that table and their matching reels were neatly arrayed on a shelf. Only fly rods and fly reels were allowed in this room. Once again Ron smiled as he thought of Ian's strong dislike of all spinning rods and reels and of how he referred to spinning reels as "those bloody infernal machines". He believed that these showy examples of engineering skill were far too technically perfect and that they did most of the work for the fisherman, leaving him requiring no real (the pun was intended) skills of his own. Ron agreed with those views of Ian's but couldn't go quite so far as he went in his passionate dislike (almost hatred) of everything too technical, too mechanical. When accused of being a Luddite, Ian willingly agreed to wear that title. He declared it an honourable title, one to be proud of; not one to be ashamed of. How often Ron had heard Ian approvingly quote Thoreau's famous warning against inventions as being merely "improved means to an unimproved end." As Ron thought of his ever more hectic lifestyle, made increasingly more hectic by all our modern electronic marvels, he felt his sympathies lean more strongly towards Ian and Thoreau's views.

A large salmon landing net and two smaller trout landing nets hung from a row of nails and a couple of gaffs hung beside them. The smaller gaff had its sharp point securely impaled in a cork from a whisky bottle. The larger, long handled salmon gaff had the distinction of having its dangerously sharp point impaled in a champagne cork as if in glorious remembrance of some notable fishing deed notably celebrated.

On the wall high above that fishing tackle was a larger than life-size African mask carved in dark ebony wood. There was something sinister about that mask. Its jet blackness was crudely carved, the entire face terribly lined and sadly furrowed. These deeply engraved lines and wrinkles hideously distorted the features. Tortured eyes and grimacing mouth seemed contorted by some unspeakable, some unbearable terror. Ron quickly turned his eyes away from that ugly mask. This morning it was uglier than ever – it all too vividly suggested his own grimly suffering hangover tortured state.

He looked at the final, and a much brighter item decorating this fantastic room – the head of a stag. That large head projected prominently on its thickly maned neck. Its wide spread of heavy antlers rose impressively to touch the ceiling. There were six neatly matching points on each antler, so that beast was a noble twelve pointer – A Royal Stag. It was the only Royal that Ian had ever shot. He had killed it before the war while swept by the lusty vigour of hot-blooded young manhood's zestful self-glorification. He had then taken on the laborious and painstaking task of stuffing and mounting its impressive head. He regarded it as his greatest work of taxidermy.

When Ian returned home after the war that noble stag's passive dignity had been rather diminished as it was turned into what he laughingly referred to as his 'miniature military museum'. The large antlers had been incongruously festooned with war trophies. There had been a long barrelled German pistol hanging from its trigger-guard; two Iron Crosses; a monocle dangling from its black ribbon; an SS officer's cruelly proud dagger and finally Ian's own Glengarry cap. That cap had been a conspicuous item with its bright red and white chequered squares, its jauntily dangling twin black ribbons and its large and silvery gleaming cap badge of the Seaforth Highlanders. Very appropriately, that badge incorporated the head and twelve pointed antlers of a Royal Stag. Ron clearly remembered the first time he had been in this room when all these items had adorned that stag. Now there were not so many. He checked over the items that remained. The two Iron Crosses still hung boastfully from their scarlet and black ribbons. At least one of these medals was entitled to boast. It was the greatest order of the Iron Cross – the Knight's Cross with Oak Leaf Cluster. It was the highest German award for outstanding bravery in battle. Not all that many had been awarded. The German army officer who had worn it and had been killed in Italy must have been a really brave soldier. The Nazi SS officer's dagger still hung from a point. Arrogantly decorated with its eagle and swastika and with the dishonourable slogan 'Blood and Honour' engraved on its hilt, that dagger sent a shudder through Ron as he thought of its evil past.

The final item now decorating the stag was more pleasant; was quite whimsical, although it too had come from a dead German officer. It was the monocle. That single eyeglass was now firmly fixed at the stag's staring right eye and its black ribbon curved in a graceful loop to an antler. That monocle gave the stag a droll appearance and yet it was surprising how little it detracted from the animal's noble dignity as it haughtily stared. With another smile Ron recalled what Ian had said, "Surely that stag is fully entitled to give such a haughty regal stare through that monocle, after all it is a Royal Stag."

"Yes, this sure is a wonderful room," Ron once more thought as he sat in silent contentment and let the room work its restful charm over him. A few times his eyes wearily closed then again flicked open. Finally, with head slumped on chest, he slumbered.

After an hour of sleep, Ron gave a loud snort and jerked wildly awake. For a few bewildered moments he stared around uncertain of where he was. Then with a smile of recognition he let his gaze wander over this wonderful den and once more happily viewed all those fantastic creatures – the fencing frog, the winking wildcat, the haughtily staring monocled stag.

Ian's cheery voice startled him out of his spellbound reverie. "How are you now, Ron? Are you feeling any better after your noisy, snoring sleep?"

"Yes, thanks, I'm feeling a good bit better. I don't feel quite so delicate and fragile now. If I was snoring I hope I didn't disturb you too much."

"Och no, it takes much more than your snoring to distract me when I'm engrossed in my creative work. Anyway, I'm finished now. I've got that fishing article ready to post. A very good morning's work well done, even though I say so myself. I only hope the magazine's editor thinks so too."

"I'm sure he will. Surely if he's a good editor, he will recognise the greatness of your work – the great work of 'Himself'!"

Ian laughed, "Och, flattery will get you nowhere, Ron."

Ron grinned, then asked, "By the way, Ian do you still have the pistol that used to hang on the stag's antler? What type of pistol was it?"

"It was a Luger, a standard German Army officer's automatic pistol. Aye, I still have it, though now I keep it hidden away in a box in the locked cupboard in my bedroom where I keep my shotgun and rifle. With all the Irish terrorist troubles just now, even here in the remote North West Highlands – the 'Wild West' – we have to keep all firearms securely locked up. Even here the local bobby checks up occasionally."

"Have you ever used that Luger? Do you have ammunition for it?"

"Oh aye, I've some ammunition. I brought back twenty-five rounds with it after the war. I've used three rounds, so – if my arithmetic is correct – there are twenty-two bullets left."

"Oh, really? What did you use the three rounds on... target practice?"

"No, definitely not target practice. Do you want to hear the story of what they were used for?"

"Yeah, I sure do. You know I like to hear your stories... as long as you're sure I'm not keeping you back from any work."

"Och no, I've done enough work for one day. You know me, I'm not all that keen on working too much."

Ian half rose from his chair and dragged it round to face Ron, then settling himself comfortably he told the story of how he had first used that Luger. Although it happened about fifteen years ago, he remembered every detail of the incident clearly.

An old crofter had approached Colin MacDonald, the local gamekeeper, requesting his help in searching for some lost cattle. These cattle, two cows with their two young calves, had been last seen near the top of the high sea cliffs at Ardoe Point. John Munro, the crofter concerned, feared that his beasts had got into trouble at these dangerous cliffs, might have got stuck down them, or have fallen over them. Colin had explained the situation to Ian and he willingly volunteered to assist in the search. Remembering previous experiences of cattle stuck in cliffs, Colin suggested, "It would be a good idea to take your Luger with you in case we have to finish off any fallen and badly injured beasts."

"Aye, certainly. That Luger's much handier than a rifle if we're clambering about on steep cliffs."

"Aye, exactly. And you can keep it hidden in your jacket's poacher's pocket if we don't need to use it."

Ian stood on a chair in his 'study', reached up and unhooked the Luger pistol from the stag's antler, then took it upstairs to his bedroom. He unlocked a cupboard and lifted out a box of ammunition. One by one he pressed cartridges into the pistol's magazine then slapped it firmly home into the butt of the pistol. He thumbed the safety catch over to safe.

As arranged, they met old John Munro at his crofthouse and after being warmly greeted by him and his semi-crippled but cheerily hearty, bright-eyed wife, the three men, with the crofter's two collies keenly accompanying them, set out to walk the rough miles towards Ardoe Point. All were pleased to have a fine, clear, dry day for this search. It was one of those bright June days when the West Highlands are at their glorious best, when the sun beamed from a cloudless sky from early dawn to late, long lingering golden dusk. A South Easterly breeze pleasantly tempered the sun's increasing warmth.

The party split up to cover more ground. Although this land they searched was not huge in area, it was wild in character and could easily hide an army, let alone a few cattle. Ardoe was a peninsula jutting out into the Minch to the North of Inveraldrory village. Around most of its shore gaunt grey rocky slabs plunged into the sea and at its furthest point the savage rock soared high to form steep and darkly intimidating cliffs. The interior of this peninsula was hardly less daunting. It was savagely broken up into many deep, boulder-strewn gullies with rocky knolls rising with fierce steepness between them. A few small lochs, darkly peat-stained and with thin, ugly, dark trout skulking in their depths, littered a number of these gullies. Many of the steep slopes were a mass of coarse, thick-stemmed, knee-high heather and the bottoms of most gullies were a bright green jungle of shoulder high bracken. Advancing like a conquering army, the bracken, that pernicious weed, was triumphantly taking over far too much of the Highland landscape.

The three humans were delighted that today they did not need to sweatily struggle through these sweltering gullies as they had often done before when searching for fox dens. Today, they could scan these gullies from the ridge tops. Any cattle in these hollows would be obvious.

Again by arrangement, the three searchers met on a conspicuous knoll near the high cliffs. None had sighted the cattle, but all had noted fresh dung and hoof marks confirming that the cows and calves had been here recently.

They sat down together. All got out and lit their pipes as they rested before searching along the cliffs. They all had the same thought – that if the cattle were stuck somewhere down the cliffs, they should be hearing them bellowing, but, ominously, they had not heard a sound. All had the same fear – that the cattle had gone over the cliffs to their deaths. Old John Munro voiced these fears then said, "I'm afraid I won't be much use searching about the cliffs, not now that I'm seventy-five years old. I'm not sae supple now with my damned rheumatics." He sighed and smiled ruefully, "Och man, it was a different story altogether when I was young and fit and foolish. When I was a boy, then a carefree thoughtless youth, I thought nothing of climbing aboot these cliffs. My brother and me used to spend lots of time gathering gulls eggs from the ledges."

"Aye, we all were foolish and fearless when we were young," Ian agreed. "When I think of some of the fool-hardy things we did it brings me out in a cold sweat."

"Aye, we were fearless then when we clambered aboot as sure-footed as billy goats." Old John paused then chuckled, "Aye man, and we climbed aboot barefooted tae. In thae days us boys went barefooted all summer. I remember how we hated the sabbaths when we were made to wear oor best boots to gang tae the kirk in."

He chuckled again, "Aye, and the mair painful and uncomfortable oor boots were the better for oor immortal souls!"

Colin removed his pipe, contentedly puffed out a cloud of smoke, then said, "Aye, we were all fearless wee devils when we were young, right enough." He smiled at Ian, "Remember when we stood on the 'anvil' here?"

"Oh aye, I remember it all right… how could I ever forget it?"

Old John looked at them in surprise, "I didn't ken you had tested yourself on the 'anvil'. I thought that test of courage had died oot sometime before the First World War."

"Aye, it had died oot right enough, but Ian and me heard about it and thought we would like to try it oorselves." Colin grinned at Ian, "I suppose we were about twelve years old then, weren't we?"

"Aye, that's right. I remember it was just after my twelfth birthday when we carried out that daring and foolhardy feat."

The 'anvil' was a wedge of dark rock, which jutted out for eight feet from the highest point of these cliffs. About five feet wide at its base, it wedged to a sharp point; it did resemble the pointed end of a blacksmith's anvil. It thrust out into airy space and beneath it was a clear drop to the sea three hundred feet below.

Generation after generation of boys from the crofting communities of Ardoe and Achairdich had, when they reached twelve years of age, stood out on that 'anvil' on one leg, holding the other leg up behind them. The longer a boy stood there the more courageous he was proved to be.

Colin and Ian told their parents they were going trout fishing at the Ardoe lochs. They did fish these lochs then climbed to the 'anvil'. They hesitated uncertainly when they saw the sheer drop to the sea. Had either boy been by himself he would have turned away in fear. As each boy looked into the other's eyes, he saw his own doubt reflected there. But neither boy wanted to be a coward. Colin pulled a penny from his pocket and said, "I'll toss you for it. If it's heads I'll go first."

The penny came down heads.

With slow deliberation, Colin returned the treacherous penny to the security of the left pocket of his grey flannel shorts – all the other pockets had holes in them. He licked his lips and gulped, then slowly, but resolutely, stepped out on to the 'anvil'.

As Ian anxiously watched, it seemed that Colin stood out there on his right leg for an eternity. Then it was his turn and that single legged stand truly was an eternity. At least they had sense enough not to look down at the alluring hypnotic movement of the sea far below them. Both kept their gaze firmly fixed on the distant, steady horizon.

Together again on safe ground, the two boys triumphantly shouted and laughed uproariously. Then they rolled together in puppyish play, wresting and struggling in mock combat. Eventually they rose and, whooping fierce Red Indian war cries, ran at breakneck speed back down to the small loch where they had left their fishing rods.

Old John again chuckled reminiscently, "Aye man, but that 'anvil' was a true test for us boys, wasn't it?"

The three men had just risen and taken their first steps towards the cliffs when they were stopped dead in their tracks by a sudden indistinct noise. They all listened intently for the sound to be repeated. It was soon repeated a few times. The bellowing of a cow drowned out the piteously uncertain bawling lamentations of a calf.

These sounds came from somewhere to the South of the highest and steepest cliff. Old John gave a grim smile, "Och well, at long last we've got something to guide us."

They hurried towards these sounds. Together they stood silently and expectantly listening while they scanned the grassy slope, which dropped steeply below them. But there was no sign of the cattle.

The cliffs here were not sheer rock faces but were perhaps even more dangerous. At the rocky cliffs at least there was solid rock to get hold of and firmly grip, but here there was no secure grip for foot or hand. The ground falling steeply away below them was all dry, slippery smooth grass with sparse patches of heather desperately clinging here and there. These heathers were kept shorn by winter's salt laden gales. Only the numerous clumps of sea pinks their flowers jauntily nodding in the sun-bright breeze, were at home in this inhospitable environment. One slip here and it would be impossible to stop oneself from sliding all the way to the sea.

John Munro shouted and his dogs barked.

They were immediately answered by loud bellowing from lower down the slope. They made out the deep bellow of one cow and the clamorous bawling of two calves. Mixed with and confused by these nearer sounds came another sound. They recognised this indistinct moaning noise as coming from another cow – a cow in grievous pain. It came from much further down the cliffs.

Very slowly, very cautiously, the three men inched their way down that slippery slope to a slight hollow fifty yards below them. There they could lie in reasonable safety and, hopefully, get a sight of the cattle.

Below them dropped a small, vertical, wall of rock. On the narrow ledge beneath it one cow and the two calves were trapped. Obviously these cattle were scared to attempt the perilous journey up from that ledge. The observant men noted the ugly scars disfiguring the steep smooth grass below that ledge where the second cow had gone tumbling down. Her despairing moans now came up to them more distinctly. They surmised she must be lying badly injured on the wide rocky ledge which they knew ran along at sea level under parts of these cliffs. They all agreed that there was no safe way they could get down to her. They also agreed that they could not just leave her lying in agony and perhaps taking days to die.

After a thoughtful silence, which seemed painfully long to those anxious, compassionate men, Colin spoke up, "Well, John, they are your cattle, how should we go about getting them up from that ledge?"

"Och, Colin, I don't want either you or Ian trying to go doon to move them. It's far too dangerous. I don't want your deaths on my conscience."

Again there was a silent pause. Sensing that old John was reluctant to come to a decision, Colin repeated, "Now, John, what are we going to do about these cattle?"

"Och man, I think there's only one thing tae try, that's to send auld Ben here doon to move the beasts."

"Aye, that's what I was thinking myself," Colin said. "It's about the only thing we can try. Is he a good steady worker with cattle?"

"Aye, oh aye, Ben's a real canny dog wi' sheep or cattle. Like me, he's getting gey auld, so he's slow and steady, not like Tam here, he's young and too keen and excitable.

After tying a restraining cord on Tam, old John sent Ben down towards the stranded cattle. At a steady unhurried pace the old collie made its sure-footed way down the steep smooth slope. Guided by its master's calm commands, it reached the far end of the ledge and with gentle firmness, backed with ancestral menace, insistently persuaded the nervous cattle to move. The large black cow led the way. Hesitantly and fearfully she clumsily started blundering up from the ledge.

The anxious men watched the cow's violent efforts with held breaths.

"Oh God… Oh my God, she's going over!" old John cried.

For some long, nerve-racking seconds the cow teetered on the edge. It seemed nothing could save her from slipping to her death. One hind hoof slithered over and sent turf cascading down. With an urgent effort her wildly groping hoof got a firmer grip and desperately heaved. Her front hoofs frantically pawed. Loudly gasping, straining every muscle, she made a final lumbering breenge. She was up.

Slowly and cautiously, she made her way up the steep grassy slope. Now here maternal instinct re-asserted itself. Turning her head she anxiously gazed back at her calf and gave a gentle, encouraging bellow. Directed by her mother's coaxing call and chivvied by the collie at her heels, the black and white calf resolutely followed her mother's tracks up from that dangerous place. She managed up without too much trouble. Her smaller size and lighter weight were a great advantage. She joined her mother and with desperate eagerness suckled her reassuring teats.

Encouraged by Ben who followed close behind her, the second calf more reluctantly started up. Soon she safely reached the others. Looking around, she pitifully bawled for her lost mother.

The tensely watching men relaxed. With a relieved smile Ian said, "Thank God that's over. That was pretty nerve-racking."

"Aye, it certainly was. It turned out much better than I dared hope," Colin replied. "For a time it was touch and go for that cow."

Old John quietly muttered, "Aye man, it was a near thing right enough."

They now had to decide what to do about the injured cow lying at the foot of the cliffs. Her loud, pathetic moans were now distressfully persistent. They all agreed she would have to be put out of her misery. There was no way they could get down to her from here. They agreed that the only way to get to her was by sea.

"Is your boat serviceable, John?" Colin asked.

"Och no man, I'm afeared she's not. She's high and dry. I'm still overhauling her." Then John brightened, "But Donald MacKenzie's boat is ready. I saw him out in Loch Doe yesterday. I'm sure we could borrow it."

"Aye, that's what we'll do," Colin said. "Ian and me will go and borrow his boat. You'll manage the cattle by yourself now, won't you, John?"

"Aye, oh aye, I'll managed fine, just fine. Anyway Ben and Tam could tak' the beasts hame by themselves from here now."

"Well then we'll leave you and hurry back to my van."

"Aye, just you do that. Just do what you think best when you get to that poor cow. Do you have a gun with you?"

"Aye, we've a gun in the van," Colin said with a conspiratorial glance at Ian, knowing full well that he had the Luger pistol hidden in his poacher's pocket. "We'll call in on our way home and let you know how we got on."

"Aye be sure and do that. The auld wife will have tea and scones waiting for you and I'll have drams poured for you."

"Och well, in that case we'll definitely call in on you," Colin laughed.

It did not take Colin and Ian long to walk back to the van. They wasted no time in setting out along the narrow, twisting road to Achairdich near the North shore of Loch Doe.

Colin parked the van and Ian and he paused for a moment to admire the beauty of Achairdich Bay. That small bay was one of the most beautiful bays in all Scotland – was perhaps the most beautiful one. Under the bright June sunshine, it was looking at its glorious best. The curving beach of pure white shell sand glaringly shimmered while the benevolent sunlight glittered the sea's gentle surface and brilliantly illuminated the water's crystal transparency. Tangles of seaweed on submerged reefs wavered their dark aquamarine blues deep in the water's voluptuous verdant green.

They went through the gate to Donald MacKenzie's croft. His wife, Flora, welcomed them at the front door. 'Himself' was away working at the peats. Refusing Flora's hospitable offer of a cup of tea, Colin and Ian rapidly explained that they wanted to borrow Donald's boat and did not want to waste any time in getting to the stricken cow.

Flora at once agreed to them borrowing the boat for this mission of mercy. "You know where the boat's moored in Loch Doe, don't you? Just you go and take it. Donald finished overhauling it a few days ago. The oars are in it and it's all fine and seaworthy."

"Good!... Thank you, Flora. We thought 'Himself' would have his boat ready. After all there should be a few salmon in loch Doe by now, shouldn't there?" Colin asked, with a broad grin.

"Salmon?... Salmon? Och of course Donald and me know nothing at all about any salmon in Loch Doe," Flora replied with a smile and an assumed air of extreme innocence.

"Och no, no, of course not!" Colin agreed with his laughter booming out. "I believe you though thousands wouldn't!"

Colin knew that Donald was a reasonable and responsible poacher. He was like Ian, neither of them overdid their poaching. They only took an occasional salmon or deer 'for the pot'. They both loved the thrill of poaching; that love flowed strongly in their blood, directly inherited from ancient hunting/fishing ancestors. They always shared their poached venison and salmon with trustworthy and appreciative neighbouring crofters. They never sold any of it.

Colin thought of how much easier his job as a gamekeeper would be if all poachers were like Ian and Donald. He and his employer, Lord Kilvert, willingly turned a blind eye to such moderate, almost innocent, traditional poaching – the continuation of the Highlander's age-old right to 'a deer from the hill, a salmon from the river and a log from the forest.' Unfortunately, many modern poachers, if they found the poaching too easy, became greedy and overdid it, looking upon poaching as a way to make some easy money and were indifferent to what vile unsporting methods they used.

As they walked along the path leading to Loch Doe, Ian and Colin heard the disyllabic rasping sounds of a corncrake loudly repeated. They smiled. They remembered how as schoolboys searching for these elusive birds which were often heard but rarely seen and whose voices seemed to come from somewhere remote from their bodies, they had decided that those damned birds must be ventriloquists.

Casting his expert eye over the meadow of gently waving grass, Colin said, "Donald's grass is in fine shape. He'll get a bumper crop of hay."

Ian agreed, "Aye, he will. Everything Donald does, he does well."

Donald and Flora MacKenzie were two of the best – but unfortunately also two of the last – of the real old breed of crofters who managed to make a contented living from their croft and from their croft alone.

Ian untied the neat knot securing the boat's running moorings, then hauled hand over hand on the green nylon rope. He smiled at seeing how eagerly the trim, freshly painted and varnished wooden boat came skimming in towards him. Its bow rode high and gave playful chuckles as it was light-heartedly slapped by the glittering ripples. Grinning at Colin, he said, "She's as keen for any wild adventure as a working terrier released from its confining kennels, isn't she?"

They got into the boat. Ian took the oars and rowed out of the small bay. As Colin sat in the stern seat he admired the neat shipshape tidiness of the boat. Then something glittering caught his observant eyes. He licked the tip of one index finger and, leaning forward, pressed the wet finger on that small silver object almost hidden in a corner of the floorboards. He held it up for Ian's inspection. He instantly recognised it as a scale from a salmon. It was the size of, and glittered like, an old silver sixpenny piece.

Ian laughed, "Now, I wonder how that managed to get there?"

"Aye, I wonder. I thought Donald knew nothing at all about there being any salmon in Loch Doe."

"Aye well, perhaps the fish just happened to accidentally leap into Donald's boat."

"Aye, perhaps!… perhaps! I suppose stranger things have happened," Colin laughed.

Both men stared thoughtfully at that salmon scale, they were thinking the same thing – that it was amazing that just as every tree's life history is recorded in its rings, so too every scale on every salmon records that fish's autobiography in its rings. By reading these rings a biologist could tell how many times a female salmon had spawned and how often it had returned to sea.

Colin flicked the scale over the side of the boat and for a second it fluttered like a lone flake of confetti.

Taking turns at the oars, they made their way down narrow Loch Doe then out of its gaping rocky mouth. In half an hour they passed under the towering dark cliffs of Ardoe Point and soon came in sight of the steep grassy slope where the cow had come to grief. There was neither sight nor sound of the poor animal. Wondering if – perhaps hoping – she had died they shouted. They were answered by pitiful moans, which guided them in towards her.

With cautious oars, Colin reversed the boat in towards a wide shelf of rock, which sloped gently into the sea. The tide was high, so most of the seaweed on the ledge was submerged with only a narrow fringe of weed exposed. This dark brown fringe gently rose, floated and disorderly spread, then, with a whispering sigh, sank again as each greenish white wave surged and then retreated. As it streamed from the ledge, the retreating water combed the seaweed's tangled tresses smoothly neat again. Above that slippery wet fringe, the ledge was dry and smooth. It appeared a suitable place for Ian to attempt to leap ashore. Further out, the sea had been calm with only a gentle swell, but in here the waves actively, restlessly, intimidatingly, surged and snarled along the starkly inhospitable shore. As Colin held the boat out from the ledge, Ian sat in the stern and studied the rise and fall of the sea. It rose and fell some five feet. It was quite daunting. A louder and more agonised bellowing moan from the cow decided Ian: "Right, take the boat in, Colin, I'll manage all right."

"Are you sure? It looks gey risky to me."

"Och aye, I'll manage fine. Take her in."

Slowly Colin inched the boat in towards the ledge. Crouching on the stern seat, Ian waited tensely poised. When the boat was at its highest point on a surging swell he leapt.

One foot landed on dry rock. The other slipped on treacherous seaweed and got soaked in the receding wave. His hands grabbed urgently as his knees thudded painfully on rock. Quickly he scrambled to his feet and got well out of reach of the next incoming wave.

While Colin took the boat out and waited, Ian climbed up the ledge and made his way around some boulders towards the sounds of the cow's moaning. After a few minutes of clambering about, he found her. When she saw Ian the cow increased her agonised moaning. She gazed at him with huge sad eyes. Those eyes were dulled with misery. Ian murmured sympathetic sounds as he examined the poor beast. She lay on her belly, tightly wedged against a large boulder. Her front legs stretched out in an unnatural fashion. Both were broken. Her chest was a bloody mess with many ribs smashed in. Towards her rear was an ugly pool of blood, urine and dung.

Obviously there was only on thing Ian could do.

The cow's distraught eyes followed his every move.

She seemed to know what he was going to do. Unbuttoning his poacher's pocket, he drew out the Luger pistol, pushed off the safety catch and slid a bullet into the breech. Pointing between the cow's pathetically pleading eyes, he took steady aim. Gently he squeezed the trigger. Instantly the poor animal was out of its misery.

The shot echoed around the high cliffs. It exploded dozens of seagulls into startled flight. Gleaming in the azure sky's sunshine, they wheeled and soared and dived like a blizzard of demented snowflakes. These raucous gulls loudly protested with a discordant cacophony of ugly sound.

A pair of herons nesting near the top of the cliffs also flew out in startled alarm. They ungainly flapped around on large, clumsy wings. Their annoyed, scolding croaks were even uglier than their usual lugubriously ugly calls. Then as they drifted back to their nest in the cliff's shade, they became a couple of huge, dark, dinosaurish bats.

Ian stood on the sloping ledge and again judged the rise and fall of the sea. Colin eased the boat in towards him. From this ledge that ceaseless surging swell looked much more daunting. Each wave seemed to surge higher and recede lower.

"Are you ready?" Colin anxiously shouted. "Will you manage all right?"

"Aye, I'll have to, won't I?" Ian yelled, sounding more confident than he actually felt.

Screwing up his courage, he poised himself ready to leap. He shouted, "Bring her in on the next wave. I'll be OK!"

Resolutely he leapt.

Fortunately the stern seat was large and strong. He landed fair and square on it then pitched forward into the boat. His hands shot out and grabbed the gunwales. His chest bumped against Colin's broad knees.

"Are you all right?" Colin asked as he heaved on the oars and urged the boat away from the foaming ledge.

"Aye, aye, I'm fine," Ian gasped.

As Colin steadily rowed the boat out from the rocky shore he laughed in relief, "Aye, well at least you jumped into the boat much neater than old Donnie did, remember?"

Ian laughed in happy remembrance of old Donnie, who had once jumped right through the thin floorboards of his boat. "Ah well, at least I didn't jump through the bottom of Donald's boat."

After a while, Ian took the oars and steadily rowed the boat back down Loch Doe while Colin made himself comfortable in the stern seat and contentedly smoked. Gently he removed his pipe and, pointing its stem beyond Ian's left shoulder, said, "I see we've got company."

Ian turned in his seat and stared. Coming steadily towards them were two large basking sharks. He stopped rowing and let the boat glide forward under its own momentum. Smoothly and silently boat and sharks slid towards one another.

From a distance both large dark triangular dorsal fins and both curving narrow tails appeared to scythe through the water with gentleness and dignified grace. But as they drew nearer those dark fins and tails gave another impression – they suggested stealthy, sinister menace. Although their brains assured Colin and Ian that those large basking sharks were harmless, were innocent 'gentle giants', which fed almost exclusively on plankton and that the close proximity of those huge fish posed no threat to them, still those rational assurances were strongly questioned by their ancestral instincts which sounded urgent, if illogical, warnings.

Ginning reassuringly at one another they sat and silently watched the two sharks sail ever nearer. Ian whispered, "They are well described in the Gaelic as "Sail Fish', aren't they?"

"Aye, they are. Those dorsal fins and those tails truly are sail like," Colin whispered... somehow it was natural to whisper in the presence of these awesome monsters.

The female shark was about twenty feet long, she sailed slightly further out than the thirty foot long male who undeviatingly held his course and glided along only an oar's length from the boat. In the clear water and bright sunlight his huge body gleamed silvery grey, his white mouth gaped cavernously wide and the five large gashes which were his gill slits constantly sieved the vast volumes of water passing through after the churning mass of plankton had been channelled into his insatiable gullet.

For a few moments, as Colin and Ian peered down at it, the shark stared up at them. Its large eye was expressionless – the men could read no hint of either fear or aggression in that coldly indifferent stare. They watched the two sharks glide away, then Ian again started rowing. "That was a most interesting experience," he said.

"Aye, it certainly was, but perhaps it's an experience we wouldn't want to repeat too often though. Not all basking sharks might be quite so inoffensively docile as those two."

"We wouldn't have had that experience if we had been using an outboard engine. A noisy, filthy stinking outboard motor would have scared those sharks away."

Colin loudly laughed at this further example of Ian's passionate dislike of things mechanical. "Och, an outboard's gey handy at times though."

He sat in silent contentment puffing on his pipe and watching Ian's steady, rhythmic, effortless rowing, then, grinning broadly, he conceded, "Aye, you're right enough, Ian, those graceful silent oars are much better than a stinking outboard... especially when it's not me that's doing the rowing!"

Ian grinned, "Och, you're getting lazy, you auld bugger; I trust you're perfectly comfortable lounging there enjoying your pipe."

Half an hour later, after securely mooring the boat, they knocked at the door of Donald MacKenzie's crofthouse.

"Come in!... Come in!" Donald cheerily cried as he ushered them into the small and cosily friendly kitchen. After warmly greeting them, his wife, Flora, went into the scullery and put the kettle on.

"You know Norman, Don't you?" Donald asked, indicating a seated visitor.

"Aye, oh aye, we've both met Norman... we've enjoyed a few good drams together," Colin laughed.

Norman laughed too, "Yes, we've certainly shared a few convivial drams."

Norman Craig unhinged his long body from the depths of the armchair and hoisted himself to his feet. He was over six feet tall, slim and wiry. His sunken cheeks emphasised his prominent cheekbones. His receding hair exposed a noble forehead. His eyes were bright with intelligence and gleamed with lively humour.

After Colin and Ian had firmly shaken hands with Norman they all got themselves comfortably seated. Soon their hands were gripping cups of tea and delicious freshly baked scones.

"I see you've been in the wars, Norman," Colin remarked.

Automatically Norman's hand rose to the top of his head and his fingers gently felt a large sticking plaster. He grinned brightly, "Yes, I had a slight argument with one of Duncan's six inch nails."

Colin laughed, "Oh, I see. Obviously you lost the argument."

Donald MacKenzie took up the story. "Duncan spent a good part of last winter building a new toilet shed for the visitors who rent out his old but and ben. He made, by his standards, a reasonable good job of it, but he did not bother to knock flat the six inch nails protruding from the walls and roof."

Norman now continued, "A fact which I did not appreciate until the first time I used the toilet. When I stood up I was impaled on one of those protruding nails. When first aid had been applied and the bleeding stopped, I borrowed Donald's hammer and knocked flat the offending nails."

"I can imagine how Duncan reacted when he was told," Ian remarked, grinning.

"Aye, exactly," Donald grinned in reply. "When I *pointed out* the dangerous way he had left those six inch nails, Duncan exclaimed, "Oh, good life, all those holidaymakers nowadays are so fussy, they want everything just so. I'm sure my toilet shed is perfectly good enough!'"

After the laughter died down, Ian said, "Oh, Norman, that would hardly have been a poetic end: A great poet found dead, impaled in Duncan's new toilet shed!"

Norman chuckled delightedly, "I thought I was supposed to be the poet about here!"

As he ate and drank, Ian once more reflected on how perfectly Norman Craig (one of Scotland's greatest living poets) looked like what we romantically expect a great poet to look like. To those who did not know him his 'lean and hungry look' might suggest an austere ascetic. But all who did know him were well aware that there was nothing in the least abstinently austere or ascetic about Norman. He passionately loved life in all its glorious multitudinous splendour.

While Flora hospitably poured more tea and passed around more scones, Colin and Ian vividly described the day's events. After relating the saving of the cow and calves and the humane shooting of the grievously injured cow, they told of their close encounter with the two basking sharks. Ian laughed, "At least we did not accidentally bump a shark with our oar as you once did, Norman."

"Yes, indeed. That was truly a memorable and unique sensation."

"You described it excellently in your poem. I think it is one of your best short poems."

Norman said nothing. He merely smiled. Perhaps he smiled in modest agreement.

Donald grinned with gentle mockery, "Och, Ian, man, what else did you expect but a great poem from Scotland's greatest poet, eh?"

Norman removed the cigarette from the corner of his mouth, exhaled a stream of smoke towards the low ceiling and depreciatingly chuckled, "Oh please, Donald, spare my blushes."

Donald laughed, "Well then, tell them that story you've just told Flora and me about your auld aunt."

"Oh, all right," Norman grinned. He stubbed out his cigarette then told that self-mocking story.

"For the last few years my wife and I have visited my old aunt once per week. She is senile and lives in a nursing home in Edinburgh. Somewhat reluctantly, and at the persistent request of the matron, I finally agreed to give a short reading of some of my poems to the more mentally alert resident of the home.

"As I entered the nursing home on the appointed afternoon I was halted just inside the front door by a dear old white-haired lady. She seemed to know me, although I could not remember having seen her before. Despite her rather geriatric appearance, she appeared reasonably alert and seemed to know what she was doing. Smiling brightly she held out her hand. I shook her hand and equally brightly smiled at her. I presumed she had been appointed to meet me and guide me to the lounge where I was to give my poetry reading.

"However, as still smiling brightly, she showed no sign of moving or of releasing my hand, I – also still brightly smiling – enquired, 'Do you know me?... Do you know who I am?'

"Her bright smile immediately vanished, was replaced by a stare of dismay. For long moments she blankly stared. Finally, agitated, she gasped, 'Oh dear me no, I'm sorry, I don't know who you are!'

"Then suddenly, like the sun coming out from behind dark clouds, her aged face brightened, her radiant smile once more beamed forth. Triumphantly she exclaimed, 'I tell you what, just you go and see matron... she will tell you who you are!'"

Once the laughter died down, Norman gave a rueful sigh, "So much for fame!"

After spending a pleasant hour in Flora and Donald's ever-hospitable crofthouse, Colin and Ian left to drive to Ardoe.

They were warmly welcomed at old John Munro's crofthouse. While John poured drams, his wife, Mary, tremulously bustled about preparing, then pouring tea. Peeved, she would not hear of them refusing to taste her freshly made scones. Their explanation that they were replete from an abundance of Flora MacKenzie's scones only made matters worse. Too late, they remembered the feud that had long existed between old Mary and Flora as to who baked the best scones. Year after year at Inveraldrory Highland Games usually one or other of them won first prize for their scones.

"Och, devil take it, you're not telling me that Flora's scones are better than mine, are you?" Mary indignantly asked as she forced a plate of buttered scones on each of them. "I've baked them specially for you, they've just come, warm and smiling, from the oven."

Resolutely they forced themselves to eat while they told of finding the unfortunate cow at the foot of the cliffs and of how they had humanely put it out of its misery. Then, diplomatically, they mollified old Mary by assuring her that those scones of hers truly tasted better than Flora's. As a reward, she insistently forced even more scones on them.

Eventually they managed to break away from the surfeit of buttered scones and drove off. Colin laughed. "I hope to God Jeannie hasn't baked any scones at home today. I couldn't face the sight of another scone!"

"Aye, I feel the same," Ian agreed. He smiled and gave a contented sight, "This is a grand way of working, we get our work well done then leisurely enjoy all the hospitable drams and scones etc. It's certainly a much better, a much more civilised way of working than the hectic way people work in cities, always watching the clock, always under pressure. I don't know how they stand it. Such a life would drive me mad."

"Aye, I know, Ian. It would drive me mad too." Colin grinned, "Och, at least here in the Highlands it's only whisky – or the fear of not getting enough of it – that's likely to drive us two mad."

After a few moments, Colin said, "I suppose you want me to drive you home to Altdour now?"

Ian nodded, "Aye, of course."

"Aye, all right," Colin gave a beaming grin, "Perhaps, if I'm lucky, I might get a dram when I drop you off at Altdour."

"Aye, man, you might… you chust might!"

Coming back to the present, sitting in his 'study' with Ron, Ian laughed apologetically. "I'm sorry, Ron, I've been going on a bit with my story. Helen says that once I start I forget to stop."

"Oh no, Ian, not at all. I sure enjoy hearing your stories."

"Anyway, that's the story of how I used that Luger pistol for the first time."

"Yeah, it's an interesting tale. What a sad end for that unlucky animal." Ron paused then repeated, "Yeah, Ian, I love hearing your stories about this place. And if I'm going to be Laird of Aldrory, as Helen predicted last night, then surely the more I get to know about the district the better. Helen was most definite when she made that prediction, wasn't she? At least that's how it seemed to me, although perhaps I wasn't completely sober when I heard her."

"Aye, you're correct on both counts, Ron. You weren't entirely sober and Helen's prediction most certainly was clear and decisive."

"Do you believe her prediction, then?… Will I be Laird in less than two years?" Ron asked.

Sensing the deep seriousness of his question, Ian thoughtfully replied, "Yes, oh yes, I believe her prediction. It is only rarely that Helen makes such a definite prediction. When she does, she is always 'certain' of its truth."

"I sure would like to hear her try to explain her 'certain' knowledge."

"Well, take my advice, Ron, don't try to question her about it. Leave it to Helen. When – and if – she wants to say more about it, she will choose her own time and her own place."

"Yes, yes, of course I'll do that." After a slight pause, Ron said, "Anyway, thanks for telling me about using that Luger pistol… I wonder if you'll ever use it again?"

Even as he asked that question the name, Campbell-Fotheringay, flashed into Ron's mind. He remembered that incident yesterday when, after he killed his stag, Ian made that remark about the loaded rifle being such a temptation if Campbell-Fotheringay should appear.

Steadily, staring at Ron, Ian repeated that question, "Will I ever use that Luger again?" The hated name, Campbell-Fotheringay, surged loud and clear in his brain.

Neither man spoke that name aloud, but each knew that it was present in their thoughts. Somehow they knew this with absolute certainty.

Eventually Ian solemnly said, "Oh God knows if I'll ever use that pistol again. I suppose the next time there's a firearms amnesty I should hand it into the police. That would put it out of temptation's way, wouldn't it?"

Chapter Five

Ron and Ian smiled as they heard the playful barking of dogs in the front garden. "Ah, here's Helen now, back from walking Glen and Corrie," Ian said.

As soon as Helen opened the door of the 'study', the two dogs came bounding in and boisterously greeted the men. Helen stood and silently surveyed Ron as he politely started to rise to his feet. "Sit down, Ron, sit down. You don't need to stand on ceremony with me. It's pleasantly polite of you though. It's nice to be greeted as a lady occasionally." Helen looked meaningfully at her husband who was firmly seated.

Smiling, she returned her gaze to Ron. Taking in his sorry dishevelled state, she asked, using the exact words Ian had used earlier, "How are you this fine morning, Ron?"

"Oh gee, Helen, I'm not too bad now. But I'm not really too good either. I'm still suffering the after effects of last night's drinking."

"Aye, you're looking gey peelie-wally."

"Pally-wally?" Ron queried.

"No… peelie-wally; very, very pale," Helen explained.

"Oh, really?… Do I look so bad? I feel a good bit better than I did earlier. It's done me good relaxing in this wonderful den of Ian's. I know of no other room like it."

"Aye, it's a unique room right enough, though it would be a lot better if it was tidied up and a heap of rubbish thrown out."

"Och, I'll get round to tidying it up sometime," Ian laughingly promised.

"How long have I been hearing that promise? It must be thirty years since I first heard it," Helen indulgently laughed in turn.

"Och, I promise you I'll tidy it up sometime… sometime within the next thirty years."

"I think the room's just fine and dandy as it is. It would lose much of its character if it was too neat and tidy," Ron declared. "I just love all those stuffed animals and birds and everything else in this den."

"Aye, that's right, I like them as well. Only Helen objected to my skill as a taxidermist," Ian said.

"Oh, really? Why was that, Helen? Don't you like those stuffed creatures? Ron asked.

"Oh, I like them fine when they're completed and on display. But it's such a hideous mess when the poor dead creatures are being transformed. But, above all, what I objected to was Ian keeping the dead animals in the large old freezer while waiting to be stuffed. Every time I opened that freezer I never knew what I would see there. I got tired of having that one-eyed wildcat glare up at me with its wickedly impudent icy wink. It was in the freezer for more than a year before Ian got round to stuffing it."

Ian grinned, "Aye, that one-eyed wildcat was the last animal I stuffed. After that Helen more or less told me to 'get stuffed' myself!"

"Aye," Helen chuckled, "I'd had enough of it. I gave him an ultimatum: either the dead animals went or I went."

"Aye, and that was, what?… about twenty-eight years ago, and you know I'm still not sure if I made the correct decision."

With playful derision Helen gave a cheeky grin and stuck her tongue out at her husband.

Ron laughed then asked, "What was the biggest animal you ever stuffed, Ian?"

"Oh, a large dog fox was my biggest undertaking and I found it large enough. It took me a long time to get it finished."

"It must be some undertaking for taxidermists in museums to stuff huge animals like elephants, mustn't it?"

Although Ron addressed Ian, it was Helen who answered. A smile brightening her voice and a twinkle gleamed in her eyes, "Aye, it must be. I suppose you could say that to stuff an elephant is truly a Mammoth task!"

Once again Ron happily gazed around this wonderful den, then said, "There is only one item I don't care for much; it's that black African mask there. Somehow it seems out of place, seems incongruous, in these pleasant surroundings." All three silently stared at it until Ron asked, "You brought it back from Africa with you, didn't you, Helen?"

"Yes I did. I worked as a nurse for three years in Africa, mostly in Nigeria, just after the war. That mask was given to me by a village chief on behalf of all his people for my help in bringing an epidemic under control. It was a special gift."

Ron could not help thinking that they might have given her a more attractive gift. He felt there was something sinister about that mask. He noticed that as Helen and Ian removed their gaze from it they exchanged a lingering, meaningful glance. He was about to ask more about that mask, but he checked himself. If there was some secret concerning it, and if they ever decided to share that secret with him, then they would do so in their own good time. He simply asked, "Did you enjoy your time in Africa, Helen?"

"Yes, oh yes. I really loved it! We were kept busy, but it was most rewarding helping those simple villagers. They were certainly very primitive but there was something most natural and 'real' in their simple existence lived so close to nature. They retained many senses and instincts and had much intuitive knowledge which most over-civilized Europeans have largely lost."

"Of course they recognised your own intuitive powers and felt you very close to them, didn't they?" Ian quietly remarked.

"Aye, they did. That was one of the reasons I got on so well with them."

"Did you not want to stay longer in Africa, then?" Ron asked.

"Oh yes! I would have loved to stay there much longer, but unfortunately the hot and humid climate did not suit me. I got quite ill and had to leave. That mask always reminds me of my time in Africa."

Again they all silently stared at the crudely carved black mask.

Some mysterious power seemed to draw their eyes to it.

Helen broke the silence, "Could you manage to eat anything, Ron? I don't suppose you've had any breakfast, have you?"

"No, I haven't... I couldn't face any food."

"Och, a hearty greasy breakfast of ham, eggs, sausage and black pudding would set you up fine," Ian suggested.

"Oh hell, Ian, don't be so sadistic," Ron gasped. His still delicate stomach queasily squirmed at the thought of such food.

"Aye, you be quiet, Ian," Helen said. "Not everyone's a hardened drinker like you, with a cast iron stomach... Perhaps you could manage some toast and coffee, Ron?"

An hour later, after they had all finished their toast and were sipping the last of the coffee, Ron asked, "What are you thinking about doing now?"

Ian grinned, "Oh, I suppose we should work in the garden, shouldn't we, Helen?... but it's too lovely an afternoon to waste working. It looks perfect for a pleasant walk. Do you fancy coming with us, Ron? The fresh air and gentle exercise should revive you?"

"Yes, I would love to. But I'd like to freshen up first." Running his hand over the sandpaper rough stubble on his chin, Ron asked, "Do you have a razor I could borrow?"

"A razor?... A razor? What's that? It's twenty-five years since I last shaved," Ian boastfully declared as he complacently ran his fingers over his proudly jutting bushy grey beard.

Ten minutes later Ron came downstairs with his appearance much improved. He had washed, his hair was combed, his kilt and stockings were neatly arranged and he had his shoes on.

"That's much better," Helen approved. "You're more like your usual immaculate self."

The dogs watched the human's preparations with keen interest. Their alertly cocked ears and gleaming eyes impatiently followed every move. With restless frustration each dog once again wondered why those humans took such an interminable time to get ready to go a walk.

Ian set an easy pace and soon all got into their stride as they followed the path that meandered along above the River Aldrory. After a couple of miles, the path parted company with the river and adventurously struck out on its own. Constantly twisting and turning, it purposefully snaked its way across the rugged, hummocky, brown and ochre heathery moor, then it stealthily slithered between steep grey crags where tenacious rowans clung amongst lichened rocks and flamboyantly flamed their proud autumn colour. Their crimson berries vied in glory with the reds and yellows and orange of the dying leaves.

Now the path split and nervously reconnoitred a few routes through an area of quaky peat bog and small, dark lochans. As the party safely, though squelchily, picked their way around one lochan whose sinister, peaty darkness suggested bottomless depths, Ron said, "Isn't it amazing how much variety there is in this countryside, even in just a few miles?"

"Aye, it is, and the scenery constantly changes with the ever changing weather, too," Ian replied.

Fleets of white clouds sailed before the warm Southerly breeze and exuberantly chased one another across the immense Highland sky. Their shadows impetuously surged across moors, sailed over lochs and playfully leap-frogged over crouching mountains. Brightened by splashes of sunshine the entire scene was a lively fluttering patchwork of glorious, ever changing light and shade.

"This pleasant breeze will blow your alcoholic cobwebs away, Ron," Helen smiled.

"Yeah, I'm feeling much better and brighter already. I sure am enjoying this walk." Then, turning to Ian, he said, "Gee, the kilt's a most comfortable garment for walking in, isn't it? I feel I could happily and effortlessly walk for miles enjoying the freedom of movement it gives and its swinging comfort."

Ian, wearing his own kilt, said, "Aye, I wholeheartedly agree, Ron, it is a fine garment, right enough. Soon, once you are Laird of Aldrory, you'll be able to wear your kilt all the time. And you'll need to add an eagle's feather to your bonnet to proclaim yourself Laird. Then you'll truly be Monarch of this 'your own, your native land'."

Both men looked speculatively at Helen, but she did not take them up on this reference to her prophecy of last night. She only smiled and said, "Aye, it's fine seeing you braw Hielanders swinging along in such jaunty style."

With real pleasure the humans and the dogs walked on, sharing – and rejoicing in sharing – the same wild countryside, although actually they inhabited quite different worlds. For the humans this was a world of bright skies, of majestic mountains and vast horizons. It was a world they consciously reacted to with keen aesthetic delight.

The dog's world was much more circumscribed. It was almost exclusively a world of scents. That path and its surroundings were a paradise of scents. Each intriguing fresh smell had to be investigated with the keenest of enthusiasm. Many voles – the short-lived prey of so many hungry predators – had left their criss-cross tracks across the path. So too had the mercilessly pursuing stoats. Once, the more rare scent of an elusive wildcat excited both dogs. Once, against the familiar background scents of heather, soggy peat, damp woolled sheep and the strong smell of red deer, came another scent; it was so strong, so overpoweringly unmistakable that even the pathetically poor human nostrils could not miss it – the pungent, musky odour of a dog fox's urine.

The path now gently sloped across another wide expanse of heathery moor. The humans happily strolled along it, now with animated talk, now in contented silent companionship. Once silence was abruptly ended by Ian shouting, "Steady Glen!... Steady!"

As motionless as a statue – a lovely black and white statue, Glen the neat Collie, stood 'pointing'. It was unusual for a Collie to point, but Glen when hardly more than a puppy had instinctively pointed as keenly as any well-trained gun dog. It had taken Ian only a little patient training to get Glen to hold his point and not rush in on the birds. Glen had helped Ron get his 'Macnab' yesterday by pointing grouse for him.

He stood with right front paw held high, tail held stiffly straight and with his entire body registered that perfect point. Only his nostrils nervously moved. Quivering, they eagerly analysed the delightful strong scent coming from the red grouse hidden in the heather in front of him.

Silently and cautiously all the others approached Glen. Corrie, the well-trained terrier, obediently kept at Ian's heels as he whispered praise, "Well done, Glen. Steady... Steady!"

Tensely expectant, they again all slowly moved forward.

A covey of grouse dramatically exploded from the heather.

As always – although expected – the suddenness of the birds' explosive flight was startling. Like spreading chunks of shrapnel, seven grouse scattered away in every direction. They sped on frantic whirring wings. They swore in guttural protest, "Go back! Go back! Go back!"

Instantly, instinctively, Ian threw his walking stick up to his right shoulder and aimed it like a shotgun at the fleeing grouse. "Bang! Bang!" he shouted. "Oh damn, a right and a left barrel and I missed with them both."

Laughing, Ron enthusiastically joined in this male, this boyish, fantasy. "Yeah, so you did. I'm disappointed in you, Ian. I thought you were a much better shot than that!"

Grinning, they both turned towards Helen. Slowly she shook her head. Secure in the superiority of her femininity she threw them a lenient smile – a bright smile, warm with indulgent maternal tolerance. "Och, I suppose boys will be boys... Will you never grow up, Ian?"

"I hope not... I sincerely hope not."

"No," Ron agreed, "I hope you never do."

Ian grinned, "No, I hope I never grow up if growing up means becoming a dull, sober, respectable and miserable old man like my brother. Surely you wouldn't want me to become like him, would you?"

"No, true enough. I certainly wouldn't. I suppose I'll just have to put up with you, imperfect as you are," Helen again indulgently smiled.

"I've never met your brother; never heard you speak much about him although he lives in Aldrory Glen quite near you, doesn't he?" Ron asked.

"Aye, he does. He and his wife live about a mile down the glen from us, but we don't see much of them. We have almost no interests in common."

"William MacLean, Ian's brother, is as different from him as chalk from cheese," stated Helen.

"Aye, and his wife, Catherine, is as different from Helen as life is from death," Ian said. "My brother was a bank manager. He lived most of his life in Edinburgh until he and his wife retired to Aldrory Glen some six or seven years ago. At one time we did not speak to one another, but now when we meet we all talk politely to each other."

"Aye, we certainly are polite; coldly, icily polite," Helen grinned.

"Oh, I find it difficult, very difficult indeed, to imagine either of you being icily polite to anyone," Ron declared.

"Och, my disagreement with William goes back many years," Ian explained. "William is two years older than me, and being the oldest brother he expected to inherit Altdour, the family croft. My father died during the war when I was in the army in Italy and so my mother kept the croft going by herself, with the help of good neighbours, until I came back after the war. Then I did most of the work on the croft with my mother helping. All this time William was working in his Edinburgh bank. He and his wife only very rarely came on summer holidays to Altdour."

Ian paused and smiled in amused recollection. "No, they did not come to Altdour often. My mother, who was a bright and cheery character, could not stand William's wife who was very dull, very respectable, and very conscious of being a 'superior' bank manager's posh wife. Anyway, my mother arranged with the Crofter's Commission that I, as her working crofter son was to inherit the croft and crofthouse on her death. Had William inherited them he would only have used, and rented out, the house as a holiday home. As you can well imagine, he was most annoyed when I inherited the croft. For many years afterwards we never saw, or had any communication with one another. However, we are now on friendly, formally friendly, terms."

"What does you brother do here, now that he's retired? Does he do any salmon or trout fishing?" Ron asked.

"Och no, not him. Even now that he's retired with a good fat pension and is very comfortably off on the proceeds of a lifetime's savings and shrewd investments, he still has only one real interest, a passion really – to ever increase his wealth. What do you make of a man who loudly declares that all his life he has read nothing but the *Financial Times* and the *Investors Chronicle*? Who boasts of it proudly instead of being ashamed of it? He and his wife are well matched; they are notorious as the meanest couple in this district. They are both non-smokers and strictly teetotal. They campaign strongly against all alcoholic drink."

Helen and Ron burst into unrestrained laughter at the passionate intensity of Ian's disgust as he spat out those last two sentences.

Ron gasped, "Obviously to you, Ian, there can be no greater condemnation of anyone than for them to be completely teetotal."

"Surely if you were like your brother and did not drink or smoke, you would have a better chance of living longer," Helen mischievously suggested, with a shrewd idea of what his answer would be.

"Och, I don't know if I would really live any longer – but I know it would damn well seem a hell of a lot longer!"

Once the renewed laughter died down Ian continued, "It's not just them being teetotal non-smokers, it's what goes with it as well. They are also most narrow-minded sanctimonious prigs. I hate their hypocrisy. True Christians are enjoined not to serve both God and Mammon, however that couple certainly manage to do just that. At least they definitely serve Mammon. I don't know so much about them truly serving God."

"I thought you didn't like to speak much about them," Helen smiled. "You're saying plenty now!"

Taking her gentle hint in good part, Ian fell silent.

"Gee, they sure sound entirely different from you two. You're hardly sanctimonious prigs, are you? Ron gleefully asked.

"I hope not!"… "No, I should hope not!" Helen and Ian answered simultaneously.

"Do they have any children?"

"Aye, they have one son, Nigel. He's studying at Glasgow University," Ian replied.

"What's he like? Does he take after his terrible parents?"

Helen said, "Oh no! Nigel's a fine lad, we both like him a lot."

"Aye, he's a grand lad," Ian confirmed, "He's usually in revolt against his parents' ways; I suppose that's to be expected, isn't it? He loves fishing. He's been out poaching salmon with me a few times. His parents think I'm a bad influence on him."

"Oh, really?"

"Aye, he takes after his uncle Ian much more than he does his own father." Helen again mischievously smiled, "Thank goodness!"

After a short pause Ron said, "I'm afraid I'm a bit like your brother. I have to spend much of my time reading financial newspapers and magazines and also like him, without boasting, my wealth steadily increases year after year."

"Aye, you bloated plutocrat, you should be ashamed of yourself," Ian laughed. "But at least you do realise that you're wasting your life and want to change it before it's too late. You know that there should be much more to life than accumulating wealth and worshipping Mammon."

"Aye, that's true. And you will change your lifestyle soon, within two years, you do believe that, Ron, don't you?" Helen, suddenly serious, asked.

"Oh, Helen, I really don't know if I believe that or not. Your prediction seems almost too good to come true, but if you are so completely certain, then yes, yes, I will believe you."

"Good! Now let's not waste any more of this lovely afternoon talking about my dear in-laws. Let's continue our walk."

Ian whistled the dogs and they left off sniffing the intriguingly strong scents and the bright yellow droppings left by the vanished grouse. Eagerly they bounded ahead of the striding humans, Glen with two small downy grouse feathers sticking to his wet black nose.

They followed the path along by the side of an attractive small burn. Lit by slanting gleams of sunshine the burn flowed brightly and cheerily, its amber water noisily gurgled round mossy stones and gently chuckled over golden pebbles.

"Does this bonnie burn have a name?" Ron asked.

"Aye, it has. It's called Aldour Burn, the burn of the otter. It's the burn that flows through our garden and gives our croft its name," Ian explained.

"Oh, really? I didn't realise that this was the same stream. Do you often see otters here?"

"Oh aye, quite often. It's obvious that otters come here 'regularly', isn't it?" Ian grinned and pointed with his stick at a neat, verdant pyramid rising on a grassy bank of the burn.

"What is it?" Ron asked.

"It is an otters' latrine."

All, especially the dogs, closely inspected that vivid green mound.

This morning's droppings, left so tidily on the very peak of the pyramid, showed up darkly against the many older droppings whose crushed and bleached fish bones glared with conspicuous whiteness in the revealing sunlight. Each dog lifted a hind leg and disdainfully showered urine over that tidy latrine.

As they walked away Ron said, "Gosh, I wouldn't have noticed that if I'd been by myself. I guess I've still a lot to learn from you, Ian, about this fascinating countryside. You don't miss much, do you?"

"No, I hope I don't. After all, I've had a lifetime's experience and observation of this land. By now I can read it like a book. I can read it as easily as you can read and understand your company accounts and all the other financial figures and jargon, most of which would be unintelligible 'Double Dutch' to me."

"You will learn, Ron. You will soon learn once you are living here as Laird," Helen stated, tantalising him again, then she hurried on before he could question her.

About a mile further on Ian noticed both dogs indulging in strange antics after they had pounced on something. As he got closer, he recognised the object that had interested them and with quiet amusement said, "Oh, poor Corrie, poor Glen, you don't care for that taste much, do you?"

The dogs were vigorously rubbing their muzzles on the grass and pawing at their mouths in desperate attempts to get rid of a strong, unpleasant taste.

"What is it? What's the matter with them?" Helen urgently asked.

"This is the matter. They don't like the unpleasant taste." Ian used his walking stick to carefully lift up a strange white object.

"What is it?" Helen and Ron asked together.

That unusual object suspended on Ian's stick looked, for all the world, like a child's glove neatly turned outside in.

"It's the skin of a toad. Both dogs lifted it then immediately dropped it as it has a most unpleasant taste. That vile taste is the toad's only defence against predators and it's usually very effective. As far as I know the otter is the only animal that has learned to deal with it. After they've grabbed a toad, the otters somehow manage to neatly skin it before eating its tasty, fleshy body."

"Gee, they sure make a very neat job of skinning it don't they?"

"Aye, they do, Ron, I suppose it's a case of an otter doing what an otter oughter do!" Ian grinned.

"What was that again?" Ron asked with a perplexed frown.

"Och, take no notice of him. He's just havering again. He's just opening his big mouth and letting his fat belly rumble!" Helen exclaimed. She then examined the toad's white skin with real interest. She felt there was something repulsive, something almost obscenely disgusting about that strange object. This was the first one she had ever seen. "Is the toad still alive while the otter's skinning it?" she asked.

"Aye, I believe it is."

"Oh, that's cruel!... Isn't that terribly cruel?"

"There is no such word as 'cruel' in nature. Surely you know that by now, Helen? Nature is neither cruel nor kind. It is neither moral nor immoral. It is simply amoral. Nature is entirely unaware of, such sentimental human terms and feelings. Those otters, and every other species, are only concerned with their ceaseless struggle for survival."

"Oh yes, I know that, Ian. You've told me that often enough. If I try to think coolly and logically, like you, then I know what you say is undoubtedly true," Helen conceded. Then, giving her quick, mischievous, child-like smile, she warmly declared, "Yet, despite what you say, I still think that otter was very cruel! I doubt if I'll ever be able to be so fond of otters in the future."

Ian made no verbal reply. He contented himself with slowly shaking his head and smiling with tolerance and affection at this further example of Helen's mind working in its profoundly feminine, profoundly illogical way.

"What do you think, Ron?" Helen asked.

"Oh, I'm saying nothing. I've heard you two discuss such questions before. I'm staying neutral."

"Coward!" Ian exclaimed as he lifted his stick high and threw the toad's skin across the burn.

"That vile taste won't harm the dogs, I hope. It's not poisonous is it?" Helen anxiously asked.

"Oh no, it's not poisonous, it's just unpleasant. The dogs will soon get over it."

They walked on and Helen was reassured by seeing both dogs run ahead and resume their usual keenly sniffing habits. The path now steadily climbed towards Cairndhu, that small rocky peak which rose steeply behind Altdour croft. Before reaching that summit the dogs, without being told, left the main path and followed a faint track through the heather, which they knew led to the small sheltered hollow where the humans often stopped and rested. As soon as she reached that pleasant spot, Helen carelessly threw herself down full length on the dry heather. Lying enjoying the young heather's springy comfort, she noted how closely the faded fawns and greens of her tweed skirt matched the heather's subtle colours. On each side of her Ian and Ron much more circumspectly settled themselves. They each neatly smoothed the pleats of their kilt under them as they sat, then they too lay back in comfort.

"Gosh, this sure is a marvellous viewpoint. It's almost exactly where we rested yesterday with the stag, isn't it? What was it you called this place, Ian?"

"Oh yes, this is where you fell asleep yesterday when you were supposed to be on sentry duty," laughed Ian. "It's called 'Caladh' – the Haven."

"It sure is well named. This spot certainly is a real haven of peace and tranquillity. Was it you who named it?"

"No. My grandfather named it 'Caladh'. He often came up here for peace and to meditate. Aye, it is a real haven, right enough."

All fell silent. All let their gaze wander over the wonderful landscape stretching enticingly before them. Craig Mhor and Craig Beag rose companionably together in the East. Small Stac Pollaidh defiantly bristled its sandstone hackles in terrier fierce display in the South, and from there the rugged heather moors of Rubha Mor stretched towards the West and stabbed a lonely peninsula out into the sea. There the Minch took over and glittered out to touch the hidden Hebrides.

Although the gaze of these enthralled humans wandered far over this huge panorama, each eye inevitably returned to and came to rest on just one mountain – Suileag. The lure of this unique mountain was irresistible. Its thrusting, fantastic shape towered in overwhelming majesty and dominated the entire landscape.

Viewed from the West, Suileag rose alone in inimitable vertical splendour and overshadowed the village of Inveraldrory. When half revealed in mist it menacingly lurked like some prehistoric monster malevolent in its lair.

Ron removed his gaze from Suileag and searched out towards the West. "We can't see the Hebrides today, can we?"

"No, we can't. They're hidden by that distant hazy mist," Ian said.

"What is it you've told me before about the Hebrides and rain?" Ron asked. "I can't quite remember?"

"Och, it's just an old joke…"

"A very old joke!" Helen interposed.

"Aye, well, perhaps. Anyway it goes as follows: If you can see the Hebrides from here, then that's a sure sign that it's going to rain; and if you cannot see them, then it is raining!"

Helen once more loyally laughed at that hoary old joke of Ian's.

Ron paused thoughtfully then said, "If your prediction does come true, Helen, then I will be monarch, or at least laird, of much of this view I'm now surveying, won't I?"

"Aye, you will be, Ron. I again assure you that you will be Laird of Aldrory Estate, and soon." Helen's voice was firm with absolute certainty.

Ron turned to Ian. "How much of this view does Aldrory Estate actually take in?"

"The – or should it be, your? – estate starts at the sea, takes in Inveraldrory village, continues up Aldrory Glen to here, then takes in Suileag and from that mountain stretches to near the foot of Craig Mhor. Some twenty thousand acres in all."

"So if – oh sorry, Helen – *when* I become Laird of Aldrory, I'll own Suileag?"

"Aye, that' right. You'll own Old Suileag there." Ian pointed and smiled, "Although surely it's ridiculous for any human to think they can actually 'own' that mountain in any real sense of owning."

"Yes, I agree, Ian, it would be a gigantic impertinence for me to think that I really owned such a unique mountain. When I buy the estate I will feel that I'm privileged to hold Suileag in trust for a short time before passing it on to the Scottish Nation via a body like The National Trust for Scotland."

Ian nodded, "Yes, that would be the correct thing to do, Ron. I can see you're going to be a great laird."

"Oh, of course he will," Helen exclaimed. "With us to guide you, Ron, you'll be the best laird Aldrory Estate has ever had."

"I hope so… I hope so. I give you my solemn promise that I will do my very best for the estate and for everyone living on it." As he made this passionately sincere promise, Ron felt all his doubts drop away. Suddenly he felt certain, as certain as Helen, that her prediction would come true, that he would be laird of Aldrory within two years. It was a strange, an exhilarating sensation, but it came shadowed with a definite sense of apprehension. How, he wondered, will this come about? How will the many problems standing in the way of him becoming laird be solved?

For a while these three humans were thoughtfully silent. They lay back in comfort and Ian contentedly puffed his pipe.

Eventually Ron broke the silence, "Suileag and all those other mountains are ancient, aren't they? Just how old are they reckoned to be?"

"They are almost three billion years old," Ian replied.

"Three billion years?… Gee, that's incredible!"

"That's what the geologists assure us. Those mountains are made of some of the oldest rock in the world – rock that is almost three thousand million years old. Through that vast expanse of time, the softer rock has been eroded away leaving those small stumps of hard rock as tombstones in memory of the immensity of time."

"That's amazing!" Ron gasped. "It's very humbling to think of such vastness of time, isn't it?"

"Aye, it is. Auld Suileag there may well exist long after our transient human species has become extinct, just as it has existed for millions of years before our conceitedly self-important species came into being."

Helen had been silently listening, and intently staring at Suileag. She now quietly, but distinctly, spoke. "It gives me an uncanny feeling to think of its age. It's awesome to think of such vast aeons of time, such titanic forces, such colossal geological upheavals. It makes all our engrossing human affairs seem so terribly petty and trivial. And yet… and yet, I feel – I know – that those vast impersonal forces in some mysterious way shape our destinies; shape them in some obscure manner, which no human can begin to comprehend. Only a very few, a few gifted – or cursed? – with special powers, can sometimes, somehow, most mysteriously tune into those obscure forces." She paused and gave a gentle smile. "It's… it's very difficult for me to state clearly what I feel. How can I describe an indescribable feeling? But I do know that those inexplicable things are undoubtedly true."

This was the first time Ron had heard Helen trying to express such deep feelings. He was impressed by the intensity of her conviction. Hers certainly was a very different world from his 'normal' world of international finance and business. Almost shuddering, he forced himself to think of that 'normal' world of his, which he had escaped from for a couple of blissful weeks. Was that 'normal' world the true reality? Was this calmer, slower, world of the West Highlands an illusion?… or was it a last lingering remnant of an ancient, a much more truly civilised reality? Ron smiled to himself as he thought of how his workaholic old father would unhesitatingly answer these questions. He now smiled at Ian, "What do you think about what Helen has been saying?"

Ian grinned, "Oh, I don't know what to think. When I was young I thought I knew all the answers; now that I'm old I'm not so sure about such things. I find it's almost impossible to believe that all us so terribly insignificant creatures can have our lives pre-determined by vast unknown forces. It just seems another example of the limitless immensity of our human conceit." He paused and smiled affectionately at Helen. "And yet I know Helen well enough by now to be certain that she does possess powers that are inexplicable. Anyway, Ron, within two years you will know if your pre-destined fate is to be Laird of Aldrory. We will all be waiting on tenterhooks for Helen's prophesy to come true."

Ron nodded wholeheartedly, "Yeah, I'll be eagerly waiting for my destiny to be fulfilled. It is very brave of you, Helen, to make such a definite prediction, to put your powers on trial in this way."

Suddenly a couple of butterflies appeared from nowhere and gaily fluttered their gaudy colours over the short heather beside them.

"Oh," Ron exclaimed. "They look exactly like the ones we saw here yesterday, don't they?"

"Aye, they do and quite possible they are direct descendants of the ones I saw as a boy here with my grandfather all those years ago."

Helen smiled, "You look very like the photos of your grandfather as you sit there with your white hair and beard and puff on your old pipe. With those butterflies fluttering about in every direction it's as if time had turned full circle, as if we were back with your grandfather again sixty years ago."

Ian slowly removed his pipe, then, as his grandfather had so often done, gently, contentedly, exhaled a stream of bluish grey smoke. Thoughtfully he murmured, "Aye, I feel something of that myself. It's a strange feeling of déjà vu." He sighed, "Ah weel, perhaps that's what most of us humans do… go round in circles and get nowhere. Or perhaps if we're wiser we get back to where our roots are and get back in touch with our ancestors."

Helen smiled. "Even this walk today has taken us round in a circle. Once we get home we'll have completed a full circuit."

"Aye," Ian said, "and what's more we'll have done the circuit in the correct way."

"The correct way?" Ron asked, "What do you mean?"

Ian laughed, "We've travelled clockwise, travelled with the sun. When they started out in their boats, all the old fishermen and crofters were always careful to turn them clockwise. To turn a boat widdershins, against the course of the sun, was considered most unlucky. Now I suppose we better get moving and head, correctly, for home and, if we're lucky, for dinner. I'm beginning to feel hungry. Of course that view usually makes me hungry, it reminds me of my favourite meal." Ian pointed at the bright glittering Western sea.

Helen smiled indulgently. She had heard this joke before – often. However, Ron rose to the bait; puzzled, he asked, "How does that view possibly remind you of your favourite meal?"

Ian replied with another question, "What is the name of that sea?"

"It's part of the Atlantic surely, part of the Western Atlantic."

"Aye, but what's that particular part between this West Sutherland mainland and the Outer Hebrides?"

Suddenly remembering, Ron triumphantly exclaimed, "Oh, of course, that's the Minch."

"Aye, that's right. That's why it reminds me of my favourite meal: my Minch and Tatties!"

Ron wore a perplexed frown until Helen explained, "His mince and potatoes."

With eyes twinkling, she turned to her husband, "Oh, Ian, I've told you before, you should tell better jokes than that, ones I don't need to explain!"

Chapter Six

That bright day was the last dry one they enjoyed for a while.

When Ian woke early the next morning he was not surprised to hear rain battering against the bedroom window. Late last night he'd noticed the wind veering towards the South West and getting stronger. He knew that wind from that quarter almost invariably brought rain driving in from the Atlantic. He also knew that, once started, that rain was most reluctant to stop. Opening his eyes, he slowly sat up in bed and watched the rain weep down the windowpanes. He listened to the wind sob and sigh around the old crofthouse's stout walls and draughtily whistle through gaps between the quivering window and the wooden frame. Reluctantly, he eased himself out of bed and into his oldest jeans and other disreputable old clothes. Gently he wakened Helen.

At nine o'clock, breakfast over, he struggled into thigh length rubber fishing waders then into his waxed waterproof Barbour jacket in preparation for going salmon fishing with Ron.

As arranged, Ron drove up and Ian dashed out into the battering storm then threw himself into the car. Jolting down the rutted narrow road they faced directly into the almost horizontally driven rain. The windscreen wipers blinked dementedly as they frantically tried to cope with the water threatening to engulf them.

Ron parked the car beside the flooding River Aldrory. The small car park was already awash with deep puddles, which were getting deeper and wider by the minute. The slim hazels and stunted birch trees bowed and shook before the blast.

Ian sighed and ruefully asked, "Do we really need to go out fishing in this bloody rain?"

Ron laughed, "Oh, Ian, surely you're getting soft in your old age. When I first knew you, a few drops of rain like this never bothered you."

"Aye, well, that's as may be. Just you wait until you're my age." Ian smiled and with forced enthusiasm said, "Och, I suppose we better get going and try to miserably enjoy ourselves."

At the first pool they expertly read the state of the river and shrewdly guessed where salmon were most like to be found in the rising spate. Ron said, "You go first, Ian. Go ahead – 'Lead on, Macduff.'"

"Aye, all right, thanks. I'll fish down through the pool quickly."

Ian lifted his fishing rod and was soon tilting that lance expertly but ineffectively at this hidden adversary, the challengingly elusive Highland salmon. The next few hours passed quickly and, despite the weather, quite pleasantly.

The rain continued to pour and the river continued to rise. These experienced fishermen knew that under such conditions there was little chance of catching salmon. However, with the unflagging optimism of dedicated fishers they fished on, ever hoping, against the odds, to meet up with at least one of those ever perverse, ever unpredictable fish which, despite the conditions, was interested in their glitteringly attractive flies.

Just as they were about to give it up as hopeless, Ron hooked a large salmon. Fresh from the sea, it was in prime condition. It struggled fiercely. It rushed across the pool then leapt high. It dived deep and sulked behind a rock.

Finally, using the massive strength of the flooded river as an ally, the salmon tore irresistibly down the pool. With his powerful rod bent in a vibrating arc, Ron applied maximum pressure but still his reel whirled and dementedly screamed as the line sliced through the dark water in urgent pursuit of the salmon. If the fish got out of the pool and into the turbulent rapids below it would escape to freedom.

Ian had anticipated this possibility. Precariously balanced on a flat, but wet and slippery rock at the foot of the pool, he alertly waited with his large landing net firmly gripped and keenly poised. Suddenly the salmon appeared on the surface splashing and struggling at the very tail of the pool. It started sliding into the wild water below. Quickly, urgently and skilfully, Ian lunged with the landing net. In one swift movement he scooped the fish into the net. The startling weight of the salmon and force of the water almost unbalanced him. He staggered. His feet slipped. Desperately he regained his balance. With the salmon securely imprisoned in the net, he leapt for the riverbank. Flinging himself on top of the struggling salmon, he quickly killed it with a few blows of a heavy stone.

Ron eagerly weighed the fish. It was almost thirteen pounds of silvery bright, firm muscled splendour. He smiled, "I thought thirteen was an unlucky number?"

"Ah well, I suppose it was unlucky for that poor salmon." Ian grinned, "It was almost unlucky for me as well, I nearly fell in as I netted it. Anyway you were very lucky to get it, Ron."

"Yeah, I know. But it wasn't only luck; it was also thanks to your skilled and daring effort with the landing net that I did get it."

Back in the relative luxury of the car they settled down to enjoy their lunch. Ron munched his dainty sandwiches, part of the neatly packed lunch provided by his posh hotel. Ian laboriously ploughed through the much coarser and thicker sandwiches he had made for himself at breakfast time.

Looking out at the depressing soaking scene, seeing it waveringly distorted by the films of rainwater flowing down the car's windows, Ian smiled, "Do you still want to be Laird of Aldrory, Ron? Do you still want to own this land of rain, storm and flood? Would you not rather retire to one of your own Sunshine States?"

"If this weather continues for much longer, I might be seriously tempted... but no, this place is where I mean to retire to. I intend to make my home in this, 'my own, my native land.'"

"Good!... good! That's what I like to hear. I'm pleased to know you're so determined to settle here. The sooner the better."

"Thanks, Ian. I truly am determined now, despite all the obstacles."

"Aye, and that bastard Campbell-Fotheringay is one of the biggest obstacles. How are we going to surmount that seemingly insurmountable obstacle I wonder?"

"Well Helen seems to have no doubt that all difficulties will be overcome, that I will become laird. Do her predictions usually come true?"

"Aye, they do. Almost invariably they do."

"It sure is amazing for her to have such strange powers, isn't it? When did you first find out about them?"

Ian took his time about replying. He silently gathered his thoughts and sorted out his memories. "I suppose the first time I had real evidence of her powers was about twenty-nine years ago, just a year or so after we were married. That first experience was not a prediction, but was just as inexplicable."

Remembering that event, Ian was surprised at how clearly the details came back to him after all those years; then he reflected that this was a clear sign of his age. It seemed undoubtedly true that as one became old it was increasingly much easier to recall distant memories, especially vivid wartime memories, than to remember details of things that had happened last month or last week. He sighed resignedly then started telling his story.

Very early one fine June morning, friends returning to Glasgow had dropped Helen and Ian off from their car at a certain point on the Ledmhor to Ullapool road. From there they set out on the path which led into the heart of the wild, unpopulated country which stretched some fifteen miles from the road to the sea in the West at Inveraldrory village. They intended to go round by the North of Suileag mountain and fish for trout in some of the many lochs scattered about in this ruggedly primitive untamed land. Eventually they would make their way back to their crofthouse at Altdour.

Morning's eager sunlight came sliding brightly round distant Eastern hills and brought with it a pleasant Southerly breeze. It was one of those blessed mornings which promise a perfect Highland June day; days which stretch endlessly in cloudless blue glory, with sunshine from earliest dawn until long lingering dusk when the sun slowly and reluctantly sinks into the Minch and leaves the Western sky painted with tremulous, golden glowing Turnerish sunset.

Helen and Ian made their way from loch to loch. Eagerly they explored and fished each fresh loch. All those lochs were new to them. Even Ian, who from boyhood had fished many of Aldrory's almost countless lochs and lochans, had not fished in this remote area before.

After two hours of walking and fishing, they came to a derelict house. It was lonely and long abandoned. At its Westerly gable the roof sadly sagged. The

94

rotting joists held the remaining tiles at a steep slope like a dark glacier and attempted to prevent any more from slithering to join the ones already littering the ground. These fallen tiles were being engulfed by a conquering growth of lush nettles.

From the skull of the once proudly whitewashed house's front wall the glassless windows blankly stared and the dark doorway vacantly gaped. In front of the doorway a couple of gateposts leaned drunkenly gateless. To the side of one post an old Rowan tree barely survived. Most of its branches were bleached white and were dry, brittle and lifeless. Only a very few brave green leaves untidily and precariously clung to life. To Helen and Ian it seemed as if, ashamed of its failure to protect this house, that Rowan had dejectedly decided to slowly die along with the slowly dying house.

Tall tough brackens rioted everywhere and aggressively encroached over what had once been cultivated ground. Beyond the house a line of Larch trees struggled to survive. Stunned and gaunt, they were in a forlornly pitiful state. Their branches stretched horizontally. Deformed by winter's Westerly gales, every tree, Muslim like, bowed towards the East.

Despite the warm June sunshine, Helen suddenly shivered, "Oh, how terribly desolate that ruined house and those dismal trees must look in dull, dreich weather."

"Aye, they certainly will," Ian agreed. "Even in this bright sunlight they don't look exactly cheerful, do they?"

"No, they don't. Oh, let's get away from here, Ian."

"Aye, all right. If I remember rightly from the map, there should be a wee loch just over that ridge."

They soon proved that he had remembered correctly. From that heathery ridge they gazed down at a small circular loch gently set in a secluded green hollow. It looked most attractive, a liquid diamond sparkling in the sunshine. Patches of Water Lily leaves dotted much of its surface. They saw a feeding trout rise.

"That looked a big trout, didn't it? Come on, let's get going," Ian eagerly exclaimed.

Within five minutes he caught a lovely trout, which weighed exactly two pounds. He admired its plump golden beauty then held it boastfully high, complacently expecting to receive Helen's praise. He was amazed to discover that she was not fishing. She was sitting on a slope above the loch. Her small body was huddled over; she held her bowed head in both hands. She was a picture of utter dejection.

"What's the matter? Why aren't you fishing?" Ian shouted.

Helen did not reply. She slowly raised her sad head and silently stared at him.

Puzzled, Ian again shouted, "What's the matter?"

Still she did not speak. Slowly and, it seemed, with a weary effort she raised an arm and weakly beckoned him to come to her.

Ian reluctantly left the loch side and strode towards that small figure again sitting with pathetically bowed head and her body wearily slumped like a half-closed clasp-knife.

"What's the matter?" he once more enquired, "Are you not well?"

Slowly, painfully slowly, as with a terrible effort, Helen lifted her head and looked up at him. Ian was surprised, and moved, to see her eyes brimming with tears. Quickly he sat beside her, put his arm reassuringly around her and drew her small body firmly to him. Slowly shaking her head she murmured, "No, Ian, I'm not ill." She paused, Ian started to speak, but Helen interrupted him. "No, I'm not ill, but I cannot fish here. I must get away from this loch."

Mystified, he asked, "But what's wrong? Why can't you fish here?"

"Oh, I don't know exactly. I just feel very, very unhappy here. There's something wrong here. There's something terribly sad about this loch."

With an effort Ian controlled his rising annoyance, "But it's a lovely wee loch. There are lovely big trout in it – look!" He eagerly pointed as another large trout rose to feed on a hatching fly.

"I'm sorry, Ian, but I must get away from here."

"Are you ill?" he anxiously asked again; he could think of no other possible explanation for her strange behaviour. He was alarmed to see her in this dejected state, so unlike her normal happily contented state. Only a short time before she had been keenly anticipating fishing this lovely small loch.

She did not answer but attempted to rise. Ian held her firmly down beside him. "Wait, Helen, let's try to fathom this out reasonably and logically. We both – but you especially – felt there was something very sad and depressing about that abandoned house, about seeing it slowly fall into ruin. It is sad to think of it having once been happily full of human life and now to see it painfully dying. Surely it's just that understandable feeling of sadness that's still with you? I can appreciate that, Helen, but it's not like you to let such a feeling get you down like this."

"Oh, you don't understand, Ian. This is a much, much, more definite feeling than anything I felt at that ruined house." She paused then hesitantly added, "But... but that desolate house is connected with this sadness here at this loch... I feel sure they are linked in some way."

"But what exactly is it that you feel? Why must you get away from here?"

"Oh, Ian, I can't explain it logically. It's a feeling I have – a deep, deep feeling. It's something entirely different from your calm, male guidelines of logic and reason which you foolishly think can explain everything in life."

Getting exasperated, Ian persisted, "But what exactly is it that you so strongly feel?"

"Oh, Ian, I feel – I know – that there's been some terrible tragedy happened here at this loch in the past. Something very sad, something involving children." Stifling a sob, she pleaded in bewilderment, "Oh, don't you feel anything of this, Ian? Don't you feel something of what I so deeply feel?"

Ian bemusedly shook his head, "No I'm sorry, Helen, I sense nothing of that at all. To me it remains just a lovely wee loch with big trout in it – trout we should be fishing for at this moment." Smiling encouragingly he pleaded, "Surely you could give it a try?"

With trembling lips Helen imploringly gasped, "Oh, Ian, do you love me?"

"Yes, yes, of course I do!" he somewhat impatiently assured her.

Then more gently added, "You know I do."

"Well, if you do love me, please, please, let's get away from this sad, sad place. Please do it without any more discussion or attempts at explanations."

Deeply moved by that desperately agitated plea, by the tears miserably overflowing her pleading eyes, by those trembling lips, Ian relented and compassionately hugged her tighter. "Aye, all right, we'll move on to the next lochs."

"Oh, thank you, Ian... I'm sorry, you must think me very foolish, but I simply must get away from this terribly sad loch." Helen smiled bravely through her tears and her face radiantly brightened in that way which Ian always found so moving.

He smiled in return, tightly embraced her and tenderly and lovingly kissed her. She eagerly returned his kisses. After a minute Ian withdrew his lips and grinned, "Come on, Helen, if you must get away from here, we better go now before you arouse me too much."

Helen's eyes smiled brightly into his, "Yes, that's what I was thinking too. Perhaps I will arouse you properly later on, when we are away from here."

Ian again grinned, "Oh, promises!... promises!"

They were only about one year married and were still passionately in love with one another. They had not had a serious quarrel yet.

Reaching into his sporran, Ian withdrew his large khaki handkerchief and offered it to Helen, saying, "Here, you better wipe your tears away."

As expected, Ian was delighted to see real laughter twinkle her eyes and brighten her voice as she refused his offer, saying, "No thank you, Ian. I'll use my own one, it's cleaner."

"Aye, I suppose it is a wee bit cleaner."

"A wee bit cleaner?... It's very much cleaner!"

Ian got the map out of the side pocket of his rucksack and studied it. "It's not far to the next loch; about half a mile over there," he pointed, "and there are two other lochs just a little beyond that."

"Oh, good," Helen smiled. She finished wiping away her tears then rose and hurriedly started out in the direction indicated.

Before following her, Ian again noted that this small 'sad' loch, like many of the smaller lochs and lochans scattered all over this vast landscape, was unnamed on the old one inch to one mile Ordnance Survey map. That derelict house was shown as a small black dot on the map but it too was unnamed. With his index finger gliding over the map he traced the route they had followed so far today. He recalled the remains of other houses they had seen. There had been that group of four or five scattered in the fertile green glen at the West end of Loch a' Chroisg. There had been two others standing alone by the side of two other lochs. All those were older ruins dating back to the times of the notorious

Sutherland Clearances. Many of those ruins were not even graced with a remembering dot on the map. Little was left of those houses but the remains of hardy grey gables, those gables which 'die last of all'. Those gauntly forlorn old gables clung on like the neglected gravestones of a cruelly dispossessed people.

Ian felt touched with sudden anger, an impotent anger joined to deep sadness as he again thought of the cruel Clearances of last century. He wondered if it was some event from those times, some particularly savage incident, which Helen had sensed and been so distressed by. Once more he pondered over those mysterious powers she seemed to possess.

As he was about to fold up the map, he noticed the name of a steep knoll marked on it a little to the East of the nearby ruined house; that name was Creagan Mor. With startling certainty he knew that was also the name of the derelict house. Creagan Mor – that name touched quivering nerves of deeply buried memory, memories from shocked boyhood.

What was it Helen had declared?… "Some terrible tragedy happened at this loch in the past; something involving children."

"Involving children!" – yes, that was it. He remembered clearly now. Although parents had tried to keep details of that horror from their own children, sad tales and awed whispered rumours had seeped out and filled eager, but dismayed, sensitive juvenile ears and imaginations.

Ian decided he would say no more about this matter to Helen until he had all the facts properly confirmed. Noting that she was now out of sight beyond the ridge, he quickly replaced the map in his rucksack and hurried after her.

Once away from that small loch, Helen completely recovered her equanimity. As they fished round the next loch, Ian was delighted to see how she was enjoying the fishing in her usual quietly composed and contented way.

Later, as they approached another loch, they disturbed three red deer hinds. Two of the hinds had young calves with them. Both alarmed mothers gave urgent warning barks then rapidly trotted off. Their calves anxiously stilted after them on long, thin, ungainly and uncertain legs. The third hind behaved differently. It started to follow the other hinds then stopped and turned to stare at those alarming humans. It gave a couple of warning barks and angrily stamped a nervous front hoof. It trotted off for fifty yards, then again turned and stared and stamped its hoof. The other hinds and calves were now out of sight.

"What's the matter with that hind?… Why is it behaving like that?" Helen asked.

Ian smiled and put a finger to his lips for silence; he whispered, "Leave your fishing rod and rucksack here with mine."

Unencumbered, they moved silently and cautiously forward through the thick heather. Helen noted that they were moving directly into the pleasant breeze so that their scent was being blown away from any animals that might be in front of them.

She was learning!

Ian halted and gazed keenly ahead. Seeing a slight fluttering movement, he smiled and pointed. Helen could not make out what he was pointing at. Even more slowly and cautiously, Ian moved forward. Helen followed. Again he stopped and pointed at the small red deer calf lying almost motionlessly curled in the protective heather just in front of them.

Helen gave a gasp of delighted surprise as she saw that entrancing small creature. Ian again put a finger to his lips in warning and they both crouched and silently admired that helpless young animal. Ian thought it had been born early this morning. It was too young to run after its mother to safety. Its only defence was to instinctively obey its mother's warning barks and to lie still in the concealing heather and hopefully remain undiscovered by any hungrily prowling predatory fox or even by the keen eyes of a high circling golden eagle. Its glossy russet coat was attractively snow-flaked with white spots. These dappled spots helped break up its outline and added further confusion to the confusing patterns made by the splashes of sunshine and fingers of shade cast over the calf by the longer heather. It was constantly being pestered by flies; it had been the annoyed flickering of its large ears which had revealed its position to Ian.

As they watched fascinated, the deer calf foolishly raised and vigorously shook its graceful head. Helen only just managed to stifle another gasp of delight as for the first time she had a clear view of the calf's huge, dark brown innocent eyes. As those alluring eyes attempted to blink flies away, its curving long eyelashes fluttered charmingly. Helen smiled as she thought how these eyelashes would turn any Hollywood actress green with envy.

After a while Ian silently indicated it was time to move away. Helen reluctantly agreed. They left that calf blissfully unaware that it had been so closely observed by those two human animals – potentially the most dangerous of all animals.

When they were well away from the calf Ian said, "That hind will soon return to her calf now that she's seen us move away." He grinned, "Well, Helen, did you enjoy that experience?"

"Yes!… Oh, yes! It was marvellous! It's the first time I've seen such a helpless young calf. It was wonderful to see it from so close up and to have it so completely unaware of our presence. That wee deer calf is truly beautiful, isn't it?"

Ian grinned, "Aye, it is. That wee deer calf is a dear wee calf!"

Helen laughed, "Oh, Ian, even someone as unsentimental as you must surely find it impossible not to get sentimental about such a helplessly innocent and beautiful wee creature."

"Aye, I admit it, I freely admit it. It is impossible not to be moved by such innocent 'Bambi-ish' charm."

With the picture of that deer calf brightly shining in her mind's eye, Helen enthused, "Oh, yes, those huge alluring eyes, those fluttering long eyelashes, those dappled white spots." With her eyes sparkling with lively happiness she exclaimed, "Oh, thank you, Ian, thank you for giving me another wonderful experience. It has really made my day."

"Good!… Good! I'm very pleased." Then with his own eyes bright with happiness and gleaming with eager amorous anticipation he again grinned, "Perhaps I'll give you another wonderful experience later on today!"

Helen brightly smiled and gaily repeated his earlier exclamation, "Oh, promises!… promises!"

Later, as they lay together at another lochside after finishing their lunch, theses promises were wonderfully fulfilled; were fulfilled to the entire satisfaction of both parties.

As they drowsily relaxed after their lovemaking, Helen, with sudden seriousness, anxiously asked, "Oh, Ian, that wee calf we watched lying in the heather will be perfectly safe, won't it? There's nothing can harm it, is there?"

Ian paused for a moment before replying. He was about to tell the truth, then wisely changed his mind. He convincingly declared, "Oh yes, it will be perfectly safe."

He was learning!

He did not want the often-unpleasant truth to spoil Helen's day. He knew that during their first few days of life, if their mother strayed too far from them, red deer calves were defencelessly at risk from predators. Each year a number of them, usually the weakest, were killed by foxes and occasionally by eagles. To these predators a deer calf was not a beautiful innocent creature; it was a temptingly alluring item of prey – so many mouthfuls of succulent food for their hungry offspring.

Before he was married he would have unthinkingly blurted out this blunt truth, but his one year of happy marriage had taught him something. He had gained some little – some very little – insight into the most mysterious workings of that most amazing thing – the female mind. Today at that 'sad' small loch, he had been given a further glimpse into an obscure area of Helen's mind.

How many other fantastic facets of her fascinating feminine mind had he still to discover?

Hopefully, Helen and he had many years of happy married life stretching before them, years in which he could gradually educate her into viewing nature in a much less sentimental way. He would get her to see nature realistically and dispassionately as he did, while still actively retaining and encouraging the power of being deeply moved by all the wondrous beauties of nature. Smiling to himself, he wryly thought, "What if Helen's feelings about nature do not change, what if through time she makes my feelings, my way of looking at nature change instead? But no, surely that was most unlikely?… and yet, and yet, he certainly would not be the first good man to be profoundly, and unexpectedly, changed by marriage."

After fishing round the last small loch, they packed up their fishing gear. As Ian eased his rucksack onto his back, he exclaimed, "Oh God, this pack's damned heavy with the load of trout." He smiled accusingly, "I hope you haven't slipped any stones into it for the rockery you're making at home?"

Helen giggled impishly, "Oh, Ian, as if I would do a thing like that!"

All day they had been following the sun as it travelled on its leisurely June course. They continued steadily towards the West on the path that would bring them directly to Aldrory Glen and to their crofthouse. For Ian this was now familiar territory. Since boyhood he had wandered over this land. He knew it intimately. He knew and loved it as his ancestors had known and loved it. As a boy, a youth, a man, he had fished the trout lochs here; had often helped gather in the scattered sheep; had poached the wary deer and the elusive salmon.

As Helen and Ian sat side-by-side and rested for a few minutes, they gazed at the impressive bulk and fantastic shape of Suileag Mountain.

"Suileag looks like some strange creature lying contentedly asleep, doesn't it?" Ian asked, "Is it an ancient, mysteriously enigmatic Sphinx?"

"Aye, maybe. Or maybe it's just a gigantic cat drowsily resting in the sunshine. I think I can hear it purring," Helen smiled.

"Well, if it's a cat, it certainly isn't a tame domesticated tabby. It's an untamed Highland wildcat. Its apparent deep sleep is deceptive, it could spring awake any second with savage, snarling teeth and fiercely unsheathed claws!"

Helen laughed, "You're letting your imagination run wild, Ian. Perhaps you've been out in the sun too long today."

His laughter joined in with hers. "Och, I don't think I'm crazier that usual, am I?"

"No, not much," she happily assured him. Then, turning suddenly serious, added, "In fact you must think it's me that's crazy after the irrational way I acted back at that 'sad' wee loch. But, you know, I just had to get away from it."

"Oh well, I don't pretend I understand your strange behaviour there, but at least we've both been wise enough not to let it spoil this glorious day."

This was true. Once away from that 'sad' loch, Helen was soon her usual contented self. Ian too had soon ceased actively worrying over that inexplicable incident. And yet, like an aching tooth that, while not really painful, constantly makes its presence felt, so the strangeness, the mystery, of that incident constantly nagged at the back of his mind.

Later that evening as they snuggled together in their large bed's cosy intimacy Ian whispered, "Well, Helen, have you enjoyed your long and strenuous day?"

"Yes, oh yes, I loved it. It's one of the best days I've ever had."

"Good! You're not too tired after it, are you? Do you just want to sleep?"

"I am a bit tired – most pleasantly and contentedly tired." Then with a chuckle she hastily added, "But I'm not too tired, Ian. I'll sleep all the better later on."

"Oh, good! But you're sure you're not too tired?"

Through the darkness he sensed the smile in her voice as she replied, "Oh, stop talking, Ian, you're wasting precious time."

He kissed her and hugged her willingly responsive body even closer to his own eagerly firm body.

Ian was wakened early the following morning by the dawn chorus. Every bird was pouring out its heart in ecstatic praise of the fresh new day. The entire garden was a rejoicing wonderland of brilliant birdsong. Ian smiled. It was much more pleasant to be wakened by this glorious sound than by the ugly mechanical clamour of the old alarm clock.

At first the dawn was tender and pale and tenuous, then morning's sunlight grew bolder and lanced through the trees and bathed everything with glowing radiance. From the top of the highest tree a song thrush led the choir of praise. From lower branches blackbirds competed with almost equal grace. Multicoloured chaffinches vigorously rattled their cheery songs while drowsy woodpigeons gently murmured tranquil croonings. A cock robin pugnaciously puffed out his proud sergeant-major chest and aggressively sentried out his first territorial challenge of the day. Unwilling to be left out of this paean of wondrous sounds a male cuckoo repeatedly hiccupped his loud, insistent unmusical call. Each discordant call was mockingly and monotonously echoed by another male cuckoo somewhere beyond the garden, while a wiser female chuckled and warbled her tolerant amusement at the noises made by these foolishly vain males.

Helen and Ian spent all that morning working in the garden. While Ian weeded the vegetable plot under the ever-watchful eye of the wooden tiger glaring out from its jungle of raspberry canes, Helen tidied up the flower beds. Before midday they felt they had done enough. Helen's thigh and calf muscles ached after her long walk yesterday. Ian felt fit enough but he was never keen on doing too much gardening, especially weeding, at any time. In fact he was not keen on doing too much of any work for too long. He had never believed that working was the main purpose in life. He only worked as much – or rather, as little – as was necessary to allow him to enjoy as much leisure as possible.

When he was demobbed from the army in the autumn of 1945, he had desired nothing but to return home to Aldrory, help his widowed mother work their croft and, quickly and eagerly making up for lost time, confirm that he had lost none of his skill at poaching for salmon and deer and at fly-fishing for the wild brown trout in the well-known and well-loved hill lochs.

Then after his mother's sudden death there had been a few blankly empty lonely years when he had drank too much, had despaired of doing anything useful with his life, had regretted not having seized the opportunity open to ex-servicemen after the end of the war to go on to a special course at a Scottish university.

Then had come deliverance. He had met Helen. Their meeting was quite romantic. It seemed as if it had been fated.

In her spare time while working as a district nurse, Helen did some painting. Inspired by the wild Aldrory countryside, she turned out some most attractive watercolour landscapes. It was while she was hanging up one of her paintings at an exhibition of local artists in Inveraldrory village hall that Ian and she had met. He was about to hang up one of his own paintings near hers. They were immediately strongly attracted to one another. It was practically love at fist sight – a thing which Ian had never believed in, had thought of as being a lot of romantic rubbish.

After six months of passionate courtship, they had married just over a year ago.

While Helen still thoroughly enjoyed her now part-time work as an assistant district nurse, she found herself increasingly attracted by Ian's alluringly seductive hedonistic philosophy of a leisurely life of quiet pleasure. And yet she, and she alone, knew that at times he had some doubts about this perhaps rather too selfish lifestyle of his. More than once while whispering confidentially together in the still blissfully novel snug intimacy of their conjugal bed, Ian had revealed that even yet, nearly ten years after the end of the war, he still wondered why he had been allowed to survive six years of war; years when death had often been all around him, when many grand comrades had been savagely killed. Tens of millions had died in that atrocious war and yet he had come through it unharmed (he smiled) apart from his minor wound.

For anyone gifted – or cursed – with an active imagination it was impossible not to ask many questions, to wonder what it was that decided who survived the war and who died. Was it, as he thought, completely random chance? Or was there some power, some preordained destiny which decided life or death? Helen was sure there was. Often in these intimate discussions she repeated her favourite quotation: "There is destiny in the fall of a sparrow!"

Ian was not convinced.

One thing he did feel strongly – that he had a duty to his dead comrades. He felt he had to live life for those comrades who had been so tragically robbed of it; he owed it to them to live life to the fullest. But what was the best, the fullest, way to live? Perhaps the easiest answer was the best – simply enjoy life. Usually this answer satisfied him, but sometimes he felt he should do something more positive with his life.

Helen encouraged him with his painting and writing; she praised his artistic talents. She grinned impishly, "And your painting and writing are a damned sight more pleasant than all your messing about with that bloody taxidermy!"

They ate their lunchtime snack in the garden and fed crumbs to the bright-eyed fearlessly impertinent tame robin. Contentedly sitting side by side they revelled in the glory of the June garden. Lulled by the drowsy drone of the languorous bees and by the sunlight's golden somnolence, they almost snoozed. Seduced by the sun's warmth, wild honeysuckle flowers opened up their creamy yellowish petals, eagerly thrust bright stamens towards the light and, with wanton abandon, poured out delicious exotic fragrance. Crazed by that voluptuous perfume, bulky, pollen-laden bumblebees swooned, rather than flew, from flower to flower in waves of sensual delight.

Helen blinked open her eyes and chuckled, "Those bumblebees are drunk. They're intoxicated with all that wondrous scent."

Ian grinned in agreement as he watched a stout bee make its unsteady way with beadle pompous dignity over a honeysuckle flower beside him. "Aye, they certainly look happily intoxicated. That one there looks as if: 'He on honeydew hath fed, and drunk the milk of Paradise.'"

A few butterflies fluttered about in impetuous, crazy fragile flight. Then on the lawn in front of them a blackbird paused with alertly cocked head. Accurately it pounced on an unwary worm. Blackbird and worm engaged in a deadly serious tug-of-war. The bird leaned back on straining legs and hauled with its merciless beak. The large red worm desperately resisted. It was an unequal struggle. The victorious blackbird chopped the violently wriggling worm into three neat pieces; small enough to fit into its fledglings' small crops, then firmly gripped them in its yellow beak. Each piece squirmed and writhed in agony.

The garden was bright with beauty, was tremulous with sunshine's eager brilliance, was alive with glorious life, but, as always, was also violently alive with relentless death.

Dainty Blue Tits ceaselessly searched through shrubs and trees, then with bulging beaks moustached with succulent bright green caterpillars, darted past Helen and Ian to their nest full of ever-hungry young.

Ian smiled, "All this desperate labour is a far cry from this morning's fine carefree rapture with which these birds welcomed the glory of the dawn, isn't it? They make me feel quite exhausted with their ceaseless activity. Unlike these birds, I think we've done enough work for today. What about strolling down to see Kate and Kenny and give them some of yesterday's trout?"

Helen smiled, "Oh, yes. Actually I was just going to suggest that myself."

"Aye, I knew you were. You see, you are not the only one with intuitive insights! Anyway I could do with some more tea; we can be sure of having many cups forced on us by good old 'Kate Kettle'."

Kate and Kenny MacLeod were their nearest neighbours. That brother and sister, both unmarried, were very good neighbours and great friends.

While Helen selected the trout to take, Ian collected the Ordnance Survey map from his rucksack and took it with him.

Today, in the bright sunshine, the front door of Kate and Kenny's ever-hospitable house stood invitingly wide open. As Helen and Ian approached it a loud commotion suddenly erupted. A cloud of about twenty small yellow chicks whirled out from the doorway. They scattered in every direction. The chicks were closely followed by four extremely agitated, wildly flapping hens. Then came Molly, the neat Collie bitch. With excited yelps she drove the hens out of the house. Finally came Kate. Gasping, red-faced and flustered, she flapped her apron furiously as she shooed more hens before her.

As the hens disappeared round the end of the house they clucked indignant protests and attempted to calmly strut with regained dignity. The Collie joyously whirligigged around like a black and white banshee as she eagerly rounded up the widely scattered chicks.

On the commodious window ledge to the left of the doorway, Kate's two old cats sat in motionless, sun-warmed comfort and silently looked on with wide, unblinking eyes. This noisy commotion had rudely awakened them. With their usual disdainful dignity, both plump ginger and white cats stared with owlish solemnity. Very obviously they strongly disapproved of all this riotous 'sound and fury'.

Kate laughed as she patted them, "Oh, Lucy… Oh, Dolly, I hope this loud racket has not disturbed your blissful snooze too much."

They replied with annoyed accusing glares and haughty enigmatic silence.

Only then did Kate notice the amused approaching visitors. Ian laughed and shouted, "I see you're having a hen party, Kate."

Her hearty laughter bellowed out and readily joined in with theirs. Her plump, buxom body shook. She was a big, jolly woman; she was as cosily warm and homely as new-baked bread. Her good-natured face beamed as she welcomed them and hurried them indoors with her inevitable hospitable cry of, "Come in… come away in. You're just in time; I've just put the kettle on."

It was her unfailing generosity with countless cups of tea, her always just having put the kettle on, which had earned her the affectionate nickname, 'Kate Kettle'. Happily, she bustled her welcome visitors into the cosily comfortable, if none too tidy, kitchen. With true delight she accepted the gift of trout.

"Where's Kenny?… Is he at the sheep?" Ian asked.

"Och no, not today. He's working in the vegetable plot."

"I'll go and have a word with him there, then."

"Oh aye, go and see him, Ian, tell him to come in for a cup of tea. Tell him he's done enough work for today." Kate smiled with gentle compassion. She was five years older than her brother. Since his nervous breakdown caused by his wartime experiences in the army she had devotedly looked after him with tender, almost maternal care.

Ian strode round to the large vegetable patch where Kenny was working – or was supposed to be working. He stood leaning motionlessly against a long hoe. He seemed in a gloomy abstracted mood. Ian could not see much evidence of him having done a lot of weeding. He did not notice his visitor until Ian spoke, "Well, Kenny, you're busy at the weeding, I see."

With a start Kenny came out of his reverie. He smiled. The warm smile immediately chased the gloomy frowns from his face. Cheerily he called out, "Oh, hello, Ian. How are you, my dear fellow?"

Ian gave him Kate's message. He needed no second telling. Carelessly he threw the hoe away and accompanied Ian to the front door, where he paused and hospitably motioned Ian to precede him, crying, "Go in… go in, my dear fellow."

This unusual expression of Kenny's always amused Ian. 'My dear fellow' was not really a Scottish expression and it certainly was not a Highland one. Kenny had never used it when they had been soldiers together during the early part of the war. It was in 1940 when the German panzers were blitzkrieging through Northern France that Kenny had shown the first signs of having a nervous breakdown. His experiences escaping from Dunkirk had made him worse. He had spent the rest of the war in military hospitals having psychiatric treatment before finally being discharged from the army. Ian thought that it must have been during his time in England being treated by army doctors that Kenny had got into the habit of using that English expression. Quite probably it had been used by some army psychiatrist – a doctor as likely as not to be in need of psychiatric treatment himself. It sounded strange coming from Kenny, spoken in his gentle West Highland accent.

After Kenny had wholeheartedly enthused over and profusely thanked them for the fine trout, they all settled down to do justice to Kate's tea and her excellent home-made scones and pancakes. Kate was the last to settle. When she flopped into her corner of the sofa, the sadly abused old springs twanged loudly in protest and Helen bounced upwards in her corner. Kate's laughter again boomed forth, "Oh, I'm sorry, Helen! You're such a light, dainty wee craitur, there's nothing of you! You didn't spill your tea, did you?"

They ate and drank; they talked and laughed. Kate and Kenny eagerly listened to the story of the wonderful day's trout fishing Helen and Ian had enjoyed yesterday. Later, Ian unfolded his map and spread it out between Kenny and himself.

"Just a minute, my dear fellow, wait until I find my reading glasses," Kenny cried as he fumbled on the paper-littered table by the side of his armchair. After carelessly scattering newspapers and magazines and an empty plate onto the threadbare carpet he smiled triumphantly, "Ah, here they are. I knew I had put them safely by."

His sister smiled indulgently, remembering the many times she had spent hours searching high and low for those elusive glasses, eventually finding them in the most unlikely places.

With his index finger moving over the map, Ian traced the route they had taken yesterday; only he started from the West and went in the reverse direction. He pointed out the various lochs they had fished. Peering through his half-moon glasses, Kenny followed Ian's exposition with deep interest. Although he no longer fished, he remarked on some of the lochs which he had fished when a boy.

"You remember those lochs very accurate, Kenny," Ian said. He was not surprised at this display of memory for he knew that, despite his nervous disorders, Kenny retained a wonderful knowledge of this district and of its history. He had an insatiable interest in, and an unsurpassed knowledge of local family histories.

Kenny smiled modestly, "Well, you know my interest in Aldrory and in its past and present inhabitants." Again peering at the map he sighed deeply, "It's sad to see so many wee black dots on this map that represent so many houses that are now merely derelict ruins."

"Aye, it's very sad, right enough," Ian agreed. He was aware that Kenny knew the names not only of all those ruined houses but also of the families who had lived in them. Much of his knowledge was stored in his quite amazing memory, but this was augmented by his store of written records, some of which had been collected by his grandfather, then had been added to by his father. Visitors from the United States, Canada, New Zealand, etc; wanting to trace their Aldrory ancestry were referred to him and unfailingly he succeeded in supplying them with accurate details of their forebears.

Ian moved his finger over the map, then deliberately held it pointing at the black dot which marked that derelict house near the small loch where Helen had been so upset. "Do you know the name of that ruined house, Kenny? We passed it yesterday when we went to fish that wee loch beside it." With bowed head Kenny carefully studied the map. When he raised his head his face wore a disturbed frown. He silently peered over his glasses at Ian. Eventually, and it seemed reluctantly, he muttered, "Yes, yes, my dear fellow, I know the name of that house."

He said no more.

Ian stared at him steadily, enquiringly and expectantly.

The silence dragged out until Kenny exhaled a profound sigh and in a subdued sad voice murmured, "The name of that house is Creagan Mor."

Kate gave a nervous start. She threw her hands to her mouth to stifle an involuntary exclamation. Helen turned and stared in surprise, but Kate said nothing, she sat rigidly still and kept her hands nervously over her mouth.

Ian broke the tense silence. "Creagan Mor... Creagan Mor," he murmured thoughtfully. "Yes, I thought that was the name of that ruined house." He then fell silent and gazed at Kenny who solemnly stared back at him.

As the uneasy silence again stretched out, Helen, with some trepidation, felt compelled to ask Kenny, "Did something very sad happen at that small loch near Creagan Mor house – something concerning children?"

Kenny did not reply. Kate tensed apprehensively.

Abruptly Kenny sprang to his feet and paced back and forward behind the sofa. The others watched him anxiously. He seemed reluctant to answer Helen's question.

After a couple of long, tense minutes, he violently threw himself back into his armchair.

Despite his sincere concern at seeing him so disturbed, Ian could not help smiling inwardly as Kenny once again loudly thudded down. That brother and sister shared the strange characteristic that they seemed incapable of sitting themselves down gently. They always either threw themselves into a chair or simply collapsed into it. Two battered old armchairs were lopsided broken-springed witnesses of their violent habit.

At last Kenny pushed his lean six-foot frame upright in his chair and rather bleakly smiled at Helen. He had, with an obvious effort, made up his mind to answer her question. His voice was quiet and impressively calm. "Yes... yes, there was a most sad, a most terrible tragedy there away back before the war. It happened in January 1924. A shepherd lived in that remote house, Creagan Mor, his name was McNeil. One day when he was out at his sheep and his wife was busy in her kitchen, their three young children were playing outside. They must have made their way to that small loch near, but hidden from their home. They must have been sliding on the ice covering the loch. Perhaps the two small boys fell through the ice, perhaps their twelve-year-old sister tried to rescue them.

Who knows?" Kenny paused, sighed deeply, then firmly stated, 'Only God knows!... Anyway, all three children were drowned."

Again he paused, closed his eyes for a few moments, then quietly continued, "About a week after the children's funeral, their mother went missing. She and her husband, both heartbroken, had been staying with relations. It turned out that she had gone back by herself to that house of sorrow, Creagan Mor, and had then drowned herself in that same small loch where her three bairns had drowned... Oh, it was a sad, a terribly sad, thing."

With closed eyes and slowly shaking head, Kenny mournfully repeated, "Sad!... Sad!... Sad!"

A solemn and thoughtful silence enveloped the room.

After a time, Kate tearfully whispered, "Oh yes, it was terribly sad. I remember as a girl overhearing our father speaking about it. We children were not supposed to know anything about that tragedy, but I heard my father tell my mother that these two funerals were the saddest ones he had ever attended. First the three wee white coffins were placed together in one grave. Then about two weeks later that fresh grave was reopened. The wee coffins were gently lifted out. The mother's coffin was lowered to rest. Then those three wee coffins were placed on top of their mother's coffin."

Kate, deeply moved by her own words, sobbed sadly. Then, lifting the apron from her lap she dabbed it at her overflowing eyes and, bravely smiling through her tears, gasped, "Oh dear, take nae heed of me, I'm just being silly. I'm making myself greet with my own sad story."

Dejectedly, Kenny repeated, "Aye, it is a terribly sad story, right enough." After staring thoughtfully at Helen for a while, he suddenly asked, "But, Helen, you've never heard of that tragedy before, have you?"

"Oh no. This is the first time I've heard of it. I certainly would have remembered if I had heard it before."

"And you've never been at that wee loch near Creagan Mor house before?"

"Oh no! Yesterday was the first time I'd ever been there. Before that I did not even know there was such a loch or such a ruined house."

For a while Kenny silently mulled over Helen's words then quietly asked, "Then how did you know that a sad tragedy involving children had happened there?"

"Oh, I don't know how I knew – I just did. I knew without any shadow of doubt. It was a very strange, but a very strong and definite feeling. I'm sorry, Kenny, but I cannot explain it any better than that."

Helen glanced anxiously, almost appealingly, at Ian. He took up the story. Calmly and clearly he told what had happened at that small loch. He explained how urgently Helen wanted to get away from that terribly sad place; how reluctant he had been to leave the large trout in the loch; how he had been persuaded to leave by Helen's deep distress. He concluded by stating, "I've tried to think of some logical explanation of how Helen knew that a tragedy involving children had occurred at that wee loch, but I've found none. There seems no possible logical explanation."

Once again that room was wrapped in thoughtful solemn silence.

Then once again Kenny sprang to his feet and nervously paced to and fro behind the sofa. Again he violently threw himself into his tortured and groaning poor old armchair. Loudly, authoritatively, impressively, he stated, "Only God – God in His infinite wisdom knows the solution to that mystery. Only God – God in His infinite compassion knows why these innocent children drowned." He paused with closed eyes for some moments, then continued, "Oh, of course it is all too human to question why God allows such things to happen, but how can we sinful humans possibly know? As the apostle said, 'How impossible to penetrate His motives or to understand His methods. Who can know the mind of the Lord?' Oh, it is not for us to question the inscrutable ways of the Almighty. Perhaps our questioning, our striving to know, was itself a sin. We must simply, blindly, trust."

All his listeners were deeply moved by the passionate intensity, the obvious sincerity, of Kenny's declaration.

Ian did not believe in Kenny's God, nor in any other god. He tactfully kept silent. He did not want to say anything that would agitate Kenny further.

Kate apprehensively watched her brother as he sat in a distracted state, eyes closed, hands tightly clasped, murmuring to himself. He seemed to be praying. She hoped that his troubled prayers would bring him peace. To ease the tension in the hushed room, Helen started cheerily telling of the many pleasant things she had enjoyed seeing yesterday. Enthusiastically she told of the beauty of the small red deer calf. She described her tremendous pleasure at being undetected by that charmingly innocent creature. Smiling, she told of the other slightly older deer calves; how ungainly they looked, as anxiously following their mothers, they lorded the shallow bay of a loch on such high stepping, high splashing, uncertain spindly legs.

All were delighted to see Kenny open his eyes and appear to listen with real interest.

Helen now told of the tremendous pleasure she had experienced at watching a pair of golden eagles soaring in majestic glory. How effortlessly they rose in stately circles, riding the thermal up-currents rising by the steep slope of Suileag's North Westerly face. How wisely these large birds conserved their energy on their leisurely soaring golden flight.

With roused interest Kenny asked questions. Helen and Ian eagerly supplied answers. As Kenny's nervous tension visibly lessened, the mood in the room palpably eased and the others relaxed.

Gently and unobtrusively Kate reached over and squeezed Helen's small hand in a spontaneous gesture of thanks for her sensitive help in easing her brother's tension. Then, lifting the large teapot, she cried out, "Oh dear, I've let the tea grow cold." As, with an effort, she heaved herself up from the sofa and made for the scullery, she laughed, "We could all do with some fresh tea. I'll just go and put the kettle on."

Back in the car, sitting beside Ron, Ian smiled as he finished his story, "So that was the first time I had real hard evidence of Helen's inexplicable powers, of her deeply sensitive intuitive senses which could tune into something – vague vibrations?… shadowy lingering memories? – that I could not feel."

"Gosh, that really was amazing, wasn't it?" Ron said, then he thoughtfully continued eating a large green apple.

For a while the only sound, apart from the driving rain, was Ron noisily biting and eagerly munching his apple. Ian removed his pipe and, with a smile, said, "You're very silent, Ron. Very thoughtfully silent. Has my story of Helen's strange powers given you food for thought?"

Ron gulped down a mouthful of apple and replied, "Yeah, it has, it sure has. I've been carefully thinking it over… I can think of no rational explanation for her amazing powers. They seem to be beyond any possible scientific explanation, don't they?"

"Aye, they certainly are."

After another thoughtful pause, Ron asked, "Does anyone else in Helen's family have similar powers?"

"Aye, her mother had something of these powers, although not so strongly developed. However, Helen's aunt, her mother's older sister, had strongly developed powers. She had the gift of second sight!" Ian grinned, "As was to be expected for anyone with that gift, she was a Highlander. Her maiden name was Cameron."

"Oh, really?" Ron, smiling, asked sceptically, "Did you get any proof of her strange powers?"

"Aye we did – or at least Helen did. She got one definite, one amazing proof of her aunt's exceptional paranormal powers… power, gift, intuitive insight, whatever you want to call it."

Ron expectantly waited for Ian to tell that story, but he laughed instead, "You're supposed to be here for the fishing, Ron, not to listen to my auld wives' tales."

"Well, do you really want to go out fishing in that?" Ron laughed in turn, pointing at the rain, heavier than ever, hammering in torrential fury against the forlorn car's weeping windscreen.

"No, I must admit I'm much happier sitting dry and cosy in here."

"Yeah, I knew that's exactly what you would say."

"Oh, did you? Are you acquiring mysterious intuitive powers too, perhaps in preparing for becoming a Highland Laird? Do you really want to hear about Helen's aunt's mysterious powers?"

"Yeah, sure I do. I'm patiently waiting. I'm all ears."

"Like Prince Charles?"

Ian gathered his thoughts together then started telling that story.

It happened early in the Second World War. Helen was a recently qualified nurse working at Strathcathro Hospital, near Aberdeen; part of it was a military hospital. On that memorable occasion she had a few days leave so she and her mother went to visit her aunt, Mrs Morag Gourlay, in Aberdeen.

The three women sat and enjoyed a pleasant morning cup of tea before setting out on a planned shopping expedition. They had the house to themselves.

110

Mr Gourlay was at work. The Gourlay's only child, John, was serving in the Royal Navy. He had been home on leave three weeks ago. His mother proudly told of how well he looked in his sailor's uniform. She breathlessly dashed upstairs to fetch her largest handbag, which held, with other treasured possessions, the latest photographs of her son. She smiled in gentle self-mockery at the foolish fond eagerness with which she got those precious photos out and passed them to her sister and niece. She listened with self-indulgent maternal pride to their loud and sincere praise of her handsome twenty-year-old son. She thought they were only giving him his due. In her, perhaps biased, opinion, there was not a more handsome young sailor in the entire Royal Navy.

Smiling fondly, she told of how John had assured her that he was in no real danger. He was now serving on HMS *Hood*, the largest, the fastest, the best battleship in the Navy. It was the mighty flagship of the Home Fleet, was the pride of the Royal Navy.

With laughter, he assured her that he was probably in much less danger than she was, after all there had been a few air raids on Aberdeen recently, whilst he was safe in that formidable battleship securely moored in the strongly protected waters of Scapa Flow in the remote Orkneys. With youth's bright eyed and fearless laughter, he told that the joke currently going around the fleet was that the *Hood* had been moored for such a long time in Scapa Flow that it was now firmly stuck on a reef formed by the thousands of empty bully-beef tins thrown overboard from that battleship.

After a fascinating half-hour with those and other photos, Mrs Gourlay carefully and reluctantly (she could happily pore over these photos for hours on end) returned them to her capacious handbag. Now the vivacious talk turned to other, and to her, much less engrossing topics.

Helen told of how happy she was working as a nurse; of how appreciated the wounded and sick soldiers were of all the nurses' conscientious loving care. With her eyes beaming and crinkling in mischievous smiles, she related some of the innocent pranks they got up to. In mid-sentence she abruptly stopped and cried, "What's the matter, aunt?"

Mrs Gourlay had been happily listening; suddenly she gave an anguished gasp and threw her hands up to her thudding heart. Her usually rosily healthy face turned deathly pale. She collapsed back in the sofa apparently in a fainting fit.

Helen anxiously attended to her. Soon her eyelids fluttered open. She was still dreadfully pale. She pointed weakly at the sideboard. Searching around inside it, Helen discovered an almost full bottle of precious pre-war brandy. A few sips of brandy brought some colour back to her aunt's cheeks.

Gasping and sobbing, Mrs Gourlay pulled a handkerchief from her sleeve and held it to her overflowing eyes. Her sister and niece gently tried to discover what was causing her such distress. Did she want them to send for the doctor? With a great effort, she slowly shook her head and gasped, "No!... No!... I don't need the doctor. He can't help me."

After a little more brandy, she whispered in an almost unrecognisable voice, a voice distorted with grief, "It's John... he's dead!... He's been killed!"

Her sister put a comforting arm around her and tried to calm her, tried to assure her that she had only had a fainting turn. "How could John possibly be dead? We know he's safe on that huge battleship, don't we?"

Helen sat on the sofa on the other side of her aunt. Her face paled as she stared with distressed eyes at her distraught aunt. Wearily, and with laborious effort, Mrs Gourlay raised tearful red-rimmed eyes and met her sister's compassionate gaze, "John has been killed. I know it. I heard him scream out for me as he died!"

Painfully slowly she turned her anguished eyes and stared into Helen's pitying eyes. "Oh, Helen, dear wee Helen, you know it's true... you believe me, don't you?"

Bursting into uncontrollable weeping, Helen threw her arms around her aunt and hugged her tightly. She gasped, "Oh, poor John!... Poor John! Oh yes, aunt, I believe you... Oh, my poor, poor aunt!"

The following day Winston Churchill, with deep emotion, announced to a stunned House of Commons that HMS *Hood* had been sunk in the North Atlantic by the German battleship *Bismark*. The BBC broadcast the grim news to a shocked nation.

A shell from the *Bismark* had penetrated to, and exploded, the *Hood's* main magazine. The resultant immense explosion blew that mighty battleship apart. Out of her crew of one thousand, four hundred only a few, a pitiful few, survived.

Two days later, Mr and Mrs Gourlay received the official telegram from the Admiralty informing them, with deep regret, that their son had been killed in action.

The sight of the telegram boy turning into their street on his way to deliver that fateful message had its usual effect on the housewives patiently queuing for their rations outside a grocer's corner shop. They had been enjoying the May sunshine; with friendly, appreciative smiles had been contrasting this pleasant warmth with the miseries of the freezing winter queues. Now, as one, they fell silent. Nervously they clutched shopping bags, purses and ration books more tightly. Every eye anxiously watched the dreaded telegram boy – that small messenger of death – to see which house he was heading for.

In synchronised slow motion all turned and watched him cycle further down the silent and traffic-less street. A few sighed in relief as he passed their house and continued further on. Those who lived at the far end of the street fervently prayed that he would not stop at their door.

A few days later Winston Churchill exultantly announced to elatedly cheering members of Parliament that the *Bismark* had been sunk by ships of the Royal Navy. The loss of the *Hood* had been triumphantly avenged. The nation rejoiced!

However, it was no real consolation to those British mothers, to those British wives, whose sons, whose husbands, had been killed in the *Hood*, to learn that

German mothers, German wives, had now lost their sons, their husbands, in the *Bismark*.

Ian's story was now ended. He relit his pipe and waited for Ron's reaction. For a while Ron remained thoughtfully silent, then he asked, "When did that happen – the sinking of the *Hood*?"

Ian searched his memory, "It was in 1941; yes, May of 1941, I think."

"I seem to remember my father talking about that sea battle. It was almost the only naval action of the entire war when battleships fired on enemy battleships, wasn't it?"

"Aye, it was. Of course, your father was in the American Navy during the war, wasn't he?"

"Yeah, he was. Although not at that time; not in May 1941. It was a bit later before the United States came into the war, you know." Ron grinned apologetically.

"Aye, I know that. I know that all too well," Ian almost accusingly replied. He grinned, "As Churchill said, 'The British people held the fort alone till those who hitherto had been half blind were half ready'."

Ron had no answer to that. He again fell thoughtfully silent, then quietly remarked, "That sure is inexplicable how Helen's aunt knew that her son had been killed in the North Atlantic immediately it happened. She knew it, what?... some twenty-four hours before Churchill made the public announcement. That was amazing! Have you thought of any possible explanation of it, Ian?"

"Well, obviously it must be some form of telepathy. Probably most scientists doubt that such a thing exists, but some keep an open mind on the subject. Surely most of us recognise, are even startled and mystified by, some slight shade of such strange telepathic powers within ourselves. Haven't we all, for no special reason, suddenly thought of someone we have not seen or heard of for a long time, only to unexpectedly meet, or receive a letter from, that person? Then surely it is hardly surprising, in fact is what we would expect, that some few, some very few people – mostly women? – have those telepathic powers in a much stronger form?

"We know how strong the invisible maternal link between mother and baby is, and when a mother has only one child then the link between them is especially strong. So perhaps it is not really so terribly strange that Mrs Gourlay, having these unique psychic intuitive powers in a strongly developed form, had telepathically picked up the anguished screams of her only son as he violently died.

"Those who are gifted with these unique senses cannot explain them. I know Helen cannot. She now just accepts them. I too have given up trying to find any logical explanation apart from a theory of mine that her powers are vague remnants of almost lost, remote ancestral senses."

Ron thought this over then said, "Yeah, I think there may well be something in that idea of yours, Ian. It's surely true that all the primitive people who lived close to nature – Red Indians, Aborigines, African tribes – all had deep affinities with their natural world through profound and mysterious senses; senses which the conquering and exploiting Europeans had almost entirely lost." He paused and grinned, "I sure look forward to when I'm the Laird and have ample leisure to study and discuss such ideas. You'll get tired of me constantly borrowing books from your wonderful library in that intriguing den of yours."

Ian laughed, "You'll be most welcome to borrow as many books as you like from my study. It will be interesting to see how your thoughts develop. I expect you will become a real Pagan like myself, but in the meantime I thought you were here for the fishing; you won't catch many salmon sitting here listening to me blethering, will you? Isn't it about time you went out into that miserable rain again?"

"That's exactly what I was thinking myself. I think I'll give the river another try before it rises any higher. What about you 'old man', are you going to continue resting here in the dry?"

"I'm very tempted to do just that," Ian grinned and peered through the flow of water distorting the windscreen. "The rain's not quite so heavy now, is it?… Och, I suppose I better come with you and have another go at the salmon. After all, there will be plenty of time for this 'old man' to rest once he's stretched out in his coffin, won't there?"

"Yeah, there should be," Ron laughed. "At least your body should have a good long rest, but I'm not so sure about your soul. Perhaps the soul of an old sinner of an atheist and a hardened poacher like you will suffer torments in Hell."

"Thanks a lot for that kind thought, Ron. However, I won't waste any time worrying about that most unlikely prospect. Anyway if my soul did end up in Hell at least it would be warm and dry. There's no rain in Hell, is there?"

"No, there should be no rain – only the evil reign of the Devil!"

As they left the car's cosy comfort and once more braved the soaking elements, Ian ruefully smiled, "Why worry about an improbable future Hell?… Surely, the grim reality of this present 'Wet Hell' is quite enough to be going on with?"

For two hours Ron and Ian doggedly but unsuccessfully fished. During that time they only once saw a fish. As they stood together just about to leave the river, having finally decided the fishing was hopeless, a salmon weighing about twenty pounds leapt high only a few feet out from them. As the salmon plunged back into the water, it sent white spray splashing over them. They smiled in rueful frustration. It was as if that fish had deliberately and disdainfully mocked their useless efforts. They smiled also in admiration of the beauty of that salmon. It was wonderful to have that sudden, unexpected glimpse of such glorious wildly ecstatic power. Strength, freedom and beauty all harmoniously blended together in that fantastic silvery leap.

Chapter Seven

At nine thirty that same evening, Ron arrived unexpectedly at Altdour crofthouse. Helen and Ian warmly welcomed him. He was soon comfortably ensconced on the old sofa in front of the cheerily glowing fire.

Soon the cork was out of a fresh bottle of Glenlivet. They had only just toasted each other, 'Slainte Math' and downed the first glorious gulp of that excellent amber nectar, when they heard another vehicle arrive.

"Oh, who can this be, at this time, I wonder?" Helen exclaimed.

"Are you expecting any visitors tonight?" Ron asked.

"No, we're not. But they are welcome, whoever they are."

As Helen went to open the door, Ian laughed, "I can guess who it is. I bet it's Colin and Jeannie MacDonald. Colin has sensed that freshly opened bottle of Glenlivet from afar and has unerringly homed in on it."

In a few moments Ian's guess was proved correct as Jeannie and Colin entered the room.

Instantly Colin's gaze lasered on to the bottle of Glenlivet. His eyes brightly gleamed. His mouth widened in a broad grin. His ruddy face beamed.

Through Helen and Ron's helpless laughter, Ian explained his accurate prediction of Colin having sensed that whisky from afar.

"Aye, well many a truth is spoke in jest," Colin jovially declared as his thunderous laughter readily joined in the general mirth.

Grinning, Ian poured a bumper dram for Colin. Jeannie followed Helen's example and insisted on a modest dram.

Once they were all comfortably settled and pleasantly started on their convivial drams Ron explained his unexpected visit. "I had a phone call at the hotel this evening from my father in New York. Some urgent business has suddenly come up and he wants me to return immediately to help him deal with it. I promised him I would return tomorrow. I've phoned the airline and have managed to book a seat for tomorrow evening. So I'll need to leave here early in the morning to drive to Preswick Airport."

"Oh, what a pity you've to leave early. You'll lose a few fishing days, and we all know how precious those salmon fishing days are to you. As it is you get few enough of them each year," Helen said with genuine sympathy.

Ron grimaced, "Yes, I know, Helen; I'll lose three precious fishing days. And, perhaps even worse, I'll lose the happy evenings sharing in this house's most pleasant company."

"Aye, and we'll all miss you also, Ron, but I don't think you'll be missing much as regards the fishing, not with the river in its present flooded state," Ian said.

Colin agreed, "Aye, that's true. And there's no sign of this bloody rain stopping. The river will keep rising for some days yet, I expect."

Ron grinned, "Many thanks for your consoling words, gentlemen."

"Gentlemen?... Gentlemen?" Jeannie laughingly queried. "I see no gentlemen here, apart from yourself, Ron."

With mock indignation, and putting on an exaggerated Highland accent, Colin grinned, "Och now, wifie, chust you hold you wheesht, ye ken fine 'Himself' there and meself here are true, are perfect, Highland Chentlemens!"

"Aye, we are chust that," Ian laughed in agreement. "We are truly a pair of Nature's Chentlemen."

"I agree Colin is certainly 'One of Nature's Gentlemen', but I have me doots if you qualify for that title, Ian," Helen quietly remarked.

"One of Nature's Gentlemen'," Ron repeated, "Gosh that's sure a grand, a fitting, title for you, Colin. Who, bestowed it on you?"

Ian replied for Colin, "It was Lady Kilvert who bestowed that title on him. She thinks very highly of him both as a gamekeeper and as a man. Every time she introduces new guests to him, she praises his skills as a gamekeeper and invariably ends by saying, 'Colin is one of nature's gentlemen'."

Colin laughed, "Aye, and I wish she wouldn't, it makes me feel a damned fool!"

"Aye, I noticed it always made you a bit embarrassed," Ian said. Then, grinning, added, "But not as embarrassed as you used to get away back in the early 1960's when there was all the publicity about D H Lawrence's novel, *Lady Chatterly's Lover* with its sexually explicit scenes of her ladyship making passionate love with her husband's employee, the gamekeeper."

Colin grinned, "Aye, that's right, Ian. I used to get quite embarrassed at times away back then when I was ghillie-ing with Lady Kilvert as she fished for salmon at Aldrory River. On fine days quite a number of summer visitors walked up the riverside path and often stopped and watched us fishing. The embarrassment occurred when they heard me address Lady Kilvert as 'My Lady'. On discovering that the lady fishing was actually a 'Lady' and that I was a gamekeeper attending her, they often, with grins of amusement, loudly and animatedly speculated amongst themselves about the relationship between that Lady and her gamekeeper – were they possibly as intimate as Lady Chatterly was with her gamekeeper? Some of those visitors were very rude with their loud laugher or knowing smiles, their suggestive comment and foolish giggles. On occasions Lady Kilvert got very annoyed at the worst, the most uncouth of those ignorant onlookers. I also got annoyed with them. I found some of their comments really quite embarrassing, knowing that Lady Kilvert must be overhearing them as well." Colin paused, gulped some whisky, then continued, "Anyway Lady Kilvert came up with a solution. She said to me, 'Oh Colin, I am getting sick of those ignorant people with their inane remarks and their uncouth manners. I'll tell you what; please no longer address me as 'My Lady'. Instead just call me 'Madam'. That should stop their remarks.' I grinned at her ladyship and said, 'Aye, madam, that's a good idea, and I'll think of myself as a ghillie, not as a gamekeeper.'

"'Good! Now that's settled, hopefully we can fish in peace.' Lady Kilvert smiled brightly as she added, 'Call me Madam' – now wouldn't that make a fine title for a musical show?'"

"And ever since then you've always addressed her as 'Madam', haven't you?" Ian said.

"Aye, that's right. And of course I call Lord Kilvert 'Sir'. He has never been too keen on being addressed as 'My Lord', at least not when he's here in the Highlands. I believe he's stricter about being called by his proper title when he's down in his estate in Suffolk, where, of course, everyone is more snobbish and class conscious."

Helen smiled, "Yes, I remember reading *Lady Chatterly's Lover*, all those years ago. It certainly was quite an eye-opener!"

"Aye, it certainly was," Jeannie agreed, "I was quite shocked by it."

"Aye, and ever since that novel was published, gamekeepers have had quite an exotic, or erotic, reputation, haven't they?" Ian laughed.

"Aye, but an unjustified, an entirely unjustified reputation, I assure you," Colin exclaimed with gleaming and twinkling eyes.

"So there was never any hanky-panky between her ladyship and you, eh, Colin?" Helen smilingly asked.

"Och no, of course not, we were both as pure as the driven snow."

Jeannie grinned at Helen and said, "Och, I suppose we will just have to believe him. Anyway from what I know of Highland gamekeepers a love of illicit sex is not their begetting sin; their biggest sin is an excessive love of whisky, whether illicit or not."

"Aye," Helen nodded in agreement and stared accusingly at Ian, "and it's not just Highland gamekeepers who have an excessive love of whisky, many crofters are just as bad."

"Och, wifies, wifies, stop blethering your damned nonsense. A love, a deep, a profound, love of whisky is nae sin – it's a blessing! Remember what good auld Rabbie said:

"Freedom and whisky gang the gither,
Tak aff your dram.''

Colin lifted his glass, tilted it high and drank deeply. He then sat back with his ruddy face glowing, a picture of perfect contentment and convivial good nature. Following his example, all the others lifted their glasses and happily drank.

"Were you out stalking with Lord Kilvert again today, Colin?" Ian asked as he set down his empty glass.

"Aye, I was. And I got bloody well soaked through again. My joints are damned tired. They're aching with rheumatics. Och, I'm getting far too old to go deerstalking, especially in this damned awful weather."

Colin threw back his head and drained his glass. Smacking his lips appreciatively he grinned, "I find the only thing that eases my rheumatics is a drop o' the craitur, or better still, a good few drops o' the craitur!"

"Och, all right, Colin, I can take a hint; again a none too subtle hint," Ian laughed as he got to his feet and took Colin's empty glass. As he refilled it, he smiled at Ron, "Didn't I tell you that Colin would sense this Glenlivet from afar and would unerringly home in on it?"

"Yeah, you sure did." Ron turned and smiled at Colin, "It must be a very highly developed sense you have. It must be a gift almost as great as some of Helen's strange intuitive powers."

"Aye, perhaps it is," Colin said, "but my sense for sniffing out whisky is nothing compared to Ian's amazing ability to ferret out alcohol. In Italy during the war he had a well deserved reputation for being our foremost expert at finding alcohol in ruined and deserted buildings."

As Ian handed Colin his generously refilled glass he grinned, "Aye, you're right. I never failed to find alcohol of some kind even in the most unpromising situations."

He raised his own refilled glass and saluted Colin, 'Slainte!' The eyes of those two old soldiers met, held steady and gleamed with bright wartime memories.

"Oh," Ron said, "you've never told me about that special gift of yours, Ian. What's the story behind it?"

Colin grinned, "Oh, Ian, have you never told Ron the famous story of your greatest, your fantastic, find of alcohol in that deserted villa North of Rome?"

"Oh gosh, no, I've never heard that story. I sure would love to, though," Ron eagerly requested.

Ian felt in a pleasantly relaxed reminiscent mood. He sensed that Colin was in a similar mood. "Aye, all right, we'll tell you that great tale. Anyway I more or less promised to tell you it that day when you got your 'Macnab'. Do you remember I reprimanded you for sleeping while on lookout duty guarding the poached stag? Then I relented. I declared the less I said about sleeping on sentry duty the better."

"Oh yeah, I remember that OK. I wondered what the story was behind that remark."

Ian grinned, "Aye, well this story explains that."

They all settled down and between them Ian and Colin told that story – one of their favourite wartime stories. Jeannie and Helen exchanged resigned and understanding smiling glances. These long suffering wives had heard their husbands tell this tale before – often.

It happened in 1944. The Italians had surrendered to the Allies and the German army was in retreat North of Rome. Colin and Ian were in a six-man patrol of Seaforth Highlanders and Lovat Scouts. They were reconnoitring well ahead of the main British army units, which were slowly but determinedly advancing Northwards. Their small patrol had been working together for some time and each soldier really knew and completely trusted his experienced comrades.

There was a difference today however; yesterday their sergeant, 'Yo-Yo' Ferguson, had been wounded and was now in a military hospital.

"What did you say his name was?" Ron asked with a grin, "'Yo-Yo' Ferguson?"

"Aye, that's right. That was his nickname."

"That sure is a strange nickname."

Colin explained, "Sergeant Ferguson was given that nickname because of the number of times he had been promoted to Sergeant and had subsequently been demoted back down to Lance-Corporal. He was promoted and demoted up and down like a yo-yo going up and down on its string; that's how he got his nickname."

Ian nodded, "Aye, he was an exceptionally brave soldier when in battle, hence his promotions. But out of battle, back in camp, he often got drunk, got into fights and caused no end of trouble, hence his demotions."

Colin again took up the story; "Our commanding officer once recommended him for the Victoria Cross after a particularly fearless act of bravery."

"Oh, really?… and did he get awarded the Victoria Cross?"

"No, he didn't. Probably his wild record prevented him getting it. He got the next highest award instead, the Military Medal."

Ian continued the tale. "Well, as Sergeant 'Yo-Yo' Ferguson was not with us, I was senior Corporal in charge of the patrol that day. After cautiously moving forward some fifteen miles we looked for somewhere convenient to spend the night. We decided on an attractive and imposingly large villa; its red-tiled roof, its clean white walls and dark shutters made a pleasant picture in the bright sunshine. It appeared almost undamaged and was deserted. Obviously it had recently been used as a German army headquarters. Metal filing cabinets were dumped in the courtyard and the remains of bonfires of documents still smouldered. Other evidence of German occupation were the overturned and smashed marble urns at the ornate entrance to the villa. As we checked through the large, overgrown formal garden, we discovered further evidence of typical vindictive German thoroughness. Every one of the dozen marble statues, nude males and females, which had lined a shady avenue, now lay tumbled and broken on the ground. German soldiers – possibly drunken – had used them for hilarious target practise. Wild bursts of sub-machine gun bullets had fiercely amputated limbs and savagely smashed the intimate sexual parts of the statues. Doubtless the drunken soldiers of the 'Master Race' regarded those nude statues as obscene works of a decadent lesser race.

"Now those barbarous Huns, having ruthlessly and boastfully inflicted their vaunted Teutonic 'civilization' on all of Europe, were in retreat and, once again, were destroying what they could not remove as plunder and loot. After thoroughly checking out the entire building for any lethal booby traps left by the Germans, our patrol split up and started on our familiar well-perfected drill. Two went scrounging for food. Two went foraging for firewood; those Italian autumn nights could get very cold after the dusty heat of the day. One was on sentry duty on the villa's high tower."

"Aye, and that left Ian on his own to carry out his special, self-appointed task," Colin said, grinning. "His vital duty was to search out any bottles of alcohol in or about the villa; if any were hidden, Ian was sure to unfailingly sniff them out."

"And did you find any alcohol in that villa, Ian?" Ron asked.

"Oh aye, I found alcohol all right – eventually. I knew there was sure to be a wine cellar in that building. As soon as I opened the cellar door there was a powerful smell of alcohol. When I went down into the cellar the alcoholic fumes almost overwhelmed me. Bottle after bottle, dozens upon dozens of bottles were smashed. They covered the entire cobbled floor. My torch beam revealed the jagged glass rising like glittering miniature icebergs out of a dark sea of wine. It was an obscene sight.

"Eagerly I directed my torch beam into all the dustily cobwebbed wine racks hoping to find at least one bottle the German soldiers had overlooked while hurriedly carrying out their mean act of spite, their denying us all those bottles of wine they could not take with them in their precipitous retreat. I did not find a single intact bottle.

"My anger steadily rose with my mounting frustration. Using every swear word I knew, I cursed those only too thorough Germans. Only rarely had I felt real hatred for the Germans. Now I hated them as I had never hated them before!

"Still swearing, I was about to leave this frustrating cellar when my torch beam, searching in a final dismal sweep, disclosed a dark door hidden in an obscure corner. My heart leapt in wild excitement. Intuitively I knew I had at last discovered a secret treasure trove.

"Eagerly I examined that door. It was strong. Its heavy oak was reinforced with large iron studs. It was firmly secured by a stout padlock. I kicked the door. I shook the padlock. I gloated, 'Just you wait. A hand grenade will soon sort you out.'

"After warning the others to expect the grenade's explosion, I hurried back down to the cellar and tied the grenade to the padlock, then pulled the pin and dashed for the safety of the stairway's thick wall.

"The explosion in that confined space was deafening. With great impatience I forced myself to wait until the smoke had cleared and the worst of the dust had settled. With some difficulty I shoved the shattered door open.

"My intuition had not failed me. A large cupboard was revealed. It was an Aladdin's cave of liquid treasures. Some of those treasures had been smashed by the explosion, but most were intact. As I inspected them, my heart thudded with anticipation. This must have been a special hoard kept exclusively for high-ranking German officers. There were wines and spirits looted from all of German-occupied Europe. Bottles of vintage Dom Perignon champagne and other excellent French wines lay side by side with vodkas from Russia and Poland; there were Italian Chiantis and Greek wines nestling with Dutch gins and schnapps.

"My fingers, eagerly delving amongst these treasures, trembled with excitement and delight as they discovered the noble crown of all this glory – two bottles of malt whisky."

With eyes gleaming brightly in glorious memory Colin laughed, "Aye, I can still clearly remember how triumphantly you charged into the kitchen where we other soldiers were assembled. You entered like a vision from heaven with a bottle of malt whisky held high in each hand. Your glorious treasures put all our modest scrounging efforts firmly in the shade."

"Aye, that's right," Ian agreed, "and when we examined those glorious bottles we discovered they were labelled, 'Property of His Majesty's Government. The War Office. For officers only.' A senior German officer must have appropriated these captured bottles for himself. It was an act of perfect poetic justice that we Highland soldiers had found and 'liberated' these precious bottles of malt whisky."

Again Colin laughed, "Aye, that grand whisky was far too good to be wasted on any damned officers, whether bloody savagely efficient Germans, sneaking cowardly Italians or snobbish English twits. We were the lads to truly appreciate it. We soon had the two corks in the fire and the whisky shared out. It did not take us six Highland soldiers long to polish off both those wondrous bottles." Colin now sat silently with a happy, dreamily nostalgic expression in his eyes as he thought of that whisky of forty years ago. How vividly he remembered every detail of that incident – that fabulous, virtually legendary, alcoholic incident.

Ian's eyes were also bright with a dreamy, far off reminiscent gleam. With real affection he too clearly remembered that wondrous whisky of long ago. He sighed deeply, "Aye, that whisky was a really glorious nectar to us poor, thirsty devils."

"Och, stop drooling over that ancient whisky, you pair. Get on with the story," Helen laughingly commanded.

Ian grinned, "All right... all right. But, you know, that was the first malt whisky we had tasted for many years. For two years in North Africa we hardly tasted a drop of whisky, so those two bottles were a really marvellous, never to be forgotten, God-sent treat for us."

"Och, I'm sure you were both all the better for being without whisky for those two years," Jeannie quietly and dryly remarked.

Colin and Ian did not demean themselves by replying to that typically feminine blasphemy. Philosophically, they wisely ignored it. They contented themselves with sadly shaking their heads and exchanging a swift glance of tolerant and amused understanding.

Ian continued the story: "Anyway, once the whisky was done, we started on the other, the less glorious bottles. We indulged in a real orgy of all sorts of drinks with our frugal meal of bully-beef, dry bread and biscuits and some juicy looted peaches. Afterwards, hour after hour, we got through bottle after bottle. Soon that large and bright kitchen, with its huge old iron cooking range with its immense ovens, and the gleaming rows of highly polished copper pots and pans hanging in neat array, reverberated to the noise of our carefree exuberant laughter and our loud and boisterous songs. Joyously we 'rolled out the barrel', carelessly 'hung up our washing on the Siegfried Line' and sensually slavered over that voluptuous lady of easy virtue borrowed from the Germans, 'Lili Marlene'.

"Traditional old Gaelic songs intermingled with some of Rabbie Burns' greatest songs and soon we were widely bawling his well-known, well-loved, most bawdy versed. Then it was a natural transition to the crudest version of 'The Ballad of The D-Day Dodgers'. That ballad was uproariously bawled out by us 'D-Day Dodgers' who were: 'Always on the vino, always on the spree.' But our voices dropped to a solemn sadness as, singing the second last stanza, we remembered many dead comrades:

"Look around the mountains in the mud and rain,
See the scattered crosses, some that have no name,
Heartache and sorrow are all gone,
The boys beneath them slumber on,
They are the D-Day dodgers who'll stay in Italy."

"Many very rude and crude suggestions were made as to what dear old Lady Astor should do with herself!"*

"Aye, we were all in fine voice that evening," Colin laughed, "until, one after another, the lads collapsed under the table. Ian and I, very slightly, more sober than them, merrily and unsteadily dragged their semiconscious bodies out of the way and left them to sleep it off in a corner where they lay with their alcohol tortured bodies moaning and groaning."

"And what about you hardened drinkers yourselves, did you eventually collapse under the table as well?" Ron asked.

"Aye, at last I passed out and Ian was left undisputed champion, the only one still managing to sit drinking at the table."

"That's right enough, Colin, but I don't think I was long in following you to the floor."

"Gosh, that sure must have been some binge. Surely even you tough, experienced drinkers must have suffered terrible hangovers after all that mixed booze?"

"Och aye, we did... we certainly did. I was coming to that part of the story, Ron," Ian said. "In the darkness of early morning my bursting bladder woke me. Not only my bladder was bursting; my head felt as if it was exploding under the vicious blows of a steam-hammer crashing and pounding in my poor, demented brain. My stomach too was in torment. Its vile contents squirmed and convulsed in terrible spasms. With a tremendous effort, I forced myself to sit up. I moaned

---

* *After the Allied D-Day landings and invasion of Normandy in June 1944, Lady Astor had suggested in a speech that the British soldiers in Italy were 'D-Day Dodgers'. 'The Ballad of the D-Day Dodgers' was Major Hamish Henderson's reply to her.*

dejectedly, 'Oh God, this is Hellish! Oh Christ, death would be a welcome relief!'

"With a supreme effort of will I forced myself to my feet and staggered across the kitchen to the door. In the shadowy courtyard I leaned against a swaying wall and thankfully emptied my almost overwhelmed bladder. Dimly seeing a low wall across the courtyard I wearily snailed my way over to it and slumped down. My stomach queasily heaved and churned. It was like a cement mixer ceaselessly revolving its semi-liquid load while its noisy engine violently thudded inside my head. I hung over the wall and my cement mixer tipped up its disgusting load. I was miserably wracked with excruciating pains.

"As I wallowed in self-inflicted agony, self-pity and self-disgust, I became aware that the morning's grey dimness was being vanquished by the sudden brightness of an Italian dawn. This vivid light stabbed another piercing agony into my demented head. In every war, dawn was a time when all sentries had to be especially alert, but our patrol had no sentry on duty. There had been no sentry all night. If a German patrol had reconnoitred here they could have killed us all while we lay defenceless in our drunken stupors, and it would have been my fault; my failure as the senior Corporal to set sentries.

"Failure to place sentries when on active service in a battlefield was one of the worst crimes any soldier could commit. If discovered, such a crime invariably resulted in the culprit responsible being court-martialled, or in some armies being shot out of hand.

"With an effort I straightened myself up, spat some more of the nauseous taste of vomit from my mouth, wiped my lips with the back of my hand, then forced myself to my feet. Slowly I crossed the courtyard and returned to the kitchen. I found Colin and two others sitting on the floor and holding their heads in moaning dejection. While they staggered to their unsteady feet and shuffled out to relieve themselves I shook awake the two bodies still lying prostrate. They swore violently. They moaned piteously. They demanded to be allowed to die in peace.

"Colin and the two others returned and slumped on to kitchen chairs. I now had a good look at them as they sat and moaned those immortal words, 'Oh God, never again... never again!' The deadly paleness of their hangover ravished faces made the dark smudges under their eyes all the darker. These half-closed eyes were bleary and bloodshot and were sunken deep in their skulls like the proverbial 'piss holes in the snow'. I tried to smile, 'My God, you three look as bad as I feel.'

"I asked them to set about brewing up some char, that ubiquitous British Army tea, strong and thick and horribly sweet with condensed milk. We all had desperate drouths and were in urgent need of some reviving tea. My mouth felt full of ashes and my tongue was coated with a layer of cement.

"I fastened on my webbing belt complete with full ammunition pouches, then hung binoculars around my neck. I explained, 'I'll go up to the tower and have a look around. Everything seems quiet enough, but I better check it out.'

"Colin raised bleary eyes and his gaze met mine. He realised that I had failed to set any sentries. With understanding sympathy he said nothing about my inexcusable dereliction of duty, instead he replied, forcing a grin, 'Aye, all right. Aye, everything seems quiet enough… apart from those two noisy buggers over there.' He pointed at the two woebegone bodies lying in the corner. They were continually moaning, belching and farting. 'They sound like a drunken orchestra crazily trying to tune up.'"

Laughing heartily, Colin interrupted Ian's narrative and explained, "You see, Big Tam's large body unashamedly gave vent to the most defiant and boastful rumbustious fortissimo farts which sounded like deep throated blasts from a tuba, while Wee Murdo's lean and wiry small body diffidently gave out high-pitched squeaking farts which tip-toed out and sounded like an ashamed and apologetic out of tune flute."

Once the laugher died down, Ian again took up the story, "Aye, I remember that well, Colin. As I picked up my loaded Sten gun and the map, I said, 'The air at the top of the tower will be a damned sight fresher than the vile stinking air in here.'

"In my sadly fragile hung-over state the steps in the high tower seemed to continue upwards interminably and were atrociously steep. At last, gasping wearily, I stepped out into the pleasantly fresh morning air. Despite the strain on my bleary eyes, I forced myself to slowly and methodically scan the surrounding countryside through my binoculars. Everywhere, all was incredibly still, silent and peaceful. It seemed unnaturally calm. I felt deep apprehension. I could not help thinking that this must be the deceptive calm before the violent storm.

"It was hard to believe that many thousands of British soldiers were deployed in the South of this sleepy landscape and that thousands of German soldiers were deployed in its North. I studied the range of mountains rising steeply from the dusty plain in that distant North. They cloaked themselves in an indistinct hazy blue; their calm beauty was dangerously deceptive for the Germans were expected to end their retreat there. They were digging in and efficiently fortifying these beautiful mountains.

"I don't mind admitting that I dreaded being part of the British force attacking these mountains. From long experience I knew how fiercely and tenaciously those tough, battle-hardened German soldiers fought. I could guess what a grim price would have to be paid in British blood before we dislodged them from these strongly defended positions. I had been lucky; in five years of war I had suffered only one minor wound. I could not help wondering how much longer my good luck would last. Might it end at these mountains?

"With a sigh I tried to put that depressing thought away. I now looked at the narrow road, dusty white and arrow straight, which passed close by this villa. I knew from the map that this was an ancient road; was part of the Appian Way, one of the many roads built by the Imperial Romans. Caesar's Legions had marched to war and to victory over this road. Now, two thousand years later, British soldiers were marching to war and – hopefully – to victory over it. And, I felt sure, in another two thousand years other soldiers of other armies would be marching to war over this same road.

"With profound sadness I thought that human behaviour has not improved much in those two thousand years, despite all our boast of progress. Perhaps our only real 'progress' was the development of weapons vastly superior to the Romans swords and javelins. With our technologically wonderful modern weapons, we can now kill many more people much more easily, quickly and efficiently. In my mind's miserably depressed mood which matched my body's tortured wretchedness, I murmured, 'Oh, Progress, what crimes are committed in thy name.'

"I had a final searching look around in every direction. All remained unusually calm. I looked again at the ruined buildings at the edge of that straight road. The map told me they had been ancient Roman barracks. With a grim smile I thought, "No doubt after a hard night's drunken debauchery many a Roman soldier, suffering an atrocious hangover, had pathetically exclaimed to his Pagan God those same heartfelt words that Christians still use – 'Oh God, never again... never again!'

"A row of five tall cypresses vertically raising their mournful darkness above a grove of gnarled old olive trees near these ancient barracks suggested to my weary mind a line of huge exclamation marks perpetually declaring their astonishment at the unending follies of mankind.

"Slowly, cautiously and wearily, I started groping down the tower's steep stairs." Ian paused, then smiled, "I'm sorry, perhaps I'm going on a bit. Am I blethering too much? Am I boring you all?"

Helen laughed, "Aye, you certainly are..."

Ron interrupted her, "No, you're not! At least not as far as I'm concerned. I love to hear your war stories, they're most interesting."

Ron, Colin and Ian smiled at one another then simultaneously raised and drained their glasses. Helen and Jeannie glanced at each other and once again exchanged understandingly tolerant smiles.

"Anyway, Ron," Ian continued, "you can now appreciate why I was so lenient with your lapse when you were supposed to be on sentry duty guarding your poached stag. I remembered only too vividly my own lapse in not setting sentries all those years ago."

Colin laughed, "At least we all learned our lesson from that drunken lapse. Ever after that incident we were always most diligent about having a sentry on duty."

"Aye, that's right, Colin. Another lesson we learned was never again to mix our drinks in the atrocious way we did then."

"Aye, yon was a really lethal mixture. It was a hellish witch's brew of whisky, champagne, vodka, red and white wines and God knows what else."

"Aye, it certainly was," Ian agreed. "I remember we even had a bottle of Benny's special liqueur."

"Benny's special liqueur? What's that?" Ron asked.

"You know, Benny Dick Tine's special drink."

125

Ron was still puzzled. Helen explained, "He means a bottle of Benedictine, the liqueur made by these monks. Oh, Ian, I've told you before you should tell better jokes that that – ones I don't have to explain."

Ian grinned, "Och, Ron's laughing at that joke, anyway."

"Aye, but he's laughing more out of pity than amusement?"

"It's only amazing that we all survived yon hellish witch's brew of alcohol." Colin relished repeating that vividly descriptive phrase. "It might well have killed any lesser men, any less experienced, less hardened drinkers than us Highland soldiers."

"Aye," Ian agreed, "and as it was it came damned near to killing a couple of our lads. Big Tam and Wee Murdo, who were thought to be about the toughest men in our small patrol, were the worst affected. It took them three days to fully recover."

Ron laughed, "Yeah, that's one thing I've also learned; that it's not wise to mix the grain and the grape too drastically together when I'm drinking."

"Aye, that's true. That's why I drink almost nothing but whisky now... malt whisky preferably," Colin said, grinning and holding up his empty glass.

"Och, Colin, man, is that another of your un-subtle hints?" Ian asked as he rose and made for the whisky bottle. "I see all our glasses are empty. I'll soon remedy that deplorable state of affairs."

Ron also rose, "No more for me, Ian, I'll need to leave now. I've still got my packing to do tonight. I want to leave early tomorrow morning for my long drive to Prestwick Airport."

Jeannie and Colin also got to their feet. Colin laughed, "No more for me either, Ian. I'll manfully resist the strong temptation. We've to be up early in the morning, too. I've another long day's deer stalking before me. I expect I'll get soaked through again. Is it still raining?... or is that a damned stupid question?"

Ron lingered for a few minutes after Jeannie and Colin had dashed through the rain to their van. He finished his farewells by saying, "Well, I'll see you about this time next year, or perhaps sooner if your prediction comes true, Helen, and I do become Laird of Aldrory."

"Och, it will come true, Ron. I assure you it will. I know you will become Laird, and soon, quite soon."

Chapter Eight

All that week and most of the following week rain continued to pour. It poured by night. It poured by day.

Driven by incessant winds, rain battered against Altdour crofthouse's old windows and set them moaning. Fierce gusts angrily rattled the roof's grey slates and shook them like a terrier shaking a rat. Cold draughts scurried from windows and slid under doors. Blustery squalls belched down the sitting room chimney and maliciously coughed choking clouds of acrid smoke into the room and sootily freckled the furniture with filthy black smudges.

Ian consoled himself that he did not have to go working as a ghillie in this atrocious weather. All the salmon fishers had left the hotel. They had been driven away, disgusted by the appallingly miserable weather and by the impossibility of fishing while the rivers were in their present tempestuously flooded state.

Aldrory River was high above its normal height. In many places it had overflowed its banks and drowned the fisher's path that straggled along beside it. The tumultuous waters were a darkly sombre coffee colour. They were stained by the tons of sour peat being washed down from high corries in remote hills, from sodden heather moors and from sadly impoverished dank glens.

The many unseen salmon moving relentlessly through the murky depths of the angry river were wildly excited, were practically intoxicated, by the fiercely stimulating challenge of the flooded waters. Fresh in from the sea, in the peak of condition, these mightily muscled silver salmon gallantly shouldered their way through the peaty waters while their furiously active gills desperately struggled to breathe in that choking soup of dark impurities.

Each morning, cumbersomely constricted by bulky waterproof clothing, Ian took Glen and Corrie for their daily walk. He found that an hour or so was long enough under these drenching conditions. Even that collie and that terrier, the keenest and hardiest of dogs, were getting disgusted by their daily soakings.

Unable to work in her beloved, but now sadly waterlogged garden, Helen contentedly employed herself in her small pottery and joyfully turned out model after model. Ian, too, took advantage of this monsoon weather to immerse himself in artistic creation. No matter how dismally depressing the weather was, his 'study' never failed to lift his spirits every time he entered it. Inevitably, his first glance was bestowed on his books. Rising shelf upon shelf they were not just hundreds of dusty volumes, they were old companions and many were well-loved friends. The stuffed animals seemed pleased to have his company. The Royal stag gave him a less haughty and more friendly stare through its monocle. The cobwebbed wildcat stopped stalking the dusty flies and bluebottles and winked him a wicked one-eyed welcome. The fencing frog and startled stoat called a brief truce to their eternal confrontation and momentarily acknowledged his presence.

He settled at the desk and laboriously hammered out a couple of short stories on the ancient 'Imperial' typewriter. He had scribbled these stories last winter and now, after revising them, hoped to get them published.

After lunch, tired of typing, Ian eagerly took up a paintbrush and was soon completely engrossed in continuing the oil painting he had started last week. Helen joined him in his 'study' and she too became absorbed in painting. As a welcome antidote to the depressing weather she revelled in creating bright seascapes. She keenly endeavoured to capture the outstanding beauty of Achairdich Bay as it basked under June's benevolent sunshine. It was difficult to do justice to the translucent beauty of the shallow sea's sensitive shades of pale greens and darker turquoises and the glossy aquamarines of submerged seaweed. And how could paint truly capture that pure white sand's blinding glare as it poured around that gently curving bay like white-hot molten metal which shimmeringly distorts solid rocks and transmutes them to flabby quivering jellyfish?

After a time Helen stood back from her painting and critically studied it. It was coming on well. She was pleased with it. She glanced across at Ian. He was entirely engrossed in painting. A warm glow flushed over her. Suddenly and clearly she once again realised just how fortunate she was. She was happy. Ian and she had achieved what few were fortunate enough to achieve – happiness and quiet contentment. In mercenary materialistic terms, they were poor. Their income from selling paintings and clay models and from Ian's short stories and articles plus his part-time work as a ghillie, was not great and was rather precarious, still, they envied no one. They had no car, no telephone, no television, no washing machine; they had, however, an abundance of home-grown vegetables and fruit and these foods were often augmented by fresh trout and the occasional salmon and venison. And somehow, no matter how short of cash they might be, there was always at least one bottle of convivial whisky in their crofthouse impatiently waiting to be shared with friends.

Feeling Helen's glance on him, Ian looked up from his painting and smiled at her. She came across and inspected his picture. She liked it. In strong, bold, vivid strokes he had one thick-trunked Scots Pine thrusting up from a steep hillside of bright glowing autumn heathers. With sincere admiration, Helen said, "Oh, I like that. It's so ruggedly strong and tenacious."

She returned to her picture. She lifted her brush but held it poised motionless for a few moments as again she felt a warm glow happily flush over her. Yes, she was fortunate; she loved and she was loved. Their passionately warm-blooded early love had, over thirty years, gradually, imperceptibly, mellowed into this present pleasantly intimate companionship. "Yes," she thought, "and even yet we do occasionally have our wonderful moments of passionate lovemaking." She smiled, "Aye, and sometimes we have our failures, usually when Ian's had too many drams, when his performance frustratingly ends, like the famous poem, "Not with a bang, but with a whimper!"

That evening, as they sat in a comfortably relaxed after-dinner mood at opposite sides of the fireplace with the two dogs contentedly stretched out between them on the deerskin rug, Helen remarked, "We haven't seen Jeannie and Colin for a while. I hope they're well. Poor Colin, I feel sorry for him having to go out stalking in all this terrible weather. He must get soaked through every day."

Ian sympathetically agreed, "Aye, he must be really sick and tired of all his soakings. I know what it's like. I've been soaked often enough in the past myself. I'm thankful I don't go helping with the stalking now nearly as much as I used to. Deer stalking's work for fit young men, not for bodachs (old men) like Colin and me."

Helen smiled, "Och, neither of you are auld bodachs yet… not quite yet."

"No… no, perhaps not. I know what I'll do, there's one sure way of getting Colin to visit us tonight." Ian went to the sideboard. He gently placed a half full bottle of Glenlivet and four glasses on the table. "Now, if that doesn't fetch Colin, nothing will!"

And, sure enough, once again that magic worked.

Shortly after nine o'clock Colin drove his van up to the crofthouse's front door and Jeannie and he were, as always, warmly welcomed by Helen and Ian.

"I see you were expecting us," Colin boisterously laughed as his gaze immediately homed in on the whisky.

"Aye, I knew that bait would fetch you. It's never failed yet."

Colin lovingly lifted the bottle and reverently examined it. "I see you've been at this whisky before, Ian, I'm surprised you've left any for me."

"Och, even I cannot finish an entire bottle by myself now. That's perhaps the worst penalty of growing old." He grinned at Helen, "Although my guid wife sometimes pointedly suggests that I suffer from another, and worse, penalty of old age."

Helen remained silent. She turned and looked at Jeannie. Both wives grinned and slowly shook their heads. Then Jeannie murmured, "I know exactly what you mean, Helen. Colin also suffers from the diminishing vigour of advancing age."

Colin ignored his wife's implied slur on his virility. He finished his examination of the whisky and beamed, "Ah well, I won't be a pessimist and mournfully say the bottle's half empty; I'll be an optimist and joyfully declare that the bottle's half full."

"Och, I'm sure it won't stay half full for long. What's holding you back, Ian? You've usually got the drams poured by now," Helen cheerfully reprimanded.

"I can't get near the blessed whisky for Colin gleefully gloating over it."

Soon they were all cosily settled and cheerfully enjoying their drams. Having noted that Colin was wearing his kilt, Helen said, "Of course, this is Thursday, this is your pipe band practise evening, isn't it?"

"Aye, it is. I was at practise for two hours. That's why we're a bit late."

"Were there many practising?" Ian asked.

"Aye, there were. There were about a dozen men and nearly twenty youngsters, both lads and lasses." Thanks to the dedicated enthusiasm of Colin and a few other keen pipers and an exceptionally gifted drummer, Inveraldrory and District Pipe Band had been re-formed recently. The village had boasted a notable pipe band before the Second World War, but that war had brought about its disbandment. "I find it surprising, but most encouraging, that so many youngsters are so keen to learn the pipes and drums."

"Aye, that must be really encouraging for you, Colin, especially with all the distractions of television and that hideous pop music to allure youngsters away from their traditional music," Helen said. "Then of course there's the separate class for beginners to learn accordion music too, isn't there?"

"Aye, so there is," Colin agreed, but with no show of enthusiasm. The accordionists and the pipers had many, usually good humoured, disputes over the relevant merits – or otherwise – of each other's music.

"You tried to learn the pipes many years ago, didn't you, Ian?" Jeannie asked.

"Aye, I did, but I made no progress with them. I'm afraid I'm just not musical."

Colin laughed, "I can vouch for that, Ian. I've heard your efforts at singing when you've had a good few drams inside you – it's not a pleasant sound!"

There was a short silence while they all enjoyed their whisky, then Helen asked with concern, "How are you coping with all this rain, Colin? Have you been stalking every day?"

Colin melodramatically grimaced and loudly groaned, "Oh aye, I've been oot every day. I had six hard days in a row last week and four so far this week. I've been soaked to the skin every time too. I'm getting damned sick of it. I despair of ever seeing a dry day again."

Jeannie grinned, "That's another reason he had to wear his kilt this evening, he hasn't got a dry pair o'breeks to his name! I've had a terrible time trying to get his clothes dry after each day's soaking." Turning to Helen, she continued, "You know how long it takes to get those thick tweed plus fours and jackets dried oot once they get soaked, don't you? It's a blessing he has a few suits of those estate tweeds or I would never have coped." With sympathy and understanding Helen commiserated with Jeannie in her ceaseless struggles to cope with these difficulties. Finally the two of them animatedly agreed in declaring, "Och, these men, they have nae notion of how much hard work and weary effort we put in looking after them so weel."

Colin grinned, "Och, never mind, wifies, you'll get your reward in heaven in due course."

"Aye, weel, we certainly won't get it here and now from you auld men, that's for sure," Jeannie grinned in reply.

Colin told of how terrible the stalking conditions were out on the hills in the relentlessly driving rain. "You know what it's like, Ian, when you're walking and climbing and stalking for sometimes as much as twenty miles, it's no use being cluttered up with heavy waterproofs, they're far too cumbersome and anyway you'd get soaked with sweat under them."

"Aye, I know, Colin, it's quite a problem deciding if it's worth wearing a light shower-proof jacket or not while stalking. This must be one of the worst spells of continuous rain we've ever had. Conditions underfoot are bad enough around the croft, they must be really atrocious out on the hills."

"Aye, they are. In all my years stalking I've never known the ground so soggily saturated. It would be nae surprise to see Noah's Ark afloat on one of the flooded lochs up in the hills."

"How many more stalking days remain before you complete this year's cull?"

"My boss, Lord Kilvert, has his last stalk tomorrow, Friday. He and Lady Kilvert then leave for Suffolk on Saturday. So I hope to God I get the weekend free. I could damned well do with a rest. I'm not as young as I used to be, you know."

"No, none of us are," Ian grinned.

"Then next week I've to shoot four stags to finish off the season's stalking. Do you want to come along with me as usual, Ian?"

"Aye, of course. I only hope the damned weather improves by then, though."

"Och, you've had much too easy a time of it staying indoors in that 'study' of yours while I've been out getting soaked day after day. It's aboot time you had a turn at getting drenched as well, you bugger, you lazy, cushy bugger."

Helen smiled, "Aye, Colin, he could do with some strenuous exercise. He's put on weight the last few weeks."

Grinning, his ruddy face beaming, Colin loudly slapped a proud hand on his stomach and said, "At least all this stalking has done me some good, my belly's lost quite a bit of surplus fat."

"Aye, I thought you were looking a wee bit trimmer," Helen said.

"More than 'a wee bit', he's a good bit trimmer," Jeannie laughed.

"He can get his kilt fastened now without such a desperate struggle. I often worried that he would have an apoplectic fit with the terrible effort he used to have to get the straps of his old ex-army kilt to fasten into the buckles at his waist. And yet sometimes I could not help laughing at him. He reminded me of my mother and her desperate struggles." Turning to Helen, she asked, "Remember my mother put on a lot of weight in her last years?"

"Yes, she did. It was partly the effects of the pills she had to take, wasn't it?"

"Aye, that's right. But she hated to be so fat. She insisted on forcing herself into a pair of old-fashioned whalebone corsets. Well, Colin's hilarious struggles to get his kilt fastened always reminded me of my struggles to get my mother's corsets tightly laced up."

Colin chuckled, "Well, I've told you before, Jeannie, you should have kept a pair of your mother's corsets for me. They would have been fine and dandy to keep my belly trim and neat."

Colin drained his glass then turned and placed it on the table beside the whisky bottle. Again his face beamed as he said, "Come on, Jeannie, it's time we were heading for home. I see the bottle's empty, so there's nothing to keep us here now."

"I could open another bottle," Ian offered.

"Och no, man, you better not. Don't tempt me: 'Get thee behind me, Satan.'" Colin's laughter once more boomed out. "Remember I've to be up early again tomorrow morning for another day's stalking and another damned soaking."

At 7.30 on the following Monday morning Calum MacLeod, as arranged, collected Ian and drove him in his, Calum's, dilapidated old Vauxhall Astra car to Glen Ardgie Shooting Lodge where they were to meet Colin and then set out for the day's deerstalking.

Calum was the thirty-four year old nephew of Kate and Kenny MacLeod. He, with his wife, Mary and their two young boys lived in a large residential caravan on Ian's croft. It was situated midway between his crofthouse and Kenny's house. They had been living in that caravan for just over one year, since shortly after Calum had been made redundant from his job as a draughtsman employed in a shipyard in Glasgow. Because of Mrs Thatcher, who – so Calum vehemently declared – had deliberately set about destroying most of Clydeside's shipbuilding and heavy engineering companies, he had been unable to find another suitable job. He had often dreamt of getting out of Glasgow and of living in Aldrory, of returning to where his ancestral roots were, that place where he had spent many happy summer holidays staying with his warmly hospitable aunt and uncle. His wife also deeply enjoyed those holidays she had shared with him. She too sincerely loved that remote and wildly beautiful land. After some initial doubts about living all year in a caravan, she agreed to the adventurous move.

Their boys, Rob and Norman, five and three years old, had taken to the country life like the proverbial ducks to water. They loved their novel and exciting new environment; loved their loving 'aunt' and 'uncle', loved Old Nell, the pony, Meg, the Collie, and all the hens and chicks. Living in the caravan was a ceaseless wonder and delight; it made life one glorious long holiday.

As he drove, Calum smiled, "You're lucky, Ian, it looks as if we might have a dry day for a change, the first we've had for weeks. It will be grand to have one day's stalking at last without getting soaked through. Mary will be amazed and delighted if I return home with dry clothes. Poor Mary, she's had a terrible time trying to get all my soaking clothes dried out in the caravan."

When Calum smiled his teeth gleamed brightly against the dense black of his thick beard and moustache. That beard, with his glossy black head of hair and his swarthy complexion, revealed the strong trace of Spanish blood he had inherited from his mother. She came from Tobermory. Four hundred years ago some of her ancestors must have interbred with survivors from the galleon, part of the storm dispersed Spanish Armada, which had sunk in Tobermory Bay. The influence of that Spanish blood was still clearly evident in a number of Hebridean Islanders.

Colin was waiting for them at the shooting lodge. They wasted no time in setting out. That day's stalking went well. Colin shot a stag before noon and they had it hanging in the deer larder shortly after two. And that was despite them having to make time-wasting detours with the laden pony to avoid the most boggy and potentially dangerous parts of the miserably waterlogged terrain.

Apart from a couple of light showers in the morning, the day remained dry and the stalkers congratulated themselves on, for once, getting back without being soaked through.

As he started the homeward drive along the narrow and twisting road, which climbed up Aldrory Glen, Calum asked, "Oh, by the way, Ian, have you heard any of the stories going around about the village shop and the garage?"

"Aye, I've heard rumours, but that's all they are, vague rumours, that the bastard of a laird is not going to renew the leases on the garage and the shop when they expire sometime next year."

"Yes, that's what I've heard. Johnnie Fraser and Bob McInnes must be very worried about it all." Robert McInnes ran the only garage and petrol pumps in Inveraldrory village and John Fraser had the only grocers shop. These premises, together with their adjoining house, belonged to Mr Campbell-Fotheringay, the owner of Aldrory Estate. He had let them out on five-year leases, but now, if these rumours were true, he was not going to renew these leases. "They've not been told anything officially yet," Calum continued, "but that's just what that bloody Campbell-Fotheringay is likely to do. Clear out more of the native Highlanders and replace them with the worst type of hideously pretentious and snobbish middle-class 'White Settlers'. He will probably sell the garage and the shop to such Southerners at prices no local can afford."

"Let's hope it won't come to that, Calum. It would be an absolute disgrace if Johnnie and Bob lost their businesses. And they and their families would lose their homes too. If they were forced out it would be a sad loss for the district."

"Yes, I know. It would be tragic! It must not be allowed to happen! It would be a complete disaster coming on top of all the houses already turned into holiday homes in Aldrory," Calum angrily declared. Getting into his stride on this familiar theme, he passionately exclaimed, "By God, the sooner every sporting estate owned by absent landlords in the Highlands is taken over by a Scottish Government in an Independent Scotland and developed for the benefit of the locals living on these estates, the better."

When living in Glasgow, Calum had been a fervent left-wing Labour supporter. He was now a passionate left-wing Scottish Nationalist.

Ian grinned, "You better not let Lord Kilvert hear you advocating the nationalisation of his Ardgie sporting estate."

Calum returned a rueful grin. His serious political convictions were, wisely, tempered by a lively sense of humour. "You're accusing me of hypocrisy, are you?... of working, even if only part-time, for Lord Kilvert, that absentee English landowner. I suppose I have to admit I'm not being all that consistent. But at least he's not too bad a laird; he does employ a number of people on his estate and is quite a good employer." He paused thoughtfully. Since coming in direct contact with Lord and Lady Kilvert and, to his surprise, finding them pleasantly friendly employers to work with, while also requiring exactingly high standards of service from all their employees, he had been forced to modify some of his long-held prejudices. He realised that these true 'gentry', these aristocrats of ancient lineage, were an entirely different and much better breed than the would be 'gentry' he had previously had contact with who, from their Highland holiday homes, patronisingly tried to act as Lords of The Manor over the local peasantry. He gave another rueful grin, "Of course I've got a wife and two bairns to think of now. Such responsibilities, such happy, if sometimes heavy, responsibilities make some compromises necessary, don't they?"

"Aye, they do. Oh, Calum, I'm accusing you of nothing except of being something of an idealist. And that's no bad thing for a young man to be. In fact, it's a poor young man who does not have some idealism."

"And what about an old man? Shouldn't he retain some of his youthful idealism?"

"Touché, Calum, touché! Aye, he should, but it's not always easy. So many bright hopes and dreams and expectations gradually die, are drowned in an ugly sea of sad reality, are sunk in the mire of politicians' broken, or forgotten, election promises. Are blighted by the false and over-optimistic promises of scientific progress."

Ian fell silent. He thought of how Ramsay MacDonald's first Labour Government had quickly forgotten its election promise to nationalize Highland sporting estates. He clearly remembered the tidal wave of euphoria as the results of the 1945 general election, the khaki election, came out, with its huge Labour landslide. Labour was going to create a Socialist Utopia in Britain. Again, Highland sporting estates were going to be nationalized, but again nothing came of this. At least that Labour government did build many Hydro-Electric schemes which brought electricity to practically every house in the Highlands. That government also very generously compensated Highland estate owners for these Hydro-Electric schemes flooding their glens and interfering with their salmon fishing.

Ian now despaired of any British government (or of any future Scottish government?) ever getting rid of privately owned Highland sporting estates. Good estate owners, better than most past owners, were all he now thought could be realistically hoped for. And yet surely it was not inconceivable that some future government might do something to encourage crofting communities to acquire and own the land the crofters worked. He no longer believed that wholesale land nationalisation was the answer; the catastrophic results of many years of complete state ownership of land in the Soviet Union were hardly encouraging.

"Oh, surely you're getting too cynical in your old age, Ian?" Calum said. "What hope is there if socialism and science have failed us? What is left? Pessimism?... Despair?... Drugs and drink?... Suicide?"

"Och, no. No, it's not as bad as that. We – some fortunate individuals – can live good, happy, contented lives. And you, Calum, and Mary, and yours boys are looking much better and fitter since you came to live in Aldrory."

"Yes, that's true. The boys have never been so healthy and happy before. They simply love it here. So does Mary, although at times she gets rather tired of the rain and of the difficulties of living in a caravan."

"Aye, I can understand that. Hopefully you'll get a house of your own before too long."

"I hope so. But the trouble is I can't afford to buy a house here now with the way prices have soared since bloody Campbell-Fotheringay started selling his estate houses to wealthy Southerners."

To defuse Calum's rising anger, Ian grinned and said, "Och, never mind, Calum, Superwoman Thatcher is going to solve all the problems of all mankind!"

Calum instantly reacted, as Ian knew he would. He took his right hand from the steering wheel and made the sign of the cross over his chest. He exclaimed, "May angels and ministers of grace defend us from the Evil One."

Ian laughed. Suddenly amusement turned to alarm. "Look out, we're nearly in the ditch!"

Calum violently swung the car back on to the road. He laughed, "You see what happens when the dreaded name of 'The Evil One' is spoken."

"Aye... I'll be careful not to mention that accursed name again when you're driving."

"Yes, it'll be much safer not to."

After last year's amazing and wonderful triumphant victory of the Falklands War and this year's (1983) sweeping electoral victory, Mrs Thatcher was thirstily quaffing the heady wine of unchallenged power; was revelling in her immense popularity in England. She was not, and had never been, really popular in Scotland.

As they neared his crofthouse Ian said, "You better not mention those rumours about the village shop and garage to your aunt and uncle. There's no point in having them worry over what are, as yet, merely rumours. Poor Kate is worried enough about the uncertain position regarding their own house."

Kate and Kenny MacLeod rented their house from Campbell-Fotheringay's Aldrory Estate. They had no security of tenure. They dreaded that some year they might be turned out of the house, or that the rent would be increased so much that they would not be able to pay it.

"Oh no... no, of course I'll say nothing to them," Calum quickly agreed.

When Calum again collected Ian early the following morning the rain relentlessly poured. It showed no sign of ever easing off.

With grim resignation the stalking party set out. Colin and Ian led the way. Calum followed them and led Nell by her long rope halter. Although getting old, that greyish-white pony was still a hardy specimen of a true Highland Garron. Steadily, willingly, sure-footedly she plodded on, seemingly completely indifferent to the driving rain. Of course, going Eastward from the shooting lodge, up long Glen Ardie, was the easiest part of the day; the rain was, as usual, sweeping in from the West, from the angry grey Atlantic and they had their backs to it. The return journey, facing into the driving rain would be much worse. None were foolishly optimistic enough to think that the rain might be over by then. Mile after mile they resolutely plodded along the narrow stalking path, which led into the heart of Argie's uninhabited wilderness. They had to make a detour round a marshy hollow where the flooded track was impassable.

"In all my years stalking over this ground I've never known the path to be flooded like this," Colin said.

"Yes, it's by far the worst I've ever known it," Ian agreed. "The land's absolutely saturated."

Soon after this, Colin decided to leave the track and climb up to a corrie that lay beyond the steep ridge above the long glen. With his vast knowledge of the deer and of this land he confidently expected to find stags there. He grinned, "At least there's one thing to be said for this bloody awful weather, it drives the beasts lower down the hill to seek some shelter."

"Aye," Ian again agreed, "we shouldn't need to climb high today."

Nor did they. They saw stags standing sheltering in that East facing corrie exactly as Colin had expected.

Calum had been left in charge of Nell lower down the ridge and well out of sight of the stags. While Colin and Ian cautiously and expertly stalked towards the deer, he patiently waited. With resigned deliberation, Nell turned her broad backside square on to the wind and driving rain. She let the lively elements tuck her long and thick grey tail snugly between her legs then stood statuesquely and stoically still while rainwater steadily dripped from her. Keeping a firm grip on the rope halter, Calum cooried doon behind a boulder and tried to summon up the fortitude to wait as patiently and stoically as old Nell did. As he pulled his hat more firmly down and his jacket collar higher, he smiled grimly and consoled himself with the thought that at least this strong wind and pelting rain kept the midges away.

Ian and Colin now lay hidden in the soaking heather within rifle shot of the stags. With the aid of telescopes, their experienced eyes expertly inspected the beasts. Colin grinned and whispered, "Look, there's 'himself' – 'The Monarch of the Glen', no less!"

The animal indicated was a magnificent 'Royal', a large, mature stag who proudly displayed a truly impressive set of antlers. These antlers carried a total of twelve points, all 'correctly' and symmetrically arranged, six points on each thick antler and the pair gracefully swept wide in a noble spread. His red autumn coat shone glossily and his lion's mane was thick around his neck. At this time, at the end of September, he was in his vigorous, virile prime.

Restlessly and nervously he trotted back and forward. The approach of the October rut, the mating time, excitedly inflamed his blood. Occasionally he stopped, shook a fountain of fine white spray from his body, lifted his head high and gave a loud, challenging, self-assertive roar. Soon these hills would echo and re-echo with the bellowing roars of lustily aggressive stags.

"He's a real beauty," Ian whispered. "Is this the first year he's been a 'Royal'?"

"Aye, it is, I've had my eye on him for a few years hoping he would grow into a 'Royal'. Last year he was only a ten pointer." Lying soaked in the heather, with the rain battering down on him, Colin wasted no more time on deciding which stag to shoot. "I'll take that auld seven pointer to the left there. He looks gey long in the tooth."

"Aye, he's a poor specimen, right enough. The sooner he's turned into venison casserole the better," whispered Ian. All this very necessary cautious whispering seemed to reinforce the feeling of warm friendship Ian and Colin had shared for so many years.

Wisely, they faithfully copied nature's process of natural selection by means of the survival of the fittest. They would kill the older and weaker stag and leave the larger more powerful 'Royal' to mate with the hinds.

Colin quickly dropped the old seven pointer with his usual accurate heart shot.

They wasted no time as they skilfully gralloched the dead stag.

Calum arrived with Nell. They loaded the carcase on to the large deer saddle on Nell's broad back. The many leather straps were wound around the stag's body and securely fastened to the saddle. The head was twisted up to keep the antlers high and well clear of the pony's body.

Plodding homeward, they faced into the wind and rain. The Westerly wind had increased in strength; it was approaching gale force. It drove the rain almost horizontally over the cowering landscape and battered it viciously into their grimly determined faces.

Colin and Ian again led the way. They picked the firmest route for the laden pony through this dreary landscape of weeping grey rocks, sodden heather and dark and squelchy peat. They followed a series of rocky ridges until the rock petered out. They started the descent towards the track below them in Glen Ardgie.

With heads bowed against the ferocious rain, Ian and Colin plodded on. They were abruptly halted by a loud shout from Calum behind them.

"Oh, Christ," Colin exclaimed, "they've gone into a bog!"

Calum and the pony had wandered a little from the exact route taken by Colin and Ian. They had suddenly plunged into a small but deep peat bog. The dangers of that bog had not been obvious to Calum's inexperienced eye – vivid green mosses grew amongst the large tussocks of grass and covered that bog with a deceptively dangerous skin. After the excessive rains of the last few weeks this small bog was a deadly quagmire.

Nell had already sunk more than knee deep. Desperately, she sucked a front leg out of the clinging bog and, with black peat splattering wildly, tried to gain firmer ground. But as one leg came up the other three sank deeper.

Calum, himself knee deep, pulled on Nell's head in urgent assistance. From firmer heather ground Colin and Ian hauled on her long rope halter. They were both much heavier than Calum, they would sink much faster than him if they went out into that bog.

The darkly churned peat, thick, filthy, fetid, was now up to Nell's heaving belly.

"Try and get the stag and saddle off her," Colin shouted.

Frantically Calum tried to unfasten the strong leather straps. He floundered out of the way as Nell suddenly made a final desperate effort to lunge out of that deadly morass. For long moments, trembling, snorting, gasping, she valiantly struggled. Exerting her utmost strength she heaved and strained.

But her best efforts were useless. Those wild struggles only engulfed her deeper in that black treacle of tenacious clinging peat. Exhausted, she gave up the attempt.

She lay motionless. She was silent but for her loud, laboured, breathing. She appeared to await her death with stoic resignation.

As Nell inexorably sank deeper, Calum ever more urgently struggled to unbuckle the straps. His cold and trembling fingers slithered over the soft leather's slimy smooth slipperiness as they followed the restraining straps down into the oozy black peat's obscene vileness.

Suddenly, commandingly, urgently, Colin shouted, "Calum, leave Nell, she's done for! Quick, get out yourself. Hurry!... Hurry!"

Calum did not realise just how deeply he too had sunk into the peat. It was now halfway up his thighs. Self-preservation instantly took command. Fear for himself replaced concern for Nell. Desperately he struggled to get free. His wild efforts were unsuccessful. The more desperate his struggles, the deeper he sank. Panic took over. With tremulous voice he shouted, "Help!... Help!... I'm stuck. I can't get out. Help me!... Help me!"

Deliberately keeping the anxiety out of his voice, Ian calmly shouted, "Don't panic lad! Quick, untie Nell's halter rope. Tie it over your chest. We'll pull you out with it."

With urgent fingers Calum loosened the rope from Nell's neck and tied it around himself. He loudly shouted, "Hurry, pull me out. Hurry!... Hurry! I'm going down!"

Colin and Ian gripped the rope and pulled. Their slipping feet slithered to gain purchase in the soft ground. Leaning hard back they hauled with all their strength, but to no avail. Calum did not move one inch towards them. But at least he sank no deeper.

Gasping, Ian and Colin rested for a few moments. Their eyes met. Simultaneously they remembered a certain wartime training. While on a tough commando course, practising landing on enemy beaches, they had been taught the best way to get out of dangerous quicksands by lying spread-eagle and 'swimming' over the sand's treacherous surface.

Clearly and authoritatively Colin shouted, "When we pull again lay your chest flat on the peat and try to 'swim' towards us over its surface. Kick up with your feet at the same time."

They started hauling on the rope, but Calum was reluctant to lower himself onto the peat. Louder, more urgently, almost angrily, Colin shouted, "For God's sake, Calum, do what I say! Get down on the surface and we'll slide you out."

Calum obeyed. Ian and Colin firmly gripped the soaking rope and pulled. After a few minutes of urgent hauling and confused floundering they felt Calum slightly, but definitely, move towards them.

"You're moving, lad," Colin gasped, "Keep struggling."

With renewed effort by their combined strength, the strength reinforced by the adrenaline surging through their blood, they pulled on the rope. The muscles of their shoulders and arms, their thighs and legs, strained as they had never strained before, not even in their utmost efforts in the tug-of-war team at Inveraldrory Highland Games.

After another few minutes of supreme effort there was a strange loud slurping, squelching, protesting sound as the oozy black peat reluctantly released its greedy grip on Calum. These ugly sounds seemed to come from a malevolent monster... from a hungry predator being deprived of its prey.

Heaving together, Colin and Ian felt Calum slide towards them. They pulled with renewed energy. Suddenly Calum's legs were free. One final heave brought him slithering over the soft peat with a wild rush. Ian and Colin fell backwards on top of one another. Rejoicing, they struggled up, grabbed Calum, and hauled him on to the firm heather. He lay absolutely exhausted. With thankful relief they flopped down beside him.

As he lay with his entire body covered in filthy dark peat Calum looked like a gigantic slimy black slug, like some loathsome creature newly evolved from Earth's first primeval mud.

After resting for a while, Colin and Ian struggled to their feet and turned their thoughts to old Nell.

While that struggle to save Calum had been going on she had continued slowly sinking. Now little more than her head and neck showed above the peat. The stag on her back bulged darkly from the evil ooze and its antlers rose like gaunt branches from a stricken tree. They moved as close as possible to her and sympathetically murmured, "Poor old Nell... Poor old girl... What a sad end you've come to."

As they stood helplessly and desolately staring at ill-fated Nell, Ian could not help imagining that there was something evilly triumphant about that dark peat bog as it so relentlessly engulfed the piteous old pony. Surprisingly, Nell had made little sound during her ordeal. Now, in answer to their murmurs of sympathy, she softly and pathetically whinnied. Her large brown eyes eloquently pleaded. Those eyes seemed enormously distended.

"There's only one thing we can do for poor Nell now, isn't there?" Ian dejectedly asked.

"Aye, I'm afraid there is," Colin solemnly said as his gaze followed Ian's to the rifle, in its cover, lying on the heather. "Let's get it over with quickly."

"Will I do it?"

"Aye, if you don't mind, Ian."

Ian pulled the rifle from the soaking canvas cover and slid a bullet into its breech. Nell's huge eyes followed his every move as he forced himself to take careful aim. Gently he squeezed the trigger.

Nell's grey head jerked back then collapsed lifeless into the dark peat. With obscene eagerness the bog began engulfing the last of its victim.

The shot startled Calum. Oozily, awkwardly, wildly, he struggled to his feet. "Oh God, what have you done?... Oh, poor, poor Nell!" He stared with dismayed eyes at what little was to be seen of Nell. Rasping sobs tore painfully from deep in his chest. Choking and profoundly distressed, he gasped for breath.

For some minutes the three men stood staring at the last of Nell. Colin and Ian stared in solemn silence. Calum was constantly shaken by violent sobs. Tears coursed from his eyes and washed clear rivulets through the peat staining his cheeks then saltily soaked into his saturated black beard.

Ian quietly moved over to Calum. Gently and compassionately he placed a hand on his shoulder. "I'm sorry, lad, there was nothing else we could do."

Calum angrily shook off Ian's hand. In a huskily distraught accusing voice he cried out, "You don't care about Nell's death. You're not in the least upset!"

Before Ian could respond, Colin diplomatically intervened, "That's not true Calum... just because Ian and me don't show visible emotion that doesn't mean we don't feel real sorrow for poor old Nell's sad death."

Calum gulped and then gasped, "Well, you... you certainly keep your feelings well hidden."

"Aye, perhaps we do, lad. That's the way we were brought up, to stoically control our feelings. Any man who gave way to excessive expressions of feelings in public was – correctly, I think – regarded as having something weak about him. Instinctively we all felt it was wrong, was disgraceful, to make an exhibition of ourselves by any too emotional display of our feelings."

"Aye," Ian nodded his agreement, "that was the true old Highland way we were brought up. I still think it is the best way. Nowadays there if far too much soppy and weepy public sentimentality instead of deeply sincere private emotion."

"Oh, I'm sorry... I'm very sorry I'm making such a public display of my sorrow, then," Calum gasped bitterly. "I hope it doesn't annoy you too much."

"Take it easy, lad, take it easy. I've told you we don't like this any more than you do. We are not unsympathetic to your feelings," Colin said. He paused, then gently asked, "Is this the first time you've seen a horse shot?"

Calum did not reply. He stood sobbingly and tearfully miserable.

"Well, is it?" Colin repeated more firmly.

"Yes, it is," he indistinctly mumbled.

"And have you ever had to kill a dog or cat or any other domestic animal?"

"No... no, I haven't."

"Well, you know, Calum, over many years Ian and me have had to put down quite a few animals; some were pets, others were farm beasts. We did not like doing it, but when there was a real reason for doing it, well we did it."

Ian again nodded his agreement. He then added, "And another thing, lad, Colin and I came through six long years of war. Being in the 'PBI' – the Poor Bloody Infantry – we were front line soldiers. We saw many violent deaths.

140

When you've seen many humans killed, it puts even the saddest death of a horse into true perspective."

Colin murmured, "Aye, and often they were our good comrades who were killed." He paused. He sighed, "And some of them suffered much worse, much longer lingering agonising deaths than poor old Nell did."

Colin and Ian's eyes met in a long silent stare. Grim memories flooded through their minds. Although forty years old those memories remained vividly clear.

For a while Calum stood silent with bowed head; silent except for the sobs that shook his body. With an obvious effort, he got his feelings under control. His sobs ceased. He looked up with tearful and sorrowful eyes. He apologised, "I'm sorry. I had no right to criticise you. Especially not after you saved my life."

"That's all right, Calum, don't worry about it," Colin said.

"Aye, forget about it," Ian said understandingly, "and anyway we would think the less of you, lad, if you had not been upset by poor Nell's death."

Calum silently smiled his thanks.

"Come on, lad, get that rope untied then we'll start for home. There's nothing more we can do here. The sooner we get started the sooner we'll get home and out of this bloody rain."

During the desperate struggle to save Calum, they had been oblivious to the rain. Now in this sad calm after that excitement they again became conscious of it as it battered with sadistic ferocity.

These words of Colin's drew Ian's attention to the rope dangling from Calum's body. It stretched away from him and lay amongst the heather in untidy sodden loops. Suddenly in Ian's imagination those grey loops were transformed – they became Calum's spilled and trailing guts. That unbidden flash of imagination had been triggered by old, ugly, wartime memories. A memory of Northern France in 1940; a moaning horse lying with coils of grey guts spilling from its split belly. A memory of Northern Italy in 1944; a moaning Seaforth soldier lying with dark guts coiling from his gashed belly. It was no surprise to see how much gut spilled from a horse's belly. It was always a shock to see how much gut spilled from a man's belly. Ian violently shuddered.

"Are you all right?" Colin anxiously asked.

"What?... Oh aye, I'm fine... I'm fine. I'm cold and miserable, that's all. I could do with a damned good dram."

"Aye, we all could," Colin wholeheartedly agreed. He turned to Calum, "Can't you get that knot untied?"

"No... no, it's pulled too tight and it's saturated, I can do nothing with it."

Calum nervously started back as Colin advanced with the razor sharp blade of his gralloching knife pointing straight at him. Colin laughed, "Och, it's all right, lad, I'm only going to cut the rope. Did you think I was going to put you out of your misery, like poor Nell?"

Calum grinned, but it was a rather forced, uncertain grin.

Ian and Colin lifted their sturdy walking sticks, settled their deerstalker hats more firmly and prepared to leave. Calum's stick and hat were swallowed in the bog. All three turned, paused, and gazed sadly at the quagmire that had so greedily enveloped Nell. The black bulge of the stag marked that evil place. The stag's antlers rose from the choking dark ooze. Their long, thin points were like bony fingers vainly raised in imploring prayer to the dismal grey sky. That louring, sad sky wept ceaseless tears – but they were coldly indifferent tears.

An hour of steady, squelchy plodding through the relentless rain brought them to a rocky gully where some of the few trees in this stark, gale swept landscape desperately struggled to survive. Grey birch trees precariously clung to life among the mass of tumbled rocks littering the gully's steep slopes. Stunted and gnarled, their lichen-covered trunks gave the impression of being soaked through to their very core. A group of rowans, red berried and vivid leaved, huddled together as if for companionship. They were the only bright splash of colour in all the grey monotony of washed out dreariness. Even the vigorously invasive thickets of tough brackens drooped their dripping fonds in utter dejection as they transformed from green life to bronze death.

"Let's stop here for a few minutes and have a smoke," Colin suggested as they neared a familiar dark boulder, which aggressively shouldered itself to the very edge of the track.

The three men sat as comfortably as possible under the huge boulder's overhang. It sheltered them from the worst of the rain. However, reluctant to be denied, rainwater seeped down through the mosses and lichens growing in wrinkles in the cold grey stone's ancient face and steadily dripped arctic cold drops on them.

Ian and Colin quickly got out their pipes and produced tobacco and matches from their waterproof pouches. As Colin puffed on his pipe he grinned, "Now isn't this the height of comfort?"

"I can think of many a damned sight more comfortable place than this," Ian smiled as he too puffed on his pipe.

Calum was a non-smoker. Although still upset by Nell's death, the strong, natural, resilience of youth, allied to insistent pangs of hunger, took over and he hauled his sandwiches out of a waterlogged pocket. He opened the plastic bag. What had been neat sandwiches were revealed as a sorry, pulpy mess of crumbs. He inspected this inedible muck with disgust.

Ian opened his mouth to say, "Give them to Nell," but stopped himself in time. They usually gave any unwanted bread to Nell. It was hard to believe that she was dead. Sensing what Ian had almost said, Calum grimaced. Scrambling to his feet, he said, "I'll just scatter these sodden crumbs outside for the birds and mice."

As Calum returned to the shelter of the massive boulder, Colin laughed, "My God, lad, what do you look like?"

Ian's laughter joined Colin's, "What do we all look like?"

Grinning, Calum suggested, "We look like three saturated, woebegone scarecrows."

"I've seen many a scarecrow looking a damned sight more presentable than us," Colin replied.

"We look like three miserable, bedraggled Froggie soldiers of Napoleon's Grand Army on its not so grand retreat from Moscow," Ian declared.

With renewed laughter Colin exclaimed, "Aye, or to put it in guid descriptive Scots, we are like three miserable drookit rats, a'clarty wi' glaur."

"Aye, and we're gey scunnered wi' a' oor stravaiging sae far fae hame," Ian added.

Not to be outdone, Calum grinned, "Aye, it's a sair trauchle, richt eneuch!"

They again laughed, then Colin said, "Aye, those are richt braw words, aren't they? It's guid to hear you, a younger generation, use them, Calum. It would be sad if sic brawly descriptive guid auld words were tae completely fa' oot o' use."

Ian and Calum nodded their agreement. Ian grinned, "Aye, it's grand tae use those auld words sometimes. I suppose we should use them much more than we do."

For a while they were silent. Ian and Colin continued smoking. Calum slightly shifted his position to avoid a persistent drip from the roof of their shelter. For the first time he really looked at the damp lichens which brightly coated much of the overhanging rock above his head. He was amazed at the variety of their colours. There were greens and greys, spots of vivid orange, and many shades of blue and purple. He smiled, "It looks as if an artist has painted those attractive abstract designs on that rock, doesn't it?"

"Aye, it does," Ian said, "I've often admired those colourful 'paintings' when we've been sheltering here."

Colin looked up at the lichens then said, "Aye, they're braw colours, but nothing like as braw as the colours on yon ceiling in Rome, remember, Ian?"

"Aye, of course I remember. How could I ever forget that unforgettable experience?" He explained to Calum, "Once in 1944, Colin and I had a few days' leave in Rome. We had a grand time. One morning we went to see the Vatican. We were most impressed by the glory of its architecture and its many wondrous sculptures. Then we were overwhelmed by the magnificent splendour of Michelangelo's fabulously glowing ceiling in the Sistine Chapel."

Ian paused then smiled, "Yes, that glory created by human genius puts these colours painted by nature on this stone ceiling to shame."

"Aye, and yon splendid building was dry and warm and aglow with sunlight, unlike this damned damp miserable place," Colin said with a rueful grin.

Calum said, "Aye, we could do with some of that hot Italian sunshine here now, couldn't we?" He grinned mischievously, "I'm very surprised that two tough, fit young soldiers as you must have been then should spend your short leave in Rome indulging in aesthetic sightseeing. I would have thought you'd have been more interested in much more carnal pleasures."

Ian laughed, "Och, it was only during the day we went sightseeing. Wisely, we devoted the evenings to much more sensual pleasures."

"Aye, the evenings were for the delights of wine, women and song," Colin grinned.

Ian's and Colin's eyes met in a glance bright with warm nostalgic memories, then Ian said, "I learned then, and still believe, that the wisest course is to enjoy both aesthetic pleasures and sensual pleasures. These diverse delights complement one another."

"Aye," Colin said, "and all those pleasures in Rome were heightened by the thought, constantly at the back of our minds, that once we returned to the battlefront we never knew from minute to minute and from hour to hour when we might get killed."

They both vividly remembered how fiercely and hungrily they had sated the urgent sexual urges throbbing through their warm young blood. The knowledge that they would soon again be in the front line, that they might be killed, put desperate urgency into all their lovemaking.

Ian smiled reminiscently, he sighed, "Aye, we had some great times with those voluptuous Roman signorinas, hadn't we?

"Aye, we had, we certainly had. Of course, we were young, fit and virile then, and under the exceptional wartime conditions we could purchase the favours of almost any Bella Donna we wanted in exchange for a tin of fifty army issue cigarettes."

"Aye," Ian grinned, "in Italy we fairly made up for our two years of enforced celibacy in the North African deserts."

Calum laughed, "Those two years must have been a sair trial for you?"

"Yes, they were," Ian laughed in reply. He was pleased that Calum was laughing, that he seemed to have got over the worst of his upset at Nell's sad death. "Yes, we were celibate from necessity, not choice. After all there's nothing to celebrate about being celibate is there?"

"No, there certainly isn't," Colin said. "Of course, bromide was compulsorily added to oor army tea to reduce oor sexual urges in the desert."

Ian grinned, "Aye, and now at oor age we could do with something to stimulate oor much reduced sexual urges!"

"Speak for yourself, Ian, speak for yourself! I'm not complaining!" Colin laughed loudly and proudly.

"Och, stop your boasting, Colin. We don't believe you."

As he knocked the ashes out of his smoked-out pipe, Colin said, "Och weel, I suppose we better get moving again. I'm getting damned cold. Sitting here in soaking clothes isn't doing my bloody rheumatics any good."

"Aye, I know," Ian agreed, "I'm damned cold myself." He paused, then grinned, "My god, how the mighty have fallen. Despite your boasting, you know the truth is that nowadays we worry more about getting rheumatics then about getting sex!"

Calum laughed derisively, "It must be terrible being old, getting stiff with rheumatics instead of getting stiff with sex!"

Colin and Ian grinned ruefully. "Just you wait, lad, just you wait," Colin said. "Rheumatics will catch up with you sooner or later in this bloody damp climate."

"Aye," Ian added, "and sooner, rather than later if the damned rain continues like this.

As they left the shelter of the boulder the allied elements of wind and rain seemed to take a sadistic pleasure in torturing them.

As Calum followed the two older men along the narrow track, he thought of and smiled over that tale of their amorous exploits in Rome. He enjoyed hearing their wartime stories. He was impressed by the depth and sincerity of the friendship that existed between them. The comradeship forged between them during six years of war was still, after forty years, as strong as ever. Probably such depth of friendship was only possible between men who had shared the dangers, the hardships, the eagerly snatched pleasures of war.

Calum had no military experience, not even post war national service. Sometimes he felt almost envious of Colin and Ian with their wealth of wartime experiences. At times he was restless at the thought that he had never tested himself in battle. Had never felt the awful thrill experienced by every young soldier as, poised on the trigger-edge of fear and excitement, he went into action for the first time. Perhaps that was a test that all young men should face? Perhaps we are all getting much too soft, much too fond of easy, lazy comforts nowadays? He had expressed something of this to Ian, who had understood and sympathised with these feelings, but had pointed out that while he would not have missed his exciting wartime adventures for anything, still he and Colin had been two of the lucky ones, they had come through the war unharmed. (Ian had laughed, "Apart from my ignoble minor wound!") It was easy for them in their old age to look back nostalgically to their wartime years, but so many had been brutally killed, had never achieved old age, and how many had been grievously maimed, either physically, or perhaps worse, mentally. And he, Calum, might have been one of these unlucky ones.

As a gust of extra ferocity cruelly drove stinging rain into Calum's face he again thought of poor Nell's sad death and of his own fear, his moments of terrible panic, when it seemed he might share the pony's fate and suffocate in that sinister quagmire. Smiling, he thought that perhaps he was being tested severely enough in the battle against the natural elements in this wild land. Yes, he decided, this was test enough to be going on with, and at least he shared with Colin and Ian the deep camaraderie of the male hunter and fisher.

They halted only once on the final part of their long and weary journey when Colin laughed and exclaimed, "I'll need to tighten my belt or my breeks will be aboot my ankles."

Ian and Calum joined in the laughter, "Aye, we'll need to tighten oor belts too."

The weight of rainwater saturating their thick, baggy tweed plus fours was dragging these garments down. The bottoms of those plus fours were hanging soggily halfway down their calves, while their thick woollen stockings were a dark, bedraggled heap around their ankles.

"I suppose I'm wasting my time doing this," Ian said as he pulled his stockings up towards his knees.

"Aye, you are," Colin laughed, "they'll soon drop doon again. I doot you'll need to use stronger elastic in your garters!"

Determinedly, squelchily, phlegmatically, they trudged onwards.

At last, they arrived at Glen Ardgie Lodge. Colin and Ian found it strange to walk past the deer-larder. There was no stag to hang and skin. Calum found it strange to walk past the stables. There was no Nell to stable, unsaddle and rub down.

They went directly to the gunroom. It did not take long to clean, dry, then liberally oil the rifle. Once it was securely locked in the metal gun cupboard they turned their attention to more pleasant and eagerly anticipated things – the three generous drams left on the gun table by Mrs Nicoll, the lodge's housekeeper. These welcoming drams were one of the traditional prerequisites of Highland gamekeepers.

Colin beamed as he picked up his glass, "We've oiled the rifle, now we'll oil oorselves."

Colin and Ian's drams instantly disappeared, were spirited away as if by magic.

Calum took little more than a sip. He made a face, "My God, that's harsh stuff. How can you knock it back like that without turning a hair? A love of such rough whisky is definitely an acquired taste."

Ian laughed, "Aye, it is. It's a taste Colin and I acquired many, many, years ago."

"Aye, and it's a taste you'll have to acquire too, lad, if you're going to be a true Highland gamekeeper and follow in my footsteps," Colin said. "And there's a very good chance that you will be taken on as a full-time trainee gamekeeper soon."

"Do you really think so?" Calum eagerly asked.

"Aye, I do. I've strongly recommended you to Lord Kilvert. You should get the offer of the job from him in the next week or so."

"Oh, that's great! Thanks, Colin. Thanks a lot."

"Och, I'm getting too old for this damned deerstalking," Colin said. "After three weeks of getting soaked through every day I'm sick and tired of it. My bloody rheumatics are giving me hell. It's about time fit young men like you took over from us auld bodachs. From next year I'm to be employed mainly as a ghillie at the salmon river."

"That's great, Colin. I'm delighted to her it," Ian said. "The ghillieing is certainly much easier than the stalking for bodachs like us twa."

"Aye, I know," Colin smiled at Calum, "I hope all this rain hasn't sickened you as well, hasn't made you change your mind about living here and becoming a gamekeeper. Do you sometimes wish you were back in a dry and cosy office in Glasgow?"

"Oh no, never! I could never settle in an office again and I could not bear to live in a city again. Despite all the rain, despite the sad death of Nell, I still love it here. I love being out on the hills in the fresh air in all weathers."

Colin laughed, "Och well, lad, that's one thing you can be certain of – you'll get no end of fresh weather here."

"Aye," Ian added, "but the trouble is it's often just much too damned fresh! Anyway, I'm glad you're still enjoying it, Calum… Ah, that's what it is to be young." Then he mischievously grinned, "Even if you did want to go back to Glasgow, there are no jobs left in that city now, Mrs Thatcher has seen to that!"

Colin and Ian laughed unrestrainedly as Calum went through his inevitable pantomime on hearing *that* name mentioned; crossing himself, he cried, "May angels and ministers of grace defend us from the Evil One!"

Colin now urged, "Come on, Calum, drink up your dram and we'll get away home." Nobly, he tried to sound convincing in these urgings, "Come on, man, drink up, you're letting the team down."

Calum took a sip then handed his glass to Colin. "I've had enough. You drink it."

Colin beamed, "'Himself' and myself will share it."

Ian laughed, "No, you drink it, Colin, your need is greater than mine."

"That's very good of you, Ian. That's a most noble act of self-sacrifice."

"Ah well, self-denial is good for the soul, isn't it?"

Colin lifted the glass, tilted his head and gulped the whisky down. Again he beamed, "Ah, that's better! Self-denial may be good for your soul, Ian, but that whisky is a damned sight better for my body!"

Ian grinned, "Och, of course we know you force yourself to drink it; we ken you take it for purely medicinal purposes."

Colin turned serious as he set the empty glass beside the two other empty glasses, he said, "I'll let Lord Kilver know about Nell's death. I'm sure he'll write Kenny a sympathetic letter on the loss of his pony and pay him some suitable compensation."

"Aye, that would be the decent thing to do," Ian said. "Of course there's the more distressing matter of us having to break the news about Nell's death to Kenny and Kate. They are likely to be very upset."

"I know. I've been worrying about that too," Calum said. "I must admit I don't fancy breaking that news to them myself."

"You won't have to, Calum, I'll do that," Ian said. "After I've had a bath and my dinner, Helen and I will go to your aunt and uncle and tell them the sad news. You could look in later in the evening to see how they're taking it."

"Yes, I will. Thank you, Ian. I'm sure Helen and you will make a much better job of telling them than I would."

Colin agreed, "Aye, it would be a difficult task for you, lad. Helen will be especially good at helping them in their distress."

Ian smiled, "Aye, that's true. Helen is never slow in ordering me to stop my poor fumbling male efforts at helping and to let her manage things in her tenderly competent feminine way."

"Aye, I know. Jeannie is exactly the same with me."

Ian said, "Try not to worry about this too much, Calum. Kate and Kenny might take the news better than we fear. After all, Kenny has been much less nervously upset for the last few years, hasn't he?"

Although giving this reassurance, Ian secretly worried that the news of having to shoot Nell might awaken tragic memories in Kenny; memories of other shot horses, of shot humans; men, women, children and even babies. It was these terrible sights that had caused Kenny's nervous breakdown forty years ago.

"Aye, and just imagine how much worse it might have been," Colin said. "For a few awful minutes we feared that you too, Calum, were going to die in that grim peat bog. God, what if we had to break the news that not only poor old Nell was dead but that you too were dead. How would we have faced your wife and bairns, your aunt and uncle, with such news?"

"That doesn't bear thinking about," Ian murmured.

As they were leaving the gun room, Colin exclaimed, "Oh God, look at the mess we've left on the floor." The water dripping from their saturated clothes had left ugly puddles all over the linoleum. "There's usually a mop inside the kitchen door, will you get it, Calum, and wipe up that water?" He grinned, "We don't want to upset Mrs Nicoll, do we?"

"No, we certainly don't," Ian smiled. "We don't want her cutting down on our drams again."

When the housekeeper was pleased with the gamekeepers she left out generous drams for them. If, for any reason, she was displeased with them, the drams were much less generous. The level of the whisky as it rose or fell in the glasses was an accurate barometer of her moods.

As Calum dropped Ian off at his crofthouse, he said, "I'll see you later on then, at Uncle Kenny's."

Ian eagerly peeled off his saturated tweed jacket and plus fours. He hung the heavy garments, each many times their normal weight, to dry in the boiler room. They immediately started noisily drip, drip, dripping onto the many layers of newspapers which Helen had, in experienced anticipation, spread over the floor.

"I hope there's plenty of hot water for a bath," he said.

"Oh, yes, it's almost boiling in the tank."

"Good!… Good! I won't be long."

"No, you better not be. Your dinner's ready, don't keep it waiting."

Ian filled the large and deep old bath with water as hot as he could bear. Slowly, gingerly, he lowered himself into it. After washing the cold rainwater out of his hair and beard he lay at full length and luxuriated in the water's steamy heat. He sighed contentedly. He pleasantly meditated that only those who have experienced being out all day in pouring rain, who have been soaked to the skin, can truly appreciate what a great sensual luxury it is to lie wallowing and relaxing in a really hot bath. Smiling, he thought, "They can keep all their modern showers; no damn shower can compare with the pleasure of this deep old bath."

After ten minutes, he reached down to the tap and ran more steaming hot water. Then he again relaxed. Although his inert body lay soaking in contented ease, his mind worried over the problem of how best to break the news of their old pony's death to Kate and Kenny MacLeod. How would Kenny react to this?

What memories the sad, but humane killing of that horse brought to Ian. What terrible memories might it flare in Kenny's easily upset mind?

As Ian peered into the bathroom's steamy obscurity, he also, almost in a trance, stared through that old cliché, 'the mists of time' to a misty scene of more than forty years ago.

Chapter Nine

White mists rose thickly from a small river in Northern France near the Belgian frontier. Though graced with the title of 'river' that sluggish water, covered in weeds and green slime, was hardly more than a wide, deep ditch. But now, in early June of 1940, it had acquired a strategic importance, had been hastily upgraded to a vital defensive line. If things went to plan, the British Expeditionary Force would halt the rapidly advancing German army along the banks of this river.

However the seven soldiers of the 6th Battalion of the Seaforth Highlanders detailed to guard one small stone bridge over the river knew only too well how rarely things did go to plan in this war. Reinforcements with artillery should have joined them yesterday morning. There was still no sign of them.

The inactive winter of the 'Phoney War' had come to a sudden end when German Panzers had, without bothering with the effete nicety of declaring war, smashed into Holland and Belgium.

That battalion of the Seaforths had marched with other British units to the defence of Belgium. They marched deep into that stricken country. Then they marched out again. The soldiers cursed their generals. They swore they were being led not by General Gort, but by the Grand Old Duke of York, although, thankfully, there were no hills here for that duke to march them up and down. "A complete balls-up!… A typical bloody army balls-up!" were some of the milder comments.

Now back near where they had started from, these seven British soldiers lay in dewy ditches on both sides of the dusty road leading to the bridge they were defending. Anxiously peering into the white mist they saw nothing, but heard a terrifying noise – the sound that all infantry soldiers, armed only with rifle and bayonet, most feared – the noise of rapidly approaching enemy tanks.

For a time the mist, as it lazily drifted from the river, thinned over the flat, damp meadows but tenaciously clung to tall poplars and thick hedgerows. The low sun momentarily revealed itself, all pale and sickly, then vanished again. The ugly rumbling, the metallic clanking noise of the German tanks got ever louder and ever more menacing.

Then as those tense soldiers stared intently from their sheltering ditches the white screen of mist wavered, thinned, then lifted. It was amazing how old clichés came true. That mist rose like a theatre curtain and revealed the stage set ready for the performance to begin. The pale sun looked weakly down like a bored and indifferent audience who had seen it all before. For thousands of years it had watched those ridiculously self-important petty humans cruelly kill one another. Now another act of that sad old farce was about to be played out.

The British soldiers saw a line of German tanks steadily trundle along the narrow road towards the bridge. Their clattering caterpillar tracks spouted dense clouds of fine dust. But of more immediate concern to Ian MacLean and his two companions in the ditch, John Kerr and Kenny MacLeod, was the one tank in the field directly in front of them. It seemed to be coming straight at them. It looked like a huge, ugly black beetle. German soldiers in grey uniforms and bucket helmets advanced on either side of the tank.

Deliberately steadying himself and taking careful aim, as he had so often done at the rifle range, Ian selected his target, held his breath and gently squeezed the trigger of his reliably accurate .303 Lee-Enfield rifle.

Shot through the heart, Ian's German soldier jerked back like a puppet violently pulled by its strings then lay motionless in the grass.

Ian selected his next target – a German soldier kneeling and firing his rifle. That enemy soldier also suddenly jerked back and lay still. He too was shot through the heart.

Ian was aware of Kenny and John firing their rifles. All the German infantry dropped into the grass and started shooting at them. The tank halted. Its turret swivelled round. The barrel of its gun pointed at them like a predator's snout keenly sniffing for hidden prey.

At the same moment as Ian shouted, "Get down!... Get down!" the tank's heavy machine-gun opened fire.

Ian sensed, rather than saw John Kerr's body being thrown savagely across the ditch. It then slithered to the bottom and lay still. Ian pressed himself flat. His body eagerly united with the earth and weeds and grass in the doubtful security of the shallow ditch while bullets thudded into the soil above him. The machine-gun swung from right to left then fell silent. Ian sighed in relief. Then he cursed as it fired again and, swinging from left to right, smashed bullets through the thick hawthorn hedge above the ditch and sent leaves and twigs showering over him. Then it finally fell silent. He wriggled along the ditch to John Kerr's body. One glance showed that John was beyond help. Machine-gun bullets had smashed into his face and blown away the back of his head. Ian closed his eyes and shut out that hideous sight. His bile rose. His stomach heaved. He vomited up his breakfast. It was awful lying being violently sick with his mouth only a few inches from the earth while vomit splashed up over his face. He urgently resisted the strong desire to raise his face up from that vile stinking mess. To give in to that instinctive desire could result in him ending up like John with half his head blown off.

He felt his white face break out in a cold sweat. He thought he was going to faint. He cursed. Sternly he told himself this was neither the time nor the place to faint. He heard Kenny MacLeod being sick on the other side of John's mutilated body. He shouted, "Are you all right, Kenny?"

"Yes," Kenny's voice came weakly back. "Yes, Ian, I'm all right."

The silence was suddenly broken by shouting German voices. Then the tank's engine drowned out all other sounds as it belched into thundering life.

Ian risked a quick glance over the edge of the ditch. Apprehension turned to delight as he saw that a curtain of white mist had again dropped down between him and the Germans. With luck, Kenny and he might escape being killed by those German soldiers, all, no doubt, thirsting to avenge their dead comrades.

"Come on, Kenny, let's get to hell out of here," he gasped. "Quick get through that gap in the hedge."

Like the well-trained soldier he was, Ian had earlier noted the gap in the otherwise impenetrable hawthorn hedge at the back of their ditch. Kenny did not move. Ian shook him by the shoulder, "Come on, Kenny, get through that gap."

Apparently in a state of shock, Kenny stared with dazed eyes. "Come on, get a move on!" Ian sternly commanded with all the authority of his lance corporal's single stripe. Kenny grabbed his rifle and staggered to his feet. Ian smiled approvingly, "Good!… Go on, Kenny, you go first. Hurry up!"

German soldiers, hearing those enemy voices, fired blindly through the mist. Some of their bullets sliced through the thick hedge dangerously close to them. On hands and knees Kenny crawled through the gap. Ian eagerly followed, "Come on, this way," he gasped. They turned away from the small bridge, which some panzers had already crossed. They ran along the narrow lane that bordered the sluggish river. The mist and the high hedge hid them from the advancing Germans.

They ran and ran, their hearts pounded, their lungs gasped, they poured sweat.

They stopped at a footbridge over the river. It was merely a wide plank with a rickety rail. Ian said, "We'll follow that lane on the other side, it's heading South, that's the way we want to go, away from the bloody Germans."

For a few miles they steadily walked along that narrow lane. It was pleasant here. There was no mist and the un-obscured morning sun glowed brightly with ever increasing warmth from a perfect azure sky. Ian gave an ironic smile, "This is perfect bomber's weather now, isn't it?"

They plodded on. The hawthorn hedge on each side of the lane was a voluptuous riot of fragrant white blossom. Here and there tendrils of wild roses and honeysuckle contorted through the hedges and boastfully added their colours and glorious scents to the scene. As if not wanting to be outdone, many butterflies light-heartedly displayed their fluttering vividness to further entrance those plodding soldiers. Ian was pleased to recognise many of these butterflies. The ubiquitous Cabbage Whites were by far the most numerous; they swarmed in drifts, like crazily mistimed snowflakes. Large and small Tortoiseshells were familiar friends. Others, burgundy red and coppery bright, he admired but did not know. He smiled; it was easy to imagine they were merely out for a pleasant stroll. How perfect this would be if there was no war. But there was no escaping the war. The drone of German warplanes, faint and distant, but a perpetual menace, and the thump of exploding bombs were a constant reminder.

At a grassy bank, Ian halted, "Let's have a rest and a fag."

It was pleasant lying all dusty and dishevelled, on that gently sloping turf with the sunshine glowing their tanned faces. They dug deep into large pockets in battle-dress trousers and pulled out cigarettes and matches. Ian offered Kenny his fags. Kenny offered Ian his.

Smoking and relaxing, Ian had the first real opportunity to think about the two German soldiers he had shot. They were the first humans he had killed. He felt no guilt. He felt no remorse. He had correctly done his duty. It had seemed little different from hitting targets of replica German soldiers at rifle ranges and, after all, those Germans were brutal aggressors. With savage ruthlessness they had invaded and conquered Denmark and Norway, Holland and Belgium, and it now looked possible that they might soon defeat France. If France fell what would happen to Britain?

He thankfully thought, "At least I did not have to use my bayonet." How often he had violently thrust the sharp bayonet into dummy straw figures of enemy soldiers. What would it be like to thrust it into a living man? "That's an experience I hope I never have," he – not for the first time – decided. (But before the war was over he, on one memorable occasion, did use his bayonet on a hated enemy.)

Ian again glanced at Kenny. He seemed fairly calm now. He certainly had been in a state of shock at seeing John Kerr violently die. Of course, John's bloodily smashed face and the scattered mess of brains and bone and blood had been a truly shocking sight. Ian shuddered at the memory. Deliberately he blanked that hideous picture out of his conscious mind. He thought of Colin MacDonald and the three other comrades who had been positioned on the other side of the road leading to the bridge; he fervently hoped that none of them had suffered poor John's terrible fate. He sat up and said, "Come on, Kenny, I suppose we better get moving again."

They lifted their rifles and steel helmets and continued down the pleasant flowery lane. They passed a few poor hovels belonging to impoverished peasants. They had been hastily abandoned and now lay sadly neglected. The only sign of life was an occasional glimpse of a lean and wary cat as it darted out of sight.

The fields were empty of livestock. From one of those deserted fields a skylark rose and thrilled the sun bright morning with vibrant song. Higher and higher he rose, louder and louder his song cascaded. Hanging almost out of sight on quivering wings he joyously warbled his transcendental glory.

Ian and Kenny halted. The listened enthralled. They rejoiced in the lark's rejoicing paean of praise.

They walked on and, once more, familiar man-made sounds took over... the distant drone of warplanes and the noise of exploding bombs.

A mile further on they heard other sounds. They stopped and listened. They soon recognised these noises as another aspect of war. On their march out of Belgium these, too, had been familiar sounds... the strange, the unique sounds made by a mass of fleeing refugees. Soon these refugees were revealed to them when the lane met a narrow road. That road stretched for miles in a straight line. It was packed with an incredible congestion of traffic, a sluggishly moving stream of fleeing humanity. These French refugees were desperately heading South, away from the victoriously advancing German army.

There were many horse drawn carts. Each cart was heaped high with precious domestic possessions – mattresses, solid dark furniture, pots and pans, food, bottles of wine. Many had coops of hungry and noisily protesting hens or geese precariously perched on top. The protests of these poultry mingled with the ugly squeaking protests of the over-laden cart's axles, badly in need of greasing, and the mournful and resentful lowing of weary and thirsty cows. Goats angrily joined this loud chorus of complaint with quavering querulous bleats. The cattle and goats were tethered to the backs of the carts. The thick layer of dust coating the road muffled the thud of the tired horses plodding hoofs as they stoically hauled their heavy loads. Most of the drooping headed horses were thin and in poor condition. The ribs of some gaunt beasts showed as clearly as the ribs of the washing boards sticking up in the carts.

The humans as they wearily trudged along were an even sorrier sight than the poor animals.

There were women of all ages: some were withered toothless crones, some were innocent virgins newly arrived at womanhood. There were children of all sizes. There were babies suckling at their mother's shawled breasts. There were many old men, all weary and stooping after a lifetime of unremitting toil on the land. It was noticeable that there were no young men except for a deformed cripple and two vacantly drooling inbred village idiots. All fit young men were in the French army. Many were being killed while fighting and killing fit young German men in a mad reversal of nature's law of the survival of the fittest.

Despondent refugees wearily pulled handcarts. Others slowly pushed heavily over-laden bicycles. Older girls pushed wickerwork prams. The babies in the prams were almost smothered under piles of blankets and linen. Young boys and girls carried pathetic bundles over thin shoulders. They were tired, thirsty and hungry. Kilometre after long kilometre their bare feet had been soundlessly shuffling through this endless road's deadening dust.

Standing watching from the side of the crowded road, Ian said, "Oh God, I feel so sorry for all those poor homeless buggers."

"Aye," Kenny agreed, "especially for all those wee, ragged, shoeless bairns. They look exhausted. I hope they get a rest soon." (Little did he guess just how soon many of those weary French bairns would get a rest – get their Eternal Rest.)

That slow, sad tide of humanity moved in dejected silence. A few of the less weary children managed to bravely smile and hesitantly wave at those two strange foreign soldiers. The adults gave apathetic glances.

A large cart pulled by two horses slowly trundled towards them. Both brown horses, dark with sweat, were fatter and in better condition than most horses in this endless procession. The cart was piled high. It was driven by an ancient, white-bearded farmer. His equally ancient wife sat beside him. Their faces were tanned a leathery brown. The old man's broad forehead was corrugated with a mass of deep, dark horizontal wrinkles. They seemed a faithful image of the countless furrows he had ploughed in his long life. Though stooped and shrunken, his body still retained impressive remnants of a powerful, thick boned frame.

In contrast, his wife was tiny. With her shrivelled features, her fragile frame and her tight stretched parchment skin she had the appearance of a dried-up Egyptian mummy.

With his toil-calloused left hand the old French farmer removed the short-stemmed clay pipe from his mouth. He spat on to the dusty road. Some spittle drooled from his lip and slid down the yellow nicotine stain on his white beard. Lifting both hands, they were as dark and grimy as the soil they had so often laboured in, he gesticulated wildly and shouted loudly and angrily.

Ian tried to follow his rapid, excited, heavily accented, rural French. Two words he could easily translate… "Kill Boche!… Kill Boche!" they were repeated over and over again.

Ian grinned, gave the thumbs-up sign and pointed at Kenny and himself, "We kill Boche!… We kill Boche!"

The old man beamed them a wide, toothless grin and his tanned face cracked all over like parched, sun-baked soil. Following her lord and master's example, the old wife favoured them with a broad smile. Her teeth flashed incongruously brightly in her aged, wizened, walnut face. She held that brilliant smile; she was inordinately proud of her expensive new set of false teeth.

Her husband now unclenched his right fist and held up three middle fingers. He repeated that wild cry, "Kill Boche!… Kill Boche!" He gasped a long and animated tirade of hatred of the Germans.

As the cart slowly rolled onwards with the old man still gesticulating and shouting, Kenny smiled at Ian, "What was all that in aid of? Why was he holding up three fingers like that?"

Before replying, Ian did some rapid mental arithmetic. He calculated that the ancient couple must be into their early nineties, in which case they were old enough to have been refugees fleeing before invading German armies three times in their lifetime. "I think he was telling us that he has seen France invaded three times by the Germans. In 1870, again in 1914, and now this time, 1940. He might very well have been a young soldier in 1870; might have fought the Prussians as they encircled Paris."

As he stared after the old couple perched high on their cart, Kenny said, "Oh, Ian, it's amazing to think that he might have fought the Germans as long ago as 1870. And no doubt his sons fought them in 1914, and now his grandsons will be fighting them again. Oh God, it makes you despair for mankind. You would think we might have learned better by now, wouldn't you?"

Ian sighed, "Aye, you would. The First World War was 'the war to end all wars', and yet here we are only twenty years later embroiled in the Second World War." He paused thoughtfully, "Aye, that remarkable old French couple truly are living history. It's little wonder that they hate the Germans. It's no wonder they want us to 'kill Boche'."

Suddenly, terrifyingly, it was not a matter of them killing Boche, but of the Boche killing them.

Diving steeply out of the glaring sun, three German warplanes accurately arrowed for that crowded road. One after the other the Messerscmidt 109 fighters flew low above the length of the long straight road. With vicious bursts of machine gun and cannon fire they indiscriminately strafed the defenceless mass of refugees. The young Luftwaffe pilots knew there was no military traffic or any motor vehicles on that road. As they efficiently carried out their slaughter the pathetic vulnerability of those despicable French peasants gave the German pilots keen sadistic pleasure. How arrogantly they proved the superior might of 'The Master Race'.

All was absolute panic. All was utter chaos as these planes sent a tidal wave of terror sweeping before them. Horses went berserk. Shying and rearing they desperately bolted. They overturned carts and dragged them into ditches or smashed them into other carts in a dusty confusion of splintering wood, whirling wheels, tangled harnesses and dangerously lashing hooves. Scraggy sheepdogs barked wildly. Terrified cows broke free of halters and galumphed away across fields, their tails held stiffly high, their hind legs kicking out behind them. Goats, too, broke free and went leaping and bounding away, their tremulous bleats joined with the cows' deep bellows and the horses' panic-stricken neighing. Hens, escaped from burst coops, scattered wildly and frenziedly protested at such undignified treatment.

Terrified children wailed and cried. Screaming mothers snatched up young children and dived into dry ditches at the side of the road. Old men and women were thrown from overturned carts. They crawled to, and rolled into the ditches.

Ian and Kenny also took refuge in a ditch. As the planes roared overhead cannon shells exploded and machine-gun bullets thudded into grass and dust and flesh. In the bottom of the ditch they pressed their bodies flat and eagerly embraced the earth in a passionately fierce act of love – the urgent love of life.

As the noise of planes faded away Ian cautiously got to his feet. Shakily, Kenny followed his example. Apprehensively they looked around. Those sheltering in this ditch seemed unharmed, but the one across the road was a scene of carnage. The plane's machine-guns and cannons had ripped along the road and along that ditch. Most of the refugees there were dead. A few survived. Terribly wounded, their agonised screams drowned the wailing of children, the sobbing of mothers, the loud laments of grandmothers.

Louder than those human sounds were the frantic high-pitched neighing screams and the deep despairing moans of grievously wounded horses.

From further up their ditch Ian saw five nuns rise and, dazed, white-faced and shaking, unsteadily cross the ugly littered road. Tenderly they helped the wounded and prayed over and perhaps brought some comfort to the dying.

Inspired by the nun's efforts, Ian said, "Come on, let's see if we can help them." Only now did he notice how badly Kenny was shaking. His face was deadly white. Ian gripped his arm and sternly, but compassionately, commanded, "Pull yourself together, Kenny. Come on, let's help them."

With an obvious effort Kenny got himself under control. His shaking ceased. Colour returned to his face. As he followed Ian towards the ministering nuns, he kept his eyes averted from the bodies of the children, women and old men that so horribly littered the ditch.

The nuns were now quietly and efficiently nursing the wounded. Ian and Kenny removed their emergency medical dressings from the special pockets in their battledress trousers and handed them to a nun. Some peasant women came and helped. They gathered blankets and sheets from upturned carts. They tore cotton sheets into bandages.

The youngest nun pressed trembling hands over her ears and screamed a torrent of words at Ian and Kenny. Ian listened intently but could make nothing of her hysterical outpourings. An older nun stood up and gently calmed the distraught young nun then pointed an imaginary gun at one of the wounded and hideously screaming horses. Ian nodded. He walked rapidly to where his rifle lay in the other ditch.

With three bullets he quickly and humanely put the three wounded horses nearest to the nuns out of their misery.

From a little further down the road came the nerve-wracking screams of another wounded horse. Ian rapidly walked towards that sound.

He recognised the ancient farmer's large cart. It lay on its side across the road. Its contents were scattered in a pathetic jumble. The two wounded horses were still attached to the cart by their hopelessly tangled harnesses. As Ian clambered round the cart an appalling sight was revealed. The horses lay together; their bellies were split open. There was a hideous mess of spilled purple/grey guts, of blood, of dung and urine. Masses of flies were gloatingly buzzing and rapturously feeding on this bounty.

One of the horses screamed loudly and piercingly. It lay on its side and lifted its head each time it wailed its high keening shriek of unbearable agony. The other horse also lay on its side but with its head flat and motionless. It gave piteously deep agonised moans. Its eye was huge: was distended in uncomprehending terror. The stench from the spilled guts was awful. Ian almost puked. He resolutely forced himself to quickly put a bullet through the brain of each horse. As he hurried away from that sickening sight, he tripped over another sickening sight. A small body lay huddled in a large pool of blood at the side of the road. It was the old farmer's wife. Ian froze and stared. He was amazed that so much blood could come from such a tiny body. Her old-fashioned black straw bonnet was askew and thin strands of white hair untidily threaded out from under it. Her mouth gaped wide, dark and toothless. Her expensive false teeth no longer proudly gleamed. They lay ugly stained with dark blood and roughly gritted with saturated dust.

Ian looked around for her husband. He soon found him. He too was dead. He lay on his back and stared blankly up at the lovely, indifferent blue sky. His white beard was darkly clotted with blood. His cloth cap was missing. Its loss revealed a large bald scalp. In contrast to his tough, leathery tanned face that exposed scalp gleamed eggshell white and eggshell vulnerable. It suggested death's bony skull that patiently waits to be revealed under every warmly living human scalp.

The old man's right arm was thrown out above his head and the fist was firmly clenched as if still defying the hated Boche. Ian felt a terrible surge of hatred for the German pilots who had carried out this slaughter of those innocent refugees. He was amazed at the strength of this feeling; he had not thought himself capable of feeling such hatred. Of course he had never before had reason to have such feelings. Suddenly he was terribly dismayed. He felt himself helplessly caught up in the vast tide of hatred this war was engendering and which threatened to drown all humanity in its evil flood.

Something pricked sharply at his conscience. He was neglecting some duty. Duty!… Military duty! His army training severely reprimanded him. He had killed five horses with five bullets. The magazine of his rifle was empty. He had failed in his duty to reload it. As he went through the well-rehearsed drill of loading a clip of five bullets into the magazine he murmured, "Oh God, I hope I don't have to use any of them to kill more horses. I'd rather use them to kill Boche." As he stared down at the dead old French farmer he sighed deeply then solemnly vowed, "I'll kill Boche for you, old man, I swear I'll kill Boche for you!"

He turned away and slowly started walking back to where he had left Kenny.

He found him slumped dejectedly with his head bowed and both hands cupping his face. He was indistinctly mumbling to himself.

Ian flopped down beside him and gently asked, "What's the matter, Kenny?"

With a weary effort Kenny raised his head. Ian was pleased to see that he was not shaking, was not pale. Then as he looked into Kenny's eyes they revealed symptoms that were worse. His eyes had a strange, dull lacklustre look. Ian gently repeated his question, "What's the matter, Kenny?"

Kenny's face took on a haggard, distraught expression, which accurately reflected his troubled mind. In a tremulously perplexed voice he asked, "Oh Ian, why… oh why, does God allow such things?" He lifted an unsteady hand and pointed. "Why does God allow those poor horses to be killed?"

"You know I had to shoot the horses to put them out of their terrible agony, don't you?"

"Oh, yes… yes, I know that, Ian. I'm not blaming you. But why did God allow their terrible agony at all?"

Ian sighed. Who could answer these questions? He remembered how as a boy, back home at Aldrory, Kenny had loved to attend to and work with the ponies on the crofts. In vague reply to these anguished questions of Kenny's, he murmured, "Oh, God knows!… God knows!" Suddenly realising the unintentional irony of these words, he repressed a sardonic grin as he queried, "Or does He?… Does He?"

They remained sadly silent for some moments, then Kenny again pointed, "And why did God allow that pure, innocent, poor wee baby to be so cruelly killed?"

"Baby?" Ian questioned. He had noticed that doll lying near the ditch.

"Aye, that wee baby there."

"It's a doll... a large doll."

Kenny slowly and solemnly shook his head and in a grief stricken voice murmured, "No, it's a baby. I saw it moving. I heard it crying. Then it died."

Ian wearily heaved himself up and went to inspect that 'doll'. It lay face down and did look like a large doll. He gently turned it over. "Oh God," he gasped, "It is a baby!"

The front of its body was a terrible mess of congealing dark blood. It seemed only about a month old.

Ian sank to his knees and bowed his head. He did not pray. He could not pray. The horrors he had seen today convinced him more than ever that there was no God, that all religion was truly 'The opium of the People'. Not a love of God, but a fiercer hatred of those German pilots filled him.

He stood up. He looked more closely at what he had taken to be the owner of the 'doll'. He saw that it was the body of a woman of about seventeen or eighteen years old. She lay on her back; at her stomach was a pool of blood. Her pale green frock was ripped and one fecund breast was exposed. Milk generously oozed from the pleading nipple. Obviously she was the mother of that baby.

Ian gently lifted the baby, laid it at its mother's breast, then enfolded her cold arms around the pathetically small and still body.

He again flopped down beside Kenny. He wiped his blooded hands on the grass before getting out his cigarettes. He put two in his mouth and lit them. Handing one over he said, "Here, Kenny, have a fag, it'll help you." Kenny nodded his thanks.

Ian lay back in the grass and smoked his fag. He enjoyed feeling the sunshine's benevolence on his face. He closed his eyes. He felt exhausted. How pleasant it would be, he thought, to sleep deeply and from that sleep pass easily and painlessly into the darker, deeper sleep of death and be free of this war, free of all hate, all fear, all worry.

He opened his eyes, sat up on his elbows and stubbed out his fag end in the grass. He smiled and with youthful resilience told himself not to be a fool. "It's bloody stupid to wish for death, I might meet it all too soon without having to wish for it." He thought of those who had met sudden, violent death here this morning. If there was no God, what then decided who lived, who died? Indifferent fate?... Blind chance? It seemed so. Sighing, he decided he'd better try and get on with the difficult enough business of merely living.

"Come on, Kenny, we better get moving. There's nothing more we can do here. Those nuns will look after the wounded and see that the dead get a decent burial." Ian rose and helped Kenny to his feet, "Come on, get your rifle and tin hat and we'll see if we can't meet up with some army unit." He smiled, "Surely we're not the only British soldiers left in all Northern France?"

Kenny docilely followed Ian as he led the way back along the lane they had followed earlier. The beauty of this lane worked its magic on Ian. After the carnage on that road the glory of the sun bright wild flowers and the heady perfume of their mingled scents was wonderful. His spirits rose. Yes, despite the worst that man can do, life was well worth living.

They left the lane and followed a narrow path through fields. Ian explained, "This path's heading South Westerly, towards the sea. We'll stop when we reach the English Channel." He smiled, "We'll swim from there."

Kenny nodded and dutifully smiled.

They clambered over stiles and passed through gates. They came to, and followed a small empty road. As they cautiously approached a junction, Ian recognised the khaki uniform and flat red cap of a British military policeman. He grinned, "Well, Kenny, this is the first time I've been pleased to see a 'redcap'!"

Again Kenny nodded and dutifully smiled.

The 'redcap' corporal ordered them to make for Dunkirk, where the navy was evacuating the British army. He pointed, "You can't go wrong, just keep heading for that smoke." Huge columns of oily black smoke were rising vertically for thousands of feet in the distance. "That's the oil tanks at Dunkirk harbour burning."

Early the following morning they stood and looked down from a sand dune at the incredible scene on the large and wide beach North of Dunkirk.

Thousands of British soldiers were crowded on to that beach. Most were waiting in orderly queues to be taken off. Slowly those well disciplined queues shuffled forward from the sands into the sea. They waded until the water was up to their shoulders, and then were helped into the small ships waiting to evacuate them. There were dozens of these ships courageously making voyage after voyage to this beach, almost always under savage bombardment from German aircraft.

Ian and Kenny went down onto the beach. It was pot-holed with bomb craters. As they skirted round a large and deep crater they saw with shock what looked like a pile of khaki-clad dead bodies. They stared aghast. Then Ian smiled with immense relief as he realised that these 'bodies' were merely an untidy heap of discarded British army greatcoats.

The beach was littered with abandoned military equipment. Army trucks burned fiercely. Half sunken ships sent up funereally palls of smoke and the oil tanks at Dunkirk harbour steadily poured out thick columns of dense black smoke.

They were about to wade out to a pleasure steamer. Ian liked the name painted on its stern, *Maid of The Channel*, when a major directing operations on this part of the beach shouted, "That ship's full. Make for one of those smaller boats. "

Wading waist-deep they pushed floating debris out of their way. As he neared a white painted motor pleasure cruiser, Ian reached out to shove more jetsam away. Horrified, he stopped and stared as he suddenly realised what this 'jetsam' was. It was dead British soldiers. Floating face down, those bodies were obscenely bloated.

Shuddering, Ian gently moved past those corpses. Then he looked round, Kenny was standing staring at those floating bodies. "Come on, Kenny, we're nearly at the boat," he shouted encouragingly.

Kenny did not move. He murmured over and over, "Oh God!... Oh God! Oh why does God allow this horror?"

Ian waded back to him and grasped his arm, "Come on, Kenny, we must get on the boat, it's ready to move off."

They were helped onto the boat. They sat huddled shoulder to shoulder on the crowded deck. No sooner were they settled when another horror burst over them. A Stuka dive-bomber came screaming out of the sun in an almost vertical dive. Every man watching that hideously wailing terrifying menace was certain that plane was coming right for him, and him alone. And when one large bomb dropped it too was aiming straight for him, and him alone. They threw arms over heads, closed eyes, cowered, and prayed. As he sat hunched in frozen immobility during those fearful seconds between the bomb being released and it exploding, Ian had a vivid flash of memory: he remembered seeing and hearing snipe displaying above the damp moors behind his home; how steeply they had dived, how loudly, how pleasantly, they had drummed. Those German dive-bombers had learned from – and how they had improved on! – those attractive diving birds. The hideous, nerve-wracking screaming wail of their sirens was one of the most terrifying noises proudly inventive men had ever perfected.

The bomb landed on the centre of the *Maid of the Channel*. It exploded. The pleasure steamer disintegrated in a huge eruption of smoke and water. A mass of debris rose high, arched gracefully, and then fell in a dangerous hail that lashed the sea's surface with cruel fury.

Something thudded on to the deck in front of Kenny and Ian. They lowered their arms and opened their eyes. They stared in disbelief at the 'thing' lying on the deck. Their shocked brains did not want to believe the evidence of their senses.

That 'thing' was a naked human arm. Sheared off above the elbow, it lay with its fingers pointing at them. Ian imagined those white, bloodless fingers deliberately pointed and accusingly asked, "Why are you alive when we are dead?"

There was a tattoo on that thick forearm. Ian studied it. A Union Jack flag was crossed with a White Ensign of the Royal Navy. A ribbon curving below the flags bore the motto, "For God – For King – For Country."

Ian felt Kenny's shoulder tremble against his own. Deep, tortured sobs racked Kenny as he stared horrified at that tattooed arm of some unfortunate British sailor.

The boat shuddered as it increased to full speed. The severed arm seemed to pulse with a ghastly life. Ian struggled to his feet and with a determined effort stooped and lifted the clammy cold flesh. He reached out and dropped the arm over the side. It sank waveringly like a dead, white-bellied fish. As it vanished into the depths Ian thought it gave a final despairing wave.

He vigorously rubbed his hand on his soaking trousers in an attempt to wipe away the horrid feel of that dead flesh. Then he struggled down beside Kenny who, sobbing and gasping, repeatedly demanded, "Why, oh why, does God allow such things?"

Ian had no easy reassuring answer to that question. He leant back and enjoyed the warmth of the sunshine on his face. He smiled up at the sun. Silently he worshipped that ancient pagan God. He smiled again and thought, "At least that God does not pretend to be a loving, caring, benevolent God. It is not a hypocrite, thank God." Ian sighed wearily. He closed tired eyes. He slept.

At Dover, Ian handed Kenny over to a gentle, sympathetic young nurse who guided him, trembling and mumbling with bowed head, to an ambulance train. At the door of the coach Ian shook his hand and said, "I'll see you soon, Kenny. Get well." He smiled at the attractive nurse, "I leave you in much better hands than mine."

Ian and Kenny did not meet again until after the end of the war, five years later. For three of these years Kenny received psychiatric treatment at various military hospitals. Then he was discharged from the army as being medically unfit. He received further and perhaps better psychiatric help at Craig Dunain mental hospital in Inverness before being allowed home to Aldrory.

In the huge army base at Catterick, three days after his return from Dunkirk, Ian met up with Colin MacDonald and others from his regiment. They were some of the few soldiers of the 51st Highland Division rescued from France. The bulk of that division had been surrounded by German panzers at St Valery and had been forced to surrender.

Ian and Colin spent the rest of the war in the re-formed 51st Highland Division and fought in all the many campaigns in the deserts of North Africa. After the invasion of Sicily came the landing at Salerno on the Italian mainland. Later they endured, and were lucky to survive, the intense horrors of the vicious fighting at Anzio beachhead South of Rome. Then came the slow, and at times savage, long campaign from Rome to the North of Italy.

Chapter Ten

Ian gave a startled jump as his vivid wartime memories were suddenly interrupted by a loud knocking on the bathroom door. It opened and Helen entered. She was preceded by their two dogs who eagerly bounded in and, placing front paws on the bath, gazed joyfully at Ian. Helen also gazed, "What have you been doing all this time in that bath? You've been ages. Your dinner is ready, it'll be spoiled if you don't hurry."

Ian smiled apologetically, "I'm sorry. I've been thinking of certain things that happened during the war and which badly affected Kenny. What happened then is linked to something that occurred when we were stalking today. I'll tell you all about it over dinner."

Helen nodded. With praiseworthy patience she nobly subdued her natural desire to be immediately informed of the details of this occurrence. Silently and solemnly she stared. Both dogs happily stared.

Ian grinned, "What are you all staring at? You would think I was some weird and wonderful public show."

Helen smiled, "Och, we're staring at nothing special. Certainly at nothing worth making a fuss over."

"Och, you didn't say that in our early married years."

"No, perhaps not, but that was thirty years ago. You had something worth looking at then, I seem to remember!"

Ian shook his head, "Oh, she's shameless, isn't she?" he asked the dogs. They activated their tails faster in eager agreement. He put a blob of soapsuds on each dog's nose then loudly and sternly asked, "Do you want a *Bath*, Corrie?... *Bath*, Glen?"

On hearing that dreaded word, '*Bath*', the dogs dropped down and scampered out with tails tucked between legs.

Again Helen smiled, "Hurry up now, Ian. I'm putting your dinner on the table in exactly five minutes."

"Oh, are you? Wouldn't you be better to put it on a plate?"

"Ha, ha... very funny! Remember now, five minutes."

"Aye, all right... all right."

When Helen closed the door Ian most reluctantly heaved himself out of the luxurious hot water and grabbed a large bath towel.

Over dinner he gave Helen the details of the sad death of Nell. He again told her of humanely shooting the terribly injured horses in France forty years ago and how witnessing these and other horrors had caused Kenny's nervous breakdown.

Blinking back her tears Helen murmured, "Poor Nell. Oh, poor old Nell. What a sad end for her." She struggled to keep her emotions under control.

Quietly, thoughtfully and compassionately she said, "You'll have to be careful how you break the news to Kenny. Telling him of having to shoot Nell is likely to revive his terrible memories of the shot horses in France."

"Aye, I know. That's what I'm worried about. That's why I want to break the news myself, instead of letting Calum do it. Young Calum has no experience of such things. He was very upset at Nell's death."

"Poor Calum. He's a kind, warm-hearted soul like his aunt Kate. She will be very upset too."

"I know," Ian agreed. "But I think she'll manage to control her distress for the sake of helping her brother. Like us, she'll be worried in case the news gives Kenny another breakdown."

An hour later they knocked at, then opened, the front door of Kenny's house. As always, they were warmly welcomed.

"Come in... come in, my dear fellows," Kenny called.

"Come in, come away in and have a cup of tea. I've just put the kettle on," 'Kate Kettle' beamed.

Kate, with her inevitable warm hospitality, urged Helen to her accustomed corner of the old sofa then she flopped down in her own sadly sagging corner. The tormented old spring once again squeakily protested and bounced Helen upwards. Kate eagerly speired for all the latest news. For some minutes Helen and she chatted. Then, sensing some unusual constraint in Ian, Kate asked, "What's the matter, Ian?... You're not saying much. Is something wrong?"

"Aye, I'm afraid there is."

Kate stared, silently apprehensive.

"It's your pony, poor old Nell. There's been an accident... a bad accident with her."

"An accident?... How bad?" Kenny asked.

"I'm very sorry to have to tell you that she's dead."

Kate gasped. Tears flooded her emotional eyes. Her hands instinctively groped for the apron on her lap and lifted it to her overflowing tears. Helen leaned over and put a comforting arm around her heaving shoulders.

Abruptly Kenny rocketed out of his chair. Agitatedly he strode around the room. Nervously he murmured and mumbled to himself. The others could make out some words – words despairingly repeated over and over: "Oh dear... Poor old Nell... Oh dear... What a calamity!... What a calamity!"

Ian rose and put a hand on Kenny's shoulder. "Come and sit down, Kenny, and I'll tell you all about it. You've a right to know what happened to your pony." He guided him back to his chair and Kenny carelessly threw himself into the depths of his groaning old armchair. Ian turned to Kate, "Get glasses please, Kate, and we'll all have a dram. We could all do with one."

He produced the bottle of whisky while Helen went into the cluttered small scullery with Kate. She quietly urged Kate to make an effort to put on a brave face to help Kenny. Hurriedly she explained Ian's fears that the death of Nell might revive Kenny's terrible memories of the horses shot in France, might even push him into another nervous breakdown. With a brave effort, Kate got herself under control. She again wiped her tears away with the corners of her apron.

Ian generously filled the glasses. As they sipped the whisky he solemnly told what had happened to Nell. He repeatedly emphasised that she had suffered no pain. He explained that her distress when trapped in the peat bog had not lasted long. He assured them that the one bullet had instantly and painlessly ended her ordeal. Wisely, he said nothing of the real danger Calum had been in when he too was stuck in the peat bog. If Kate and Kenny knew of this they would worry about him every time he was out deerstalking. Instead, Ian warmly praised the noble efforts Calum had made to try and save Nell.

During Ian's discourse, Kate unobtrusively dabbed at her tear-filled eyes with her indispensable old apron. Helen encouraged her to sip more of her almost untouched whisky. They all anxiously waited for Kenny's further reactions.

For a few minutes he sat silent with closed eyes. Then, feeling all their sympathetic eyes fixed on him, he opened his own eyes, sighed deeply, looked steadily at each of them in turn, and then murmured, "I'm all right now. Don't worry about me. I assure you I'm all right, my dear fellows." He took another sip of whisky and added, "Poor Nell... Poor Nell. She was a fine pony. We will all miss her. But at least she had a painless death." He stared steadily into Ian's eyes and quietly asked, "Do you remember the horses you shot in France all those years ago, Ian?"

Ian tensed. He felt Kate and Helen tense in dread anticipation. This was what they all feared, the flaring revival of the terrible experiences which had ruined Kenny's life.

"Aye, I remember them," Ian gently confirmed, wondering what was coming next.

"And you remember all those old French peasant men and women, those mothers, those children, that wee baby, all hideously and ruthlessly killed by the Germans?"

"Aye, I remember them all."

"Well, there is only one explanation of these terribly cruel killings – it was God's will!"

Ian opened his mouth to protest, but checked himself just in time.

Kate and Helen silently and apprehensively waited. They had never heard Kenny mention his horrifying and obviously unforgettable wartime experiences before.

"Yes, it was God's will," Kenny gravely repeated with absolute certainty. "All the millions killed in the war, all the horror, the misery, the grief, were all part of God's will. All part of God's inscrutable scheme of things. All part of His fantastic design – a design so unimaginably vast that it is completely incomprehensible to us petty humans. No human – not even the best, the wisest – can possibly hope to even begin to understand the meaning of it all. We must just humbly and uncomplainingly accept everything – the seemingly bad and evil along with the good – as all being part of God's divine will."

The three solemnly intent listeners were deeply impressed by the obvious sincerity of this belief of Kenny's. Ian thought, "Yes, Kenny certainly has got complete faith in his remote and inscrutable God, but it seems a terribly arid, a terribly blind joyless faith." Then he thought it was all very well for Kenny to pronounce so assuredly about God's divine will, but what about God's divine love? How did that fit into His scheme of things? With an effort he stopped himself from asking that question aloud.

Perhaps Kenny sensed Ian's unspoken question: quietly, but steadily he continued, "It's equally impossible for us – for any human – to understand how God's love, His divine love, is expressed through all those killings, but it is. It is expressed through them just as surely as through all the many gloriously wonderful things we readily recognise and joyfully accept as direct expressions of His Divine Love. After all, we know that truly 'The Lord moves in a mysterious way, His wonders to perform,' don't we?"

For a time Kenny stared steadily and silently at Ian, then said, "That's the truth, you know, the simple truth." He sighed deeply, "It has taken me many years, many sadly wasted years, to discover it. You... you do see the simple truth of this... of this, His Divine Truth, don't you, Ian?"

"Aye," Ian immediately and unkindly thought, "the simple truth for simple minds, perhaps?" For some moments he stared at Kenny without answering. He could not believe in his inscrutably unknowable God. He could not believe in any God. His wartime experiences had confirmed his atheism. He found it impossible to see a sign of any God – certainly not any benevolent loving God – in the hideous horrors of war. He remembered the words written on so many British war memorials, 'To the Glory of God and in memory of those who died, 1914–1918.' How could all those deaths possibly be to the Glory of God? He recalled being taught in religious lessons at school that God had created the universe for His Glorification. That didn't seem a very worthy object for a Supreme God, did it?

He could understand, and sympathise with Kenny's fatalistic belief that whatever occurs must occur and there is nothing we can do about it, but he could not believe in his Supreme God who directed fate. Surely we humans are not important enough to merit the guidance of a supreme all-powerful God? And what about free will?... Couldn't we change things by our own efforts? Ian wryly reflected on how he had argued about such questions when he'd been much younger. Now he was older – and wiser? Or was he merely being a hypocrite as, for Kenny's sake, he convincingly lied, "Aye, it must be true, Kenny, it must be the simple truth, or there is no meaning to life at all."

He consoled himself with the thought that if sometimes, for a good reason, it is correct and necessary to lie to others, it is vital never to lie to oneself – to do so is surely despicable.

Kenny smiled, lifted and drained his glass, then reproachfully held it out. Ian quickly refilled it. All four sipped their drams. Three thankfully, but silently, celebrated Kenny having taken the news of Nell's death so well.

There was a knock at the door and Calum MacLeod entered. He stood hesitantly beside the door. His face, what little of it that was not concealed by his bushy black beard and the tangle of jet hair falling over his forehead, was lined with worry.

All evening he, and his wife, had been worrying over how Kenny would react to the death of Nell. He was amazed and delighted to see his uncle smile a warm welcome and call out, "Come in, my dear fellow, come away in."

Then his aunt confirmed the pleasantly relaxed atmosphere by cheerfully crying out, "Sit down, Calum, sit down. You're just in time for a cup of tea. I was just about to put the kettle on again."

Calum's worry lines vanished as he smiled affectionately at 'Kate Kettle'. He beamed around at all the smiling and welcoming faces then laughed, "I don't suppose you'd take any notice if I said I don't need any tea, aunt?"

"No, I wouldn't!… Everyone is always the better of a good cup of tea."

"Och, he'd be much better with a dram," Ian laughed as he rose and poured out a small dram. Tea was Kate's infallible remedy for all the world's ills, just as whisky was Ian's. Over the years they had had many friendly disputes over the relevant merits of each remedy.

"Here lad, drink up that wee dram. I know you don't drink much, but that whisky will do you good." Glancing meaningfully at Kenny, Ian smiled, "We are all having a celebratory wee dram."

Calum raised his glass and happily toasted the company, "Slainte Math."

All eagerly returned that toast then Kate struggled to her feet and made for the scullery despite Calum's repeated declarations that he needed no tea.

Helen laughed, "Oh, Calum, you know what she's like; no power on earth can stop good old 'Kate Kettle' from making her endless cups of tea."

Kenny chuckled; his face glowed as he enjoyed the convivial company and the pleasant whisky. Quietly he asked Calum, "Do you remember old Molly, the pony we had before poor Nell?"

"Oh yes, of course I remember her. As a boy on holidays here with you, I often got rides on Molly, just as in turn my own wee boys got rides on Nell."

"Aye, that's right, my dear fellow. Molly was a fine pony, but perhaps we kept her too long. Probably we should have had her put down before she became such a poor, crippled, blind and helpless invalid. Perhaps we were un-intentionally cruel in keeping her alive so long."

Kenny sighed deeply, sipped his whisky, then gently said, "At least poor Nell had a quick and painless end, she did not suffer all the terrible cruel indignities of extreme old age. So you, Calum, or none of us, should be too upset at her sudden death,"

"Yes, that's true… that's very true, uncle. Poor old Nell did not suffer much at all." Calum gulped. He felt an emotional lump in his throat, not only at the thought of Nell's death, but also at the realisation of his uncle Kenny's natural goodness in suppressing his own sad feelings in order to help him, Calum, get over his upset.

After everyone once more enjoyed Kate's keenly pressed hospitality, Kenny fell soundly asleep, deeply slumped in his battered old armchair. Despite Kate's protest, her visitors prepared to leave. Calum said, "I'll need to get back to Mary. I said I wouldn't be long. She'll be worrying about how the news of Nell's death has affected Uncle Kenny. She'll be delighted when I tell her how well he's taken it."

After Calum left, Kate warmly thanked Helen and Ian for coming to break the news to Kenny and her. "It was very good of you to spare Calum the ordeal of having to tell us."

Ian said, "Anyway, Kate, we're delighted that Kenny took the sad news so well and that he seems to have got over the worst of his nervous upsets."

"Aye, thank God, he's improved a lot over the last few years." Kate fervently agreed. "He no longer has those terrible bouts of depression which so prostrated him in the past."

Ian nodded, "It's wonderful that he has, at last, found satisfactory answers to the profound religious uncertainties that so troubled him."

Ian thought of that blind acceptance of an inscrutable God and all of His mysterious workings, which Kenny had found and which seemed to have brought him something like a reasonably serene peace. I certainly cannot believe in Kenny's God, but that's not important, what is important is that his belief brings him peace. And, after all, who am I to dispute his beliefs, or to say whether they be false or true?... Oh, I suppose most humans need to believe in something. I don't suppose it really matters if our beliefs are true or not, as long as we do sincerely believe in them and live up to them. He grinned in self-disparagement; yes, I suppose we all need some illusions and perhaps I have the greatest illusion of all – the illusion that I have no illusions!

Eventually Helen and Ian managed to tear themselves away from Kate's sincere and protracted thanks. They scurried for home through the pouring rain.

Chapter Eleven

October came in and brought with it yet more gale-driven rain. Then almost unbelievably, came ten glorious days of pale blue skies and benevolently beaming sunshine. Each morning on the hills and in the higher glens there was a keen hoarfrost. It sugared the dying yellow grasses with sparkling life and gaily candy-flossed the thick heathers.

The bright dry weather and the clean, delicate feel of frost stimulated the rutting stags to an even keener mating frenzy in these, 'The Days of the Roaring'. By day and by night their loud challenging bellowings echoed amongst the autumnal hills. Some nights the stags' deep-throated rumbling roars behind Altdour croft kept Helen from sleep. Often Ian's snores as he lay asleep by her side sounded like answering roars. When, exasperated beyond endurance, she wickedly jabbed a vicious elbow, as sharply pointed as a challenging stag's antler, into his defenceless ribs he angrily roared awake and gave a real stag-like bellow.

On one of those blessedly windless frosty evenings Jeannie and Colin MacDonald arrived at Altdour. For a minute they stood with Helen and Ian outside the croft house door listening to the roars of stags reverberating and savaging the countryside's frost-clamped silence.

Once all were comfortably settled around the cosy sitting room's blazing fire, Helen, chuckling heartily, merrily complained of often being kept from sleep by the roaring of the stags combined with the snoring of her husband.

Jeannie laughed, "You have my heartfelt sympathy, Helen, I know exactly what it's like to be kept awake by those sounds. I don't know which is worse, the snores of Colin or the roars of the stags."

Ian grinned, "Och, Jeannie, it might be much worse. What if you were kept awake by the snores of the stags and the rutting roars of Colin?"

Tears of laughter twinkled her eyes and her jolly cheeks glowed as Jeannie cried, "Och, it's many a long year since I've heard Colin roaring with rutting lust… he's almost beyond all that nonsense now!"

"Och, I'm not quite beyond it yet. I'm not too old to not occasionally rise to the occasion," Colin indignantly declared.

"Oh aye, occasionally… very, very, occasionally!" Jeannie chuckled.

"I know how it is," Helen laughed. "Ian's exactly the same."

After exchanging a rueful glance with Colin, Ian grinned, "I think it's about time we changed the subject; this is getting much too personal."

"Aye, so it is," Colin quickly agreed. "I'll tell you our news instead. We called in to see Kate and Kenny MacLeod on our way up here tonight. We had a message to deliver from my boss, Lord Kilvert."

Laughing, Helen asked, "I don't suppose you happened to get a cup of tea from Kate, by any chance?"

"How did you guess?... Surely it's impossible for anyone to go to 'Kate Kettle's' and not be hospitably drowned in an ocean of tea."

Colin continued his story. "I took letters from Lord and Lady Kilvert to them. These letters expressed their sorrow at the sad death of the pony, Nell, while she was hired out for the deerstalking on their Ardgie Estate. Lady Kilvert wrote an especially sympathetic letter. Lord Kilvert enclosed a cheque in compensation for the loss of Nell. He also ordered me to arrange for Flora, the estate's oldest pony, to be given to Kenny as a replacement for Nell once the hind stalking is finished."

Ian said, "That's very good of him. Kate and Kenny will be delighted. They would feel lost without a pony. All their lives they, and their parents before them, have always had at least one pony."

"Aye, I know. They are gey pleased at getting a replacement for Nell. This was to be old Flora's last stalking season anyway. As you know, she is a fine steady and gentle beast. She will be perfect for Kenny and Kate and, being white she even looks like poor Nell."

Jeannie had been listening patiently, now she smiled and said, "Well, that's that all explained, now I can tell you our other news, Helen, our great news…"

Helen interrupted, "Has Sheila had her baby?" Sheila MacDonald was Jeannie's daughter-in-law. Helen knew that she was expecting her first child about this time. "Is it a boy?"

Jeannie beamed, "Aye, it's a fine sturdy eight pound boy. He was born yesterday. They are both doing fine."

Ian jumped up, grabbed the whisky bottle and quickly re-filled all their glasses. "This calls for a celebration. We must wet the head of your first grandchild."

"Do you know what they are going to call him?" Helen asked.

"Oh aye, it's all arranged. He's to be called Colin, after his grandfather." Jeannie smiled fondly at her husband, "'Himself', there, pretends not to be excited, but really he's as proud as Punch to have a grandson at last and to have him called Colin."

Jeannie and Colin's married daughter, Alison, was a nurse in Inverness; she had no children. Their son, Alasdair, was, like his father, a gamekeeper. Now, after a four-year wait his wife had produced a long hoped-for child.

The whisky bottle rapidly emptied. Vivacious talk and hearty laughter once more delighted the cosy small room.

Two hours after those ever welcome guests had left, Helen lay sleepless by Ian's side in the familiar comfort of their conjugal bed. She sighed resignedly as her husband's all too habitual snores loudly snorted and gurgled from his open mouth while his body lay relaxed in untroubled sleep. How she wished she could drop off to sleep as quickly and effortlessly as him.

Somewhere high on Cairndhu a large, proudly antlered stag roared his aggressively defiant challenges at lesser stags. From a safe distance these younger stags warily answered that dominant beast's challenges. But always, afraid and frustrated, they turned tail and ran when he furiously charged and angrily drove them away from his jealously guarded harem of hinds.

Helen sighed again and pulled the bedclothes higher over her ears in a vain attempt to smother all the annoying sounds, animal and human. She settled herself with patient resignation to pass the time as easily as possible. From long experience she knew that sleep might not overcome her for an hour or two yet. She often found this sleepless, dreamily drowsy state quite pleasant. As her tired body gradually relaxed her mind was free to roam and soar. Freed of all conscious constraints her subconscious set out on limitless, rudderless voyages over oceans of memory and over uncharted Freudian seas of vivid, at times delightful and erotic, at times grotesque and frightening, fabulous fantasies.

But tonight she managed to control her mind. She thought with pleasure of Jeannie and Colin's happiness at the birth of their first grandson. She brightly pictured that sturdy, healthy, lustily howling newborn baby boy. That happy picture suddenly flashed to much sadder scenes. With overwhelming sadness she again clearly remembered the pathetically small and horribly deformed baby boy she had given birth to twenty-seven years ago. For a few heartbreaking minutes her son whimpered with faint, strange, animal-like noises. He weakly struggled. Then he died.

After the passage of so much time the memory of that birth and death no longer bled with the keen, sharp-toothed stab of severe grief. Yet it was never quite forgotten. It remained as something like a faint dull ache, a lingering, haunting grey ghost of sadness.

Occasionally, as now, that old ghost escaped from time's dark shadows and flared to vivid life. Helen's mind was no longer in control. Old memories took over. She relived that nightmare time.

As they nursed Helen with tender care after her long and agonising confinement, compassionate nurses and doctors gently suggested that it was perhaps just as well that her hideously deformed baby had not lived. Hiding his own grief, Ian, too, tried to persuade her of this. But nothing could console Helen to her grievous loss.

For a few weeks she lingered in a terribly weak state, shattered both physically and mentally. She hovered close to death.

Twice Ian was called to her bedside in the shivering pre-dawn hours, that dismal time when all life is at its lowest ebb. She was not expected to live through the approaching dawn.

How small, how sad and frail her body looked under the white sheet and blanket, it hardly raised a mound in what seemed a vast snowy waste of bed.

However, a huge indomitable spirit was concealed in that tiny, terribly weak, terribly shrunken body.

Gradually, stubbornly, she physically recovered. Infinitely slowly she put on a little weight. After a month she was allowed home to Aldrory. Ian tenderly and lovingly looked after her. The doctor and district nurse regularly and caringly attended her. Friends and neighbours thoughtfully helped.

Day after day, week after week, she sat slumped apathetically in her armchair by the fireside. She brightened when 'Kate Kettle' called and, with her boisterous laughter booming, related the latest local gossip. Jeannie and Colin Macdonald also managed to cheer her and spark some weakly smiling reaction. But after every visitor left she again sank into an apathetic state.

Although being careful not to show it, Ian gradually despaired of Helen ever truly recovering her spirit. When he saw how even their two collie dogs, bemused and saddened by her inexplicable lethargic state, and whom she had so deeply loved, could not bring her out of that distressing condition he doubted that anything else could.

One morning, four months after Helen lost her baby, as Ian helped her settle into the armchair, he was surprised to see her gently smile. She whispered, "I've had enough of this misery, Ian. I know how to end it."

"To end it?" He gasped in alarm. "What do you mean?"

Again she managed to smile, "Oh, don't worry, Ian, I don't meant to end this misery by ending my life. No, I mean just the opposite... I intend to truly live once more."

With amazed delight Ian beamed, "That's great, Helen, that's great! How can I help you?"

She stared steadily at him, "You must do one simple thing for me; do it without asking any questions, will you?"

"Yes, yes, of course I will. What is it?"

"Bring that black African mask from your study and hang it on the wall opposite me where I can sit and see it. Then take the dogs out for a good walk. Come back in two hours, not before."

"But... but why? What's the point of bringing that ugly mask in here?"

"Oh, Ian, please, please, if you love me just do what I request and ask no questions. I assure you I know what I'm doing. I promise I won't do anything foolish while you're out. I will not leave this chair. I will simply sit here and, when you come back, I assure you I will be better. I will be back to my normal old self."

Convinced by the assured intensity of her words, Ian unhooked a painting from the wall opposite Helen and hung the ugly ebony black African mask into its place. "Are you sure you will be all right?" He anxiously asked as he prepared to leave with the dogs.

Helen gave an impatient frown, "Yes!... Yes! Take the dogs and go!"

The dogs thoroughly enjoyed the two-hour walk, but Ian worried that he had done wrong by leaving Helen alone for such a time.

Apprehensively he entered the front door. The house was absolutely silent. With heart-thudding trepidation he opened the sitting-room door. The two collies bounded ahead of him.

Helen sat where he had left her. He saw at a glance that she was changed. She was the lively, vivacious Helen of old. With a tender hand on each dog she lovingly caressed and warmly welcomed them. The madly excited collies could not contain their wild joy.

172

Ian looked on with emotion. With a beaming face and a lump choking his throat he walked over to Helen.

She smiled brightly up at him, "Did you have a good walk? I know the dogs did."

"Aye, I enjoyed the walk fine." He smiled down at her, "You're looking much better, Helen, are you feeling better?"

"Yes, I feel much improved. Physically I'm still rather weak, however my body will soon recover now that my mind has recovered." She smiled up at him again and that smile instantly vanquished the last of her deep dark lines of misery, which for the last four months had been, 'writ in moods and frowns and wrinkles strange' over her face. That smile also lit up and mischievously sparkled her eyes in the old familiar way, which Ian knew and loved so well. She murmured apologetically, "I'm sorry to have been so depressed these last few months, Ian. I must have given you a horrid time. Have you been terribly worried about me?"

Ian nodded and smiled fondly, "Aye, I've been very worried about you Helen, but no longer. You are better now, thank God."

"Thank God!... Aye, thank God... but which God, I wonder?" Helen stared fixedly at the African mask hanging on the wall facing her. "Thank that Pagan God, perhaps?"

Ian gazed at that ugly mask then, puzzled and slightly apprehensive, asked, "What do you mean? What has that thing got to do with your recovery?"

"It has everything to do with my recovery. Why do you think I asked you to hang it there?"

Ian slowly shook his head and smiled, "I've no idea. But I now know you well enough to realise that when you get one of your strange, illogical ideas or feelings or intuitions or whatever you call them, then all my poor reasoning male logic can do is stand back in awed wonder."

Helen smiled affectionately at him like a mother with her bemused child. "Why, don't you sit down and I'll tell you all about it?"

Ian sat on the broad arm of the chair. He put an arm around her shoulders and drew her to him. He bent over and kissed the eager lips raised to his. She snuggled contentedly into him, grinned, then commanded, "Now look at that mask"

For a while they both stared silently at it.

"Do you see anything different about it, Ian?"

"No... no, I can't see anything different. Do you?"

"Yes, I do. I certainly do!... It has more lines – lines of deep grief – around its mouth and eyes. It is wearing my grief on its face. It has willingly taken that unbearable burden away from me and left me happy again."

Before Ian could question this absurd impossibility, Helen hurriedly explained, "When I was leaving Africa after helping nurse many native villagers through a severe epidemic, one of the chiefs gave me that mask as a gift, a very special gift. That chief was a great leader of his tribe. He possessed strange powers. Most Europeans regarded him as a witch doctor and thought his powers mere primitive superstitions, if not downright trickery. I didn't. He predicted that I would work in a wild part of my own country and be married there and live happily with my husband." She paused and chuckled, "It sounds like a fairy tale, doesn't it?"

"Aye," Ian laughed "a fairy tale that came true when you married your handsome, braw Hielander."

"Aye, perhaps," Helen grinned, then continued, "But the village chief also told me that I would have one tragedy in my life. He said that I should try to overcome my grief by my own effort of will; but if I couldn't succeed then by staring uninterruptedly and with my utmost concentration at that ebony mask for exactly one hour my grief would transfer to it and I would once more lead a happily contented life."

Ian lifted his gaze from her and again stared intently at the ugly mask. He said nothing.

"It happened exactly as he said it would," Helen went on. "At the end of one hour of concentrated staring I felt my load of grief and dejection leave me. I was again happy. I saw…" She paused, then in smiling deference to Ian's masculine logic, altered that to, "I thought I saw new lines of grief appear on the hideous lined and tormented ebony mask. Do you believe me, Ian?"

"Oh, of course I am delighted to see that your load of sorrow and distress over the death of our baby has been lifted from you; but whether that mask is wearing your grief, well I don't know about that. It… it just seems impossible." Ian paused thoughtfully, then asked, "Helen, have you ever read the novel, *The Picture of Dorian Gray*?"

"No, I haven't… why?"

"It's just that that strange book by Oscar Wilde deals with the idea that some human emotions and wishes, if felt deeply and passionately enough, can sometimes, somehow, be transferred to inanimate material objects. In the novel they are transposed to, and amazingly alter, an oil painting, a portrait. The subject of the portrait, a handsome youth, fervently wishes that he may retain his youthful beauty forever and that all the ugly lines of age and debauchery be transferred to the portrait. His wish is granted. He does not change. The portrait, hidden away, becomes a disgusting, loathsomely lined and wrinkled record of hideous debauchery."

"I'll need to read that book sometime." Helen's eyes twinkled, she chuckled, "But I assure you, Ian, the lines I transferred to that African mask were not lines of wild debauchery."

Ian laughed, "No, of course not! We've had many wonderful times of glorious sexual passion together, and hopefully we'll have many more in the future, but they hardly amount to wild debauchery. But the idea's the same; in your case they were lines of grief which you transposed to that mask."

Helen smiled inwardly as she noted how Ian now seemed to be accepting the truth of that 'impossible' happening. She asked, "Does the novel explain how such things happen?"

"No… no, it gives no real explanation." Ian smiled, "Except that they come about through making a pact with the Devil."

"Oh, Ian, I assure you I haven't made a pact with Auld Nick!"

Ian chuckled, "I wouldn't put it past you, you wee devil." He hugged her closer and gently kissed her. He straightened up and smiled, "Oh, Helen, I almost believe that what you believe is actually true, that your grief is transferred to that mask."

Her eyes impishly twinkled, "You're learning, Ian, you're learning."

"Do you want to leave the mask hanging there?"

"No. It has served its purpose. It is not exactly cheerful, is it? You can put it back in your room again."

"Good! That seascape painting of yours is much more pleasant."

Ian hung the black mask in its usual place in his 'study'. Not for he first time he wondered what state the native artist had been in when he carved that grotesque mask. Not a very happy state surely? He must have deeply felt many of the cares, agonies and horrors that afflict humanity, and he had hideously enslaved his feelings in those multitudinous lines and wrinkles deeply scarred around the sensual mouth, the leering eyes and the severely frowning brow. But surely there were no more lines than before?

He stood back and stared intently at it. Yes, of course it was unchanged… Or was it? Were there possibly more lines now? No… no, of course not! Once that idea was in his mind it was all too easy for his imagination to run riot. Could the mask really possess some talismanic power? The African chief believed so. Helen believed so. Could he believe so?

If the notes of a singer's voice, hitting a certain pitch, can break glass; if magnetic waves can move inanimate metals, then is it not possible that certain unique human mind waves can change some types of inanimate materials? Had this really happened to that mask?

Can mind change matter?… Can anguish re-shape atoms?… Can't faith move mountains? Ian smiled in self-mockery, he had any number of questions; he had no definite answers. Once again he fell back on his favourite quotation, 'There are more things in heaven and in earth that are dreamt of in our philosophy'.

Lying in bed, still trying to get to sleep, Helen smiled thinking of how often she had heard Ian recite that quotation during their thirty years of contented marriage. The death of their baby and her inability to have any more children was the only tragedy in her life. Yes, she thought, she had much to be thankful for. She had her fine husband and her finer dogs. She had this cosy home, her attractive wild garden, and all around stretched the landscape, dotted with trout loch, which she loved.

She sighed contentedly; yes, she truly had much to be thankful for.

A burst of exceptionally loud and abrasive snoring from Ian jerked her out of those mellow reflections. She was about to jab an exasperated elbow into his ribs when another memory halted her. She remembered what the young widow, only thirty-four years old, had said to her shortly after her husband had been drowned

175

when his lobster boat sunk a few miles along the coast from Inveraldrory village. The distraught widow had sobbed, "Oh, when I think of how annoyed I used to get at Norman's loud snoring. How often and how angrily I used to waken him up. Oh, how I wish I had him sleeping beside me again – I would never complain of even his loudest snoring again."

So Helen thoughtfully refrained from deploying the sharp and vicious weapon of her elbow, instead she gently shook Ian. Mumbling and grumbling, still asleep, he turned towards here. His stertorous snores ceased. Helen snuggled into his body's familiar comforting warmth and gave a contented sigh as she finally drifted into sleep. Drowsily she repeated, "Yes, *I do* have a lot to be thankful for."

Chapter Twelve

The Aldrory countryside cowered miserably like a cruelly beaten dog as it was relentlessly lashed by November's ice-toothed winds and numbing slithery sleet. The mountains and high moors of Ardgie, suffocated by smooring snow and ceaselessly assaulted by gales and blizzards, proved the truth of that name's meaning, 'The Windy Heights'.

This dreich month, with its equally dismal companion, December, were the dreariest months of the year. Sadistically, they cruelly thrust their raw misery deep into the marrow of stiff, rheumatically aged bones. Old people shivered, coughed, snuffled and wheezed through the last weary weeks of the dismally dying year.

Helen and Ian spent most of these drearily dull short winter days busily and creatively employed in pottery, workshop or 'study'.

After turning out a dozen or so clay models of attractive Highland animals, which experience had taught were very saleable to tourists, Helen would allow her imagination loose rein and create a couple of fabulously grotesque creatures. These wildly improbable monsters were like escapees from the surrealistic world of that weird and wonderful artist Salvador Dali. Whenever, with self-disparaging smiles, she showed these creations to Ian he praised her painstaking efforts then laughed and shook his head, "If these creatures give a true insight into what goes on in that wee head of yours, then it must be an amazing phantasmagoric world you have tucked away in there. A psychiatrist would have a wonderful time trying to psychoanalyse it. I gave up trying to logically fathom out its mysterious workings many years ago."

While Helen was engrossed in her pottery, Ian busied himself in his workshop making walking sticks etc, or in his 'study' writing short stories, articles and poems. The time passed quickly, productively and happily for them both.

Some days, Ian was enlisted by Colin MacDonald to help with the hind stalking. Usually there was little, or no, pleasure in being out on the hills stalking at this time of year, often in the most appalling weather. However, it was a necessary task. The numbers of red deer hinds had to be kept under control and the stalking and accurate shooting of them by experienced gamekeepers was the only practical, humane method of doing this. If large numbers of hinds were not shot each year many of them would die a long, lingering, painful death in late winter or early spring from lack of sufficient fresh grazing. Even with the annual culling, in a severe wet winter and a late spring many red deer carcases littered Highland hillsides and moors.

There were simply too many deer roaming the Highlands. Aldrory district suffered more than many places as a direct result of the landowner, Campbell-

Fotheringay's ruining of the estate and by him employing no gamekeepers to carry out an effective programme of deer culling. In ever increasing numbers deer were raiding crofter's vegetable plots and even in Inveraldrory village (a part of his estate) people were suffering from his years of deliberate neglect, as deer were now starting to raid and cause havoc in flower gardens. High and unsightly deer fences had to be erected to protect all gardens.

Things were not quite so bad on Lord Kilvert's neighbouring Ardgi Estate. He employed Colin MacDonald and other gamekeepers who between them managed to keep the deer numbers on that land to reasonable levels.

Often Colin and Ian, with Calum MacLeod helping, left the Land Rover parked by the main road, which swept along by the North shore of seven miles long Loch Ardgie, and then set out in the estate's boat with its powerful outboard engine. They crossed near the centre of the loch to the remote, uninhabited and little visited South shore. November's miserable weather drove the deer down from the high hills and made it a less difficult and arduous task to locate them, shoot them, and drag the dead hinds to the waiting boat.

One morning the stalking party again set out. It was a really miserable morning. The dull, overcast sky was as cold and grey as slate. Rain and sleet had washed all colours out of sky and hills and moors. Everything was a uniform dull monochrome. The only splash of colour was the burns, which, pouring in furious spate down steep hillsides, were glaring white gashes like chalk strokes violently slashed down a blackboard.

They headed for Torr an Eilein. That island, thickly clothed with gnarled old Scots Pines, was a conspicuous landmark. As he steered the boat Calum said, "It's amazing how well the islands on this loch are covered with trees while most of the land around it is completely treeless."

Ian withdrew the pipe from his mouth – Colin and he were tranquilly enjoying a smoke before the hard work began. "Aye, that's right, Calum, it just shows how well the trees survive when they're free from the destructively hungry mouths of sheep and deer."

Colin, too, removed his pipe, "Aye, without so many sheep and deer the Highlands would regenerate their native woods again."

Ian laughed, "But if there were no deer you would be out of a job, Colin."

"Och, I'm retiring soon anyway, so that wouldn't bother me. I'll quite happily leave it to young Calum here to take over and sort out the future."

Calum grinned, "I look forward to that. I would like to see a better balance between deer, sheep and native trees." He shoved a hand in one pocket of his new waterproof jacket and brought out a fistful of bright red Rowan berries. "You see I'm a good disciple, I'm faithfully following the fine example set by you two old-timers."

Together they laughed, "Well done, lad. Obviously we can safely leave the future in your well-trained hands."

Colin had started that grand and unusual habit. Ian soon copied him. Now Calum was keenly continuing their good work.

It was a few years after the end of the war when, working as a gamekeeper again, Colin got into the habit of taking a handful of Rowan berries with him when he was out on the hills and moors in the autumn. At any suitable place not too accessible to sheep and deer he left some of these berries. Now amongst rocks and boulders, from steep screes, from cracks and ledges on small cliffs, from moist sides of miniature ravines, small Rowan trees tenaciously struggled to survive and grow.

Thanks to Colin's and Ian's efforts hundreds of young Rowans grew amongst these more inaccessible and remote corners of the starkly wild landscapes of Ardgie and Aldrory. They had started this unofficial, unscientific effort at conservation through their love of, and observant knowledge of, this, their ancestral land. And these efforts commenced long, long, before ecology, the environment and conservation had been heard of by most people; and certainly long before these things became the 'in thing'.

As Calum returned the berries to his pocket, Ian laughed, "Thank God we didn't have to spread these Rowan berries in the same way as the blackbirds do, by swallowing them then passing out the hard stone in our shit."

Colin's ruddy face beamed, his stout body shook as he too laughed, "No, it would be a gey difficult job doing it that way. To shit the stones into many of the awkward places we've put the berries we would have needed to have been devilish braw contortionists."

As they lounged in the boat, enjoyed smoking their pipes, enjoyed the laughter and each other's company, Colin and Ian kept a warily experienced eye on the weather. They well knew how suddenly, how dangerously, the treacherous November weather could changed, how quickly this large loch could be whipped into a roaring fury. Calum kept an attentive eye on those knowledgeable old men as well as on where he was steering the boat.

Colin pointed with the stem of his pipe, "I don't like the look of that."

"No," Ian agreed, "nor do I. And it's coming towards us at a fair lick."

"Aye, it is." Colin turned to Calum, "Head for the Chief's Islet over there; we'll shelter at it for a wee while."

As he swung the boat towards the small rocky island, Calum queried, "The Chief's Islet? Which chief?... and why that wee island?"

Ian grinned, "You should be ashamed of yourself, Calum, you, a MacLeod, and you don't know that some of your ancestral clan chiefs are buried on that islet."

When they reached, and securely tied the boat to the islet, Calum, eagerly jumped ashore to explore it. He did not take long. Only a few scrubby bushes grew here and some piles of stones marked the MacLeod Chief's neglected and almost forgotten graves.

Calum quickly scrambled back into the boat and huddled down beside Colin and Ian who were already well cooried doon with backs to the storm, which now viciously engulfed them. Sky and hills, islands and loch disappeared as a smothering, greyish blanket of ugly sleet relentlessly descended and covered, men, boat, and ancient graves.

Thrusting numbed hands deeper into jacket pockets, Colin grimly grinned, "Perhaps your ancestral chiefs are better off than us, Calum, at least they won't be feeling this bloody freezing sleet where they are, deep in their graves."

"No, they won't. Although I wonder just how deep their graves are. This island looks pretty solid rock, doesn't it?"

"Aye," Ian answered him, "I noticed that the first time I landed here. I don't suppose the graves can be very deep. Of course that doesn't matter on this remote island. That's why they were buried here in the distant past; where no hungrily marauding wolves could dig the bodies up."

Ten minutes later the sleet stopped, the dull clouds swept away and a pale and watery sun tried to smile down.

The three men rose, shook soaking sleet from their clothes and wiped persistent drips from noses. With telescopes they methodically scanned the gently sloping hills rising from the South shore of the loch. They quickly pinpointed three separate herds of hinds. Like themselves, these deer had been waiting miserably hunched, for the storm to pass over. Like themselves, each beast shook sleet from its coat. Each vigorously shaken misty-spray glittered in the pale sunlight with a fine, rainbow brightness.

Colin said, "We shouldn't have much trouble getting within range of these hinds. We better use the oars from here in, we don't want the noise of the outboard to disturb them."

Ian willingly got one of the long, double-handed oars out. Calum took the other one.

Colin sat comfortably in the stern seat. He again got out, filled, and then lit his favourite old pipe. When it was drawing to his entire satisfaction he sighed contentedly, settled himself even more comfortably and beamed benevolently at the straining oarsmen.

Ian grinned, "Are you sure you're perfectly comfortable there? You might do something while we're sweating our guts out; you could sing us a sea shanty."

Colin laughed, "No, I'll be a Highland bard and entertain you with a story. Have you heard of 'Donnie Disgrace' and his encounter with the Duke of Sutherland, Calum?"

"No, I haven't. The mere mention of those hated Dukes, with their notoriety over the Sutherland Clearances, is enough to make my blood boil."

"Aye, I know lad." Colin grinned at Ian, "Of course you remember 'Donnie Disgrace', don't you?"

"Oh aye, certainly. He was a great character, a real auld worthy. He was one of my boyhood heroes with his wild, devil-may-care eccentric ways, his poaching skills, his boisterous laughter and his un-quenchable love of whisky."

Calum exploded a burst of laugher, he gasped, "My God, that vivid description perfectly fits more than one man in this boat!"

Their laugher unrestrainedly joined in with his. "Aye, I suppose it does... Aye, nae doot we're in the same boat as auld Donnie." Once he regained his composure Colin told the story of 'Donnie Disgrace'.

It happened a few years before the First World War. Donnie Sutherland was a crofter living in Aldrory Glen. The salmon filled River Aldrory (and in those days it really was filled with salmon) flowed irresistibly close to his croft. Donnie delighted in outwitting the gamekeepers guarding the river. Time after time, using the utmost ingenuity, he snatched a salmon almost from under their noses and got clean away with it. Some of the younger gamekeeper were secretly tolerant of, and amused by, Donnie's exploits, but the head gamekeeper, Ewan Grant, hated him and vowed to catch him red-handed some day and have him jailed.

The Duke of Sutherland was having a holiday salmon fishing, deerstalking and grouse shooting on his sporting estates of Aldrory and Ardgie. Late one afternoon as he was walking away from the River Aldrory with his 'tail' of retainers behind him, Grant carrying his Grace's fishing rod and two younger gamekeepers carrying the four salmon his Grace had caught, they met, they almost bumped into, Donnie Sutherland as he came round a sharp bend on the path beside the river. Both parties stopped and stood staring at one another. Donnie stood none too steadily, his breath reeked of whisky, obviously he had been happily partaking of a few drams.

"Where are you going? What are you up to?" the Duke loudly, commandingly, demanded to know.

Anger flared in normally placid Donnie, he was not accustomed to being spoken to like that. "Och, I'm taking a walk up by the river, as I've every right to do."

"Oh, going poaching, are you? Going poaching on my river?"

"Your river? Your salmon? Your land and your sun and sky, I suppose? You own everything, don't you?"

His Grace flushed with anger; he too, was not accustomed to being spoken to like this. With bad grace he ignored this outburst and turned instead to his head gamekeeper, "Search him, Grant. No doubt he has a gaff or a net hidden somewhere about his person."

"Yes, your Grace," Grant obsequiously replied. He carefully laid down his master's fishing rod then eagerly, expectantly, gloating, stepped up to Donnie.

Donnie innocently held out his arms, "Go on, search me. Search me as much as you like."

Almost trembling with disappointment, Grant reported, "He's got nae poaching gear on him, your Grace."

"Are you sure?… Oh, doubtless he has it hidden somewhere nearby." Angrily his Grace snarled, "Haven't you got it hidden, you… you, what's your name?"

"My name is *Mr* Sutherland, your Grace," Donnie over-politely announced.

"Well, Sutherland, isn't your poaching gear hidden nearby?"

Swaying slightly Donnie tried, not entirely successfully, to look completely innocent, "No it isn't. I don't know what you're talking aboot."

As baffled, the annoyed Duke started to walk past Donnie, he commanded, "Well, Sutherland, don't let me see you here again on my land."

Stepping in front of him, Donnie stopped his Grace. "Your land?... Your land? By rights it's as much my land as yours. Your accursed family stole it from us, your ain clansmen and handed it over to your bloody sheep."

The Duke tried to walk on but again Donnie stopped him and loudly and passionately asked, "Aye, and what aboot all the clansmen who for centuries fought and died for their clan chiefs, shouldn't their descendants have received more consideration from your family?"

Increasingly annoyed, his Grace vehemently snarled, "Do you think the Chiefs didn't fight too? My family fought for centuries to gain and hold this land."

"Oh, did they now?" Donnie excitably cried, "Well, I tell you what I'll do – I'll fight you for it here and now. Come on!... Come on!"

While the Duke and his gamekeepers looked on in amazement, Donnie wildly threw off his tweed jacket, raised and clenched his fists and advanced on his Grace in a boxing posture, loudly shouting, "Come on!... Come on! Raise your fists and fight like a man!"

With his fists actively jabbing the air Donnie circled around the Duke with what he fondly imagined was an experienced boxer's bouncily agile fancy footwork but was in reality more a staggering, uncertain soft-shoe shuffle. He repeatedly challenged, "Come on!... Come on! Fight like a man!"

Each time the Duke tried to get away, he found Donnie determinedly blocking his way. "Oh, damn it," his Grace cried in exasperation, "I've had enough of this ridiculous nonsense!" He turned to his gamekeepers, "Grant, Fraser, MacLaren, apprehend this drunken oaf and frogmarch him to Inveraldrory police station. I'll go ahead and alert the village policeman. I'll have this obnoxious wastrel charged with being drunk and disorderly and threatening physical assault."

"Yes, your Grace," Grant keenly replied, delighted at the prospect of Donnie Sutherland being jailed at last.

As the 'keepers grabbed Donnie the Duke strode disdainfully away, Donnie shouted after his retreating figure, "Your *Grace*?... Your *Grace*? You're nothing but a *bloody disgrace*, your Grace!" Delighted with this expression, he repeatedly called out, "Aye, you're nothing but a bloody disgrace!"

"Och, be quiet you damned fool," ordered head 'keeper Grant as the two younger 'keepers firmly held Donnie by his arms.

"Och, bugger you, Grant, you arse-kissing toady. I'll no' fight with you; I want tae fight the organ-grinder, no' his bloody monkey!" This insult struck home especially keenly as Grant was all too aware of the nickname his enemies had given him, "The Hairy Ape". He certainly was very hirsute with his large beard, his bushy eyebrows, hairs growing from ears and nostrils and thickly matting the backs of his hands. With mischievous glee Donnie added, "Och, I suppose you're mair a bloody hairy ape than a damned monkey, I'll grant you that, Grant!"

Grant swore at him then turned furiously on the two 'keepers who could not prevent themselves from grinning. "What the hell are you twa laughing at? You'll hae something tae laugh aboot if I get you sacked, won't you?"

They instantly fell solemnly serious. This was no light threat. The possibility of losing their jobs was truly no laughing matter for those young men. They had their wives and bairns to think of. If they lost their job, they also lost the 'keeper's tied estate house and if the Duke was displeased with them, they might well be blacklisted and find themselves unable to get employment on any other estate.

Donnie was duly charged, tried and sentenced. He spent fourteen days in Dornoch jail.

While he was in jail the story of him challenging the Duke of Sutherland to fight for his land swept over the entire county. By the time the story, expanding by word of mouth, had, like the ripples from a stone thrown into a loch, reached Caithness, Ross-shire and Inverness rumours and wild exaggerations had done their inevitable work; Donnie had not only challenged the Duke to physical combat but had actually fought and vanquished his Grace. He had knocked him unconscious with a powerful uppercut. Then with his right foot planted firmly and triumphantly on the horizontal Duke's chest had loudly proclaimed himself indisputable victor and therefore, by right of conquest, the rightful new laird of all Sutherland.

It had taken a large posse of policemen and gamekeepers to overcome and arrest Donnie. Then when they revived the aching Duke, there was nothing in the least graceful about his Grace's language as he furiously swore to get his revenge on his assailant. How ardently he wished for the powers his ancestors had ruthlessly enjoyed a few centuries ago – Donnie would be hanging from the nearest tree by now.

Rumour's fictions are always much more intriguing and lively than dull reality. Simple truth tastes all the better for being seasoned with romance's spice.

When Donnie was released from jail he found he had become a living legend. He received a hero's welcome when he returned to Aldrory. Innumerable drams were forced on him and countless admiring toasts drunk to him, 'Donnie Disgrace', as he was now firmly nicknamed. He proudly retained that name until his death at a ripe old age.

By the time Colin finished this story the boat had reached the gravelly South shore of Loch Ardgie. He ginned, "Oh, I'm sorry, Ian, I was going to take a turn at the oar."

Ian also grinned, deliberately he broadened his speech, "Och, were you, man? I thought you didna seem ower keen to take ower ma oar."

After beaching the boat they silently and cautiously made their way along the shore, all the time keeping out of sight of the deer grazing on the slopes above them. They passed the ruins of the stone jetty and the many grey gable ends that gauntly rose and marked the sites of old croft houses scattered about Tubeg Bay. They went along by small Loch a' Mhuilinn. Then as they started up the concealing hollow where the Mhuilinn Burn flowed down to join the loch, Ian asked, "Is this familiar territory to you, Calum?... It should be."

"Yes... yes, of course it is. We're almost at Mhuilinn Mor, the big mill and house where my ancestors lived until they were cleared out in 1816."

A few minutes' walk brought them to these ruins. Water, flooding dark, murky and peaty and miserably cold, still eagerly rushed down the mill-lade but now turned no mill-stone. One large old circular stone lay flat and was half overgrown with grass and smothered over with drooping bronze bracken. Tumbled walls and lichened gables were all that remained of the mill and house.

Calum smiled at Ian, "It was a much brighter day the first time I was here. Do you remember that lovely June day when, as a youth, I came here with Helen and you?"

"Och aye, I remember it fine. After your Uncle Kenny told you about this old mill and the ruined home of your ancestors we got no peace until we brought you to see them for yourself."

"I hope I wasn't too much of a nuisance to you."

"Och no, not at all. Helen and I really enjoyed yon day. We had a lovely walk in along the path from the West end of Loch Ardgie and I seem to remember that we all caught quite a few trout."

"Yes, we did. You were very patient with me, helping to improve my skill, or lack of skill, at fly-fishing. My casting definitely improved. That day was the best one of that holiday."

"And what did you think when you saw the ruins here at last?" Colin asked.

"Oh, I was thrilled. Of course my youthful head was full of all sorts of romantic notions of kilts and claymores, of stirring pipe tunes and the clash of battle. I imagined all sorts of exciting things having taken place here." Calum smiled self-mockingly, "Och, probably I had much too avidly read far too many of Scott's, Stevenson's and Neil Munro's wildly adventurous Highland novels. When I see these ruins now, when I'm a bit older... and perhaps a bit wiser?... the emotions I feel are anger and sadness."

"Aye," Colin agreed, "There is something terribly sad about all those ruins here."

"Aye, especially on a miserable dreich grey day like this. You can almost feel the misery oozing out of those sad, neglected auld stanes," Ian said. Then he grinned, "Och, we're getting awful maudlin, we'll be shedding tears next." He smiled at Calum, "And you know, as we get older, even when we're in our old age, it is no bad thing to retain something of our youthful romantic notions. Life is gey drab without some romance, without some idealism, without some high, imaginative aesthetic aspirations." Remembering previous occasions when he had been much less positive about being able to retain youthful enthusiasms, he smiled ruefully, "There endeth the lesson for today."

Colin pointed at a few small Rowan trees growing amongst the ruins and along the side of the burn, "Those are my imaginative aesthetic contributions to this sad and lonely place. Hopefully they will survive and be growing long after I am dead."

"I was going to ask if you had seeded some of your Rowan berries here," Calum said. "Do you mind if I drop some of my berries about here too?"

"Go ahead, lad, no one has a better right than you to do so; but spare some for the wee ravine higher up the burn, the ones I dropped there have not survived. Perhaps yours will thrive better."

Calum's pocketful of berries was soon disposed of as they cautiously followed up by the burn towards the hinds. Within the concealment of this hollow, deeply gauged out by the burn over thousands of years, it would have been a very difficult task to stalk unseen up this fairly open and featureless slope to within rifle range of the deer.

Lying on the edge of the hollow they again brought their telescopes into play. One herd of hinds was about half a mile above them and another herd was about the same distance away to their left. Fortunately the hollow of a tributary burn gave hidden access to the deer on the left. Also, as they had noted earlier, the wind was steady from the South East and carried the obnoxious strong scent of these humans away from the deer.

After studying the hinds, Calum noted the menacing black clouds moving towards them, he quietly remarked, "It looks as though we're in for another storm of sleet soon, doesn't it?"

Colin winked at Ian, "He's learning… he's learning fast. I was just going to comment on that approaching storm myself."

Ian grinned, "Aye, and so was I."

Colin quickly decided the stalking tactics, "I'll go after these hinds above us; you take Calum and go after the other ones, Ian. We should be in position within fifteen minutes. When I fire, you fire too, okay?"

"Aye, fine. Hopefully we should get them before the storm blots out everything again."

And so they did – just!

Ian gave Calum his rifle, "You take the first couple of shots as soon as Colin fires, then pass the rifle to me."

Colin fired. His hind dropped dead.

Calum fired twice. Two hinds dropped dead.

A few moments passed. The hinds stopped running, stood motionless and looked back. Colin fired again. Another hind died. Ian took a quick but accurate shot and a fifth hind fell, also shot through the heart.

After these final shots the remaining hinds stopped for nothing. They fled at full speed up the slope with their hoofs spraying a delicate fine mist from the grass and heather. To the left a party of about twenty stags urgently followed one another up a narrow track on steeper ground. Their pale rumps showed up brightly in the weak sunshine. To the stalkers they looked like the white splashes of a flooded Highland burn impossibly defying nature by cascading uphill.

Quickly, expertly, they gralloched the five dead hinds.

Colin was pleased at getting five hinds in one day. "We'll soon get the cull over at this rate," he said. "The quicker we're finished with stalking in this awful weather the better I'll be pleased."

"Aye, it really is bloody awful weather," Ian agreed as the dark clouds swept low over them. He grinned, "Or should that be, bloody offal weather?" The slanting, smothering, vicious sleet again drew its miserable opaque curtain over the entire scene.

They started dragging the first three hinds to the lochside. Fortunately the route was mostly downhill. At least the sleet, which was slobberingly and vindictively freezing their hands and faces, did some good. It slushily covered the ground and made it easier for the hind's bodies to slide along behind the strenuously hauling men. Thankfully these hinds were considerably lighter than the stags.

Beside the boat they quickly untied their ropes and set out back up the hill through the thick sleet to the other two dead hinds. Slithering down the treacherously slippery slushy slope, they hurriedly dragged these hinds towards the waiting, but unseen, sleet-shrouded boat.

By the time they again reached the shore it seemed to them that these dead deer mysteriously increased in weight as the thin ropes dug ever deeper into their aching shoulders.

They wasted no time in loading the five carcasses into the boat; nor, at the North shore, did they waste any time in getting them unloaded, dragged to, and dumped into the parked Land Rover. The desire to get out of the miserable, freezing, vicious sleet was a great incentive to speed. An even greater incentive for Colin and Ian was the thought of the drams poured by the housekeeper at Ardgie Lodge and set out awaiting them on the gunroom table.

"Come on, let's go. It'll soon be dark," Colin said.

"Aye," Ian grinned in agreement, "it'll soon be dark as the inside o' a big black cat!"

186

Chapter Thirteen

Dreary November slowly crept with crabbit sulkiness into dark December.

At least the dying year's final month brought with it the promise of mid-winter festivities.

Helen and Ian did not bother much with Christmas. Wisely, they husbanded their energies for the New Year celebrations. They celebrated Hogmanay's ancient and openly and honestly pagan festival with a sincere and unashamedly Pagan enthusiasm, which put the horrid hypocrisy of so much of modern over-commercialised Christmas festivities to shame. For many years they shared their Hogmanays with Jeannie and Colin MacDonald. A happy ritual of having dinner together on New Year's Eve had evolved. On alternate years they went to each other's house for the convivial festive meal and stayed until after dawn on the first day of the new year.

This time it was Helen and Ian's turn to have dinner at Arduplan, the MacDonald's home. That small, old, sturdily walled gamekeeper's cottage stood isolated, an oasis of warm humanity defiantly set in the surrounding wilderness of heathery moors and steep hills. The nearest neighbour, an estate shepherd, lived two miles away. Happily and eagerly they set out to walk from Altdour croft on the path leading directly to Arduplan. With their two dogs in advance, they followed along above the River Aldrory, crossed by the footbridge, then continued over the moor which stretched almost to the door of Arduplan.

Had the weather been bad, Colin would have collected them in his van, but today the weather was glorious. Three days ago there had been a slight fall of snow, then a keen frost set in. The frost still held the thin powdering of snow in its crisply firm grip. This was one of those, unfortunately all too rare, perfect West Highland winter days. The beauty was breathtaking. All was calm and glittering bright. As if trying to make amends for past dourness, the sun on this last day of December gallantly tried to put some suggestion of warmth into its wintry smile. The arching sky's cloudless blue faded to a paler blue as it neared the earth then became a diaphanous milky white which met and confusingly merged with the far horizon's range of snowy hills.

Under these perfect conditions the nearer mountains slid themselves even nearer. Ever majestic Suileag excelled itself. It rose ever more imposingly, its sheer steep crowned with a sprinkling glory of snow and ice. More than ever it dominated.

On the highest part of the moor Helen and Ian halted and gazed around. After a few wondrous silent moments Helen gasped, "Oh, it's glorious! It's beautiful! It's one of the most perfect views I've ever seen."

They delighted in the silence, in the breathless stillness; all earth, all water, even the cloudless sky, was held firmly immobile in frost's keen grip. This calm perfection was especially welcome after the weeks of driving sleet and howling gales.

They walked on accompanied by the pleasant sound of their boots merrily crunching through the path's thin covering of crisp firm snow. Reaching the final heathery ridge they stopped and looked down on Arduplan.

Helen smiled, "It looks real cosy down there in its sheltered hollow, doesn't it?"

"Aye, it does. Aye, it's a truly snug wee hoose."

"Come on then, let's hurry down to enjoy its unfailing warm welcome," Helen urged.

Ian glanced at his watch, then at the descending sun hanging low in the West. "There's no hurry. It will be well worth waiting for a few minutes to see the sunset from here before we drop down to Arduplan."

They did not have long to wait. Before it sank into the sea, the mid-winter sun joyously sparkled the snow with a diamond bright glitter then warmly glowed everything in ephemeral splendour. The moors, the near mountains and distant hills blushed rosy shades of pastel pink. The Western sky caught fire; it flamed and flared. It glared burnished golds and gleaming yellows, it smouldered pale mauves and violets.

Suileag eagerly caught and passionately reflected the sunset's last splendid brilliance. For a few wondrous moments its inexorable steepness gloriously pulsed with fierce, fevered volcanic reds.

Helen and Ian stood transfixed. Silently they stared in awed wonder. The last lurid gleams of the dying sun rouged Helen's cheeks whore bright. Slowly her lips formed themselves into a warm smile. Her eyes gleamed brightly in her rapturous face. Gently she murmured, "Oh, that was wonderful! What a fantastic sunset!"

"Aye, it certainly was. Who could fail to have their senses, their 'soul', thrill at such an awesome display of beauty?"

As dusk's shadows lengthened the frost immediately increased its grip. Both humans imagined they could actually hear the keen frost stealthily consolidate its hold. Joyfully they hurried down the steep sloping path towards Arduplan.

They met Colin outside his house. He had just finished locking the hens up for the night and feeding his two fox terriers at their kennels. After the cheery greetings were over, he said, "You go away in, Helen, and see Jeannie while Ian and me put your dogs in the spare kennel."

"Aye, all right," Helen replied. "You don't need to tell me where Jeannie is; she'll be slaving over a hot stove, as usual."

Colin beamed, his hearty laughter bellowed out, "Aye, that's right. However, did you ken, Helen?"

As he spread fresh straw inside the kennel, Ian again enjoyed breathing its delightful sweet scent, which seemed to hold and give out the glory of sun-warmed summer days. After brushing a few stray wisps of straw from their clothes, the two men started towards the house.

Gleaming brightly through dusk's shadowy dimness the lights from Arduplan's windows gave a cheery promise of hospitable welcome. So too did the glorious, the uniquely distinctive scent of the peat smoke languorously rising from and hovering over the small house.

As he entered the warm, cosy sitting room where the peat fire genially glowed, Ian called out a merry greeting to Jeannie in the scullery, then added, "My, Jeannie, that's a real grand smell coming from in there. No need to ask what's cooking."

"Och, it's nothing special," she modestly disclaimed. "You'll just have tae take pot luck."

Ian laughed, "Oh, Jeannie, we know your 'pot luck' of old: it's always a mouth-watering pot of luscious culinary gold."

Helen chuckled her wholeheartedly approbation, "Aye, that's true, Ian, you expressed our feelings well, and in rhyme too!"

While Colin was happily pouring out two drams and two sherries, Helen and Ian were busily employed in taking off their boots and putting on shoes. Ian had carried these shoes in his rucksack along with some gifts and – the vital item – a bottle of whisky.

Colin laughed, "You would think you were going tae kirk. That's what the auld folk used tae dae after walking miles to kirk in big boots or wellies. They changed into their sabbath shoes before entering the House of God."

"Aye, I know," Ian grinned, "but I'm sure it'll be much more entertaining here than in any kirk."

Jeannie came out from the hot and steamy small scullery. Her rosy cheeks were flushed brighter than ever. Soon they were all comfortably seated. Once the first toast of 'Slainte mhath' had been given and the first gulps swallowed, their first comments, as usual, were on the weather. Helen vigorously described the joy of their walk and the glory of the sunset in today's perfect conditions. "Aye, the weather really was perfect," Ian said. "It is great to have such clear, calm frosty conditions, especially after all the awful weeks of gales and sleet."

"Aye, that was real course, savage, treacherous weather," Jeannie said.

"Aye, yon was real Campbell weather," Colin grinned.

"Oh, Colin MacDonald... Colin MacDonald, will you never forget, never forgive, the Campbells?" his wife gasped through her laughter. Then, turning to Helen, she excitedly exclaimed, "Have you heard the news about Campbell-Fotheringay?"

"No... no, we haven't heard anything about him. What has that damned laird been up to now?"

Colin interrupted, smiling, "How can you expect to hear all the latest news when you don't have a television or a phone in your house?"

Helen laughed in reply, "Och, one way or another we hear the news sooner or later."

"Aye," Ian agreed, "we find that that hearing things a day or two late doesn't make any real difference. Anyway we do have our old wireless to keep us in touch."

Colin grinned, he deliberately broadened his accent, "Och man… man, you're chust a thrawn auld bugger, with your damned auld-fashioned 'wireless'."

Unable to restrain herself any longer, Jeannie dramatically burst out with her news, "Campbell-Fotheringay is being investigated by the London police for murder!"

"For murder?" Helen and Ian gasped together.

"Aye, for murder," Jeannie confirmed, fair delighted with the sensation her startling announcement was causing.

"You didn't tell me about this when we were outside, Colin," Ian said.

"No, I ken I didn't," he replied, grinning at his wife, "I promised Jeannie I would say nothing. I agreed to let her tell you. She was fair cock-a-hoop at the thought of what a fantastic piece of news she had to disclose."

"Aye," Jeannie said, "I was praying that no one told you the news before I did. I was wanting to surprise you!"

Helen laughed, "Well, you've succeeded. You've certainly surprised me."

"Aye, me too," Ian agreed. After thinking for a few moments, he added, "Although I suppose we shouldn't really be surprised. Campbell-Fotheringay is such a rotten bastard that it is not out of character for him to commit any crime, not even the worse of crimes – murder."

The others nodded in agreement, then Helen asked, "But what happened? Who has he murdered?"

Jeannie told the story as reported on the television news and in the newspapers.

There had been a party at Campbell-Fotheringay's flat in London's fashionable Mayfair. Some twenty people had been there, mostly young people connected to 'showbiz'. It seemed it was a really wild party, an orgy of unlimited drinks, drugs and sex. During the course of it, sometime in the early morning, a nineteen-year-old girl had fallen to her death from the third storey balcony of the flat.

There was confusion over what had happened. Campbell-Fotheringay claimed to have been alarmed at seeing the girl leaning dangerously far over the balcony railing. He had dashed to try to pull her to safety, but he was too late, she toppled over just before he reached her.

At least two witnesses claimed to have seen him push her over the railing.

She has been a girlfriend of Campbell-Fotheringay's, but recently he had given her up. There had been many violently acrimonious scenes between them in public.

This girl who had met such a violent death was the daughter of a Tory Member of Parliament who had been a junior minister in Mrs Thatcher's government. She had also been an actress with a minor role in a popular TV 'soap'. These facts accounted for the large amount of media coverage her death was receiving.

"The police will have a difficult task to establish what really happened if all the witnesses were 'high' on drugs and drink, won't they?" Ian asked.

"Aye, exactly," Colin agreed, "that's probably why he'll get away with it, even if he did commit murder."

"Aye, trust him, the rotten bastard, he will get away with it, I bet," Ian savagely exclaimed.

"Och, don't worry, Ian, he will get his just deserts sometime sooner or later; if not for this crime then for something else." Helen stated most convincingly. She turned to Jeannie, "Has he been arrested and charged with murder?"

"Oh no. Not so far. According to the news he is merely, 'assisting the police with their enquiries'."

"I bet he did it, and I bet he will get away with it too, the rotten bastard!" Ian vehemently repeated.

Helen glanced uneasily at him; she again worried that he was getting too obsessive in his hatred of Campbell-Fortheringay.

Jeannie and Colin sensed her unease. There was a short silence then Colin's voice boomed out, "Och, this isn't a very cheerful subject for New Year's Eve, is it?" Turning to his wife he asked, with a rueful grin, "Isn't the dinner aboot ready yet, wifie? I'm gey hungry, I haven't eaten much all day. I've been starving myself in preparation for tonight's special dinner."

As Jeannie got to her feet she laughed, "Och, trust you, Colin, you're aye thinking aboot your stomach."

"Aye, and there's plenty o' it tae think aboot," Ian laughed.

"Och, it's gey empty the noo, anyway," Colin beamed as he complacently and loudly slapped his strong hands over his large belly. "There, did you hear it boom like an empty big bass drum?"

Ten minutes later the four of them were happily seated around the old, solid oak kitchen table, which had been pulled out into the centre of the room. Joyfully, and in the case of Colin and Ian, very eagerly, they all dipped their spoons into the large plate of steaming hot Scotch broth set before them. After a few spoonfuls, Ian paused and declared, "My, Jeannie, that's real braw soup. No one can make guid auld Scotch broth like you do."

Helen, too, joined in with sincere praise, "Aye, that's right. It really is great broth, Jeannie. It has something special – a unique taste that I can never quite manage to achieve in my broth."

Jeannie, her honest rosy cheeks beaming, modestly exclaimed, "Och, it's nothing special. I just make my broth the way my mother made hers; real thick, with plenty o' guid home grown vegetables in it."

Ian laughed, "There certainly are plenty o' vegetables in it, my spoon can stand upright by itself!"

While the others were speaking, Colin concentrated on keeping his spoon industriously moving from plate to mouth and from mouth back to plate. Pausing for a moment with the full spoon halfway to his mouth and with his eyes gleaming brightly, he declared, "Aye, it is a braw broth. It's too damned good to waste time talking about it. The best praise we can gie it is to sup it all up and leave oor plates scraped clean."

Soon all their plates were empty. All refused Jeannie's offer of second helpings. Ian grinned, "We have tae leave room for what's to follow. We know how generous your helpings of venison casserole are."

And so they were.

"Reach oot and help yourselves," Jeannie hospitality ordered as she placed a generously heaped dish of large potatoes on the centre of the table.

While Helen stretched out and took a potato, Colin laughed, "That's what I love tae see – laughing tatties!"

Although they had heard him say this on many similar occasions, the others dutifully joined in his laughter as they eagerly helped themselves to the 'laughing tatties'. That steaming heap of potatoes, boiled in their skins, joined in the festive spirit and – as Colin described it – split their sides with laughter. They were those great old favourites, King Edwards. They appetizingly flaunted their succulently white, dry and floury crumbling flesh from their burst skins.

Like all the other vegetables, those potatoes were home grown and fresh from Arduplan's highly productive, expertly and lovingly tended kitchen garden. The venison too was, in a sense, home grown. Colin, with Ian's willing assistance, had shot a mature hind on the moors a mile or so behind his house. After hanging for three days in his barn that venison was in prime condition for Jeannie to transmute it into this excellent, mouth-watering casserole.

After a few minutes of silence – a silence broken only by the loud clatter of busy knives and forks and the hearty munching of food – Helen laughed, "Oh, Jeannie, we don't get much conversation from those men-folk o' oors, when they're so greedily eating, do we?"

"Och no, we certainly don't. Obviously there's nothing the matter with their appetites."

Ian momentarily paused in his chewing and grinned broadly, "Our hearty eating is a noble tribute to the excellence of your cooking, Jeannie."

Jeannie smiled at Helen, "I think they truly do like that food."

Colin's mouth was delightfully full, his ruddy cheeks bulged, with knife and fork poised, out of use for a few moments but held ready for further assault, he gulped down his mouthful of glorious food and exclaimed, "Och man, you can keep all yon foreign muck – all those fiery curries, all those sweet and sours, yon fancy Chinese foods in their ridiculous dainty wee dishes; none o' them can compare with this simple, honest, guid auld Scots food so generously set before us."

Half an hour later their plates lay empty… all were scraped clean, all were completely, nobly and appreciatively empty.

Ian sighed with deep contentment, "It's truly a grand thing to be blessed with a healthy appetite. Eating good food is surely one of the greatest pleasures in life… perhaps the greatest? It's the only pleasure that lasts our entire life, isn't it? It starts when we are babes suckling our mother's milk and lasts right until we are geriatric, with no other pleasure left us."

Nodding in agreement, Colin added, "Aye, but hopefully the real pleasure o' drinking drams well remain with us too, even when we are geriatric."

Colin and Ian helped carry the dishes into the small scullery. As Jeannie and Helen tied on aprons in preparation for washing up, Colin, standing by the sink, asked, "Can I be of any further help to you?"

Jeannie grinned at Helen, "He doesn't sound all that enthusiastic in his offer of help, does he?"

"No, he certainly doesn't. Nor does Ian seem very keen to help, either."

Ian was lingering at the entrance to the scullery. He was casting longing glances at the bottles of whisky and the cigars lying waiting in the sitting room. He thought they looked sadly neglected.

Jeannie laughed, "Och, just get oot o' my scullery, Colin. There's little enough room in it for just Helen and me. There's certainly no space in here for you with that huge belly of yours. It's aboot time you went on a strict diet again."

Colin beamed, "Aye, maybe I'll go on a diet right enough... but only after I've finished off all the broth, venison and tatties remaining in these pots there. Anyway, I don't think my belly is really all that huge, it's just a wee bit bloated after that grand dinner."

"Oh, get out o' here and let me in to the sink. You two men go and have your smoke, Helen and me will soon clear up in here."

Colin needed no second telling. As he squeezed past Jeannie he laughed, "Good, that's what I hoped you'd say."

Jeannie grinned good humouredly at Helen, "Och, men!... Aren't they useless these men?"

"Aye, they are... they certainly are! I don't know why we women bother with them at all."

As Colin moved into the security of the sitting room he chuckled, "Och, wifies, stop blethering such nonsense. Ye ken you women would be completely lost without us men."

Helen and Jeannie disdained to reply to that blatantly blasphemous male chauvinism. They contented themselves with exchanging meaningful, condescendingly superior feminine smiles.

As they set to and started washing up the dishes, Jeannie said, "I don't like seeing a man working at the kitchen sink. I don't think it's really a man's place, do you?"

"No, I don't," Helen glanced into the sitting room to make sure they were not being overheard. "I think there's something terribly sissy about any man who likes working in the kitchen or doing the housework."

"Aye, I agree... it's hardly work for a real man, is it?" Jeannie smiled, "Alison gets annoyed at me, she says I'm far too old fashioned." (Alison was her twenty-six year old married daughter.) "Och well, perhaps I am. Anyway I prefer my old fashioned ways; I'm happier with them, and at my age I'm not going to change my ways just to be in the fashion."

"No nor am I. And all those new fangled feminist ideas which destroy the old, well-established roles of husband and wife don't seem to bring much happiness or contentment to their modern 'with it' marriages, do they?"

"No, they don't… they certainly don't. What with all their divorces, separations, living with 'partners', re-marriages and all that nonsense, they can hardly have much contentment. I feel sorry for the children of those broken marriages, with the security of their home and the love and care of both their parents suddenly shattered. It must be terribly upsetting for them." This time Jeannie peeped into the sitting room and, after satisfying herself that the husbands were not listening, quietly, confidentially continued, "To tell the truth we've been most fortunate with our men, haven't we? We've both had thirty years of happy marriage. That's much more than many – if any – of the young ones are likely to have."

"Aye, that's true, we really have been most fortunate with our men folk." Helen smiled roguishly, "But, of course, it would never do to tell them that."

"Och no!" Jeannie gasped, shocked at the very idea, "Och no, of course not!"

Contentedly they continued their work in the scullery. They felt happily enveloped in a cosily conspiratorial atmosphere of true, deep, feminine friendship.

Ian and Colin had comfortably settled themselves at either side of the fireplace. Each lovingly caressed a glass of whisky in one hand and urbanely embraced a cigar with two fingers of the other hand. Elegant columns of bluish/grey smoke lazily rose towards the low ceiling and with amiable condescension mingled their luxurious aroma with the plebeian scent of the peat smoke modestly spiralling up from the cheery fire.

Above the mantelpiece hung one of Ian's large oil paintings, a gift given many years ago to Jeannie and Colin. It was a faithful copy of Landseer's 'Monarch of the Glen'. The Royal Stag stared masterfully and majestically around him, a true 'Monarch of all he surveyed'. With the passage of time, peat and tobacco smoked had darkened the painting to a mellow Rembrandt like quality; that was how Ian described it; unkinder critics declared the red-bodied stag was ruddy well kippered.

"Ah," Ian contentedly sighed, "Life has its compensations, hasn't it?"

"Aye, it has," Colin readily agreed as he took another gulp of the fine mellow malt whisky then drew strongly on his affluent cigar. He settled himself even more comfortably in his deep armchair, stretched his legs further out towards the peat fire, blew out an euphoric cloud of smoke, grinned and winked at Ian, "Aye, man, life certainly has its compensations."

A while later, their glasses drained, their cigars smoked out, they rose and surrendered the fireside armchairs to Jeannie and Helen, as, rolling down their sleeves, they came through from the scullery.

"My, those men were gey comfortable in here," Helen remarked.

"Aye, they were, but now it's our turn tae put oor feet up," Jeannie smiled.

Soon all four were comfortably settled and each easefully nursed a glass of whisky. How strongly all in that cosy small room felt the heart-warming glow, the deep camaraderie, of their informal friendship. For thirty years those two contentedly married couples had been sincere friends, while Colin and Ian's friendship went even further back – right back to earliest schooldays.

Suddenly Helen exclaimed, "Oh Jeannie, you promised to tell us about your Christmas holiday. Now we're all settled together again, let's hear all about it."

With willing eagerness Jeannie and Colin between them told of the pleasant four days they had spent with their son, Alasdair, his wife Sheila, and their three-month-old baby. This baby boy, Colin, was there first grandchild. They were delighted with him.

Jeannie explained to Helen in detailed and, so it seemed to Ian, somewhat excessive length, all the wonders of her grandson's marvellous features. Lovingly she described the colour of his eyes and hair, the strength and sturdiness of his limbs, the glory of his winning smile. There had never been a baby like him!

Colin patiently waited for her fresh grandmotherly enthusiasms to run their course, then started telling Ian of the marvellous dinner they had eaten on Christmas day, of the fantastic amount and variety of drinks they had consumed.

Colin's thirty-year-old son, Alasdair, was also a gamekeeper. He had never desired to be anything but a gamekeeper. Colin was undemonstratively delighted that his son was following him and his grandfather and great-grandfather to become the fourth generation of gamekeepers in the family. Such a family tradition used to be fairly common in the Highlands. It was now rare. Colin secretly hoped that his grandson would in due course become the fifth generation gamekeeper in the family. Probably this feeling was a simple desire for something like permanence in this all too impermanent life. He felt the reassuring continuity of the successive generations of gamekeepers to be a fundamentally fine thing in this time of too much, too rapid, change. Or, he wondered, was his increasing dislike of so much change merely another sign of his ageing?

His son had repeatedly told him how different, how much better, this estate he now worked on was compared to all other estates he had experience of. Colin had been amazed to learn the truth of this for himself.

For more than two years, Alasdair MacDonald had been employed, one of four gamekeepers, on a sporting estate in Wester Ross. This large estate was owned by Mr Jan Van Hoogstraeten, a Dutch multi-millionaire. During the eight years he had owned the estate, he had spent large sums on improving it. He was a keen sportsman and conservationist. Under his guidance, by a strictly selective programme of extensive culling, the excessive numbers of red deer on the estate had been reduced. As a direct result, and by judicious, and expensive, winter feeding, the remaining healthy herds of stags and hinds were greatly improved in condition and weight.

On other parts of the estate miles of high fencing had been erected to exclude deer. In these fenced off areas whole new forests of native Highland trees were thriving.

Being a good landowner, that wealthy Dutchman had wisely not neglected to improve conditions for the members of the human species living on his estate. No expense had been spared in improving the houses of all his estate employees. New bathrooms, better kitchens and extra bedrooms had been added. Whenever possible local builders had been employed. Old grey slates were used to keep the traditional character of the houses. A number of entirely new houses had been built. These timber homes were of solid log construction. They too blended well with the wild landscape. A few secluded holiday chalets had also been built, each with its rowing boat on an adjoining trout loch.

That Christmas holiday was the fist time Colin and Jeannie had visited their son and his wife since they had moved to this estate. After driving up the twisting five mile private road leading to the estate's imposing, many turreted, grey stoned Victorian style shooting lodge they continued for another quarter mile to Alasdair's attractive new log house. Once the warm greetings and the loudest of the wild gushings over the baby were over, Colin and Alasdair stood gazing through the lounge's large window at the magnificent view across a tree-lined loch to the imposing Torridon mountains. Freshly snow covered, these steep mountains shone most impressively in the glaring winter sunshine.

When informed by their son that they were invited by Mr & Mrs Van Hoogstraeten to Christmas dinner at the lodge, Jeannie and Colin's startled reaction was exactly as their son and daughter-in-law had expected. They were astonished at this most unexpected invitation.

"Oh, we can't have dinner with the gentry in the big house!" Jeannie instantly declared. "We would feel completely out of place there with them."

"Alasdair and I are going," Sheila said.

Relieved, Jeannie grinned, "Oh well, in that case Colin and me will stay here and baby-sit with wee Colin."

"Oh no you won't," Sheila smiled in reply, "I've got the baby-sitter all arranged. You're both coming with us to have dinner with the 'gentry' in the 'big house'."

"Yes," Alasdair confirmed, "you're coming with us. The boss – Mr Van Hoogstraeten – and his wife are looking forward to meeting you both. You'll find them very friendly and unassuming." He addressed his father, "You've brought your pipes and kilt with you, haven't you?"

"Oh aye, I have. When you phoned you told me to be sure to bring them."

"Good! The boss will ask you to play your pipes sometime. Although Dutch, he's keen on encouraging Scottish music and traditions. In some ways he's more Scottish than many Scots." Seeing that his parents were still apprehensive at the thought of dining with 'the gentry', he tried to reassure them by explaining that all the gamekeepers employed on the estate, with their wives, would be sharing that Christmas dinner with them. "When we're all together like that the boss, and his wealthy Dutch guests, make no difference between 'the gentry' and 'the commoners'. You'll be amazed at how quickly they put you at ease. And there will be great food and even greater drink at that dinner." Grinning at his father, he added as an extra inducement, "There will be an unlimited supply of the very best mature old malt whisky."

This last tempting bait was irresistible. Colin beamed at his wife, "Och, Jeannie, I think we should force ourselves to go!"

Resignedly, Jeannie sighed and slowly shook her head, "Och, I don't suppose wild horses could keep 'himself' away from that dinner now."

"No, nor drag him away once he gets started on the malt whisky," Alasdair laughed.

After being introduced to Mr & Mrs Van Hoogstraeten and their friends, a Dutch Count and Countess, and to the gamekeepers and their wives, Jeannie and Colin were comfortably seated with them all in the large lounge of the shooting lodge. They soon felt completely relaxed in the pleasantly informal atmosphere. The generously filled glasses of vintage champagne helped, in no small measure, to engender the feeling of companionable friendship.

After all had helped the Van Hoogstraeten's personal Dutch chef carry the laden dishes through to the dining room and all, including the chef, were seated at the massive antique oak table, many bottles of excellent red and white wines were quickly emptied and played their part in further enlivening the happily friendly mood.

Once all the wonderful food was eaten and the dishes disposed of in two large dishwashers the party returned to the comfortable lounge. The brightly gleaming eyes of the Highland gamekeepers gleamed even brighter as generous drams of mature whisky were poured... the real drinking was now about to begin. The toast of 'Slainte mhath' was again heartily given, whisky was gulped, lips were loudly and appreciatively smacked. Havana cigars were handed round. More wood was heaped on the glowing fire. Laughter rose louder. Eager talk got more animated and as the hours happily flew by got less distinct, got joyously and carelessly slurred.

Jeannie continued the story of their Christmas holiday by asking, "Remember that time with Lord and Lady Kilvert when they showed us their fishing and travel cine-films? Remember how, although quite pleasant, it really was very formal with all of us constantly being on our best behaviour?"

"Oh yes, I remember it fine," Helen said. "It was just too formal to be truly enjoyable, wasn't it?

"Aye, exactly," Jeannie said. "Well, it really was amazing how completely different that dinner with those Dutch millionaires was. There was nothing in the least snobbish about them; no hint of any class divisions and it certainly was not in the least formal. We were a Jock Tamson's bairns' the-gither."

Colin nodded his agreement then warmly enthused, "Aye, and the Dutchman was much more generous with his drinks than Lord Kilvert was yon time. Och, yet despite that meanness with drinks, Lord Kilvert isn't a bad employer. There are a lot worse lairds than him."

"Aye, that bastard, Campbell-Fotheringay, for one!" Ian exclaimed. "Isn't it sadly ironic that of those three lairds the best one obviously is that Dutchman; the second best is Lord Kilvert, an Englishman; the worst, by far the worst, is Campbell-Fotheringay, a Scotsman?"

"Aye, it is," Colin said. "Although of course Campbell-Fotheringay is only partly Scottish. He's half English and half Scots. Aye, and unfortunately his

Scots blood is the worst of Scottish blood – is damned, devil tainted Campbell blood!"

Jeannie shook her head, grinned and once again asked, "Oh, Colin… Colin, will you never forget or forgive what the Campbells did to your MacDonald ancestors in Glencoe? After all, it happened nearly three hundred years ago."

Colin grinned, "All right… all right, I'll say no more about that infamous massacre carried oot by those Campbells: or Cambeuls, as is their correct Gaelic name, which, as you ken, means 'those of the twisted mouth'.."

Jeannie, Helen and Ian burst into loud laughter. Then Ian asked, "I suppose those twisted mouthed Campbells all speak with forked tongues, do they Colin?"

"Aye, they do, they certainly do?" Colin replied. Then self-mockingly, laughed at the foolish solemnity of his reply. "Anyway," he continued, "Alasdair has done real well for himself by getting taken on by that wealthy Dutchman. Did I tell you aboot the special treat the retiring gamekeeper, who Alasdair took over from, got from his boss?"

"No, you didn't, Helen said, "what was it?"

"Well, in addition to getting a good retirement pension and a generous farewell bonus that 'keeper got an all expenses paid holiday of a lifetime. He flew on a specially chartered executive jet from London direct to Miami as a guest of Mr Van Hoogenstraeten, who was on a business-come-pleasure trip to Florida. While the Dutch millionaire attended to his leisure interests in Miami and Orlando, that gamekeeper explored the Everglades National Park. Then the next seven days he spent as a guest of his boss on a large and luxurious motor yacht cruising in the Caribbean. A smaller boat was also chartered for big game fishing. The quality and the unlimited quantity of the food and drink on that yacht was, to that keeper at least, truly exceptional. He was treated as an equal as he swam and fished and ate and drank with his boss and the other wealthy guests."

Jeannie now took up the story, "Aye, and that's not the only outstanding holiday the Dutchman arranges for his employees. Every summer the head gamekeeper and his wife fly to Greece and have the use of their boss's private yacht, complete with crew, to go sailing amongst the Aegean islands."

"Oh, that's amazing," Helen exclaimed. "Alasdair certainly is most fortunate to have such an exceptional boss. There can be very few bosses, very few landowners, like him. I can never imagine any of the wealthy British upper class gentry being so outstandingly generous, being so outstandingly democratic and so completely un-class conscious."

Ian had been listening silently and thoughtfully, he now spoke up, "Aye, I agree it is amazing, is almost incredible, to hear of such a good laird. I only wish to God there were many more like him."

Colin nodded, "Aye, man, it would be chust braw to have a laird like him, wouldn't it?"

"You know," Helen said, "hopefully that Dutch millionaire might be the start of a new, a much better, type of Highland estate owner." Warming to this theme her voice rose excitedly, "If our horrid laird, Campbell-Fotheringay, is a murderer, is charged and found guilty, is jailed for years, then surely his Aldrory Estate will be put up for sale. That would be Ron MacDonald's chance to buy it. We know how keen he is to own the estate, to own the actual land which his ancestors were cruelly and shamefully driven from last century. He would be an excellent laird. He would put new hope, new life, new prosperity into the place."

Fired by her enthusiasm, Ian eagerly agreed, "Aye, Ron would be a great laird. He would transform the estate. He…"

Colin interrupted him, "Is he really rich enough to buy the estate? Do you really think he will?"

Helen instantly answered, "Yes, he is!… Yes, he will!"

Impressed by her certainty, the others silently waited for her to continue, but she said no more. She lifted her glass, smiled enigmatically, and then sipped her dram.

Chapter Fourteen

Now, one hour before midnight, the cosy small sitting room at Arduplan was arranged ready for the many expected Hogmanay revellers. Chairs had been brought in from bedrooms; the solid oak kitchen table was placed against the back wall and was heavily laden. There were bottles of whisky and cans of beer. There were innumerable plates heaped high with sandwiches, with Jeannie's home-made scones and oatcakes, with shortbread and black-bun.

Grinning, Ian said, "That sturdy old table is groaning under its gargantuan hospitable load of food and drink."

"Aye, there's enough to feed an army!" Helen agreed.

Well pleased, Jeannie smiled modestly, "Och, if we have our usual flood of visitors after midnight we'll soon get through that lot."

"My, this crowdie cheese of yours is really excellent, Jeannie," Helen enthused as she ate a small piece. "Surely you'll win first prize at the games next summer with it. Auld Maggie's crowdie can't win it every time, can it?"

"Och, we'll just have to wait and see if I can beat Auld Maggie at last," Jeannie said, then openly and honestly added, "I hope I do."

For the last two years Auld Maggie Gunn's crowdie cheese had won first prize at the home-made products competition at Inveraldrory Highland Games. The judges remarked on her cheese having some special unique flavour that set it apart. From the judges, and from everyone else, Auld Maggie jealously guarded the secret of how her crowdie acquired its special flavour. Jeannie's crowdie had twice won second prize.

Later, as they all again sat around the glowing peat fire, Jeannie dreamily murmured, "I think this is the best part of the Hogmanay celebrations; the four of us having a few quiet drams, happily reminiscing and once more re-telling the familiar old tales."

"Aye, and some of us forever re-telling the same old jokes," Helen said, smiling accusingly at her husband.

Ian smiled back, "Ah weel, I suppose it's inevitable that after thirty years together we have heard each other's jokes, each other's stories, over and over again."

"I agree with you, Jeannie," Helen said. "Each year I increasingly enjoy these quiet few hours before all the noisy exuberance after midnight. Och, I suppose it's just another sign of us all getting old, isn't it?... us delighting in this calm before the storm."

Colin laughed, "I enjoy these quiet hours too; but I still like to keep up the guid auld traditions. I love to noisily greet the new year and to hospitably welcome many first-footers into oor humble hame."

"Aye, it would be terrible if all the grand auld traditions were to die out," Ian agreed. Then, grinning slyly, remarked, "I notice you've not got any bottles of Colonel Moorcoomb's famous Barley Wine set out on your hospitable table, Colin.

"No, I haven't. I think that Barley Wine of his is only worth drinking when there's nothing better to drink."

Ian nodded, "Aye, that's true. Remember the first time the colonel gave us a bottle of that Barley Wine? He thought he was bestowing a very great benefit on us, didn't he?"

"Aye, he did… Aye, I remember it fine," Colin laughed.

It had happened about ten years ago. Colonel Moorcoomb and his old friend Major Wisden, rented one week's salmon fishing on the River Aldrory from Lord Kilvert each year. Colin and Ian usually ghillied for them.

Inevitably, that retired colonel and major were known as "Morecambe and Wise". At times they were almost as funny as that famous comic duo. They both had a fine active sense of humour and they and their ghillies shared many a laugh together. They certainly were not typical English "officers and gentlemen". There was nothing in the least snobbish about them. They both came from the North of England, which probably explained their lack of snobbishness. They really enjoyed getting away for a while from their sun-loving wives – or, as the colonel ungallantly called them – "their fire-breathing dragons". The wives went off together to much hotter and drier climates than the Scottish Highlands.

Colonel Moorcoomb was fortunate enough to own a small brewery. It had been owned by his family for many generations.

That year, at the end of the first day's fishing, the two ghillies waited at the parked cars before they all left the river. Eagerly and expectantly they watched the colonel open a cardboard box and lift out a small bottle. He smiled at Colin and explained, "This is a new line we have developed at my brewery. It's a special strong beer called 'Barley Wine'. It's very strong and very bitter."

He handed the small dark bottle to Colin.

Colin carefully inspected it. It was very small, about the size of a 'Babycham'. It looked tiny; it seemed to have shrunk, as it nestled in the palm of Colin's large hand.

"That one bottle of Barley Wine is equal in strength to a double whisky," the colonel enthusiastically extolled. "Now, what would you like, Colin, that bottle of Barley Wine, or a dram?"

Colin took his time about replying. He slowly turned the small bottle over in his powerful hand and thoughtfully continued to inspect it. Slowly he raised his eyes and silently gazed at Colonel Moorcoomb. His mouth broke into a broad smile. His eyes twinkled.

The colonel, Major Wisden and Ian waited patiently for Colin's well-considered reply. Knowing him, they expected him to come out with some appropriate humorous remark.

They were not disappointed.

"Och well now, Colonel," Colin said in a slow, deliberate, judicious voice, "I'm sure a *wee* bottle of your Barley Wine would be very nice... *after* a double whisky!"

Once again Colin and Ian laughed heartily at that well remembered story. Jeannie and Helen joined in the laughter. "We've heard that tale many times, haven't we, Helen?" Jeannie asked.

"Aye, we have... many, many times!"

"Och well, it's a story well worth the re-telling," Ian grinned. "And as a reward we both got not one, but two, wee bottles of the colonel's special Barley Wine after getting a good dram first. The colonel and the major were really tickled by your reply, Colin."

The final hour of the old year passed quickly and pleasantly as they laughed over other old, well-loved, re-told tales.

The large old wooden 'wag-o'-the-wa' clock which had been Jeannie's mother's, continued relentlessly scything time with its smooth swinging heavy brass pendulum. To and fro... to and fro, it ceaselessly swung as it had swung through many lives, through many generations. Gathering up its energy it wheezily cleared its throat then coughed out tremulous gobs of sound. Twelve times it coughed then, exhausted by the tremendous effort, fell into weary, scything slumber.

All jumped to their feet and warmly saluted one another, then Colin and Ian hurried to a bedroom. Ian lifted the shotgun and two cartridges while Colin gathered up his set of bagpipes. Keen to welcome in the new year in the traditional old Highland way, they strode a few yards out from the front door.

Ian raised the shotgun to his shoulder and fired one barrel high into the calm frosty air. That shot sped the sad old year on its way. He fired the other barrel. That shot loudly and joyously welcomed in the bright new year.

Rudely awakened, all the dogs in the kennels violently leapt and savagely barked. Their barking drowned out the noise of the hoofs of alarmed stags and hinds beyond the high deer fence as they crunched through the crisp frozen snow. Ian and Colin watched these shadowy semi-tame, winter-fed deer as they stampeded off in a panic and disappeared into the moonlit night.

Colin inflated the bag of his pipes and started playing. Although large and thick, his strong fingers danced with surprising lissom grace over the holes of the chanter. Fortunately the rheumatics increasingly affecting his legs had not spread to his fingers.

Jeannie and Helen stood at the door and happily listened as Colin played through a variety of lively pipe tunes. After five minutes he stopped and they all waited expectantly listening in the sudden still silence.

They had not long to wait.

With sudden sharp precision two shots again startled the frozen moon-bright landscape. They were followed almost immediately by the sound of an accordion repeating some of the tunes Colin had played.

They smiled at one another in the frosty dimness and Colin said, "Good old Jamie, he, too, keeps up the old traditions."

That shepherd, Jamie Gordon, with his wife, Bella, were their nearest neighbours. They lived two miles away. Almost invariably they were the first visitors at Arduplan after this noisy New Year ritual had been performed.

Less than ten minutes later the cheery tooting of a vehicle's horn announced their arrival.

Bella and Jamie Gordon uproariously invaded the room and overflowed it with a tempestuous flood of boisterous high spirits.

Noisily, warmly, sincerely, they all greeted one another. Jamie was a jovial barrel of a man. He was middle-aged and of medium height. His cheery deep voice and unrestrained laughter proclaimed his lusty enjoyment of life. He was well matched in his wife, Bella. She was a vivacious merry creature who enjoyed a joke and un-maliciously revelled in discussing all the latest local gossip and scandal. Her stout figure was getting increasingly stout, or – as she insisted, with her homely face dimpling into smiles – was just getting "pleasantly plump".

Her husband agreed. Slipping an arm around her voluptuous waist he hugged her to him and merrily declared, "You're ay getting ever mair temptingly plump an' cuddlesome, ye ken."

For a moment Bella smiled up at him with tender affectionate eyes, then cheerily cried, "Och, stop it… stop it, you muckle great gomoral!" As she pushed him away her loud laugher volcanically erupted from the heaving slopes of her ample bosom.

When they were all seated with a glass in one hand and food in the other, Helen remarked, "That's a lovely wee locket you're wearing, Bella."

With childlike innocent enthusiasm Bella replied, "Aye, it's bonny… it's real bonny, isn't it?" She unfastened the chain and handed the locket to Helen, stating proudly, "It's real gold ye ken. It was Jamie's maithers. It opens up and there's a bonny wee picture o' his maither an' faither inside, see."

After Helen and Jeannie had admired and suitably praised her golden locket, Bella complacently fitted the chain around her neck and adjusted the locket so that it rested comfortably on her vast bosom.

Ian smiled at her, "That locket's real gold, is it?"

"Aye, it is. It's pure gold, ye ken."

For some moments Ian stared at it as it rested so snugly in the hollow – more a wide valley than a neat cleavage – between the impressive mountain peaks of Bella's fecund breasts. Grinning impishly he said, "Well, in that case all I can say is (imitating an American accent) 'There's gold in them thar hills'!"

Shaking her fist at him, Bella exclaimed, "Oh, you cheeky deil!" then her laughter burst out and joined in with all the other laughter cascading around the room.

Soon she was eagerly and excitedly gossiping about the latest scandal of Campbell-Fotheringay, with his wild orgy of drink and drugs and sex leading now, possibly, to a horrendous murder. "Although whit else can a' body expect wi' a' they awful carry-on's doon in London – yon sinful den o'iniquity?" she gleefully asked.

Later, each time new visitors arrived, that scandal was again brought up, was again animatedly discussed and Campbell-Fotheringay's excessive, licentious, probably murderous, indulgences once more roundly condemned. Then the question of what would happen to his Highland estate if he actually was a murderer and was given a long jail sentence was repeatedly speculated upon. All, to a greater or lesser degree, would be affected by what became of him and of his Aldrory Estate.

Four visitors more concerned than most were two middle-aged married couples, the Frasers and the McKinnons. John and May Fraser had the only grocer's shop in Inveraldrory village. Robert and Anne McKinnon had the only garage and petrol pumps in the village. They rented their shop and their garage from Campbell-Fotheringay. Over the years they had tried to either purchase these properties outright or hold them on a long lease, but Campbell-Fotheringay always curtly refused them these requests.

The short leases on the garage and the shop expired at Martinmas (November) in this fresh new year of 1984. The McKinnons and the Frasers were increasingly worried by constant rumours that Campbell-Fotheringay was intending to sell both these properties to wealthy incomers at prices which they, the locals, could not afford. Most of his estate houses had already been sold in this way.

Anne McKinnon quietly confided her increasing fears to Helen and Ian. They tried to reassure her. Eventually, Helen grasped Anne's hand, stared steadily into her eyes, and with convincing certainty stated, "Things will work out all right, Anne, I assure you they will. Try not to worry about it."

Anne was most impressed. She stared silently and wonderingly at Helen.

"Aye, lass, don't worry. What wee Helen says is true. Yon damned Campbell laird will get what he bloody well deserves before long." Old Murdo Munro had been intently listening; he too spoke with profound conviction. Old Murdo was really old; he boasted of being ninety-four years of age, although his family thought him only ninety-one. A retired gamekeeper, he was, and revelled in being, a real 'worthie', one of the all too few individuals of unique character left in this age of so much dull conformity. Suddenly he grinned widely, proudly revealed his bright new set of false teeth, and complained, "Och, but this is gey dreary talk for Hogmanay. Come on Anne, lass, gie us a cheery sang."

Smiling, she refused, "Och, no, not yet, Murdo, I've not had enough whisky yet to get me going. Later, once I'm properly lubricated, you won't get me to stop."

"My accordion's oot in the Land Rover, you ken; I'll fetch it in an' gie you a braw tune or twa," Jamie Gordon eagerly volunteered.

Melodramatically, Colin loudly, groaned, "Och man, you better chust leave your damned accordion where it is, oot in the Land Rover. That's the best place for it – unseen and unheard!"

This was a familiar old dispute. Colin loudly claimed the bagpipes as the best of musical instruments and pretended to despise the accordion. Jamie vehemently praised the accordion and pretended to despise the bagpipes. This friendly and lively controversy dated from the first time these men met, nine years ago, when Jamie had moved from his native Aberdeenshire to work as a shepherd on Lord Kilvert's Ardgie Estate. "Och, Colin, man, you're haivering," he laughed. "You don't appreciate braw music brawly played on the greatest musical instrument – the accordion."

Grinning broadly, Ian intervened, "Och, Jamie, I suppose you'll next be claiming that tartan you're wearing is the tartan of the greatest Scottish regiment, eh?"

Jamie was wearing his ex-army Gordon Highlanders kilt. Ian and Colin were dressed in their old Seaforth kilts.

Again Jamie laughed, "Aye, of course! The Gordon's are the best regiment, everyone kens that."

This inter-regimental rivalry was another long-standing, light-hearted dispute between them.

"Och, anyway, you were never a real soldier, Jamie, you only served a short time in National Service after the war. Colin and I were real soldiers who did real soldiering during six long years of war."

Jamie threw up his arms, "Och, man, I gie up… I surrender. Could I help it if I was born too late to fight in your war?" He paused, then jovially grinned, "But onieway I'll be playing ma accordion later on whether you like it or no, ye ken that, don't you?"

Helen beamed at him, "Aye, that's right, Jamie, I love your playing. It takes me back to the guid auld times when I was a quinie in Aboyne many, too many, years ago."

Ian smiled at her, "Och, trust you couthie North East buddies to gang up together."

These familiar friendly disputes were halted by more visitors eagerly and noisily entering and being sincerely and vivaciously greeted. Glasses were again unstintingly filled; more toasts were given and drunk; sandwiches, oatcakes and shortbread were insistently pressed on all the guests. The excellence of the food was again emphatically and loudly affirmed. Cheerful animated talk and honest hearty laughter ceaselessly rang out.

Another two carefree hours of convivial happiness timelessly passed, two hours of freely circulating whisky, and now it was no longer a matter of persuading anyone to sing; it now was impossible to get anyone to stop singing.

With keen enthusiasm Jamie Gordon went through his extensive repertoire of Bothy Ballads. Some were bowdlerized versions fit for polite society, but most were original unashamedly bawdy ballads he had learned as a loon, then as a bachelor shepherd in rural Aberdeenshire. He put his entire heart and soul into each song. Roaring out with uninhibited lusty zeal he kept his audience in fits of laughter.

Then, despite Colin's good-natured protests, Jamie brought in his accordion. "Ah weel," Colin grinned, "I supposed I'll just have to put up with your damned noise for a wee while, then when it gets too much for me I'll get my pipes and play some real music outside."

Even Colin, who loved pipe music, had to admit that the bagpipes were rather overpowering if played in such a small room.

Had anyone in that room been entirely sober they might well have found Jamie's hearty accordion playing a bit overwhelming, but as it was they thoroughly enjoyed his lively toe-tapping music and they raised exhilarated and inebriated voices in cheerful song more or less in time with his jaunty playing.

After a time Colin slipped out of the room. He collected his bagpipes and took them outside. Standing a short distance from the front door, which he left open, he sent a spirited reel drunkenly reeling across the frozen landscape's ghosty whiteness.

The strange, unfamiliar sound amazed more than one fox and other stealthily unseen nocturnal prowlers. It stopped these wary animals in their tracks and held them mystified with alertly cocked ears.

In a noisy, vivacious group everyone poured out of the house and formed a wide circle around Colin who, stimulated by this appreciative audience, played better than ever.

After the sweaty warmth of the gregariously crowded room, the freshness of the calm frosty air was invigorating.

"Och, I feel a' this fresh air going tae ma heid!" Bella Gordon unsteadily giggled.

Jamie, having lost his audience, belatedly came staggering out with his accordion still strapped to his chest.

After a few more minutes of solo playing, Colin paused, took the charter from his mouth and grinned, "All right, Jamie, I'll relent. You can join in and we'll play together."

As Colin started up again Jamie enthusiastically joined in. Despite all the drams he had taken, his fingers danced over the accordion's keyboard as vigorously and accurately as ever.

Helen remarked on this to Bella, "I think Jamie plays better when he's a wee bit fou, doesn't he?"

"Aye, he does. Although I'm sure he'd play even mair brawly if he was sittin' doon. A' the whisky has fair gone tae his feet!"

While Jamie was in complete control of his fingers, his feet had an unruly mind of their own. The more he tried to stay in one spot the more they led him astray. One moment he was almost bumping into Colin, the next, staggering back, was in danger of falling into a ditch. No matter how much he swayed and staggered he never once stopped playing, and never ceased beaming a benevolent smile on his happy audience.

Colin, too, never once ceased playing, not even when smartly stepping out of the way to prevent Jamie colliding with him.

Ian smiled as he tried to imagine what a weird and wonderful cacophony of discordant sounds would issue from the bagpipes and from the accordion if they did bump together and collapse to the ground.

After ten minutes they both stopped playing. Colin laughed, "The dogs don't seem to think much of oor music, do they?"

All the time they had been playing the dogs in the kennels had kept up a noisy chorus of protesting barks and mournful howls.

"No, they don't," grinned Ian. "They're very astute music critics!"

Helen sympathetically murmured, "I feel sorry for the poor dogs. I'm afraid they won't get much sleep tonight."

Colin again laughed, "No, nor will we, I'm pleased to say."

Jeannie smiled, "Aye, and the poor hens won't get much sleep either. They're having a gey disturbed night tae."

Made restlessly uneasy by all the loud, unusual sounds, the hens, safely locked in their shed, cluckingly scolded and nervously fluttered. Their lord and master, the large glossy black rooster, occasionally gave querulously half-hearted crows in vain efforts to disguise his own nervous unease and maintain his pompous macho pride.

Jeannie cordially started ushering all the visitors back into the house. "Come on, come away in. I'll make some tea. We've lots of sandwiches to finish yet."

Her female visitors politely, but unconvincingly, murmured, "We should be going now, Jeannie. It's not fair us keeping you up all night."

Colin would not hear of any of them leaving, "Go on... go away in. There's plenty o' whisky to get through yet, as well!"

That last remark decided the male visitors. With cheers and uproarious laughter they unsteadily charged towards the open door. Old Murdo Munro, despite his ninety-plus years, determinedly led the way.

The women folk smiled and sighed understandingly at one another, then, with some slight show of reluctance, followed in after their men folk. What was left of the night was given over to the splendid full moon. Its translucent light flowed like clear liquid and bathed the wintry landscape in a fine silvery sheen.

A quieter, but no less happy and convivial hour passed as they drank tea and eagerly ate sandwiches, oatcakes and Jeannie's excellent crowdie cheese. Old Murdo Munro took advantage of this quiet lull to re-tell one of his oft told tales. He always prefaced his tales by asking, "Did I ever tell you the story aboot...?" This time he asked, "Did I ever tell you the story aboot the time I took yon bloody Jerry, Kaiser Bill, oot stalking?"

Although his audience had heard this story many times, they cheerily expressed their desire to hear it again.

With this encouragement Murdo happily got into his stride. "Aye weel, yon Kaiser Bill – he wasn't the real Kaiser, ye ken, but that was what I called him – came for a stalking and fishing holiday here before the last war, aboot 1934, I think. He was a big, square heided Prussian Baron. He was called Baron Von Fokkeroff, or some sic bloody stupid Jerry name."

Old Murdo chortled with spiteful glee. His listeners knew of, and understood, his hatred of Germans, for two of his brothers had been killed in the First World War, and he himself had lived through the nightmare horrors of those years of terrible slaughter. Then his oldest son had been killed in the Second World War. He continued his story, "Ah weel, yon baron rented Ardgie Lodge for a month.

He brought his wife and *eight* bairns wi' him. He also brought twa nannies and a puckle o' other servants. Weel…"

Ian interrupted him, "Did you say he had eight bairns?… *eight* children of his own?"

"Aye, that's right. He had eight bairns."

"Och well," Ian grinned, "in that case obviously that *baron* was not *barren*, was he?"

Not understanding Ian's joke and rather annoyed at the interruption, old Murdo hurried on with his story. "Ah weel, on my first day oot stalking wi' Kaiser Bill we spied a puckle o' stags on the far side o' Corrie Dheirg. We climbed doon a bit and, hidden by a wee ridge, approached the stags. It should hae been an easy stalk, only I suddenly saw a hind lying on that ridge. She was one o' thae very alert auld hinds… whit dae ye call them, again?"

"An old matriarch," Ian answered. "Or, a better description, an auld bugger o' a dowager."

"Aye, that's right… 'an auld bugger o' a dowager'," chuckled old Murdo. "Aye, weel yon dour deevil o' a hind fair spoiled oor easy stalk. She would see us if we went onie further forward. I told Kaiser Bill this and pointed her oot tae him. Through my telescope I could see her clearly, but that stupid Jerry, even wi' his muckle expensive telescope, couldna see her. I told him exactly where the auld hind wis lying on the ridge, but the damned fool still couldna spy her. Wi' bloody Prussian arrogance he declared, 'There is no hind there! It is only large stone you are seeing.'

"That fair got ma dander up! I said tae him, 'Weel, I've been stalking in these hills for ower thirty years and I've never seen a stane like that before. It's a gey queer stane!'

"'Vot do you mean?' Kaister Bill angrily demanded.

"'Weel, Baron, it's the first time I've ever seen a stane waggin' its lugs!'"

Old Murdo joined in the general laughter with unrestrained enthusiasm. Suddenly his top set of new false teeth shot out of his mouth. With amazing accuracy they landed in the tumbler of whisky he was lovingly holding at his lap. (He had resolutely refused to drink tea when whisky was available.) He fished them out and replaced them in his mouth. Chortling merrily he announced, "Oh man, ma new wallies taste real braw noo!"

Once the tea was drunk and most of the food eaten the whisky was again generously poured.

Soon freshly lubricated voices were again loudly and joyously raised in song. Jamie Gordon, having been persuaded to leave his accordion with Colin's bagpipes in the bedroom, revenged himself by insistently singing a series of ever more bawdy bothy ballads. Once again his uninhibited, uncensored songs made the audience helplessly weak with laughter.

For a short time auld Murdo Munro unsteadily stood and quaveringly sang well loved, though uncertainly remembered, old Gaelic songs. Then, exhausted, he collapsed into his comfortable armchair in the place of honour by the peat fire and immediately fell asleep. Soon his regular wheezy snores were keeping time with the wheezily swinging pendulum of the ancient clock on the wall above his head.

"Come on, Colin, let's hear some o' Rabbie's great auld songs now," Ian – backed by all the others – loudly demanded.

Colin was easily persuaded, he drained his glass, got to his feet and stood squarely in the centre of the room. For a few moments he beamed around at all those friends surrounding him, then, with his broad face brightly flushed and glistening with sweat, raised his deep bass voice in 'A Red, Red Rose'. To her slight embarrassment, but secret pleasure, he kept his gleaming eyes firmly fixed on his wife, Jeannie, as the rich timbre of his expressive voice movingly rendered that wonderful love song. After that he sang a succession of Burns' great songs, ending, patriotically, with 'Bruce's March to Bannockburn'. His audience enthusiastically joined in that inspiring song and sent it thundering around and around the convivial small room.

As he wiped the sheen of sweat from his brow, Colin gasped, "Come on now, Ian, it's your turn to gie us your party piece."

In his whisky inspired jovial mood, Ian was not loath to do his bit to entertain the company. He struggled to his feet and said, "Like guid auld Rabbie, I'll wish:

"That I for poor auld Scotland's sake
Some usefu' plan or beuk could make,
or sing a sang at least. "

Looking around his happily expectant audience he chuckled, "But I'll have pity on you all. I'll spare you the torture o' me 'singing a sang'...."

"Thank the Lord for that," Colin exclaimed in a dramatic stage whisper, "we've a' endured the agony o' your efforts at singing before!"

Grinning broadly, Ian continued, "Aye, anyway I'll gie you some o' Rabbie's poems instead." With loud enthusiasm he fairly accurately recited some of Burns' best loved poems, including 'Holy Willie's Prayer' and 'Tam O'Shanter'.

Once the noisy applause died down other voices, now eagerly free of all constraints, burst forth in song.

May and John Fraser's spirits left their bodies where they were jammed into a corner by the door and went gaily stepping out by Loch Tummel and Loch Rannoch on 'The Road to The Isles'.

Although Colin sat with an arm thrown affectionately over Jeannie's shoulders, in spirit he and his wife were out with their favourite song on the heather moors, striding amongst 'The Wild Mountain Thyme.'

Not to be outdone, Bella Gordon was, with a voice quivering with emotion, sending 'The Star O' Rabbie Burns' brightly soaring into orbit.

Gradually the mountain thyme withered and faded; the Westering road arrived at its journey's end and only Rabbie's irrepressible immortal star continued to blaze forth.

As everyone in the room joined in and sang Bella's song with honest emotion Ian felt uplifted; he murmured two lines from 'Tam O'Shanter':

"Kings may be bless but Tam was glorious,
O'er a' the ills o' life victorious!"

Smiling, he thought, "Aye, that's exactly how I feel, victorious over all of life's many ills." It was a wonderful feeling. He smiled benevolently on everyone in the room and on the entire human race.

Through a misty whisky haze of happiness he tried to count the number of people crammed into this noisily sweaty gregarious small room. He soon gave up. So many had arrived; so few had left. All through the night cars had arrived, all with cheerily winking headlamps and merrily hiccuping horns. Every new visitor was unfailingly greeted with genuine and un-abating warmth.

Influenced by the songs and poems of Burns, Ian knew that there was one more visitor in this room – Rabbie himself! His presence was unmistakable, was distinctly, solidly, palpable to Ian. Rabbie was completely at home in this convivial company; he eagerly joined in their drams, their songs, their jolly fellowship. He cast an appreciative expert eye over the lassies. These unpretentious revellers, these crofters, shepherds, gamekeepers and their wives were descendants of the same good old Scottish peasant stock as he was himself.

"Aye," Ian thought, chuckling, "Auld Rabbie is at relaxed ease here. He's much more at home here than he would be at any modern Burns Supper patronised by the grand, the great and the unco guid. What a wonderful satirical poem he would write if he could see one of those formal Burns Suppers graced by the imposing presence of a God-like Lord Provost; packed with a monstrous regiment of petty wee councillors, all pompously puffed up with vast self importance; crowded with worldly wise mercenary business men, all hoping to cultivate potentially useful contacts by exchanging the 'correct' handshakes.

"And what," Ian wondered, "would Rabbie make of the even more monstrous regiment of their unco respectable wives?" All these women so acutely conscious of, so jealously guarding, the correct pecking order, like hens haughtily fussing around their farmyard midden.

How loudly, how unconvincingly, that august company praise 'Auld Scotia's Bard'. How eagerly they acknowledge his greatness – it's safe to do so, that poet is two hundred years dead, there's no danger of having to dig in your pockets to help relieve his want. He can conveniently be forgotten until the hypocrisy of next year's elaborate Burns Supper and its abundance of whisky again provide 'a laxative for a' loquacity'.

These musings of Ian's were interrupted by the noisy arrival of yet another car-load of visitors. He wondered how any more could possibly manage to squeeze into this already tremendously overcrowded room. He knew that Jeannie and Colin would never turn anyone away. He smiled, "Och, they'll manage in somehow – perhaps the walls will expand. Aye, that was the secret, these hospitable walls forever expand."

Now he actually saw these walls and this room expand: saw them enlarge into a glorious ever-expanding universe of brightness, of song, of honest laughter, of sincere friendship. He saw Rabbie's dream come true, saw all men universally joined in noble brotherhood.

Vaguely, dreamily, he smiled, then sighed, "Oh, would that ever come true? Was it merely a rosy, whisky inspired dream?"

Overflowing with noisy cheerfulness, four boisterous newcomers bustled into the welcoming house. Violent explosions of laughter again shook the room. As, somewhat unsteadily, Ian rose and held out his hand to greet them, he laughed and, to their amused mystification, assured them that, "Yes, it was true; yes, the room was expanding. Yes, there actually was an ever expanding universe of song, of laughter, of friendship!"

Chapter Fifteen

It was four days later and the bright fires of Hogmanay celebrations were dying to smouldering dust. Most humans were wearily getting back to normal life.

Skippers of fishing boats, shepherds, crofters and gamekeepers resumed their regular pre-breakfast routine of inspecting their barometers. All tapped the glass with anxious fingers as they saw with foreboding how mercurially the mercury had dropped since last night. Each barometer was pointing to 'Storm', and, ominously, was still dropping. In different words these men thought the same thing: "I doot we're in for a bit o' a blow... It looks like dirty weather ahead... We're in for a real savage storm, I doot."

Before noon the last lingering pleasantness of the frost's calm was finally destroyed by the wind rising towards gale force.

Fishing boats turned and fled from the deadly menace of the wind as it came thudding in Arctic gusts from the North West and agitated the dark sea to dangerously high, fast racing crests.

The boats thankfully scurried into the shelter of Inveraldrory harbour. Fishermen crowded into the welcoming sanctuary of the Seamen's Mission and resignedly left the storm to do its worst.

Dusk descended early and darkness allied its menace to the force ten gale. With each long dark hour the wind got even stronger. By midnight gusts of over one hundred miles per hour were flinging vicious volleys of rain screaming almost horizontally over the cowering landscape.

Few animals and even fewer humans slept soundly that night. For Helen it was by far the worst, the longest, the most frightening sleepless night she had ever experienced. She lay miserably listening to the storm interminably battering against Altdour. Even that solid old crofthouse's thick walls seemed to shake. And yet even in the midst of her miserable weariness she thought with sympathy of the sheep and deer lying huddled in soaking misery on the bleakly exposed moors and hillsides. Her misery was nothing compared to theirs. She envied the hibernating creatures. She imagined the hedgehog curled in a tight ball, snug and barely breathing, under its thick covering of dry leaves. She pictured – not so pleasant a picture – the sinister adder tightly coiled in deathlike sleep, coldly indifferent in the depth of its dark cave.

As she snuggled ever closer into the reassuring warmth of Ian's solid body and felt his beard tickle her face, Helen whispered in his ear, "Perhaps these are the wisest creatures, the ones that hibernate all winter."

Ian was not – not after thirty years married to her – in the least surprised by Helen's strange remark coming entirely unheralded in the deep dark of the night. He drowsily replied, "Aye, perhaps they are, Helen, but we don't do too badly either, do we? We go into semi-hibernation during the worst of the winter months and get on with our indoor creative work."

He put an arm around Helen and held her close. He tried to get to his longed for sleep, but even he, normally the soundest of sleepers, could not ignore the storm ceaselessly howling and fiercely battering against the house. Loose old slates on the roof persistently clapped and clattered and rattled like the chittering teeth of a shivering swimmer. The wind sighed and mourned in the eaves. At gable corners fierce eddies wildly whirled then gyrated higher with mad banshee screams and wails. Pages of newspapers stuffed between the wooden frame and the sash-window stopped the bedroom's old window from rattling but did not quite prevent the tempestuous wind from draughtily penetrating. These insistent draughts whined and slobbered like angrily frustrated predatory beasts.

Shortly after 4am when all human life reached its lowest ebb, the North Atlantic's gale increased to hurricane. Sea devoured land. Awesomely united, these overwhelming elemental forces, sea and wind, madly orchestrated themselves to a final tremendous crescendo of "sound and fury" which to humbled, terrified, trembling humanity seemed to threaten the imminent end of the world.

When dim grey dawn eventually came sluggishly slithering over the battered landscape it confirmed to Helen and Ian that the crofthouse and the old stable behind it were undamaged. Helen grinned, "Your ancestors certainly knew how to build really substantial houses, didn't they?"

"Aye, they did. They built not just for themselves but for generations to come."

They explored the garden; littered with broken branches and carpeted with a thick layer of twigs, it was a sadly woebegone, bedraggled sight. A few of the taller birch trees lay uprooted and seven or eight mature firs by the boundary fence were flattened. They were amazed, and delighted, to discover that all the large old Scots Pines outside the garden had survived. Ian smiled, "How tough those rugged auld buggers are. They'll outlive the pair o' us by many a lang year, nae doot."

He pointed at Altdour Burn above them, "Cairndhu's wee waterfall is acting crazy."

Normally that burn dropped as an attractive small waterfall down the steep rocky slope of the little crag – but not now.

Today, perversely, the water in that little waterfall did not fall – it rose!

The wind had moderated, but it still blew a wild gusty gale, which hammered square on to the crag. Each gust grabbed the wee burn's peaty water as it trembled on the precarious lip of the cliff; grabbed it and, like a terrier with a rat, shook it, then threw it high in a glittery white fountain before disdainfully tossing it aside in a drenching fine spray which saturated the surrounding heather.

It was only later, when they learned of the destruction the storm had caused that they fully realized just how fortunate they had been to have suffered so little damage.

Some houses had lost most of their tiles and the driving rain, pouring in, soaked through attics and bedrooms. Many static caravans, which their owners had thought securely anchored, ceased to be static; were torn from restraining ropes, were rolled over and over and smashed to pieces. An ugly litter of thin aluminium sheets and fluttering fibreglass insulation was scattered far and wide.

Three of the seine-net fishing boats moored in Inveraldrory Bay and a few smaller boats had been torn free and smashed on to the rocky shore. The battered wrecks of these boats littered the South shore of the bay. They rose and fell, rolled back and forward, groaned and sighed as the wild surf surged and receded and surged again and constantly broke over and played with their gashed and splintered victims with what seemed like spiteful glee.

Many garden sheds simply disintegrated and disappeared. A wooden hen house was blown into the sea and sailed like a modern Noah's Ark, with some hens desperately clinging to it, across the bay. The hens were blown off and, fluttering like demented autumn leaves, flew for a short distance before being drowned. All along the uninhabited rocky South shore of Inveraldrory Bay masses of seaweed were thrown in high heaped, contorted dark tangles far beyond the normal high tide line. Scattered amongst the seaweed was a vast variety of stranded flotsam: broken planks and other wreckage from shattered boats; nylon fishing nets with their bright orange, their greens and blues intertwined in intimate clinging coils; countless smashed fish boxes; the ugly debris of demolished sheds and caravans; the saltily soaked and bedraggled bodies of hens. These dead hens were not wasted; nature saw to that. It transformed what for the hens was unmitigated disaster into a glorious bounty for the hungry, winter-lean foxes keenly scavenging along that storm littered shore.

The highest tide, goaded by gusts of 130 mph, had so mangled and mutilated pebble beaches that they were now unrecognisable. Houses near these beaches had their windows thickly coated with salty whitewash and their garden lawns, where not covered with pebbles, were bleached white, while the few remaining leaves of evergreen shrubs were black, shrivelled up tea-leaves.

After having their candlelit dinner (not through indulging in a romantic notion, but because they, like thousands of others, were without electricity) Helen and Ian went early to bed. Both were tired after their long, sleepless night. Again tonight as darkness fell the wind rose and now it was gusting to gale force. Hugging Ian close in their bed's cosy intimacy, Helen said, "Oh, I hope it doesn't get as bad as last night. I'm real weary, I could do with a decent sleep."

"Aye, so could I," Ian said and reassuringly added, "It won't get as bad as last night. That was exceptional. It certainly was the worst gale – or hurricane – I've ever experienced. Hopefully it's only once in a lifetime that it gets like that."

Helen smiled in the darkness, "I hope so. Once is enough, is more than enough. The 'normal' gales we get here every winter will seem like moderate breezes compared to it." (With gusts *only* reaching sixty to seventy miles per hour it did indeed seem quite peaceful that night.)

214

"Aye," Ian murmured, "the savage power of the vast elemental forces we experienced last night certainly humble us. They make all our brave human endeavours seem very puny and petty, don't they?"

Westerly gales of rain and sleet and fierce Easterly blizzards alternated with one another through January and into February, then the middle of February brought its usual, its most welcome change. The wind veered to the South East. It stayed set from that quarter for the next few months. With sharp, ice-edged keenness that wind swept the sky clear of all dismal dull grey clouds. Week after week the reawakened sun glowed with ever-increasing warmth from the pale, milky blue sky.

Ian, as usual, was recruited by Colin to help with the heather burning. It was pleasant to be out on the dry hillsides in the crisp thin clear air and eager sunshine. There was something primevally rewarding about lighting fires and seeing the flames creep along and greedily consume the thick old heather. It was easy to understand the primordial wild joy his remote ancestors must have felt as they torched the ancient Caledonian forests to drive out menacing packs of wolves and the more dangerous wolfish packs of human enemies. He imagined how these Pagans must have revelled in their orgy of fire raising as they watched their fires soar high in all consuming whirlwinds, saw old Scots Pines exploded into huge flaring resinous torches then cascade demonic showers of sparks that spread to fresh dry undergrowth and kept the uncontrolled fire roaring along in fine style. They must have felt a huge surge of pride, an intoxicating sense of their own vast cleverness as they conquered fire's awesome power and used it for their own grand purposes.

Ian enjoyed the comradeship of working with Colin and with Calum MacLeod. They were a good team who worked well together. They had improved on their ancestors. They tried (and usually succeeded) to keep their heather fires under strict control.

On the dry, South facing gentle slopes of the grouse moors beyond large Loch Ardgie they burned out patch after patch of the oldest heather.

At each suitable place they lit a line of flames about fifty yards wide then allowed the gentle breeze to lead the flames up the heather slope while they, using fire-brooms they had made from birch twigs, beat out the flames on both sides of the burning patch. This left only the front line of fire actively advancing. When this had gone far enough they set about these flames. Beating from left and right they met in the centre and extinguished the last of the fire.

These black patches gaped like ugly scars disfiguring the wounded hillside. The infliction of such wounds was justified, was necessary. By midsummer those smouldering scars of black ash would be transformed to patches of vivid green. But next Spring they would be verdant velvet carpets of fresh young heather shoots which were the essential tender food for hungry red grouse chicks.

Some slopes of older, thicker heather were left unburnt to provide winter shelter and nesting cover for the adult grouse.

Colin, Ian and Calum were sitting together, all eagerly eating their lunchtime sandwiches. They complacently studied the burned black patches stretching along the slope below them. Colin gave a satisfied smile, "That's a good morning's work we've done."

For many years Colin had dedicatedly managed this grouse moor. He had conscientiously burned patch after patch in strict rotation. He had eliminated all too old, too thick and tough heather. Those gentle slopes were now a perfect mosaic of fresh, vigorously thriving heathers at different controlled stages of growth. He was rewarded by observing a steady increase in the stock of healthy grouse on this moor.

"Aye," Ian agreed, "we made a good job of it. Those patches are in a nice neat row."

"Yes, they're a very satisfying sight, right enough," Calum said.

"Aye, and you'll reap the benefit of this work in the years to come, Calum, after Ian and me are retired," Colin said.

"I hope so. I eagerly look forward to continuing your year of fine work once you're both enjoying your well earned retirement."

Ian and Colin exchanged glances, they knew they shared the same thought: that it was good, was heartening, to see a young man so keen to be a gamekeeper, especially when so many local young men were only too keen to leave the Highlands, seduced by the (false?) lure of the cities.

Calum leant back on his elbows and raised his face to the sunshine; sensually he revelled in its luxurious warmth. "I am really enjoying being out on these moors in this pleasant weather," he grinned, "and with this pleasant company. It's interesting and satisfying work. It's great to be paid for doing what you enjoy doing." Smiling, he gazed around the vast landscape, "It's almost unbelievable that I now have this wonderful country – those hills, this moor, the lochs, the rivers – as my workplace."

Sympathetically and understandingly Ian smiled at Calum's warm enthusiasm, "Aye, it's a much better workplace than a drawing office in a Glasgow shipyard, isn't it?"

"It certainly is! I could never go back to being stuck indoors again!"

Ian grinned, drolly winked at Colin, then said, "Oh, well, in that case you must thank Mrs Thatcher for getting you on your bike and making you move here, Calum."

Laughing, Calum once more performed the facetious pantomime he went through whenever that name was mentioned: he made the sign of the cross over his chest and cried out, "May angels and ministers of grace defend us from the Evil One!"

Having finished their sandwiches, Colin and Ian lit up their pipes and smoked with quiet contentment. Calum grinned, "I would have thought you'd had enough smoke from the burning heather without wanting any more."

"Och, but this pipe smoke's quite different. It's most pleasant to relax and quietly enjoy a good pipe," Colin said, between puffs.

"Aye, it is," Ian confirmed as he blew out a cloud of smoke. "Sitting enjoying a leisurely pipe is one of life's great pleasures. And anyway we didn't have any trouble with heather smoke this morning. We've had an easy time so far today."

Colin nodded, "Aye, we have. But you know, it's not always as easy as this, Calum. There are times when it all goes wrong. That's when you learn all about the choking heather smoke."

Ian and Colin remembered desperate times when heather fires had got out of control. Remembered a gentle breeze, like today's, suddenly rising to a howling gale; remembered an unexpected change in wind direction taking their fire, defiantly self-willed, on exactly the opposite course from the intended one.

At these times the wind eagerly fanned fires to a blazing fury and swept hungry tongues of flames leaping and roaring along at a frightening speed, consuming everything in their path. How highly the savagely hot flames leapt as they roared up steep slopes of thick old heather. How violently they exploded straggling, tinder dry old gorse bushes into soaring furnaces.

How swiftly flames swept over dry stretches of yellow mat grass; how quickly every large tussock of bent grass burst into flame, whoomed high, then instantly died. How pungently the smouldering grey ghosts of incinerated grasses gave out their sharp smell – the scent subtly different from the distinctive primordial scent of heather smoke.

They well remembered many a suddenly eddying gust driving flames and smoke shrieking towards them. They remembered urgently staggering back, choking, gasping, coughing, their sweatily flushed faces sootily freckled with black smudges, their eyebrows scorched and Ian's beard singed and smoking, their mouths and throats parched sandpaper dry. Now, sitting beside Colin and Calum, Ian ran his hand over his grey beard and smiled, "I've had this beard singed a few times; it's been left frizzled and giving off a strong pungent smell more than once."

"Aye, I know," Colin laughed. "I remember saying to you that I thought it was only the King of Spain who got his beard singed."

Laughing, they recalled shared schooldays, shared history lessons about Sir Francis Drake, Cadiz, and the Spanish Armada. In those days Highland children were taught almost nothing about Scottish history, most of their lessons were about English kings and queens. They were taught only in English. The use of Gaelic was forbidden in school and was most strongly discouraged.

"Do you remember Miss Grant?" Ian asked.

"Aye, of course! How could I ever forget her? Even yet, after all these years, whenever I hear her name the palms of my hands tingle and glow with remembered pain. God knows how many times she viciously belted us boys with her cruel tawse merely for the crime of using a Gaelic word in her class."

"Yes, I know, Colin, I'm exactly the same," Ian said. "To us boys she was just a terribly feared old battle-axe. Now, looking back, we realise she was a terribly frustrated virgin, an old maid, who sadistically relieved her bitter, spiteful frustrations by mercilessly belting us defenceless young males.

"Of course, like many women of her age, she lost her fiancé... had him cruelly killed in Flanders during the First World War. Now that we understand her better we can sympathise with her, can't we?"

"Aye," Colin nodded, "I can pity her now; then, when I was a boy, my only pity was self-pity... pity for my poor smarting and stinging hands."

Ian turned to Calum, "Anyway, lad, you've yet to experience a heather fire that's really got out of control; yet to see a flood of fire advancing and leaping over a hillside, spreading and roaring like some savage beast malignantly alive with rage."

Colin smiled, "Aye, Calum, you've not yet had your clothes strongly, lingeringly smelling of heather smoke."

After fighting a really fierce fire, it was amazing how tenaciously that powerful and unmistakeable scent of heather smoke clung to clothes. It especially liked and lovingly clung to tweeds. Colin's and Ian's thick tweed plus fours and jackets had often been deeply impregnated. Months after the heather burning, if their tweeds got damp, the dampness again brought out that unique, not unpleasant, smoky, tweedy scent.

Ian stared at Calum's bushy, glossy black beard, he grinned "You won't be a real Highland gamekeeper until you've had the wild flames scorch that beard of your chin."

Calum laughed, and, defiantly jutting his arrogant beard, exclaimed, "Och, I don't fancy that. I would hate to lose this beard. It's taken me many years to cultivate it to this perfect size and shape."

"Och, never heed what Ian says, lad, you can keep your beard virgo intacta and still become a real gamekeeper," Colin assured him, grinning widely. "Aye, I'm sure you'll be a real Highland gamekeeper, although an unusual one if you remain practically teetotal; after all, Highland 'keepers are not exactly noted for their teetotalism, are they?"

"No, I should damned well hope not!" Ian exclaimed, "It'll be a sad, sad, day if they ever are!"

Colin laughed, "Aye, I know... I agree. But, damn it, man, this talk o' teetotalism is gey dry work. I could do with a drink. My throat's fair parched."

"As parched as that time ghillieing with the Admiral?" Ian gently asked.

Colin grinned in reply, "Aye, almost... almost!"

Calum listened with amusement as between them they told the story of the miserable Admiral.

It happened a good many years ago.

Lord Kilvert asked Colin and Ian to take an elderly retired Admiral out fishing on the loch at Ardgie Shooting Lodge. Although that attractive loch contained many brown trout, the Admiral was not interested in these fish. He was a fanatical salmon fisher, dedicated to catching salmon and nothing but salmon. He despised all lesser fish, regarding them as vermin.

Colin and Ian each took an oar and rowed against the strong wind up to the far end of the loch.

They turned the boat and guided it to drift over parts of the loch where, from long experience, they knew there was the best chance of catching salmon. As the admiral expertly cast his salmon flies and drew them enticingly through the waves the overburdened black clouds racing low overhead released their heavy load of water. The rain pelted ferociously. The wind madly increased its demented howling.

Time after time Ian and Colin manfully strained at the oars to persuade the reluctant boat to battle against the stormy waves and the shrieking gale and win to the far end of the loch. Hour after hour the Admiral, ignoring – perhaps even perversely enjoying – the atrocious weather, stubbornly fished. Although they saw quite a few salmon vigorously leap high and wildly splash back into the waves, the Admiral failed to catch a single fish. During all his hours of fishing he had not seen or felt even one salmon show any interest in his skilfully fished flies. He could not understand it. Gradually he grew dejected and despaired of catching any salmon today. His temper, never the most serene, rapidly deteriorated.

Colin and Ian could not understand his lack of success either. Obviously he was a highly skilled and experienced fisher. There were many salmon in the loch, and they knew that today's conditions with stormy waves usually excited the salmon and enticed them to eagerly and, sometimes it seemed even playfully snatch at the fisher's flies. Although they could not understand the salmon's lack of interest these old ghillies were not really surprised by it. All their years of experience had taught them many things about salmon, but the most certain thing they had learned was how uncertain these noble fish were. They were the most unpredictable of creatures. Quite often when, as today, conditions seemed perfect no salmon were caught, and yet sometimes under the most unpromising of conditions they were caught. Probably the major factor accounting for their unpredictability was the fact that these alluring, and all too often exasperating fish, ceased to feed once they entered fresh water.

As, once more, they rowed up the loch the rain battered heavier than ever and the wind increased to gale force. The Admiral's annoyed exasperation had grown increasingly evident. However, as he huddled under his soaking oilskins in the stern seat at least he had a pleasant consolation that Colin and Ian did not have. Now and again he drew a large silver flask out of a pocket and consoled himself for his most disappointing fishing by taking a hearty gulp of excellently mature malt whisky. After each generous gulp the flask was returned directly to his pocket. It was never once offered to the ghillies as they strained and sweated at the oars.

Finally, with still no success, even the Admiral, that crusty old veteran of many a stormy ocean, had had enough. With rainwater dripping from his bushy eyebrows and running from his whisky inflamed bulbous nose, he curtly barked, "Turn the boat around. Head for the jetty. This fishing is hopeless! I'm wasting my time!"

Quickly, willingly, Colin and Ian expertly turned the boat. There was an anxious moment when the boat was broadside to the turbulent waves. It rolled wildly and shipped a load of cold water. Then the bow came round and they were safe.

The boat now responded like a greyhound released from its trap. It leapt forward and joyfully raced before the storm as if it knew it was heading homeward to the security of the sheltering jetty.

No strenuous rowing was now required from Ian and Colin, they needed to do little more than guide and encourage the boat on its keen flight. They now had ample leisure to minutely observe every move the Admiral made as, once more, he produced the silver flask, unsealed it, and raised it to his mouth. He gulped deeply. He lowered it, paused for a few moments, then raised it again. Tilting his head back he lifted the flask high and poured the last few drops of whisky down his throat.

Colin, having given many un-subtle hints, such as staring longingly at the flask and licking his parched lips, again cursed that miserable Admiral under his breath and fervently wished he'd choke on those last few drops of whisky. Instead, the Admiral brought out his already filled pipe and a box of matches. Huddling forward for shelter, he struck match after match. All failed to light on the damp box. Purple faced with annoyance he swore irritably, "Oh, God damn it, is there nowhere dry on this damned boat where I can successfully strike a match?"

Ian glanced at Colin and, noting the roguish gleam in his eyes, waited expectantly for his reply.

Quietly and gently Colin drawled out his answer, "Och, well now, Admiral, you could try striking a match on the back of my throat... it's certainly dry enough!"

Once the laughter subsided, Calum asked, "How did he react to that subtle hint of yours, Colin? Did you get a dram from the Admiral once you got ashore?"

"Hell no! There was not the least suggestion of a dram from him, afloat or ashore. He was annoyed at me. He hardly spoke to us at all after my gentle hint."

"Aye, and we never even got a tip from him after rowing for all those hours in that gale and getting soaked through, too," Ian vehemently added.

"Aye, that's right. Although we didn't miss much by not getting a tip from him. We learned later that his usual tip to a ghillie was a half-crown."

"Really? He gave half a crown, that's what?... only two shillings and sixpence?... as a tip?" Calum cried in disbelief. "How very generous! He must have been a real miserable bastard."

"Aye, he was, he certainly was," Colin wholeheartedly agreed. "Thank God not many of the 'gentry' are as bad as him."

Ian laughed, "No, he certainly was not an admirable Admiral!"

Chapter Sixteen

While the fine spring weather remained bright and dry Ian, Colin and Calum were kept busy at the heather burning. Some days, though continuing dry and bright, were made impossible for burning by the strength of the wind.

On some of these days when it was impossible to go heather burning, Ian dug over the vegetable garden. He determinedly dug despite his freezing fingers and a constant drip at his nose. Invariably he was closely accompanied by a bright-eyed hungry robin. Hunger overcoming fear, the robin bravely landed on his outstretched hand and snatched the offered worms.

Suddenly Helen shouted from the corner of the house, "Come in, Ian, your lunch is ready."

She shouted only once, then, shivering, turned and dashed back indoors.

Ian only needed telling the once. He stabbed the spade firmly into the soil and left it. Immediately the robin perched on that fine vantage point and, with cocked head and keen eyes, eagerly searched for worms in the fresh dug earth.

When Ian entered the sitting room, Helen was kneeling in front of the roaring fire with both hands stretched towards the leaping flames. A dog sat at either side of her. Turning her head she gasped, "Oh, that's a bitter freezing wind. You must be frozen, Ian."

"Aye, it is a bit raw out there." He grinned, "It's a real 'lazy wind', isn't it?"

Helen smiled as she remembered her puzzlement on first hearing Ian use that description of a freezing wind many years ago. She pictured a 'lazy wind' as being a pleasantly balmy summer breeze softly whispering amongst tremulous aspen leaves, certainly not as a bitterly freezing winter wind. Ian had explained, "A 'lazy wind' is a bitterly cold wind, one so lazy that it declines to go all the way around a human body, but instead slices straight through."

"Aye, it certainly is a real 'lazy wind'," Helen agreed.

Dry, bright and warm weather lasted for much of April. The heather burning ended before grouse and other ground-nesting birds started preparing their nests. Then the almost inevitable happened on the twenty-fifth of the month. Warm spring abruptly ended and snowy, sleety, miserable winter returned. In the North West Highlands the first lambs are born at exactly that time, so this annual return of winter is resignedly known as 'The Lambing Snows'.

After a ewe gave birth it struggled to its feet, shook the layer of slushy wet from its wool, and, with the warmth of its urgently licking tongue, fought a desperate battle against the thickly falling freezing sleet.

Each year Helen's heart bled for the poor shivering lambs. Covered with soaking snow the young lambs huddled miserably against their stoic mothers and desperately tried to steal some reassuring warmth from them. They despairingly bleated with weak, tremulous voices. Perhaps they wondered why they were exposed to this cruel environment. Perhaps they wished themselves back in the cosy warm comfort of their mother's womb.

To Helen it seemed cruel that they should be born into such miserable conditions. Each year she expressed her concern and always heard Ian make the same reply. "Aye, I agree, Helen, it does seem cruel, but we know it's nature's way. It's all part of nature's first and greatest principle – the survival of the fittest. Any lambs that are too weak will simply not survive. And of course, as you well know by now, there is…"

"There is no such word as 'cruel' in nature," Helen said, interrupting him. "Oh, I know… I know, Ian, you've told me that often enough."

Despite his clear-sighted understanding of the correctness – indeed of the profound goodness – of nature's cruel seeming ways, Ian willingly assisted Helen as she did her utmost to help the weakest lambs survive. They had no sheep of their own. Ian had inherited his mother's flock, but had not kept them long. For him sheep gave no reward, financial or any other, worth the effort of looking after them. Yet he unstintingly helped his neighbour, Kenny MacLeod, look after his sixteen ewes. As Kenny had no croft of his own he kept his sheep on Ian's croft. Many of Kenny's ewes were gey lang in the tooth and often required human help with their difficult births. At lambing time Ian accompanied Kenny on the vital morning and evening rounds of the ewes.

All were agreed that it was a good thing that Kenny had his sheep to keep him occupied. He had always retained his interest in them except during the worst of his bouts of post-war depression.

Each morning and evening, while Ian and Kenny were doing the rounds of the ewes, Helen visited Kenny's sister, 'Kate Kettle'. With maternal instincts thrilling in a flood of love they went through the pleasant procedure of preparing to feed two very weak lambs. Each lamb was the weaker of two sets of twins. Carefully they heated the milk to the correct temperature, sometimes surreptitiously added a drop or two of whisky, then poured it into two baby feeding bottles complete with rubber teats.

How they rejoiced when a weakly lamb grew stronger and ever more insistently demanded more, ever more milk. How tearfully they grieved when a weakly lamb grew ever weaker and was found one morning huddled in the terrible stiff cold stillness of death.

One evening, Helen noticed that Kate was not as cheerful as usual, she smiled, "What's the matter, Kate, you seem rather subdued, is something wrong?"

"Oh, I'm sorry, Helen, I'm just being silly. It's just that I can't help worrying about all the rumours going around about Campbell-Fotheringay not going to renew the leases, or going to impose huge rent increases, on his estate houses. I had two visitors this afternoon and they talked about little else."

Helen nodded, "Aye, I've heard these rumours as well, but that's all they are, just rumours, there might be no substance to them, you know."

"Aye, that's what I keep telling myself, but still I can't help worrying. Of course I try not to let Kenny see that I'm worried, but what if it was true? What if the rent on this house was greatly increased? We simply couldn't afford to pay it. What would happen then? Oh, any worry like that would drive Kenny distracted, it could bring on another nervous breakdown." Kate paused, lifted her indispensable apron and wiped anxious tears from the corners of her eyes. "Oh, I'm sorry, Helen, I'm being foolish again. Oh, how lucky Ian and you are to have the security of your crofthouse. You are protected by the Crofters Commission aren't you?… no landowner can increase your rent unreasonably, can he?"

"Yes, I know; it's a great thing to have the security of the croft. It's just a great pity your father did not have a croft of his own to pass on to Kenny and you."

Kate's father had worked for Aldrory Estate before the war under its previous owners. After his death, Kate and Kenny were allowed to continue living in the 'tied' estate house, paying a rent, which was increased every five years. It would be terribly cruel if they were turned out and the house sold to wealthy incomers.

Helen knew that some others on the estate were also getting increasingly worried about the uncertainty over their leases. She did not mention this, instead, grasping Kate's hand with both of hers, she stared steadily into her worried, tear glittering eyes and quietly and convincingly said, "Don't worry, Kate, I feel – *I know* – that things will work out all right for Kenny and you. Don't ask me how I know… I just do! You believe me, don't you, Kate?"

Kate, remembering many previous instances of Helen's strange, inexplicable powers, felt a touch of fear. She sensed something alarmingly like witchcraft. Summoning up a slightly tremulous smile she replied, "Yes, oh yes, I believe you, Helen, thank you… thank you. You've taken a load of worry off my mind."

They both gave startled jumps as the front door was noisily thrown open.

With relief they heard a babble of excited, high-pitched children's voices. They laughed.

Two small boys burst into the room, wildly exclaiming, "We've come to feed the lambs!"

"Yes, Auntie Kate, I'm going to feed Lucy," the oldest boy cried.

"And I'm going to feed Donnie," shouted his younger brother.

Coming in behind the boys, their mother laughed, "Don't make so much noise. Don't get too excited, boys!"

Mary MacLeod was the wife of Kate's nephew, Calum, and Rob and Norman were their five- and three-year-old sons.

With both boys eagerly running ahead they all made their way to the outbuilding, which housed the lambs. A corner was made into a comfortable, straw layered pen. As the boys shouted, the lambs shakily got to their feet and unsteadily stretched themselves. They hungrily and plaintively bleated and tottered on long, spindle-shanked legs, which hardly seemed strong enough to support even the slight weight of their skinny bodies.

Eagerly, though gently, they were lifted by the brothers. Seated side by side on a bale of straw each boy lovingly held and fed his lamb.

Young Norman chortled a gurgling laugh, "Look at Donnie's tail. It's going faster than Lucy's, isn't it?"

"No, it isn't! Lucy's going faster... see!" indignantly shouted Rob.

"They're wagging at the same speed," their mother stated, smiling with well-practised diplomatic skill.

As each lamb urgently sucked the rubber teat its tail frantically signalled ecstatic pleasure. Both bottles were quickly drained. The boys cuddled their contented lambs and went into fits of giggles each time a lamb gave a loud, frothily white burp.

Calum MacLeod drove up just as Kenny and Ian arrived back at the house. For a few minutes they all stood outside cheerfully blethering. Then 'Kate Kettle' laughed and made a slight variation to her usual announcement, "I'll just go in and put the kettle on."

Rob tugged urgently at his father's jeans, "Dad, Dad, can we take Meg to find eggs?" His Uncle Kenny answered, "Aye, Rob lad, wee Norman and you can go with Meg to search for eggs." He smiled down at his small collie and she, with cocked ears keenly listening, smiled up at him. "Well, Meg, what are you waiting for? Go and fetch your basket."

Dashing into the house she emerged a moment later with a shallow basket firmly gripped by its curved handle. The boys excitedly accompanied her round to the back of the house. Calum and Ian followed more leisurely. Kenny went with the three women into the house.

A steep rocky knoll rose close behind the house. Its near side was a jumbled confusion of boulders with a dense mass of thick, old gorse bushes rioting amongst them. These savagely spiked bushes formed an impenetrable jungle; at least they were completely impenetrable for humans, but Kate's hens found them an excellently secure and sheltered roosting and laying place. And Meg, the neat small collie, had little trouble in penetrating under the jagged bushes in search of the hens' eggs. She now gently laid down the basket at the foot of the knoll. Then, urged on by the boys, though she needed no urging, with experienced skill slid her trim body under the gorse bushes and glided out of sight.

Ian and Calum waited patiently beside the basket. The boys waited much less patiently, they kept peering into the gorse jungle in search of Meg. Occasionally a hen's squawking protests indicated the unseen presence of Meg as she diligently searched for fresh eggs.

Soon she appeared with an egg tenderly held in her mouth. Wee Norman eagerly stepped forward to take it from her, but his big brother caught him and angrily commanded, "Leave Meg alone! She'll put the egg in her basket."

With gentle care Meg laid the egg on the layer of dry sphagnum moss snugly lining the basket. With smiling eyes she looked up to be praised.

"Well done, Meg," Calum cried encouragingly, "Now go on, fetch more eggs."

Gurgling with laughter the boys joined in, they pointed and with eager, high-pitched squeals cried, "Fetch, Meg… fetch!"

Twice more Meg appeared carrying an egg. With infinite care she placed them neatly on the soft green moss cupped within the basket. Rob chuckled delightedly, "Look, Norman, Meg's made a bird's nest."

Norman stared with wide-eyed wonder, "What kind of bird's nest is it?"

Rob looked questioningly up at his father. Calum smiled, "It looks like a wild swan's nest, I think." He in turn looked at Ian for confirmation.

"Aye, that's right. It's a swan's nest."

Meg again disappeared into the gorse bushes. She seemed to be searching deeper into the heart of the wilderness. Suddenly a cock wren burst out from the gorse and perched on a boulder. It loudly scolded Meg as she searched alarmingly close to the nest where his silently apprehensive mate sat tightly on her clutch of tiny eggs.

Ian smiled, "Isn't it amazing what a loud sound comes from such a small bird?"

Calum lifted Norman to let him see the small, dull brown, noisy wren. "Why is its tail sticking up?" Norman asked.

"Its tail always sticks up," his father replied.

"Oh, does it?… Why?"

Calum looked appealingly at Ian who laughed, "I'm sorry, Norman, I don't know why it always sticks up. It just does."

The three-year-old boy gave first his father and then Ian a long, contemptuous stare of disappointment. He had thought those wise grown-ups knew everything.

Fortunately just then Rob excitedly shouted, "Here's Meg coming back."

This time she carried no egg, but looked gey pleased with herself as she stood by the basket and assiduously licked her lips.

Ian bent down and examined her mouth and jaws. Fresh yellow yolk was guiltily sticking to her chin. "Oh, you rascal, Meg, you've found and eaten another egg, haven't you?"

She did not attempt to deny her crime. Her eyes grinned mischievously up at Ian and her tail gently waved with an air of quiet self-satisfaction.

Ian laughed, "Och, Meg, you're well nicknamed, 'Meg the Egg'. No wonder your hair is so wonderfully glossy. A raw hen's egg per day keeps your coat in perfect condition, doesn't it?"

Calum laughed in turn, "I suppose she thinks she well deserves that reward for fetching these other eggs from where no one else can reach them."

"Aye, I expect she does," Ian agreed. Grinning he stroked his bushy grey beard, "Perhaps we should start taking a raw egg each day too, Calum; they would put a real gloss in our beards, wouldn't they? And I remember reading that raw eggs also have strong aphrodisiac qualities."

Calum laughed and complacently stroked his thick, jet-black beard, "Och, my beard's glossy enough as it is and, unlike you, I've no need for any aphrodisiacs. I'm virile enough without!"

"Oh, stop your damned boasting, Calum. It's all right for you at your age, but once you reach my advanced years you are glad of any damned stimulant you can get."

Norman and Rob knelt beside Meg and examined the telltale yolk staining her chin. Their father handed them clumps of damp moss. "Here, boys, wipe her chin clean."

As they joyfully carried out their ablutions on the gentle and patient dog both boys gleefully chanted, "Oh you rascal, 'Meg the Egg'."

When they finished, Rob looked up at his father and, with eyes bright with laughter, chuckled, "That's a good *joke* about the *yolk* on 'Meg the Egg', isn't it, Dad?"

Without being ordered, Meg gently lifted the egg-laden basket and proudly carried it into the house. As the two men and the two boys followed her they saw Kate outside the front door. Calum gaily cried out to his aunt, "You're not by any chance going to tell us that you've just put the kettle on, are you?"

'Kate Kettle's' laughter exploded, "No, for once I'm not! I was going to tell you that I put the kettle on half an hour ago and now the tea's all ready for you."

From his battered old armchair in the kitchen Kenny's voice loudly and hospitably bellowed, "Come in, my dear fellows, come away in."

Sitting drinking her tea, Helen unobtrusively studied Mary and Calum MacLeod as, with their two boys between them, they contentedly reclined on the old sofa. She thought they made a most pleasing picture of a happily healthy perfect family. With his glossy black hair and beard and tanned complexion Calum suggested glowing, virile male strength. Mary, too, had abundant glossy black hair, which swept in natural waves to her shoulders. Her cheeks rosily glowed with vital young beauty, with vigorous health, and with the wonderful contentment of fulfilled motherhood. The gleaming blood red of her smiling lips owed all to nature and nothing to the unnatural artifice of lipstick. Norman and Rob had inherited their parents' dark hair and now, after being out in the cold wind, the generous heat of the hospitable kitchen fire was flaming their chubby cheeks to the brightness of the glowing coals.

Suddenly, for an intense moment, Helen felt a keen stab of terrible sadness. She suffered a fierce, unworthy pang of jealousy. Her frustrated maternal instincts felt a deep regret that she had no children like those lovely boys of her own. She was, once more, poignantly reminded of the loss of her baby all those years ago.

Something drew Helen's gaze away from that contented family to Kate, who sat beyond the sofa. She, too, was motionlessly gazing intently at that young family. A sure intuitive instinct told Helen that Kate was experiencing similar feelings to her own. She knew that poor Kate was suffering a terrible regret that she was an 'old maid'; that she had never had a lover, nor a husband; never had a child of her own. In confirmation of this, Kate suddenly threw her hands up to her mouth to stifle an anguished sigh.

Feeling Helen's searching gaze on her, Kate turned her head and gave a sad, woebegone smile. A few moments later her usual cheery smile again took over.

No one else in the room seemed to have noticed this secret silent exchange of sad feminine longings. Certainly none of the males, animatedly talking amongst themselves, had.

Helen smiled consolingly to herself as she thought, "At least, I have a good husband. At least, I've known the ecstasy of true, deep love."

"The boys are fair thriving in this Highland environment, aren't they?" Ian remarked to Calum. "They have a grand time feeding the lambs and helping Meg fetch the hen's eggs. It's an excellent life for them; far better than their old life in Glasgow."

Calum heartily agreed, "I don't suppose they would ever be happy in Glasgow, or any other city, after leading this fine healthy natural life here."

He paused and looked meaningfully at his wife, "I know I could never settle in Glasgow again."

Mary smiled at him, "Och, it's all right for you… you're working outside most of the time, but I'm often stuck in the caravan all day with the boys. I get a bit tired of it when it rains and blows day after day, as it did much of the winter. I don't look forward to another winter in the caravan, especially after our terrible disappointment over the house old Ferguson promised us."

Calum reached over, took her hand and squeezed it sympathetically, "I know, Mary, I know. That was a big disappointment to us all. Hopefully something else will turn up before long." He grinned reassuringly, "Aye, I'm sure something, perhaps something even better, will turn up soon."

Mary smiled lovingly at him, "Aye, I sincerely hope so too."

John Ferguson, a lean and mean and taciturn elderly crofter who lived a mile down Aldrory Glen from them, had verbally promised to sell Calum and Mary a semi-derelict house he owned on one of his crofts. This old house occupied an attractive site just off the peat track on the hillside overlooking the glen. They had keenly looked forward to doing up the house and transforming it into a comfortable home.

Then, a month after receiving that promise, Mary and Calum heard that John Ferguson had sold that old house to a wealthy English solicitor at a price far higher than they could possibly afford. They were still upset and angered and felt bitterly betrayed by Ferguson reneging on his promise to them. And – rubbing salt into their wound – was the knowledge that the house would become merely one more summer holiday cottage.

When Ian met old Ferguson after hearing that upsetting news he had angrily accused him of having been greedily 'bought and sold for English gold!!' This was not the first time Ferguson had let unreasonable selfish greed override generous initial promises.

Helen spoke up in an impressively firm and assured voice, "Yes, Calum, like you I feel that something will turn up soon. In fact I'm sure that it will." She looked steadily at his wife, "Try not to worry, Mary, I assure you things will work out all right – and soon."

For some moments there was a profound silence in the room. All were deeply impressed by Helen's assured certainty.

Suddenly Rob's voice sang out, "I don't want to go back to Glasgow! I don't want to leave Meg!" He was lying on the dusty carpet with his arms around Meg. He lovingly hugged the gentle collie tighter.

Wee Norman now piped up, "No, and I don't want to leave Dolly!" Dolly was the old ginger cat contentedly purring in his lap. "And I don't want to leave Lucy and Donnie." Those were the weak lambs they fed every day.

"No, I don't want to leave Donnie and Lucy, too! And I don't want to leave Flora, too!" Rob urgently added. Flora was the pony that had replaced poor old Nell.

Their mother smiled lovingly and indulgently on them, "All right, all right, boys, none of us will go back to Glasgow." She smiled at Helen, "I just pray that you are proved correct, Helen. I don't think I could face many more winters in the caravan."

Helen sympathised with her. She had often visited Mary in the caravan during the past winter. She vividly remembered how its frail aluminium walls shivered and shook under the fierce gales and how loudly the rain battered against windows and how dementedly it hammered on the fearfully thin roof; it sounded as if some malignant giant was drumming with impatient fingers, angrily demanding admittance.

Only the numerous wires and ropes Calum had festooned over the large residential caravan kept it secure through the wild gales. Each time she tripped over one of these ropes Mary cursed and wearily complained that she felt like a fly enmeshed in a spider's web.

During the worst of January's hurricane they had abandoned the caravan and slept, or tried to sleep, in the welcome shelter of Kate and Kenny's solid old house. Each dawn they anxiously peered out of the bedroom window and were delighted, and amazed, to see their caravan still intact.

"I assure you, Mary, you won't have to spend many more winters in your caravan," Helen said, again with impressive certainty. Then, not wanting Kenny to get too disturbed by her solemn declarations, she quickly changed to a lighter, more cheery topic.

Later, as they were preparing to leave, Calum said to Ian, "Well, what do you think of our friend Campbell-Fotheringay now? (Campbell-Fotheringay – what a damned name; what a bloody mouthful!)"

Yesterday's newspapers reported that a Coroner's Court in London had decided the tragic death of the young woman who had fallen (or been pushed?) from the balcony of Campbell-Fotheringay's Mayfair flat had been an accident and that no one could be held responsible for her death. The coroner had solemnly indulged in his usual platitudinous homily on the irresponsibility of young people mixing drugs and drinks together.

"Och, it's what I expected. Trust him to get away with murder!" Ian said, "Or am I being too cynical? Perhaps poor Campbell-Fotheringay is as innocent as a lamb."

Calum smiled cynically, "Ach aye, nae doot he's as innocent as a new born lamb. It's just a pity he's not as dead as mutton." Then, with rising anger, he continued, "Now he'll be free to carry on as Laird of Aldrory; be free to continue his hellish policy of devastating this estate. The terrible thing is that there seems nothing anyone can do to stop him. It's monstrous that in this day and age an evil landowner like him can do as he likes. It's as if we were in the 1880s instead of the 1980s! Oh God, it makes my blood boil! At times I feel I could happily kill him myself – it would be a justifiable action surely? It would merely be a good riddance to bad rubbish, wouldn't it?"

"Aye," Ian thoughtfully replied, "I suppose we could make out a convincing case that to kill Campbell-Fotheringay would be an action where the good ends justified the evil means, couldn't we?"

Ian noticed that Helen was staring silently, intently, and it seemed, uneasily at him. He thought he detected apprehension and foreboding in her intense eyes.

He now glanced anxiously at Kenny. Obviously his nephew's wild outburst had upset him. He sat slumped in his dilapidated old armchair with his eyes tightly shut. He was muttering nervously and indistinctly.

To relieve the tension, Ian grinned, "Aye, I know how you feel about him, Calum. He makes me very angry as well. Aye, our laird is truly an evil one – almost as evil as your friend, Mrs Thatcher, the 'Great Evil One' herself, eh?"

Kenny opened his eyes and thankfully joined in the general laughter as Calum relaxed and went through his invariable performance whenever that name was mentioned. Crossing himself, he merrily cried out, "May angels and ministers of grace defend us from the Evil One!"

Chapter Seventeen

After returning from one of the lambing rounds with Kenny, Ian sauntered by himself through Altdour Croft's wild garden before he went indoors. The tranquil calm of this sheltered garden was a real delight after having been coldly and boisterously buffeted on the exposed, windswept moors. With renewed gratitude he once more admired his grandfather's foresight in planting the efficient windbreaks of fir trees around the crofthouse and garden.

A clump of larch trees appeared all wintry gaunt and bare, but as he got nearer he saw with pleasure that they were tentatively touched with the first faint signs of Spring. All the thin branches were veiled with a delicate pale green mist as the tiny fresh needles daringly peeped forth.

Moving on, he admired a few early primroses, which modestly revealed their tender pale yellows amongst a mass of wood anemones that whitened the ground under the trees like a late lingering snowdrift.

Ian took hold of the slender branch of a young silver birch and examined it closely. Less confident that the defiant larches, each reddish-brown bud, thickly swollen and minusculely tipped with green, impatiently waited for warmer sunshine before daring to burst into leaf. Ian imagined he felt faint stirrings in the slender birch branch as if it was tremulously alive with the exciting awakenings of spring. He smiled. The trees, the shrubs, the woodland flowers, the entire garden, smiled with him. All nature happily thrilled in keen anticipation of the bright, warm, May days coming soon.

After two more miserable days the 'lambing snows' ended. May took over and, fulfilling its promise, brought warm sunshine and gentle calm. The smiling warmth put fresh life in the lambs. Almost with disbelief they revelled in the sunshine. It was such a fantastic contrast to the vile, shivering, miserable weather they had been born into and was all they had known up to now. Singly, or in small groups, they leapt, they ran, they bounced in a delightful madness of riotous joy.

The warmth persuaded fresh grasses to joyously thrust forth. This tender lushness sent ewes on a thankful orgy of gluttonous eating. Spring comes late to this Northern land, but when it does arrive it explodes its sudden generosity unstintingly. Unfortunately it also frees weeds from their long winter sleep and shoots them in joyous life with wild abandon. It was a busy time for Helen in the flower garden and for Ian in the vegetable plot.

Ian was also kept busy at the peat cutting. Kenny assisted him at this work. Calum often came with them and his help, his keen young strength and vigour was much appreciated by the two older men, for that peat cutting was hard, laborious work which got harder and back-torturingly more toilsome as one got older.

Early one morning Ian rose and, as usual, crossed to the bedroom window and studied the weather. It was another glorious day. The fresh risen sun was already glowing with golden warmth from a cloudless sky. Giddy with the delicious delights of spring every bird in the garden was a loud, vibrant rapture of song. Each bird strained its utmost to outdo all rivals.

Ian turned towards the chair where his peat stained jeans and other working clothes lay. He stopped with hand stretched out towards them. He turned and smiled down at Helen, "Och, damn it, we aren't going to waste all this glorious weather working, are we? Come on, get up and we'll go fishing."

Helen sat up in bed and with a chuckle pointed to the tweed skirt she wore on their fishing expeditions. "I knew you were going to say that this morning. I put that skirt out ready last night before you came to bed."

While he buckled on his kilt, Ian laughed and slowly shook his head. "Och, Helen... Helen, you're uncanny. You always ken what I'm thinking. You know it before I know it myself." It really was quite disconcerting how she seemed to so effortlessly read his mind. Smiling, he thought it was just as well he had no guilty secrets he wanted to hide from her – how impossible that would be.

By one o'clock they had fished round three small lochs and were now at a larger loch. Before settling down for lunch they removed their boots and stockings then paddled in the loch. Despite the pleasant sunshine the water was icily cold. Helen gasped and ran ashore. Ian soon followed. He sat beside her and laughed, "My God, Helen, how the might have fallen! Age has fairly caught up with us. Remember when we used to swim in these lochs and never found them too cold?"

"Oh aye, I remember fine, but that was many years ago... far, far too many years ago!"

It was most pleasant to lie on the gentle slope of short grass and feel the sunshine gradually put warmth back into their refreshed, but numbed feet. They happily ate their lunch. The two dogs, having gobbled the generous scraps, turned around a couple of times then flopped down with contented sighs and settled to sleep.

Helen, too, sighed. Contentedly she murmured, "Aye I remember many pleasant fishing and swimming days of long ago." She smiled affectionately at Ian. "I remember one particular day... one truly perfect day."

"Oh, Helen, how did you know I was remembering that perfect day as well?" He grinned, "I was thinking of the perfect lovemaking we made that day."

"Oh, trust you to remember that!"

Smiling, Ian reached over and held her hand. They lay back and drowsily let reminiscent dreams wing them back twenty-nine years to that June day at another loch.

Somehow – surprisingly – Ian had never got round to fishing that high and remote hill loch before. Now, after hearing its sublime beauty and its fabulous trout praised in almost awed whispers by someone who had recently fished it, and spurred by Helen's equal keenness, he decided it was high time this inexcusable neglect was rectified.

Before six on a perfect June morning they left home in the dilapidated old Ford van, which Ian owned at that time. They drove through sleepy Inveraldrory village, along the single-track road by large Loch Ardgie, then up the side road, which laboriously clawed its way up a high ridge. There were some worrying minutes wondering if the straining van would make it up the steepest bends, but, gasping, and leaving flakes of rust and the occasional nut or bolt in its wake, it gallantly clambered on and victoriously gained the summit. The road now meandered along a high plateau. Reaching a certain point they parked the van.

An hour later, sitting resting almost a thousand feet higher, they looked down on the distant van, which had shrunken to a red 'Dinky' toy abandoned by a careless child. Beyond the van the empty road continued its lonely journey over long Highland miles of desolate moor before it dropped steeply to the sea. It did not stop at the rocky shore but, as if in suicidal despair, plunged straight in and drowned itself at Kyledu Ferry, here the aggressively restless waters of a narrow sea loch bit deeply into the grimly resisting land.

Helen and Ian steadily climbed up through a wilderness of steep heather slopes and over stone littered grey ridges. They passed a few lochans lurking secretly in rough folds and rocky crannies of this harsh, primeval landscape. Refusing to be seduced by the doubtful charms of these dark waters they determinedly pressed on towards their much brighter distant goal.

Ian again sat and studied his tattered, pre-war, one inch to one mile Ordnance Survey map. He smiled reassuringly, "This is the final climb, Helen. Our loch's just over this ridge."

"Och, you've been saying that for the last few ridges. I hope to God you're right this time."

"I am… I am. I'm sure of it. You'll get your reward over this ridge, I assure you."

Helen's eyes glittered roguishly, "Och well, I look forward to getting my reward at last – perhaps I'll get more than one reward before the day's over, eh, Ian?"

"Aye, probably you will!" Grinning, and remembering previous glorious outdoor 'rewards', Ian's eyes sparkled with love and amorous anticipation. They were well rewarded when they reached the top of the ridge and gazed down on their eagerly longed for goal. The smallish loch cosily nestled in its high and remote fresh green corrie, which in turn sheltered beneath the curving ridge of Glas Bheinn. That ridge rose five hundred feet above the loch and its steep sides were pale with many screes of grey stones which hung suspended in space and time like fossilized avalanches. The entire place was a rarely visited Shangri La.

The surface of the loch sparkled enticingly in the benevolent June sunshine, but all was not peace in this haven. The ceaseless battle between life and death was glaringly evident. It was being inescapably played out before their eyes. About twenty black-headed gulls were behaving noisily and erratically. Many large trout were rising and dimpling the loch with silvery rings. Dozens of large, pale green mayflies were hatching out and gently floating over the loch's surface. The trout were going crazy voraciously feeding on this succulent fare.

The gulls were going even crazier as they frantically swooped and snatched helpless mayflies from the water.

With almost trembling fingers they assembled their fishing rods. Ian exclaimed, "My God, I've never seen gulls behaving like that before. It's amazing. They're acting like swallows."

These streamlined black and white gulls soared high, momentarily hovered with shimmering wings, then swooped and skimmed over the water with accurately snatching beaks. While their ceaseless movements were dizzyingly impressive, they did not have the inimitable effortless grace and beauty of swallows and there certainly was nothing remotely swallow-like in their constant cacophony of bad-tempered squabbling and raucous swearing.

"Have you ever seen so many mayflies?" Helen asked.

"No, never. We better get fishing before the hatch is over."

But, instead of decreasing, the mayfly hatch increased. As they cast out their artificial dry-flies which resembled the natural flies, more and more mayflies appeared on the loch's surface. Flotilla after flotilla, they daintily sailed like a miniature yachting regatta. Their gauzily translucent upright wings acted as sails which urgently utilised the faint breeze to steer them towards the safety of the high green reeds that lined part of the shore. Few of these vulnerable mayflies seemed to make it to the sanctuary of these reeds, most fell victim to gluttonously excited gulls and trout.

This was trout fishing at its best. The excitement was intense when one of those large trout rose and snatched your enticingly floating dry-fly. The instant the deceived trout realised its mistake it went wild. That strong, wily, hard fighting wild brown trout tore unstoppably across the loch then suddenly leapt high – a glorious golden gleam arching bright in a cascade of crystal spray.

The fisher's line hissed and sliced through the water in urgent pursuit. The madly revolving reel screamed its wildly thrilling song. Crazed nerves no longer ended at trembling finger tips... they spidered out and spun their delicate thread through the joyously quivering and bending rod and along the taut vibrating line. Human nerves are in direct touch with the nerves of the hard fighting trout; are in direct touch with the nerves of our re-awoke, our un-remote fisher/hunter ancestors.

Immersed in sublimely timeless time, the perfect hours passed perfectly unnoticed by Helen and Ian.

Eventually, pangs of hunger alerted them to a sense of time.

Before having lunch they lay out and admired their catches. These large trout were beautiful. All had deep, plump bodies and neat small heads. They glowed a bright golden yellow and were attractively freckled with large red spots.

"Oh, they really are lovely, aren't they?" Helen said. "They're like gleaming bars of gold."

"Aye, they are lovely and they're far more precious than any actual bars of gold!"

Helen nodded in eager agreement, "Aye, trout like these and silvery fresh salmon are almost the only creatures which really retain their beauty after death. I think there's something sad about a dead grouse or deer!"

"Aye, I suppose most creatures seem sadly pathetic when dead. Humans are the saddest of all. Once dead we lose all dignity. I think the saddest aspect of all the dead human bodies I saw during the war was how terribly insignificant they looked. They were like thoughtlessly discarded puppets. It was difficult to believe that only a short time ago they had been full of life, full of energy, full of hope." Ian paused and sighed, "It was no different if they were British or Germans or Italians. It made no difference what rank they were. We soldiers had a saying, 'the body of a dead general stinks as badly as the body of a dead private'."

As she looked down at the neatly arrayed dead trout, Helen gently murmured, "I suppose some people – the anti-blood sports fanatics – would condemn us for having been cruel to these trout, wouldn't they?"

"Aye, they would, but they would be wrong. I am convinced that the hunting/fishing instinct is one of the most deep-rooted instincts in man…"

"And in women… at least in some women," Helen smiling, interrupted.

"Aye, in some women too," Ian diplomatically agreed, "and I feel sure it would be a disastrously black day for mank… for humankind, if fishing and shooting were ever to be banned."

"Aye, I wholeheartedly agree with you, Ian. It is always wrong to go against our deep natural instincts, isn't it?"

"It is, it certainly is. To do so only results in sad, unhealthy frustrations."

Helen laughed, "At least we don't suffer from my frustrations, sexual or any other. Not as long as you live up to your promises, that is."

"I will!… I will! I promise you I will!"

As Ian placed the trout in a waterproof bag, Helen said, "You know, Ian, I've been thinking that even if we were being cruel to those trout they, and the gulls, were in turn being every bit as cruel to all those innocent mayflies, weren't they?"

Ian laughed, "Aye, they were… they certainly were. Trust you to think of that, Helen. Of course Nature does not recognise such a concept as 'cruelty'. All its ceaseless killings, no matter how savage or how painfully prolonged, are merely a normal part of its dispassionate rule that each creature, each species, must constantly struggle to survive."

For some moments they stood thoughtfully silent then Helen smiled, "Let's not spoil this lovely day discussing such things. I'm going to look at those wild flowers." She pointed at a jumble of scree and grey rocks on a steep slope above the loch. "It looks a wonderful natural rock garden."

And so it was. There were many bright clumps of sea pinks (at 2,000 feet, quite a home on this hill, far removed from their usual salty haunts). There were yellow trefoils spreading over screes like streaming golden honey, and rare, gentle, mountain-avens peeped shyly out from behind age-weathered stones.

"Oh, it's glorious, it's a botanist's wonderland," Helen enthused. She sat on a large grey stone. Ian sat beside her. They gazed near and far. Mountains rose steeply in the South and West. To the North, space stretched to infinity. Behind hidden Kylesdu Ferry appeared hazy ridge after hazy ridge of almost uninhabited wilderness, which stretched to the gaunt, storm-tortured cliffs of Cape Wrath.

After a few silent spellbound minutes they rose together and hurried towards their rucksacks at the lochside.

"Do you want lunch now, or what?" Helen asked.

"Oh, I'd much prefer 'or what'!" Ian grinned, then added, "Although actually I was thinking about have a swim. That water looks very inviting, doesn't it?"

"Aye, it does. I was just about to suggest us going swimming myself."

"Of course we've no swimming costumes with us, you know."

"Aye," Helen grinned impishly, "I know. We'll just have to swim nude, won't we?"

After the initial plunge, the first gasping shock, the loch water did not seem too cold.

They swam together then companionably floated on their backs and with thrashing legs fountained sparkling foam of greenish white spray. Then leisurely, almost motionlessly, they floated and idly stared at the vastness of the serene azure sky.

Helen giggled, "Is the sun staring down at us I wonder?"

Ian laughed, "If it is, not doubt it's amused at what it's seeing. No wonder it's benevolently smiling. Certainly old Suileag is impertinently staring down at us. Look, see him peering over that ridge there."

The highest summit of that distant mountain lifted its steeply rounded dome above a nearby ridge.

"Aye, I can just glimpse auld Suileag – he's a real Peeping Tom, isn't he? It's impossible to escape from his watchful stare anywhere in this district. It's a good thing I'm not over modest, some women would be quite embarrassed at having him rudely staring at their naked bodies."

"Aye," Ian agreed, "he's a real rude, lewd, lustily gloating auld Pagan devil, right enough."

Helen stood waist deep in the water and with both hands swept her wet dark hair from her face and smoothed it back over her head. This action lifted her firm small breasts smoothly upwards. Ian stood near her and admired those glistening breasts. With keen appreciation he noted the drop of water delicately clinging to each nipple and glittering like a crystal tear. He smiled, "Och Helen, you're a most temptingly alluring wee mermaid standing there like that."

"Oh well, if I'm a mermaid you must be a merman… that must surely be your 'codpiece' I'm seeing just under the surface there."

"Enough of this fishy talk!" Ian laughed. "Are you going ashore?"

"Aye, I've swam enough. Are you coming for lunch, or what?"

Laughing, Ian again replied, "Och, I'd much prefer 'or what'!"

For a while they lay on the short grass and contentedly let the sun's warmth dry them.

"I'm nice and warm now," Helen gently murmured.

"Aye, so am I. In fact I'm getting really heated up!"

Helen raised herself on both elbows and looked at his aroused body. She giggled, "Aye, I can see that... Oh, Ian, what are you wasting time for?"

For answer he rolled over and clasped her naked body to his naked body. Gasping with pleasure their bodies intertwined and became one flesh.

Later, drowsily satiated, they languidly ate and drank. Wisely, they leisurely protracted the sensual pleasures of eating and drinking. Their naked bodies revelled in the benevolent sunshine as it poured a Pagan benediction over them. All nature languorously relaxed in midsummer's pleasant midday torpor.

The hatch of mayflies was over. Undisturbed by any rising trout the loch's flat surface calmly slept. Even the gulls, those greediest of birds, for once were satiated. They rested in a silent row along a gravel shore.

Helen smiled. "With their black heads and white bodies these gulls book like a piano keyboard stretched over that shore."

"Aye, they do. And what do those two wagtails look like?" Ian pointed to the pair of pied wagtails perched on stones near them. These attractive birds had also gorged on mayflies. Their crops bulged alarmingly. Their long, usually ever active tails now only occasionally managed a half-hearted flick.

"They look like a couple of wee clockwork toys with their mainsprings run down, don't they?"

At the end of their un-hurried meal, Ian finished chewing a final mouthful of bread, then smiled at Helen and quoted:

"Here with a Loaf of Bread beneath the Bough,
A flask of Wine, a Book of Verse – and Thou
Beside me singing in the Wilderness –
and Wilderness is Paradise enow."

"Oh, how romantic... how surprisingly romantic coming from you, Ian."

"Aye, I know. I must be getting a bit soft in the head."

"It must be the influence of this perfect place and this perfect day."

They lay contentedly and companionably silent, then Helen happily murmured, "Yes, this remote Ardgie wilderness truly is 'Paradise enow', isn't it?"

"Yes, it certainly is."

For a while they were again drowsily and contentedly silent. The serene silence was ended by Helen going into a fit of giggles.

Ian turned and lazily opened one enquiring eye, "What's so funny now? What fantastic notions are going through that crazy wee head of yours?"

Still giggling, her eyes roguishly gleaming, she gasped, "What is that line of poetry you often quote about 'a thing of beauty'?"

"Oh, it's from Keats' poem, 'ENDYMION':

236

"A thing of beauty is a joy for ever:'
Its loveliness increases; it will never pass into nothingness but..."

"Yes," Helen interrupted, "yes, that's it: 'A thing of beauty is a joy for ever'. That line came un-summoned into my mind as I was looking at your naked body; at a certain part of your naked body – your penis."

With complacent male vanity, Ian glanced proudly at that organ as it drooped in flaccidly relaxed ease. Smiling into Helen's eyes, he asked, "Well, what about it? What has it got to do with that line of great poetry?"

"Och, no doubt I'm just being crazy again, but as I gazed at your penis this fantastic thought suddenly came to me: That thing may well be 'a joy for ever'... but it most certainly *is not* 'a thing of beauty'!"

For some astounded moments Ian was struck dumb.

Eventually, he slowly shook his head and cried, "Oh, Helen... Helen... Helen, trust you to come up with the most crazy ideas."

Sparkling eyes gazed into sparkling eyes. They burst into uncontrollable laughter. Their bodies shook. They wept unrestrained tears of joy. Helen gasped, "Och, we're crazy... we're crazy!"

"Aye, we are... we are, thank God we are!"

Ian rolled onto his side, put an arm around Helen and once more drew her naked body to his naked body. For a while they continued to shake with laughter; then inevitably the inevitable happened and more urgent passions took over. Helen's body warmly responded to the aroused eagerness of Ian's body. "You're not too tired, are you?" he murmured.

"Oh, no... no... no!" She giggled, "I'm eager to sin again!"

"Aye, so am I. Anyway, as we're married our lovemaking is nae sin. It's a pleasure sanctified by God, by church and state."

"Mmm, I know. But even if we weren't married, surely in this perfect place, under these perfect conditions it would simply be a sin not to sin?"

"Aye, it would. It would be a grievous sin against nature for us not to lovingly make love."

Helen giggled, "Oh, I love making love out in the open air like this. Somehow it seems so wonderfully natural."

"Aye, it is. It's the most natural thing in the world. And, thank God, at this time of year, under these glorious conditions, there are no damned midges to spoil our lovemaking." Ian grinned, "What's more, while making love in this remote mountain paradise there's no danger of us frightening the horses as we're doing it!"

Helen gave a puckish hobgoblin grin, then smiled into Ian's eager, hotly gleaming eyes, "Enough of this talk... let's have some action... some magic action."

Enfolded together they again wondrously became one flesh. Their coalescent bodies now shook not with laughter, but with the wonderful, the ridiculous, the ecstatic madness of love. Swept by vast tides of tempestuous passion, they moved together – moved together in undulating waves of ecstasy.

Gasping, sweating, moaning, they climaxed in a wildly magnificent volcanic eruption of fantastic pleasure.

Later, exhausted and fulfilled, they lay side by side flat on their backs. Only their hands touched and, faintly trembling, eloquently communicated their love. Drowsy eyelids drooped and lethargic bodies contentedly drifted towards sleep. They – Helen especially – loved this thrilling calm after love's wild, passionate, excitement. Lingering in the long, sweet aftermath, a delicious languor caressed her body.

Ian smiled as he heard Helen gently and happily sigh. Then he experienced a strange, a wonderfully strange, sensation. He felt himself – his soul?... his spirit?... his psyche? – released from his drowsy body. He rose... he floated. Free of his flesh, he gazed down on his own body as it lay completely relaxed beside Helen's apparently sleeping body.

His floating spirit quivered as delicately as the faint tremors of tender aspen leaves sensing, rather than actually feeling, the merest hint of a breeze. He felt his Pagan soul gloriously unite with all nature. It had a radiant affinity with nature's universal vastness. It was at one with the sun and the sky, the mountains and moors, the loch and the trout, the gulls, wagtails and mayflies. Helen was an integral part of him; he was an integral part of her.

These powerful pantheistic feelings were glorious; they profoundly transcended any narrow religion's arrogant dogmas and limited visions. Nothing seemed any longer remote or mysterious. He was in intimate touch with the Infinite. He was in communion with the palpable purity of beauty. He felt it needed only a little – a very little – effort on his part and he could master all mysteries; could gain all knowledge; would know the Ultimate Universal Truths, but he was too blissfully relaxed, too dreamily content, to bestir himself to make the least effort.

For an immeasurable space of time he was rapt in ecstasy... was in a transcendental state of bliss.

Then suddenly, with no consciousness of any returning movement, he was back in his body lying on the grass beside Helen. She turned her head and smiled radiantly at him. "You've returned, have you? That was a glorious experience, wasn't it?"

Without thinking, he smiled and nodded, "Aye, it most certainly was." Then, startled and mystified, he asked, "How did you know? Did you have that same fantastic disembodied experience at the same time as me?"

"Yes, I did."

"You've had such experiences before?"

"Aye... oh aye, quite a number of times. And you?"

"Only once, and that was nothing like so vivid, so wonderful, as this time."

"Aye, I know, Ian, I know. Mine was the same."

He stared at her in amazement and for a while lay still in thoughtful silence.

Helen accepted her wondrous experience as an ineffable gift; a gift she could not understand but which she thankfully enjoyed. She knew that such mysterious, mystic visions belong to realms beyond the reasoning, logical brain.

Ian's masculine mind attempted to find some logical reason for his wondrous experience. Painstakingly he tried to intellectually analyse what had happened to him. He remembered the words of some philosopher he had once read: 'The Mystical Experience is distinguished by its Ineffability'. How, therefore, could he possibly describe the indescribable, or explain it, in poor, halting, stammering words?

Helen's enquiring voice interrupted his thoughts. "Most of those who have had such a mystical experience believe they've been in touch with some Deity; been in contact with their own particular God, don't they?"

"Aye, they do, but I didn't. Did you?"

"No... no. I felt in a state of bliss, but did not feel in touch with any specific God."

"I was the same. It was a wondrous awe-inspiring feeling but was not specifically a religious feeling. If there was a God involved, it definitely was a God of Pantheism, an all-embracing godlike force of universal unity."

Once more they fell thoughtfully silent.

Ian recalled how he had felt just before that glorious experience. After their wondrous lovemaking he had lain sensuously replete. Not only his sexual instincts, but all his instincts were satisfied. Having eaten and drank, he was not hungry, was not thirsty. The demands of his ancient hunting/fishing instincts had been well fulfilled and, conscious of the wild beauty surrounding him, his aesthetic desires were also satisfied.

He wondered if it was because all his physical needs were completely satisfied that his 'soul' had been able to float free of his body and have that unique mystic experience. Mystic? He questioned that possibly pretentious word, but no other word better described that experience.

As he shared these thoughts with Helen, Ian suddenly grinned, "We know that many saints and would-be saints have attempted to reach a state of mysticism through asceticism; through renouncing all physical pleasures, through striving for many years with austerity and chastity and the severe mortification of the flesh, don't we?"

"Yes, we do. What about it?"

"Well, wouldn't it be supremely ironic if we've discovered that the best, the easiest, the most direct route to deep spiritual experience – to mysticism? – lies *not* through renouncing the flesh and all physical pleasures, but by *indulging* the flesh and being satiated with physical pleasures?

"You must admit it's a most alluring idea. The true way to bliss lies not in *denying* the senses, but in *satisfying* the senses!"

"Aye, it is... it certainly is," Helen said. She chuckled, "I don't suppose your brother or his wife would agree with this theory, would they?"

"No, they most definitely wouldn't. They would be shocked. They would be more convinced than ever that our two souls are earmarked for Eternal

Damnation. With their narrow Calvinistic outlook they regard almost all pleasures, even the most innocent of natural pleasures, even the highest of aesthetic pleasures, as sinful."

Helen sighed, "It must be terrible to be like that, to see sin in even the greatest, the most beautiful works of art humans have created. Surely if anything raises humans higher than the animals it is our ability to create wondrous works of art."

"Aye, I know, Helen. But you agree that my idea is a most tempting, a most alluring hedonistic theory, don't you?"

"Oh aye, I do… I do."

"And my way is obviously much more enjoyable than any narrowly ascetic saintly way, isn't it?"

"Oh aye, it is. Somehow I could never imagine you leading an abstinent, austere and chase saintly life, Ian."

"No. Nor could I, thank God!" He chuckled, "Although from what I've read of the lives of the saints most of them only turn ascetic as they get older after having led a sinfully debauched life. I remember being impressed by Saint Augustine. He understood the urgent need to satisfy our sexual passions. As a young man he keenly pursued women. At least he was honest as, struggling with his strong sexual impulses, he pleaded to God his Libertine's Prayer: 'O, Lord, please make me chaste… but please, Lord, not yet… not quite yet'"

Helen laughed, "Oh well, I hope the time's far off when *you* start chasing after chastity, Ian."

Ian grinned as he once again glanced down at his flaccidly relaxed genitals with complacent pride, "Oh, don't worry, Helen, I have no intention of turning chaste in the near future. For me to be chaste would be a terrible waste of those precious God-given treasures, wouldn't it?"

Time leisurely stretched itself timelessly out as they lay in silent, companionably intimate contentment. Dreamily, they drowsily drifted in and out of soothing sleep.

Happiness – shared exultant happiness – permeated them. They were happier at that moment than they had ever been. Both knew to live as they were now living in contented harmony with one another and with oneself, and with one's chosen environment, was the highest, the truest, way of living, and Helen had another source of happiness. She would share this secret with Ian later. Ian and she wanted a baby, and, sensually and blissfully aware of Ian's semen oozily moist deep, deep, inside her, she was certain that she would conceive today. That would be the perfect culmination of this perfect day. Hugging her joyous secret she smiled radiantly: she could not conceive of not conceiving!

Eventually, Ian glanced at his watch and reluctantly said, "I suppose it's about time we started moving."

They decided not to fish any more but to leisurely make their way back to the waiting van. "It would be foolish to spoil this perfect day by being over greedy for fishing, wouldn't it, Ian?"

"Aye, it would." He grinned, "And anyway the best of the fishing's over."

No mayflies were hatching and the satiated trout were not rising. The greedy gulls had departed. The breeze had died and left the loch's surface glittery calm; left it mirror still except when, from nowhere, a playful swirling cat's-paw of wind came and skittishly kittened across the water for a short distance then vanished. The somnolent air was drugged with sunlight.

Taking many enjoyable rests, they unhurriedly made their way over the long, rough, heathery Highland miles. Fortunately this homeward journey was all downhill.

Their dilapidated old van was also pleased that its return route was down the steep hill it had so laboriously climbed in the morning.

As they cruised down the final slope into Inveraldrory village, Ian smiled at Helen, "Do you fancy having dinner at 'Hamburger Harry's'?"

"Oh yes, that would be great. I wasn't fancying having to cook dinner when we got home, not after this lovely, but long and strenuous day we've had."

"Aye, it would be a great pity to spoil this perfect day. Anyway, it's about time we tried 'Hamburger Harry's' new restaurant, isn't it?"

Harry Williamson – or 'Hamburger Harry' as the locals had nicknamed him – had for the last few years been selling hamburgers and fish and chips from his van in the village. Last winter he had bought a shop, then converted it into an attractive small restaurant.

Soon Helen and Ian were comfortably seated at one of the rear windows of the restaurant, which looked out over the estuary of the River Aldrory and across Inveraldrory Bay. They had finished their excellent Scotch broth and were well into the haddock and chips (the haddock fresh from the local fish market) when Ian stopped eating and quietly said, "If you turn your head slowly to the left, Helen, you'll see something interesting."

Mystified, Helen turned and stared out of the window. She gave a gasp of delight, "Oh, it's the white otter!"

A large, pure white male otter had emerged from the waters of the estuary. With smooth, silent, sinuously effortless movements it undulated over slippery, seaweed draped rocks. The four pound grilse it firmly carried drooped from both sides of its mouth like a large silvery white moustache and the doomed young salmon's tail frantically wriggled in ineffectual protest.

The otter settled on a dry slab of grey rock only a few yards from the restaurant's windows. Helen continued starting with boundless delight. Ian had seen this white otter before, but this was Helen's fist sight of it. For the last six months or so it had become a fairly familiar sight in the estuary and bay. The older and more superstitious fishermen liked to see it as they set out from Inveraldrory harbour. They believed the ancient legend that a white otter brought luck and good catches. These fishermen rewarded it with gifts of fresh fish when they returned to harbour bountifully laden.

Helen and Ian watched fascinated as the otter, with very obvious voluptuous pleasure, methodically chewed through the thickest 'middle cut' of the grilse's delicious, bright red trembling flesh.

Then some loudly approaching people disturbed the otter. It lifted its head and stared. The next moment its streamlined body slid with sleek boneless grace over the rocks then noiselessly glided into the water and disappeared without a splash, with hardly a ripple.

"Oh, what a lovely sight," Helen exclaimed. "That white otter has made this perfect day even more perfect."

"Aye, it has," Ian said, delighted with her glowing delight.

Back home at Altdour they quickly got through the unavoidable chores. While Helen prepared the dogs' food, Ian expertly gutted and beheaded the trout. He then dumped the pailful of heads and guts on the compost heap. Many seagulls, scenting that enticing fresh offal, appeared from nowhere and impatiently clamoured to get at it. As Ian threw the sheet of corrugated iron back on top of the compost heap, he mockingly laughed at the gulls, "Is that *awful* of me, denying you a feed of that luscious *offal*?"

He laughed again and shook his fist as a spray of white excrement splashed down and just missed him. It was tempting to think that had been a deliberate attack on him by the large, angrily frustrated herring gull. Certainly the baleful glare from its jaundiced eye as it swept low overhead seemed full of icy fury.

Helen and Ian soon got themselves comfortably ensconced in their deep old armchairs on either side of the fireplace. The tired, well-fed dogs contentedly stretched out on the deerskin rug in front of the unlit fire. Ian's favourite old pipe was drawing well and Helen was enjoying, as a special treat, a relaxing cigarette. They each held a generous dram. Helen took an appreciative sip then sighed, "Oh, Ian, this has been a really perfect day."

"Aye, it has. It's a day we will remember for the rest of our lives."

And, twenty-nine years later, as they lay side by side at this other loch, that prediction of Ian's proved correct: they did remember that far off perfect day. They clearly remembered every wonderful detail of it.

Happily, Helen reminiscently murmured, "Yes, that certainly was a perfect day at the Green Corrie Loch all those years ago. It must be, what... almost thirty years ago."

"Almost thirty years?... That's amazing. It hardly seems thirty months, let alone thirty years."

Helen, smiling, stared at Ian. Smiling, he stared at her. Each noted the signs of age in the other. Ian's white hair was getting thinner; his beard was turning from grey to white. Helen's still abundant, still rather unkempt naturally curly hair was pure white; many crows-feet were deeply etched at the corners of each eye, they crinkled as she smiled; they were – as she declared with rueful good-natured resignation – laughter lines and not lines of age. She grinned, "Despite my age, I don't feel old. It's strange, you know, but I hardly feel any older than I was on that perfect day all those years ago."

"Aye, I know. I feel exactly the same. It's hard to realise that to strangers, to youngsters, we must appear an old couple." He smiled, "I suppose one thing that does betray our age is us now finding the loch water too cold to really enjoy paddling in let alone swimming in."

Helen squeezed his hand, which was gently holding hers. Again she grinned, "Aye, and another thing which betrays our age is the fact that we're content to lie side by side now and do nothing more than hold hands." Her eyes twinkled, "Quite a change from that day, eh?

Chapter Eighteen

Three days after that fishing trip, Helen and Ian were once more relaxing in their old armchairs by the fireplace when Colin MacDonald's van drove up to the front door. Jeannie and Colin were heartily welcomed, were soon comfortably settled and hospitably provided with drams. Colin apologised for calling so late. "It's after ten o'clock. We won't stay long. We've all to be up early tomorrow morning."

"Och, you'll stay long enough for a cup of tea," Helen said, as she moved towards the scullery.

Colin explained their late visit, "I had a phone call from old John Munro; he's had a few lambs killed by foxes, and this evening he saw a large fox trotting off with a freshly killed lamb. It made off in the direction of yon large cairn where we found the fox den last year, remember, Ian?"

"Aye, oh aye, I remember that place fine. So you think foxes are using that den again this year?"

"Aye, it looks likely. I promised to go tomorrow morning and search for the foxes. Do you fancy coming along with me?"

"Aye, certainly. I'll give you the pleasure of my company." Ian glanced with unspoke accusation at Helen as he said, "A day chasing after foxes will be much more interesting than a day spent weeding the vegetable garden, as someone had planned for me, won't it?"

Colin laughed, "Aye, it will. Anything is more interesting than that damned weeding!"

Every year Colin – like all Highland gamekeepers – was kept busy during spring and early summer searching for fox dens. Every known den had to be thoroughly inspected by the fox-terriers and, if occupied, the foxes ruthlessly and efficiently dealt with. Apart from going round all the fox den sites on his own beat, covering thousands of acres of Ardgie Estate, Colin received many requests from crofters to search their outlying croft lands for savagely marauding, lamb plundering foxes.

As they drank their tea Jeannie and Helen pleasantly gossiped and with keen anticipation looked forward to their day out tomorrow, when their mutual friend, Mrs Margaret Yeats, who had a guest house in Glen Aldrory, was taking them in her car on a shopping expedition to Inverness. Margaret Yeats' husband, John, was a talented artist and photographer. His landscape paintings and photographs of local scenes sold well. He also sold some of Helen's clay models and some of her and Ian's paintings in his shop and gallery.

Later, Jeannie remarked, "I see our friend the laird, Campbell-Fotheringay, is back again; I saw him in the village yesterday. He's looking terrible. He looks old and ugly and debauched. He had two young blondes with him, one hanging on each arm."

Helen grinned, "No wonder he's looking debauched!"

"Aye, he must be slowly killing himself with an excess of drink, drugs and sex," Jeannie said. She gave a slight shudder, "Oh, he's a horrible man."

"Aye, it must be a terrible thing to be hooked on drugs," Colin remarked.

Helen smiled, "I notice you don't condemn him for indulging in drink or sex."

Colin raised his glass of whisky and grinned at Ian, "Och, I don't suppose we can fairly criticise him too much for his drinking, can we?"

"No... no," Ian laughed, "I doot that would be a case of the pot calling the kettle black, wouldn't it?"

"And what about sex? What aboot his blonde young whores?" Jeannie asked.

Both men hesitated to reply; eventually Ian winked at Colin and said, "Och well, perhaps we can't condemn him for that either, can we? After all we are not pure angels, are not exactly innocent virgins ourselves, are we?"

Colin's laughter thunderously boomed out, "No... no, we are not innocent virgins – thank God!"

Jeannie and Helen disparagingly shook their heads and exclaimed, "Och, men!... men!" But their laughter heartily joined in with the men's.

After taking a good gulp of whisky, Colin said, "If Campbell-Fotheringay is slowly killing himself, is committing a form of slow suicide, well you have to admit that it is a pleasant way to do it, through drinking and fornicating!"

"Aye," Ian agreed, "that must be a good way to go." Then he more seriously added, "But that method of suicide takes a long time and in the meantime that bastard is ruining this estate. If he's killing himself then the sooner he does it the better; the better for everyone on the estate. I only wish he would kill himself quickly – before someone is tempted to do it for him!"

For some moments there was a solemn silence.

Then Helen laughed, "Och, Ian, perhaps Colin and you are just jealous of him... jealous of him with all his beautiful young blonde dolly-birds."

Punctually at seven-thirty the following morning, Colin again drove up to Altdour croft. Jeannie transferred to Mrs Yeats' car which had arrived a few minutes earlier. Helen also got into the car. As she settled herself, Margaret Yeats asked, "Are we all ready? Have we got everything?"

"Yes... yes, we've got everything."

Then suddenly Helen exclaimed, "Oh no, wait, I've left my shopping list. Will you get it for me, Ian, please? It's on the kitchen table, I think."

Ian rapidly glanced over the shopping list. Without surprise he noted that the first items were for tapes of classical music, including some piano concertos, Helen's favourite music. More mundane items, such as food and clothes were relegated to lower down the list. He grinned, "Here it is, Helen, although from what I've seen of it, it's not so much a shopping list... it's more a Chopin, Liszt!"

Laughing and waving as the car moved away, Helen shouted, "Aye, it may be a 'Chopin, Liszt', but when we 'girls' are away in Inverness don't you two 'boys' go and get yourselves 'Brahms and Liszt'!... Don't come home the worse for drink!"

"As though we would!... As though we would!... Anyway we've never been 'the worse for drink' – we've always been the better for drink!"

As Colin and Ian prepared to set out from the Munro's crofthouse at Ardoe in search of the marauding, lamb-killing fox, old John Munro insisted on going with them. His wife tried to dissuade him. Ian and Colin were not too keen on him accompanying them either. He was about eighty years old and his eyesight was not too great. However he was determined, so they gave in with good grace. John's wife, Mary, was not so gracious in defeat. As she saw him off at the door she sighed in exasperation, "Did you ever see the like?... Och, you're a thrawn auld bugger. Be careful now... be careful!"

"Aye, aye, I'll be careful. I'm no' a bairn, ye ken."

"Oh no? Then why do you so often act like one?"

As the men went round the side of the crofthouse out of sight and hearing of Mrs Munro, old John sighed loudly and meaningfully, "Och, wummen!... och, thae wummen!"

Aglow with deep understanding and warm male companionship the three men grinned at one another. There was no need for further words, instinctively they were allies united in the age-old masculine struggle with women.

As they strode along the wide peat track that led into the heart of wildly rugged Ardoe peninsula, Ian and Colin kept a wary eye on old John's shotgun. That dangerous weapon swung around in every direction as he pointed out some feature in the landscape then related an ancient legend connected with it. More than once they both received an almost indecently intimate view up the menacing ends of the barrels of his erratic and – hopefully – unloaded shotgun. Exchanging amused slightly apprehensive glances they knew they were thinking the same thing: that old John's gun posed a far greater threat to them than to any fox.

They eventually arrived safely at the end of the track and took a short rest. Colin encouragingly said, "You're managing fine, John. I only hope I'll be as fit as you at your age."

"Och aye, I'm still gey spry! I'm not too decrepit yet, although tae hear that auld wifie o' mine you'd think I was halfway in my coffin!" He gave a wide, almost toothless, almost boyish grin, "Och perhaps she wishes I was in ma coffin; na doot she would get some peace then!"

Laughing heartily, Ian exclaimed, "Och, John, you're an incorrigible auld bugger!"

Colin gleefully added, "Aye, John, you're a disgraceful auld bugger of a bodach!"*

---

* 'bodach' – old man

246

Old John chuckled delightedly. As they started out again he grinned, "Och, man, but I'm fair enjoying this outing with you twa lads. It's real braw tae get away frae the cailleach* for a wee while."

They climbed up and along a rocky ridge then dropped down into a steep-sided gully. Steadily and cautiously they worked through that rough wilderness. Despite the sunshine glaring from the cloudless May sky, the wind, set steadily from the North, had a cold edge to it. Channelled through that narrow gully it sent ripples shivering over the thick heather and, terrier-like, shook and worried the tall, lush fonds of bracken.

When they arrived at the large cairn of tumbled boulders where foxes often had their den Colin whispered to the old crofter, "Will you stay here, John, and cover this area in case a fox breaks out through that bracken? We'll go further on and cover the rest of the cairn."

They left him comfortably settled on a convenient large smooth stone with his shotgun held alertly across his lap. Colin had checked that gun and, finding it unloaded, had diplomatically suggested it might be a good idea to load it now.

Ian and Colin laboriously ploughed their way through the wilderness of thick old heather which filled the gully below the steep cairn. To the cursing, sweating, struggling men it seemed as if the tough, woody heather stems were maliciously alive and evilishly determined to trip them up at every step.

Reaching positions where their guns could cover all the large cairn, they released the wildly impatient fox-terriers. Keenly eager, the three dogs darted for the cairn. As usual, Colin's old terrier, Dirky, led the way. Although the oldest he was still the keenest. His raggedy torn ears and battle scarred muzzle were evidence of his many encounters with foxes. He was a tough, experienced, wily fighter; a valiant opponent for even the largest and most powerful of foxes. Colin's younger terrier, Rory, eagerly followed close behind Dirky. Ian's terrier, Corrie, struggled to join them.

All the dogs were soon lost to sight in the confusion of jumbled boulders. Only their excited yelps, getting fainter and fainter as they went deeper and deeper underground, indicated their whereabouts.

With shotguns at the ready, Ian and Colin alertly and expectantly waited. They did not have long to wait.

Less than a minute after the terriers vanished underground a large fox bolted out from between two huge boulders above where Colin was waiting. Pellets from his first shot splattered harmlessly against rock. His second shot accurately struck home. Hit squarely in the chest the fox was thrown on its side. For a few moments its body quivered and its legs jerked spasmodically. Then it lay in the unnatural stillness of death. It had met a much more merciful death than many of the savage deaths it had inflicted on helpless lambs.

The terriers squabbled over and worried the body of the fox until they were sternly ordered away. Ian and Colin inspected the body. It was a large, strong male fox in the prime of condition.

---

* 'cailleach' – old woman

After they searched amongst the mass of boulders and found no evidence of the place having recently been used as a fox den, Colin said, "It looks as if that fox was on its own. If there was a vixen and cubs hidden in this cairn the terriers would be down after them."

"Aye, they've lost interest altogether," Ian agreed, "so it must have been a lone rogue male fox without a mate."

"Aye, and we know that often such lone rogues cause more havoc than a dog fox hunting to feed his vixen."

"I wonder if it's their frustrated sexual instincts that make such lone foxes go on killing sprees?"

"Aye, it could be… it could well be." Colin suddenly grinned, "We can understand how those poor frustrated male foxes feel, can't we? Remember our time in the deserts of North Africa during the war? With no females for hundreds of miles we sometimes felt pretty wild with frustration, didn't we?"

Ian laughed, "Aye, we did… despite the bromide in our tea, we certainly did! Aye, it's no wonder that frustrated male foxes often go on wild killing sprees."

After searching about for some more time, Colin, said, "Och, I suppose we better go back to old John, he'll be wondering how we've got on."

Ian picked up the body of the fox by the tail and Colin lifted another smaller body, then they carefully clambered down through that steep chaos of primeval rocky litter.

Old John Munro impatiently awaited their return. He grinned as Ian threw the body of the fox down beside him. "Och, well done, lads… well done."

Eagerly he inspected the body. Even in death, as it lay stretched out on its side, that large, mature, male fox was a beautiful animal. In the bright sunlight its fresh summer coat shone, all glowing red and gleaming bronze, and its long and bushy tail was attractively tipped with a pure white brush.

John quietly soliloquised, "Och, man, but you're a richt bonnie beast. It seems a shame we had tae kill ye."

Without a word, Colin disclosed the small body he had been hiding behind his back and threw it down beside the fox. It was the remains of one of John's lambs. That mutilated small carcase was pathetic. In places its curly white wool was darkly stained with dried blood; its tail and both ears – those tasty titbits – had been chewed off.

For a moment John stared at the remains of his lamb then, savagely kicking the dead fox, angrily exclaimed, "Oh, you cruel bugger!… Oh, you filthy brute!… Och, you're an ugly, ugly, deil!"

Colin's laughter boomed out, "By God, John, you quickly changed your tune!"

Ian and Colin decided to check out two sites, at the furthest point of Ardoe peninsula, which foxes had used as dens in previous years. Old John, feeling rather tired, thought he better make his own way home and not slow the fitter men. As they parted, he hospitably stated, "The cailleach will have fresh scones ready for you when you return and I'll have drams waiting for you."

They thanked him, they grinned, "That's a grand inducement for us to hurry through our work."

Finding no trace of foxes at the first site, they made their way along the cliff tops and cautiously passed above the smooth, steep grassy slope where, years ago, they had helped rescue John's stranded cattle.

Colin smiled reminiscently, "You did real well that time, Ian, when you leapt ashore from the boat, humanely shot the grievously injured cow, then managed to leap back in again."

"Aye," Ian laughed, "but I was a lot younger and fitter then. I doubt if I could do it now."

"Aye, oor limbs were a sight mare supple then. And we weren't troubled wi' rheumatics, either."

Grinning at one another, they sighed deeply. They sighed at the terrible swiftness of the passing of the years; they sighed foreseeing the increasing onset of the ailments, the aches and pains, the weaknesses and indignities of old age.

A little further on they clambered down a slightly less steep rocky gully to where, sometime in the remote past, a huge slice of dark cliff had collapsed and left a mass of rocks crazily jumbled all over the slope. In the sea below, one gigantic sharp-toothed boulder rose at low tide and jutted high like a starkly fossilized iceberg.

All the terriers, again led by Dirky, eagerly disappeared down the narrow entrance to a dark cave.

Old Dirky soon returned. Colin grinned at him, "Well, Dirky, nothing doing in there either, eh? It's been a disappointing day for you, I'm afraid."

Dirky shook himself violently then lifted his leg and disdainfully piddled at the entrance to that uninteresting, fox-less cave. He threw his master what seemed an annoyed, accusing glare.

Colin laughed, "I'm sorry, Dirky, it's not my fault we've not found more foxes for you to fight today."

Ian laughed too, "Aye, obviously he's very disappointed with you, Colin."

The other two terriers emerged and the entire party started on the homeward journey.

With the dogs leading the way, they walked along the track that led to John Munro's croft. As they approached a blind corner there was a sudden, startling, noisy commotion. The terriers yelped and hastily scattered as a dark blue range rover came roaring round the corner. Colin and Ian jumped clear as the vehicle skidded and slithered to a shuddering halt. Its horn blared noisily and angrily.

After assuring themselves that their dogs were unharmed, Ian and Colin approached the range rover. Only now did they recognise the driver – Mr Campbell-Fotheringay, the laird of Aldrory Estate. Two beautiful young blonde women were squeezed in the front beside him.

In an aggressively loud voice Campbell-Fotheringay shouted, "Why aren't those damned dogs under control? They nearly put me in the ditch! What are they doing on my estate anyway, eh?" He now recognised the two men. "Oh, it's you, MacLean, is it? What are you doing here? What are you poaching this time, eh?"

Ian swung his shotgun up on to his shoulder with its barrels pointing harmlessly to the sky. He put his right hand on the door of the range rover and stared in at Campbell-Fotheringay. "I'm not poaching. We're doing your damned work for you."

Campbell-Fotheringay ignored him. He turned to Colin, "And you, MacDonald, what are you doing here on my estate, eh? You've no business to be here."

With an effort, Colin kept quiet and reasonable as he explained, "Mr Campbell-Fotheringay, Ian and I are here at the request of a local crofter to search for foxes which have been killing his lambs."

"This is *my* estate. You are not employed here. You have no right to be here unless *I*" (he strongly emphasised the 'I') "give my permission for you be here, MacDonald."

"If you employed gamekeepers to look after your estate there would be no need for Ian and me to be here searching for foxes." As Colin said this he too lifted his shotgun from the crook of his right arm and swung it out of the way on to his left shoulder with the barrels, like Ian's, innocently pointing at the sky.

"Don't you dare try to tell me how to run my estate, MacDonald," Campbell-Fotheringay almost screamed. "And don't think you can intimidate me by threatening me with your gun."

Before Colin could reply Ian passionately interjected, "The only way you're running your estate is running it into the ground… ruining it… running it to disaster!"

"I don't need any damned ignorant know-all crofter like you, MacLean, to tell me my business either," Campbell-Fotheringay shouted furiously. His fat, putty pale face suffused with anger, it turned an ugly, bloated, purplish hue. The veins on his forehead bulged. His mean little eyes blazed hatred. "There are far too many lazy crofters on my estate like you, who are good for nothing but poaching my salmon and my deer." He paused for breath, then gasped out, "And you, MacDonald, you're supposed to be a gamekeeper, why are you working hand in glove with this notorious poacher, eh?"

With a great effort Colin kept his anger under control, reasonably calmly he repeated, "Listen, Campbell-Fotheringay, we're not poaching, we're doing your work for you. We're killing vermin on your estate. You should employ gamekeepers of your own to do this work."

Ian again quickly and passionately interjected, "Aye, and you yourself, Campbell-Fotheringay, are the worst vermin on this estate… you are the vermin who should be killed!"

The bloated wee laird positively screamed, "Are you threatening me?" He turned to the silent blondes sitting beside him, "Remember what he said. Remember his threats. You are both witnesses to his threats." He then glared at Colin, "I've told you before, MacDonald, don't you dare try to tell me how to manage my estate."

Colin's anger now got the better of him, his ruddy face darkened, his eyebrows lowered, his eyes glowered, "Och, you damned wee squirt, Campbell, don't you shout at me like that. This isn't the nineteenth century, we don't have to bow down and humble ourselves before the likes of you any more."

"I'll report this insolence of yours to your employer, MacDonald. We'll see what Lord Kilvert has to say about this threatening insolence."

"Och, Lord Kilvert is a real gentleman; I know he hasn't much use for the likes of you."

"Oh, is that so? Well, we will see about that, I..."

Once again Ian interrupted, "It's true what Colin said. This isn't the nineteenth century. The sooner we get rid of obnoxious, petty wee bastard bonnet lairds like you the better."

Campbell-Fotheringay's bloated face bulged even more furiously. It grew a darker shade of purple. His small eyes vanished, engulfed in ugly folds of fat. Ian, remembering that Helen always described those eyes as being "horrid wee mean and shifty piggy eyes," thought how accurate her description was. He did look like an ill-tempered pig as he screamed, "The sooner we get back to some nineteenth century discipline and strict values the better!"

"By God," Colin exclaimed, "that's cool coming from you! Who are you to talk about discipline and strict values? You... you debauched wee bastard of a bloody Campbell, with your drugs and your fancy 'whores'."

Before Campbell-Fotheringay – speechless with wrath – could gather breath to reply, the young blonde sitting next to him grabbed his arm with both hands and cried out in a loud and affected drawling English accent, "Oh Tony, da'ling, don't waste any more time with those yokels. Let's move on, it's getting cold sitting here." As he turned and gave her a sickly smile, the other blonde indistinctly muttered something about, "Those obnoxious, uncouth peasants... Let's go, Tony!"

Campbell-Fotheringay complied with their requests. Perhaps he was secretly pleased to be persuaded to do what he wanted to do – to get away from those two very angry and potentially dangerous men. As he wound up the window, he glared at Colin and shouted, "I'll remember this, MacDonald. I'll remember your damned insolence!" He put the Range Rover into gear and drove off.

Colin and Ian stood looking after the retreating vehicle. The ugly black pulse of hatred violently throbbing through their veins gradually subsided. They grinned at one another. "That was quite a confrontation," Ian said.

"Aye, it was... It sure was. He didn't like me calling him a debauched wee bastard with his drugs and his whores."

"No, he didn't," Ian laughed, "and he didn't like you calling him a 'bloody Campbell', either. I thought it was going to come to another clan battle between the MacDonald's and the Campbell's. I noticed that at first you politely called him 'Mr Campbell-Fotheringay', then you dropped the 'mister'. Then you dropped the 'Fotheringay', so that you were calling him 'Campbell'; then finally, 'Bloody Campbell'; and you spat out those final two words with real venom."

Colin laughed, "Aye, I suppose I did; I wasn't really conscious of it though. It must have been my ancestral MacDonald blood speaking."

"Aye, and speaking about venom reminds me of the old saying: 'It is the bright day that brings forth the adder'. Well, this bright day brought forth a real vile, venomous viper in the shape of that bastard, didn't it? Anyway, I was thankful that you had unloaded your shotgun a while ago; had it been loaded I would have worried that you might have been sorely tempted to use it on that venomous bastard!"

Again Colin laughed, "I had the same thought about you, Ian. It was reassuring to remember that your gun was safely unloaded too."

"I also thought it a good thing you weren't wearing your kilt either, Colin, if you had been, you might well have drawn the sgian dubh from the top of your stocking and stabbed that dagger into that ugly, fat, pig throat of his!"

"Och, Ian, don't put such ideas – such dangerously attractive ideas – into my head."

The bantering tone they had been using suddenly died. They stood silent and motionless. They stared into one another's eyes. The thought of stabbing daggers into throats immediately conjured up two incidents from wartime Italy. The subconscious worked its deep, dark, profound alchemy and – un-requested – floated certain pictures on the surface of the minds of those old comrades. Despite (or because of?) the passage of forty years, these pictures were vividly clear: Ian going wild with his bloodied bayonet; both of them silently, stealthily, slitting throats of German sentries.

These pictures from the past made them wonder if there might be something mysteriously and sinisterly prophetic in those last few words of theirs – might they be seeing a picture of the future? They felt the touch of something eerie… a suggestion of Highland second sight?

Ian shook himself free of the trance-like state, "Helen should have been with us; with her sensitive, intuitive feminine senses she would have more clearly understood these vague sensations we both felt."

"Och man, it's just as well she's not here. It's best not to be able to see into the future."

They were again silent for a few moments then Colin gave his usual beaming grin, "Come on, let's get going. In twenty minutes we will be at John Munro's croft, and he's got drams waiting for us there."

They started off. The tireless terriers again keenly lead the way, but the two men easily kept up with them – the thought of the waiting whisky put fresh life, a fresh spring, in their striding feet.

Soon they were comfortably ensconced in the Munro's crofthouse; soon the first drams were downed; soon the glasses were refilled. Old Mary Munro poured the hospitable tea and urged them to do justice to the heaped plates of her home-made crowdie cheese and thick scones. "Sit in… sit in! The scones are this minute made. I've just taken them, all warm and smiling, from the oven."

As they happily ate and drank, Colin and Ian told the story of their fierce encounter with Campbell-Fotheringay.

"Ochone, ochone," Old Mary lamented, "it's terrible how that laird's ruining this estate."

"Aye, it is… it is," Old John angrily agreed. "The bastard deserves to be done away with, it would be a good riddance."

"Oh hush, John," said his wife, "don't say such things. It is not for us to decide such matters. He will get his just desert in due time, when The Good Lord decides."

"Aye, weel, I wish The Good Lord would decide soon."

"Oh, be quiet, John, be quiet."

Diplomatically Colin spoke up; sincerely and whole-heartedly he praised Mary's scones and especially her crowdie cheese. Secretly delighted, she modestly protested, "Och, my crowdie's nothing special now. At my age I can't make it the way I used to."

"Aye, we're a' getting auld; a' getting burdened we' failing powers," John toothlessly mumbled as he dipped a biscuit in his tea.

"Aye, we are… we are, sorrow take it!" His old wife sighed then asked Colin, "Is Jeannie entering her crowdie in the Inveraldrory Games again this year?"

"Oh aye, she is. But I expect Auld Maggie Gunn's special crowdie will win first prize once again."

"Aye, perhaps it will. I wonder what it is that gives her crowdie that special flavour the judges always remark on?"

"I wonder?… I wonder? It would be most interesting to discover her secret, wouldn't it?"

After dinner that evening, Helen and Ian sat relaxing by their fireplace. After her long journey to and from Inverness and the hectic shopping spree, Helen was exhausted; or, as she expressed it, was 'fair puggled'. Ian sympathised, "Aye, you look a wee bit wabbit, Helen. I always find a day spent – a day wasted – in a car or in a city most exhausting. It's an entirely different feeling from the tiredness – the pleasant tiredness – I experience after a long, strenuous day out on the hills."

However, Helen's exhaustion did not prevent her from frequently rising from her chair to play and replay the tapes she had bought. Ian laughed, "You fairly keep Chopin and changing these tapes around, Helen."

In the silence as she once more changed a tape they heard a vehicle stop at the front of the house. Ian looked out of the window. "It's the police Land Rover. The policeman's coming to the door."

"Forensic Fred?"

"Aye, Forensic Fred."

They smiled at one another; smiled at that apt nickname for the local policeman. His correct name was Norman Frederick Sutherland, but that formal name was rarely used locally. To all and sundry he was, and always would be, 'Forensic Fred'.

His father had been the Inveraldrory policeman. Even when at primary school Fred had only one ambition – to become a policeman. At senior school his favourite books were detective stories. Sherlock Holmes was his hero. Fred secretly dreamed of wearing a deerstalker hat and smoking a curving, large bowled, meerschaum pipe.

He joined the police force and served in Glasgow. He was very impressed by a course on forensic science applied to detective work. He transferred to the Highland Police Force and served for many years in Stornoway. His loud, resonant voice acquired something of a lilting Hebridean accent there. Eventually, to his delight, he was appointed village policeman at Inveraldrory.

He was popular, but the locals were quick to note an idiosyncrasy he had: his habit of claiming that, "There is no crime that forensic science cannot solve." A wit nicknamed him, 'Forensic Fred'. That name tenaciously stuck to him. There were rumours that he kept a large magnifying glass and a microscope hidden somewhere in the police station and that he still hankered to be another Sherlock Holmes.

Ian genially greeted him, "Come in, Fred, come away in."

The policeman smiled and ducked his head as he came through the doorway into the cosy sitting room. His vast bulk overwhelmed the small room. He was six feet four inches tall and weighed over sixteen stone. His solid body was all heavy bone and firm muscle.

Helen felt tiny as his huge body towered over her. She winced as they shook hands. Her dainty hand was lost in his massive one. Laughingly she protested, "Oh, Fred, you don't realise your own strength!"

"Sit down, Fred, sit down. Are you here on official business or is this a social visit?" Ian asked.

"Och, let's say it's chust a bit of both."

"Och well, in that case can I offer you a bit of a dram?"

Fred loudly laughed, his deep voice boomed out, "I shouldn't really, but it's nice to be offered a drink. Aye, I'll take a dram, but make it a wee one, chust a wee one."

As the policeman moved towards the sofa the old floorboards creaked and sagged under his formidable weight. The glasses neatly arrayed on the large sideboard trembled together as if awed at the terrible majesty of the law.

The old sofa deeply sagged; its flattened springs suffered grievous bodily harm from the massive weight of the policeman's 'too, too, solid flesh'.

When Ian handed him a dram, Fred repeated, "It's nice to be offered a drink. I wasn't offered one at the place I've just come from."

"Oh, and where was that?"

"At Campbell-Fotheringay's Aldrory Lodge."

"Oh well, enough said. What else would you expect at that bastard's?"

The policeman grinned, "Och well, Ian, I must admit I don't have any great liking for him myself. However, I had to go and see him. He phoned me earlier this evening and more or less demanded my immediate presence. When I got there he started raving about being threatened by Colin MacDonald and you this afternoon. He claimed the two of you had halted his range rover at gun-point and menaced him and his companions with your shotguns."

As Forensic Fred recalled that scene at Aldrory Lodge he again felt a surge of anger at the way he had been treated.

Mrs McPherson, the old, semi-alcoholic housekeeper/cook, had shown him into the drawing room. The large room reeked of smoke, and not just tobacco smoke. His suspicious nostrils thought they detected the smell of cannabis. Quickly and observantly he looked around. None of the room's occupants were actually smoking at present. What had been an attractive, comfortable room was now dustily neglected; like its owner it was run down and going to seed.

Campbell-Fotheringay did not rise to greet the policeman. He remained sprawled on a huge settee of faded and stained floral patterned chintz. One arm was carelessly thrown over the lovely young blonde who voluptuously draped herself around him. A second blonde lay at the other end of the settee. They all held, and frequently drank from, tall, well-filled glasses.

Two men lounged on a smaller settee at a far wall. Self-engrossed, they seemed to take little notice of the others. Forensic Fred summed them up at one glance: they were a couple of slim and effete 'gay' show-business 'luvvies'.

Campbell-Fotheringay stared up at Fred and silently surveyed him with insolent indolence. His small, ferrety eyes looked astonishingly shifty. Mean, suspicious and restless they did not hold Fred's steady gaze. With what seemed a weary effort he forced something that resembled a smile over his podgy features and petulantly exclaimed, "Oh, there you are. So you've arrived at last, have you, constable?"

"Yes, sir, I'm here to take your statement about your accusation of being threatened by firearms."

"What do you mean my 'accusation'? I'm telling you facts, constable."

Fred pulled out his notebook and biro, "Very well, sir. Now calmly and clearly please tell me those facts."

Not very calmly and not very clearly, Campbell-Fotheringay poured out a loud tirade of accusations about having been held up, threatened at gunpoint by Colin MacDonald and Ian MacLean. Finally, exhausted by his ravings, he raised his glass and eagerly drained it. He held out the empty glass. The blonde beside him drawled out, "You refill it for him, dahling Virginia, I'm much too comfortably ensconced here to move."

"Oh, all right," Virginia peevishly exclaimed, "I'll do anything to please our great lord and master."

Giving Fred a bright, provocative smile she languidly raised her legs from the settee. Deliberately she alluringly and seductively revealed the long slim thighs beneath her shortish frock.

Fred stared. He gasped. He could not be sure if the enticing vague darkness at the top of her thighs was a pair of dark panties or not. He frowned and hastily averted his gaze.

Virginia giggled delightedly, "Oh, you're blushing, big boy, you're blushing!"

Deliberately he ignored her. Determinedly concentrating all his willpower on his official business he stared at the jottings in his notebook. But his flesh had a will of its own. He was uneasily aware of excited stirrings at his genitals.

Virginia sensed his unease. She laughed merrily and mischievously, "Oh, am I getting you embarrassed, big boy? Am I getting you excited?"

"Oh, for Christ sake, Virgie, shut up!' screamed Campbell-Fotheringay. "Get me my drink, for God's sake! This is serious business. Being threatened by guns is a serious affair, isn't it, constable?"

"Yes, sir, it is."

"Oh, I suppose you better sit down, constable, I'm getting tired of staring up at you."

The blonde draped around the laird lazily drawled something that sounded like, "Yeah, Tony, he's making the room damned untidy, standing there."

Virginia handed Tony his refilled glass. Ungraciously taking it, he did not thank her. After alluringly rearranging herself in her corner of the large settee, she smiled brightly at Fred and patted the place beside her, "Come on, big boy, sit beside me. Surely a huge handsome hunk like you is not frightened to sit beside poor, innocent little me?"

Fred wisely ignored that seductive offer. He sat in a large armchair on the opposite side of the huge, ornate, impressively carved marble fireplace.

"You're awfully far away over there, big boy, why don't you come and sit beside me?" Again she invitingly patted the settee.

"Och, I'm fine where I am, thank you."

"Are you frightened of me? Are you frightened of all women? You're not like them, are you?" She indicated the two self-absorbed men on the settee near the door. "You're not 'gay', are you, big boy? That would be a terrible waste of such a gorgeous hunk of beefcake."

Without consciously willing it, Fred's deep voice deepened as he angrily and emphatically declared, "No, I'm certainly not 'gay'! If it's any of your business, I happen to have a wife and two young children."

"Oh, all right, big boy, I believe you. Keep your shirt on!"

The other blonde giggled, "Knowing you, Virgie, you would much rather take his shirt off, wouldn't you?"

Virginia brazenly laughed, "Yeah, I'd like to take not only his shirt, but his entire uniform off. You know I always go for men in uniform and love to strip them of their uniforms."

Irritably, Campbell-Fotheringay shouted, "Oh, for Christ sake, you two, shut up! Leave him alone!"

Again, Virginia giggled, "I'm not touching him – unfortunately!"

"Oh, for Christ sake, shut up!"

She pulled a face, but obeyed.

Campbell-Fotheringay once more started ranting about being threatened by the armed men. At length Forensic Fred interrupted him, "Now, sir, do you want to bring charges against them, or don't you?"

For a while longer he blustered and raved. Finally he reluctantly conceded, "No... no, I suppose not. It would be difficult to prove that charge, wouldn't it?... despite me having those two witnesses."

"Yes, it would be difficult to prove your allegations, sir." Fred could not help somewhat spitefully adding, "I don't think these *ladies* of yours would make very impressive witnesses."

"Constable, don't you be impertinent. Your Chief Constable is a friend of mine, you know," Campbell-Fotheringay blustered, "I've a good mind to report your insolence to him."

Fred was not intimidated by this threat. It only made him angrier. Controlling himself, he calmly replied, "Your being a friend of the Chief Constable is entirely irrelevant to these enquiries."

Although he made this firm statement sound convincing, Fred knew that it was not quite accurate. He was only too well aware that there were 'wheels within wheels'; he knew that the 'old-boy network' was still powerful and that the 'correct' handshake was obscurely, but powerfully, influential.

He also knew that his Chief Constable was often invited for a few days salmon fishing, grouse shooting and deer stalking by many of the Northern lairds. Seemingly he genuinely delighted in these sports and was a fairly reasonable and decent man. But, by all reports Fred had heard, his wife was entirely different; she was supposed to be a snobbish bitch who delighted, not in the sport, but in boasting of being a friend and guest of the titled and wealthy estate owners. She was a notorious name-dropper.

"Anyway, sir," Fred continued, "as you are not bringing charges against them, that's the end of the matter for now." He put his notebook and pen away. "I'll see Colin and Ian this evening and hear their version of the story."

"Oh, so it's Colin and Ian, is it? Not MacDonald and MacLean, eh? No doubt they are friends of yours, but I'm sure you won't let that friendship influence you in any way."

Fred ignored that sarcasm. He stood up. "I'll be in touch with you again, sir, after I've interviewed *Colin* and *Ian*." (He deliberately emphasized the 'Colin' and 'Ian'.)

"Oh, very well... very well, constable, go and see your friends," Campbell-Fotheringay exclaimed dismissively as he lifted and again drained his glass. "Anyway, it's time for our dinner. As a matter of fact you've been keeping us from it, you know," he peevishly added.

"Oh, I'm sorry, *Sir*!" Fred could not resist adding, "Don't bother to get up, *Sir*. I'll see myself out, *Sir*!" He emphasized each 'Sir' with heavy irony. As he strode towards the door one of the effete men cooed, "Ooh, isn't that handsome big policeman most attractively masterful when he's angry?"

Virginia's laughter rippled out, "Oh, just you leave him alone, Arnold, that gorgeous hunk is mine."

Fred halted at the door and glared at Arnold. He read the black print on his tee shirt, 'Proud to be Gay'. He read the other's proclamation, '...So am I!' "My

God," he thought, "what bloody idiots! 'Proud to be gay?' – what the hell was there to be proud about a man having sex with another man?"

Fred firmly banged the door shut behind him. He stood in the hall. He sniffed. From the kitchen regions came a strong smell of burning food. Suddenly the loud clatter of a dropped cooking pot reverberated, followed immediately by vehement curses in English and Gaelic. He recognised the angry voice of Mrs McPherson. She sounded none too sober. Grinning, he thought, "I doot she's been at the cooking sherry again."

As he opened the front door Fred smiled vindictively, "I doot the bloody laird and his cronies will have to wait a while yet for their dinner – for their burnt offering."

Standing on the steps he looked around. It was sad to see the state of neglect and decay in the shooting lodge and the surrounding garden. All the tattily peeling doors and windows desperately needed painting. Many slates were missing from the steep roofs and round towers, and damp stains darkened the walls. What had been smooth lawn was now an unkempt wilderness, disfigured with large tussocks of matted grasses and by entire landscapes of pretentious mountain ranges created by armies of ever-active moles. The flowerbeds had long since been completely taken over by rankly rioting weeds.

It was a perfect May evening. The sunshine's glowing warmth persuaded the rampant wild honeysuckle to unstintingly give out its exquisite scent. Fred breathed in deeply. The evening air felt wonderfully pure and wholesome after the vile degenerate atmosphere of that room he had just left.

From massive old Scots Pines wood pigeons languidly cooed and collared doves drowsily joined in the murmuring chorus. From topmost branches song thrushes competed with vibrant blackbirds. Somewhere a high, hidden, solitary skylark joyously trilled and embraced the entire world with cascading glory.

With startling suddenness the deadly menace of a darting sparrowhawk silenced these birds. With expert precision that ruthless raptor clamped sharp talons on the least alert blackbird. It was all over in a few seconds. A screech of terror, an explosion of feathers, and the hawk, clutching its victim, was out of sight while a few small downy feathers were still lazily drifting towards the ground. Pigeons clattered away on loud clapping wings. These wings clapped in self-applause, in self-congratulation that they were not that dreaded predator's victim.

For a moment the sudden death of the blackbird saddened the policeman – but only for a moment. He was well aware that such deaths were an integral part of natural life – were part of nature's wholeness. That blackbird had lived a good life in its correct environment. A short life, but a real life. Its death had been swift and clean.

How different, he thought, from those humans he had just left, with their 'sophisticated' lifestyle – that 'life' which was more a slow, degenerate death. He remembered his short time in London and his years in Glasgow; he recalled vast, sprawling, housing estates and immense high-rise flats. How utterly different that hideous urban ugliness was from the wild beauty of this untamed

Highland landscape. Little wonder that so many condemned to live in the grim, soulless, unnatural environs of huge cities found their only refuge in drugs and alcohol. Only drinks and drugs could give them soporific sleep and opaque dreams and visions.

When Forensic Fred finished giving an edited version of his interview with Campbell-Fotheringay, Ian angrily exclaimed, "Oh, he's a lying bastard! Colin and I never threatened him with our shotguns. And anyway our guns were unloaded when we met him." Calming himself, he gave the attentive policeman a full and accurate account of what had happened. He concluded by stating, "Colin will confirm the truth of my version of these events."

"Aye, I'm sure he will. I will call on him later this evening and chust be checking." Forensic Fred took a sip of whisky then grinned at Ian, "Your account sounds much more convincing and reliable than that laird's wild rantings and ravings."

Both listeners had a shrewd idea of what the policeman, discreetly concealing his private opinion, thought of Campbell-Fotheringay. They had no doubt he felt the same as them – felt a deep loathing for the degenerate laird.

Helen asked, "Is he actually going to bring charges against Colin and Ian?"

"Och no. Not now. At first he stormed and blustered about charging them, but eventually he thought better of it."

Helen smiled, "I'm sure you helped him change his mind."

Fred grinned, "Aye, well, I did my bit to dissuade him."

"Did he threaten to report you to your Chief Constable, by any chance?"

Fred stared at her in amazement. "Aye... Aye, as a matter of fact he did chust that. But how did you know, Helen?"

"Och, I just guessed it. Knowing what a venomous reptile he is, I thought it was just the sort of sneaking, malicious mean threat he was likely to make."

Fred nodded and said, "Oh, I see." Although appearing to accept her simple explanation, he had secret doubts. He was very superstitious. In public he succeeded in hiding much of this failing – this weakness? – but he could not hide it from himself. Over the years he had heard many tales of Helen's inexplicable powers, and, despite the cheery friendliness she always showed him, he could not help feeling rather in awe of her.

Helen and Ian exchanged a quick, meaningful glance. They guessed Fred's feelings. Ian smiled inwardly as he remembered Fred's father and grandfather. They had been very superstitious and very frightened of anything in the least supernatural. Obviously Fred had inherited not only their physical strengths but also their superstitious weaknesses.

Helen sensed Fred's awe, his fear of her strange powers. She was quietly amused. He was so large and strong; she was so small and petite. She giggled within herself as she pictured him as a huge elephant frightened of her, a tiny mouse. Suddenly, unaccountably, she felt a violent flood of warm, maternal instincts. She had a crazy notion that he needed her motherly love and protection. Secretly smiling, she scoffingly dismissed the ridiculous idea.

Glancing at the policeman's empty glass, Ian asked, "Another dram, Fred?"

Struggling up from the depths of the twanging relieved old sofa, Fred grinned, "Och no. No thanks, Ian. Remember I'm on duty. I'll go and see Colin MacDonald now." Thanking Helen for the tea and Ian for the dram, he laughed, "Your hospitality was much better than the hospitality I didn't receive at the laird's."

"Aye, I hope it was," Ian grinned, "I should damned well hope it was!"

Chapter Nineteen

June came in and brought day after day of glorious weather. Eagerly, from early dawn to late lingering dusk, the sun shone from a cloudless sky.

Every crofter, every shepherd, every gamekeeper was employed outdoors. Wisely, all made the most of this weather. All were well aware that once this protracted dry spell ended it might be long enough before they were blessed with such a spell again.

Helen and Ian spent every possible minute outdoors. Both their faces were attractively tanned. They, Ian especially, thought it a form of sacrilege to waste any of the precious sunshine by being indoors. He revelled with a truly Pagan joy in the pleasure and beauty of each brilliant day.

Some days they had to work in the garden; the weeks of sunshine and drying Easterly winds did little to check the rampant growth of virile weeds.

But many days they went trout fishing.

Setting out in the cool of early morning they walked and climbed to various hill lochs. The trout they caught were a bonus; their deepest delight was simply in being together in this wild landscape under such perfect conditions.

So – aglow with deep, hedonistic pleasure – many long, idyllic June days passed idyllically.

Once they fished large, attractive Loch Crocach. As Ian rowed the boat past a certain island he smiled at Helen, "Remember this island?… remember the first time we were here together?"

"Yes, of course I remember; how could I ever forget it?"

On their first fishing trip to this loch, almost thirty years ago, Helen had known nothing of this loch. Ian, deliberately, told her nothing of its history and legends. He was discovering and – unsuccessfully – attempting to find some logical explanation for her mysterious power. He intended to secretly test these powers at Loch Crocach.

After fishing all morning amongst numerous small and densely tree-covered islands in a large bay, Ian said, "I'll row back up the loch and, after lunch, we can fish that part of the loch."

As they neared a large, lushly green island he smiled, "I badly need a piss! What about you, Helen?"

"Aye, I'm needing one as well."

"We'll land on that island, alright?"

After relieving themselves, Ian suggested, "What about having lunch on this island?"

With alert, but carefully hidden keenness he awaited her reply. Her reaction was as he suspected it would be – she provided further proof of her amazing powers.

"Oh, no, Ian, I don't fancy having lunch here. Let's go somewhere else."

"Oh, why? What's wrong with this island?"

"Oh, I'm not sure. I just don't like it here. I don't feel comfortable here."

Ian stared at her. He made a strong effort to keep the knowledge of this island which he possessed, but which she did not share, deeply hidden in the depths of his mind where she could not find it. But she found it.

"You know something about this island, don't you, Ian?… Something you haven't told me about."

"Aye, I do. But before I tell you what I know will you please try to explain to me what you feel about this island?"

For a few moments Helen hesitated; she slowly, silently, deliberately looked around the lush green island. "Oh, Ian, it's hard for me to put my feelings into words. I… I feel terribly uncomfortable here. I know it looks a pleasant fresh green place, but… but it possesses an eerie atmosphere… it's as if sad, restless souls were uneasily confined here."

Ian's jaw dropped, his mouth gaped wide. He stared at Helen in speechless amazement.

She smiled, "You look as if you've seen a ghost, Ian!"

He pulled himself together, he managed a grin, "No, Helen, it's you who's seen, or sensed, ghosts!"

"Now tell me what you know about this island."

"Aye, right. Well, the name of this place is Suicide Island. A number of suicides and at least one murderer are buried here. As you know, murderers and suicides were not allowed to be interred in graveyards in the past, they had to be buried in un-consecrated ground. In the Highlands they were usually buried on islands where their tormented souls were unable to travel over the surrounding water."

"So this island is haunted?"

"Yes, it's reputed to be haunted."

Flames of anger flushed Helen's cheeks as she accused Ian of bringing her here under false pretences, of unfairly using her.

"I'm sorry," he apologised, "but there was no other way I could carry out that experiment; the ghosts would already have been planted in your mind. Now I'm astounded at this further proof of your uncanny powers. Please forgive me, Helen."

She did not relent immediately. As Ian rowed the boat away from the island he tentatively asked, "Don't you notice something else strange about Suicide Island?"

She remained ominously silent.

Hesitantly, perhaps foolishly, he pointed and said, "Look, Helen, isn't there something strange about that island?"

Slowly, reluctantly, she turned and stared at Suicide Island. After a tense silence she aggressively stated, "No!… I don't see anything strange about it!"

Ian recklessly persevered, "Think of all the other islands on this loch."

Again she turned and stared. Suddenly, her anger forgotten, she animatedly cried, "Oh, of course, there are no trees growing on that island!"

"Aye, exactly!"

Every island on the loch, apart from Suicide Island, was – in marked contrast to the treeless mainland – thickly covered in trees. Birches, hazels, rowans, willows and aspens crowded them all. Every small rock, jutting darkly from the water, willingly played host to the small rowans, which gallantly struggled to survive on their stark environment.

"Why is that, Ian? Why do not trees grow on Suicide Island?"

"I don't know. I have never found any logical explanation. That island, covered in lush grass, should also be covered with trees, but not one tree grows there. It is very strange. It is abnormal."

Helen stared at Suicide Island for a while then quietly but firmly stated, "As there is no normal explanation for that island being treeless then obviously the true explanation must be in the paranormal."

As Ian nodded in agreement, he wished he could accept the 'truth' of Helen's statement as confidently, as calmly, as unreservedly, as she did.

Now, thirty years later, they were fishing Loch Crocach again, and still not one tree grew on Suicide Island. There still was no logical explanation for this abnormality.

Often, at the end of the glorious June days, Helen and Ian strolled through the garden to the front gate, leant companionably on it and admired the fantastic magic of the unhurried sunset. The sun lingered far beyond the Hebrides and slowly, reluctantly, descended towards the glittering Atlantic and suffused and pulsed the oceanic sky with golden glory. The constantly changing colours were the gentle evening's only movement; all else was breathlessly still.

In what seemed an awed whisper Helen said, "The sky is being lovingly brushed by the delicate touch of angel's wings." With an impish grin she glanced sideways at Ian; she had a shrewd idea of how he would react to such whimsical fantasy.

He returned her impish grin, "Oh, Helen, you can fly with your angels. I'll soar with the godlike genius of the magnificent 'Sun of God' – Turner!"

Over the years Helen and Ian had tried to capture the wondrous glory of such sunsets in paint. They were never satisfied with their efforts. They had ruefully agreed that it took a genius like Turner to do justice to such glorious golden sunsets.

Helen's eyes twinkled, "Oh, Ian, we're both on the side of the angels!"

Once more Colin and Jeannie MacDonald called late in the evening at Altdour Croft. Once more they were comfortably settled with drams in their hands and Colin again requested Ian's help in searching for plundering foxes.

"Whose lambs have they been killing this time?" Ian asked.

"Not lambs… hens! Auld Maggie Gunn has had all her hens killed by foxes which got into the hen run," Colin explained.

"Oh, poor Auld Maggie. She'll be terribly upset. She's very fond of her hens, isn't she?" Helen said.

"Aye, she is," Jeannie confirmed. "She loves all her animals: her dogs, her sheep, her hens, but especially her large tribe of cats."

"Aye, that's right," Colin laughed. "I think she's much more fond of her cats and other animals than she is of people…"

Helen interrupted, "Perhaps that's understandable!"

"Aye, it is. I feel sorry for poor Auld Maggie," Jeannie said. "She's not had much of a life, has she?"

The others nodded in sympathetic agreement.

"No," Ian said, "and now, like most local old maids, her only pleasure, apart from her animals, is in being miserable at dreary Calvinistic prayer meetings."

Grinning broadly, Colin said, "Aye, and we can be sure of one thing, Ian: we won't get a dram from her. That pleasure is strictly forbidden – that pleasure is a grievous sin! She's vehemently teetotal."

"Aye, I know. Of course that's hardly surprising, considering the terrible time she had with her father and then with her alcoholic older brother."

With gentle irony Helen quietly said, "Och, the pair of you sinful reprobates will be all the better for going without drams for once."

Jeannie nodded in amused agreement. Colin and Ian silently grinned at one another and dismissively shook their heads.

Later, as they all stood at the open front door, Colin said, "It's a pity you don't have a phone, Ian, it would save me having to drive over here every time I've to get in touch with you."

"Och, I've managed fine all my life without a phone; I'll manage the rest of my life without one, too."

"Och, you're a right stick-in-the-mud; a… a… what do you call it?"

"A Luddite?… Aye, I am a Luddite, thank God!" Ian laughed, "Anyway, what are you complaining aboot, man?… if I had a phone you wouldn't get your dram, would you?"

"No, by God, that's true. Aye, nae doot you're best withoot a phone after all, Ian!"

Early the following morning the noise of Colin's van disturbed the innocent, yawning brightness of Aldrory Glen as he collected Ian.

They drove through Inveraldrory village and left it drowsing in gentle feline bliss under the spell of the perfect June morning. They sped along the fine, wide new road, which ran along by the North shore of Loch Ardgie. Now and again they caught glimpses of the narrow, old single-track road. Ian smiled as he looked down on that abandoned road where it collided and twisted in a series of sharp bends. "It looks like a huge black adder forever wriggling through that thick heather, doesn't it?"

As he glanced out of the side window, Colin grinned, "Aye, I suppose it does. Your imagination's still strong, Ian. Perhaps it's as well my imagination isn't so active; we'll be safer if I keep my mind on the driving."

Ian laughed, "Aye, that's true. When I had my old van, years ago, Helen was never happy with my driving. She worried that I didn't concentrate properly, that I often let my imagination lead me dangerously astray."

They passed a shallow bay on Loch Ardgie that was dotted with small rocky islands. Each was untidily crowned with a few ruggedly gaunt old Scots Pines. Once again Ian admired those grimly tenacious trees as they resolutely survived on what was little more than bare rock. On their horizontal branches and flattened tops they flaunted their scanty greenery like tattered, but boldly defiant banners which challenged the fiercest winter gales to do their worst.

Soon the van was slowly bumping up the rough track which climbed to Maggie Gunn's isolated croft.

As Colin and Ian got out of the van Auld Maggie came round the end of her crofthouse. She was accompanied by three cats and numerous kittens. Immediately they caught sight of the strangers all the cats turned tail and bolted out of sight. Other cats briefly appeared at the open front door then instantly scurried back inside.

'Auld Maggie', although known by that name for a good number of years, was not really so very old. She was only a few years older than the two men. They remembered her from school days at Inveraldrory when she had been in a higher class than them. Thin and of medium height, her white hair, her lined, careworn sallow face and her serious, almost melancholy manner made her older than her actual years. The sombre, dowdy, dark clothes she always wore added further years to her age.

As she greeted the two men they sympathetically noted the whiteness of her face and the redness of her eyelids; they – correctly – surmised that she had had a long, sleepless, weeping night. They expressed their sincere sorrow for the slaughter of her hens.

"Have they all been killed?" Colin asked.

"Oh yes!… yes! At least almost all of them have."

"How many did you have?"

"Twenty-one… exactly twenty-one, plus the cockerel. Plus a lot of young chicks." Maggie sighed deeply and tears of misery flooded her eyes. "Now only three hens are left and the poor cockerel. Those foxes, those… those dirty evil brutes, killed all the others. They even killed all the innocent wee chicks."

Ian and Colin again expressed their deep sympathy. From long experience they knew that most young chicks, even if they escaped the foxes snapping jaws, died from the shock – the absolute terror – of such an experience.

"We'll go and have a look at the hen run before we go after the foxes," Colin said. "It's round by those birch trees, isn't it?"

Auld Maggie nodded, "Aye, it's over there." She pointed and tremulously added, "I won't come with you. I can't face seeing all my poor slaughtered hens again. It's much too sad a sight."

It truly was a pitiful sight. Hens and chickens' bodies were scattered all over the hen run. At corners of the wire netting fence many hens had been trapped as they frantically fluttered to escape and their torn bodies lay in ugly heaps. Stickly saturated feathers were a repulsive soggy mess in the pools of congealing blood and small chicks were almost unrecognisable – they lay like crumpled and sodden yellow dusters. Noisily buzzing flies and bluebottles revelled in the mess.

The morning breeze gently played with the loose, dry feathers, which were scattered everywhere. Occasionally a stronger gust ruffled the feathers of some dead hens and for a moment it seemed as if life was again rippling through them.

Some hens lay decapitated, their heads snapped off by the foxes. The bodies of two hens were stuck high in the fence. Their heads and necks hung limply outside the wire netting while their bodies hung inside. Obviously they had tried to force their way through the netting in a desperate attempt to escape.

Colin and Ian sighed grimly as they inspected this scene of carnage, which the morning sunshine brightly disclosed in all its horror. The door of the wooden henhouse hung open; they went inside. As their eyes adjusted to the dim interior they saw more slaughtered hens. They did not stay long in that smelly charnel house.

Colin said, "More than one fox carried out this slaughter."

"Aye, it looks like the work of two foxes; a dog fox and his vixen."

"That's what I think. It wouldn't be so bad if they only killed and took away one hen each, but this wholesale slaughter is terrible."

"Aye," Ian agreed, "such wanton blood lust is atrocious; it's unforgivable."

Colin grinned, "So you won't have any qualms about killing the foxes?"

"No, I certainly won't!"

They now inspected the fence. Almost hidden by thick clumps of gorse, they discovered where the foxes had entered by digging under a weakness in the fence.

"Come on," Colin said, "let's get going. The sooner we find and ruthlessly kill those ruthless foxes the better."

They collected their shotguns from the van then released the impatiently eager terriers. All this time these terriers had loudly, angrily, frustratedly, been answering the fierce barking challenges of Maggie's frantic dogs which were locked away in an outbuilding.

Two hours later the men and terriers reached and checked out an old fox den. It was soon obvious that it was not being used this year.

An hour and a half of steady walking and sweaty climbing brought them to the next known fox den, two thousand feet up on the long and stony grey ridge of Ben Bhreac. By the excitement of the terriers and the evidence of scattered hens' feathers, this den was obviously in use. Further searching quickly revealed more evidence that confirmed the foxes' guilt. A hen's head and neck, a wing and a lamb's woolly tail were the scattered playthings of fox cubs. Grouse, hens' and gulls' feathers lay on the grass and littered the surrounding heather. Fresh droppings of adult foxes and of well-grown fox cubs were lying here and there. It was a typical untidy fox slum.

Colin grinned, "There's no holding the terriers back now, they're going mad straining at the leash."

"Aye! Well, let's, 'Cry, 'Havoc', and let slip the dogs of war'," Ian quoted.

Sometimes they had to wait for a long time for the foxes to bolt and be shot and for the terriers to get to and kill the cubs, but this time it all went easily and quickly. In less than one hour the dog fox and the vixen had been accurately shot and cleanly killed and three well-grown cubs had been killed by the terriers and their bodies dragged out from the den.

As they stood and looked at the five bodies, Colin said, "Auld Maggie will be pleased to have the slaughter of her hens avenged like this."

Ian nodded in agreement. As he got older he was becoming less keen on killing. But he was a realist; he had no time for excessive, ill-informed soppy sentimentality. There had to be some killing. In nature death was an integral, an essential, part of life.

Colin grinned, "We may be getting to be bodachs right enough, but when it comes to shooting, there's nothing slow about our reactions, is there? Many a much younger man might easily have missed these fast bolting foxes."

"Aye, that's true. Our many years of experience stand us in good stead."

As they neared Maggie's croft Colin smiled, "I'm looking forward to getting a drink at Auld Maggie's. I'm gey thirsty."

"Aye, it'll be fine and dandy to get a drink – even if only tea."

"Poor Auld Maggie; she's not had much of a life, has she?" Colin compassionately remarked.

After leaving school, Maggie helped her parents run their isolated croft. She loved working with the animals. She was an excellent milker. Gently crooning ancient Gaelic milking songs she got more milk from the blissfully relaxed cows than her mother (secretly jealous) ever managed.

Maggie was also excellent at the lambing. Many a weakly lamb owed its life to her devoted loving care, and many ageing ewes got through their difficult births thanks to her skilled help.

When she was twenty-one, Maggie got engaged to Donald Mathieson, a crofter's son and a part-time lobster fisherman. They looked forward to getting married in a few years' time.

Then had come the Second World War. Maggie's fiancé went into the Royal Navy. Her younger brother, John, joined the Seaforth Highlanders. Maggie worked harder than ever on the croft helping to produce urgently needed food in those years of desperate food shortages.

Then came disaster. Her brother was killed in Italy. Two months later her fiancé was drowned in the North Atlantic.

For many wearisome long months Maggie was devastated by the tragic blows. Day after day she wept for her fiancé and her brother. At night, when exhaustion finally brought sleep, it was a nightmare haunted restlessness full of tortured visions of Donald's bloated body floating face-down in the lonely wastes of the North Atlantic and of John's mutilated body lying in the dreary dry dust of remote Italy.

Slowly – oh, how painfully slowly – she got over the worst of her grief.

For twenty years she looked after her parents. They never really got over the death of their youngest, their favourite son. Her father increasingly sought consolation from the whisky bottle. After his death her mother became much more selfishly self-pitying. Her demands grew ever more imperative, her whining complaints ever more frequent.

Although she tried not to admit it, Maggie found her mother's death a vast relief. She revelled in no longer being at anyone's beck and call. Gradually her weariness lifted and her health improved. For a few years she knew quiet contentment with all her animals. She almost dared to be happy. But all too often her Calvinistic conscience uneasily questioned if happiness was not a sin. She guiltily feared that this pleasant state could not last.

All too soon her fears were realized.

The wife of her older brother, Andrew, suddenly died in Glasgow and he decided to return to the family croft, which was legally his. Maggie had no say in the matter. Once more she was at the beck and call of an unappreciative relation. She was inconsiderately treated as an unpaid housekeeper.

As Andrew Gunn grew older his dour, solitary drinking grew ever greater. What had been a controllable habit rapidly became a compulsive necessity. He turned into a morose alcoholic. Maggie had a terrible time looking after him; hers was a thankless wearisome task helping him through the worst of his dark depressions. Eventually, after a few severe bouts of delirium tremens, he died in Graig Dunain mental hospital in Inverness.

Maggie desperately tried not to admit that his death was a vast relief. Once more she almost dared to look for happiness with all her loving, her sane, her wise animals. But again she uneasily questioned if happiness was not a sin.

While her brother's death brought her exhausted body the physical rest it urgently needed, her conscience brought anguish to her soul as she lay sleepless in her lonely bed. A terrible sense of guilt crept over her. Had she done enough for her parents? Had she done enough for her brother? Had she loved them, despite their faults, as deeply, as sincerely, as a true Christian should? Hadn't she been secretly thankful when they finally died? She succeeded in hiding her guilt from others, but could not hide it from herself. She certainly could not hide it from her omniscient God who saw into the utmost depths of every sinner's guilty soul.

She became much more devoutly – but also much more narrowly and intolerantly – religious. She passionately preached against the Devil and all his works. She directed her most vehement prayers against the Devil's chief Highland ally – whisky.

After putting the terriers and the unloaded guns in the van, Colin and Ian approached the open door of Maggie's crofthouse. A black and white cat appeared in the doorway. At the sight of the men it immediately panicked. It dashed into a passage between the door and the stairway. Its legs were a

268

confused blur of motion as its frantic paws tried to get purchase on the polished, slippery linoleum while its body remained obstinately stuck in the same position. For a few fantastic moments the poor cat was a ludicrous caricature of a crazy cartoon cat.

At last, slithering and slipping, it made it to the stairs. It flew up them. On the tenth step it stopped, turned, and indignantly glared at the men who were bellowing with mocking laughter. Then, wrapping its regained dignity around itself, it turned and slowly and sedately continued up the stairs.

Maggie Gunn hospitably ushered the men into her kitchen. "Come in… come away in. I've got some food ready for you."

As he saw the well-laden table, Colin exclaimed, "Oh, Maggie, you shouldn't have gone to all this trouble for us."

"Och, be quiet… be quiet, 'twas no trouble at all. Sit down… sit down the pair of you. How did you get on? Did you find these foxes?"

"Aye, we found them all right. And we killed them all right." Between them they gave her a full account of their success.

Maggie listened intently. When they finished she cried out, "Oh, good!… good! I'm delighted that my poor slaughtered hens have been revenged. I praise the good Lord that those evil devils of foxes won't kill any more hens again."

"No," Colin agreed, "nor any more lambs."

"Aye, that's true – the Lord be praised!"

Maggie hurried into the scullery. She reappeared holding a large teapot. Suddenly flustered, she giggled, "Och, I'm stupid, I forgot to put tea in the pot. I'm sorry to keep you waiting. Just you read those tracts I've put out for you. I won't be long."

Ian and Colin grinned at one another. They guessed that Auld Maggie was old-maidishly excited at having two male visitors violating the prim neatness of her tidy kitchen. They picked up the leaflets from their plates. Un-enthusiastically they glanced at those Christian temperance tracts. They winked at one another. They could not take the temperance message seriously.

As Maggie placed the teapot on its brass stand on the table and then carefully pulled the woollen tea cosy, shaped like a ginger cat, over it, she asked, "Well, have you read your tracts?"

Colin tactfully replied, "Aye, Maggie, we've glanced at them. The trouble is we don't have our reading glasses with us to read them properly."

"Och well, in that case take them home with you and be sure to read them and take their message to heart."

They neatly folded the leaflets and put them in their pockets. "Aye, we'll be sure to do that, Maggie," Ian untruthfully promised.

"Good!… Now you can have your food and tea." Ian took her up on the hospitable offer; his hand reached for the sandwiches. Just in time it stopped as Maggie continued, "Will you be saying the grace, Colin?" (She knew better than to ask Ian, that hopelessly unregenerate heathen, to say grace.)

"Och no, Maggie, you give the grace, I'm sure you're much better at it than me."

"Oh, very well; I'll just say a few words." Although she replied with quiet modesty, she was secretly delighted to have this captive audience to preach to.

She bowed her head, tightly closed her eyes and started saying grace. With solemn expressions both men bowed their heads, but they kept their eyes open and stared hungrily at the food spread out under their noses – so near and yet so far.

Maggie's 'few words' expanded into a good number of words. Her short grace became a long prayer. There seemed to be an awful lot of sin, an awful lot of miserable sinners, an awful lot about the terrible evils of strong drink, in her prayer.

With startling suddenness Ian's stomach rumbled.

He ashamedly lifted his head and furtively glanced at Maggie. Her head remained deeply bowed, her eyes remained tightly shut; ignoring that rude bodily noise she steadily continued saying grace. Ian now looked at Colin, sitting at the opposite side of the table. Colin, too, had raised his head and glanced at Maggie; he quickly grinned and winked at Ian. The wink and grin were joyously returned.

Auld Maggie's grace flowed fervently and unendingly on and on.

Ian smiled as a grace he had heard queasy soldiers use on a wartime troopship during stormy weather suddenly surfaced in his memory:

"We thank thee Lord, as we now sup;
And we'll thank thee again
If we don't bring it up."

Staring at the forbidden food heaped untouched on the table, oh how he wished Maggie's grace was as short and sweet. Now it was the turn of Colin's stomach to complain of its emptiness. At first, almost apologetically, it made a few hesitant high-pitched squeaks and squeals; then, gathering courage, it gave a series of loud rumbles, which rudely echoed around the room.

The men dared not raise their heads. If their eyes met, the desperately restrained internal laughter trembling through their bodies would burst out. Such laughter while she was saying grace would mortally offend Auld Maggie; it would be a terrible insult not only to her, but to her God. It would be blasphemy.

However, Maggie could hardly ignore Colin's stomach's impolitely unsubtle hint. She abruptly ended her grace with a loud, "Amen. Amen." The men thankfully joined in that 'Amen'.

With a hint of annoyance, she ordered, "Hand over your cups."

After pouring the tea, she relented and said in a friendlier tone, "Now help yourselves to what the Good Lord has provided."

Both hungry men did full justice to Maggie's generous spread. They wasted no precious eating time on finicky, over-polite, fancy table manners. The heap of sandwiches quickly diminished, or, as Colin jovially declared, "They're just melting awa' like spring snow thawing frae a drystane dyke."

After the sandwiches were finished, Maggie urged her scones, oatcakes and crowdie cheese on her visitors. Noting Colin's empty plate she said, "Come on, Colin, eat up. Have another scone and more crowdie."

"Och, I've had two scones already, Maggie."

Her careworn face suddenly brightened as she smiled, "Actually, you've had three, ye ken... but who's counting?"

Colin and Ian heartily laughed. They felt a surge of warm compassion for poor auld Maggie. In that unexpected, untypical touch of humour they detected a glimpse of how much happier, how much brighter a person she might well have become if only life had been a bit kinder to her.

Later, she still continued to press food on the men, but with distinctly less keenness. She was torn by a conflict between the demands of traditional Highland hospitality and a desire not to encourage the sin of gluttony.

Her face flushed brightly, her hands fluttered nervously, her entire body quivered with embarrassed delight as she basked in the sincere and repeatedly expressed praise that Ian and Colin bestowed on her home-made scones, oatcakes and, especially, her crowdie cheese.

"Your crowdie has a unique flavour like no other crowdie I've ever tasted," Colin once more enthused.

"Och, I'm sure your wife makes crowdie *almost* as good as mine!"

Both men smiled as they noted the emphasis she put on the word 'almost'.

Having finished eating, they sat on at the table and drank more tea. Ian glanced around at the many pictures in the clean, but cluttered, kitchen. Most were framed black and white photos of Maggie's parents, her brothers, and more distant relations. The others were sombre Victorian drawings of dismally dull scenes full of grey mists and gothic ruins. One exception to this general dullness was a brightly coloured print of Saint Francis of Assisi. He was depicted standing with outstretched arms and with numerous birds fearlessly feeding from his hands. Dainty small deer, lambs, sheep and donkeys gazed up at the saint with adoring eyes.

Ian remembered being in Assisi for a short time just after its liberation. He found it a dirty, smelly, unpleasantly rundown place. He found no evidence that gentle Saint Francis's humane teachings, his loving care of animals, had had any effect on the impoverished peasants in the district; they still cruelly overworked their underfed and overloaded donkeys.

Noticing Ian looking at the bright print, Maggie gently smiled, "Saint Francis was a great man. His wonderful love of all animals inspired the animals to love him in return." She paused and gave a troubled Calvinistic frown, "But I have never been able to understand how God allowed such a great man to be so misguided as to be a Roman Catholic."

Ian nodded and smiled but said nothing. He never ceased to be amazed at how believers could be so certain that their own particular religion, their own narrow cult, was the only true faith and all others were woefully wrong. Surely those who have such belief in their own undeniable rightness can have little or no imagination. When Ian heard them expound their convictions with such absolutely certainty, he was always reminded of the fond Scots mother proudly declaring as her soldier son marched past with his regiment: "They are a' oot o' step except oor Jock."

Ian's gaze now wandered up the large, old fashioned fireplace opposite him where a 'wallie dug' sat at each end of the high mantelpiece and with insipidly simpering silly expressions kept a friendly eye on the many gaudily painted tin tea caddies neatly arrayed between them. Higher yet, in the place of honour above the mantelpiece, hung two large pictures of equal size. Both these solemnly framed black and white photos had mourning ribbons of black crepe stretched along their tops and hanging down their sides.

The photo on the left was of Maggie's younger brother, John. It showed him as a sturdy, bright-faced smiling youth proudly dressed in his Seaforth Highlanders' uniform. The other photo showed Maggie's fiancé. He too was smiling bravely. He too wore his Royal Navy uniform with youthful pride.

Maggie noticed Ian looking up at those old photos. She quietly remarked, "Later this year it will be exactly forty years since poor John and Donald were killed in the war."

Ian gently replied, "Forty years?... It hardly seems possible."

Colin turned in his chair and looked up at the photos. "Aye, it's unbelievable that forty years have passed since then."

"Aye, I know," Maggie solemnly nodded, "but it's only too true. 1944 to this year, 1984, is exactly forty years, isn't it?"

Ian sympathetically murmured, "That was a very sad time for you, Maggie."

"Aye, it was. It was a terribly sad time. I can never forget it. I can remember it as clearly as if it happened only yesterday." Maggie fell silent. She sat absolutely still and stared at the faded old photos. She was wrapped in a dark shawl of sad memories.

Colin and Ian also sat uneasily still and silent. They felt deep sympathy for Auld Maggie. Suddenly Ian had a feeling, an almost guilty feeling, that she was secretly accusing Colin and himself of having survived the war, while her (worthier?) brother and her fiancé had been killed. He sensed her questioning, 'Why?... Why had they been killed?... Why had those others survived?

Ian and Colin had often discussed those insoluble problems. Why had some comrades been killed in their first action? Why had they themselves survived six long years of war and safely come through many fierce battles?

With an effort Maggie dragged her eyes from the pictures and stared sadly at her visitors. She sighed deeply, "I must accept that it was God's will – God's inscrutable will – that they died. Oh, I know it's a sin to doubt His divine purpose, but even yet, even after all this time, I still find it difficult to accept the need for their deaths." Those old, but still painfully deep and raw wartime wounds forced a sob to her throat and tears to her eyes.

She bravely gasped, "Och, don't heed me; I'm just being silly!" She hurriedly snatched up the teapot and gently shook it. "Och, I'm getting so forgetful. It's empty. I forgot to fill it again, and I could do with another cup. You two will be all the better of another good cup of tea as well – 'the cup that cheers, but does

272

not inebriate' – unlike the whisky which I'm afraid the pair o' you are still much too fond of."

Getting to her feet she moved towards the scullery. Abruptly she halted and turned round; her gaze went back to the photo of her brother. Tearfully she murmured, "I'll never forget the kindness of both of you writing to let my parents and me know that when John was killed in Italy he died instantly. The knowledge that he did not suffer any dreadful lingering pain helped us all to cope with our grief over his death."

She turned and hurried into the scullery. Colin and Ian's eyes met. They silently gazed at one another. They knew that they were thinking of the same thing – the secret knowledge that they would keep forever hidden from poor Auld Maggie Gunn.

They had lied to her and to her parents with their assurances that her brother, their son, had died instantaneously. Their convincing, well-intentioned, consoling lie was entirely justified; it had been only one of the many, many thousands of similar consoling lies sent to grieving next-of-kin during the war.

The truth about John Gunn's death was harrowingly different.

Chapter Twenty

1944 was a momentous year.

It was a time of titanic struggles. It was a year of decisive battles. The outcome of these battles shaped the course of future history.

Millions of Russians and Germans were savagely fighting and brutally dying on the Eastern Front. The Red Army was victoriously driving the German invaders out of Russia. As Stalin proudly proclaimed to a wildly ecstatic (and captive sycophant) audience, "Soon, very soon, the only German soldiers left on Russian soil will be dead German soldiers!" Being the consummate politician he was, he managed by implication to bestow much of the credit for this glorious success on himself, on his inspired military leadership.

Huge British and American armies had invaded Normandy, had liberated France and Belgium and were driving the German army out of Holland.

Allied bombers were devastating German cities. The Germans' 'secret weapons', the V1 flying bombs and the V2 long-range rockets, were killing thousands in London.

All across the (not-so pacific) Pacific Ocean American and Japanese warships and aircraft savagely fought for mastery of that vast ocean. American marines suffered grievous losses as they captured island after island, all vital stepping-stones on the path to Japan.

The British 14th Army (the forgotten army) fought the Japanese in the steaming jungles of Burma.

The world had never seen war on such a gigantic scale.

Colin MacDonald and Ian MacLean were part of another almost forgotten British army – the 8th Army, the 'D-Day Dodgers', in Italy. Although the scale of the fighting here was comparatively small, the hardships and dangers were real; death was just as terrifyingly final here as anywhere else.

The German army retreating up the length of Italy towards the formidable Northern mountains was like a wounded beast making for its lair. Although outnumbered by its relentless pursuers and getting weak from loss of blood it was always dangerous; at any time, usually when least expected, it could turn and savagely hit out.

One thing slowing the advance of British and American armies were the many land mines left by the Germans. These anti-tank mines and smaller anti-personnel mines were skilfully buried in dusty plains and in muddy mountain passes. Complementing these mines were the countless ingeniously hidden lethal booby traps set in deserted buildings.

Despite the utmost – and quietly heroic-efforts of Allied sappers to clear these mines and booby-traps, these devilish devices steadily reaped a grim harvest.

At least, if the victim got medical help in time, the anti-personnel mines did not usually kill – they 'merely' blew off a foot or a leg!

Then some junior German army officer in the Ordnance Corps thought that those anti-personnel mines were not very efficient – surely they could be improved, be made to kill instead of merely wounding? His recommendations duly passed up through the regular channels. High-ranking officers acted on his ideas and soon civilian engineers, teutonically proud of their technical skills, eagerly and quickly transformed these ideas into practical results.

Their improvement was quite simple. They fitted a powerful spring to the anti-personnel mine. Now, when stood upon, it did not explode on the ground but sprung up and exploded at stomach level. It efficiently killed its victim by disembowelling him. A great improvement!

The proud German engineers eagerly tested their improved Teller mines on human guinea pigs in concentration camps. Delighted with the gory results, they sent their perfected mines to Italy for field trials.

Ian and Colin's mixed unit of Seaforth Highlanders and Lovat Scouts was one of the furthest forward of all British army units. They were also one of the first to be warned of this new 'improved' Teller mine. These soldiers swore with weary resignation – hadn't they enough to worry about without this grim new danger?

Major Ferguson was briefing his officers and senior non-commissioned officers. They crowded around the table where the map was spread out. He pointed to a small town on the map. "That's our objective for tomorrow, gentlemen. It's only nine miles away, it shouldn't take us long to reach it. Intelligence reports say the Jerries cleared out of it yesterday."

Sergeant-Major Buchanan asked, "What's the name of the town, sir?"

The major smiled, "I'm not quite certain about the correct pronunciation of that Italian town. What do you think, Sgt-Major?"

The Sgt-Major leaned over the map. He read the name "ARSOLI". Straightening up, he grinned broadly, "I'm sure the men will know how to pronounce that name, sir. No doubt they'll make many bawdy comments when we tell them they're heading up to Arsoli tomorrow."

And they did! The soldiers listened with unrestrained glee as the Italian name was rather uncertainly pronounced by the grinning Sgt-Major. That name strongly appealed to their earthy sense of humour. All the ribald jokes and smutty suggestions put them in a lively mood as they set out shortly after dawn en-route for Arsoli. They saw no Germans, nor any signs of activity in the small town; they dared hope that, for once, intelligence information was correct and it had been abandoned by the Jerries.

They fervently hoped that this calm would continue; but, not allowing themselves to be foolishly lulled into a false (and potentially fatal) sense of security, they advanced slowly, silently and cautiously.

Suddenly, Ian felt unaccountably uneasy. He had a strong sense of foreboding. Then, twenty yards to his left, there was a small, distinct, sharp explosion.

Ian's body – and Colin's nearby one – were instantly lying flat and pressing into the dust. Their bodies had not been directed by conscious thought but by sensitively acute survival instincts.

The noise of the explosion was immediately followed by a far worse sound – a terrible, nerve-racking scream of anguish.

It hardly seemed possible that such agonised screams could come from a human throat. They sounded like the screams of a trapped and tortured animal's unbearable pain.

Colin and Ian got to their feet and hurried towards the screams. They dreaded to think what they would find.

Their worst dreads were realized.

The screams were coming from one of their comrades, one of their younger and less experienced comrades, Private John Gunn.

The sight of him stopped them in their tracks. They stared aghast. The young soldier had stood on one of those 'improved' anti-personnel Teller mines. He was disembowelled. His hands desperately clutched at the hollow, filled with ugly dark blood, where his stomach had been. His mutilated intestines lay around him in a filthy mess of purple and grey coils.

Colin and Ian, those tough, battle hardened 'old sweats', paled and felt their bile rise. With a determined effort they got themselves under control – John Gunn urgently needed their help.

Kneeling beside him they put down their Sten guns and pulled out emergency medical dressings from their trouser pockets. They tried to remove John's hands from his ghastly wound, but they refused to be moved. They gave up the attempt. They realised that such a huge wound was beyond their help. Even the most skilled surgeon could have done nothing. They returned the medical dressings to their pockets.

John stopped screaming. He seemed unconscious. Colin gasped, "There's nothing we can do for him. Will you stay with him, Ian, and I'll go and get a medic orderly; he'll give him morphine."

"Aye, right, Colin, but hurry… for God's sake hurry!"

Ian sat beside John; he put his arm around his shoulders, lifted his agonised head and rested it against his own chest.

Ian stared after Colin as he jogged away with his clumsy boots erupting small explosions of dust. Repeatedly his khaki figure appeared and disappeared in and out of an olive grove's neat patterns of light and shade. He anxiously prayed that none of those sinister Teller mines lurked in Colin's path. His attention was torn from that vanishing figure by a violent shudder convulsing John's body. With renewed comradely compassion he tightened his grip around John's shuddering shoulders. He hoped that even in his terribly shocked state John would realise that he was not alone.

John appeared to surface from the deep depths of his dark ocean of severe shock. His eyes, glazed and tortured with pain, turned slowly and searchingly up towards Ian's face. With an anguished effort he whispered, "Is… is… is that you, Colin?"

Ian bent his head down to hear better, he replied, "No, John, it's me, Ian."

"Who?"

"Ian… Ian MacLean, you know me, don't you?"

John managed the suggestion of a grim ghost of a smile as he murmured, "Och, aye, Ian… Corporal MacLean… I know you… you drunken auld bugger!"

Ian forced a smile, but a lump choked his throat and hot tears stung his eyes.

After a short silence another violent tremor shook John's body. He sobbed and gasped, "Oh, Ian… I… I don't want to die!"

"You won't die, John. You won't die."

For a moment John's eyes stared with searching, imploring, interrogation into Ian's eyes.

Ian was conscious stricken. He feared John was seeing through his too ready, his too glib lies. He feared that despite – or because of – his shocked state, John might have some heightened awareness of what was a lie, what was the truth.

With a desperate effort, Ian forced true sincerity and deep reassurance into his well-intentioned lies. He tightened his grip around John's shoulders, stared steadily into his stricken, appealing eyes, and firmly repeated, "You won't die, John. You won't die. Colin's gone for the medics. They'll be here soon. They'll give you morphine. The doctors will soon patch you up."

Ian was pleased to see that his convincing lies seemed to be getting through. John again bravely tried to smile, then murmured, "Oh, Ian… I… I'd like to go home."

"Don't worry, John, you'll soon be flown to Blighty. You'll soon have lots of beautiful young nurses dancing attendance on you."

Ian imagined that John's eyes brightened for a moment, then another violent shudder shook his body and, groaning loudly, he again sank into his own lonely hell of anguish, shock and pain.

A number of times as he sat holding John's dying body, Ian thought he had actually died. He face was a ghastly colour – the pale, yellow, ugliness of a dead toad's belly. His cheeks seemed to be collapsing inwards. He hardly seemed to be breathing.

Ian's attention was distracted by a sudden swift movement beyond John's body. A small, dark green lizard scurried over the dust. Vanishing into the dark shade of some sombre shrivelled shrubs it left a tiny track in its wake. Ian smiled as he thought, 'Biologists assure us that such a reptile is far below us clever humans in the evolutionary scale, and yet that primitive little lizard doesn't need to worry about exploding a mine and having its guts blown out'.

The incessant loud buzzing of hundreds of black flies now drew Ian's attention, against his will, to the hideous sight of John's guts lying in the dust. Despite the greedy flies obscenely coating the revolting mess, he was sure he detected a slow ripple in those warm guts as if bacteria were still urgently carrying on its vital work. A noisy mass of flies swarmed in the bloody hollow where John's hands still determinedly attempted to hold his non-existent stomach together.

A few lines from one of the First World War poets (he could not remember which) hammered in Ian's brain:

"In a great mess of things unclean,
Sat a dead Boch; he
scowled and stunk
with clothes and face a sodden green..."

He sighed despairingly, "O God, will we never learn? Will we never give up killing?" Knowing how resolutely and bravely most German soldiers fought, he sometimes despaired of the war ever ending, or, at least, of him surviving to see the end of it.

John's body gave another violent tremor. He groaned piteously. A wave of hatred surged through Ian. He felt black hatred for the German engineers who had perfected the Teller anti-personnel mine. No doubt they were inordinately proud of having brought that mine to maximum efficiency. But of course it was not only the Germans who keenly devised and perfected ever more efficient weapons of death. All industrialised nations were guilty. Much of mankind's greatest efforts in this century were directed towards producing ever better weapons to ever more efficiently kill ever more people.

Ian wearily wondered if his hatred was a cover to hide another emotion... an emotion he was reluctant to admit to himself... fear... real deep fear. He knew that he should wish John to be released from his suffering by death. He should... and he truly did and yet he could not help the cowardly thought that as long as John precariously clung to life then he had an excuse to sit in safety beside him. But once John was dead there would no longer be that excuse. He would have to move, and once moving perhaps it would be his turn to step on one of those terrifyingly perfected Teller mines.

Not for the first time during this war, Ian cursed his too active imagination as he vividly pictured the horror of stepping on one of those mines. How hideous that fraction of a second between the mine being released and it exploding at waist level. He could feel his belly being ripped open; he could see his guts splattering out; he could...

Suddenly his sixth sense saved him from further imagined horrors. It stridently warned him of someone approaching. Consciously he had seen or heard nothing, but he instantly reacted to that warning. He checked that his loaded Sten gun was to hand, then searched for movement in the olive grove. He saw two figures appearing and disappearing in the light and shade. With relief he made out their khaki uniforms. As they came nearer he recognised Colin and Sergeant Smith, their senior medical orderly. Obviously they too did not want to risk stepping on a mine; Colin was leading and he cautiously kept in the footprints he had made earlier. Sgt. Smith walked close behind Colin.

The sergeant glanced at John's hideous stomach wound. He slowly shook his head. Kneeling, he felt for the pulse in John's neck. There was none. He felt the unmistakable cold, clammy touch of death on him. Again he shook his head.

"He's practically dead. I could give him morphine, but there's no point. He's not suffering now. He can't live more than another few minutes."

In less than a minute Sgt. Smith's prediction proved correct. A few final spasms contorted John's body then he gave a terrible coughing, sighing, choking sound – that sound which tears at the nerves of even the most hardened and experienced listeners – the death rattle.

Sgt. Smith reached out and gently closed John's blankly staring eyes. "His ordeal's over. No need to hold him now, Ian. He's now held in the cold, unfeeling clutch of death."

Ian slowly eased John's head – his suddenly death heavy head – from against his chest and gently placed it on the dusty ground. Awkwardly he scrambled to his feet and straightened and stretched to ease his cramped muscles. Colin handed out cigarettes. He struck a match and lit the sergeant's and Ian's fags. He blew out the match and with a fresh match lit his own fag. They all smiled but said nothing; they knew it was bad luck to light three fags with the one match. – ridiculous superstition?… Aye, probably, but it was best not to tempt fate. Having survived five years of war they felt they needed all the luck they could get to continue to survive to the end of the war. They sat together and smoked. Ugly black flies crawled on John's bloodied lips, explored his gaping mouth, vilely intruded up his nostrils and tried to force themselves under his closed eyelids. Sgt. Smith sighed, "Oh well, at least those bloody flies don't bother him now."

"No, but they bother me," Colin said. He rose, waved the flies away and gently spread a clean – a reasonably clean – khaki handkerchief over John's face.

As they smoked their second fags, Ian said to Colin, "We'll need to write to John's parents and give them the usual reassuring lies; tell them that their son died instantaneously and did not really suffer much."

Colin nodded, "Aye, it's the least we can do for them."

Sgt. Smith also nodded, "Yes, I've had to write a few of those reassuring letters myself. Those consoling lies are fully justified, they do help bereaved parents or wives in their grief."

Suddenly the sergeant loudly and violently let out a stream of the vilest swear words he knew. Almost shamefacedly he apologised, "I'm sorry!… I got carried away! This is the third victim gutted by those bloody Teller mines I've attended recently. Is it any wonder I curse the bloody Germans who made them?"

"Aye, they certainly are hellish weapons," Ian agreed.

"Was it your poet, Burns, who wrote about man's inhumanity to man?" asked Sgt. Smith who came from Yorkshire.

"Aye, it was," Colin replied: "'Man's inhumanity to man makes countless thousands mourn'!"

"Only thousands mourning?" the sergeant asked, doubtfully.

"Aye, when Rabbie wrote that poem wars only killed thousands, or tens of thousands; then in the First World War millions were killed; but now, in this bloody war, tens of millions have died and the killing's still going on," Colin said with grim despair.

They were all sadly silent for some moments, then Ian, with solemn irony, murmured, "Ah, well, that's Progress for you!"

Ian was startled out of these memories by Auld Maggie addressing him. He tore his mesmerised gaze away from the picture of Private John Gunn. "Oh, I'm sorry, Maggie, what did you say?"

"I told you to hand over your cup. I've made some fresh tea."

As they drank, the subject of the local laird, Campbell-Fotheringay, arose; his evil policies and his vile personal iniquities were roundly condemned. Ian angrily declared, "I cannot help hating him. I've rarely felt such hatred for anyone before."

Gently, but determinedly, Maggie rebuked him, "Oh, Ian, I can understand how you feel, but it's wrong to hate anyone. We must try not to hate any of God's creatures."

"Not even savagely marauding, hen-killing foxes?" Colin asked, grinning.

Maggie managed to return his grin, "Och well, Colin, we are all human… all too human. There is a limit to our tolerance and those terrible foxes go far beyond my limit." She continued her plea, "No, Ian, you shouldn't hate him. Only God has the right to judge such an evil sinner as him." Her voice rose as she passionately declared, "God is not mocked! Campbell-Fotheringay will get his just deserts in due course!"

"Aye, and the sooner the better!" Ian fervently exclaimed.

"Oh no!… Oh dear me, no! It is not for the likes of us to decide when or how he will be punished. Only God can decide that. A wrathful and yet a righteous God will, in His own good time, using His own chosen instrument, strike him down. He will be justly punished for his grievous sins, for all his dreadful whoremongering."

Colin and Ian were silent. They were impressed by Maggie's absolute certainty. (Afterwards – in view of what happened later that year – they remembered, with something like awe, how profoundly prophetic her passionate words turned out to be.)

Maggie smiled with a brave attempt at Christian forgiveness, "Och, I suppose he is his own worst enemy."

Ian laughed, "Oh no he's not… not while I'm alive!"

The cheery tooting of a vehicle's horn startled Maggie. Flustered, she leapt to her feet, "Oh, dear me, is that the grocer's van?… Oh, dear me, I forgot all about it!" She snatched up her shopping bags and purse then dashed out to the grocer's mobile shop.

Colin smiled at Ian, "If you're quite finished eating we better head for home and, hopefully, for a dram."

"Is that a promise?" Ian asked as, spurred by that incentive, he gulped the last of his scone and crowdie cheese and washed it down with the remains of his tea.

In the passageway Colin halted outside the slightly open door of the bathroom. "I'll just go in and have a piss."

Ian looked in at the mobile shop and spoke to Angie, the driver. Almost immediately Colin joined them. He hadn't been long in the bathroom. They thanked Maggie for her hospitality and made their farewells.

As Ian got into the van beside Colin he saw that he was full of some wild excitement, which was kept under control only with the greatest difficulty. "What is it? What's the matter?" he asked.

Colin's broad and ruddy face was now vividly alive with suppressed laughter; it beamed brightly, it bulged amazingly, it seemed about to explode into uncontrollable mirth. With a supreme effort he only just managed to gasp out, "Wait. I'll tell you when we're away from here."

He put the van into gear and started down the track. He tried to concentrate on the driving, but after a few moments he could no longer restrain his laughter – it exploded out and thunderously shook his entire body. Such glorious unrestrained laughter was infectious. Ian's laughter joined in with Colin's. "I wish I knew what we're laughing at," he gasped.

Laughing uncontrollably, Colin merely shook his head – he could not speak.

Out of sight of Maggie's crofthouse, Colin pulled into a passing place at the side of the track. He switched off the engine. Now his pent-up laughter could be freely released. Torrents of laughter roared from his heaving belly and shook his shoulders. They boomed and reverberated around the van. Ian's laughter again joined in. Their combined laughter shook the van. The three terriers in the back joined in the noise with uncomprehending yelps and questioning whines.

"It would be nice to know what we're laughing at," Ian again gasped.

For a time Colin did not reply – he couldn't! Then he wiped the tears of laughter from his gleaming eyes and his flushed cheeks and, with a desperate effort, managed to exclaim, "I need to go out… to go out for a piss."

"Aye, so do I," Ian said.

As they stood relieving themselves at opposite sides of the van, Ian said, "I thought you went for a piss at Auld Maggie's?"

"Aye, so I did. But I didn't have one there."

"Oh?… Why?"

"That's what I'm laughing at – the reason why I didn't have a piss in Auld Maggie's bathroom."

With renewed laughter, with his eyes again overflowing with joyous tears, Colin collapsed into the driving seat. Ian got into the passenger seat. "Oh, come on, Colin, for God's sake share the joke with me."

In reply Colin asked, "Did you enjoy the crowdie cheese you had at Maggie's?"

"Aye. Aye, I did. Why?… Didn't you?"

"Oh aye, I did… then! But I now wish I hadn't eaten so much of her crowdie. My stomach's feeling a wee bit queasy. How's your stomach?"

"It's fine… it's fine. Why? What's wrong with her crowdie?"

"Well, Ian, you ken that Auld Maggie's crowdie always wins first prize for its unique flavour, don't you?"

Ian nodded, "Aye."

"Well, I've discovered the secret of that unique flavour." Colin could hardly continue for his renewed laughter; making a gallant effort he explained, "I couldn't have a piss at Maggie's because... because her fresh made crowdie cheese was... was in a muslin bag hanging in, and dripping into her lavatory pan!"

"No!... You're joking, Colin, surely you're joking?"

Colin shook his head, his face beamed, he gasped, "That's the truth, I assure you that's the absolute gospel truth!"

"Oh God, no wonder her crowdie has such a unique flavour!" Once again unrestrained laughter burst forth, then Ian ruefully moaned, "Oh God, I wish I hadn't eaten so much of her special crowdie."

"Why?... Is your stomach beginning to play up, too?"

"Aye, it is. It feels a bit queasy now."

"Och, never mind, a few good drams will soon settle oor stomachs. Och, I suppose we better get going and head for those drams." Colin grinned, "And you know, in fairness to Auld Maggie, I don't think she uses that lavatory pan for much else but her crowdie. I ken she has an outside lavatory round at the back of her house."

Ian also grinned, "Aye, even so, I don't think conditions in her bathroom will be exactly perfect for crowdie making. I don't suppose they'll comply in every detail with all the ridiculously stringent food hygiene regulations imposed by Brussels."

Colin nodded, "No, but yet I've never heard o' anyone being ill after eating her crowdie."

"Apart from us!" Ian laughed, "and that's only because we know where her crowdie's been. It only shows what power imagination has – proves the truth of mind over matter."

As he drove along the main road Colin said, "Just wait till I tell Jeannie that she'll need tae hang her crowdie in the lavatory pan if she wants tae compete with Maggie's special crowdie."

"I bet she won't believe you. She'll think it's another o' your tall tales."

"Aye, I know; but I'll convince her of its truth, eventually." (And he did – but Jeannie stubbornly persisted on hanging her dripping crowdie over a clean basin in the scullery). Colin smiled, "I suppose we should keep the secret of Auld Maggie's unique crowdie a secret, shouldn't we?"

"Aye, I suppose we should. We shouldn't tell anyone, apart from our wives."

Their eyes met. Those eyes were bright with fresh laughter. They knew that this discovery was far too good a story to remain secret for long.

Sure enough, in less than one week the tale of the secret of Auld Maggie's special crowdie swept through the entire district. As the story was joyfully told and re-told in house after house it expanded with many ludicrous, colourful additions as witty men hilariously spiced it with inventive, whisky inspired embellishments.

Poor Auld Maggie Gunn was the only person in the district who did not know that her great crowdie secret was no longer a secret.

Chapter Twenty-One

July brought rain, midges and tourists. The tourists were welcomed and the salmon fishers, if no one else, welcomed the rain. The ubiquitous midges got no welcome. These tiny tormenting devils drove some of the less hardy, frantically scratching tourists away.

Ian was kept busy working as a ghillie with the salmon fishers. Helen was employed part-time helping her friend, Margaret Yeats, cope with all the work at her busy guesthouse.

On one of their days off, Helen and Ian took advantage of the dry and warm morning to go trout fishing. At mid-day the weather changed. Heavy black clouds built up in the West and with slow, but grimly determined tenacity, approached them. Soon these clouds loured menacingly overhead. Wearying of carrying their irksome burden of moisture they released it in a savage deluge.

The two fishers frantically struggled to pull on and fasten their waterproofs. With rapidly lessening enthusiasm they continued fishing while the rain unremittingly poured. Eventually Ian ruefully grinned, "Oh, to hell with this, Helen, come on, let's head for home."

Helen's face brightened, "Aye, that sounds a good idea. There's no pleasure in this, is there?... and poor Glen and Corrie are getting fair drookit."

The collie and terrier were pictures of abject misery. Ian laughed, "Trust you to be more concerned aboot the dogs than aboot us poor humans!"

Keener than ever, the dogs led the way home. As they passed a lochan, Ian grinned, "Oh, Helen, we're fair showing our age, scurrying for home like this, aren't we? Remember that time we got caught in a thunderstorm? We didn't turn tail and run for home then. We madly enjoyed swimming naked in this lochan in the warm downpour."

Helen giggled, "Aye, we certainly reacted very differently then. It must have been at least twenty-five years ago. Oh, we were young and foolish then... now we're not so young and – perhaps – not so foolish!"

On that fishing trip of so many years ago the perfect weather seemed firmly set and they took no waterproofs with them. The Gods punished them for their foolhardy audacity. Massive purple/black clouds built up and obscured the sun. Approaching thunder loudly rumbled over the hills and reverberated around the glens. Soon it was violently rumbling overhead. Then the rains came. First came a few heavy, sullen drops – the scouting outriders of the rapidly advancing main army. Then came an absolute deluge. It was as if a tap had been turned full on. In a few minutes their clothes were soaked through.

The trout, always acutely sensitive to changes in atmospheric pressure, went deep and became sluggishly inactive. The fishing was now hopeless. Helen smiled, "Perhaps, like me, they've got a headache."

They set out for home. After an hour of weary walking through the pouring rain and the oppressively humid atmosphere, they halted at a dark lochan. "This is a strange, unreal world we're in, isn't it, Ian?" murmured Helen. "It's such an eerie purplish light."

"Aye, it is. It is. It's certainly not the normal everyday world. There's something definitely surrealistic about it."

The compressed space between sodden earth and the low, heavy clouds held a unique, an unearthly light. All ordinary colours of the grasses, the heathers, the rocks, were killed, were smothered in a strangling pall of mourning purple. The flat surface of the lochan was inkily black. Huge raindrops splattered like buckshot over it.

With a sudden determined effort, Helen threw off the dismal effects of the strange atmosphere. Grinning widely, she also began to throw off her sodden clothing.

Ian gasped, "What are you doing?"

"I'm going for a swim."

"In this weather? In this rain?"

They had swum in this lochan before – but always in bright summer sunshine.

"I'm terribly sweaty. I fancy a plunge in the lochan. With this warm atmosphere the water should be just right – cool enough to invigorate, but not cold enough to freeze. Come on, Ian, aren't you joining me?"

"You're crazy!" Ian shouted as he started peeling off his saturated clothes. "Och, I suppose I'm as crazy as you, Helen!"

"Aye, I hope so… I damn well hope so!"

Madly they plunged, they swam, they splashed.

Coming rushing through the shallows towards Ian, Helen wildly shouted, "Oh, Heathcliff!… Oh, my Heathcliff!"

Ian instantly joined in her madness: he rushed forward loudly shouting, "Oh, Cathy!… Oh, my Cathy!"

In a glorious commotion of spray their naked, pluvially gleaming wet bodies came together with a strange squashy smacking sound. They hugged each other tightly. "What a queer noise. What did it sound like?" Helen gasped.

Ian grinned, "Like a large flounder being slapped on to a fishmonger's marble slab."

Helen giggled, "Oh, Ian… Ian, that's one of the things I love about you – you say the most romantic things!"

For reply he hugged her even closer, lifted her off her feet and whirled her round and round. Their two collies excitedly joined in this hilarious madness. Ceaselessly barking, they splashingly cavorted around those crazily cavorting, ever unpredictable humans. Helen happily cried, "Oh, we've got the poor dogs as daft as ourselves."

Hand in hand they rushed out of the water and threw their soaking bodies on their soggy clothes. Helen laughed and gasped, "Oh, we're crazy!... We must be really crazy to carry on like this."

"Aye, we are, thank God!"

"Why, 'thank God', Ian?"

"Because it proves we're sane. The only really sane people are those who occasionally do crazy things."

"Oh, in that case we certainly are sane – very, very, sane!"

For a little time they lay happily silent while the unrelenting rain drummed warm, impertinently exploring fingers promiscuously over their naked bodies.

"Come on, Helen, we better get moving. The sooner we get into a hot bath the better."

"It's hardly worthwhile getting into those soaking clothes, is it?... apart from our boots and stockings."

"Oh, Helen, we better put some clothes on even if they are wet through and gey uncomfortable."

"Why? Surely there's nothing wrong with going naked here where there's no one to see us. And anyway I want to continue the unique pleasure of having this warm rain flowing over my bare body. It's a wonderful, a fantastic feeling, isn't it?"

"Aye, it's a rare sensual experience, I agree, but still I think we better put some clothes on for the journey home." Ian grinned. "Suppose we met my prim brother – or worse, much worse, his straight-laced prudish wife?"

Helen's eyes twinkled impudently. She gave a slow, sly, elfin smile, "I'm just trying to imagine her disbelieving shocked expression if she saw us returning, both naked, to Altdour."

Laughing, they started to pull on sodden stockings and soaking boots. Ian stood up and tightly buckled the heavy weight of his saturated kilt around his waist then bundled his other clothes into the rucksack.

"Och, if you're being such a spoilsport I suppose I'd better put on some clothes as well," Helen complained. "But, like you, not too many." She pulled on her soaking tweed skirt and securely fastened it.

"Is that all you're putting on?"

"Aye, Ian, again like you I'm going topless!"

Ian slowly shook his head and gave a wide grin, "Aye, all right, let's get going."

Later, in the small wood which sheltered their home, as they walked under the dejectedly dropping, sadly dripping branches, a couple of half-hidden small birds energetically shook their damp feathers then with cheery voices tentatively tried out some notes of a bright song. They rejoiced that the fierce downpour was over. The thunder now rumbled and grumbled, snarled and growled in the distance like a bad-tempered dog.

"What are those birds?" Helen asked.

Staring at her bare breasts, Ian laughed, "Very appropriately, they are a pair of great tits."

Helen joined in his laughter, "Well it's a good thing the weather's so warm, otherwise it's a pair of blue tits you'd be seeing!"

Chuckling, they cautiously made their way to the front of the crofthouse. As expected, no one was about. They quickly entered. "You have your bath now, Helen." Grinning, Ian added, "And you don't need to tell me; I know the first thing I've to do... dry the soaking dogs – correct?"

Helen smiled as she made for the bathroom, "Aye, that's right. You're learning, Ian, you're learning!"

Twenty-five years later, as they once more passed that dark lochan in pouring rain they behaved differently. Cluttered in bulking waterproofs they hurried on. They were not tempted to swim in it. Ian solemnly voiced their thoughts, "Ah yes, age makes a big difference to how we act, doesn't it?"

One evening, a few days later, Ian's nephew, Nigel MacLean, visited Altdour. Helen and Ian warmly welcomed him.

"Here are the books I borrowed from you, Ian. I'm sorry I've kept them so long. I didn't manage to read them all, I was too busy studying for my final exams.

Nigel was the only child of Ian's older brother, William. He had recently completed his studies at Glasgow University.

Ian glanced over the titles of the returned books. He felt a thrill of pleasure at the safe return of those 'lost sheep', which had been borrowed more than a year ago.

Nigel was staying with his parents at their home in Aldrory Glen. He had promised his mother he would spend at least two weeks with them. He intended to keep that promise, but it was quite an effort. He would stay no longer and would leave with real relief in a few days time.

"Where are you going?" Helen asked, "back to Glasgow?"

"Yeah, to Glasgow, but just for a week or two, then I'm going with a friend to India for some time – months or years, who can tell?" He grinned widely, youthfully pleased at the vagueness of his exciting plans.

"You'll be studying philosophies, be searching for knowledge, be looking for the true meaning and purpose of Life, eh, Nigel?" Ian asked.

"Yeah, that's exactly what I hope to do. I'm really excited about it. Surely there's nothing more worthwhile than to search for the Absolute... to – hopefully – discover the Ultimate Truth?" Nigel's eyes eagerly gleamed and his cheeks brightly glowed with youthful enthusiasm.

"Aye, but the difficulty is to know which Ultimate Truth is the True Ultimate Truth. There are as many Ultimate Truths as there are religions, aren't there?" Moved by Nigel's warm, infectious, idealism Ian did not want to be too cynical, too discouraging, he smiled, "Anyway, I agree it's a grand – the grandest, the noblest – task you've set yourself. I – Helen and I – sincerely wish you every success in your noble quest."

"Thank you – but you know, my quest is not so unique. I'm only following the trail blazed by many hippies away back in the 1960s."

Ian nodded, "Aye, I know. Aye, lad, you're wise to travel and see something of the world while you're young."

Nigel gave a cheeky, boyish grin, "I wish you'd persuade my parents of that and of the wisdom of my plans."

"They disapprove, then?"

"Yes, of course they do. Did you expect anything else?"

"No, not really."

Ian and Helen exchanged a quick glance. They knew that Nigel's mother had set her heart on her son becoming a Church of Scotland minister and his father had wanted him to follow in his footsteps and become a bank manager. Both had been disappointed. Nigel had absolutely refused to study religion and theology or finance and economics. His reflective, artistic nature led him to the humanities and he had recently graduated with an Honours degree in Classics. He expected to become a teacher – but not for a while yet. The lure of the East beckoned. His spirits soared as he anticipated exploring the magic, the myths and legends, the mysticisms, of India.

Helen said, "I'm afraid Ian and I have no influence with your parents, Nigel. They strongly disapprove of our hedonistic lifestyle. Although we live near them we don't see much of them."

Nigel grinned, "Yeah, I know. I don't blame you for seeing little of them. I find it quite an ordeal to spend two weeks with them, these couple of weeks seem more like a couple of months."

Ian nodded understandingly then said, "I'll just put these books back in my 'study'."

Nigel and Helen followed him into that untidy room. While Ian lovingly replaced the books in the correct places on the crowded shelves, Nigel eagerly gazed around at the one-eyed wildcat on the dustily cobwebbed window ledge, at the small green frog keeping the astonished stoat at bay with its sharp sword, at the royal stag superciliously staring through its monocle. He exclaimed, "Oh don't ever change this room; it's perfect, it's wonderful!"

Helen laughed, "Aye, Nigel, you always loved this room. As a wee bairn and then later, as a schoolboy, you liked nothing better than playing here!"

Nigel rather shamefacedly said, "Yes, I seem to remember quite often screaming in a tantrum at my mother that I loved this house of yours much better than my own home." He paused, he grinned, "Actually, I still do!"

Ian returned his grin, "Aye well surely for anyone with imagination, especially a child, this house is much more interesting than your terribly house-proud mother's spotlessly tidy, sterile, bookless place?"

"Yeah, it is… it certainly is."

Later, as they sat around the fire and enjoyed their tea and drams, Helen asked, "What happened to your hand, Nigel?"

A large plaster covered the back of his left hand. "Oh, it's nothing much: I cut it on barbed wire while helping Kenny MacLeod remove an old fence and put up a new one in its place."

"Oh yes, 'Kate Kettle' told me you were helping her brother with the fence. Kenny would be pleased to have your assistance. No doubt you were well rewarded with many cups of tea from good old 'Kate Kettle'."

Nigel gave another boyish grin, "Yeah, I sure was. She forced innumerable cups on me. I've never drank so much tea in my life before."

Ian laughed, "Aye, and when you're working with Kenny there's always another hazard: you have to beware of the tools he carelessly throws about."

"Yeah, I soon discovered that! I had often to smartly leap away to avoid the hammers and saws he violently threw aside."

"It's just a pity old 'Stirling Ross' isn't active: he and his Land Rover would soon have removed the old fence for Kenny." Ian grinned, "Aye, and he would have removed the new fence as well!"

Nigel listened with amusement as Ian told the almost legendary story of 'Stirling Ross' and the new fence.

It happened a good many years ago.

Donald Ross worked as a part-time postman delivering mail to the houses scattered throughout Aldrory Glen. Through summer's sunshine and sweaty heat and through winter's gales, snow and sleet, Donald plodded up the glen with unvarying pace.

Then it was decided the mail would be delivered by van. Undaunted, Donald, over fifty years old, rose to the challenge. He bought an old Land Rover and set about teaching himself to drive. Fortunately he had his croft land and the peat track behind his house to practise on. With wild exhilaration he traversed every inch of that land – to the great alarm of, and grave danger to, his sheep.

A neighbouring crofter, an experienced driver, gave Donald a driving lesson – once!

A Royal Mail driving instructor came from Inverness and gave Donald a driving lesson – once!

That instructor returned to Inverness with badly shaken nerves. He had considerable experience of wildly erratic driving by blissful, carefree characters from the 'Wild West' Highlands, but Donald surpassed them all. The culmination came when he made an emergency stop. It happened at a bend on the narrow road, which crawled up Aldrory Glen. When Donald – eventually – got the Land Rover stopped, the instructor found himself staring down a steep, boulder-strewn slope to a lochan far below. The Land Rover trembled on the very edge of the drop. The instructor urgently grabbed and pulled up the hand brake.

Donald politely apologised, "Och now, I'm sorry, I forgot that hand brake again." He smiled disarmingly, "Och well, never mind, it doesn't matter much… that brake doesn't work very well anyway."

The instructor, his nerves – like the Land Rover – on edge, shouted at Donald to get out at his side. Donald reluctantly clambered out, exclaiming, "Oh, good life, what's all the fuss about?"

The instructor nervously persuaded the Land Rover away from the edge. Before thankfully setting out for the normality of civilized Inverness he told Donald that he had no hope of becoming a Royal Mail driver.

A greatly disappointed Donald could never understand why he had been failed as a postal driver, after all, as he often declared, "Och now, there's nothing much to this driving; I find it comes quite naturally to me."

Once, after a few dramas, Donald Ross disclosed that he greatly admired the motor racing driver, Stirling Moss. That champion driver was then at the peak of his success. Donald also foolishly disclosed that when younger he had harboured secret ambitions of becoming a motor racing driver.

That was it! He was immediately given the nickname 'Stirling Ross'.

After failing the driving test he only used his old Land Rover on his own and neighbouring crofting land. His neighbours, and the local policeman, agreed it was much safer not to have him drive on a public road.

The Aldrory crofters erected a fine new fence on the boundary between their crofts and the outlying common grazing land. Stirling Ross offered to remove the discarded old fencing wire and posts with his Land Rover.

The crofters stood well clear as he reversed his beloved old Land Rover towards the heap of rusty wire and rotting posts. He violently jammed on the brake and, to the great surprise of all onlookers, the vehicle shuddered to a halt at, but without going through the new fence.

The old wire and posts were loaded into the back of the Land Rover. Again the crofters stood well clear as Stirling, with some effort, clambered behind the steering wheel. The tortured gears made their usual bad-tempered snarling growls as Stirling, like a determined lion tamer, persuaded them to reluctantly obey his fierce commands. The Land Rover jerked forward, halted, then jerked forward again, then halted.

Angrily, Stirling thudded the full weight of his large right foot on the accelerator. The overwhelmed pedal cowered on the floor while the engine lustily roared and the vehicle raced forward.

It dragged the new fence with it. Neither Stirling, nor the other crofters, had noticed that the towing hook at the back of the Land Rover was entangled in the new fence.

Like a zip fastener being rapidly unzipped, post after post was torn from the ground and dragged along by the fence wire.

The crofters ran for safety.

Eventually Stirling got the vehicle stopped. He clambered out. He stared in disbelieving dismay at the havoc caused to the new fence. "Oh, good life... oh, good life," he stammered.

To the other crofters that exclamation seemed somewhat inadequate.

"Oh, God damn it, man... damn it to Hell, Donald, look what you've done! Didn't you feel the fence dragging behind you?"

"Och now, there's not need for that swearing at all," Stirling indignantly gasped. "After all I was chust trying to help you."

"Och, God damn it, Donald, why didn't you stop at once when you felt the engine straining?"

Stirling pushed back his cap and scratched his head, "Och now," he slowly drawled, "I did think she did seem a wee touch sluggish... so I chust stood on the gas... gave her more of my boot!"

The crofter glanced at Stirling's huge, cumbersome, size eleven wellingtons; despite his anger he could not help smiling. "Aye, and, by God, you've got plenty boot to give her, haven't you?"

"Och, man, there's no call at all for such unkind personal remarks."

Again, the crofter smiled, "Oh, Donald, you deserve to feel my damned boot on your damned backside!"

Ian remembered how, many years later, he had helped clear out Stirling's untidily cluttered crofthouse. Stirling had been an old bachelor living by himself. Sorting through the life-long accumulation of rubbish, Ian wondered if he would come across a secret hoard of erotic 'girlie' magazines, as he had done more than once before when clearing out other old bachelors' houses.

But this time he was disappointed.

He did come across Stirling's secret hoard of magazines – but they were not erotic. They were motor racing magazines. They included a few old ones with special features on his worshipped hero, Stirling Moss.

At the end of Ian's story, Nigel laughed, "Yes, it would have been fine to have had old Stirling and his Land Rover to help us."

"Did you cut your hand on rusty wire, Nigel?" Helen asked. "That could be dangerous. Did you get an anti-tetanus injection?"

"Oh yes. You know what my mother's like; when she learned that I'd cut it on rusty wire she insisted on my going to Doctor Cairns for an anti-tetanus jab."

Ian grinned, "Aye, I suppose it's safer to get that jab, right enough, although not everyone would agree with the need for it."

"Oh no? Who wouldn't think it necessary?" Nigel asked.

Before Ian could answer, Helen laughed, "You've played right into Ian's hand, Nigel, you've given him the excuse to tell another of his old stories; one I've heard many times."

"Aye, but perhaps he hasn't heard it."

Nigel smiled and said, "I won't know if I've heard it until you start telling it, Ian. Even if I had, I still like to listen to your retold old tales... in fact, I think you should write a book about them."

"Aye, so do I," Helen said.

Warmed by this encouragement, Ian settled himself even more snugly in his comfortable old armchair, took a generous gulp of whisky and said, "I intend to... I assure you I do intend to." He then started telling the story of 'Penicillin Pete'.

This story, once again happened a good number of years ago.

Peter Norman MacInnes was an old crofter living in Aldrory Glen. He was a bachelor, and since the death of his unmarried sister, Janet, he lived alone. Peter

MacInnes was eighty-nine years old and was remarkably fit and active for his age. He had been a regular soldier in the Cameron Highlanders. He had fought in the Boer War. He was – he revelled in being – a 'Character', one who still enjoyed a dram and a good laugh. He did not enjoy, did not bother much with, such drearily uninteresting things as housework or too much washing of either his clothes or of himself. His sister had kept house for him and he had, at her insistence, shaved once per week on the Sabbath morning so as to be reasonably neat for going, again at her insistence, to Kirk. Since her death he had neither shaved nor gone to church. He felt all the better for these twin neglects.

Old Peter shared his untidily neglected crofthouse with one companion – his thirteen-year-old collie, Rab. Dog and man suffered from failing eyesight, and occasionally, when the man tripped over the dog or the collie was stood upon, they snarled and swore at one another.

On one particularly dull and miserable November day, Rab was lying contentedly stretched out warming his old bones in front of the kitchen fire. He was sound asleep. In the dimness of the late afternoon gloom his master accidentally stood on one of Rab's outstretched legs. Instantly the old collie sprang from deep sleep to self-defence. Instinctively it snapped at Peter's ankle.

The startled old man cursed and staggered to a chair. Ashamed of his inexcusable deed, Rab apologetically sidled over to his beloved master and begged to be forgiven. He was.

As Peter examined the wound there was a knock at the door, it opened, and Doctor Cairns stepped in.

"Oh, it's yourself, doctor, come away in," Peter called as he attempted to hide his injured ankle behind his other ankle. The doctor observed his action. "Is there something wrong with your foot, Peter?"

Doctor Cairns was the local general practitioner. Based at the surgery in Inveraldrory village, his practice covered a vast area. Capably and conscientiously he single-handedly attended to his widely scattered patients. Whenever he called on any of Peter's neighbours he made a point of looking in on the old man. The doctor knew how reluctant the thrawn auld bugger was to request his assistance. He admired his toughness and his self-reliant independent spirit. He wished that some of his younger patients, frequent visitors at the surgery, were half as tough as old Peter. "What's wrong with your foot?" he asked again.

"Och, it's nothing much, doctor, just a wee bit scratch at ma ankle." He explained what had happened.

"You'd better let me have a look at it, any dog bite is potentially dangerous."

"Och, it's nae worth botherin' wi', doctor."

The doctor insisted. Peter reluctantly revealed his injured foot.

"Take your sock off," Doctor Cairns ordered.

"Ma sock is off, doctor."

Startled out of his professional calm the doctor exclaimed, "Good God, I thought that was a black sock on your foot!" Peering more closely through the dimness he saw that the foot was shadowed with dirt. Recovering himself, he said, "I'm sorry. It's so dim in here, I can't see properly. Let's put the light on."

As he went to the doorway and switched on the light a startling thought came into the doctor's mind, "I wonder how many baths old Peter's taken since his sister's death?" While he cleaned away the dirt and blood from around the wounded ankle, Doctor Cairns secretly smiled to himself as he answered his own question, "Damned few... if any!"

And yet despite the unwashed state of that tough old man's body and clothes he remained much fitter than many a carbolicly clean man half his age. "*Despite his unwashed state?*" the doctor wondered, again smiling to himself, "No doubt old Peter, like quite a few other old people in my practise would tell me that they keep their fitness and health *because* of their unwashed state. They claim that too many baths or showers just wash away the body's natural defences." As a young and up-to-date physician, Doctor Cairns could not agree with their theory – it was ridiculous. (And yet he was to thoughtfully remember this stoutly asserted belief of those old people when, many years later, he read a persuasive article in a medical journal written by an eminent microbiologist. The scientist argued that taking too many hot showers or baths was likely to reduce the body's natural defences by reducing the amount of necessary bacteria on the human skin: this bacteria should be left to get on with its intended task of dealing with the skin's dirt.)

"That's the bite cleaned now. It's not deep, it's not bleeding much."

"Och, doctor, I told you it was only a scratch. I'm sorry to gie you all this trouble."

"It's no trouble," the doctor replied as he spread antibiotic powder over the injury and then covered it with a large plaster.

Rab, the ashamedly contrite old collie, sat and anxiously looked on as the doctor attended to his injured and generously forgiving master.

Doctor Cairns hid a smile as he said, "You can put your sock and shoe back on now, Peter. I'll go to my car and get a syringe for an anti-tetanus injection."

As he turned, the doctor patted Rab and smiled, "Oh, you old rascal; what do you mean by biting your master?"

Peter was delighted to see the doctor in such a pleasant mood. "Och, he couldn't help it. He didn't mean it. It's gey good of you to gie him an anti-tetanus jab."

Doctor Cairns stared in astonishment. "What are you talking about, Peter? The anti-tetanus injection is for you."

"Och, doctor, I don't need onie injection. Go on, gie it tae Auld Rab."

The doctor opened his mouth to argue, then, thinking of the filthy state of Peter's foot, he lost his customary professional dignity; he burst into loud laughter. "By God, Peter," he gasped, "Aye, right enough the poor dog is probably in much greater need of the anti-tetanus injection than you are!"

Old Peter heartily joined in the doctor's laughter, then said, "Instead o' onie injection I'll tak the best medicine... a dram... a damn big dram! You'll tak a dram we' me, won't you doctor?"

Automatically Doctor Cairns started to refuse; he had a strict rule that he never drank while on duty. Smiling he relented. He would break his own rule this once. "Thanks, Peter, but make it a very wee dram."

Peter thrust a full bottle and an empty glass at him, "Here, doctor, help yourself, tak as much or as little as you want."

"Thank you, Peter." Furtively he examined the glass – it looked none too clean. "Oh, well," he thought, "what the hell! Hopefully the strong neat whisky will kill off all germs in the glass."

Cheerily they toasted one another, "Slainte Mhath!" The whisky burned its way down the doctor's throat. He gasped and grimaced, his eyes watered. "By God," he thought, that should certainly kill all known germs!" He managed a smile, "Did you make that whisky yourself, Peter?"

"Och no, doctor. It's a gey puckle o'years since I had ma ain whisky still."

After taking another big gulp of whisky, old Peter sighed contentedly. He was not in the least discomposed by its raw strength. "Sit doon, doctor, sit doon. Mak yourself at hame."

They sat down at the kitchen table and Peter leaned comfortably on a corner of it. Doctor Cairns inspected the littered table and gently eased his chair away.

"Whit's the matter, doctor? Mak yourself comfortable there."

"I'm fine, Peter, I'm fine."

While Peter was engrossed in lovingly gulping more whisky, the doctor scrutinised the untidy table. It was a truly amazing mess. Probably it had not been really cleaned since the death of Peter's sister. The oilcloth cover looked as if it had originally been chequered with red and white squares, but it was difficult to be sure, for most of it was now covered in a mass of fungi-like growths. There were lively moulds of many colours – sickly greens; pale blues; revolting yellows and un-regal purples. There were patches looking as if they were touched with white hoarfrost; other spots luxuriously sprouted what looked like an old man's five-day stubble of grey beard. A brown china teapot; jars of marmalade and of various jams and sauce and pickle bottles all securely fitted into their own invariable places and rose like islands set in this weird, fantastic, science fiction landscape.

"Oh, Peter, don't you think it's about time you got a new table cover, or gave this one a really good scrubbing?"

The old man stared at the doctor in genuine surprise, "Why?... Whit's the matter wi' it, man?"

"Oh, Peter, it's a disgrace! It's absolutely filthy!"

Old Peter glanced at the table then fixed the doctor with a baleful stare. "Och, man, I'm fair surprised at you. Surely as a doctor, a man o' science, you should ken that thae fungi growths are gey guid for you." He grinned broadly and proudly, "Och, doctor, don't you ken that I discovered penicillin long before yon Doctor Fleming did?"

Doctor Cairns again burst into unrestrained laughter. Eventually he managed to gasp, "Oh, Peter... Peter, you're incorrigible!... you're absolutely incorrigible!"

As he drove home the doctor suddenly remembered that penicillin had been derived from a green fungi-like mould. He continued his journey in a pleasantly amused, but an increasingly thoughtful mood.

Ian grinned as he finished his story, "So that's how old Peter MacInnes acquired his nickname, 'Penicillin Pete'."

Laughing, Nigel asked, "Did he suffer any ill effects from being bitten by his dog?"

"Och no, not him, not that tough old bugger. And, amazingly, his poor old dog was none the worse for having taken a bite at his master's grubby ankle."

Chapter Twenty-Two

The month of August was the height of the tourist season. Its high point was the Inveraldrory Highland Games. All eagerly looked forward to this event. All fervently prayed that the weather would be kind on that special day. The games were being held on a Friday. On the Tuesday, Wednesday and Thursday it rained. Apprehensively the games officials peered out at Friday's grey and doubtful early morning sky. Were all their months of painstaking voluntary work going to be ruined by yet more rain?

But the Gods relented. Before nine o'clock the clouds dispersed and bright sunshine dried out the grass and the sagging tents and large marquees at the games field. By eleven the sun was hot but was pleasantly tempered by a moderate South Easterly breeze. Conditions were perfect.

When, in mid-afternoon, Helen and Ian arrived, they were delighted with the bright and cheery scene. After all the dreary days of rain how vivaciously the sunshine now enlivened everything and everyone. The entire place was a lively riot of colour. Gaudy flags flew from marquees and tents, from buildings and tall flagpoles. The line of old sycamore trees at the edge of the games field was festooned with gaily fluttering festive buntings. The fishing boats in the adjoining harbour were kaleidoscopically dazzling with their gleaming varnish and paint, their heaps of blue, green or orange nylon nets; many were 'dressed overall' from bow to stern with lines of multicoloured marine flags. The happy crowd parading around the field was also brightly coloured. The women were delighted with the all too rare opportunity to display their bright summer frocks but, for once, their charming splendour was eclipsed by the brightness and glamour of the peacock proud men's kilts of varied and vivid tartans.

While the eyes were delightedly dazzled by all this colour, the ears were entertained by the sounds of the pipe bands, by single pipers, and by Scottish tunes insistently thumping out from the carnival in the far corner of the field. Voices rose high and happily in this noisily gregarious community. French, Dutch and German tongues and a variety of accents, Australian, English and American, mingled with the Scots tongue of the locals in a cheery confusing babel. The only unhappy voices were those of agitated seagulls that raucously and querulously expressed their displeasure at all this inexplicable human activity, which had taken over their resting and roosting field beside the harbour. However, these gulls got their reward later when they greedily scavenged the litter of food scattered around the field.

Refusing to be kept out of all the multitudinous sensual delights, Ian's and Helen's nostrils sniffed and keenly analysed the promiscuously mingling smells. The sweet and homely scent of fresh mown grass vied with the distinctive paraffin and diesel tainted air of the harbour. From the shore the fresh, high-heaped tangled coils of dark brown seaweed impregnated the breeze with a sharp, tangy iodine taste. Older, slowly rotting seaweed insistently gave out their strong, rude, briny breaths.

Helen and Ian made slow progress going around the games field. Every few minutes they met, and stopped to talk to friends. All was convivial talk and laughter. Everyone was in a festive mood. All continually congratulated one another on enjoying such perfect weather. They met Jeannie and Colin MacDonald. Colin was having a short respite from playing in the local pipe band.

Jeannie said, "We're on our way to the home-baking and home-product tent. The judges should be giving their verdicts soon. Are you coming along with us?"

"Aye, certainly," Helen replied. "Hopefully we'll see your crowdie cheese beat auld Maggie Gunn's this year for a change."

"I wonder if the judge has heard the story of auld Maggie's crowdie hanging dripping in her lavatory pan?" Colin asked with his face beaming and his eyes twinkling.

"I expect she has," Ian grinned. "How will it effect her judgement, I wonder?"

The large tent was fairly crowded. The judges had not yet arrived, but were expected any minute.

They went to the table where the crowdie cheeses were set out awaiting judgement. Auld Maggie Gunn was hovering there keeping a watchful eye on her crowdie and anxiously looking out for the judges. She greeted them and they stood talking. They all turned and stared as there was a sudden noisy commotion at the entrance to the tent.

Jeannie and Helen smiled and Colin and Ian grinned as they saw the reason for the disturbance, but auld Maggie tut-tutted loudly and disapprovingly as Jamie Gordon came reeling in. As soon as that burly shepherd caught sight of them he came unsteadily staggering forward with outstretched arms. As loudly as if shouting orders at distant collies, he bellowed greeting in his warm and couthie Aberdeenshire accent.

"How are ye, ma bonny wee Helen?" he shouted as he lifted her off her feet and hugged her to his massive chest.

"I would be fine if ae could breathe!" she gasped. "Put me doon before you crack a' ma ribs!"

After greeting Jeannie almost as warmly, he shook hands with Colin and Ian. His laughter boomed out, "Ae see yer still wearing thae damned Seaforth kilts; why don't you wear the kilt o' the best Highland regiment – the Gordons – like me?"

Colin laughed in reply, "Och away, man, we've heard, and ignored, those stupid blethers of yours before."

Ian's laughter joined in, "Aye, Jamie, we ken you blether a lot o' nonsense. You just open your mou' wide and let your muckle great belly rumble!"

Grinning, Jamie turned to Auld Maggie, "And how are ye, Maggie?"

"Och, don't speak to me. You're drunk, man, you're disgustingly drunk!"

Jamie laughed as if she had paid him a great compliment, "Aye, I suppose I'm gey fou."

"O, man, you're as fou as a puggie!" Ian exclaimed.

"Och, Ian, man you're just damned jealous that you're nae as fou as me!" Jamie again turned to Maggie, "Weel, Maggie, is your crowdie cheese gaun tae win first prize this year again?"

"Aye, I hope it does. I expect it will!" She firmly declared, with no hint of false modesty.

All expectantly waited to hear what Jamie would say next – he was well known for his witty remarks when he was fou.

"Och weel, Maggie, if ye win this year again we'll a' ken it's nae flash in the pan! You'll fair deserve tae be flushed wi' success!"

These jovial and emphatic words and the uproarious laughter they caused, made Maggie realise that the secret of where she hung her crowdie was no longer a secret. Deeply mortified and wildly angered she desperately wanted out of that tent and away from those, as she thought, cruelly laughing fools. She raised her hand to Jamie's broad chest and gasped, "Oh, get oot o' my way, you... you drunken oaf!"

Normally her slight shove would have had as little impact on Jamie's vast bulk as a butterfly landing on the broad back of a Clydesdale horse, but, unsteady with drink and laughter, it caught him off balance. He staggered backwards. He bumped against, then thudded onto, the trestle table laden with home-made crowdie cheeses and large sponge cakes. The table promptly collapsed under his considerable weight. He landed on his back with his legs in the air.

With eyes wide in disbelieving amazement at the shocking sight revealed to her, and aghast at the havoc she had caused, Auld Maggie raised a hand to her mouth to smother a scream. She then started to hurry away. After a couple of steps she turned and revengefully shouted, "If I deserved to be flushed wi' success you should be flushed wi' shame! You're a disgraceful drunken fool, Gordon!" Then, tempted by some impish devil, or stirred by memories of Chaplin's slapstick films, she stooped, lifted a large, almost intact sponge cake at her feet, aimed it, then threw it at Jamie Gordon.

By now Jamie was sitting up, his face was brightly flushed – with shame?... with shock?... with whisky? – probably with a combination of all three. His kilt was neatly rearranged and now he stared foolishly at his laughing audience. He silently registered open-mouthed astonishment as the cake struck the side of his face. The sponge cake slid to the floor and left his cheek lathered with cream and jam. Gently, as if in slow motion, jam and cream slithered down to his chin. He shaved some of this clinging lather off with his fingers then tentatively licked the cloying sweetness. Now, his insouciant nature reasserting itself, he happily lifted and eagerly started eating the sadly battered sponge cake. As he thrust handfuls of cake into his mouth he noticed the local Church of Scotland minister, the Reverent James Sinclair, and his wife, moving away; they seemed the only two in the crowd who were – like Queen Victoria – not amused. Their faces wore sternly disapproving frowns.

Jamie Gordon jovially shouted after them, "Never mind, Mrs Sinclair, never mind; yer sponge cake deserves first prize again this year. It's braw!... It's real braw!"

As, stumbling, almost blinded by her agitation, she hurried away from that hateful tent, Auld Maggie nearly bumped into a stout woman with two young children. She only recognised the woman when she cheerfully asked, "Have you seen that man o' mine onie where, Maggie?"

"Oh aye, I've seen that man o' yours, Bella," Maggie gasped indignantly. "I've seen far too much o' him! He's a damned disgrace! You should be ashamed o' yourself letting him oot in that indecent state!"

Bella Gordon stared stupefied, "Whit are ye talking aboot, Maggie? Whit's happened? Whit indecent state?"

"Och, ye ken fine." Auld Maggie's voice rose higher; almost hysterically she screamed (to the vast amusement of all within earshot). "You should be black ashamed o' yourself allowing him oot wi' nae drawers on!"

Maggie hurried away. Bella stood motionlessly staring after her – she was, as she described it later, "fair dumbfoonered".

After a while she tightened her grasp on the hands of her young son and daughter and said, "Come on, bairns, we better go an' find that fool o' a faither o' yours and see whit daft ploy he's been up tae this time."

As she hurried into the large tent she was relieved to see all the cheery faces – nothing serious could have happened surely? Then, catching sight of her husband, she gave a frightened scream; he was sitting on a flattened table, surrounded by a mess of food, and apparently covered in blood. Hurrying towards him she gasped, "Oh, Jamie, whit's happened? You're a' bloody!"

For a moment Jamie stared at his wife, puzzled, then laughed, "Och na, Bella, it's na blood, it's jam. It's strawberry jam – an' it's damned braw!" He grinned at his children, "Come on, bairns, come an' get some o' this braw food."

Bella's laughter boomed out as the boy and girl sat on either side of their father and eagerly shovelled sponge cake into their mouths. Turning to Helen, she asked, "Whit do ye thin o' ma three bairns?" With eyes sparkling she cheerfully added, "Aye, and Jammie there is the biggest bairn o' a', the muckle fool. Whit daft ploy has he been up ta that's upset poor Auld Maggie Gunn sae much?" Her genuine concern at Maggie being so upset clashed with her puckish love of innocent fun.

When Helen explained what had happened, Bella was convulsed with helpless laughter. She almost collapsed alongside her three bairns. "Poor Auld Maggie," she gasped as tears of merriment flowed unchecked down her plump rosy cheeks. "Oh, poor Auld Maggie... an' her such a prim old maid, tae!"

After leaving the tent, Helen, Jeannie, Colin and Ian continued walking around the games field. They had not gone far when Ian exclaimed, "Here's my friend coming."

"Aye, I see him," Colin said, "your friend, my friend, everyone's friend."

Mr Campbell-Fotheringay was approaching them; he had a blonde, leggy young lady possessively clinging to each arm. Despite the heat of the August sunshine, all three were wearing heavy, waxed waterproof jackets, thick tweed breeches and cumbersome green wellingtons. Obviously they were desperately acting the part of posh and superior huntin', shootin' and fishin' county gentry. The blondes vied with one another in making piercingly loud remarks in frightfully pretentious high-class accents. Recognising Ian and Colin, they threw them haughty stares. Campbell-Fotheringay's pale puggy face darkened and his shifty small eyes narrowed even more as he glowered at the two men. They disdainfully scowled back at him.

Two slim, long haired young men completed Campbell-Fotheringay's party. One was dressed in pale pastel blue slacks and shirt while the other was a blush of rosy pinks. Gold chains glittered around elegant necks and dangled from thin wrists. As they swanned along with light and dainty tread they smiled at one another, delighted at the stir they were causing amongst the unsophisticated Highland yokels.

They certainly provoked many comments, mostly amused disparaging ones from the younger locals and scathing caustic ones from affronted older people who tut-tutted with severe Calvinistic frowns.

Once that party passed, Ian saw old – over ninety years old – retired gamekeeper, Murdo Munro. He leant with hunched shoulders over his stout shepherd's crook and gripped it with tremulous, age-blotched hands. These arthritically deformed claw-like hands were as knottily gnarled and twisted as the roughly carved handle of the hazel crook. He stared, mouth hanging open and eyes wide, in undisguised disbelief after these two flamboyantly effete men.

"What do you think of those two, Murdo?" Ian shouted.

"Oh, hello, Ian." Murdo grinned and chortled, "Och, I'm damned if I ken whit tae make o' them. They're gey queer… gey queer, a' the gither!"

Ian laughed delightedly, "Och, Murdo, you've spoken much truer than you realise. Aye they certainly are 'gay'; aye, they certainly are 'queer'!"

"Are you enjoying this sunshine, Murdo?" Jeannie asked.

"O aye… aye, it's fine." He lifted his head and gazed at the cloudless blue sky, "Aye, but I doot it won't last long; I doot we'll pay for it later!"

Smiling, Ian thought, "Murdo's typical of so many old Calvinistic Highlanders for whom there is something definitely sinful about openly and thankfully enjoying the sensual pleasure of warm sunshine." How often, after about three consecutive dry and sunny days, he had heard such old people solemnly declare, "Och, we could be doing with some rain… the ground's gey dry!"

They left old Murdo and happily continued strolling along. Another party was coming towards them. They recognised Lord and Lady Kilvert and their oldest son, his wife and their two children and the middle-aged nanny with their baby in her care. They were an interesting, and instructive, contrast to Campbell-Fotheringay's party. The ladies were comfortably dressed in attractive summer frocks.

The gentlemen were in slacks and shirtsleeves, each had his tweed jacket draped over an arm; that was as far as their concession to informality went. Even in this August heat they 'correctly' wore quietly unobtrusive ties.

In their unassuming, well-modulated voices they greeted them with sincere friendliness. For five minutes the members of the two parties chatted pleasantly together. Smiling, Lord Kilvert said, "Well, Colin, let's hope we get weather like this tomorrow for the Glorious Twelfth."

"Aye, sir, let's hope so. It would make a pleasant change from last year's rain."

This games day Friday was the eleventh of August, so tomorrow was the Glorious Twelfth, the start of the grouse-shooting season. 'The Twelfth' was a major annual event on all Highland-sporting estates, which carried a reasonable stock of grouse.

Lady Kilvert smiled at Colin and Ian. "I hope your enjoyment of this games day won't be too curtailed by us all having to be at the grouse shooting tomorrow."

Colin laughed, "Ah well, madam, as we've to be up bright and early tomorrow morning, I doubt Ian and I will have to curtail the amount of whisky we drink today."

"I'm sure you'll both be none the worse of that," Jeannie quietly and dryly remarked.

Lady Kilvert laughed, then, looking pointedly at her husband and her son, said, "No, I'm sure all our husbands will be none the worse for taking less whisky today!"

The wives, natural allies, smiled and nodded their agreement while the four husbands, those other natural allies silently, looked at one another and resignedly shook their heads.

The two parties now went their separate ways.

Jeannie and Helen and Colin and Ian all agreed that Lord and Lady Kilvert were a pleasant couple, were unpretentious true gentry. They resumed sauntering around the field. They made slow progress. Every few minutes they met, and stopped to talk with friends. Many gamekeepers and crofters had travelled far to be here today. Some would not meet again until next year's games. Eagerly, loudly, laughingly, they exchanged all the latest gossip, all the most memorable fresh tall tales. Poor Auld Maggie Gunn and the saga of her special crowdie cheese featured prominently and uproariously in these tales.

Moving on, they saw yet another party approaching them. Warmly they greeted – and were greeted by – Kate Kettle, her brother Kenny, their nephew, Calum MacLeod, his wife, Mary and their two young sons, Rob and Norman. Calum was resplendent in his new kilt of MacLeod of Harris tartan; his large jet-black beard jutted proudly. His uncle Kenny was wearing his best Sabbath suit. The warm sunshine playfully teased the camphor smell of mothballs from the dark cloth.

"Oh, what a crowd here today," Kate gasped. "We're meeting all our friends – it's lovely!"

"Aye," Helen laughed, "anyone who is anyone is here today."

The boys were desperate to get to the carnival at the far side of the field. Their parents willingly took them there while Kate and Kenny stayed with the others and watched the heavy events taking place on the games field. Eight ponderously waddling muscular 'heavies' freely sweated and loudly gasped as, straining and heaving, they contorted their huge bodies in fierce struggles to put the shot, toss the caber and throw the heavy hammer. The massive local policeman, 'Forensic Fred' Sutherland, was conspicuously eager amongst all those keen competitors. He had won many prizes in previous years and was determined to win more today. He was also secretly pleased, dressed in dark green kilt and glaring white vest, to have this opportunity to show off his impressive physique.

Jeannie admiringly gazed at him, she smiled, "It's reassuring to see the strong arm of the law so impressively revealed, isn't it?"

"Aye, it is," Helen agreed, "and it's also good to hear the voice of authority so loudly and decisively bellowed."

Displeased at something or someone, 'Forensic Fred' was shouting orders across the field. His resonant voice rumbled up from deep within his broad chest and, thundering forth, was clearly heard above the music of individual pipers and the discordant noises blaring from the carnival.

Kate Kettle laughed, "Aye, Fred's fair got a powerful voice. He bawls like a bull, doesn't he?"

Noticing the roguish twinkle in Helen's eyes, Ian intuitively guessed what she was going to say. He grinned, "I think you better cover your ears with your hands, Kate, and not hear the shocking thing Helen's about to come out with."

Puzzled, Kate looked innocently and enquiringly at Helen.

Helen laughed, "I was just about to remark that probably the reason Big Forensic Fred *bawls* like a bull is because he's got *balls* like a bull!"

Kate burst into uncontrollable laughter, her cheeks flushed. Automatically she reached down for her apron to throw over her face, but for once she was not wearing it. She covered her face with her hands instead. Through the laughter, through the smothering hands, she indistinctly gasped, "Oh Helen… Helen, you say the funniest things! I never know what you'll come away with next."

She looked to see how her brother was taking this risqué joke. Kenny had turned his back on them and, perhaps not too seriously, was disapprovingly exclaiming, "Oh, what talk, my dear fellows, what talk!" However, his shoulders shook with suppressed laughter.

Again they walked on, again they met another party coming towards them. There were sincere greetings on all sides. The party consisted of just three: Johnnie Fraser, Bob McInnes, and Norman Craig. Norman, one of – if not *the* – greatest of living Scottish poets, was as usual, spending much of the summer in this district.

There were increasingly persistent rumours that Campbell-Fotheringay was not going to renew the leases on Fraser's shop or on McInnes's garage. Both men were very worried about the possibility of losing their businesses and their attached houses. However – thanks no doubt to "inspiring bold John Barleycorn" – no sign of this, or any other worry was evident on Johnnie's or Bob's face today.

Bob McInnes was Chieftain of the Games this year. They had been celebrating this notable event. He proudly strutted, a fine figure in his highland outfit, and carried the long cromach, engraved with his name and presented to him as Chieftain, as impressively, although perhaps not as soberly, as a newly appointed bishop with his large, ornate symbolic crosier.

As they heartly congratulated him on his appointment, he forced a bottle of whisky on them. Kenny and then Colin lifted it, toasted the Chieftain, then drank. As Ian lifted the bottle he said with feeling, "It's great… it's really great, to have a local, a native Highlander like you, Bob, as Chieftain of the Games this year. You well deserve the honour. You deserve it much more than most of the Sassenachs and the pretentious petty wee 'bonnet lairds', wi' an eagle's father proud in their bonnet but wi' nae bawbees in their sporran, that we've had as Chieftains in the past."

Colin nodded in agreement then said to Norman Craig, "You've done well in the trout fly-casting competition, Norman; you're in the finals now, aren't you?"

"Yes, I am. I play the final match in about ten minutes."

Casting for distance and accuracy with trout and with salmon fly rods were special events at these Games.

"I hope you win it," Colin said.

"Aye, I hope so, too," Ian said. He grinned, "Nae doot you'll be in special training for it?"

"Yes, of course I am," Norman replied. "Can't you see that I'm specially training?" With gleaming mirthful eyes and beaming face he indicated the cigarette held in one hand and the bottle of whisky firmly gripped in the other, "I can think of no better training than this, can you?"

"No, of course not!… No certainly not!" Colin and Ian replied together. Resolutely, manfully, and most unusually, they refused more whisky.

"We have to be up early tomorrow for the Glorious Twelfth – the start of the grouse shooting," Colin explained.

"Oh, bugger the grouse! Come on, Colin, man, drink up!" urged Johnnie Fraser as he generously thrust his bottle of whisky at him.

An announcement came over the loudspeaker requesting all members of the pipe bands to report to the bandsmen's tent. Colin grinned, "Saved by the bell! I'll need to head there now… there's no rest for the wicked."

The bandsmen's tent rapidly filled up with pipers and drummers. With hopeful, but foolish, optimism they eagerly searched through wooden and plastic crates for any remaining whisky or beer. They were disappointed. All the considerable amount of alcohol which had been in this tent was already in their stomachs. To qualify as a good piper, two special attributes were required – extra capacity lungs to inflate the bagpipes and an extra capacity stomach to absorb vast amounts of whisky. Colin qualified perfectly on both counts.

The last parade of the massed pipe bands was the grand finale of the Games. Once it was over the happy crowd started slowly melting away.

Chapter Twenty-Three

The 'Glorious Twelfth' dawned gloriously. It promised another day of endless sunshine – and it kept that promise right through to dusk's lingeringly reluctant darkness.

Shortly before 9am a convoy of cars and vans, led by Lord Kilvert's silver Rolls Royce, swept out from Ardgie Lodge and headed for the grouse moors.

Soon they were driving along by the shore of large Loch Ardgie, which calmly glittered and distortingly reflected the surrounding hills. Then, after passing under the steep limestone cliffs of Inchnadhu, they arrived at the moors. The humans quickly disembarked. All were keen and eager, but their eagerness was nothing compared to that of all the excited dogs.

They set out. They were an impressive sight. The gentry were dressed in expensive, but unassuming, tweeds. The four 'guns' carried their own shotguns – the Rolls Royces of shotguns – handmade (and made to measure) Purdey's or Holland and Holland's. Their dogs were also worth a small fortune – all Kennel Club registered thoroughbreds.

Even the gamekeepers and ghillies were impressively dressed today. All wore their best plus four suit of Ardgie Estate's fawnish tweed. This pattern of tweed was kept exclusively for this, Lord Kilvert's sporting estate. They wore ties, and their boots or sturdy brogues were highly polished. They kept up the old tradition of being well turned out on this special day. It reminded Colin and Ian of their army years with all the bullshit entailed in a commanding officer's parade and inspection. Earlier, at the shooting lodge, they had noticed Lord and Lady Kilvert casting a discreet, but keen and pleased eye over them.

Conditions were perfect today. A slight but steady Easterly breeze gently flowed over the three-mile long ridge of gently sloping, well-managed heather moor. They divided into two parties with a setter working ahead of each party. Each setter methodically ran in wide sweeps back and forward through the heather, efficiently quartering the ground in front of the advancing 'guns'. The dog's nostrils keenly analysed every scent carried on the steady breeze. They disdainfully ignored all scents but one – the incomparably exciting scent of elusive grouse hidden in the heather. It was a pleasant sight to watch these well-trained dogs, guided by a gamekeeper, effortlessly working the ground.

The hillside over which Colin was guiding a large, black and tan Gordon setter was a huge stretch of bell heather out in full bloom, a beautiful spread of gently slopes and undulating waves of blushing pink. Each step he took through that exotically flowering heather puffed up a cloud of pale pollen dust which filled his nostrils with a delicate, a deliciously sweet, honey scent. He enjoyed this alluring subtle scent but was not so pleased to notice that all the work he had put in early this morning giving his boots a high, a sergeant-major approving polish was nullified by the pollen dust which now thickly covered these boots and transmuted them to a dull grey.

Boots and pollen were forgotten as Tweed, the Gordon setter, got a 'point'. He stood statuesquely still with his right foreleg raised. He accurately pointed at the grouse he scented but could not see in the pink heather somewhere ahead of him.

The two guns – Lord Kilvert and his son – took position on either side of Colin and Tweed. Lady Kilvert, her daughter-in-law, and two other guests stood further back. Ian, burdened with a fully laden cartridge bag and an, as yet, empty large game bag, waited with Calum MacLeod who was similarly burdened and who held two other setters which impatiently waited their turn to search for grouse.

When all were correctly positioned, Colin allowed Tweed to advance on the grouse. The setter cautiously advanced with his body, from eagerly questing nostrils to the tip of his outstretched tail, a straight line, a line pointing with arrow accuracy at the silent and motionless grouse hidden ahead of him. In impressive slow motion, each paw was gently lifted and even more gently placed a little further forward. Ancestral instincts urged him to dash wildly at these annoyingly elusive birds, but inbred training held him back. Colin whispered gentle words of praise and encouragement as he slowly advanced at Tweed's side. While keeping an alert eye on the dog and on the heather in front of him, he also kept a wary eye on the keen 'guns' on either side of him. He made sure that they remained slightly ahead of the setter and himself. From long experience he knew how dangerous it was for gamekeeper and dog to get even slightly ahead of the sometimes rather trigger-happy 'guns'.

With that suddenness which, although expected, is always so startling, a covey of grouse bombed up from the pink heather. Violent wings fanned a mist of dusty pollen as nine plump birds exploded away. The 'guns' held fire for a few seconds. They gave the birds a fairer chance of escape. They gave themselves more difficult, more sporting shots. Four shots blasted out. Five grouse fell dead. As they disappeared in the distance the remaining birds cursed and cried, "Go back!... Go back!... Go back!"

Lord Kilvert's first shot had killed two grouse. His spaniel eagerly found, retrieved, and handed over his three birds. His son's black Labrador retrieved his two birds; that dog's glossy black coat was now dandruffed by the heather pollen to a dusty ghostly grey.

The five grouse in turn were handed over to Ian. He put two in his game bag and gave three to Calum, grinning, "There, lad, that's them fairly divided; you're a lot younger and fitter than me!"

By noon all the 'keepers and ghillie's game bags were heavily bulging. All the 'guns' had had a good morning's sport. By now the August sun was glaring hot. The refreshing breeze had completely died away. Although still keen, the dogs were getting exhausted; they lay and violently panted.

The decision was taken to rest and have an early lunch. They made their way down towards the parked cars. Seeing them approaching, Lord Kilvert's chauffeur, Jack Morris, put the bottles of beer in a burn to cool. He then got out the baskets of packed lunches prepared earlier by the housekeeper and the butler for the 'gentry'.

Soon all were lying resting, relaxing, and drouthily enjoyed the beer. Although all were stretched out on the heather, they were not lying together. The 'toffs' lay in one group, while the 'keepers and ghillies lay in another group at the 'correct', respectful, traditional distance from 'The Quality' in accordance with the strict rules of etiquette decreed by posh society.

The sun beat down. Hazy layers of quivering heat ovened up from parched heather and slabs of solid rock lost their solidity, they dissolved into shimmering uncertain ghosts of themselves. Sweat-soaked shirts got even sweatier. The poor dogs panted ever more violently. When all the beer and some of the food were disposed of, Lady Kilvert rose and came towards the 'keepers. Colin got up and approached her.

"I think it's far too hot – much too hot for the dogs – to do any more shooting today," Lady Kilvert said. "What do you think, Colin?"

"Aye, madam, I agree it's much too hot. And anyway, with no wind now the dogs wouldn't be able to get a proper scent."

Colin saw Lord Kilvert coming to join them; he noted something most unusual about his lordship, something he had never seen before in all his almost thirty years of working for him.

Colin smiled brightly at Lady Kilvert, "And, madam, there's something more, something much more positive, that proves it's far too hot to do any more shooting today."

"Oh, is there really?... and what's that, Colin?"

If possible, Colin smiled even more brightly; he stared steadily at Lord Kilvert, who was now standing beside his wife. "Well, madam, the fact that Lord Kilvert has removed his tie is final positive proof that it's exceptionally hot, that it's much too hot to work the dogs."

Lord Kilvert burst into explosive, unrestrained guffaws of laughter. He gasped, "That's a good one, Colin!"

Lady Kilvert laughed too, but not so uproariously. Colin was not quite sure if she laughed with – or at – her husband, who now hurried to his guests and exuberantly repeated Colin's remark about the significance of him, for once, removing his tie. The guests, too, exploded into boisterous laughter.

As Colin (who, like all the 'keepers and ghillies, had long since removed his own choking tie) sat beside Ian he winked and whispered, "I thought my remark was funny... but no' as funny as a' that!"

Soon all the humans and dogs were embarked in the cars and vans and heading for home.

Two miles beyond Inchnadhu the convoy was halted by a large lorry broken down and skewed across the road. The road was completely blocked and was expected to remain so for at least an hour.

Overcoming his annoyance at the delay, Lord Kilvert ordered his chauffeur to turn the car and make for Inchnadhu Hotel. He smiled, "We could do with more refreshments. You'll all be my guests at the hotel."

Once the 'gentry' were supplied with drinks, Lord Kilvert ordered whiskies or beers for all the 'keepers and ghillies – all except Colin. Grinning, he said, "Just lemonade for Colin, I think. I suspect he had too many drams at the games yesterday." Then with a wink at John Murray, the hotel owner, he cheerfully ordered, "Oh, go on, make it a double whisky for him, the old reprobate."

Again the party was divided into two groups, each having separate tables. After a few minutes, Mr Murray, hovering at Lord Kilvert's elbow, discreetly murmured, "Shall I send a bill for the drinks to Ardgie Lodge, my lord?"

"What?... What?" His lordship gasped. "No... no, I'll pay for them now." He reached for his jacket, then remembering, exclaimed, "Oh, damn, I've no money with me!"

His son and the other gentlemen offered to pay. "No!... No! I invited you here as my guest. I will pay," Lord Kilvert decisively declared. He turned to his chauffeur and asked, "Will you let me have £25 – Jack?"

Jack Morris – he was the only one who *was* drinking lemonade – got up and stood beside his employer at the bar. He knew that his lordship rarely carried money about with him; more than once he had heard him remark that a pound note in a pocket or wallet was lying shamefully idle, earning no interest.

Jack had spent much of his working life in Lord Kilvert's employment, as his father had done before him, first as a general driver and then as a trusted chauffeur. When he and his father, also Jack, had both been driving for Lord and Lady Kilvert some wag had named them "Morris Senior" and "Morris Minor". Although he knew how his employer hated to be kept waiting for anything, Jack deliberately did not hand over the requested £25 until he drew two notebooks from his jacket pocket and carefully consulted them. He then painstakingly wrote in them. In the notebook entitled "Expenses – Rolls-Royce", he neatly entered '£25 – transferred to miscellaneous expenses'. Then in the 'Expenses Miscellaneous' notebook he entered '£25 – from R-R expenses. Lord K refreshments – grouse shooting'.

As he somewhat impatiently waited, his lordship turned to his guests and smiled, "Ah, I only wish all the accountants employed in my businesses kept their books as accurately and conscientiously as Jack keeps his!"

After a pleasant twenty minutes, Colin quietly said to Ian and Calum, "I think we better have a look at the dogs."

The van containing the setters had been carefully parked in the shade of a large chestnut tree. Despite this shade it was hot in the van. They took the panting dogs out and led them to the nearby small river.

As they returned the setters to the van they noticed Lady Kilvert standing outside the back door of the hotel. After being at the toilet she had come to check upon how the dogs were faring. She smiled and waved, then returned indoors.

Colin winked at his two companions, "That's what I expected. I knew she would come out to check up on the dogs."

Ian grinned, "Aye, you can tell she's real gentry. That class of people are always much more concerned for their dogs and horses than for humans."

"Are they all like that?" Calum asked. He did not have their long experience of 'The Quality'.

"Oh aye, they are all like that," Colin replied. "Some prefer dogs to horses; other prefer horses to dogs, that's about the only difference amongst them all."

"Aye, that's true," Ian confirmed, "although, as usual, there's always the one exception that proves the rule. Remember that story we heard after the war, Colin, about a certain lady in her Inverness-shire estate?"

Between them they told Calum the almost unbelievable story.

At the start of the war, in September 1939, a certain lady was left in charge of the family estate. The owner of the estate, her brother, Sir James – (remembering, the old army adage, 'No names – no pack drill', they did not give his name) was in the army, as were his younger gamekeepers. Two old 'keepers came out of retirement to help for the duration of the war. That slightly eccentric lady had a large collection of Shetland ponies and various breeds of dogs.

Fearing that it would be impossible to get food for all her animals and, like many others at that time, expecting imminent German air raids with poison gas, she ordered the two old gamekeepers to shoot almost all her ponies and dogs.

Reluctantly, but obediently, they carried out her orders. These old gamekeepers, born when Victoria's Empire was at the height of its power, had been brought up to unquestioningly obey orders from their 'superiors'. 'Theirs was not to question why; theirs was to do – or die!'

When they first heard this story, Colin and Ian found it impossible to believe. For a true lady to order the deaths of her ponies and dogs was extremely out of character for that class of person. The teller of the story, a young gamekeeper, an ex-Lovat Scout, assured them of its truth.

Colin grinned, "Aye, it's amazing, right enough. In my experience of that class o' people most of them would prefer to keep their dogs and ponies and order the shooting o' their decrepit auld gamekeepers."

Shortly after this, they noticed that traffic was again moving on the road. Their convoy of cars and vans was soon in motion. The broken down lorry had been towed to the side of the road and one lane was clear. The Inveraldrory policeman, 'Forensic Fred' Sutherland, was directing traffic. The Rolls Royce stopped and Lord and Lady Kilvert exchanged a few pleasant remarks with him; they thanked him for getting the road clear. As they started to drive away, the policeman drew himself up straight and snapped them a crisp salute in farewell.

Colin halted the van beside him and Ian exclaimed, "My God, Fred, that was a real smart salute you gave the gentry in the Rolls. I hope we get a salute like that too."

The massive policeman laughed, "You'll get the salute an auld bugger of a poacher like you deserves – a two fingered salute!" He straightened up and extended two rudely mocking fingers.

As the van moved off, Ian laughed and shouted, "Oh, charming!... Charming!"

Chapter Twenty-Four

For eight more consecutive days the sun beat down. Delighted – and astonished – tourists revelled in the August heatwave.

When September gustily swept in it brought heavy Atlantic showers, which foreshadowed the approach of autumn's gales and winter's storms. It also brought confirmation of the rumours of degenerate Campbell-Fotheringay's threatening storm of yet more evictions from his disintegrating Aldrory Estate.

John Fraser received a solicitor's letter informing him that his lease on the grocer's shop was not going to be renewed. Robert McInnes received a similar letter regarding his lease of the garage premises. They were instructed that the shop and garage, with the attached houses, were to be vacated within three months.

Early in the evening, two days after these letters had been received, a violent knocking at the front door startled Helen and Ian and sent their dogs into a barking frenzy. The sitting room door flew open and Calum Macleod stormed in. He was in an extremely excited and agitated state.

"What's the matter, Calum?" Helen asked.

With an effort, he gasped, "Here, Helen, read this." He handed her a large stiff white envelope.

Helen's face clouded as she read the letter. "Oh, he can't do that! He... can't turn them out just like that!"

Ian impatiently took the letter from her. It was from the same Inverness solicitor; it informed Kenny and Kate MacLeod that they could no longer rent the estate house they were at present living in. They had to vacate it within three months.

Ian silently folded up the letter and slid it into the envelope. For a few more moments he said nothing, then, loudly and vehemently, shouted, "The bastard!... That Campbell-Fotheringay bastard!... The bastard should have been bloody well strangled at birth!"

He drew breath then opened his mouth to continue shouting, but, becoming aware of Helen steadily and purposefully staring at him, he desisted. Helen's eyes glanced at Calum then returned to again stare at Ian. He got her message. Calum's face had gone paper white, the pallor emphasised by his beard's glossy black. His entire body trembled. He looked ready to faint.

"Sit down, Calum. Sit down there," Ian commandingly ordered, pointing at the sofa.

Calum unsteadily obeyed. Despite her deep concern, Helen could not help smiling to herself at seeing how wildly Calum threw himself onto the old sofa; obviously he had inherited this habit from his Uncle Kenny and his Aunt Kate.

"I'm sorry," he apologised, "I've got myself into a terrible state over this. It's terrible to think they can be turned out of their home like this!"

Ian had been busy with the whisky, "Here, Calum, take this dram. I know you don't drink much, but it'll do you good. Go on, drink it up, lad."

Again Calum unsteadily obeyed. Colour came back into his face, his trembling ceased.

"How are Kate and Kenny taking this news?" Helen anxiously asked.

"Better... a wee bit better than I expected."

"Oh good! Of course they've – we've all – been fearing this since Johnnie Fraser and Bob McInnes received their notices to quit a couple of days ago."

Calum nodded, "Yes, I know. I saw Johnnie and Bob earlier today. They're doing everything they can think of to resist Campbell-Fotheringay. They've taken legal advice and phoned our Member of Parliament. The MP and the lawyer, although sincerely sympathetic, hold out little hope of being able to do much, apart from possibly getting permission for them to stay on longer, six months instead of the three months."

"And Kenny and Kate will be in the same position," Ian said.

Calum nodded again, "Aye, exactly."

"But surely even he – that bastard – can't just throw them out of their home into the wilderness!" Ian's anger rose as he pictured this happening. "By God, is this the nineteenth century?... Is this the bloody Highland Clearances all over again?... Are we all to just sit back and let this happen?... Are we going to do something about it?"

Fanned by Ian's anger, Calum's excitement flamed. He jumped to his feet and paced to and fro behind the sofa (again, how like his uncle, Helen thought), "Yes, yes, Ian, I feel like you... exactly like you... but what can we do?"

Ian forced himself to calm down, he even managed a haggard grin, "Aye, there's the rub! What can we do?"

Helen smiled up at Calum, "Sit down, Calum. Finish your dram and let's calmly think if there is anything we can do. What about the media?... Surely the press and television would make a sympathetic story out of this?... out of this continuation of the Highland Clearances?"

"Oh yes; Johnnie and Bob have arranged that; some journalists and a television crew are expected tomorrow."

Ian smiled cynically, "Oh aye, nae doot they will make a good sob story of it, make it a nine-day – or nine-hour – wonder, then forget about it – as will the Great British Public."

"Then what can we do?" Calum despondently asked.

"I think the best thing we can do at this moment is to go and see how Kate and Kenny are," Helen quietly and sensibly said.

Fifteen minutes later they were all seated in Kenny's kitchen. As always, Kate warmly welcomed them even though her eyes were red-rimmed and her cheeks tear-stained. Despite their protests, she insisted, "I'll just go and put the kettle on."

Kenny was resting in his bedroom. He came down when he heard, or sensed, the tea being made. He looked tired and wan and a strange light glittered in his eyes. Helen thought she read intense excitement, and something more – wildness, a restless defiance, in those gleaming eyes. She fervently prayed it was not the glittering madness of religious fanaticsm, gone out of control. He, too, welcomed them with his usual words, but not his usual heartiness, "It's good to see you, my dear fellows."

He threw himself into his long-suffering armchair then silently accepted the tea and scones. They all ate and drank in a subdued mood. Kenny gobbled his food and gulped his tea; he was the first to finish. For a few minutes he lay back with closed eyes. He mumbled indistinctly.

Suddenly he opened his eyes and sat up. He stared steadily at Ian and spoke loudly and clearly. "I had a weird nightmare – or rather, a vision – when I was resting on my bed just now." He paused, took a deep breath, then related his 'vision'. "I saw a straggling procession of Highlanders slowly and despairingly making their way to sailing ships which waited like ugly predatory monsters to swallow them up. The sky was black with the pall of burning thatches. These people – men and women, sinless children and babes – were being ruthlessly herded by devils, by blood-red devils.

"Then the thick smoke blacked out the scene. When the picture cleared I saw a pathetic procession of French refugees slowly shuffling along crowded, dusty roads. They were ceaselessly harried by huge vultures. These ugly creatures swooped and viciously pecked out eyes and slit open bellies of humans and horses.

"Then smoke again blotted out the scene. This thick, oily smoke came from the burning oil tanks at Dunkirk. When it cleared I saw an amazing scene. I saw all of us in this room, and your wife and two wee boys, Calum, and Johnnie Fraser and Bob McInnes, complete with their wives and children; I saw them all as clearly as I'm seeing you now, Ian. We were all teetering at the very edge of an immense cauldron filled with boiling tar. The evil black surface of that tar belched large bubbles, which burst and threw stiflingly thick sulphuric fumes into our faces.

"The Devil was trying to push us all into that hideous cauldron. He jabbed and thrust at us with his three-pronged fork. His body was blood red, but… but his bloated face was white – was a slimy snail white – it was the ugly face of Campbell-Fotheringay!

"He was just about to succeed in pushing us over the edge when the Archangel Gabriel swept down and with his glittering sword smashed the Devil's fork to pieces with a loud, victorious clash."

Kenny paused, he managed to grin, "The noise of my walking stick falling with a loud clatter onto my bedroom's wooden floor woke me up. I was startled. I was sweating. But I rejoiced. The Archangel Gabriel had come as a messenger from God. Oh, my dear fellows, I had been vouchsafed a message – a vision – from God."

Again Kenny paused and sat silent. His eyes glowed with unearthly brightness; he appeared to be in a trance. His audience was silent and motionless; all were impressed and deeply moved, but also apprehensive over the excited and delicately balanced state of Kenny's mind.

Kenny came to with a violent start. Gently and benignly he smiled on them all. "Yes, my dear fellows, I have been graced with a message from God. The message is clear: I – we all – have to fight against that vile sinful devil, Campbell-Fotheringay! We must fight the good fight with God's help – 'Man proposes, but God disposes'. We would simply be doing the Devil's work if we unresistingly allow that evil laird to turn Kate and I out of our home. No, with God's help, he won't get rid of us as easily as he thinks."

Kenny jumped to his feet as he made that impassioned statement. All followed his example. All were too excited to sit still.

"Yes... yes, Uncle Ken and Aunt Kate, we'll all help you to stay on here; we'll all do our utmost to help you fight this... this good fight!" Calum exclaimed with eager excitement.

"Aye," Helen immediately agreed, "Ian and I will do anything we can to help you stay here. You know that, don't you?"

Ian added his wholehearted agreement, "Aye, we – and everyone in the district – will support you in your struggle to resist being evicted, Kenny."

"Thank you... thank you, my dear fellows," Kenny said, deeply moved.

Once more drying emotional tears with her faithful old apron, 'Kate Kettle' unsteadily laughed as she hurried towards the scullery, "Oh, this calls for a wee celebration; I'll go and put the kettle on!"

Later that evening, as he lay in the familiar cosiness of the conjugal bed, Ian murmured, "Kenny and Kate seem amazingly determined to resist Campbell-Fotheringay's attempt to evict them, don't they?... But I'm fearful of how well they will stand up to all the worries and stresses of having that bastard laird and his lawyers and perhaps even the police harrying them over their staying on, their squatting, in their home. It could easily drive poor Kenny into another nervous breakdown – might well push him over the edge." Thoughtfully he repeated "Push him over the edge? That was a weird dream (or vision?) that Kenny had, wasn't it? That part about the French refugees proves how his experiences in 1940 are still vividly remembered, still deeply effect him, even after forty years."

"Oh, don't worry about the stress being too much for Kenny, I feel sure it won't come to that," Helen said. "I think, no, I'm sure, that something decisive, something violent will happen before then and that my prediction about Ron MacDonald becoming laird will come true soon."

Ian felt a nervous tremor flutter over Helen's petite body as she snuggled closer to him. "Oh, Ian, please don't ask me any more about it. Hold me tight and let's get to sleep."

He obeyed. As he held her body to his he felt her gradually relax. Together they relaxed. Together they eventually slept.

Chapter Twenty-Five

Three days later, not being required for the ghillieing, Ian unexpectedly had a day free.

There was heavy rain early in the morning, but by nine-thirty it stopped and the sky cleared. "I think I'll take the dogs for a walk along by the river. Do you want to come?" he asked Helen.

Eagerly she agreed to accompany him. Then, suddenly, unaccountably, changed her mind. Decisively she stated, "No, Ian, I won't come with you. I'll stay at home. There's something I want to do."

Knowing how she loved to walk the dogs, Ian was surprised at her refusal. He asked, "What are you going to do?"

She hesitated; she was reluctant to reply. At last she said, "Oh, it's a clay model I'm making, I want to complete it this morning. It's... it's a special model."

Ian gave a puzzled frown. It was strange that she should prefer working on a model to walking the dogs. "Are you sure?"

"Yes!... Yes! Take Glen and Corrie, go on, don't keep them waiting any longer, they're getting gey impatient."

The collie and the terrier keenly followed this exchange. Having heard the word 'walk' they, once again, could not understand why these humans took such a time to fulfil the promise of that magical word.

At last the front door opened and the dogs bounded out. Ian started to follow them. He was abruptly halted by Helen's urgent voice, "Oh, Ian, be careful, be very careful at the river. Be especially careful at that ugly dark pool I've always disliked."

"Poll Dubh, you mean?"

"Aye, that's right, the Black Pool."

"And why should I be extra careful there?" he asked with a smile.

"Oh, Ian, please, please, take my request – my warning – seriously."

Ian was deeply impressed by her fervour. He solemnly nodded, "Aye, all right, Helen, I'll be very careful there, I promise you I will."

"And, Ian, watch the dogs carefully. Don't let them go near the edge of that dangerous pool. Keep them well away from it, promise me you will."

Again he nodded and faithfully promised.

Ian happily made his way along the path that ran above the river. The sunshine's warmth, after the early morning rain, enticed out many fresh, clean, subtle scents. The distinctive odour of damp soil mingled with the resinous tang of fir trees, and, further along, modest bushes of bog myrtle shyly suggested their faint scents. Ian pulled a handful of these smooth wet leaves, crushed them in his fist, and then inhaled the pungent, pleasant (and midge deterring?) aromatic fragrance.

Aldrory River was running high and fast. Casting his expert eye over each pool, Ian decided they would be difficult, but not impossible, to fish at this height of water. However, on this stretch of the river, owned by Campbell-Fotheringay, no one was fishing. Ian appeared to be the only human moving in this pleasant scene of tree-dappled light and shade and glittering, foaming water.

But, as he neared Poll Dubh, the scene changed and with it, remembering Helen's warning, his mood changed.

Here the riverside was thickly planted with dark firs, which cast a dense, dismal shade. No birds sang here. No wild flowers grew here. Nothing but sinister slimy fungi lived and thrived in this dank, damp, dark place. A deep layer of dead pine needles shrouded the path and smothered the sound of Ian's footsteps as, with foolish apprehension, he hurried through this dreary place.

He arrived at Poll Dubh with increased unease. He was being stupid, he was allowing Helen's warning to nervously influence him. With a deliberate effort he calmed himself. He thought only of the salmon, which should be resting in the depth of the pool.

He found it easy to understand why Helen had never liked this part of the river. Poll Dubh was a deep dark pool which, perpetually cloaked in sunless shade, formed the lower end of a deep ravine through which the river wildly rushed as if frantic to escape from this doleful place. The path brought Ian out from the fir trees at a point thirty feet higher than, and immediately above, the tail of that dark pool. An iron ladder, securely fastened to the almost vertical rock face, led down to a narrow rocky lower path only slightly above the river's swirling surface. Ian did not descend that ladder; instead he lay flat on his stomach, firmly gripped the iron supports rising above the ladder and peered down into the depths of Poll Dubh. He knew that salmon usually rested there after having fought their exhausting battle up through the series of rapids, which tempestuously rushed and roared below this pool.

It was difficult to see the salmon in that dark, sunless pool. Even Ian's experienced eyes at first could see none, then the water's surface momentarily calmed and he spotted about ten fish lazily and companionably resting together. Quickly the water's turbulence again drew its concealing veil over them.

As he continued staring over the ravine's sheer edge, Ian occasionally saw a restless salmon move slightly upstream, then, panicking, urgently turn and resume its old position in the flotilla. Smiling, he noted how effortlessly the peat-stained water's alchemy transmuted these turning fish from their natural silver to bars of gleaming gold.

Then another movement caught his eye – a warning flash of red!

Someone was slowly moving along the narrow lower path. They were coming down through the ravine below where Ian lay hidden with only his head revealed. Cautiously he slithered back so that even less of his head could be seen from below. With intense curiosity, he watched that figure in its bright red nylon jacket as – completely unconscious of Ian's presence – it got nearer.

Suddenly, startlingly Ian recognised that figure. His heart thudded loudly and violently. Curiosity transmuted to hatred.

"It's him... it's that bastard, Campbell-Fotheringay!" He peered even more intently. There was no mistaking that hated figure. "What's he doing here? He's not fishing. Is he on his own?" Ian observantly searched up and down that lower path; there was no one else on it. He turned his head and looked behind him to where Corrie and Glen patiently and obediently sat further back on the top path where, keeping his promise to Helen, he had left them. Obviously no one had disturbed these alertly watching dogs. "It looks as if the bastard's here by himself," Ian thought, as his gaze returned to that despicable laird who was now standing immediately below him at the bottom of the iron ladder with one hand gripping it.

"By God," Ian gasped with wild excitement, "he's coming up here!"

As soon as Ian and the dogs left her, Helen hurried to the small pottery where she fashioned her clay models. She stood and critically studied one fresh model standing by itself on the bench. She was quite pleased with it. Its small stout body was an exact replica of the human male it represented, but she was not pleased with the head, she had not caught a convincing likeness of the human face's loathsome ugliness.

She sat, lifted the model and rapidly worked with nervous fingers on the soft clay.

As – still unseen – Ian intently watched him, Campbell-Fotheringay stood for long uncertain moments holding onto the ladder and irresolutely looking around him. At last he moved. He did not climb the ladder. Slowly and carefully he continued his way along the narrow rock ledge by the side of the river.

With a gasp Ian expelled his breath. He smiled. He had not realised how intensely he had been holding it. While his body relaxed his mind was in turmoil. Was he pleased or not at seeing that obscene enemy of his, whom he loathed with something like obsessive hatred, move away to safety?

At last Helen was pleased with her frantic efforts. It was not perfect, but that ugly bloated face was now instantly recognisable above the clay model's bloated ugly body. She lifted it and hurried out of the pottery and into the crofthouse.

Ian again gasped as he saw Campbell-Fotheringay halt, hesitate, then turn and come back up-river. He instantly knew why his enemy had turned: at this height of water the lower path would be impassable further down the ravine. He smiled. It seemed that nature was working to return his enemy to him. Or were other forces – other much more mysterious forces – working to return his enemy to him? Had some strange unknown power arranged this chance meeting in this wild and lonely place?

Chance meeting?... Chance meeting? Vividly he remembered Helen's warnings: "Be very careful at the river; be especially careful at that ugly pool,

Poll Dubh. Please take my warnings seriously." Had Helen sensed this – not chance – but predestined meeting?

Gasping, Helen climbed the steep stairs to her bedroom. She wildly rummaged through one of the side drawers in her dressing table. Impatiently she pulled the drawer out, turned it upside down, then with nervous eagerness searched through the varied contents scattered on the carpet.

"Oh, bugger it, it's not there," she cursed.

Sue upturned the other side drawer. Kneeling, she urgently scattered many packets of nylon tights, a variety of combs and plastic hair curlers, a large brown envelope which burst and cascaded an avalanche of old black and white family photographs; then she came across two 'Mars Bars' (intact but rather fusty). "How did they get there?" she wondered. Finally, desperately, she conjured up a magician's bright blizzard of multicoloured headscarves and dainty handkerchiefs.

"Ah, at last!" she exclaimed, grabbing a large hatpin. This pin had been given to her by her old aunt; it was of formidable length and had a Tay pearl of impressive size adorning its blunt end.

Campbell-Fotheringay again paused undecidedly at the foot of the iron ladder. Ian was again uncertain if he wished that hated enemy to return along the lower path, the way he had come, to safety, or not.

"Oh God, if he does climb up, what will I do? Should I silently leave, taking the dogs, so that he'll never know I've been here? Or, should I... should I what?" Staring down at Campbell-Fotheringay, Ian clearly remembered Kenny's nightmare. That laird, dressed in his red jacket and with his pale, toad-like loathsome bloated face, was unquestionably the evil Devil described by Kenny. Ian grinned as he noted the red belt hanging loose from the back of his jacket, "He's even got the Devil's tail!"

Campbell-Fotheringay grabbed the iron ladder with both hands and started climbing.

Helen hurried into Ian's 'study'. The Royal stag threw her a haughty stare through its monocle; the one-eyed wildcat cast her a solitary glare; the alarmed stoat and the fencing frog momentarily forgot their deadly quarrel and spared her a questioning glance. Ignoring them all, Helen stood beneath the ugly, ebony black African mask hanging on the wall. She stared at it with steady, unblinking eyes. It unblinkingly stared back at her. She raised the clay model in her left hand and held high the fearsome hatpin in her right. That sharp weapon was quiveringly posed ready to strike.

Ian's heart pounded. His pulse raced. Adrenaline surged through his blood. It roared through his veins as wildly as the river's flooding madness through the narrow ravine.

How laboriously, how slowly – as if in a slow-motion film – Campbell-Fotheringay climbed up that vertical ladder. Despite the noise of the rushing river and the pounding of his own heart, Ian clearly heard the laboured panting of that debauched and obviously badly out of condition laird.

Ian's right hand urgently groped for, found, and firmly gripped a heavy stone. It fitted neatly into his large hand as if designed for it. His mind was a confused commotion of feelings. Wild excitement jostled with deep apprehension and fear. He was fearful of the violent action he was about to take; then, suddenly blindingly, he knew he was not a free agent. He knew this violent action was beyond his control.

As Ian looked down – looked down physically, morally and metaphorically – on painfully slowly ascending Campbell-Fotheringay, he thought the bald white dome of the top of his skull was like a rotten turnip waiting to be smashed to a mushy pulp. He could not see much of the podgy pale face beneath the skull, but the fat white fingers as they clammily crept from rung to rung had the look of already belonging to a drowned and bloated corpse.

Ian's left hand gripped the iron rail more and more tightly. His straining knuckles gleamed whiter and whiter. Slowly he raised his right hand and held the heavy stone firmly poised.

Helen started to fiercely jab the long hatpin at the clay model. She stopped in mid-action. She hesitated for a moment then resolutely jabbed it down again, but at a different part of the model.

At last Campbell-Fotheringay's skull was level with Ian's chin. Warned by some instinct, the laird looked up in sudden alarm. His small, shifty eyes snapped open as widely as they could. They stared with shock and fear and disbelief into Ian's eyes, which, for a breathless moment, unflinching stared back with unbridled hatred.

As Campbell-Fotheringay opened his mouth to shout, Ian smashed the heavy stone with the full strength of his right arm on to the exact centre of that exposed forehead.

Campbell-Fotheringay's head snapped back. His hands clawed wildly at empty air. His body fell backwards headfirst. It thudded on the narrow rock ledge then tumbled with a resounding splash into the water.

Ian glimpsed the body sweep round a jutting black rock, then vanish into a maelstrom of white foam and splashing spray.

Ian's grip relaxed on the iron rail, colour came back into his knuckles. His heart and pulse steadied to their normal beat.

He still held the heavy stone – that stone-age weapon – in his right hand and his arm tingled with the intense shock, the savage thrill, of the fierce impact of stone against bone.

Now his entire body tingled. He was swept by a thrill of excitement and of apprehension. He felt the cold touch of fear, but also the hot thrill of something wildly, primitively, ecstatic. Vividly he remembered when he had first felt such emotions during the war, on his first time in action.

He examined the stone; there was no blood on it or on his hand. He threw the fatal stone far out into the river.

He rose and turned. The two dogs greeted him. "What are you doing here? I ordered you to sit back there." The rebuked dog's tails drooped. Ian instantly relented, he laughed and caressed them, "All right… all right. It was my fault anyway, you heard me shouting, didn't you? You thought I was shouting for you."

He knew he had shouted some words as he struck with that stone. He remembered the exact words he had used, and, with another vivid flash of memory, recalled when he last used these Gaelic words in anger. On that occasion his savage killing (with a bayonet) had been sanctified by war, but this time he had committed murder. Yes, there was no escaping it – he was now a murderer!

And yet he did not feel like a murderer. He felt his killing of Campbell-Fotheringay was completely justified. He was certain this killing had been preordained – or was this merely an easy excuse for his murderous action?

As he continued caressing Corrie and Glen he smiled and thought, "At least the dogs don't see any difference in me; they don't turn from me as a murderer."

Again smiling, he thought of how passionately Helen believed that dogs had a sure and unfailing instinct that told them which humans were good and which evil. "Aye, I've passed the test of the dogs alright, but what about Helen?… What will she think when I tell her I'm a murderer?" He paused thoughtfully, "But I won't need to tell her. She will already know!" He knew with sudden absolute certainty that Helen was already aware of what had happened at Poll Dubh – that dark pool which she always so disliked and felt to be shadowed by sinister forces.

As Ian approached his croft he saw Helen leaning on the wooden garden gate. He smiled as he strode up the rutted narrow road towards her. "She's getting gey auld looking," he thought with affection and some surprise. How glaringly white her hair was. He felt he was seeing her – really seeing her – for the first time in many years. How easy it was for a married couple that were always together to go through the years without really noticing the changes age was relentlessly working on their spouse. "How old is she?… Three years younger than me, that makes her sixty-one. Not so very old." Again he smiled to himself, "I bet Helen's looking at my white hair and beard and thinking I'm getting gey auld looking."

He gave a puzzled frown; it seemed strange and foolish to have such inconsequential thoughts when perhaps he should be full of remorse and apprehension after having committed murder.

The dogs caught sight of Helen and rushed to wildly greet her. She greeted them with warmth that equalled theirs. Vivacious smiles swept all signs of anxiety from her face and illuminated her cheeks with warm, loving brightness. Around her beaming eyes radiated a maze of merry wrinkles.

As Ian leaned beside her on the gate, Helen stared at him intently for a while then said, "You met Campbell-Fotheringay at the river… at Poll Dubh."

To Ian it did not seem a question, more a statement. "Aye, I met him there."

"He's dead."

Again more a statement than a question. "Aye, he's dead!"

He was not surprised by her knowledge. She was not surprised by his lack of surprise.

As they sat facing one another in their comfortable old armchairs at either side of the fireplace, Ian gave Helen a detailed account of what happened at Poll Dubh. When he finished, he rose and picked up a clay model from the untidily littered small table beside her chair. He sat again and studied the model. It was an exact likeness of Campbell-Fortheringay. The large hatpin projecting from the centre of its forehead gave it an incongruous appearance, linked it to the mythical unicorn and to the other fabulous creatures Helen was so fond of creating.

"It's a striking likeness, Helen, when did you make it?" Ian smiled at the unintended irony of his description, 'a striking likeness'.

Helen also smiled, "Oh, I made it yesterday, but I was not entirely satisfied with it, I finished it off this morning."

"That was what you were doing instead of walking with the dogs and me?"

"Aye, that's right, Ian. I felt... no, I knew... I had to complete it this morning."

Ian silently continued studying the ugly small model. The accurate ugliness of the bloated body, the podgy face and the mean, pig-like eyes was amazing – was amazingly repulsive. He shuddered slightly. "You knew what was going to happen at the river this morning?"

With quiet solemnity, Helen replied, "Yes, I knew there was going to be a violent death at that dismal place, Poll Dubh. I was certain – or almost certain – that Campbell-Fotheringay was going to die there." Her face clouded with remembered perplexity, "But... but, I had to make sure it was him who died, so I made that model and stuck that hatpin in it."

"Ah well, you were wise tae 'mak siccer'."

After another silent pause, Ian asked, "Why did you stab that hatpin into its forehead? I thought pins were usually stabbed into the hearts of models?"

"I started to stab it into the model's heart, then something stopped me and directed it into the centre of its forehead." She asked – or stated – "That's where you struck him... in the centre of his forehead?"

Ian nodded solemnly, "Aye, in the exact centre of his forehead."

They fell silent. The only sound was the wheezy breathing of the two dogs lying sleeping in a patch of sunlight behind the old sofa.

After a while, Ian asked, "Did you happen to note the time when you stabbed that pin into the model?"

"Helen nodded, "Yes, I glanced at the clock immediately after I'd done it."

"Well, what time was it?"

"It was exactly twenty-two minutes past eleven."

Helen stared her unspoken question at Ian.

He nodded, "Aye, Helen, it was eleven twenty-two when I smashed the stone on his forehead!"

They sat motionless and soundless. They stared steadily into one another's eyes. They had no idea how long they sat and stared.

'Normal' time had ceased to exist. 'Normal' reality no longer applied.

The dull, worldly life of normality's mundane everyday affairs was suspended – had been replaced. Aye, but replaced with what?

Even while lost in this timeless and unreal (or more real?) trance-like state a part of Ian's brain urgently tried to analyse what was happening; tried to comprehend what this strange new 'reality' was.

He felt this silence, this stillness, to be intensely and mysteriously alive. With awe and a touch of fear he knew himself to be surrounded by powerful unknown forces – unknown, but undeniable forces, which, if they could be tapped into – as Helen seemed to have done – could direct the course of human events. Not visibly, but inwardly, he shivered under the renewed icy touch of ancestral fears.

As his Pagan ancestors whispered their primitive, their illogical, beliefs and superstitions through Ian's nerves, that logically reasoning part of his perplexed brain tried to assure him of the falseness, the foolishness, of these primitive messages. But he was not convinced by logic's assuring voice. Like his ancestors, like Helen, he knew that 'nature' at its deepest, its most elemental, held mysterious 'truths' that could not be explained by science.

That eternity of silence and stillness startlingly ended.

The spell was broken by a sudden, a frightening, loud, eerie, banshee howling.

These high-pitched demented sounds froze Helen's and Ian's blood. The hairs at the back of their necks rose.

Those hairs madly thrilled and tingled as the crazy howling got louder.

Suddenly Helen's consternation turned to relief. She laughed and pointed. From her chair she could see the two dogs where they sat beyond her end of the sofa. Both had their heads thrown back and were loudly and mournfully howling their hearts out. Glen, the sensitive collie, had started the howling, then Corrie wholeheartedly joined in.

Ian stood to see the dogs. His laughter merged with Helen's. "What's all that unearthly noise for, you two?"

Both dogs stopped howling. They joyfully bounded to be petted.

"They must have felt something of what we felt," Helen said.

"Aye, they must have."

"And obviously they're glad to be back to a 'normal' atmosphere again."

"Aye," Ian laughed, "and so am I!"

Grinning merrily, Helen got to her feet and said, "Let's get a bite of lunch, then take them out for another walk. The sun's shining. We must put the dark events of this morning out of our minds; they are done and finished with. The future is now much brighter."

Ian smiled his wholehearted agreement, "Aye, the outlook for Aldrory and its people certainly is far brighter now that Campbell-Fotheringay is dead."

That evening 'Forensic Fred' Sutherland, the local policeman, called at Altdour crofthouse.

Once his massive body was settled on, and was cruelly torturing the poor old sofa, and he held – at his insistence – only a modest dram dwarfed in his huge hand, he explained the reason for his visit. "You've heard of Campbell-Fotheringay's accidental death at the river today, haven't you?"

Helen and Ian nodded and murmured confirmation that they had. (Ian mentally steeled himself to tell as few lies, and to tell them as convincingly as he could, in reply to the further questions he guessed the policeman would ask. It was a task repugnant to his honest nature, but an ordeal he did not shrink from.)

"Aye, well I'm chust checking up by asking if you happened to be at the river today by any chance, Ian?" The policeman grinned widely, "I won't enquire if you were poaching salmon; all I want to know is did you see Campbell-Fotheringay at the river?"

Ian wisely kept to the truth as near as possible. "Aye, I did happen to be at the river, but not poaching; believe it or not. I was merely walking the dogs. Admittedly I did have a good reconnaissance for salmon in the pools. Aye, and I did see Campbell-Fotheringay, but only for a minute at Poll Dubh, then he went his way and I went mine."

"Was he fishing?"

"No. He, too, seemed to be merely on a reconnoitre at the river."

"Aye, that confirms what the young ladies," Forensic Fred again grinned, "his seductively attractive dolly-birds at Aldrory Lodge told me. Seemingly he was having another look at the river before deciding if he should sell his salmon fishing rights. Doubtless he was wanting to raise more money to spend on his drugs, drink and fancy young whores. Aye, it seems a straightforward case of accidental death."

Ian noticed the policeman now staring fixedly at the small clay model of Campbell-Fotheringay on the table. He lifted it and held it out to 'Forensic Fred'.

"What's that?"

"Oh, it's just another of my foolish whimsical models," Helen answered, "like those ones there." She pointed to a couple of fantastic, fabulously surrealistic creatures on the table beside her.

Irresolutely and uneasily the policeman took the model. Cautiously he examined it. Helen was pleased that she had removed the pearl hatpin from its forehead. "It… it looks something like Campbell-Fotheringay, doesn't it?"

"Aye, Fred, I suppose it does," Helen admitted.

"It… it's almost like a voodoo model of a victim. All it needs is a pin sticking in its heart."

"Aye, I agree, it is something like a voodoo model," Ian said quietly. "But of course, Fred, there is no possible way that model, admittedly looking something like Campbell-Fotheringay, can have any connection with his accidental death, is there? Surely the utmost efforts of forensic science would be unable to find any link between these two things."

'Forensic Fred' smiled a ready, but a rather forced, uncertain smile. "Oh aye, Ian, of course any connection is absolutely impossible!"

"Yes, believing in a connection would be like believing in ghosts." Ian grinned mischievously, "Of course none of us here believe in ghosts, do we, Fred?"

Eagerly the policeman exclaimed, "No... no, of course not." He took a sip of whisky, then, grinning with disarming self-mockery, said, "No, Ian, I've never believed in ghosts... but I've been scared of them all my life."

Helen reached out for the clay model. With haste, and obvious relief, Fred handed it over.

"Oh, Fred, I forgot to congratulate you on receiving your medal," Helen said. Ian added his warm congratulations to hers.

Fred had recently been awarded the Police Medal of Gallantry in recognition of his bravery at a car accident.

Late on in the evening of the Inveraldrory Highland Games, Fred, in the police Land Rover, saw the headlights of a rapidly approaching car. He pulled into a convenient passing place on the narrow road winding up Aldrory Glen and waited. But the car never passed him. To his horror he saw it fail to take a sharp bend and go tumbling down the steep slope below. Amazingly, it missed the many boulders littering that slope and ended on its roof, with its lights still blazing, in the cushioning softness of a peat bog.

After phoning for the doctor and ambulance, Fred grabbed his large torch and clambered down the slope to the upturned car. Two young local couples, none exactly sober, had been in the car. One couple managed to struggle clear, but the other couple, apparently unconscious, were trapped under the car. The air was urgent with the dangerous stench of spilled petrol.

Fred saw that the unconscious couple were lying half in and half out of the car. He tried to drag them clear, but the weight of the car trapped them. He urgently shouted at the freed, but shocked couple, "When I lift the car you pull them clear, right!"

They nodded and stooped to help. With his back against the car, Fred slid down and groped in the clammy soft black peat with his huge hands, got a grip on the car and heaved up with all his massive might. Gasping and straining, he put desperate effort into the struggle. Reluctantly the oozy peat released its grip and the car rose a few inches. His nerves and muscles screaming with the effort, Fred raised it six inches and held it while, with difficulty, the trapped couple were dragged clear.

Thankfully he lowered the car and eagerly eased his aching hands free.

He had just completed pulling the unconscious couple well clear of the wrecked car when it exploded into flames.

Helen and Ian heard the story of the policeman's brave feat of strength from one of the people involved in the accident.

"Aye, Fred, you well deserve the medal," Ian said.

Fred thought so himself, but, smiling, he modestly concealed his secret pride and said, "Aye, perhaps. But, you know, not everyone was greatly excited by the accident. Auld Donald 'Archie' Ross, in his crofthouse a few hundred yards away, was wakened by the noise of the accident. With leisurely deliberation he pulled on his breeks and big wellies then strode over at his usual unhurried pace.

"As he gazed at the blazing car and then up the steep slope to the road, he pushed back his cap, scratched his head, and murmured, 'Oh, good life!… good life!' Then, turning to the shocked and injured lying on the ground, he quietly and calmly enquired, 'Did you coup?'"*

Later, after the policeman left, Helen smiled and said, "Good old Forensic Fred. I like him. Somehow he mysteriously awakens my maternal instincts. Foolishly, I feel I should protect and mother him. He's so massive, so overwhelmingly strong, such a brave giant when faced with any normal incident requiring strength and brute force; and yet when it comes to anything suggestive of the paranormal, or the supernatural, well he's still just a wee bairn feart o' the dark."

That night as they again lay in the cosy conjugal intimacy of their bed, Helen whispered, "You know that Campbell-Fotheringay's death was fated, don't you, Ian? There's absolutely no need to feel any guilt over having killed him."

"Aye, I know, Helen. Believe me, I feel no guilt. Like you, I am convinced that his death was predestined, was inevitable.

"Oh, it was… it was! Believe me it was! The fact of him, most unusually, being at the river by himself, and of you being alone there too, and of you already being in position at the top of the ladder when he climbed up it, were not all just coincidences, you know."

"No… no, I don't suppose they could be."

Sensing the note of doubt still lingering in his voice, Helen convincingly continued, "Oh, Ian, you were merely the instrument – the predestined instrument – that caused his death. You are no more guilty than I am, believe me."

Startled, Ian vividly remembered what Auld Maggie Gunn had said about Campbell-Fotheringay that day when her hens had been killed by the foxes: "A wrathful and yet a righteous God will, in His own good time, using His own chosen instrument, strike him down." How profoundly prophetic her passionate words now seemed. He repeated, "Using His own chosen instrument." He smiled in the darkness, "So I was merely the instrument of God?… But what God?… A Christian God? Or some other unknown 'God'?" He lay thoughtfully silent for some moments, then, drawing Helen comfortingly close in to him, repeated, "No, Helen, I assure you I feel no guilt. Killing him was like ridding the world of vile vermin! I am sure that, like my killing of Nazis during the war, it was fully justified. The truth is that the world is a better place with that obnoxious man dead!"

"Yes, I know, Ian, I completely agree with you. No tears will be shed over his death. Now let's get to sleep – to sound, clear-conscienced sleep."

And they did. Soon they were both in deep, undisturbed slumber.

---

* 'Coup' – to overturn.

324

The Inverness pathologist's report on Campbell-Fotheringay's body found that its multitudinous injuries had been caused by it being violently smashed against rocks by the force of the flooded river. It appeared to be a straightforward case of accidental death. The police and the procurator fiscal agreed and a finding of 'death by misadventure' was duly recorded.

Chapter Twenty-Six

A few days after Campbell-Fotheringay's death, Colin MacDonald drove Ian MacLean home after having been ghillieing at the salmon fishing with Lord and Lady Kilvert and their guests. Colin reversed the van into the turning place outside the closed gate at Ian's croft. He switched off the engine then turned and stared steadily and solemnly into Ian's eyes. Ian enquiringly gazed back. "What's the matter, Colin?"

"There's something I want to ask you, Ian... something very serious."

With a flash of insight Ian guessed what the question would be, "All right, ask away. I promise I'll give you an honest answer."

"Ian, did you have anything to do with Campbell-Fotheringay's death?"

This was the question Ian expected. Calmly he asked in reply, "What makes you ask that, Colin?"

"Och, I don't know exactly, it's just a strong feeling, an intuition I have that you are in some way responsible for his death. And I know how intensely you hated him."

Ian grinned, "I wasn't the only one who hated him, you know."

"Aye, I ken that fine," Colin said then said silently and expectantly waited.

"Aye," Ian quietly admitted, "I had something – had everything – to do with his death!"

Slowly, calmly, and in detail, he told Colin what had happened on that momentous day.

When Ian finished his confession Colin said nothing. He pulled out his pipe, filled and lit it, and in thoughtful silence smoked it. Ian followed his example.

When both pipes were almost smoked out, Ian asked, "Well, Colin, aren't you going to say something? Is my confession of having committed murder going to end our friendship?"

"No... no, not at all! It'll make no difference to our friendship, Ian. Our friendship is too old, too deep and firmly rooted, to be destroyed by what you've done. I know the murder you committed was done for the highest of motives; was done to save Kate Kettle and Kenny, and the others, from being evicted from their homes; was done to save Aldrory Estate from decaying into utter ruin. I suppose your action raises the age-old question about ends and means, doesn't it?"

Ian nodded, "Aye, it does. The question is: can a good end justify the evil means that bring it about?"

"Aye, that's it, Ian. I really think that in this case, especially if Ron MacDonald does now buy Aldrory Estate and sets about repairing the terrible damage Campbell-Fotheringay had done to it, then yes, the evil – the murderous – means are fully justified!"

"Yes, I'm also convinced they are." Ian was deeply moved by Colin's endorsement of his act of murder. "Thank you, Colin, thank you for your reassuring understanding."

Colin gave a quick grin, "Ah weel, Ian, you certainly solved the problem of what to do about Campbell-Fotheringay... even if your solution was a wee touch drastic!"

Ian returned Colin's grin, "Oh, I agree it was extremely drastic, but there was no other way. It was the only possible way to stop his terrible, his – if it doesn't sound too melodramatic – his nefarious evil plans, and, you know, I did not plan his murder; no, despite my hatred for him, my drastic act was completely unpremeditated. And, of course, I did not do it for any selfish personal gain either."

"Aye, I ken that, Ian." Quietly, musingly, Colin said, "It was very strange Campbell-Fotheringay and you meeting like that at the river, both of you alone and no one anywhere near to witness what happened. It was queer you being in a position like that at the top of the iron ladder, too. The chances against that happening must be very, very, great." He paused thoughtfully, "It was almost as if that meeting was fated to happen. Surely it could not be merely coincidence that you should both have been at Poll Dubh at exactly the same time?"

Ian was delighted to receive this further confirmation of Helen's conviction that this death had been fated to happen. "You have just said, in almost exactly the same words, what Helen said about his death."

"Oh, so you told Helen about killing him?"

"No!... I didn't have to! She already knew he was dead. I merely confirmed it to her." He hesitated, then decided to say nothing about the hatpin impaled clay model Helen had made. "She accepted his death as being predestined; as me being merely the instrument of fate."

"So only the three of us know of your involvement in his death?"

"Aye, only Helen, you, and me, know. What about Jeannie? Will you tell her?"

"No... no, I'll say nothing to her. The fewer who know the better. She would not want to know about your guilt anyway, Ian."

"My guilt?" Ian queried. He frowned, "Aye, of course legally I am guilty of murder. I suppose I should feel some guilt, but I don't; I feel absolutely no guilt at all." He paused and gathered his thoughts. "Oh, of course I've broken the law by killing him. But I'm convinced there are some occasions when it's right, it's essentially correct, to break the law."

"Aye, I suppose there are."

Ian asked, "Remember July 1944?... Remember the German Army officer's Bomb Plot to kill Hitler? Had they succeeded (as they almost did) then, under German law, they would have been guilty of having carried out an illegal act of murder. Yet surely if ever a violent act of killing was fully justified that murder of Hitler was justified... would have been a good, a morally correct act?"

"Aye, of course," Colin agreed. "But surely Campbell-Fotheringay, with all his vile faults, was nothing like as bad, as evil, as Hitler?"

"No… no, not quite!" Ian grinned. "But isn't the principle the same? Those German army officers tried to kill Hitler before he dragged their country down to utter ruin. I killed Campbell-Fotheringay before he brought this part of our country to utter ruin."

Colin nodded his understanding and agreement.

For some moments they smoked in silence, then it was Colin's turn to remember. He asked, "Remember that time in Italy when you deliberately did not shoot a young German soldier you had in your sights?"

"Aye, of course I remember."

Ian was a sniper lying by himself on a sun-parched arid slope overlooking a narrow path amongst Italian foothills. Suddenly he saw the movement of a solitary grey figure. His telescopic sight clearly revealed the German soldier. Ian's finger curled around the trigger. He held his aim, his breath, his finger. The thin German soldier was very young – a mere youth. A mere youth?… Aye, but a Hitler Youth?… a fanatic young Nazi? That thought tightened on the trigger. Kill him! Do your duty! But no, still Ian let him be and intently observed his every move. The German soldier stooped at a trickle of water beside the path and drank from cupped hands. He filled his aluminium water bottle, straightened up, fastened the water bottle to his belt then lifted his rifle and slung it over his right shoulder.

To Ian it seemed that the German had lifted his rifle with some reluctance. Smiling, he thought, "Am I being foolishly indulgent because of that German's obvious youth?" He sighed, took his finger from the trigger and watched the German walk out of sight.

Days later, still undecided whether his act of mercy had been a good and decent act or merely a very foolish one, Ian relieved his feelings by telling Colin about the incident.

Now, forty years later, sitting beside Ian in the van, Colin said, "That's still the unanswered question: did you do right or wrong by letting that young German soldier live? Might he later have killed British soldiers, perhaps even some of our own good comrades?" Colin paused then reminiscently continued, "Anyway, I remember after you told me, in strict confidence, about the incident, I said, Oh well, Ian, you took the God-like decision that the young German soldier should live instead of die; so perhaps sometime in the future, long after this bloody war is over, you will be entitled to again act God-like and to justifiably kill someone. Perhaps the two acts will cancel one another out. Well, it now seems that thought of mine has come true."

Ian nodded, "Aye, it does seem that your prophecy has been realised, Colin. Doesn't that seem further proof that my act of killing Campbell-Fotheringay was an act fated to happen? By not killing that young German soldier I broke British Army Law. By killing that hated laird I broke British Civil Law. Aye, the one act does seem to neatly balance up the other act, doesn't it?"

"Aye, it does. Although I suppose most people would see a huge difference between killing in war and killing in peace. One is an act of duty, the other an act of murder."

"Oh, I know, Colin, I know!... But, after all, is there all that much difference? Don't you remember what Auld Rabbie wrote about war and murder in his poem, 'Thanksgiving For a National Victory'?"

"I can't quite remember it," Colin grinned, "But nae doot nothing on earth will stop you quoting it, Ian."

"Aye, well I'll just recite a few lines as best I remember them:

"Ye hypocrites, are these your pranks,
to murder men and give God thanks?
Desist for shame, proceed no further,
God won't accept your thanks – for murder! "

"At least we're not hypocrites. Surely it would be utter hypocrisy to pretend sorrow for Campbell-Fotheringay's death?"

Their pipes were smoked out. They knocked out the ashes on the outsides of the van's doors and then refilled and relit their pipes. As he leisurely puffed out lazy clouds of aromatic smoke Ian asked, "Do you remember..." Grinning, he interrupted himself, "We seem to be full of auld men's wartime memories today, don't we, Colin? Resolutely he continued, "Do you remember what I shouted when I bayoneted yon SS soldier?"

"Oh aye, I remember a' the vile swear words you shouted!"

That action had been short, sharp and deadly. No quarter had been given. No prisoners had been taken.

A young German soldier with both hands held high and a white surrender handkerchief waving in each hand slowly walked towards the small patrol of Seaforth soldiers. Colin and Ian, experienced veterans, lay still and alertly covered that approaching German with their Sten guns. Out of the corners of their eyes they saw with dismay four of their young and inexperienced comrades, only recently arrived in Italy, rise and, foolishly trusting, move forward to capture the German and proudly make him their first prisoner.

Ian's urgently shouted warning was drowned by the loud hammering of a Schmeisser machine gun. Heavy bullets thudded into agonised flesh and effortlessly smashed through the thickest of bones. The four young British soldiers savagely died.

Too late, Ian and Colin opened fire on the treacherous German. He had already dived over a protective wall.

Keeping out of sight of the German machine gunners, Colin and Ian crawled along a ditch to the shelter of a dried-up riverbed. There they met Captain Stewart with his patrol of twenty men. They explained what had happened. The captain cursed. The message he had just received from battalion intelligence warning him there was a unit of an elite SS regiment – all its indoctrinated soldiers fanatical and ruthless Nazis somewhere near his Seaforth patrol, had come too late for him to alert all his men, especially the young novices. With angry passion he addressed his soldiers. "We must find and kill those SS bastards! We must avenge our treacherously slaughtered young lads!" Staring directly at the youngest, most inexperienced soldiers he clearly and emphatically said, "Take this lesson to heart… Never, never, trust any SS soldiers, even (or especially) with a white surrender flag. Always remember they are untrustworthy – they are as untrustworthy as a politician's promise!"

There was a low rumble of agreement from the British soldiers.

Outrage and lust for revenge mingled with apprehension and outright fear. The more experienced soldiers knew only too well what a dangerous task they were letting themselves in for – still, it had to be done! Some secretly silently prayed. Some loudly cursed the treacherous bastard Germans.

Strangely, for no order was given, all those Seaforth soldiers threw away their tin hats and replaced them with their Balmoral bonnets, complete with stag's head cap badge. All seemed collectively to reject reason's logic and obey ancestral Highland instincts.

While a few pinned down the Germans with fire from the front, most of the Seaforths, using the concealment of the river bed, got behind the enemy position and attacked from the rear. The fighting was fierce and bloody. Captain Stewart threw hand grenades into the German's machine gun position. The three machine gunners violently died.

The noise of battle suddenly ceased. The fighting seemed over. An eerie, uneasy silence reigned.

With startling suddenness a German soldier rose and desperately ran. He was ten yards from Ian. Instantly he swung his Sten gun round and pressed the trigger. Only two shots blasted out. The magazine was empty. He threw the gun aside, drew his bayonet from its scabbard and ran after the German.

The German soldier fell. Whether wounded or tripped, Ian neither knew nor cared. The German's right hand urgently fumbled for the Luger pistol in its holster. He glared at Ian with scorching black hate.

Ian threw himself on top of the German and plunged the bayonet into his chest. It neatly sliced between ribs and went in deep. Gasping, ignoring the spurting blood, Ian withdrew the bayonet, raised it high, and again plunged it into the heaving chest. Again and again he raised it; again and again he plunged it in with manic ferocity. Ian was no longer a civilised, compassionate human being. He was a primitive unreasoning savage who brutally exulted in this barbarous fury of violence. Each time he plunged the bayonet in he exploded a shout of triumph. His eyes blazed with mad hate. His choking breath came in wild gasps and gulping sobs. Blood and sweat coursed down his face and dribbled from his trembling chin.

The young German's eyes had lost their glare of fanatic hatred; had lost their expression of arrogant Nazi pride. They were filled with the weaker, but more human, emotion of terrible fear. With amazed surprise he realised he was dying.

As, kneeling and straddling the dead German body he madly continued to plunge his bayonet into its soggy mess of a chest, Ian gave a sudden startled jump. He, too, experienced a frantic rush of fear and amazed surprise as he felt his right wrist and arm being firmly seized and held. He heard Colin's voice commandingly shout, "Stop it, Ian!... Leave him alone. He's dead!... The bastard's dead!"

As he glared up and met Colin's authoritative stare the mad blaze of hatred faded from Ian's eyes. Relief replaced fear.

Determinedly, Colin eased the bayonet out of Ian's violently trembling hand. "Come on, Ian, give me it. You've done what had to be done with it. He's dead."

As he held the bloody bayonet in his own hand, Colin stared down at the dead young German SS soldier. "Aye, you did well to kill him, Ian, I think that's the bastard who came out with the false white surrender flags."

Colin helped Ian to his feet, "Come on, Ian, we'll sit and rest and have a fag."

As Ian unsteadily walked away, Colin picked up the dead German soldier's cap. For a moment he studied its proud, silver, death's-head SS badge, then used the cap to wipe blood from Ian's bayonet. He threw the blooded cap down beside the corpse and stooped to read the proudly assertive slogan on the large badge on the corpse's leather belt. Beneath the eagle bravely protecting the evil swastika were the words: 'Gott Mit Uns'. Colin smiled ironically as he translated: 'God With Us!'. "Oh God... Oh God," he thought, "what crimes are committed in Thy name!"

As they sat and smoked, the battle tension gradually eased. Their adrenaline ceased to flood, their nerves calmed and Ian's trembling lessened. After they lit up their second fags Ian managed a rather uncertain apologetic grin, "I'm sorry I behaved like that with my bayonet. It was an ugly thing to do, to continue stabbing him even after he was dead, wasn't it?"

"Aye, it was. But it was understandable. We were both on edge after seeing those four lads of ours treacherously killed."

"Aye, I know, Colin, and after all it's the first time I've lost control of myself during all this bloody long war." He grinned more assuredly, "And I'll do my damnedest to make sure it's the last time too!"

The German's bloody body, lying not far from them, lying in the terrible stillness, the impenetrable silence of death, was an irresistible magnet attracting hundreds of black flies. Loudly buzzing, they actively swarmed in a keen and ugly mass.

The German blood saturating Ian's uniform attracted other flies. Cursing and swiping at the persistent pests, he exclaimed, "Oh, bugger off... I'm not a corpse... not yet!" Savagely he smacked at flies tormenting his blood-streaked right cheek. Two squashed dead flies fell down his ugly stained khaki shirt to the dusty ground.

Mysteriously summoned, a couple of apposite lines surfaced from his subconscious:

"As flies to wanton boys, are we to the Gods,
they kill us for their sport."

Was that true?... Are we humans merely playthings of the Gods? To Ian, thinking of the British and German soldiers who had been killed here today, it seemed like it. Again he pondered the mystery of what decided who lived, and who died, in war. Are the Gods playing with me? Are they stringing me along, letting me think I'm going to survive this bloody war, only to swat me dead just before it does finally end? How cruel were all these deaths, and – cruellest of all – was the knowledge of how unimportant, how meaningless they were in any profound view of nature and of man's place in the universe. Ian knew how little his death would really matter. If he was lying there with those other bodies the sun would continue indifferently in its set course while he turned to dust. And yet how stridently, how persistently, his selfish human egoism cried out in denial of the meaninglessness of his own life, of his own death.

Colin's voice suddenly broke into Ian's thoughts. It was not his usual powerfully deep voice; it was a strangely muted emotional voice. Ian hardly recognised it as, with infinite compassion, it murmured a few simple heartfelt words: "Those poor lads... those poor young lads. How sad... how terribly sad."

As, forty years after that wartime incident, Colin sat in the van beside Ian, he repeated, "Aye, Ian, I remember what you shouted when you bayonetted that SS soldier. You shouted every vile swear word you know at the top of your voice, and, after five years in the army, you knew many!"

Ian grinned, "Aye, I suppose so. But don't you remember me shouting something else?"

"What?... Oh aye, now I remember. You shouted something in Gaelic. What was it again?"

"I shouted, 'Ba's no beatha!' – the war cry of my clan, the MacLean's."

"Oh aye? And what does it mean?"

"Ba's no beatha! – Death or Life! An appropriate thing to shout when you're killing your enemy, don't you think? And I shouted it again as I smashed that stone on Campbell-Fotheringay's forehead. I don't think I shouted any swear words then, but I certainly yelled out that war cry again; the dogs, sitting further back, heard me and came to investigate. On both occasions I did not consciously shout it. That ancient war cry arose subconsciously from my ancestral past."

After a few moments of thoughtful silence Colin nodded, "Aye, Ian, I don't suppose any of us can entirely escape from our ancestry, even if we wanted to, can we? When we add to our Highland ancestry (our savage fighting clan spirit deliberately fostered by the Highland regiments) the army training we received on how to most efficiently and ruthlessly kill our enemies, and then put that training into practise for six long years, it's hardly surprising that I'm not shocked by you committing one more death – even though the law calls it murder."

"Thank you, Colin. I repeat I too feel no shock or sense of guilt over his death. After all why should Campbell-Fotheringay's life have been held sacrosanct when the lives of all those millions of victims of the war were not?"

"Aye, I agree. There was no valid reason why his vile life should be spared." Colin could not prevent a broad grin beaming out, "And, after all, he was a Campbell, wasn't he?"

Ian laughed, "Aye, he was a Campbell. And you know, Colin, it wasn't just your MacDonald clan who suffered from the Campbells, the MacLeans suffered too. The MacLeans fought as Jacobites against Campbells in 1715 and 1745.

And after Culloden, the Duke of Argyll took over all the MacLean lands in Mull, Morven and Duart. He made the MacLeans landless for forty years."

It was Colin's turn to laugh, "You certainly know your clan's history, Ian."

Ian grinned, "Aye, I do… almost as well as you know yours." He glanced at his watch, "Good life, we've been sitting here for nearly an hour." He opened the van door, "Come on, we better get going. All this talking has made my throat gey dry. I could do with a refreshing dram. You better come in and have one, too, Colin."

Colin readily agreed, "Aye, one, or two, drams will be most acceptable." He again beamed broadly, "I was beginning to despair of you ever suggesting it, Ian!"

Ian laughed then said, "Thank you for being so understanding, Colin. I'm delighted that my confession of my… my murderous act has made no difference to our friendship."

"No, it hasn't… I assure you it hasn't. After everything we've been through together, in war and in peace, our friendship is too precious to allow his death to end it. Oh of course your act of murder was a criminal wrong. But I don't think it was morally wrong, Ian, in fact, like you, I believe it was a morally justifiable act." Colin paused, then – his ancestral MacDonald blood speaking – added with a grin, "Aye, and I repeat, after all, your victim was only a *bloody Campbell*, wasn't he?"

Chapter Twenty-Seven

Late on the following Saturday evening, the sound of a car driving up to their front door disturbed Helen and Ian as they sat on either side of the cosy small sitting room's blazing peat and log fire.

"Who can that be at this time?" Ian asked as he heaved himself up from the comfort of his deep old armchair and made for the door.

"I expect it's Ron MacDonald," Helen said.

Ian stopped and turned and stared. He opened his mouth to question her, for they were not expecting a visit from Ron, who, as far as they knew, was in New York. He had had to cancel his usual fishing trip this summer because of his father's serious illness. Ian, thinking better of it, said nothing. He closed his mouth and hurried to open the door.

A minute later he ushered a beaming Ron MacDonald into the small room. Ian, too, was beaming as he firmly and delightedly held high the two bottles of malt whisky Ron had eagerly thrust on him. As Helen warmly welcomed Ron, Ian got busy with one bottle and three glasses.

Soon all were comfortably seated and, after toasting one another with cries of "Slainte Mhath!" were enjoying the malt whisky's mature excellence.

Both Helen and Ian noticed Ron's nervous air of barely concealed excitement. They refrained from commenting on it, although, with a touch of rising excitement themselves, they wondered at it.

Smiling, Helen gently and sympathetically remarked, "You're looking gey peelie-wally, Ron. You look as if you've had a stressful time lately."

"Yeah, I have, Helen. I've had a hell of a stressful time!" He paused and took another large gulp of whisky.

"How's your father now, Ron?" Ian hesitantly asked.

"My father's dead," Ron exclaimed. "Dad died four weeks ago."

While Helen and Ian murmured the conventional condolences, Ron had another large and soothing drink of whisky.

Ian and Helen followed his example and for long moments all three silently drank.

Ron put down his empty glass and, appearing more calm and composed, repeated, "Yeah, I've had a real stressful time recently. I've got lots of exciting things to tell you." He smiled, "If you had a phone I would have rung you with my news, but I've been far too busy to write you."

"We've got exciting news, too, Ron," Ian said.

"Oh, really?… and what's that?"

"Be quiet, Ian. Let Ron tell his news first," Helen sternly reprimanded,

"Oh, aye, all right. Go ahead, Ron."

"Yeah, well my first news I've already told you – the death of my father. I wrote three months ago and told you of him suffering a massive stroke; well he never recovered from that stroke. It was terrible seeing him lying completely paralysed. All his life he had been so active, had been a tremendously hard worker – a real workaholic. Now he could not even speak. Only his eyes, with their desperate mute pleadings, their soundless screams, revealed the mental anguish he was in.

"It was a relief when he eventually died. A relief to himself, to me, to my younger brother, to all who knew him." Ron paused, there had been a tremor in his voice; with a determined effort he controlled his emotion. "Well, even before Dad's death I received a couple of bids for the small but very successful financial business he had built up throughout his life. I had helped him run and expand the business and now I was the sole inheritor of it. Then another even more generous and tempting offer came in. All these bidders were ruthless predators, ugly vultures, descending on their prey even before it was quite dead.

"Anyway, after Dad's death I sold out." Ron again paused, he smiled disarmingly, "What with my own investments, the money I will receive for the business and will inherit from Dad, I find myself a wealthy man. A man of wealth and leisure."

"An enviable position to be in," Ian remarked.

"Yeah, I know. I do try to appreciate my good fortune, but so far, ironically, I've been far too busy – busier than ever – to really feel its wonder. But, anyway, that's why I'm here tonight. I came over with the international loans director of the bank that bought Dad's business. I've to introduce him to my contacts in London, Edinburgh and Aberdeen and to help him finalise a big and complicated loan which I was negotiating with English and Scottish banks for some North Sea oil companies. I've left him in Aberdeen to worry over the details while I took the chance to have a short break with you this weekend."

"We're glad you did. We're delighted to see you, Ron," Helen said. "Have you booked in at the Inveraldrory Hotel?"

"No, I haven't. I came direct here to see you both first."

"Oh good! In that case there's no need to go to the hotel. You're most welcome to stay here with us. The spare bed's ready and waiting for you."

"Oh, really? Many thanks, Helen." Ron grinned, "I was hoping you'd say that… it almost seems as if you were expecting me."

Helen gently smiled, "Aye, well, perhaps I was."

Puzzled, Ron gazed enquiringly, but when she said no more he continued with his news. "The next exciting thing I've to tell you is that I'm no longer married. My wife has left me for a wealthy yacht-owning boyfriend she's been having an affair with for years. They are living together in the Caribbean. My divorce proceedings are in the hands of my lawyer. You remember my now ex-wife, Cynthia, don't you?"

When Helen and Ian nodded, but diplomatically said nothing, Ron continued, "Yeah, well you know what she was like; she was a stupid, selfish, snobbishly pretentious bitch! I'm much better off without her."

"No," Ian now freely admitted, "we were not all that impressed with her that one time she was over here with you."

"Aye," Helen agreed, "I think you are well rid of her, Ron."

While Ron had been talking, Ian had unobtrusively refilled all their glasses. They now quietly and thoughtfully sipped the whisky.

"So, Ron, there's no obstacle to prevent you becoming Laird of Aldrory Estate now?" Ian asked.

"No... none! Or at least, Campbell-Fotheringay, the present hated laird, is now the only remaining obstacle preventing me from becoming Laird.

"Campbell-Fotheringay is no longer an obstacle," Ian quietly stated. "He's dead!"

"Dead?" Ron shouted. He jumped to his feet. "Dead?... When?... What happened to him?... What's happening to Aldrory Estate?"

"That was our exciting news, Ron," Helen said. "There is now nothing to stop you becoming laird within two years, as I predicted."

Ron flopped down. He tried to contain his excitement as Ian told of Campbell-Fotheringay being drowned in Aldrory River. Helen admired how skilfully Ian omitted telling of his own decisive part in that 'accident', without actually telling any direct lies.

Once the first shock of this unexpected news had somewhat subsided, Ron's astute business brain got to work. "I'll phone the Estate Agents in Inverness tomorrow morning and get details of the sale of Aldrory Estate. I know..."

Laughing, Ian interrupted him, "Tomorrow's the Sabbath, Ron, all the unco guid, God-fearing burghers of Inverness will be at kirk, or in bed nursing their hangovers."

"Oh, darn it, I forgot all about tomorrow being 'the Sabbath'." Ron thought for a few moments. "If it's all right with you, Helen, I'll get up very early on Monday morning; I'll try not to disturb you, and I won't need any breakfast. I'll call in on the Estate Agents in Inverness on my way back to Aberdeen."

"Och, Ron, you won't leave this house on Monday morning, no matter how early, without a good breakfast inside you," Helen declared.

"Thanks a lot, Helen. That's very good of you. Anyway, I've been told, in strict confidence, by various banking contacts in Aberdeen that Campbell-Fotheringay has Aldrory Estate heavily mortgaged and deeply in debt to the Bank of Scotland. Now that he's dead the bank will want to sell off the estate as quickly as possible. Hopefully, there shouldn't be any real difficulty about me buying it."

At seven on Monday morning, after they had all enjoyed a good breakfast, Helen and Ian saw Ron off outside their front door. As he got into his hired car, Helen cheerfully declared, "The next time we see you, Ron, you will be Laird of Aldrory."

"Yeah, I hope so... I darn well hope so. I plan to be back soon. I haven't managed a single day's fishing so far this year. I'll do my damndest to get at least one day on the River Aldrory with you, Ian, before the salmon season's finished."

And he did. Ron returned fifteen days later and got two days' fishing on the River Aldrory. He was delighted to catch three salmon in that attractive river which, laughingly, he now called, "My River… or at least my part of the river." (Lord Kilvert still owned the top three miles of the five and a half mile long river). One of Ron's salmon was a lovely 12 lb hen fish. As she was heavy with spawn he gently returned her to the water where, bemused but unharmed, she quickly recovered and eagerly continued her rudely interrupted urgent journey to her ancestral spawning redds.

The two silvery fresh cock salmon were killed and Ron generously gave them to Helen and Ian. Delightedly, Helen invited Ron to dinner on the Saturday, "We'll have the largest salmon then, I'll give you a better meal than you'd get in the posh hotel you're staying in."

"Oh, really?" Ron said, then, grinning, added, "Yeah, I'm sure you will, Helen."

Helen had a happily hectic time organising the dinner. She was hospitably determined to do her guests proud. Jeannie and Colin Macdonald eagerly accepted the invitation to share in the dinner. They knew from past experience how delightfully the expertly cooked and delicious tasting fresh wild salmon would melt in their mouths.

When Helen set the large dish in the middle of the laden table in Altdour crofthouse's cosy, small sitting room there were cries of praise and admiration. "My, Helen, you've done us real proud again," Jeannie genuinely enthused. "You've excelled yourself!"

"Yeah, Helen, you sure have surpassed yourself this time," Ron wholeheartedly agreed.

The entire 9lb salmon lay cooked to perfection on a bed of silvery tin foil. Knobs of home-made parsley butter steadily melted and spread their glorious golden benevolence over the salmon's bright red, mouth-watering lusciousness. Bunches of dill, leaves of bog myrtle and scatterings of thyme garnished the fish, which was entirely encircled by a chain of delicately thin slices of lemon.

For some moments, held spellbound by the food's beauty, by the feast's succulent promise, all silently stared at the large, thick salmon. Then Ian grinned, "It looks like a stout Lord Provost with his gold chain of office barely able to confine his swollen chest's pompous pride."

Colin laughed, "Aye, and that salmon looks so bonny set oot there it almost seems a shame to carve it up."

"I gathered, and I put that wild mountain thyme on it especially for you, Colin," Helen chuckled.

All the others laughed; they knew that "The Wild Mountain Thyme" was Colin's favourite song, the one he passionately rendered whenever he had partaken of a good few convivial drams.

"You can sit and admire the salmon as long as you want, Colin, but I'm going to eat it now," Ian said.

Laughing boisterously, Colin eagerly held out his plate, "I said it almost seemed a shame to cut it up, but not quite, I'll help you demolish it, Ian. I'll force myself to eat it!"

Later, well into his second helping of salmon, potatoes and vegetables, with beaming eyes and full mouth, Colin remarked with compassionate pity, "Och, I feel real sorry for a' thae poor, sair misguided vegetarians. Imagine refusing to eat such delicious God-sent food as this braw salmon!"

"Aye," Ian readily agreed, "I hardly think a vegetarian soya burger could possibly compare with this really excellent salmon; this noble gift from the Pagan Gods of hunting and fishing."

Later again, as the two wives patiently waited for Ron and their now almost replete husbands to finish off the food on their refilled plates, Jeannie smiled and said, "These men have done full justice to your great cooking, Helen. There's hardly a pick left o' that salmon."

Nor was there – little remained of that once magnificent salmon but its large, bare, neatly ribbed backbone. "Aye," Colin beamed, "we've fair picked the bones clean. That white backbone's now fit tae be a mermaid's comb."

As, once again, both wives waited for their husbands to finish eating – this time their chocolate gateau and ice-cream – Jeannie suddenly gave a gasp of surprise as she glanced at the clock, "Good life, look at the time; we've been sitting at dinner for over two hours!"

"Aye, I know," Ian enthused, "it's great! That's the truly civilised way dinner should be eaten, leisurely and appreciatively and shared with good friends."

"Yeah, I wholeheartedly agree, Ian," Ron said. "It's a terrible insult to the cook, and shows no appreciation of all her hard and noble work, to greedily bolt down her excellent food without properly, lingeringly, tasting it. Such behaviour is uncouth and uncivilised.

"Once I'm installed as Laird of Aldrory I eagerly look forward to sharing many leisurely, convivial, dinners with my good friends (here he happily stared at each of them in turn) at my comfortably renovated and hospitably welcoming Aldrory Lodge."

"We all look forward to that as well," Helen said.

"Aye," Ian grinned, "we'll be sure to keep you to that promise, Ron." He then turned to Colin, "What's the matter, Colin?… don't you agree… don't you think it's great to spend more than two hours eating?"

"Aye, oh aye, I've faired enjoyed this really braw long dinner." He complacently slapped his bulging stomach, "My belly's fair rejoicing. It…"

Beaming, Jeannie interrupted him, "Aye, that belly of yours is nearly bursting apart the seams o' your auld kilt again, even after I've already sewn them up. I've told you before, you ought to go on a strict diet."

"Och, wifie… how dae you expect me to go on a diet when Helen tempts me with such a braw dinner?" Jovially he continued, "I was going to remark that it was a bit o' a shame to spend quite so much time eating when most o' that time could have been devoted to the more precious pleasure o' drinking that sadly neglected Glenlivet instead."

338

"Oh, Colin… Colin," chortled Ron, "you're priceless, you're completely priceless!"

Everyone helped carry the dirty dishes into the overcrowded small scullery. "For this once I'll break my rule and leave the washing-up till the morning," Helen authoritatively decided. "It would spoil the dinner to do that work now." She grinned, "Ian can do the washing up tomorrow morning."

"What was that you said, Helen?" Ian, busy pouring whisky, asked with a smile. "I didn't quite hear you. I'm getting a bit deaf, you know."

Hardly had they got themselves settled, all eagerly and appreciatively sipping generous drams and the men enjoying luxurious cigars, when this pleasant after dinner relaxation was disturbed by the loud and cheery tooting of a car's horn.

"Oh, that'll be Calum and Mary MacLeod and the boys. We told them to come here after dinner this evening," Helen explained. "I hope they've brought Kate Kettle and Kenny with them. It'll do their aunt and uncle good to get out for the evening after the worrying time they've had over the threat of being turned out of their home."

"Yeah, well there's no danger of that happening now; not with me becoming the new laird," Ron said.

Helen and Ian warmly welcomed their six new guests and happily urged them into the house.

For a time the crowded small sitting room was a noisy bedlam of loud, cheerful and sincere greetings. Kate Kettle's hearty laughter merrily joined in with Colin's beaming and booming vivacity. Kenny firmly shook hands with Jeannie, Colin and Ron. With the load of worry that had depressed and agitated him now lifted, he was in fine form. He seemed more cheerful than he had been for many years. He eagerly enquired of each, irrespective of gender, "How are you, my dear fellow? I'm delighted to see you again."

Mary and Calum more quietly, but just as sincerely, greeted, and were greeted by everyone. Their boys, six-year-old Rob and two years younger Norman, were shyly constrained in this crowded world of boisterously noisy adults.

Extra chairs were brought in. More drams were poured. More toasts were loudly given and happily drunk. The boys, lying on the floor, were soon engrossed in the board games they had brought with them.

Once again all had barely got themselves comfortably settled when the cheery tootings of a vehicle again disturbed then. Helen recognised the lively sounds, "Oh, it's the butcher's van. I forgot all about him."

She hurried out and soon returned with her purchases and the butcher. The stout and jovial local butcher cheerily greeted everyone. He was introduced to Ron. After making a not very convincing play of refusing Ian's offer of a dram he relented. Loudly he toasted them all, 'Slainthe mhath', then he gulped half the generous dram down. He, too, smacked appreciative lips; he, too, sincerely, almost reverently, declared, "My, but that's a real braw malt whisky."

"You're late on your rounds tonight. You must be real busy," Jeannie dryly remarked with a quiet smile.

"Och, no. Business is gey poorly. It's nothing like it used to be. I remember when, years ago, in summer there were queues o' visitors every morning at my shop and at the bakers and grocers. It's nothing like that now. I miss a' the cheery customers I used tae get during the Glasgow Fair Fortnight. I used tae have a rare crack with them a'." He took another gulp of whisky then grinned, "But there was one cheery auld Glasgow wifie this July I had a few good jokes with."

His audience listened expectantly. The butcher was as well known for his jokes as for his quality meat. He continued, "Well, the auld wifie asked me if my oranges were real Sevilles. "Och aye, wifie, my oranges are genuine Sevilles; I only sell the best. I sell nane o' yon foreign muck here!" She then admired some o' my best steak, "Och, mister, that looks real braw prime meat. Is it awfa' dear?"

"Och naw, missis," I assured her, "it's nae awfa' deer – it's awfa' coo!"

The ruddy-faced butcher's laughter rang out at his own jokes more loudly than anyone else's.

After the butcher left they all enjoyed a peaceful half hour of quiet relaxation, of pleasant chatting, and, on the part of Colin and Ian, of quietly determined drinking. Then the noise of an approaching vehicle once more disturbed then. "Who can this by now, I wonder?" Helen asked, smiling, as she rose and, with Ian, made for the door.

They warmly welcomed the new visitors; They were Jamie Gordon, the shepherd on Ardgie Estate and his wife, Bella.

"Och, we didn't ken you were having a party," Bella gasped as she saw all the other guests already crowded into the small room. "We just thought it was aboot time we visited you, Helen, we haven't seen you for months, ye ken."

"Aye, I know, Bella, I was thinking about you just this morning. I was hoping – was expecting – to see you soon. We're delighted to have you both visit us again. We'll soon make room for the two of you."

"Aye, surely you'll manage tae squeeze in twa neat wee craiturs like Bella an' me," roared Jamie as, following his wife's large, homely and comfortably buxom figure, he moved his solid bulk into the centre of the room.

They were introduced to Ron MacDonald, the only person they did not know. They were somewhat awed on being told that Ron was going to be the new laird of Aldrory Estate. However Ron soon put them at ease with his customary American style of friendly, enthusiastic informality.

Colin beamed at Jamie, "I'm glad you didn't know aboot this party, Jamie, or nae doot you would have brought that damned squeeze-box o' yours that you misguidedly call a musical instrument. We're spared that ordeal, thank God!"

"Och, I suppose I'll have to endure that awful noise you make with those damned bagpipes o' yours instead, won't I?" James asked with a good-natured laugh.

Ron, too, laughed, "Oh, never mind what he says, Colin, I'm keen to hear you play your pipes again. I love bagpipe music. I'm going to learn to play them once I'm settled in as laird."

"That's great, Ron" Colin said. "You can join wee Rob. I'm giving him some tuition with the chanter." He turned and smiled at the boy, "Did you bring your practice chanter with you, Rob?"

"No," Rob murmured, "no, I forgot to bring it."

His mother fondly chuckled, "You mean you were too shy to bring it, weren't you?"

"Gee, it's a pity you didn't bring it," Ron said. "But never mind, once Colin has taught you to play the chanter you can teach me, eh? Is that a deal, Rob?"

The boy shyly grinned up at 'The Laird' and violently nodded his head.

"Meantime, I want to hear Colin playing his pipes," Ron demanded.

"Och aye, I'll play them soon, after I've had a few more drams. I play them much better then."

"Aye," Jamie laughed, "and they sound a damned sight better tae your listeners when they've had a guid few drams tae!"

Ian spirited up, and generously filled, another two glasses. He handed them to Bella and Jamie, who had managed, with much laughter and squeezing, to get themselves seated on the overcrowded and sadly sagging old sofa.

"The more the merrier!" Jeannie laughed.

"Aye, the more the cosier!" Katie Kettle cried.

"Aye, as long as we've a' got room tae lift oor drinking hand," Bella bellowed, "that's a' that matters!"

Mary and Calum MacLeod got themselves comfortably seated on the floor beside their two boys who were helplessly giggling at the antics of the amusing adults.

Kenny, languidly stretched out in Ian's armchair by the fireside (he was the only person granted the great privilege of sitting in 'himself's' chair), said little; he contented himself with beaming benevolently on all the merry company and now and again encouragingly and approvingly exclaiming, "That's right, my dear fellows, that's the style, drink up!... drink up!" He was not backward in taking his own sage advice!

Helen, discreetly sipping her modest dram, also benevolently smiled around on the happy guests, their obvious happiness warmed her with a gentle glow of deep contentment.

Ian glanced at her and they exchanged a quick, private smile; he too was happy to see all their guests so happy. For a few solemn moments he thought of his act of murder which had made this happiness possible, had brought this deserved contented security to Kate and Kenny, had ended their miserable anxiety over the threat of eviction; had brought a much more secure future to Mary and Calum and to their boys; had enabled Ron to achieve his dream of regaining his ancestral roots and of improving the prospects of all those on his Highland Estate. Although employed by Lord Kilvert on his Ardgie Estate and therefore not so directly involved, the other four guests might in the future also benefit from Ian's illegal deed. Meanwhile they were honestly and unselfishly happily aglow in the reflected happiness of those others, just as Helen and he were. Yes, he again assured himself, my savage act truly was justified. That one death, that entirely un-mourned death, has brought much happiness and peace of mind. Yes, my conscience is clear, my killing of Campbell-Fotheringay was like my killing of Nazis during the war, a fully justified deed.

Another general loud burst of laughter hurled Ian out from his inner thoughts and back amongst the happy company.

The generous drams flowed. The unnoticed hours flew. Whisky-loosened voices rose higher in animated talk, in song and ever-louder laughter. Colin often marched to and fro in the garden playing his pipes. Good old Kate Kettle eagerly helped Helen put the kettle on and soon tea, sandwiches and scones were hospitably handed around, were appreciatively accepted and quickly disposed of.

"Whit, nae shortbread or black bun, Helen?" Jamie roared. "Whit kind o' Hogmanay is this?"

"Aye, it's just like Hogmanay, isn't it?" Jeannie merrily agreed.

"Aye, it's gey hard… it's near impossible, tae believe it's only three months tae Christmas and New Year," Kate said. "It only seems a few months since last Christmas."

"I ken," Colin said, "it's just further proof of us a' getting gey auld."

"Aye, it's incredible, it's disconcerting, how quickly the time passes," agreed Ian.

There was a short silent pause while all the older people nodded and sighed in solemn agreement.

Rob and Norman looked on with puzzled, frowning faces, they could not understand those old adults; to these young boys the three months of waiting till Christmas was an unimaginably long immensity.

The silence was ended by Jamie's mighty laugh, "Och, anyway, it's just as weel to enjoy a few guid dress rehearsals like this before the real Hogmanay gallops up on us like a wild kelpie and droons us in a loch o' whisky."

"Gosh," Ron enthusiastically declared, "I sure look forward to spending my first Highland Hogmanay with you all here this year."

Helen smiled, "That's great, Ron. You can stay with us; the spare bed will be ready and waiting for you."

Mary MacLeod, unaccustomed to drinking much whisky, had many uncontrollable fits of giggles as she merrily joined in the evening's joviality. It was a real treat for her to get away from the caravan for a while and to be with all those genuine friends. With lively, though un-tuneful eagerness she loudly joined in the singing. Her husband, Calum, not much of a whisky drinker either, was also benignly feeling the effects of all his drams. His impressively large, bushy black beard showily jutted and exuberantly wagged in accompaniment to his loud and keen, but also rather out of tune, singing. Anxious to keep the good old Scots songs alive he delighted in joining in as, in turn, Colin and Jamie went through their extensive repertoires, (Colin fairly set the 'Wild Mountain Thyme' vigorously blooming). And each time Bella sent 'The Star o' Rabbie Burns' sparkling into blazing orbit, Calum's unbridled enthusiasm matched hers. As the night wore on and the whisky continued to flow, they got ever more sentimental and maudlin in their rendering, in their homage to their beloved hero.

The food and tea helped partially sober Mary and Calum as they sat together on the carpet, leaned against the rather unsteady wall, and beamed around with benevolent grins. Mary suddenly noticed that she could not see her youngest son. Anxiously she asked his older brother, "Where's Norman?"

Giving a mischievous grin, Rob crawled over the carpet and pointed under the table behind the old sofa. "There's Norman!" He delightedly giggled.

The small boy was curled up and asleep in the dog's wickerwork basket. He companionably shared the large, comfortable bed with Glen, the Collie. One arm was affectionately stretched over the good-natured dog. Corrie, the terrier who normally shared the basket with Glen, lay outside with tolerant though occasionally sighing, resignation.

As, smiling, Calum gently lifted his sleepily protesting son out of the basket, his uncle Kenny laughed unrestrainedly and merrily declared, "Och, Norman, my dear wee fellow, you are far too young to be found lying senseless under the table!"

"Aye, Norman, boy," Colin said, "you better leave that space under the table for us older, but perhaps not wiser, adults."

"Oh dear, what time is it?" a suddenly conscience-stricken Mary asked. "It must be long after the boys' bedtime. Oh Calum, we'll need to take them home and get them tucked into bed."

"I don't want to go to bed. I'm not sleepy," Rob stoutly declared while he desperately attempted to stifle another insistent yawn.

As he snuggled cosily into his father's arms, little Norman, not to be outdone by his older brother, managed to blink open heavy eyes and defiantly state, "No, I'm not sleepy, too! I don't want to go home. I want to stay with Glen."

The fondly smiling parents were as obviously unwilling to leave the ongoing festivities and retreat to their isolated caravan as their boys were. The thought of going at this hour, in the dead of night's dreary darkness, to that coldly lonesome caravan was most un-alluring.

"I suppose Jamie and me should be heading for hame tae," Bella said. Despite her best effort she failed to make this suggestion sound convincing.

Her husband cast her a disapproving frown, "Och, Bella, we're gey fine where we are. I'm sure Helen and Ian don't want rid o' us. They would tell us if they did!"

"Aye, we would… we certainly would," laughed Ian.

"What about your two bairns, Bella, is someone looking after them?" Mary asked.

"Oh aye, my sister an' her man are staying with us for twa days. They're baby-sitting for us tonight."

With a bright smile, Helen came to the rescue, "Och, there's no need for anyone to leave. The boys can stay here in the big spare bed tonight, Mary. They'll be no trouble."

Rob's face beamed, his eyes and voice desperately pleaded, "Oh yes, Mum, let us sleep here, please… please!"

Despite his sleepiness, wee Norman caught the excitement of his brother's eagerness. He forced open his eyes and added his pleading to Rob's.

"Oh aye, all right, you can sleep here," their mother, easily persuaded to do what she really wanted to do, smilingly conceded.

Excitedly, Rob went up to Ian, "Uncle Ian, can I get a book to take up to bed with me?"

"Aye, of course you can. You know where my library is, don't you? Just run there and get a book."

As Rob ran to the door his brother demanded to be set down. With desperate urgency he ran after Rob into the enchanting room across the passage.

"I think the book's just an excuse for them to get into that 'study' of yours, Ian. I well remember how, as a boy, I loved to get into that unique and fascinating room." Calum laughed, "Aye, and I still love to go into it!"

"I should hope you do, Calum. Something would have gone seriously wrong with you if you had entirely lost your great childhood love of that room. Surely every adult with any 'soul', with any imagination, must try his utmost to retain something of the feeling of wonder, of magic, that room gave him in his childhood. To lose that magic, that wonder, is to start withering to the grave."

"The Child is father of the Man, eh?"

Ian grinned, "Aye, exactly Calum."

From the comfort of 'himself's' deep old armchair, Uncle Kenny smiled up at them, "That's right, my dear fellows. You know what the Good Book says, don't you?... 'Unless you go back and become like little children you shall not enter the kingdom of God'."

They entered Ian's 'study'. They halted. They grinned. "Och well, obviously Rob and Norman are completely captivated by this room's magic," Calum said.

Norman was on his knees gazing wonderingly at the fencing green frog as it defiantly kept the amazed stoat at bay with its large, sharp, darning needle sword. The young boy held his face close to these amazing animals and studied them with riveted attention. He passionately admired the bright-eyed wee frog for its astounding bravery and resolution.

Rob, with all an older brother's two vast years of superiority, disdainfully and elaborately ignored the silly wee frog. He pretended to despise it; oh, it was good enough to childishly amuse his kid brother, but was unworthy of his much more mature attention. Instead, motionlessly transfixed, he stood and gazed at the impressively large head of the Royal Stag high on the wall. He unblinkingly stared and bravely returned that noble, if somewhat dusty and moth-eaten, beast's vastly superior monocled stare.

As more of the adults crowded into the gloriously unusual room, Calum, cheerily asked, "Well boys, do you like this place?"

His youngest son instantly answered with ecstatic eagerness. "Oh yes, Dad, it's magic!"

"Yes, Dad, it's magic," Rob confirmed. "It's like a... a wizard's magic den!"

Ron laughed triumphantly, "There, Ian, the truth from the 'mouths of babes and sucklings!' I've always told you this room is your den, not your study!"

"Aye, all right, Ron, I give in. I surrender. I accept the bairn's proof. From now on this room is my den."

"Your magic den, Uncle Ian?" Rob quietly and shyly asked.

"Aye, Rob, my... and childhood's magic den."

Norman wanted to be held up to see the stag properly. His father lifted him.

"Are those your medals, Uncle Ian?" Rob asked, pointing at the two iron crosses hanging on their ribbons from the stag's antlers.

"No, Rob, they're medals taken from dead German officers during the war."

Staring wide-eyed, Rob asked, "Did you kill any Germans, Uncle Ian?"

"Aye, oh aye, I killed some Germans."

"Oh... why?" wee Norman asked.

At loss for a suitable answer, Ian hesitated then said, "Oh well, you see, Norman, I had to. Those Germans were trying to kill me."

"Oh... why?"

"Because Uncle Ian was trying to kill them!" Colin jovially intervened. Smiling, he reminisced, "I remember when our son, Alasdair, was a bairn just wee Norman's age he asked those same awkward 'whys?' in this room."

Calum laughed, "Yes, and I believe I asked exactly those same 'whys?' in here, too."

"Oh well, let's hope that by the time Rob and Norman grow up, no soldiers will be killing other soldiers," Mary fervently said.

The others murmured, "Yes, let's hope so." But the more experienced older ones murmured it with much less hope of that pious wish of Mary's ever coming about.

"By the way, talking about medals, did Colin and you, Ian, get awarded any special medals for your long and gallant war service and your," here Ron grinned, "noble war wounds?"

Ian grinned in reply, "No, Ron, we got no special medals, we only got the usual campaign medals: the 1939–45 star, the North Africa star and the Italy one. No, we didn't get the Victoria Cross and bar."

Ian winked at Colin, and on cue, Colin took up the hoary old army joke. "No, we didn't get the highest award, the VC and bar – all we got was VD and scar!"

Thankfully the puzzled boys did not understand that joke, did not share in the adult's laughter.

"Come on, boys, let's see what books we can find you," Ian said. "One's with lots of pictures of birds and animals, eh?"

"And of fish and fishing?" Rob, a keen, but novice angler, asked. Ten minutes later, Mary and Helen led the boys, each firmly grasping two books, upstairs to bed.

More and yet more pleasantly unmeasured carefree hours flew by. All the happy revellers in the crowded small room floated along on a billowing ocean of conviviality. This ocean had its high crests, had its low troughs. The crests were boisterous with song and laughter; the troughs were subdued with sleepy snores. Ian described it as, "A joyous time of boozing and snoozing."

Colin and Ian were not guilty of the habit – the crime? – of snoozing. This drinking time was too precious to waste on sleep. While others snored, they happily retold the well-loved old tales, once more laughed over the familiar old jokes. Although they had drunk much more whisky than anyone else they showed no sign of insobriety. They were steady on their feet and their voices were un-slurred. Only the vivid, steamy, furnace glow of their enlarged scarlet faces and the gleaming brilliance of their eyes revealed to anyone knowledgeable in the ways of Highland drinking the impressive, or reprehensible, amount of whisky they had enjoyed.

Once again Helen and Kate handed around gratefully received, and slightly sobering, scones, sandwiches and tea.

When all had finished eating, Mary giggled, "What are we going to do now?... go home?"

Her suggestion was greeted with jeers and loud derision. Ron was vocal in leading the protest, "Gee, no, Mary, none of us want to go home." Turning to Colin he demanded, "Come on, Colin, it's time you played your pipes again. You promised to play something special, didn't you?"

"Aye, I know I did. I was playing it when you were sound asleep; your snores were a damned sight louder than my music!"

"Oh gee, Colin, you don't expect me to believe that, do you?"

Colin beamed good-naturedly, "Aye, all right, I'll play something special, something I've composed for you, Ron."

Ron sat up. He gasped. "Oh, really? Have you actually composed a pipe tune for me?"

"Aye, I have. Here it is, Ron. It's a tune to celebrate you becoming the new laird." He handed over the handwritten musical score. "Keep it. It's a present to you. We've all signed it."

Ron was deeply moved. He keenly examined the score. It was entitled, 'Aldrory's Welcome to The New Laird'. He excitedly jumped up. "Gosh, thanks, Colin. Thanks a lot. Thank you all. I sure will treasure this wonderful present." He warmly shook Colin's hand. "Come on now, let's hear this tune expertly played by its great composer."

As they all started to move towards the door, Ian instructed, "Everyone take their dram with them and we'll drink a toast after Colin's played his tune."

There were gasps of surprise as they discovered that the reign of the long dark night was over. It was dawn – that strange, uncertain time which was neither truly night nor yet truly day. How still, how solemnly and mysteriously still, were the shadowy loutish trees as the silent battle was fought between light and dark. The entire garden was suffused with a dim, mournful light.

Slowly, reluctantly, night conceded victory to dawn's luminous grace, to its eager, translucent freshness. The defiantly exultant notes of Colin's jaunty new pipe tune completed the rout of ugly night and vague insubstantial things became benignly solid.

As – by popular demand – Colin again played 'Aldrory's Welcome to The New Laird' a shaft of sunlight beamed almost horizontally in from the East and lit up the group of ancient Scots Pines on the slope behind the garden. The Eden fresh golden glowing light put new life into those gnarled and rugged and grimly tenacious old trees. The flaked grey bark of thick trunks received a transfusion of warm red blood and the upper branches blushed a lively virgin pink while the bottle-green pine needles were transmuted to an iridescent purplish sheen. Those noble old trees were now a magically glowing hymn of praise to the glory of the newborn day.

To wild acclaim – especially Ron's – Colin finished playing. With his bagpipes tucked under his left arm he gratefully accepted his well-filled glass from Ian.

Rob and wee Norman had been wakened by the pipes. They stared out of the bedroom window, then, breathlessly anxious not to miss all the fun, came cascading down the steep stairs.

Norman, cosily cocooned in a tartan rug, was lovingly held by his tired but happily content mother. Rob, also snugly wrapped in a warm rug, was securely held by his fondly smiling father. Each boy firmly gripped a glass of lemonade in his uncovered right hand.

When all were silent, Ian raised his dram high and loudly proposed a toast: "Here's to Ronald MacDonald, the new Lair of Aldrory… and here's to a new dawn for Aldrory."

Chapter Twenty-Eight

Three years have passed.

Three times skeins of spring-excited geese have arrowed high overhead, have driven their sharp wedges through the vast empty skies, accurately heading for the Magnetic North.

Three times eider ducks have returned to sheltered sea bays and enchanted them with the sad sweetness of their delicate crooning.

Three times swallows have unerringly returned to the familiar cosiness of their nesting sites inside Altdour Croft's old stable and have thrilled the air with ethereal beauty.

Three years have passed since Ron MacDonald became the new laird, became the owner of the twenty thousand acres of Aldrory Estate. He lived up to his promise. He was the best laird Aldrory had ever had. Aldrory was now a more prosperous and secure place for the increased numbers who lived and worked there.

On a perfect evening in May 1987, Helen and Ian, with their two dogs again eagerly leading the way, strolled down the rough track through the front garden. They passed the two mysteriously alert sentinel rowan trees, both delicately clad in fresh, tender, green. Then they passed the even more delicate pale green drooping grace of silver birch trees. They leaned on the welcoming security of the old gate's sun-warmed wood. Ian struck a match and once again leisurely enjoyed the simple, deep, pleasure of getting the tobacco in his favourite old pipe well alight.

Swallows gracefully swooped around the trees and low above their heads. They smiled at one another. They breathed a gentle, a perfectly synchronised sigh. They were happy.

Although he was now, at 67 years, an old-age pensioner, passing time had made little difference to Ian's appearance apart from turning his hair and his ever more bushy beard a purer white. Helen, too, was little changed; perhaps her petite body seemed a little more frail, perhaps there was the suggestion of a slight stoop.

As their gaze wandered over the attractive scene spread out before them they thought of the welcome developments in Aldrory Glen.

Although its thick shelterbelt of trees hid Aldrory Lodge from them, they knew how Ron, spending freely and whenever possible employing local tradesmen, had had that shooting lodge extensively renovated, redecorated and refurnished. He had turned one large room into a combined study and library and here all his father's luxurious sets of handsome, leather-bound books were attractively arrayed and, at long last, were being keenly taken down and lovingly read.

Ron had also spared no expense in getting the lodge's shamefully neglected gardens back into shape. The overgrown old flowerbeds were cleaned up and were blooming. The walled vegetable and fruit garden was again productive.

A cook/housekeeper was employed and her husband worked as gardener/handyman. A younger man was employed as assistant gardener and, during the fishing and deer stalking seasons, as ghillie and pony-man. His attractive 'partner' was also employed; she helped in the lodge and, being a passionate horse lover, helped look after, and was allowed to ride, the two stalking ponies.

Two gamekeepers were employed on the estate. One of these was Calum MacLeod. Rapidly gaining experience, he was being groomed to become head gamekeeper when the older 'keeper retired in a few years' time. After his Uncle Kenny died from a massive heart attack two years ago, Calum and Mary and their two boys had, at her urgent request, moved in with his aunt, Kate Kettle. Their caring, loving, if at times rather too lively, company helped Kate get over her deep grief for the death of her brother. Later, Ron generously bore much of the cost of building on a 'granny flat' to the end of the house. Comfortably ensconced in the independence of her own place, Kate Kettle was forever putting on the kettle in her neat, small kitchen and contentedly pouring innumerable hospitable cups of tea.

It was also Ron's financial help, together with government grants and loans, which enabled Calum and Mary to have a holiday chalet built near the large residential caravan which had been their home and which they now rented out to visitors.

From where they lazily leant against the garden gate, Helen and Ian clearly saw that new chalet and, looking further down the glen, they saw other new buildings.

The old, large and rambling Church of Scotland Inveraldrory Manse (which had been built when a minister could afford to employ a number of obsequious and miserably paid servants) was put up for sale as soon as a neat modern bungalow, full of (at the minister's wife's insistence) labour-saving devices, was built to replace the old manse. Ron immediately bought the manse. It too was extensively and expensively renovated. The old tables and coach house were altered and greatly extended. Now buildings had been, and were still being, built on the glebe land close to the old manse. This complex of buildings was now a different type of spiritual centre; a place devoted to developing and encouraging native Highland artistic and cultural talents and awareness.

Ron had been most impressed by the talents and keenness of the teachers and students at the Gaelic language and cultural centre in Skye. They inspired him to set up this centre in Aldrory. Its first year had been a great success. There were more applications than available places. New classrooms and extensions to the hostel accommodation were now being built. Ron had been amazed and delighted at the number of young people keen to learn about and keep alive the old traditions of Highland bagpipe, fiddle and clarsach music. They were also determined to keep the Gaelic language and ancient folklore alive.

Although finding it a difficult language to master, Ron resolutely attended the beginners' Gaelic class. He was more successful in learning to play the bagpipes under Colin MacDonald's patient tuition.

Colin, too, was now a retired – or rather a semi-retired – pensioner. In addition to his state pension he received a reasonable, though hardly generous, pension from Lord Kilvert. However, Jeannie and he also enjoyed the benefit of living rent-free in a house on his lordship's Ardgie estate. This small house was conveniently nearer to Inveraldrory village.

Colin, becoming ever more a (usually) uncomplaining martyr to the cruel torture of the rheumatism in his legs, was delighted to be free of the exhausting demands of West Highland deer stalking with its many tiring miles of walking and climbing, its constant soaking rains and its crawling through soggy peat bogs. He was well content to hand over these 'pleasures' to younger, keener and fitter men. He sometimes helped as a ghillie at the much less demanding salmon fishing. Thankfully his fingers were, so far, only very slightly affected by rheumatics and he spent many happy hours teaching piping to local children and to pupils at the new cultural centre.

Jeannie, too, taught for some hours each week at that centre. While other tutors looked after the more abstract and aesthetic pleasure she attended to the more physical and sensual, but no less real, pleasures of food and eating. She happily passed on her extensive knowledge of, and practical skills with, traditional Highland cooking. Her sumptuous dishes were made from the simple wholesome ingredients, which had been widely used by all Highland housewives until the recent past. Her own favourite was her really thick, really nourishing, Scotch broth, with all the vegetables from their own organic garden. Colin's favourite was her mouth-wateringly delicious venison casserole.

To young housewives keen to acquire something of Jeannie's skills it was a revelation to see what a tasty and filling meal she could make from a few large herring when these humble, sadly neglected, almost despised, fish were thickly coated with real oatmeal and expertly grilled.

Her most difficult challenge was to persuade younger women that gutting and cleaning fish and even gutting and skinning rabbits or hares, was not really such a terribly revolting task. Demonstrating her skills with a sharp gutting knife and her strong, dexterous fingers she repeated her granny's saying; "If your bairn's, your man's and your ain bellies are rumbling badly enough wi' hunger you'll soon forget onie fancy ladylike qualms aboot gutting fish an' skinning beasts."

Jeannie willingly shared her knowledge of Highland herbs, berries and seaweeds. She sometimes made nettle soup and, more rarely, soup made from a variety of seaweeds.

Colin, notoriously conservative in his eating habits, occasionally tried a few spoonfuls of his wife's nettle soup, but resolutely refused to touch her seaweed soup.

He well knew how explosively violent certain seaweeds' laxative properties were!

Over the years, Ian and Colin had often laughed with unrestrained reminiscent mirth as they recalled a certain incident involving this powerful property of seaweeds.

It happened in the fateful summer of 1939 shortly before they were called to the colours with their Seaforth Highlanders Territorial Army unit. Finlay McPherson, a sixty-four year old bachelor, was the butt of their mischievous youthful ploy.

Despite his married sister's deep misgivings and frequently repeated warnings, old Finlay was determined to end his lonely bachelor state. He was going to marry the thirty-one year old woman who helped with his housework. She, with scheming, voluptuous allurement, assured him that the thirty-year difference in their ages was of no importance. After a final furious row, old Finlay's sister washed her hands of him, declaring, "There's no fool like an old fool! You can stew in your own juice!"

Finlay secretly worried that his vital old juices might not rise to boiling point. On his stag night binge he un-soberly ashamedly admitted his fears of not being able to satisfy his young bride on their wedding night.

"Och, don't worry, Finlay, we'll fix you up," Colin solemnly assured him. "Ian and me will prepare a sure tonic for you, one made from my granny's reliable auld recipe."

Concealing his merriment, Ian joined in, "Aye, Finlay, that sex tonic is made from herbs and nettles and berries. Just you drink a glass of it on the evening of your wedding night and you'll be fine. It's guaranteed to put lead in your pencil!"

Finlay innocently and sincerely thanked them.

Trustingly he drank the 'sex tonic' they gave him early on his wedding night.

Colin and Ian hid behind a drystane dyke at the back of Finlay's crofthouse. While they expectantly waited they kept company with a half bottle of whisky. They did not have long to wait. The back door suddenly opened and then loudly banged shut. Peering over the dyke they grinned delightedly as they saw old Finlay desperately rush to the outside lavatory. His bare and scrawny shanks gleamed wanly pale in the moonlight. He was wearing only a pair of un-laced boots and a collarless grey flannel shirt. The long tails of his thick shirt flapped wildly above his knees as, with the seaweed in that special 'sex tonic' wildly erupting its laxative effects in poor Finlay's churning bowels, he pulled the lavatory door open and dashed inside.

Ian and Colin valiantly struggled to suppress their laughter as they heard thunderously loud noises come from the lavatory and then saw old Finlay reappear and hurry back to his house.

They comfortably resettled themselves behind the dyke. Their whisky was almost finished when they heard the back door once more urgently open and saw poor old Finlay again dash for the lavatory.

When he had finished and was opening the house door, Colin and Ian could not longer restrain themselves. They burst into loud laughter. Colin shouted, "Oh, Finlay, it's a terrible pity your wedding night is spoiled!... It's a shame it's sae wet and windy!" Loudly, hilariously, Ian joined in, "Aye, Finlay, it's a right pity you've got the back door trot!"

Shaking his fist at them, Finlay furiously shouted, "Och damn you, you young deils!... Wait till I get hold o' you, you pair o' bloody buggers!"

His frustrated young bride's plaintive voice quavered from the bedroom window, "Oh, Finlay, who's there? Who are you talking to? What's keeping you? Come up to bed at once!"

Submissively her new 'lord and master' started to obey. Then, holding the house door open, he hesitated. With angry curses he frantically shambled back to the lavatory. The bang of the slamming door was almost immediately echoed by a dramatic explosion inside the lavatory.

The insistent sound of loud, intensive hammering disturbed the lovely evening's peaceful calm. Lazily leaning on the garden gate, Helen and Ian smiled. They were pleased with further evidence of the encouraging regeneration taking place in Aldrory. Helen said, "The builders are fairly working late at Nigel's place, aren't they?"

"Aye, they are. They're fair getting on with that building."

They stared at the Lilliputian figures crawling over the skeletal triangular timber ribs of the roof of the large extension rapidly rising at the back of an old house further down Aldrory Glen. Although welcome, this particular development had, for Ian, a certain sadness, for it came about through the death of his older brother, William. There had been no great love, no deep communion, between the brothers; still Ian had felt William's death surprisingly strongly. Of course, as one gets older, the death of anyone you know is always a shock; is a grim reminder of how tenuous is your own grip on life.

The last eighteen months of William MacLean's life had been painful and distressing. He had been diagnosed as having cancer. Extensive tests discovered the cancer to be malignantly widespread and inoperable. He had, understandably taken the news badly. He was incensed that he, a lifelong teetotaller and non-smoker, had cancer in his lungs, his stomach, his liver, while his dissolute brother, Ian, a lifelong drinker and smoker, kept in robust health. It was grossly unfair. Why had God so unjustly inflicted this curse on him? It was enough to make him, who had been a convinced and assiduously practising Christian all his life, despairingly doubt the truth of the loving kindness of God, or even of His very existence.

During some of their distressful discussions, Ian, despite his sincere compassion for his dying brother, could not help being secretly amused at the immense irony of him, a convinced atheist, trying as convincingly as he could to assure his brother that, after all, his atheism might be wrong, there might be an afterlife in which William would enjoy heavenly bliss. And another – a terribly sad – extra irony, was that poor William, a convinced Christian, was now, when faced with the stark reality of imminent death, having terrible doubts. Trembling, stammering, and with his anguished eyes pleading for reassurance, he asked, "Oh, Ian, what if you've been right all the time and there's... there's no God? What if my lifelong beliefs are… are nothing but… but foolish illusions?"

Deeply moved by such anguish, Ian, as forcefully as he could, reassured his brother. "Oh no, William," (William never allowed anyone to call him 'Bill') "your God must exist. It would be too cruel of Him to allow all who believe in Him to be so grievously misled."

When death finally, and mercifully, claimed William it left these profound – or profoundly ridiculous – questions unanswered. It always does.

William MacLean's son, Nigel, came home from India six months before his father died. These months were a terribly stressful time for him as he helplessly witnessed his father's slow, painful death, his protracted dying made worse by his ever increasing resentment of the unfairness of him being afflicted with this hideous, this undeserved, disease, his increasing hatred of those in robust health, his deeply despairing religious doubts. Nigel, a non-believer, was too young, was too openly and honestly sincere, to be able to reassure his father with the palliatives of a hope which he himself could not honestly believe in.

His father's will left Nigel the family home in Aldrory Glen and most of his investments. Nigel was now well off. His mother already owned their comfortable flat in Edinburgh's fashionable Morningside and was also well provided for.

Now came the strain of living with his grieving mother. Nigel suspected her grief of being more a conventional show of what was expected of a new widow rather than being a sincerely felt emotion. There was a steady, at times violent, conflict between Nigel's honest youthful intolerance of, and his mother's passionate belief in obeying societies conventions, of always doing the 'correct' things. There were many acrimonious scenes, inflamed by their vastly different natures, as house-proud Mrs MacLean endeavoured to keep the house, which was no longer hers, neat and spotlessly clean.

It was an immense relief to them both when she went to live in her Edinburgh flat. There she would enjoy a strictly conventional life in the dour respectability of Morningside.

Nigel was excited by the cultural centre Ron was developing at the old manse. Early on during his time in India, he had thought it would be wonderful to establish a Buddhist centre back in Aldrory Glen. How eagerly he had studied and had tried to believe in that alluring religion. He had been greatly impressed by the deep, simple goodness and profound, unworldly, wisdom of most of the Buddhists he had studied with. But yet he could not believe. He found that the appalling poverty of the mass of the population forced him to agree with Karl Marx, that "Religion is the opium of the people."

Sorrowfully, he remembered how heart-breakingly terrible had been the despair of other Indian friends, devout Hindu disciples of Mahatma Gandhi and his passionate advocacy of Peace and non-violence, when they discovered that their country (and Pakistan) were going to devote unlimited resources to developing their own atomic bombs.

Nigel now despaired of and was becoming cynical about all religions. He was learning!... or was he losing his way?

Under the guidance of Ian he had learned to discuss serious subjects seriously, but also to enliven the seriousness with wit and humour and – above all – whisky. He remembered Ian saying, "As I get older I feel increasingly sure that the comedian's frivolity is much wiser than all the priest's theology. I'm also sure that Groucho Marx was a much greater man than Karl Marx. Karl's theories unfortunately brought misery to millions. Groucho's inspired genius brought laughter to millions, and, fortunately, his old films still do."

Nigel mirthfully told of how when returning home from India he had spent a couple of nights with a friend in the Ibrox district of Glasgow. They went to a public house not far from Rangers football stadium. Obviously most of the drinkers in this pub were supporters of the famous local football team. Blue and white scarves were conspicuous. One typical Glaswegian, short, stocky, and with pugnaciously jutting jaw, came over to them; he addressed Nigel, "A've no' seen you here afore, Jimmie."

"No," Nigel replied, "this is my first time in this pub."

"Aye, that's whit a thought. A wid ha' remembered ye if you'd been here afore."

He stared at Nigel with bleary bloodshot eyes then raised his pint glass and took a deep satisfying gulp. Lowering the glass he wiped his mouth with the back of his hand then gave a loud, appreciative burp.

Nigel was prepared for the next question. It came as expected. "Seen as you're a stranger here, Jimmie, whit a want tae ken is... are ye a Protestant or a Catholic?"

Nigel gently smiled, "No, I'm neither! Actually I'm a Buddhist."

His interrogator was momentarily taken aback, "It's a' very weel saying you're a bloody Buddhist, Jimmie... but whit a want tae ken is... are you a Protestant Buddhist or a Catholic Buddhist?"

Despite what he had light-heartedly told that Glasgow bigot, Nigel was not a Buddhist. He found the belief that every creature, even the humblest insect, had an immortal soul and an inviolable right to live, absolutely impossible to believe in. Smiling, he wondered did every Highland midge have an immortal soul?... Was it morally wrong to kill one midge?... Was it a sin? He doubted if even the most devout Buddhist would be able to refrain from viciously swiping at a savagely tormenting cloud of these tiny terrors. Anyone who could endure their maddening attentions with stoic equanimity must indeed be a saint.

Nigel also found it impossible to believe in that other tenet, which was a core belief for most Buddhists and Hindus – reincarnation.

He clearly remembered how, during one of their many discussions, Helen had emotionally and most movingly told of when, as a young student nurse many years ago, she had witnessed the drawn out agony and then the terrible death from meningitis of a lovely three-year-old girl. That harrowing experience shook her belief in there being a God. How could a God, whom Christians assure us is benevolent, is a God of loving kindness, have created that hideous disease, meningitis? Why did He create that ghastly evil which attacked the spinal cord and then the brain of innocent young children? How could He inflict that terrible torture on these innocents? How could he listen to them screaming in agony hour after hour, day after day, until a desperate dose of morphine killed them and mercifully ended their unbearable suffering?

Sobbing compassionate tears, Helen passionately declared, "If there is a God, he's got a lot to answer for! How will he ever be able to look these tortured children in the face? Will he beg their forgiveness"

There was a solemn silence, then Ian, remembering some of the sights he had seen in Germany at the end of the war, said, "Aye, and wasn't Jesus supposed to have protectively ordered, with deep, tender, compassion, 'Suffer the little children to come unto me?' Well, where was Jesus during those terrible years when thousands – hundreds of thousands – of innocent children were suffering in the German Concentration Camps before being callously and methodically 'disposed of' in the gas chambers and furnaces?"

Again there was a solemn silence, which Ian again ended. He thoughtfully remarked, "There is only one doctrine which explains these terrible evils inflicted on innocent children – reincarnation; the belief in the transmigration of each individual soul from life to life in an almost endless progression. Those children were suffering for the vile evils they committed in previous lives. After suffering for these sins in existence after existence they will eventually, having atoned for them, reach a state of near bliss – a state of Nirvana." He paused, he smiled, "It's just a great pity that most Europeans, including myself, find it utterly impossible to believe in this."

"I know," Nigel said. "I'm the same. But, in India, I couldn't help being terribly impressed by how deeply the doctrine of reincarnation was believed in. How utterly certain those millions were of its absolute truth."

"Aye, I know, Nigel, I can understand you being so impressed by that," Ian said. "But, of course, the fact of vast numbers believing in anything is absolutely no guarantee of its truth, is it? After all, not so many centuries ago almost everyone was convinced that the Earth was flat and that it was the centre of the Universe, with all the other stars revolving around it. We don't think that's true now, do we?" He grinned, "Although no doubt some still do."

Helen had regained her composure; now, putting her handkerchief away, she grinned impishly, "I thought 'Nirvana' was a soothing ointment?"

Grinning in turn, Ian replied, "Aye, well in a sense that's exactly what it is."

Having given up his dream of opening a spiritual centre in Aldrory Glen, Nigel, instead, was in process of establishing a practical centre for outdoor activities. Two holiday homes had come up for sale and Ron, the new laird, bought one. An estate gamekeeper and his wife now lived in it. Nigel bought the other one. It was conveniently close to his own home. This second house was being extended and turned into a backpackers' hostel. He also bought a mini-bus, which now brightly and proudly carried the name 'Suileag Safaris' on its sides. An attractive young lady, whom he at times gaily called, 'my good friend', or, more formally, 'my housekeeper', but whom Helen laughingly referred to as, 'Nigel's bidie-in', now shared Nigel's home and bed. She also keenly shared in taking parties on walking and climbing safaris throughout this district's fascinatingly unique, untamed element wilderness.

As they continued leaning on the garden gate, Ian repeated, "It's really great to see all this regeneration taking place in the glen."

"Aye, it certainly is," Helen enthusiastically agreed. "But come on, it's time we were heading home."

As they walked side by side up the track, which gently climbed through the garden, Helen smiled, "I swear this slope is getting steeper with each year that passes."

Ian grinned, "Aye, I was just thinking that myself!"

Chapter Twenty-Nine

On the following Sunday Ian and Colin met, as they often did on the Sabbath day of rest, at the River Aldrory. Colin strolled up the path from Inveraldrory village, while Ian leisurely sauntered down from Altdour Croft. Sometimes their wives accompanied them, but not today. Their only companions on this pleasant Sabbath in late May were the three terriers and one collie. As they stood talking they were surprised to see two large, open, brightly coloured golf umbrellas bouncing up the path towards them.

They silently exchanged wondering glances. They looked at the sky. A thin drift of hazy cloud was passing over the blue sky. It slightly shaded the bright sunshine. They held out upturned palms. A few light spots of rain were drifting down, they hardly moistened their hands, and yet this slight rain, more the suggestion of rain rather than real wetness, was making those approaching figures huddle under their large umbrellas.

Colin grinned, "You would think it was raining, wouldn't you?"

"Aye, you would think it was pouring. I wonder who those big softies are?"

They made no further comments, for the owners of those glaring umbrellas had almost reached them. Ian and Colin observed them closely. They were two young men. Both looked to be in their late twenties, both were tall and heavily built, both showed incipient signs of developing bulging bellies. They were sweating profusely, each burdened with a monstrously large pack. From an outside pocket of each pack a large plastic bottle of natural spring water protruded.

As Ian and Colin cheerily greeted them the young men halted, laid down the still erected umbrellas, removed their packs and greedily drank from the plastic bottles. They generously offered Colin and Ian a drink of the bottled water. Politely they refused. Colin laughed and pointed to the attractive small burn beside them, which flowed clearly and merrily down to the river, "There's plenty just as good – or better – water there for us to drink."

"Oh, but is it safe to drink untreated water?" anxiously asked the larger of the young men, a German from Hamburg, now working in Scotland.

"Aye, oh aye, it's perfectly safe. Ian and me have been drinking burn water for over sixty years and it's never done us any harm. Aye, and it's grand with whisky, tae!"

The second young man, a Scot from Glasgow, laughed, "I'm sorry, we've no whisky to offer you, we're both practically teetotal."

They replaced the bottles, heaved on their packs, lifted the gaudy umbrellas and with them held above their heads as protection from the almost non-existent rain, continued on their way.

Ian and Colin stared after them. The young men glanced back at those strange, white-haired old men so quaintly dressed in faded old ex-army kilts and tattered tweed jackets. The young Glaswegian, complacently aware of all his fashionable and expensive backpacker's clothes and equipment, grinned, "What do those two, odd, ancient characters look like?… Like a Scottish version of *The Last of The Summer Wine*?"

Ian grinned, "What do those two young men look like cowering under their huge umbrellas?… big Jessies?"

"Aye, they do. Just imagine if, when we were their age, we, or any young man, had been seen using an umbrella, he would have been wildly jeered at and laughed to scorn."

"Aye, I know. We would have been ashamed to have even thought of using an umbrella."

"These young men, these supposedly tough backpackers, don't seem in the least self-conscious or even remotely ashamed of using them, though."

"I know, Colin, I know. That's what I find the saddest thing of all."

"Aye, it's sad to see how youngsters seem to have degenerated since the war. Just think of how tough the likes of that young German's father was if he was a soldier in the war. We knew all too well just what tough fighters those Germans were, didn't we?"

"Aye, we did. Aye, and we were gae tough ourselves then, too."

Suddenly, Colin laughed, "Good God, Ian, we must be getting fair auld. It's a sure sign of old age when you go on about how much the younger generations have deteriorated, isn't it?… Come on let's go and get a seat and a smoke."

They steadily climbed up the path to one of their favourite resting spots, a pleasant heathery knoll with fine all round views. The sun was again brightly shining as they and their dogs got comfortably settled and the men leisurely went through the pleasantly familiar process of preparing to smoke their pipes. Colin grinned and pointed, "The rain must definitely be off; I see even those sadly degenerate backpackers have taken doon their damned ridiculous umbrellas."

As Colin struck a match he again grinned, "I'm sorry, Ian, I should have called them hikers, not backpackers; you don't like that modern word, do you?"

"No, I don't. I think it's a terribly ugly word."

"You're like Auld Maggie Gunn…"

Ian laughingly interrupted, "Good God, man, I damned well hope I'm not!"

"You're like Auld Maggie Gunn." Colin repeated, "You don't like new words, or old words to change their meaning. Jeannie and me met her yesterday in the village; she was talking to Mrs Bruce, the schoolteacher. Young Mrs Bruce kept talking aboot the school and all her kids. Eventually Auld Maggie interrupted her, "Oh, Mrs Bruce, I didn't ken you kept goats."

"Goats?… Goats? I don't keep goats, Maggie. Whatever made you think that?"

"Och, it's just hearing you speak so much aboot a' your kids, ye ken. I always understood that goats had kids and that humans had children!"

Laughing, Ian exclaimed, "I'm glad Jeannie and you had such a gay time with Auld Maggie. Of course I use the word 'gay' in its correct, original meaning, not in its perverted modern sense!"

By now both their pipes were going perfectly. They lay back in contented ease and gazed about them. The peak of Suileag rose high above a nearby ridge. That ancient mountain's steep domed summit was clear, was sun-bright, was mysteriously, mystically, appealing. They silently stared at it. Suileag – remote, ageless, indifferent – ignored those two staring humans.

That unique mountain was now under the care of the National Trust for Scotland. Gifting it to that excellent organisation had been one of Ron MacDonald's first acts on becoming Laird of Aldrory. He had also given generously to have a derelict shepherd's house near the mountain turned into a climber's bothy. The legal formalities required to gift that mountain had been completed fairly quickly as Ron had only to deal with the one body.

It was a different matter entirely in his desire to hand over most of the crofting land he now owned to the crofters living on and working that land. The complex negotiations to bring this about had been going on for two years. Ron had not realised just how many organisations he would have to deal with. Apart from the crofters themselves and the Crofters Commission, the County Council, the Countryside Commission, the Nature Conservancy and the Red Deer Commission were all involved. Even the Royal Society for the Protection of Birds, who had a small reserve on the crofting land, was keen to put its oar in. Only now did Ron appreciate the truth of the old definition of a croft as being, 'a smallholding in the Highlands completely surrounded by red tape'.

Ron was wise enough, and had wealth enough, not to allow himself personally to be entirely swamped under by the endless paperwork. By now he had discovered that the greatest advantage of having wealth was, if correctly used, the wonderful freedom it gave its owner. It enabled him to hire experts; solicitors, estate agents, bankers, etc, to do the dreary, tediously dull work for him and leave him largely free to do the things he enjoyed doing.

As they contentedly smoked, Colin said, "When Jeannie an' me were in the village yesterday we were pleased to see how well Johnnie Fraser's getting on with the extension to his shop. I'll be a great wee supermarket when it's completed."

John Fraser had bought his grocer's shop and the adjoining house from Ron. Now, with security of ownership, he was ambitiously extending the shop.

"Aye, we saw that ourselves the last time Helen and I were in the village. We also noticed that Bob McInnes is building an extension to his garage."

Robert McInnes, too, had bought his garage business with its adjoining house from Ron. He had also increased his share of transporting fish from the prospering Inveraldrory fish market by the purchase of two large new refrigerated trucks.

"The entire district has fair benefited in the... the what?... three years... since Ron brought the estate, hasn't it?

"Aye, Colin, it has. And I'm sure there are more benefits to come. I know Ron has a few more developments in mind." Ian drew deeply on his pipe then slowly and steadily jetted a stream of smoke into the calm air. As he watched the blue smoke lazily disperse he smiled, "And I don't think it's merely an insubstantial pipe dream to hope that what Ron's doing on Aldrory estate will set a shining example. An example that will be repeated on other estates through the Highlands."

Colin thoughtfully smoked for some moments then quietly said, "You brought all this about, Ian... or at least you made it possible for it all to come about, didn't you? That one violent act of yours, the killing – the murder – of Campbell-Fotheringay cleared the way for Ron to buy the estate, didn't it?"

"Aye, it did."

"We haven't spoken about that act of yours since shortly after you committed it; do you mind if we speak about it again, and this time probably for the last time?"

"No, I don't mind in the least. Go ahead, Colin, say anything you want."

"Well, firstly, Ian, does your conscience trouble you at all over that... that murder you committed?"

"No, it doesn't. It did not trouble me then; it doesn't now; it never has done in the time in between."

"You feel no pangs of guilt?"

"No, none, absolutely none. I have not lost one minute's sleep over it I assure you, Colin."

"There's still only the three of us – Helen, you and me – know of it, is that right?"

"Aye, that's correct: only us three." Ian grinned, "After all, it's hardly a thing to shout about from the rooftops, is it?"

Colin was pleased to see how easily Ian discussed this matter. "What about Helen?... Doesn't she mind? Has she never been upset over it?"

"No, never! She was, and still is, convinced that that violent act was fated, was predestined. She is certain that I was merely the chosen instrument of fate." Ian had a sudden vision of that clay model of Campbell-Fotheringay with the large hatpin sticking out from the centre of its forehead; had that model, that sharp pin, decided Campbell-Fotheringay's fate? Had he, Ian, truly been the guiltless instrument of fate? He again decided against telling Colin about the clay model. He repeated, "No, I have no feeling of guilt. After all, I feel no guilt about the Germans I killed in the war. Do you, Colin?"

"Och no, of course not! We were doing our duty, were helping rid the world of a vile evil, weren't we?"

"Aye, exactly! And I feel the same about killing that bastard Campbell-Fotheringay.

"I'm sure no one wept for his death. His parents and his brother were dead; his wife had acrimoniously divorced him years ago and his daughter had killed herself with drugs and drink. And I don't suppose his two fancy young whores lost much time in getting themselves fixed up with a new sugar daddy."

"No, Ian, I don't think you have anything to feel guilty about." Colin drew deeply on his pipe then continued, "You know, Ian, I can't understand all this talk about some of our soldiers feeling guilty at having killed Argentinean soldiers during the Falklands War. I think it's ridiculous they should feel any guilt for doing their duty, doing what they were trained to do."

"Yes, I know. I think it's deplorable. And, after all, our servicemen in that war were entirely professionals, not unwilling conscripts. Surely there must be something unfulfilled about a professional, a career soldier, spending more than twenty years in the army and never once seeing action, never once testing himself in battle?"

"Aye, he would be like a fireman spending a lifetime in the fire brigade and never once fighting a fire."

"Aye, exactly! And another thing I deplore is all this nonsense about soldiers requiring special psychological, 'counselling' after their 'traumatic' experiences. My God, Colin, we received, we needed, no 'counselling' after all our many 'traumatic' wartime experiences, did we?"

Colin nodded, "No, we effortlessly took everything in our stride. Aye, we unflinchingly carried out even the most horrible acts when necessary. Remember that short, intensive commando course we were sent on? Remember how we were trained to creep up on German sentries and silently slit their throats? Remember the one, the very hazardous, occasion we put that training into practice?"

"Yes, of course I do."

"Aye, and even though that was quite a harrowing experience, still, afterwards, we lost no sleep over it, we felt no guilt over it."

"No, of course not! And another thing (those old soldiers were fairly getting into their stride) there's now a lot of nonsense talked about the terrible trauma of coming under, or having caused, what do they call it?… Oh yes, 'friendly fire'. My God, you would think soldiers had never accidentally killed and wounded their own troops before. I don't suppose there's ever been a major war when this hasn't happened."

They both clearly remembered the time, during the German counter-attack on the Anzio beachhead, when they had come under artillery fire from British guns. They had less clear memories of when, in a confusion of billowing smoke, shrouding mist and heavy rain, they had fired with mortars and machine guns on vague, shadowy, menacing figures which later turned out to be other British soldiers.

They accepted these incidents for what they were – unfortunate accidents. All tried to learn from these accidents; all did their utmost to ensure they were never repeated, but, wisely, they again lost no sleep over them, felt no guilt over them.

"I wonder how well the young men of today would cope with such a long and savage war as we," here Ian grinned, "…and a few others – endured?"

"Not very well, I doot." Colin also grinned, "How the hell would they manage withoot their umbrellas?"

For a moment those grinning old veterans stared at one another then burst into loud laughter.

"Och, Ian, there we go again, disparaging the younger generation. We'll need to stop it."

Gradually the laughter faded and died, but their mirth lingered long in their bright gleaming eyes. For a while they again smoked in happy silence, then Ian quietly quoted two lines of poetry:

"Our deeds still travel with us from afar,
And what we have been makes us what we are."

"And what exactly is that supposed to mean?" Colin asked.

"Och, it means that we cannot escape from our past; that our past shapes us. Our six years of war, all those killings we carried out, all the times we were almost killed, are still with us. They make us very different from the younger generations who have never known war. They cannot begin to understand what our experiences were like."

"Aye, that's how I feel when I'm talking to youngsters; I feel there is a... a barrier of incomprehension between us.

"Aye, and, sadly, it's an insurmountable barrier. They just cannot understand how we coped with all those 'traumatic' experiences, how we came through them all and emerged at the end of the war as mentally undisturbed, perfectly normal people."

"Aye," Colin grinned, "I suppose we are 'perfectly normal', aren't we?"

"Aye, we are. Or perhaps we are normal *and* perfect?"

"'Normal *and* perfect'? Och I very much doot if either of oor wives – oor poor, long suffering wives – would agree with that description!"

"No, I don't suppose we really are 'perfect', are we? I suppose we must admit to at least one fault: our love of – perhaps excessive love of – whisky."

Colin grinned his agreement. "Aye, man, that's true. Aye, but ye ken that 'fault' has given us more pleasure than all oor virtues – oor many, many, virtues – lumped together, hasn't it?"

Again they laughed. Again they contentedly continued smoking. After a while Ian said, "I suppose it's all those wartime experiences of ours that enable us to view one more violent death – my killing of Campbell-Fotheringay – in a calm, un-shocked light; a different light from how all those with no experience of the savagery of war would view it."

"Aye, I'm sure that's true, Ian. Aye, and I'm sure that drastic act of yours is definitely one case where the ends do fully justify the means!"

Ian nodded his agreement and warmly smiled his thanks. They were comfortably enveloped in sincere friendship. That friendship was, after forty years, still glowingly alive with wartime's deep camaraderie.

Eventually, when his pipe was smoked out, Colin said, "You know, Ian, I've been thinking…"

"Oh, congratulations, Colin, but don't overdo it. Don't strain yourself!"

Colin good-naturedly chuckled and repeated, "I've been thinking that to most of those who know you as a basically good and decent human being, that violent act of yours, if they knew of it, would seem very out of character; they would surely find it impossible to understand."

Ian nodded, "Aye, I suppose many people find it incomprehensible how such apparently conflicting and extremely contradictory traits can exist in the one person and yet that individual can present a harmonious whole." He paused, then asked, "Remember when we were in Germany just after the end of the war?"

Colin laughed, "What, more old soldier's memories, Ian?... Yes, of course I remember."

"Remember Belsen?... Remember it and the other concentration camps we were taken to see?"

"Aye, of course."

"Remember one particular camp – I think it was Buchenwald – the camp used by the German army medical service?"

"Aye, of course," Colin repeated, wondering what relevance this had to what they had been discussing.

"Well, that's where we fully realised just what vastly different traits could exist together in seemingly normal, well-educated people, wasn't it?"

Like most British soldiers, Colin and Ian had been taken to see the horrors of the German concentration camps. Most decent people, until shown the appalling truth, found it hard to believe that a modern European race – a race that boastfully proclaimed their highly civilised state – could inflict such barbarously hideous horrors on their fellow Europeans. After Belsen and another large camp, the sickened British soldiers thought there could be nothing worse for them to see – they were mistaken!

They were taken to a smaller camp where many medical 'experiments' had been carried out. There they were again assaulted with that now familiar, all-pervading, revolting smell – the disgusting stink of death, the even more disgusting stench of evil.

Again they saw lines of scorched and blackened ground where the prisoners' wooden dormitories had stood. They, and the filthy mattresses and verminous bedding, had been soaked with petrol and burned down – had been cleansed by fire. But nothing could cleanse the evil lingering about the intact gas chamber and intact furnace where the victims not wanted for medical 'experiment' had, with methodical ruthless efficiency, been disposed of.

Beside the gas chamber was the room where the prisoners had been stripped before being forced into the lethal 'showers'. It contained the usual pathetic heap of 'trophies'.

There were many sets of false teeth; there were individual teeth containing gold fillings; there were many pairs of spectacles; there were a few swollen, pale fingers cut off for the gold rings, which were too tight to remove. There was a tangled pile of human hair. Coarse grey tresses from old women mingled with the thicker, darker locks of younger women. Coils of glossy dark hair, which had been crudely, sadistically, shorn from wailing, terrified girls littered the dank concrete floor. There was an adult's artificial leg. There was even one glass eye. That pale blue eye seemed to macabrely stare from the obscene heap with desperate mute appeal.

The British soldiers were taken to the adjoining operating theatre. At first glance there seemed nothing out of the ordinary about the two operating tables, which their guide, a Major – a British army doctor – grouped them around. The Major said nothing, he waited for some soldier to ask the inevitable question: "What are all those straps hanging from those operating tables for, sir?"

"They were to constrain the patients… or rather, the victims." Like an actor allowing the tension to build, the Major indulged in a dramatic pause before he explained. "Yes, gentlemen, those straps constrained the victims while the German army doctors carried out their hideous experimental vivisections of the living human guinea-pigs."

The Major slowly looked around this latest mixed batch of experienced British soldiers. He again noted the expected expressions come into their toughened faces – the usual reaction of puzzlement, of disbelief.

The uncertain silence was broken by a tall, burly sergeant who asked in a disconcertingly shrill high-pitched voice, "Were these victims given any anaesthetic before being experimented on?"

"No!… None! They were completely un-anaesthetised!"

A corporal asked, "But, sir, how did they stand the pain?"

"They didn't! They passed out when the pain got too bad. On these occasions nature was more humane than the inhuman human experimenters. Nature mercifully dropped these victims into deep unconsciousness, or into the deeper, the more merciful unconsciousness of death. They were expendable. There was an unlimited supply of victims for those heartless German doctors to experiment on."

The Major led the silently subdued soldiers down a corridor and into a large comfortable lounge. "This is where the German doctors and nurses relaxed in the evenings after carrying out their inhuman operations during the day. It's a nice room isn't it?"

The puzzled soldiers vaguely nodded.

"Those are nice table lamps aren't they?" asked the strangely smiling Major. "I'll just switch them on. Do you like the lampshades?"

The light from the two large table lamps brightly gleamed through the transparent pale yellow shades and countless pinpoints of light glittered from tiny holes in both shades.

"Very attractive, eh?… Very pretty, eh?"

The even more puzzled soldiers stared silently at the peculiarly smiling Major. They wondered why he was showing them two table lamps. A couple of Glaswegian soldiers, tough wee privates in Glasgow's own regiment, the Highland Light Infantry, glanced at one another and exchanged quick grins. As articulately as words these grins said, "What is that stupid bampot of an officer showing us bloody lampshades for?… What does he think we are – Big Jessies?"

Eventually the burly sergeant asked, "What are those lampshades made of, sir?"

The major paused before replying. When he had his audience's full attention he dramatically announced, "These lampshades are made from human skin!"

There were gasps of shock. He waited for the visible tremors of horror and revulsion to still before elaborating, "Yes, gentlemen, these lampshades are made from skin taken from the tragic human victims of these… these diabolical German doctors and nurses, these professionals who were supposed to be devoted to relieving human suffering, not to deliberately cause human suffering. These monsters almost make me ashamed to be a doctor!"

He walked across the hushed room to a gramophone. He gently lowered the needle-head on to the record, which was already in place. The heroic glory of Beethoven's wondrous third symphony surged through the room. Enthralled, the major listened intently; as always, he was deeply and sincerely moved by the awesome beauty of the music. Only a few of the soldiers appreciated classical music, the others wondered why they were being forced to listen to it.

After five minutes the major, with real reluctance, forced himself to turn the gramophone off. He again smiled his peculiar smile, "Well, gentlemen, aren't those hideous lamps and that glorious music strange companions to find together in this room?" He paused, then explained, "Those diabolical German doctors and nurses, after carrying out their ghastly operations and experiments on their poor un-anaesthetised victims all day with untroubled consciences then spent many of their evenings in this comfortable lounge. Here they relaxed and listened to classical music. Many of them were often genuinely moved to tears by the sheer beauty of Beethoven's music. I speak German. I helped interrogate them, I, too, love Beethoven's music. I find it impossible to understand how they could be so sincerely moved by the aesthetic beauty of great music – as I am convinced they were – and yet be so callously indifferent to the terrible suffering they caused in their evil, inhuman work. I find it utterly bewildering that such incompatible traits should exist together in apparently reasonable normal human beings.

"What about you, gentlemen?… Can any of you 'gentlemen' understand it or explain it?"

All the soldiers silently pondered these questions; but Ian, despite the seriousness of the occasion, could not help being secretly amused by the major. He noted how that class-conscious English 'officer and gentleman', as he addressed his un-gentlemanly audience of non-commissioned officers and lowly other ranks, pronounced the word 'gentlemen' with inverted commas around it.

No one could provide answers to the major's questions. Like him, they found such inconsistent behaviour astounding. It was almost unbelievable that those cultured music-lovers could be the same unfeeling brutes that carried out these vile experiments; who made – for macabrely perverted amusement? – these lampshades.

Those experienced, battle-hardened British soldiers could understand 'normal' war, they had seen plenty of it, but what they had witnessed in these concentration camps was something hideously different.

It was pleasant for Colin and Ian to come back from those forty-year-old, still vivid, ugly memories to the lovely scene spread all around them. Quietly they gazed about; their experienced, observant eyes took in every detail of the heather moors, scattered with Birches, Rowans and Scot Pines; of the rugged ridges; of the distant hills; of dominant Suileag, presiding with vast indifference over this glorious landscape.

It was pleasant to breathe the fresh wholesome purity of the Highland air after those memories of the vile stink of death, of the stench of evil.

It was *not* so pleasant to feel the burdensome weight of those forty years descend on their bodies; feel those years rheumatically ache in their backs, their hips, their knees.

But they were not quite finished with those old memories, for – quietly and thoughtfully – Ian said, "Our visit to that concentration camp forced me to realise just what vastly different traits can exist in any one person.

"So my murder of Campbell-Fotheringay is not really out of character for me. And I suppose that without some inconsistencies, some ambiguities, most humans would be much less interesting characters."

Colin nodded, "Aye. And I suppose our greatest ambiguity, Ian, one we've often discussed and which, after forty years, is still unresolved, is our attitude to war – to 'our' war. Oh, of course there is no doubt what a terrible thing that war was; it was the worst horror humans have ever inflicted on themselves. And yet to us inexperienced, and in many respects ignorantly innocent young men, going to war, with the prospect of seeing foreign countries, was a thrilling adventure. We, and most who came through the war safely (if they are honest about it) found it an unforgettable experience – an exciting, a toughening, a character-forming experience which we would have hated to have missed."

"Aye, that's true, Colin. Oh, of course all the hideous horrors, all the devastating madness, of that war was terrible, but the whole nation, the entire population, were united, were wholeheartedly working and fighting together in a common purpose. And don't most people really prefer the easy road of communal madness to the hard path of individual sanity?

"And despite all 'our' war's horrors and its miseries, at least we actively lived during it. Aye, if we had been killed, at least we *had* lived! In today's lost society how many – how few – have ever been deeply, meaningfully alive? Damned few, and getting fewer with each passing generation! So many do not so much live as merely exist."

Ian paused, he grinned, "I'm sorry, Colin, I'm going on a bit, aren't I? I'm getting carried away with the heady, intoxicating exuberance of my own verbosity!… It's just that I feel it a terrible shame that so many lead such dull, petty, sordid little lives, when life should be – can be – so much finer and brighter and nobler."

Colin laughed, "Aye, Ian, I've certainly heard you spout aboot such things more than once before! Aye, we are fortunate that oor entire lives have been lived in this wild Highland countryside. We always have been, we still are, in close touch with nature."

"Aye, we are a consciously alert and aware elemental part of nature. And our 'souls' also live through our arts and our crafts too." Ian paused, he grinned, "As you know, Colin, I have long since given up pondering over the question: Is there life *after* death?... I am convinced that the important – the vital – question is: Is there life *before* death?... Aye, we are fortunate to live where, and how, we do. Aye we do truly and meaningfully live. And, hopefully, we will continue really living for a puckle o' years yet."

They companionably smoked in silence for some moments then Ian said, "No doubt it's a terrible, a sad, a most unpleasant and unpopular thing to suggest, but perhaps society, getting too soft and decadent, needs the occasional savage spur of war to direct it to the true realities of life, to again appreciate the true creative potentials of peace.

"After all, Europe's almost ceaseless wars did not prevent Europeans from producing vast amounts of great art, did they?"

Colin quietly asked, "Aye, but wouldn't they have created a lot more great art if they had enjoyed many centuries of peace?"

Ian had speculated on this before. He had his answer ready. "Aye, perhaps they would... but perhaps they wouldn't. Think of the example of Switzerland. That country has had five hundred years of peace, and what have the Swiss contributed to European art and culture in those peaceful centuries? – Nothing but the cuckoo clock!"

Laughing Colin glanced at his watch then said, "Och, I suppose it's aboot time we started heading for home now that oor second pipe's smoked oot." As, leaning on his stout stick and laboriously struggling to his feet, he loudly complained, "Oh, God damn it, I'm fair stiff after sitting sae long. My joints aren't near as supple as they used to be."

With less effort, Ian also struggled up from the springy bed of soft young heather; he smiled and sighed, "Aye, we're both getting gey auld and a sight less sprightly. Still, Colin, as long as your fingers are supple enough to play the pipes and lift a glass o' whisky tae your mou', things are not too bad."

They now noticed the distant figures of a man and a dog on the path. They thought they recognised John MacAulay, a retired postman whom they quite often met here on their Sabbath stroll. Colin asked, "Is that MacAulay over there?"

Ian pointed at Glen, his black and white sheepdog, and grinned, "No... that's ma collie over there!"

With tolerant good humour Colin once again dutifully laughed at this old joke of Ian's.

Taking leave of one another they leisurely and contentedly started walking to their respective homes.

Chapter Thirty

The brilliant June sunshine beaming through schoolroom windows brought no pleasure to nine-year-old Rob MacLeod – it brought cruel torture! He felt as trapped as the two angry bluebottles noisily buzzing in frustrated incomprehension against the smooth, warm, transparent surface so mysteriously denying them their freedom.

Today a more terrible torment of anxiety was added to the usual torture of being imprisoned in this dusty, bookishly stuffy room while, with all his soul, he longed to be at joyous active play or be trout fishing in the benevolent sunshine and the freedom of the exhilarating summer air. Every day since last Sunday the sun had endlessly shone from a perfect cloudless sky. It was now Friday morning. He was in an agony of suspense. After being forced to waste this week of sunshine confined in the hateful schoolroom, would, as so often seemed to happen, the weather change to cloud and rain at the weekend? And tomorrow was not just a normal Saturday, it was the first Saturday in June, it was to be a very special day – if the weather held. Uncle Ian had promised to take him, and his younger brother, Norman, to fish a special 'secret' small loch which held lovely large trout.

Rob silently and fervently prayed to unknown Gods that the weather would hold. He woke before five on Saturday morning. He leapt out of bed. Desperately he rushed to the bedroom window and flung open the curtains. His heart leapt with joy. At this time of year, in the far North, there is little real night; often the weak dusk and the strong dawn almost merge. The sun was already shining. The air was already vibrant with birdsong. Sunshine's bright benediction was eagerly dissolving dawn's lingering crepuscular glow.

"What are you doing, Rob?" His brother's sleepy voice querulously asked.

"I'm looking at the sun. I'm listening to the birds. It's great! Come and see!"

As Norman joined him at the window, Rob grinned, "It's a great day for going fishing, isn't it?"

Norman laughed and loudly and excitedly gasped, "Oh yes, it's magic!… it's magic!"

"Be quiet, Norman. Don't wake Mum."

His seven-year-old brother was instantly contrite. "Oh, I'm sorry. Mum's not quite well, is she?"

"Yes, she's well, it's just that she's going to have a baby. We're going to have a baby sister in four months' time." Although he imparted this information to his young brother with all the vast superiority of his two extra years of life, Rob could not really understand what was happening to his mother. He had seen cats fat with, then give birth to kittens, that seemed quite natural, but that his mother should have a baby growing in her stomach was most puzzling, was difficult to believe. Eagerly, but with some trepidation, he longed to grow up, to enter, to understand, the strangely complex and mysterious world of adults.

Norman was puzzled too. How could his mother possibly know what was going to happen in four months' time? Four months was an immensity of time. Today was all-important. "Uncle Ian won't forget to take us fishing, will he?"

"Oh no, he won't forget."

Nor did he. At nine o'clock the fishing party set out. It was a family excursion; the boys' parents, Mary and Calum, went with them, as did Helen with Ian. Although five months pregnant, Mary MacLeod was determined not to be left behind. For her sake they took the longer but much less steep path along by Aldrory River and across the moors. The wildly excited boys and the ever-keen dogs eagerly and noisily led the way. Ian and Calum strode along together, each willingly burdened with a rucksack loaded with fishing tackle and food for the entire party. Helen and Mary, enjoying each other's happily intimate, gossipy feminine company, brought up the rear.

How impatiently the boys waited with those, to them, inexplicably slow and unexcited adults when they frequently sat and rested, instead of hurrying forward to reach and fish that exciting 'secret' loch.

When they left the path and started climbing a gentle, heather slope, Ian and Calum saw a herd of about a dozen stags running off over the ridge in front of them. Calum pointed and shouted to Rob and Norman, again eagerly leading the way, "See the stags, boys!"

The boys halted and stared in the direction their father was pointing. "Where?... Where?"

"They've just disappeared over that ridge. You're too late."

"Och, that's not fair! I want to see the deer," Rob loudly complained.

"Yes, so do I, too," Norman plaintively echoed.

Calum laughed, "How do you expect to see deer when you're making such a noise, eh?"

"We'll be quiet now... Yes, we'll be very quiet," the brothers promised.

Their father smiled indulgently, "A bit late now, isn't it?"

"Och, never mind, boys," Ian said, "if you do keep quiet we might see more deer at the 'secret' loch."

Before they reached the loch Ian halted and pointed, "What are those birds, boys?"

With effortless grace two large birds were turning in high, lazy circles.

"Are they eagles?" Norman eagerly shouted.

Rob scornfully corrected his kid brother:

"No, stupid, they're buzzards!"

"How do you know?" Norman indignantly demanded.

"Can't you hear them calling?... Only buzzards call like that."

"Like what?"

"Something like cats mewing."

"Is that right, Uncle Ian, are they buzzards?"

"Aye, Norman, they're buzzards. There's no mistaking that plaintive mewing." Then Ian smiled and, wishing to cheer the disappointed boy, said, "Aye, but in a way you're correct, too, Norman, for these buzzards are now also known as 'The Tourists Eagles.'"

In the West Highlands most locals have long since give up correcting tourists as they excitedly tell of seeing 'eagles' perching on fence posts and telephone poles. With concealed quiet amusement they let these tourists revel in their happy illusions and have tolerantly christened these buzzards "The Tourist's Eagles".

As Ian expected, there were deer at the 'secret' loch. There usually were. They were attracted to this spot by the sweetness of its lush, lime-enriched grass. Weathered outcrops of soft limestone rock thrust bleached skeletal elbows up all around the loch and formed a small island of fertility defiantly set in the surrounding vast ocean of hard, sterile, two billion year old Lewisian Gneiss.

There was a herd of hinds and young calves and a separate group of stags. All were lying resting after having been keenly grazing since early morning on the delicious grass. How leisurely, how contentedly, these ruminants chewed the cud. Under the influence of the warm, benevolent June sunshine heavy eyelids dropped over drowsy eyes. Having recently moulted out of their dull, rough and thick winter coats these deer were now resplendent in the bright, gleaming, reddish garb of summer. The stag's new, fast growing antlers were cosily cocooned in tenderly smooth protective 'velvet'.

But not every deer was complacently and drowsily un-alertly relaxed. One old, grey-haired matriarch was, as always, watchfully alert. Although lying down and happily chewing, she – the oldest hind – nobly resisted the alluring temptations of heat-induced sleep. Resolutely she kept her eyes wide. Suddenly her ears registered a faint, unusual sound. She reacted immediately. With amazing agility for such an old beast, she leapt upright. For long moments, standing statuesquely still, she intently stared.

Lying watching these deer, wee Norman had been too excited to keep silent. The hind had heard his exclamations. She now heard Rob angrily tell his young brother to be quiet. Not waiting to hear or see any more she gave one loud, harsh, alarm bark then turned and fled. Every other deer instantly leapt up and urgently followed after the 'auld dowager'. Although fleeing with desperate urgency these deer moved with what seemed effortless ease and with charming grace. "Oh, we're sorry to disturb your pleasant after dinner snooze," Helen laughed as the panic-stricken deer vanished over a ridge.

"Yes, it's most unkind of us to startle them like that, isn't it? I hope the sudden fright doesn't give them indigestion," Mary exclaimed, joining in Helen's laughter.

"Come back, boys, come back!" Calum shouted as Rob and Norman excitedly started running after the deer. "They'll be miles away by the time you got the top of that ridge."

"Aye, come on, lads, let's see if you can catch a couple of big, braw trout," Ian shouted.

The boys returned and eagerly helped assemble the two fishing rods. They listened intently as 'Uncle Ian' patiently explained why he was selecting the one particular patter of artificial dry fly to fish with today, out of the many patterns in his fly box. Fishing conditions were far from perfect. The sun blazed from the pale, milky-blue, cloudless June sky and pierced through the scintillating translucent water to clearly illuminate the sand and pebbles on the bed of the small loch.

"The limestone makes the water brilliantly clear, doesn't it?" Calum remarked.

"Aye," Ian said, "it's quite different from the lochs in the peat moors; there the water's dyed a gleaming whisky-gold. In this limestone loch the water's – to use the old cliché – gin-clear."

Helen puckishly grinned, "Och, Ian, trust you to aye be thinking o' alcoholic spirits!"

Only when a slight breeze gently ripped the loch's surface was it worthwhile casting the artificial mayflies to – hopefully – entice some trout to rise.

After an hour with no hint of a trout, Norman and Rob's interest began to wane. The more immediate and much more urgent need for food and drink took over. They sat beside their resting mother and 'Aunt Helen' and their hungry clamour was quickly, and pleasantly, stilled.

Urgent yells from Ian and their father catapulted both boys to their feet and flung them round the loch to where the men's rods were bent in wondrous arcs under the pressure of large trout.

Ian handed his rod to Rob who skilfully fished the large, strong-fighting trout. For interminable breathless minutes all life was one glorious, quivering anguish of wonder and heart-stopping suspense. Eventually Ian scooped the trout into his landing net.

Calum handed his rod to wildly excited wee Norman and, while trying to calm him, helped him fish the high leaping trout. Suddenly, as Calum held his landing net in the water, Norman screamed in desperate dismay, "Oh, Dad, it's come off! I've lost it!"

The fly had come free. The released rod sprang upright. Tears swamped Norman's eyes. His father triumphantly lifted the landing net, the large trout was securely imprisoned in the net. Norman's face transmuted from bleakest woe to brightest joy. "Oh, Dad…" he shouted his thanks, his wonder, his admiration, "Oh Dad… that's magic!"

Both trout were quickly killed. Rob weighed his, "It's exactly one kilogram," he boasted.

"One kilogram?… One kilogram?… What's that in real weights?… in good old imperial pounds and ounces?" Ian laughingly demanded.

"About two pounds," Calum replied, then winking at his sons, said, "Isn't Uncle Ian a real old stick-in-the-mud?"

"Yes, Dad," wee Norman delightedly giggled, "He's a real old dinosaur!" As Uncle Ian shook his fist at him he firmly hugged his 1lb trout to his chest and laughingly ran to boastfully show it off to his mother and Aunt Helen. Rob ran after him.

The suitably impressed women praised the large, plump trout with rewardingly loud and genuine enthusiasm. Mary and Helen exchanged quick, quiet smiles; their smiles were full of secret understanding – these womenfolk were well practised in the gentle art of unstintingly praising their triumphantly returned hunter/fisher men-folk. As Calum and Ian joined them, Helen, with a bright grin, again enthused, "Well done, boys; that's a real fine brace o' braw trooties."

"Aye," Ian laughed, "they are really braw trooties."

The men settled themselves comfortably beside their wives. Ian, rising to Helen's bait, told the tale of another brace of braw trooties.

It happened a good number of years ago. One summer, a seventeen-year-old lad was employed on Lord Kilvert's Ardgie Sporting Estate as pony-boy/ghillie. The sturdily strong lad was keen and enjoyed the work. There was only one snag: he was a loon of sound Aberdeenshire farming stock and his rustic Doric dialect was so broad that the West Highlanders had difficulty in understanding him. The English gentry could hardly understand a word he spoke – he seemed to speak an unknown foreign language.

One evening Lord Kilvert met the loon, John Forbes, as he was returning to his bothy beside Ardgie Lodge. The lad had been trout fishing. "Well, John, did you catch anything?" asked Lord Kilvert.

With eager, quick excitement the loon loudly and enthusiastically replied, "Och aye, sur, I caught twa braw trooties, ye ken!"

His Lordship, barely comprehending a word of this reply, smiled pleasantly and, hoping he was saying the correct thing, politely murmured, "Oh, well done John… jolly good show!"

Rob and Norman loved the loon's vivid description of his trout. Kneeling beside, and proudly gloating over their own trout, they repeatedly chanted, "Aye, they're twa braw trooties, ye ken!"

To the smiling adults the boys seemed to be kneeling in worship and singing a litany of praise. When Calum suggested this Ian agreed, "Aye, and with childhood's instinctive inbred wisdom, they are not praying to any modern Christian God, but to a much more ancient God – to the, in my opinion, much more true and valid Pagan God of hunting and fishing."

They lay back in relaxed ease and ate and drank. They revelled in the Pagan glory of warm sunshine caressing their faces. Quietly, comfortably, all felt they had achieved a glory of true living.

Calum chuckled, "Oh, this is undoubtedly much better than working, isn't it?"

"Aye, man, it certainly is," Ian immediately agreed. He grinned, "Work is a thing I've never been too keen on…"

"Aye, we ken that alright," Helen interrupted.

Grinning even more, Ian ignored her interruption and continued, "It's much more pleasant to sit here and get our knees browned again after the dreary, long winter."

Mary smiled, "Yes, it's grand to feel the sunshine again." After glancing at her pleasantly warm bare legs she stared at her two sons. She practically purred with maternal pride at seeing her boys so happy and so radiant with health.

"Rob's and wee Norman's legs are getting as brown as berries, aren't they?"

The boys were wearing shorts; Helen wore a light skirt and Mary had on a loose-flowing, flower pattern frock, which inconspicuously accommodated her pregnant figure. Calum wore his MacLeod tartan kilt, while Ian had on his faithful old, and getting very faded and shabby, Seaforth Highlanders kilt.

As they – mainly the males – finished off the food the adults idly and contentedly gossiped. Mary mentioned that, while shopping in the village yesterday, she had met Bella and Jamie Gordon.

"Oh, how are they?" Helen asked, "I haven't seen them for ages."

"Oh, they're fine. They seem to be very busy just now."

"Aye," Ian said, "this is a busy time for all shepherds."

"Yes, but on top of that they're having a lot of work done in their house," Mary explained. "They're getting a new kitchen and bathroom installed."

"Jamie's doing some of the work himself," Calum said. "He's worried about how he'll manage to get the large, heavy old iron bath out before he can get the new bath in. Seemingly the stairs to the bathroom and bedrooms are very narrow, steep and awkward."

Ian nodded, "Aye, they are." Grinning broadly he suggested, "Jamie should get Auld Murdo Munro to sort out that problem for him."

"Auld Murdo?" Calum queried. "I didn't know he knew anything about plumbing. He's a retired gamekeeper, isn't he?"

"Aye, he is, but he did a bit of plumbing once – and once only!"

Smiling, Calum and Mary stared enquiringly. Helen also smiled, "Och, don't encourage him. I recognise the signs; he's leading up to another of his old stories."

"Well, we love to hear Ian's amusing old tales," Mary said. "Don't you?"

Helen gave another smile, a good-natured, indulgent smile, "Oh aye, I like fine to hear his stories – the first time. It's no' sae fine tae hear them repeated umpteen times though."

Mary laughed, "Och, don't heed her, Ian, go on, tell us your story."

Needing no further encouragement, Ian eagerly plunged into his tale.

It was set in the early 1960s. A mains water supply had been installed and was being piped to almost every house in Aldrory. Amongst those taking advantage of this novel new innovation was Duncan Mathieson, a middle-aged bachelor crofter living at Achairdich, a few miles from Inveraldrory village. Duncan had bought a second-hand bath, toilet and wash-hand basin. He was quietly confident that he could install them himself and thus save paying a plumber's extortionate charges.

One day, as he was busy converting a small bedroom into the new bathroom, Duncan had a visit from Murdo Munro, the old, semi-retired gamekeeper. Murdo had been ferreting and shooting the all too abundant rabbits infesting Achairdich's sand dunes. He gave Duncan two large, plump rabbits. Then Duncan led the way up the steep, narrow stairs, past the sharp, awkward bend, and ushered Murdo into what was going to be a smart new bathroom. Duncan proudly displayed and loudly extolled his great plumbing efforts. With suitably flattering enthusiasm Murdo admired Duncan's efforts, although he secretly thought the workmanship very crude. Still, he reflected with an inward smile, I suppose for good old Duncan the results will be good enough. Everything Duncan did he enthusiastically proclaimed as being 'good enough'. The neighbouring crofters held different views on how 'good' Duncan's 'enough' was. They had nicknamed him 'Duncan Good Enough'.

Pointing to a corner where he had lifted the floorboards, Duncan, with uncharacteristic modest doubt over his own abilities, said, "I'm not quite sure about how to set about cutting through that plaster and lath there. That's where the big soil outlet pipe from the lavatory pan has to go."

Murdo had a sudden brilliant idea, "How big has the hole to be?"

Duncan widely cupped his hands, "Oh, about that size should be good enough."

Giving an enthusiastic grin, Murdo exclaimed, "Just you wait here, Duncan; I'll solve that problem for you in a couple o'shakes o' a lamb's tail."

Murdo returned a minute later. He had his shotgun with him. Duncan eyed the gun with alarm, "Good life, man, what are you going to do with that?"

"Och, don't worry, Duncan, I know what I'm aboot."

Holding the muzzle of the gun six inches from the lath and plaster he confidently declared, "It'll just blow a neat hole the size you want through the ceiling."

Duncan scratched his scalp and doubtfully asked, "Are you sure? It won't make too big a hole, will it?"

"Och, no! Trust me, Duncan, it'll be fine and dandy. Now stand back and I'll fire."

He held the shotgun firmly and pulled one trigger.

The noise was shocking! It was deafening and the thick cloud of dust was choking!

They hurried down the steep stairs and entered the kitchen. Coughing and spluttering they peered through the dense mist of white dust. Duncan stood aghast. Despairingly he exclaimed, "Oh, good life!... good life! Look, half the ceiling's doon!"

This was an exaggeration. Not quite half – perhaps a quarter – of the kitchen ceiling was missing, was covering the furniture and floor in a thick layer of plaster, lath and dust.

"Oh, good life, look what you've done, Murdo," Duncan loudly lamented.

Murdo silently stared at the havoc his bright idea had caused. Apologetically he murmured, "Och, Duncan, man, I'm sorry. I'm sair sorry. I don't ken whit to say. I'm dumbfoonered. I'm fair dumbfoonered."

For some minutes Murdo made no further reply to Duncan's continuing laments and angry recriminations; finally, having had enough, he muttered, "Och, never mind, Duncan, look on the bright side."

"The bright side?... What bright side?"

"Och well, Duncan, you were worrying aboot how you were going to get that heavy bath up those steep and awkward stairs, weren't you?"

"Aye... aye, I was. But what's that got to do with this... this Devilish mess?"

"Och well, Duncan, all you need to do now is bring the bath in here, tie a rope on it and pull it straight up through that hole in the ceiling into the bathroom."

Ian smiled as he finished his story and added, "So if Jamie Gordon needs help to get his new bath into the bathroom he should see Auld Murdo. He and his shotgun will soon solve that problem for him."

After another half hour of lazily contented ease, Mary said, "I think I'll start for home now. I've had enough of lying in the sun for today."

"Are you feeling all right?" Calum anxiously asked.

"Yes, oh yes, I'm fine. I'll just slowly meander home."

"Do you want me to come with you?"

"Och no, Calum. I don't want to spoil your, and the boys', day. Just you four 'boys' stay as long as you want."

"I'll come with you, Mary," Helen said. "I've had enough of the sun for now, as well. We'll just pleasantly make our leisurely way home together."

As they set out at a comfortably easy pace, Mary and Helen quietly enjoyed the cosily intimate feminine camaraderie of each other's company. They intuitively relished its subtle difference from the friendly companionship of the previous mixed male and female company.

On one of their frequent rests, Helen asked, "Have you decided the name of your baby girl yet?"

"Yes, I've finally made up my mind. I'm going to call her Catherine."

"Catherine... Cathy... Catherine MacLeod." Helen judiciously tested the name. "Yes, I like it. It will suit her fine."

Neither Helen nor the mother to be had any fears that the baby might not be a girl. Helen had convinced Mary that it would undoubtedly be a girl to perfectly complete her family.

Helen smiled, "Have you been reading *Wuthering Heights*, Mary?"

With startled surprise Mary gasped, "Yes, I've just finished reading it. How did you know?... Oh, that's a foolish question... you would know, Helen!"

"Aye, I just guessed it."

"Guessed it? More than just guessed it, I think. Oh, of course the name 'Catherine' was a clue, wasn't it? Yes, that fantastically strange and wonderful novel did influence me, I admit."

"Aye, exactly. That's what I thought."

"Another name I like and thought of giving the baby was 'Iona'. It's an attractive and unusual name, isn't it? Mrs Iona Bruce, the young schoolteacher, is the only one I know who has that name."

Helen grinned. "Do you know how she got that name, 'Iona'?"

"No, I don't."

"It's quite a romantic story really. Her parents decided that if they conceived a baby girl on their honeymoon they would name her after where they spent the honeymoon. They spent most of their honeymoon on the Isle of Iona, hence their daughter's name."

"Oh yes, that really is most romantic."

A more mischievous grin puckered Helen's mouth, "When I told Ian that romantic story he paused and thought then remarked, "All I can say is, it's a damned good thing for the lassie that her parents did not spend their honeymoon in Achiltibuie!"

When Mary's merrily ringing laughter quietened down, Helen contritely apologised, "Oh, I'm sorry, Mary, here I'm telling another old story after me scorning Ian for spouting all his old stories so often. I hope they don't bore you too much."

"Oh, no, Helen. It's great to hear those old tales; it would be sad if they were lost and forgotten."

"Are we going to do any more fishing, Dad?" Rob asked once the two women left them.

Calum looked enquiringly at Ian, "What do you think?"

"Och, I think it would be a waste of time under these conditions." The sun beat down heavily and relentlessly; there was not a breath of wind; the surface of the loch was as flat and motionless as a silvery sheet of burnished steel.

"We were amazingly lucky getting these two trout. I have not seen a mayfly hatch or a trout rise since then." He now addressed the boys, "And anyway it's best not to be too greedy. That wee loch can't have all that many trout in it; let's be happy with what we've got and leave the others for another day, all right?"

Both boys nodded in not too enthusiastic agreement.

Sensing their disappointment and remembering his own keen boyhood enthusiasms, Ian smiled and winked at the boys, "I tell you what we'll do: you've seen and fished this secret loch, well now we'll go and explore a secret cave."

Norman and Rob gasped, then chorused, "A secret cave?"

"Aye, a large, limestone cave where your ancestors lived nine thousand years ago."

"Nine *thousand* years ago?" the amazed boys again chorused. They stared with wide-eyed, open-mouthed wonder. With a touch of trepidation wee Norman asked, "Are there any ghosts in the secret cave?"

Ian clearly remembered the one and only time Helen had gone into the cave. How definitely, how uneasily, she had sensed the presence of 'ghosts' in the gloomy cave's dark dimness. Ancestral pagan voices eerily whispered vague, coded messages at her. However Ian smiled reassuringly, "No, Norman, there are no ghosts in the cave."

Rob scornfully laughed at his young brother, "Och, don't be a silly big baby frightened of ghosts." With excitement and perhaps just a hint of apprehension, he then asked, "Are there any skeletons in the secret cave?"

Ian laughed, "No, there are no skeletons in the cave either, but lots of bones have been found in it; bones of bears and reindeer and lynx which used to live here and which the cavemen hunted, killed, and ate."

Tremulous with wonder, Rob said, "Oh, did they really?"

Wee Norman said nothing. He intently studied his father's glossy black beard and hair, then with equal intensity stared at Ian's hair and beard. How pure white that head of hair was. The brave bushy beard was also pure white – apart from that funny, yellow nicotine stained smudge at the left corner of the mouth. It was strange how old Uncle Ian looked compared to his father; why was his hair so white when dad's hair was so black? Suddenly he asked, "Oh, Uncle Ian, did you see the bears and reindeers living here when you were a boy?"

Indignantly he wondered why they all laughed at him.

"Och, Norman… Norman, I may be gey auld, but not as auld as that – not quite!"

After having, with eager, excited happiness thoroughly explored the mysterious and creepy secret cave, but having discovered no ghosts or skeleton or even bones, they returned to the secret loch. They collected their rucksacks and fishing rods then started on the homeward journey.

Ian again winked at the boys and smiled, "I think we'll go this way and we might discover another 'secret' place."

He led the way down by the small burn that flowed out of the loch. After a few hundred yards the burn disappeared underground.

"Where's the water gone to?" the boys wanted to know.

"We'll just wander down this lush glen and see if we can find it again," Ian said.

Half a mile further on they found it at the top of a small and attractive grassy hollow. The pure water playfully gurgled and bubbled up out of the porous limestone ground. It formed a small stream, which soon became a waterfall. The water joyfully slid down a gentle slope of smooth rock thickly covered with dark green, velvety soft moss into a small but deep pool thirty feet below. The virgin stream, the limpid pool, all un-tainted by peat's sullying amber, glittered their crystal transparency to perfection under the glory of the June sunshine, its brightness glaringly brighter after the secret cave's sombre gloom.

Some young rowans and birches added their gentle beauty to this beautiful secluded spot.

They all stopped and stared. Ian smiled, "Well, we've found the burn again, boys. Do you like this secret place?"

Together, Norman and Rob loudly enthused, "Oh, yes!… Yes, it's great!… It's magic!"

"This is our secret waterfall, our secret water slide and secret swimming pool where Colin and me and other boys used to slide and swim during the school holidays." Ian paused and grinned, "Of course those far off pre-war summers, were real summers. The sun shone endlessly week after week, month after month then – or so it seemed."

"Oh, Dad, can we swim and slide here?" Rob asked.

"Oh yes, Dad, I want to, too. Can we? Can we? Please, Dad, please," Norman urgently pleaded.

"Aye, why not?" Calum laughed. "The water looks really tempting, doesn't it? I'm going to slide and swim with you. What about you, Ian?"

Before answering, Ian bent down and put some fingers in the water. Beside him a small rowan was also bending over the stream. Some of its slender branches delicately combed the water's surface, while on higher branches clusters of white blossoms unstintingly gave out their lovely, sharp sweet scent.

Again Calum laughed, "Like you, Ian, that rowan's testing the temperature of the water with its delicate fingers."

"Aye," Ian laughed in reply, "and nae doot, like me, it's finding the water damned freezing. So, I think I'll stay out of the water, I'll stay high and dry."

"Coward!" Calum jeered as he started removing his boots and stockings. The boys already had theirs off and were hurriedly throwing off their remaining clothes.

"Och, I never felt the water cold at your age, lad, but just you wait till you're my age. Once you're over sixty and are, all too rapidly, approaching seventy, then with each year that passes, the hills get steeper and the water gets colder. No, I'll go up to that knoll there and sit in the sun and smoke my pipe. Just you lads enjoy yourselves, there's no hurry."

Ian had not walked many yards before loud shrieks stopped him in his tracks. He turned and stared. He grinned. The boys shrieks of shock as their naked bodies encountered the cold water were followed by explosions of laughter as their father inelegantly slid down the mossy waterfall and splashed wildly into the pool beside them. There were many more loud bursts of laughter as they splashed one another then raced back up the slope and slid down again.

With keen, boyish enthusiasm Rob, wee Norman and their father wholeheartedly and unashamedly paganly gloried in the innocent but deeply sensual pleasure of that long, mossy, silky smooth slide and the exhilarating, gasping plunge into the clear pure chill of the deep pool.

Reaching the grassy knoll, Ian quickly and comfortably settled himself. He soon had his favourite old pipe companionably going. The sun, that other blessed old companion, was warm on his face. He sighed contentedly.

As the three humans slid and splashed and joyously played, Ian was irresistibly reminded of other playful creatures he had watched many years ago – a family of four otters. It was winter and a covering of fresh soft snow blanketed the landscape and smoothed away all harsh outlines. Hidden at a vantage point across the narrow loch, Ian observed the adults lead the way. They slid on flattened bellies and outstretched legs. With broad heads they snow-ploughed a steep track down to the dark, calm water of the loch. Their two half-grown youngsters impatiently jostled for place, then with wild excitement followed the parents down the exhilarating snowy slide. Time after time all four slid, swam, climbed back up and slid down again. Their carefree joy was palpable.

Ian had watched enthralled.

Another explosion of yells and laughter returned him to the present. The pool was a white fury of spray and of high leaping, high kicking bodies. Ian smiled as he compared these humans with the otters. How much more graceful the otters were; how elegantly they slid into the water then effortlessly undulated out of it. And how very much quieter they were!

A sudden, an unexpected, a most welcome silence set Ian's gaze free. He lifted his eyes from those three happy humans and looked beyond the opposite ridge to where Suileag steeply reared its awesome might. That unique mountain was inescapable. Today, as always, it impressively and majestically completely dominated this wild landscape.

The steady glare of afternoon sunlight revealed the mountain in vividly clear naked detail and effortlessly and playfully moved it nearer to Ian.

He smiled warmly. Once more he greeted Suileag – welcomed him as an old friend. At one time, when much younger and much fitter, he had climbed Suileag annually. It had been something of a pilgrimage. But the two climbs he particularly remembered were separated by six years – six years of savage war.

In July 1939, before being called up in his Territorial Army unit, he had climbed Suileag by himself. Sitting at its domed summit he wondered if this would be his last visit. A European war seemed inevitable. No doubt his regiment would be in the thick of the fighting. Would he survive? If he did, he promised himself (and old Suileag) that one of his first acts after the war would be to return to this summit.

In October 1945 he kept that promise. He sat on top of Suileag... he sat on top of the world. Silently he thankfully rejoiced. Then this pleasure became tinged with sadness as he thought of all his comrades who had been killed in the war. How incredibly lucky he had been to have come through all the fierce battles unscathed (apart from his ignoble minor wound!) Why had he survived when they had died?

For a time he was burdened under the weight of their deaths. Then he brightened. He gloried in the wild beauty of the landscape – his own ancestral homeland – spread all around him, with startling utter certainty he knew his true purpose now was to live life to the full. He had to live it not only for his own sake, but he must live life for those dead comrades too.

Forty-two years had passed since then, and, yes, he had lived life to the full. He thought of how incredibly quickly his life was passing. Soon it will be over. He stared at Suileag. What is the span of any human life compared to those ancient rocks, not just millions, but billions of years old? We only have:

"One Moment in Annihilation's waste,
One Moment of the Well of Life to taste..."

As he got older he increasingly felt the terrible sadness of the briefness of each individual life. Increasingly he understood why most humans cannot accept the shortness, and for many, the pointless insignificant emptiness of their life; who cannot face life's stark, often ugly, reality without some religion's consoling promise of an immortal afterlife. He sympathetically understood their need for this reassurance, but he could not believe in the validity of any of the world's many religions.

Another loud burst of laughter from the three humans so uninhibitedly glorying in their wild, watery, pagan play startled Ian out of his pleasantly drowsy tranquil state of reminiscent contemplation. He smiled happily and indulgently. It was good to hear laugher disturb the lonely silence of this remote place.

He again admired the lush greenness of this small glen, which the gin-clear burn so richly watered with its peat free, lime generous goodness. Of course, his nature-wise ancestors had realised and utilised the bounty of this place's uniqueness. From where he sat Ian could make out the faint mounds, the bright green outlines, of what had been the walls of a shieling. He knew there were more of those smothered over emerald green outlines further down the gradually widening glen. He thought of how gratefully the small black cattle must have relished this lush summer pasture after each winter's long, lean, hungry weariness. How they must have put on weight and gloss at these bountiful high shielings. And how the young Highland men and women tending these cattle must have enjoyed living in the shielings, far from the severe strictness of their elder's disapproving Calvinistic frowns. Ian smiled tolerantly as he thought of how many autumnal weddings had, of necessity, followed on naturally from these happy shieling months of summer.

Now only the deer and some sheep benefited from this lush bounty.

Ian sighed as he thought of how sadly empty and desolate was this depopulated country.

Shadowed with nostalgic sadness his mind's eye saw the limestone cave, saw it actively occupied by his ancestors nine thousand years ago; it saw the remains of the broch on the seashore at Clachghuirm, saw that circular dry-stane tower being used some two thousand years ago; it saw the pathetic, crumbling remains of a castle on its lochside promontory, then saw it as it had been when it was the formidable stronghold of proud MacLeod chiefs. He actually saw the faint green ghost of that shieling across from him and he imagined the many others scattered over this high land. He vividly pictured the all too numerous rickles of stones and gaunt, lichen covered gables which lingered on with grey, tombstone sadness and marked the lonely almost forgotten sites of what had once been populous Highland communities.

Ian again sighed. He had got himself into a mournful mood. He removed the pipe from his mouth and examined it. With a rueful grin he complained, "Och, damn it, even my auld pipe's gone out on me too."

Busying himself with refilling his favourite old pipe Ian once again wondered if he would see a meaningful reversal of that dismal tide of depopulation in his lifetime. He hoped so... he fervently hoped so. But was that hope realistic? In his present mood, he doubted it. But would there never be a reversal? He could only hope there would be – and not too long after he was dead. Suddenly a stanza from *Omar Khayyam* came into his mind; it was one he had, more than once, quoted to Helen:

"Ah Love! Could thou and I with Fate conspire
To grasp this sorry scheme of things entire,
Would not we shatter it to bits –
And then remould it nearer to the heart's desire!"

His spirits rose. He thought, "Och well, at least – with Helen's mysterious help – I've done my bit; I conspired with fate to get rid of Campbell-Fotheringay. Thanks to that decisive, fateful act of mine and to Ron MacDonald's ongoing developments, Aldrory Estate has started to regenerate, has started to build up its population and, hopefully, this is only a start."

As Ian struck a match, lit his pipe and once again quietly revelled in the tobacco's subtle, mellow comfort, he was startled by a sudden extra loud burst of laughter from Calum and the boys as they once more slid, plunged and splashed with exhilarating carefree abandon. Their uproarious laughter completed the rout of the last lingering remnants of his melancholy. He beamed a wide smile.

He happily thought, "Yes, as long as the pure innocence of childhood's spontaneous laughter sounds loudly enough around the world then there yet remains some hope for us humans."

There was another explosion of laughter from Rob and wee Norman. That laughter did not just fade away. Ian heard it ripple out and sweep in joyous waves Eastwards over all of Sutherland; Northwards over all of Caithness and Southwards over all of Ross-shire and Inverness-shire. It swept unabated ever further South, yes, even over Argyll, the stronghold of the Campbells!

Ian had an ineffably wondrous vision of all those sadly depopulated glens and straths once again happily populated. Loudly and distinctly he heard all those fertile straths and sheltered glens once more echo and re-echo with that most glorious of sounds – the sound of children's carefree laughter.